MURDER MOST UNUSUAL

MURDER MOST UNUSUAL

MICHELLE SOMERS

THRASHER
PUBLISHING

A WORD FROM THE AUTHOR

Welcome inside my sometimes frightening, always romantic mind.

I hope you enjoy *Murder Most Unusual* – sequel to my debut, award-winning novel, *Lethal in Love*.

These stories are set in Melbourne, Australia, so please note that boots are only footwear when they're not associated with cars. Rubbish bins are for trash, car parks are parking lots, firies are firemen and ambos are paramedics and/or ambulances. Toilets, bathrooms and loos are restrooms, bums are butts and avos are afternoons or avocados, depending on context.

And as for spelling, anything that looks strange reflects how we do it Down Under – S's are Z's and double-L's are single-L's.

And anything else? Well, that's deliberate too.

That said….

Thank you for choosing to read Chase and Stacey's story.

I hope you enjoy it!

Michelle Somers

*To Danny, Josh, Nathan and Gabriel
– my biggest, loudest, most ardent fans.*

ABOUT MURDER MOST UNUSUAL

When the line between fact and fiction is blurred, a sadistic killer is born.

Author Stacey Holland lives in a fictitious world where the mortality of her characters is governed by a tap on her keyboard.

Homicide detective Chase Durant's cases are real and gritty and one wrong move could be his last.

When their two worlds collide, and fiction melds with fact, can they fight the attraction raging between them, all-the-while fighting the killer determined to destroy them both?

Prologue

They make it look so easy in books. Murder the victim, move the body.

Stacey Holland adjusted her grip on the mannequin and puffed the hair from her eyes. Squinting through darkness, she shrugged off the wish to be somewhere else. Warm wouldn't hurt. The Bahamas. Or curled up on her couch, a good book in one hand and a spiced cider in the other. And a tub of the best choc-chip cookies in the universe.

Instead, she was Arctic-blast cold, plotting the perfect murder for her perfect manuscript. Because nothing less than perfection would do.

Damn the drill of her mother's voice. *Fame's not won from the back-row seats, my girl. Get out there, get dirty and get it right.*

She scrunched her nose against the crack of mud on her skin. Yep, if nothing else, she ticked that last box, tenfold.

A cow mooed in one of the far paddocks and another answered its call. The chill night air sliced through her wet clothes, labour's sweat covering her skin, a trickle running down her collarbone and falling between her breasts.

She tightened her grasp on the fibreglass hand, breathed deep and heaved. Planting her gumboots into the rain-soaked grass, she braced, leaned back, used every last kilo that usually made her despair but now gave her leverage.

Plop.

The ground slammed hard against her butt. If she'd shed those extra inches the fall would've hurt a helluva lot more. As it was, the jar slammed her tailbone and juddered up her spine.

Mud soaked through her jeans.

Great.

Goose pimples pricked her skin. Needled her blood. Chilled her bones. She shuddered. Slumped toward her bent knees. Stuck.

Her choc-chip-cookie obsession prevented her from slumping

further than a few inches forward. Her head dropped to her palm, the squish against her forehead barely registering on her *icko-meter*. What was a little more mud?

She'd never been a "why me?" kinda girl, but now was as good a time as any to start. On paper the corpse would have moved.

Reality's a killer. Her lips twitched.

So, why am I butt-deep in what better be mud?

Because death and despair are my fictional friends. And simply, superbly delicious.

The snort left her lips before she realised it had formed. It didn't matter that the alliteration was as ridiculous as her ass dancing the hippo-shuffle through mud puddles and paddies.

Cold shivered through her body, a sensation chased closely by a sharp, "so what?" shrug. If it took mud-dancing to reach bestseller status, then she'd schlep a whole vat of mud back to her car.

Her heart skipped a heady cha-cha through her chest. She grinned, shook herself off, slithered and squelched her way to her feet. Her butt still protested, but it could have been worse. Could have been her arm broken, not the mannequin's.

She brushed the muck from her hands, then crouched and clicked the ball joint back into its socket. Too thunderous for stealth. But thankfully, no one was around for miles.

Not that it mattered. She wasn't doing anything wrong. *Much.*

Not long now.

Light winds fluttered the leaves above, eddying musty scents through the air. A promise of more rain.

He squinted through his night-vision lenses, his steel-tipped boots planted firmly in the muck.

A head-lamp bobbed through the black – distant, indistinct, like a lone firefly in search of its mate.

He dropped the binoculars, letting them hang from his neck, drawing on his cigarette, watching the smoke curl upward and mingle with the frostbitten sky.

Expectation slinked like a wild dingo up his spine. Stealthy.

Ravenous. *Insatiable.*

A crack echoed through the paddock. He tensed, cigarette dangling between his lips. The faraway yellow flickered, bobbing its leisurely way toward the barbed boundary fence. Then a car door slammed. Another.

Dark swallowed the light. An engine growled then dulled as a double-wide beam tore through the ankle-length grass.

He pressed back, tree bark pricking his neck like a goad of conscience, had he been prone. The headlights bounded through the entry paddock until swallowed by the shadows.

His nostrils flared, drawing in smoke and icy anticipation.

Ten minutes of darkness ensured she wouldn't return.

Stacey Holland. Author extraordinaire.

The beat of his heart quickened, the heady scent of imminent death pricking his senses. She thought she knew loss. Pain, even. She didn't know shit from shitake. But she'd learn soon enough. He was one hell of a teacher.

And soon she'd lap up every one of his lessons. Would drop to her hands and knees at his feet, greedily begging for more.

His lips spread wide, the smile of a lover seconds before satisfaction.

He stubbed his cigarette into the ground. Dropped it into a zip-lock bag and into his pocket. It paid to be careful. Others had been caught with less evidence.

His ute wasn't far. A hundred metres or so away, behind the hay barn. He opened the boot and wide eyes stared out from the cramped plastic-lined interior.

'Showtime.'

He withdrew a tiny bottle from his pocket, grinning as the man shrunk further back like a steer roped and ready for a butcher's knife. He found the racing pulse at his neck. Felt the blood course its tribute through the body for the last time.

'It's useless wasting your energy, trying to change destiny. You can't. Fighting will only prolong the pain.' He snatched the blue collar and dragged him closer. 'Be a good boy and I might let you go. What do you say?' He didn't wait for an answer. Truth? He didn't care. Either way the man would die, the method already prescribed.

He patted his inside jacket pocket. The knife hadn't moved.

Palm braced against the man's temple, his thumb and forefinger folded back the eyelid. Clear liquid spilled from the nozzle onto the red-rimmed iris, pooling at the edges as if clamouring for escape. There was none.

He pressed harder against the sweat-soaked temple, stalling movement that might see the liquid spill free. He didn't have to wait long. Life's force raced its death march through the trembling flesh until it could run no more. The body spasmed, stilled. The pulse at his neck sprinted erratically, then stopped.

Extracting the body from the boot was easy. It hung limply over his shoulder, still limber, still warm. Muscles flexed, he steadied, then began the trek. Only a kilometre to the spot she'd chosen for him.

Only a kilometre to her scene of the crime.

2 days later ...

It's just research, you nut.

Rain streamed down Stacey's hood, plops the size of elephant's tears dripping onto her already sopping face. She rolled her eyes and huddled further under the building's narrow eaves.

Try telling that to my heart.

Driving tight fists deep into her pockets, she blew, but no amount of puffing dislodged the hair plastered across her cheek. She relented, dragged a hand out and pushed the strands back, before returning her frozen fingers to the warmth.

Somehow imagination helped romance flow easily onto her pages. Suspense was a different, prickly-thorn-in-your-butt story. Hence the reason she stood outside Detective Chase Durant's precinct, sodden and shivering, in the wettest May on record for twenty years, trying to still her senses before she bowled inside and had to unglue her tongue from the roof of her mouth. Again.

He did that to her. *Why?*

She'd never been a sucker for broad shoulders and fathomless blue eyes. Or a smile that made her knees fold like the billows of an accordion. She wrote sexy detectives, and he happened to be a *particularly* sexy detective, in the flesh. Maybe that was it. Or her overactive imagination getting the better of her. Or maybe she needed to take Shazz's advice and get out more.

Either way, wavering outside his place of work wouldn't catch her anything but a cold, something she needed less than his amused tolerance and a desire to prove she deserved otherwise. It didn't matter how he viewed her, as long as she left today with enough info to finish her book.

Another bracing lungful of frost and her hands left their warmth for the two-way double doors. Her palm connected with the glass and it sprung outward, driving her back. She stumbled, overcorrected, propelled forward into a solid mass – strong arms, warm, spicy scents, and muscles both delectably superhuman and male all at once.

Murphy's Law chuckling at her expense.

Chase's fingertips dug into her upper arms, pushing her back. 'Lurking outside police stations now, are we Stacey? Hoping to catch a killer? Or maybe a detective?' Humour tumbled across his lips, calling her resident kittens to romp and roll across her stomach lining. 'I guess it's your lucky day. You found one.'

She stepped back, giving the kittens a stern back-in-your-basket warning. Chase yanked her from the path of a passer-by and she toppled back into his body.

Firm, muscular, warm …

Before she became too comfortable or kidded herself that she'd enjoy the wrap of his arms and the press of his lips too much, he dragged her through the station doors.

Her skin tingled, not from cold.

She shrugged free of his grasp, tossing the rain from her hair, avoiding his gaze. There it was again, that amused forbearance she hated so much. It hauled her back two-and-a-half years. Made her feel worthless and small, and left her questioning how far she'd come.

And whether she'd ever really moved on from being nothing at all.

Stacey's lips tightened like a bow seconds before the arrow's fired.

Chase's first impulse was to lean across and drown in the scent of honeysuckle and woman. His second was to get the hell away before he did something stupid. Like kiss her.

'What are you doing here, other than wreaking havoc on everyone within bomb-blast range?'

One-and-a-half metres of curvaceous irritation uncoiled, like a taipan ready to strike. 'You bowled me, buddy, not the other way round!'

He bit back a retort. Rolled his shoulders and winced.

His troubles were no fault of hers, and projecting them only added guilt to his ever-growing dung-pile of emotions.

Still, that didn't change the fact that Stacey Holland was trouble, with her dripping blonde ringlets, bright pink cheeks and wet ruby lips. He had no time for distractions. The Night Terror had struck again, killing a friend. That was his focus – that and stopping the bastard before he murdered again. That and showing he deserved his lead role on the case.

He had so much to prove.

The second hand on his watch hacked at the last threads of his patience. 'I have to go.'

'But we have a meeting.'

'Tomorrow.'

'Today.' To prove her point, she shoved her mobile in his face.

He read: *Appointment. Detective Durant. 1.30 p.m.*

The words were a mental slap about his head. As if things weren't bad enough, his memory had become another dud bullet in an already dwindling chamber.

He pushed the phone away.

She snatched her hand back as if his fingers were the last thing she wanted against her skin. Or maybe they were the first?

He couldn't help it. Her reaction tugged a dry smile to his lips. 'Appointment? Don't you mean *date*?'

'This is work, not pleasure!'

Red flooded her face and he bit back a laugh. 'Ouch! Yet another slap to my ego. If you're not careful, I might think you don't like me.'

She had that startled deer look – wide eyes, ready to bolt – and his laughter slipped into a chuckle. 'Work and pleasure aren't mutually exclusive, you know.'

'They are for me.'

'Live a little, Stacey. Life's too short.' Which reminded him. His real appointment awaited. He side-stepped and pushed open the door. 'Call and we'll make another time.'

She scampered up beside him, didn't notice the puddle until she ploughed through it, splashing water halfway up his leg. *Great!*

Water plastered her trousers to her calf, but she didn't seem to notice, or care. 'Can't we at least walk and talk at the same time?'

His right arm spasmed. Reason enough to end things here. His squad believed he was following up on a lead and he didn't need some ditsy romance writer catching him on the lie. He stopped, and pulled her in before she pitched into a lamppost. How the woman survived her day without him was a mystery. Wide green orbs stared up through the rain, her lips parted and ready …

He released her and stepped back. *Not now.*

'I'm busy in the real world, solving real problems, catching real killers. I don't have time for pretend.' He glanced at his watch. *Dammit, if he didn't move, late would be an understatement.* No brisk walk to clear the cobwebs now.

He raised his hand to a passing taxi and sighed inwardly when it pulled into the curb. He brushed past her and this time she didn't follow. 'Call me and we'll have that date. Just not today.'

Her frown deepened. No sense of humour – that was her problem. And he had neither the time nor the inclination right now to help her find one. Stacey lived in a fairytale world where princes rode in on white horses and the damsels they saved were young and perfect and innocent; where life always ended with a happy ever after.

Fiction. He wasn't fool enough to think life even remotely resembled that.

His fist clenched in his lap as he tried to hold it steady.

That didn't mean he was willing to give up hope.

Chapter One

11 months later ...

*...**A**nd the RuBY winner is ... From Mishap to Murder, Stacey Holland!*

The Cloverleaf Ballroom erupted in a frenzy of applause, friends and associates standing, cheering. Celebrating. For her.

Champagne bubbles clogged in Stacey's throat. She knocked back another mouthful to wash them down, and spluttered.

Great move, Einstein.

Shazz slapped her none-too-softly on the back and she almost leapt from her seat.

'Ouch!'

'Complain now, thank me later,' her friend whispered. 'At least you're no longer choking your way toward cardiac arrest.'

Stacey straightened. Damn, she was right! Who knew bubbles scared the same as hiccups?

Romantic Book of the Year.

She won.

Difficult to move past the whirling spinning wheel that was her thoughts.

Shazz pulled her out of her seat and into a hug. 'Go get'em, Stace. Romance Writers of Australia's biggest award, and it's yours. This is your moment.'

It was. One she'd envisioned since her leap into romantic suspense three years ago.

Agent, Beth Samuels – "Morticia" to her friends – unfolded her lithe frame from her chair and sandwiched Stacey's hand between her bony ones. 'Well deserved. You aced it this time.'

Rita Hayden, her editor, flicked back her fiery bob before wrapping Stacey into her curvaceous frame. 'I knew you had it in you.'

Ethan Miklem tugged her into a not-so brotherly embrace, his low whisper delivering a gopher-trail of goose bumps across her neck.

'Another rung on your ladder to success. I'm glad I get to share it with you.'

People wanted to hug her, shake her hand, tell her she'd done good.

She'd been trying to tell herself that for years. Now perhaps she'd believe it.

Her head whirled and she gripped the back of a chair.

She'd avoided going heavy on the alcohol all evening for just this moment. A RuBY nomination was the Australian romance authors' equivalent of the Oscars. No mean feat. Exciting. Elating. Thrill-the-pants-off-overwhelming.

RWA President Jermaine Hart had pitched into the lead-up and Stacey had thrown caution all the way to Antarctica. This was *the* moment – a stepping-stone toward New York Times best-seller status.

Recognition. *Validation.*

Reason her mother had to be happy now.

She blinked, champagne effervescing through her blood and into her brain.

Jermaine's speech had her biting nails she'd never bitten before, and steadying her nerves had become more pressing than the need for temperance. She'd grabbed Shazz's second glass of bubbly and downed the lot in one hit.

She hadn't considered the subsequent steam-train rush of alcohol to her brain.

A path cleared before her.

Paper scrunched in her palm. Her speech.

Daubing moisture from her eyes, hoping her mascara was as waterproof as professed on the label, she made her careful way to the stage through the cheering crowd. Over-polished marble and stiletto heel collided. She tottered, caught her breath, adopted a nothing-to-see-here-but-drunk-woman-in-heels smile, then continued toward the stairs. The hellish heels transformed the remaining metres into a marathon.

Don't trip. Don't trip. Don't trip.

She made it past stair number one. Only four more to go.

Don't trip.

The toe of her borrowed Armani sandal caught on the second step and she pictured Shazz's cringe, her protect-those-shoes-with-your-life speech forever engraved in her mind.

'Got you!'

Jermaine grabbed her arm and guided her up the remaining stairs.

Air whooshed from her lungs as she made it to the podium, all vital body parts miraculously intact. Jermaine pressed the award into her hands and she didn't hear a thing past that moment. The angular-cut glass felt cold and unnatural, heavier than it looked. She tried not to think of how the shards would scatter if it were dropped.

Great murder weapon.

Not an ideal time for plotting.

She stared out at the crowd of upturned faces, an entire litter of kittens prancing through her chest. *Everyone out there is on your side. They want you to win.* Her editor's words. Comforting in theory, not so easy to remember under a bright spotlight and five-or-so hundred pairs of eyes.

She rested the award on the slanted wood, smoothed her crumpled speech with her free hand, cleared her throat and launched in before the tentative grasp on her nerves slipped.

'As many of my oldest friends will attest, I've been dreaming up bad guys and bad boys since I was old enough to appreciate the difference.'

Chuckles rippled through the audience, providing her with courage enough to stem the waver in her voice. 'I've always felt that authenticity is the key. Every piece of action, every murder that makes it into my books is performed until I'm satisfied it's plausible. If I can't do it, I don't write it.'

She looked up from her notes. *Big mistake.*

Cut glass dug into her palm as she lost herself in familiar eyes of tropical blue. Butterflies joined her resident kittens, tangoing in tandem across her stomach.

Breathe.

Oxygen dragged into her lungs, diffusing the jitters.

How dare he! Trespassing on *her* day, *her* moment. Making her all fuzzy and warm and melty in front of her friends.

No!

She clenched her jaw, ignoring a heartbeat that would challenge the most rigorous Riverdancer. The racing heartbeat wasn't him. It was the champagne.

Awareness was not allowed in places that shouldn't be aware. Not over Detective Chase Durant.

Her grip on the award tightened. She stared at her crumpled speech and forced the scrawled black into focus.

'My characters are everyday people who get caught in not-so-everyday circumstances. They're true and honest, they hurt, but they always mend. Such is the way of romance, a genre which gives so much pleasure to so many of our readers. It's why we as authors push through the uncertainty, through the pain, the tears. But this moment, accepting this award, makes every tear, every heartache worth it, because it says that in some small way I've touched the hearts of the people out there. And as writers, that's all we ever strive to do.'

This time when she looked up, she avoided the front row's far left table.

'My list of thank-yous is long, but I'll try to make it quick. First, I'd like to thank …'

Before she knew it, her speech was done, the crowd was standing and concertina legs were carrying her back to her seat. His table stood in the opposite direction to hers, so avoiding him should have been easy.

Her gaze met his. Deep, probing, accusatory.

'What happened up there?'

Stacey snapped her attention to Shazz. *Safer.*

She dropped into her seat. 'Chase Durant happened.'

The presentations wrapped up and wait-staff descended on the room with trays of chocolate berry mousse and crème brûlée.

'He's here?' Shazz swivelled in her seat, an excited oh-my-god-I-just-saw-Hugh-Jackman shrill in her voice.

Stacey grabbed her arm. 'Don't be so obvious.'

'Oh, like you?'

'Very funny.'

'Not so if the look on your face is anything to go by. Why do you let him rile you?'

'Oh, let's see, because he thinks I'm a flake and a disaster. Plus, last time I asked him for help he fobbed me off.'

'Wasn't he working some serial killer case at the time? I'd say that's reason enough for not being as *available* as you'd have liked.' Shazz winked on the word "available", as if that bugged Stacey more than the info she'd needed for her now award-winning novel. It *so* wasn't. 'Far as I can see, with the way his eyes superfix-follow you, the only disaster in this equation is his emotions.'

Damn, she couldn't help it. Shazz's words had that fuzzy feeling back again. She bit her lip rather than ask her for more.

'Forget about him. He doesn't matter.'

She said the words with a toss of her hand. Even turned to the table and smiled at Ethan across the swanky chocolate centrepiece. But as others joined them and drew her into another round of hugs and congratulations, she knew the words were a lie.

Her speech was so close to a confession, its sweetness glazed his tongue.

She was brazen, he'd give her that. And too goddam sexy in the green, filmy get-up that clung and revealed and … well, *revealed*.

The Muscle Man deep in conversation with her seemed to think so. His palm brushed her upper arm as he leaned in. She gazed into his eyes, didn't pull away.

Chase pushed out of his seat. Time to clear his head, of her, in the dress. *Out of it.* He tossed back his lemon, lime and bitters. Better if it was whiskey. Only this was work, albeit off the clock. He had a hunch and he had to follow wherever it led. Which meant keeping his head.

Focus. Not easy with a certain strawberry blonde needling at his concentration. But he'd prevailed under worse pressure. And there were worse things than surveilling Stacey Holland.

Even if she was willing to kill for a good story.

His glass clattered onto the table. Difficult to believe the woman could plan, let alone execute a murder. But too many indicators pointed her way and until he could rule her out, she was stuck fast under his radar.

And Muscle Man's, it seemed. The bastard could barely tear his eyes off her.

With a growl, Chase headed for the double glass doors leading out to the rose garden.

'What the hell are you doing here?'

His hand paused on the cold of the glass, then pushed, and he slipped through, toward the scent of roses, leaving the plush scent of honeysuckle behind.

The door opened behind him, as he knew it would.

'Chase?'

Even angry, her voice contained a lilt that tugged at his gut. Low.

He turned to meet her flinted-green glare, her face a soft contrast of shadows under the muted lighting. So not the face of a murderer.

He crushed the thought before it wheedled its way through his reserve. He'd worked homicide long enough to know murder had many faces, some of them just as exquisite as the one looking up at him now.

'Funny how fate keeps crossing our paths.' He grinned.

'Does "pull the other" ring any bells for you?'

The daggers in her expression said she missed the humour.

One day he'd see her laugh.

Another thought to bury. And he'd heap on weedkiller, just to make sure. He had no business making the stern Stacey Holland laugh. Enjoying the view, on the other hand, was free fodder, and who in their right mind would pass up such a bargain? He indulged in a slow perusal of that dress close-up, enjoying the way her skin flushed, the red disappearing beneath her strapless neckline.

His spike in temperature had everything to do with spring moving toward summer, and nothing to do with the view. Or his reaction to it.

He switched focus from his reaction to hers. 'Why am I here? To celebrate the success of women in writing, of course.'

'Something I'm sure your date is most grateful for.' She frowned the moment the words left her lips, the grate of her voice matching the porcupine-prickles in her stance.

His grin couldn't help but widen. His "date" was busy networking inside, and Gracie's bestie. And while dating his sister's friends was something he'd partaken on occasion in the past, this, right now, was work.

That didn't mean he couldn't enjoy it. 'Jealous?'

She even snorted cute. 'I write fiction, I don't live it, detective.'

'You called me Chase before.'

'And many other things, but I think for all intents and purposes "detective" is fine.'

He stepped in. 'Why? Because it helps you keep your distance?'

She tottered backward on those ridiculous heels. Heels that made her legs go on forever, tempting a man to explore and dream and want. He reached out and the only way to steady her was to pull her in. He was a practical guy, after all.

Her chin tilted up, the set of those plump raspberry lips unimpressed, even whilst the green of her eyes became overtaken by black. By a need almost equal to his.

'Why are you really here, *detective?*'

She pressed every single one of his buttons, and he was tempted to press back – hard. Against the wall, on the carved wooden bench …

A life without living is worthless. Why his father's words came to him now, he had no idea. He was all too familiar with the weight of regrets.

Damn!

Killer she may be, but cold she was definitely not.

Why was he there? 'For this.'

Her lips parted, an invitation in any language. He accepted like the gentleman he was. She tasted of chilled champagne and strawberries dipped in dark chocolate mousse. His hands moved from her waist to her hips and he pulled her in closer still. Just as he'd imagined doing back when she bowled into his precinct almost a year ago on the pretext of research.

His heart gunned like a V8 eating up ground on the Grand Prix's home straight. Her mouth moved tentatively under his and he groaned. *If only she wasn't …*

He jerked back. *What? A cold-blooded killer?*

What the hell was he doing? Angling to be her next vic?

Kissing a murder suspect wasn't the stupidest thing he'd ever done, but it ranked pretty damn close. Even if he found her to be innocent, fraternising within an investigation was taboo, and could spark the end of a career.

He took another step back, ignored the draw of her body, the memory of how damn fine she tasted. Distance meant sanity, something she sucked from him like a succubus drew life from its victim.

Some moves were inexcusable, regardless the excuses. 'That should never have happened.'

'Damn straight, it shouldn't!' Her bottom lip trembled, as if she were vulnerable. Hurt. Despite the fact she'd kissed him back.

He had a crazy desire to do it again, to kiss her pain away. His right wrist began to tremble. He stilled it with his other hand and turned away. He was not weak. Life would not do that to him. He dropped his hand. *She* would not do that to him.

He turned back. Now she looked pissed. Well, she could take a frigging number.

'Nice speech up there. I hear there are writers who'll do pretty much anything for their craft. Is that true?'

She caressed the green stone nestled between her breasts and he imagined those same fingers slowly caressing him. His groin tightened.

Was she doing it on purpose?

She licked her lips and he almost groaned out loud.

'How far would you go to close a case?'

He shook his head. 'That's not the same thing.'

'You think not?' He dragged his gaze from her hand to her face and hated the knowing look she shot him. 'Do you love your job, detective?'

His fist clenched. Not as strong as he'd have liked. 'I can't imagine doing anything else.'

'Then we're a lot alike because neither can I. And if I need to go the extra mile to turn a good story into a great one, I'll do it. Even if it means talking to a cranky detective.'

When she smiled, the right side of her mouth quirked and her eyes filled with mischief, *knowing,* as if she held a secret. It made him want to know it, want to get it from her in any way he could.

He gritted his teeth. 'I'm not cranky.'

She arched her brow. 'Did I say you were?'

'You said–'

'I know what I said. It's what you assumed that I find interesting. You think you're the only detective I know?'

Time to pull the rug back under his feet from where she'd dragged it. 'You were telling me how far you'd go for a good story?'

'More to the point, does it bug you that I might know more than one detective?'

Barely two seconds passed between his question and hers. She was deflecting. Well, it took two to ping-pong and he was an ace at the backspin and block.

'From memory, last time you wanted help around interrogation techniques. Well, here's a quickie, no charge. Stacey Holland, where were you on the evening of Thursday, fourteenth of May?'

Her glare suggested he hunt for lost marbles. The hand on her hip suggested he watch out for thin ice. 'I'm not sure where you're going with this, but how would I know what I was doing eleven months ago?'

'A knee-jerk response about seventy per cent of suspects give first-up. Now think, what was happening in your life around that time?'

Her brow furrowed, then cleared. She bit her lip and he pulled his gaze north of temptation.

'I was finishing *From Mishap to Murder*. So, I guess I'd have been writing.'

He nodded. 'Now what if I told you the fourteenth was the first dry night after a week of solid rainfall? In fact, it was the wettest May on record for the past twenty years.'

He spotted the moment she remembered and tried to act like she didn't. Her frown frosted over, her expression clouded, and her gaze dipped beyond his left knee. 'I was researching a scene for my book.'

'What scene was that?'

Her head jerked back. 'What's this really about?'

'Helping you.'

'Can we at least be honest?'

'You first.' He rolled his hand.

She watched like it was bug-infested, or riddled with leprotic boils. 'You think I'm lying about something?'

'You tell me.'

Air puffed through her lips disturbing the blonde wisps slung low over her brow. Then she rolled her eyes in that typical stop-yanking-my-chain look. 'Why are you really here?'

He searched her expression. 'I'm on a case.'

Her reaction was immediate – a war between curiosity and feigned disinterest. If he'd been a gambler, he'd bet all his chips the writer in her would triumph.

She wavered before moving closer, winning him his bet amidst a flurry of honeysuckle and heat. 'Anything interesting?'

Funny, but this time he'd swear she wasn't holding anything back. Or maybe the awkward-and-absurd act concealed a damned good liar.

'Only if you view murder that way.' Still no reaction. She was good. Better than. Her talents were wasted in books when she could easily have graced the widescreen. 'But it's an ongoing investigation and off limits.'

'That's a shame.'

'Undoubtedly.' His hand spasmed and he clenched it before it started to shake. 'I should get back to my date.'

Her poker face didn't span past masking murder. It seemed that jealousy was harder to hide.

Her palms smoothed over her thighs and only a dead man would miss how the material hugged every curve she'd pressed against him when they'd kissed.

'See you around, Stacey Holland.'

She tilted her head. 'You know one thing I believe in less than fate?'

He raised his brows.

She raised hers in return. 'Coincidence.'

Chapter Two

'I'll take one, no, make that two metres of the three-strand rope. And this.' Stacey dropped the fishing line onto the counter and dug into her bag.

'Going fishing?'

Heat flooded her face. She ploughed around for her purse, looking anywhere but into eyes that stripped every scrap of sense from her brain.

Was the confounded man stalking her? Today of all days, with her shoddy pre-weight-loss tracky dacks and hoodie.

Not that her wardrobe or the frizzy wildness of her hair should matter.

It didn't matter.

'Maybe.'

'No maybe about it.' His voice was as dry as her not-so-honey-blonde split ends. 'Fishing tackle, boat anchor rope. That smells of fishing to me. Can I come?'

She slanted her gaze upward of denim and muscle-hugging cotton until it met with eyes fifty shades of irritating and irresistible. Her heart rate spiked. Why'd the devil have to look so damn hot in blue?

Her fingers contacted the smooth leather of her purse. She dragged it out, shooting Chase what she hoped was a cactus-wilting glare. 'You may think you're funny, but it's just delusion.'

'Ouch! That's a kick right where it hurts.'

'I'm sure you've enough ego to spare.' She pushed the items across the counter to Burt, or so his nametag said. It also said he was there to help in any way he could. Shame that didn't extend to tossing an overzealous detective out of her life. 'No doubt I have fate to thank once again for bringing you to Hook, Line and Sinker the exact moment I happen to be here. Are you stalking me, detective?'

Burt leaned in, no pretext of anything but lapping up their

exchange. Her glare did nothing but elicit a wide grin from both men.

Burt's behaviour, she could understand. Their "conversation" had to be reels more riveting than fishing-talk. Chase, on the other hand, had no excuse. His hip rested against the counter, his arms folded across a chest she'd experienced up close and personal only a week ago.

The gleam in his eyes said he knew exactly the effect his presence had on her equilibrium. 'And why would I do that?'

Flames swept across her face. All she needed was for him to add one plus one and come up with a window. This was anger, not attraction.

'Boredom?'

'You underestimate yourself, Stacey. You are anything but boring.'

She slapped her card against the payWave reader, then stuffed her receipt and purchases into her bag. Time to leave Burt and his over-eager interest behind. If she was lucky, Chase would take her none-too-subtle hint, stay put and keep the other man company.

She strode to the exit and pushed through the heavy wooden door. Her luck had to come in at some stage. Just clearly not today. The wind whipped about her hair as Chase joined her on the footpath.

She gathered the frizz-ridden strands in one hand, holding them back so she could see. 'Okay, let's get this awkward stuff over with. If you're angling for a date, forget it. I don't date.'

The blue in his eyes deepened. Then his lips curved upward and she locked her knees for fear of crumpling like a house of matchsticks to the ground.

'*Interesting.*'

At least the cold on her cheeks provided a reason for the red. 'Not really. Just reality.'

'Yet nothing exists for no reason. Why don't you date, Stacey?'

Heart conga-drumming in her ears, she lifted her chin. 'Why do you need to know?'

'Curiosity.'

'Just as well you're not a cat.'

His gaze narrowed. 'Otherwise you'd write me into one of your books?'

'I don't kill cats.'

'But you do kill people?'

'With a pen.'

He cocked his head. 'Painful death.'

'Like this conversation.' She backed up. 'I have somewhere else to be, so goodbye *detective*. And next time you have an inclination to follow me, don't. Just for the record, you're not my type.'

The wind urged her on as she turned and strode away. If wishes were guaranteed, that'd be the last she'd see of Detective Chase Durant.

Congo heartbeats amped up to techno.

'I wasn't angling for a date.' His laughter pranced about the wind, meandering playfully through her mind. 'And just for the record, you're not my type either.'

Gloved fingertips *bump-bumped* across rows of spooled fishing line, dry thuds matching the dry empty thud of his heart. Dust eddied and unsettled, drifting downward and showering the muddy brown of his steel-tipped boots.

Red bloomed across her cheeks. Through cracks in the shelving he could see she was riled. Flustered. A wildcat on heat. Over an idiot detective who wouldn't recognise a clue if he rammed it up his tight ass and lit a match to it.

He flicked the grime from his gloves, then turned his head, found sudden interest in the array of rods as the bitch stormed past and slammed through the store's front exit.

Dick on a lead, the pig-cop followed. Her voice grated through the glass, anger and denial in one overwrought outburst. Her trembling body told another story. She wanted him. Wanted him to fuck her until she couldn't remember her name, or his.

It would be her downfall. Always picking the wrong man.

The fishing line slipped easily into his pocket. Strolling the aisle, he added sinkers to his basket. A packet of hooks joined his pocketed nylon. He smiled at the young assistant straightening a display. She flushed, smiled back, invited. *Tempted.*

He headed for the ropes, ignoring the weighty need that filled and tightened his balls. His path was set. Straying, no matter how sweet, was not an option. Not yet.

He fingered the nylon strands. His gut told him the climbing rope would be better, but he picked up the three-strand anyway. It was her choice. The drama, the deliverance, the death. Her choice.

All but the finale, the last bow. They would be his.

Stacey threw her bag onto the table and her body onto the couch.

After she'd tossed the flowers from her front doorstep into the trash, curbing her breath and her temper all the way. She wasn't stupid enough to believe that Brad's fortnightly delivery signified more than control. Three years divorced and he was still manipulating her and her emotions. Still making her feel small and insignificant, and a damned laughing stock.

Something the entire male population seemed intent on these days. Or at least the male population she came into contact with. *Very close contact.*

The thought flicked a switch and heat flooded her body.

Damn!

Had she just made a blithering fool of herself?

Of course she had. Hence the reason – well, okay *one* reason – she didn't date. She could write a relationship in a matter of hours, minutes even. But give her a real, live man and she couldn't connect enough words to start a shopping list.

Idiot!

She banged her head against the back of the couch. Relief factor – zero. And now her head was a bass drum in a marching band.

What had seemed the most logical explanation for his turning up every which way the past week, was wrong. Very wrong. He didn't want to date her.

You're not my type either. Her heart did that little dive-bomb thing that came latched to the feeling labelled *idiot.* Of course, a man like Chase Durant wouldn't fall for someone like her. Not with a choice of clichéic willowy blondes or stunning redheads like his partner. And that was a good thing.

He was too close to the kind of man she'd sworn to stay clear of.

Memory clutched her chest, squeezing until she thought her ribs might shatter. Her father. The yelling. The hurt. The last time he walked out their front door. The reasons he left her behind and never turned back. Brad's control. His need to change her a rejection itself. Thoughts she'd mulled and turned over time again, cutting deep into old wounds.

Neither man deserved her energy, her time. They'd robbed too much of both already.

She plucked a loose thread till it unravelled, the hole growing in sync with her unease.

Why have you been following me, detective?

Since the awards dinner, something niggled. Something in their exchange made little or no sense. Something past the kiss she would not think about.

She crossed her legs, clenched her thighs. *Mind out of the rose garden and into reality.*

What date did he mention? May fourteenth? In seconds she was at her desk, tapping her keyboard. A lead weight slammed her chest. She clicked on the link. Dropped her jaw all the way to the overworn cream carpet.

It was a joke. It had to be a joke.

The front page headline slashed that theory to shreds.

Nine Knife Slasher Strikes Again.

The more she read, the deeper she fell into a fictional world that was *From Mishap to Murder*. A fictional world she'd created which had suddenly become real.

No!

No-no-no-no-no-no-no-no-no.

This wasn't happening. In Hollywood, yes. Melbourne, Australia? No way. Not with her story. Her murder.

Her head spun, a spinning-top off its trajectory and heading straight for trouble.

Oh, god! Was that it? Chase believed she was a murderer. That she killed to make her murders authentic?

She stumbled up from her chair and dashed for the bathroom. *Do not vomit. Do not vomit.*

She made it to the toilet bowl just in time. A sinful waste of toast, eggs and perfectly seasoned avocado.

She dropped to the floor, jarring her knees, her nerves.

Bile lurched in her stomach and surged up her throat.

Whoever said positive affirmations worked didn't know shit from sugar-free strudel. They sure as hell never worked for her. She was better off without them. And him.

He'd kissed her, for what? Not because he was attracted. *Oh, no.* He'd kissed her for a confession, for her to trust him and tell him she killed people.

She gagged. Waved farewell to another lot of good cuisine. Probably last night's Thai tofu and noodle salad. She rinsed, then wiped her mouth with a wad of toilet paper, tossed it into the bowl and flushed.

She'd acted out her book, then someone had gone and acted it out for real. As if her book were a prescription. *A recipe for murder.*

Great name for a TV crime show, not her life.

Comprehension shuddered through arms and legs that struggled to push up from the floor. Slowly, shakily, she stood. *He* knew. That whole conversation, the flirtatious chit-chat, the supposed advice for her novel … He knew and not once had he let on. He'd followed her, led her to believe he was interested …

A sluice of cold water over her face and a vigorous rub of the towel replaced anger with disgust.

Since when was seduction a prescribed interrogation technique of Melbourne police? All the time she'd worried over trespassing on private farmland, he'd been looking to convict her for murder. Naive fool that she was, she'd read his continued presence as interest. How he must have laughed after their exchange outside the store. How he must be laughing still.

Only this was nowhere near funny.

Clutching the white marble sink, she blinked at the mirror. *Coincidence.* A pale reflection of herself nodded back.

Once the cops looked closer, the murder would appear nothing like her scene. There'd be differences. *Big differences.* Then the police would have no choice but to continue hunting for the killer elsewhere.

It didn't matter that she didn't believe in coincidences. She didn't believe in love either yet, like yesterday's trash, it was littered all around her.

The pound against her skull mushroomed until she thought her head would explode.

She'd make Chase see sense. Self-preservation aside, she had an obligation. If the police were looking at her, it left the killer free to kill again. *If* that was his plan. Something she didn't doubt. She'd researched enough psychopaths to know gratification killers rarely stopped at one. It was her responsibility to change that. Fast. Whatever the consequences.

Which meant a visit to Chase's precinct and a long conversation. The thought of seeing him made her skin burn. The burn lower and deeper she chose to ignore.

Luck dangled the entire weekend before her. Time enough to prepare for their confrontation, and time enough to stew. Still, come Monday, only one more exchange and she'd sever him from her life forever. Like the sharp, clean rip of a scab from a healing wound.

It wasn't as if she'd done anything wrong, so what on earth could he do?

Arrest her for mannequin murder?

Chapter Three

Two weeks.

Two aching, agonising, endless weeks until he discovered whether the only career he'd ever wanted was about to end. Starting the moment he stopped procrastinating and took the stupid blood test. Chase slammed his fist against his desk and immediately regretted it. Pain shafted up his arm. The sound echoed through the precinct and more than a few heads popped up before he glared them down.

'You okay?' Jayda Thomasz peered at him over her desk. The only squad member impervious to his mood.

He scowled.

Avoiding her grilling, green-eyed scrutiny, he grabbed his coffee only to drop it back down. His hand fell into his lap and trembled against his thigh.

'Why wouldn't I be?'

'Only you can answer that.' She bit her lip in that *I'm-about-to-make-things-awkward* way of hers. 'Are *we* okay?'

'Sure.' The word shot out fast and gruff, and any hope she hadn't noticed was dashed by the *are-you-serious* bite of her glare.

She visibly bit back a tirade that only a year ago would have flayed him full force. 'I know life's crazy at the moment, what with the wedding and all. But you're my partner and friend. I'd hate for things to be weird between us.'

'No weirdness here.' He shot her what he hoped was his usual grin. 'Life's a rainbow on an LSD trip. You hooking up with a reporter, on the other hand …'

She didn't look the least bit pissed with the dig. An indication that the whole lovebug thing had bitten her bad. Not that he cared past being happy she was happy. Eleven months ago, his interest had been a fumble for distraction – more a "what if?" than an "I seriously want you in my life" scenario. He didn't seriously want anything in his life.

Anything but the job, that is.

And now he hadn't a clue where his life was headed …

She flipped and twirled her pen between her fingers, a new trick courtesy of lover boy. 'I'm meeting Seth for a drink. Why don't you join us?'

'Pass.'

'You're not still pissed about that whole Night Terror thing?'

Was he pissed? Her butt-head fiancé had bulldozed Chase's rescue op. An officer had been stabbed, Chase had been forced to shoot the serial killer before he filled Seth's numb-skull with a round of lead. And, for his troubles, he'd won a first-class chewing out from Hackett.

Bet your ass he wasn't all fuzzy and friendly about the guy. Considering he *knew.*

He flexed his fingers. Hated they felt useless and weak. He'd told no one. Not even Gracie. Why worry his sister when his fears could be groundless?

But sniffer dog Seth had discovered what he'd tried his damnedest to hide – symptoms that could spark the end of his career. The man was a ticking grenade with a dodgy pin. As of yet, he hadn't shared anything with Jayda. Who knew how long that would last?

'You can't avoid each other forever. You're my partner, he's my fiancé. You're both a big part of my life. I'd like for us all to get along.'

One big, fucking Brady Bunch happy family.

He pushed an all-is-raindrops-on-roses-hunky-dory grin to his lips. 'Distance makes the heart grow fonder, right? Who knows, in time I'll be as crazy-in-love as you are.'

Her internal eye-roll was as clear as the dry in her voice. 'If nothing else, your sense of humour hasn't improved.'

Project deflection successful. Now to focus on what mattered.

He shuffled through the papers on his desk to open the coroner's report on William Huffey.

The body – nine stabs to the chest, right hand wired into a Boy Scout salute – lay soldier-stiff and straight in a paddock out on the Dresden's cattle farm. The Nine Knife Slasher's third and last victim before he disappeared eighteen months ago.

Something about the scene tugged at his subconscious. What the hell was it? 'I might stay back and take another look at the Huffey murder.'

'Last I heard, the case was cold since the NKS vanished. Has something new surfaced?'

He mentally crossed every crossable limb of his body. 'No. But I figure fresh eyes might find something we missed.'

She tutted. 'Once upon a Friday night, you'd have a date.'

'Once upon another time you'd rib me for playing around.'

'Now you don't play around enough.'

He quirked a brow. 'You're asking me to play?'

She did that pretty blush thing where every bit of exposed skin flamed, from her shirt neckline to the roots of her Ferrari-red hair. One thing hadn't changed since Seth muscled his way onto the scene – she was still an easy tease. And Chase still loved seeing her flustered.

She tugged at a stray red strand. 'Not asking, suggesting. With someone else. I mean, there must be plenty of women out there more than willing to go out with you.'

'Such a glowing endorsement.' His hand clenched in his lap. 'My last almost-date ended up dead. Forgive me if I'm not all gung-ho to try again.'

The words stripped colour from her face, rushing moisture to her eyes. If he could have bitten back every idiotic blunder, he would. 'Damn, Jayda! I'm sorry. I didn't mean–'

'To remind me the Night Terror killed someone I loved? It's not as if I'm likely to forget.' Pain rasped her voice like a saw carving live flesh. Then her eyes flashed with kick-ass strength that had seen her face a psychopath and survive. 'What I don't get is why you haven't dated since.'

'No reason.'

'Chase Durant. You can't bullshit me. Something's up, has been for months. Much as you say you're okay, you're not. You need to talk about it.'

Things were so much easier when she didn't talk – before she fell in love, went all goo-goo eyed and changed, dissecting everything, including him and his perceived open-for-discussion social life.

The file on his desk suddenly nabbed his interest. As did the coffee stain on the top right corner. 'Look, it's as simple as the opportunity hasn't come up.'

Jayda switched attention to the front desk. Her expression screamed *a-ha* while her mouth kicked up into a wide grin. 'Well, don't look now, but opportunity just walked in the front door.'

He looked. His temperature spiked, his gut tightened. And that wasn't the only thing.

Windblown hair, cheeks flushed with red, Stacey Holland was talking to Sam in that animated way of hers. Then her lips pursed and she indicated in his direction.

He turned back to Jayda, nerves as taut as a string stretched to its limits. 'She's a suspect.'

'For what?'

'A hunch I'm following in Huffey's murder.'

Hurt filled her expression. 'I thought you said there was nothing new. What hunch?'

'I didn't want to tell you until I had something.'

'Since when do we keep our partner out of the loop?'

The string snapped. 'Not sure, Jayda. You tell me.'

Her breath hitched.

It was a low blow, but this was one train wreck he couldn't avoid. Easier to keep the distance than let people in.

Jayda's palms slapped against her desk and she pushed up out of her chair. *Mission accomplished.*

'You're still sore about *eleven* months ago? Get over it, Chase. And yourself.' She grabbed her jacket and bag. 'I refuse to apologise again. Tell Hackett I'm following up a lead. And don't bother to call me until you get that head of yours out of your ass.'

She stormed toward the exit, bowling past Stacey, almost knocking her over in the process. Not that the woman needed help. She managed clumsy all by herself.

Jayda was right, of course. He was an ass. Funny thing was, he'd long gotten over her working the Night Terror case without him. Was over her falling for another man. He was even over discovering a friend had betrayed him in the biggest way possible.

There was nothing that made him so angry he wanted to punch the wall until his fist came out the other side.

Nothing but the possible time bomb hanging over his head – a debilitation that had robbed his mother of a normal life and his father of every dream so he could be her carer, twenty-four-seven. Degeneration of his muscles until justice and the fit of his gun in his palm were a distant memory.

He wanted to yell. Fight. Do something so stupid he'd lose sight of everything that made his life feel over.

'We need to talk.' Honeysuckle taunted his senses.

He slammed the file closed and flipped it over. Why did her voice make him want to forget with her?

Mind out of the ridiculous.

Stupid, but not *that* stupid.

His eyes meandered up fitted black pants, a barely covered midriff and cleavage that made him want to see more. He liked her curves, liked that she looked all woman, not skin and bones as if she starved herself half to death to fit fashion.

Her skin flushed the colour of cotton candy. Who'd knock back an offering of the sweet, sticky sugary stuff? 'You've changed your dating policy?'

'If I did, you're not the one I'd be talking to.'

'Wow, woman. That bite of yours kills.'

'Nothing I do *kills*.' The pink fled her face and her gaze darted the precinct. 'Don't you have an interrogation room or somewhere we can go?'

'Ah, to be alone.'

'To *talk*.'

'More research?'

'Of sorts.'

Fun as it was to tease her, she looked ready to explode.

He stood and grabbed his jacket from the back of his chair. 'Coffee?'

'I don't do coffee.'

'A woman who doesn't do coffee or dates. Interesting.'

'For heaven's sake, Chase, I'm not here for psychoanalysis.'

'Well, I need a drink. So if you need to talk, you'll have to humour me.'

He wove through the bevy of desks, nodding but not stopping until he'd made it through the front door. The idea was a spur of the moment, and even now he didn't know where he intended to go with it. Only that he didn't want their "talk" taking place with his squad around.

After all, there was still a possibility that she was innocent.

Yeah, right.

That was head number two talking.

Even if she didn't commit the murder herself, she was somehow tangled up in this mess. The evidence dictated it. Very rarely did evidence lie.

'This is work.' Her voice wavered.

He turned to find her hesitating in the doorway.

'There's a great bar two blocks down.' He started walking.

'I don't want a date. I want a conversation.'

'You're really hung up about this date thing.'

Her heels clacked unevenly on the sidewalk behind him. Why'd she wear the ridiculous things if she couldn't walk in them? They weren't the Stacey he imagined, the one who dressed for her pleasure not others. The shoes didn't fit. Only purpose they served was to make her legs longer. And for that, he couldn't complain, unless she broke an ankle over the damn things.

She tugged his sleeve. 'Can you at least slow down?'

'I thought you were in a hurry to talk.'

'I–'

Dull weight smacked into the base of his spine. He stumbled, her legs tangled with his, her fingers scrabbling at his back, ending any chance he may have of regaining his balance. As the ground rushed up to meet him, he rolled to protect his wrist, leaving his left elbow to crunch against the pavement.

'Shit!'

She lifted her head from his hip.

'Oh, god! I'm sorry, I'm so sorry.'

Pain knifed up through his arm and his elbow throbbed. 'Don't tell me this was another bloody scene in your book!'

She pushed herself up, and he shouldn't have noticed how the top two buttons of her shirt had popped. The woman was trying to kill him and woody was up? He was a darn sight sicker than he first thought.

'I don't kill people for research!'

He dragged his gaze to hers. 'You could have fooled me.'

He rolled onto his good arm and tried to manoeuvre into a sit, more distracted than he should have been at her fumbling fingers refastening her top. The last button popped into place and she offered her hand. He ignored it.

She let it drop to her side. 'Perhaps if you'd cut the comedy and we'd talked inside, you'd know the truth without all this.' Her arm waved at his sorry ass still sprawled like insect splatter on the pavement.

He rolled onto his knees and pushed himself onto his feet. Not the most graceful of moves, but it beat setting up camp and staying.

'Let me help you.' Again, she offered her hand.

'Oh, you've helped way more than you need to already.'

'These heels–'

'Are ridiculous. You need to stop trying to be something you're not.'

He steeled whatever patsy part of him felt sorry for the hurt in her eyes. The person deserving sympathy was yours truly. What the hell damage had she just done?

His head spun and his elbow throbbed like a jackhammer battering to break free. She grabbed his other arm, steadying him. 'Let me at least get you to a hospital. My car's just back a block.'

He shrugged her off. 'I'm not getting in a car with you. My self-preservation's not done for yet.'

'You're not very funny, you know.'

'I wasn't intending to be. Thanks to you and your footwear,' he gestured to weapons that Vic Police should list as prohibited and dangerous, 'I'll be stuck behind a desk for the next week, maybe more. That's as far from funny as an electric eel up my ass.'

'I said I was sorry.'

'Did you say that to William Huffey before or after you stabbed him?'

Her mouth opened, as if to deny it. He swayed. She clamped her lips, and this time when she took his arm he let her.

'Would you prefer I call an ambulance?'

'No!'

Her scepticism was well deserved. But last thing he needed was a bunch of ambos digging around, discovering the truth. If word made it back to the squad …

'Stacey!'

They turned in unison, her hold on him breaking.

Muscle Man. Great.

Electric blue eyes slid the length of Stacey's body. Chase's did the same, only then taking in her grazed palms and the blood-stained knee peeking through a tear in her trouser leg.

'Hell! What happened?' Muscle Man's gaze gobbled every inch of her, like a starving man presented his first meal in months. He caressed her elbow. Stood closer than necessary.

She didn't pull away.

The tendons in Chase's neck stretched like a hangman's noose about its victim.

'Ethan.' She tippy-toed and kissed his cheek. 'I tripped. Nothing major.'

'Looks major to me. Let me take you home.'

There was something too familiar about him. About the way he looked at Stacey. He was too Herculean, unshaven, with overlong black hair and even blacker eyes.

He grinned, and the white of his teeth set off a tan that defied possibility mid-winter. 'I'm a whiz at first aid.'

The sparkle in her eyes lacked reserve. 'You're a whiz at most things, but I need to take Chase to a hospital.'

'Chase?' Only then did he seem to notice Stacey wasn't alone. He glared down at Chase, as if *he* were to blame. The buffoon obviously didn't know Stacey that well.

Her gaze darted between them, as did her hand. 'Ethan, Chase. Chase, Ethan.'

Muscle Man's chest swelled as he extended his hand. Chase supported his arm and nodded.

'Broken?'

'Possibly fractured.'

His gaze returned to Stacey. 'Why don't I take you? My car's not far.'

Another winning smile saved for buffoons only. 'I can manage. Thanks for the offer, though.'

'How's research on your new book? Need any help?'

Cherry flooded her cheeks as she turned to Chase. 'Ethan's a fireman. He helped out with my character, Sebastian, in my last book.'

'Although he wasn't quite what I'd pictured when I read it.'

'He was a little unusual, wasn't he?'

'Off the wall, I'd say.' He grinned. 'But I happen to like *off the wall*.'

Again she seemed flustered.

'How about tea sometime this week?'

'Can I call you?'

'I'll count on it.' Muscle Man's teeth glinted in corny toothpaste-commercial white.

Enough was damn well enough. Any more lovey-dovey chitchat and he'd puke.

He ground his jaw. 'Time we were gone.'

Her gaze flew to his. 'Of course.'

The great lump of muscle dropped a kiss on her cheek. 'Make sure you call.'

She nodded, watching as he left.

Chase stepped into her line of sight. '*Fine.* Drive me to St Vincent's.'

She pulled back and stared through lashes so long they dragged his gaze to hers. 'St Andrews is closer.'

'Do you want to help or do I need to call a cab?' He had no intention of talking her through why the larger hospital was the better option. Why he couldn't risk being recognised at the smaller St Andrews.

'Fine.' She huffed, but she hunted her keys out of her bag. 'Can you walk or should I bring the car around?'

'You've damaged my arm, not my legs. I can walk.'

'Suddenly the big, strong man? I wasn't questioning your manhood.'

'Great. Because my manhood's just fine.'

She snorted. 'Good grief! Are you for real?'

'I was about to ask you the very same thing.' His arm burned like someone had stuck a knife deep into the bone and was slowly twisting. He clutched it to his chest and tried to remember if he'd read about injuries accelerating onset. Nothing came.

'So, tell me how you did it.'

She blinked, all wide-eyed and I'm-not-a-serial-killer innocent. 'Did what?'

'Subdued a man twice your size and then stabbed him to death.'

Chapter Four

Afusion of antiseptic and eucalypt burned Stacey's nostrils. Her chair was cold and hard, and she wrapped her arms round her body to stop the shivers from burrowing deeper.

What she'd do for a good, old-fashioned bawl about now.

Both knees burned. Blood oozed down her leg, clinging to the ripped polyester of her favourite black pants. Her palms stung. Her head throbbed. She had to be the biggest klutz on the planet. Hell, why stop there? Universe.

Although, if the idiot hadn't forced her into following him outside, the whole disaster would never have happened.

She glared at the closed curtain of his emergency cubicle, willing a thousand termites to infest his armpits. It was an hour since the nurse had led him there, but not before he'd ordered Stacey to take her disastrous presence to a universe where she couldn't cause any more havoc. The man had attitude, capital A. Was like an eel that snatched at your leg and, once attached, refused to let go.

She'd ignored every jab about her and murder. Much as there were moments she was tempted to prove him right and finish the job Shazz's ridiculous heels had started.

That was a conversation for later when she could be sure he wouldn't arrest her for assault of a police officer. She wouldn't put it past him. He was pissed enough.

Well, so was she. He'd accused her of murder, then made jokes and wanted to take her out for a drink. No wonder her inexperienced wires were tangled and she'd thought he was interested.

Much as she'd love nothing better than to go home and nurse her wounds, inside and out, she wouldn't leave until she'd set him straight. Then she could wipe the stick of him from her hands forever.

'Don't tell me you're still here?'

He may have been pale, his arm all splinted and supported in a sling, but he'd far from lost the detective-in-a-dung-heap attitude.

She pushed up from the chair to meet him eye to eye. 'How else would you get home?'

'Feeling guilty, are we?'

Regardless of blame, he had a diabolical cheek. 'Feeling crabby, are we?'

'You just sprained my arm, so yeah, I'm not spinning cartwheels.'

'It's not broken? But, that's great!' The knots in her shoulders loosened. About time today she had good news.

'Can the Pollyanna routine. The last thing I'm feeling is all bouncy and joyful.' He winced, then huffed. 'Fine. Let's get this over with.'

'Meaning?'

'Take me home.'

'So you believe I'm not going to kill you?'

He headed for the exit, barely sparing her a glance. 'No, but right now I'm too damn tired to care.'

She blinked back tears that had no right to fall. His whole dismissal and lack of belief hurt. Weird when the man was nothing but a source of information to her. And not even that lately.

She ran to catch up as he strode through the double sliding doors. 'I'm a writer, not a killer. The only power I wield is with my keyboard.'

'Evidence says otherwise. Funny, but I never saw the pattern until I read your book.'

'You read my book?' Why did the knowledge warm her and make her nervous all at once? Then his first sentence railroaded the second. 'What pattern? The fact there's a real murder similar to one I wrote?'

'No, the fact that you have three murders in your book and I have three dead bodies that match.'

You will not be sick again!

She swallowed, then couldn't help it. She squeaked. '*Three?*'

Chase stopped at the car. Dusk had claimed the sun and the wind picked up, whipping her hair about like a cat 'o nine tails. Her fingers couldn't have pushed the unlock button even if she'd held the controls in her shaking hand.

He glowered at her across the green bonnet. 'What's the plan now? Freeze me to death?'

Her chin jerked up. 'When will you get it through your

Neanderthal skull that I'm not a murderer?' Murderous thoughts not included. The man tempted her beyond belief.

She found the keys, pressed "unlock" and yanked the door open, slipping behind the wheel. The engine was on by the time he'd manoeuvred into his seat, more than a few choice words leaving his lips as his elbow bumped against the console.

She didn't offer to help with his seatbelt. He was so determined to paint her as the bad guy in this scenario that he could damn well suffer.

Finally the buckle clicked into place and he turned his blackened gaze to her. 'I'll believe you're innocent when I see cold, hard evidence.'

Oh, to bite back! But the ride would be unpleasant enough without her adding to the tension, regardless what she thought of his evidence-gathering capabilities. And her temper was too heated to prevent those bites from surfacing, no matter how much she tried to suppress them. Instead, she checked the rearview mirror and reversed out of the parking spot.

His head dropped back against the headrest and he closed his eyes. 'I'm in South Melbourne. Turn right.'

She turned left.

His eyes shot open. 'Your *other* right.'

It was that tone he used to make her feel stupid and incompetent. She hated that it worked. It always did when she was on unfamiliar ground.

In two years of marriage, Brad had it aced.

She wasn't sinking into that muddy pit once again, least of all with someone who meant nothing.

She clutched the steering wheel and gritted her teeth. 'Sarcastic as well as crabby? You might want to toss the attitude. Unless you'd prefer to get out and walk?'

'I might have to if you can't tell your left from your right.'

'How on earth do you lug that colossal chip on your shoulder around?'

He almost looked repentant. *Almost.* The slip was so brief it might never have happened.

He sighed. 'I'm tired, I'm sore and I have a killer to catch, regardless whether they're in the car with me now or not. *Please* take me home.'

Fingers from his good hand pinched the bridge of his nose and some little part of her heart softened. He had to feel like crap. Not that it excused his rudeness or his pigheaded stance on her alleged guilt. Or the blatant non-existence of an apology for all of the above. Regardless, she couldn't help but feel sorry for him. When he wasn't ragging on her there were times he appeared quite normal. Pleasant, even.

'There's a box of ibuprofen in the glove compartment.'

'I don't want drugs, I want you to do what you offered while most of my limbs are still intact. Take. Me. Home.'

And then there were times he acted like the biggest ass on the planet.

'Sure. But there's something I have to do first, and it can't wait.'

He peered through the window. 'Where are we going?'

'My place.'

His glare burned head to toe as she manoeuvred the car into her driveway.

'To finish me off? Or perhaps you're angling for that date after all.'

The engine shuddered as she cut it and shot him a look he couldn't possibly mistake. 'When hell freezes over ring any bells for you?'

For the first time since his fall she sensed a smile. 'Oh, you say that, but do you really mean it?'

She released her seatbelt, then did the same to his. 'Time to get out.'

He clipped it back in. 'I'll wait here.'

'Not if you want me to drive you home.'

His scowl returned.

She didn't give him time to cut her down again. 'I want you to believe I'm innocent and you want evidence. Well, everything you need is inside. Just give me five minutes, then I'll take you home. I'll even tuck you in if it makes you feel better.'

Blue-almost-black eyes bored into hers. Then he unclipped his belt.

Before he could change his mind, she jumped out of the car and rushed round to open his door. She didn't offer to help and he didn't ask for it, getting out awkwardly before following her up the stony path.

They passed under the bare old eucalyptus, its leaves smattering the cobbles, no doubt a consequence of the recent gale-force winds. Other trees nearby were almost bare. Autumn's frost had come a season early.

Flowers bordered either side, bedraggled and wilted, although the weeds seemed to thrive just fine. Funny she hadn't noticed before now. Or maybe, not so funny. When was the last time she'd felt the cool damp of dirt on her hands? Fed their hungry roots with blood and bone or topped up with a good dousing of water? She could barely recall.

Writing immersed her, always had, so that nothing outside existed until the moment she typed those wondrous two words – the end.

Something she should be working toward right now instead of justifying herself to an arrogant, egotistical, he-man who undermined how far she'd come the past three and a half years.

Shaky fingers scraped key against metal. Nerves from stress, not his presence.

She didn't bring men home.

Correction. Chase wasn't *men,* he was a detective and he thought she was a killer. Important to remember that.

She stepped inside and sensed his warmth at her back, his spice enveloping her as she crossed the living room floor.

'What the fuck!' His weapon was out, his stance braced to kill.

Her gaze followed the point of his gun.

'Don't shoot!' She leapt between him and the old fashioned hat stand, waving her arms, her heart pounding hard like a buffalo stampede. Yeah, right. That'd stop a bullet, no problem.

Chase didn't quite drop his gun, but his grip loosened.

Breathe.

Rubbing her palms down her skirt, she fought the wither of his glare and edged her shaky way toward the stand and the green python who'd comfortably wrapped himself around it. 'Cuddles, baby. What are you doing out?'

Chase stepped back, wide eyes darting left then right. '*That thing* is in your house intentionally?'

She ignored the nark in his voice. '*That thing* is a green tree python and, yes, his presence is intentional. He's a pet.'

Stacey sanitised her hands before touching the cool skin, sliding her palms down until she could lift him gently from the stand. His tail coiled with loose familiarity around her wrist.

The hand holding the gun twitched. Action Man was nervous? Over a snake?

'Put that thing away before you prematurely discharge all over my living room.'

His grumblings would have better suited a building site than her living room but, small mercies, he did what he was told. After taking another step back.

'I presume you have a permit?'

She willed her eyes not to roll. 'Like any law abiding citizen.'

Chase snorted and she tossed a glare his way before blocking him from her vision. Her heart racing and her spine as taut as a rubber band at snapping point, it wasn't the best time to be handling one and a half metres of pure, restricting muscle.

She steadied her breathing and focussed on Cuddles. 'How did you get out, mister?'

The answer was obvious when she reached the terrarium. The front sliding door was ajar, the lock engaged but not connected. She must have been in such a hurry before leaving that she failed to perform her morning check and recheck routine.

Sloppy. When it came to Cuddles, sloppy wasn't an option. Luckily he'd found his favourite perch rather than a way out of the house.

'I had you pegged as a cat lover.'

She lowered the python into his home, allowing him time to slither out from her arms. 'Midnight spends his days outside.'

'Midnight?'

'My cat.'

'You have a cat?'

'You can't sleep with a snake.'

It was one of those moments. *Did I really just say that?*

She closed the cage, double checked the door and all four clasps on the mesh top, before she turned around. By then the burn on her face had cooled.

'Let's get this over with.' Heart still racing, she headed for the hall.

With a final glance at the closed terrarium, he followed.

'Any more snakes that I should be aware of?'

'No, just the one.'

'One too many,' he muttered.

When she reached the door under the stairs, she stopped.

He moved in until her nostrils brimmed with spice. 'Having second thoughts?'

She bristled. Did the man have any switch other than insufferable? 'Of course not.'

The handle turned easily and she took a deep breath. The room below was sacred, private. A place where magic happened and her stories were built. Allowing Chase to see what no one else had, allowing him into the machinations of her mind, shouldn't have mattered. Nothing right now should matter, past proving her innocence.

Get over yourself, Stace.

She flicked the light switch. It fizzled.

'Damn!'

'What's wrong?'

'The light bulb's gone again.'

'Convenient.' His voice was dry, disbelieving.

Insufferable. 'Hold on.'

She stepped inside, feeling her way through the darkness at the top of the stairs before locating what she was after. Light rammed her dilated pupils as she stepped out. She screeched, raising her hands, backing away from the gun barrel levelled at her chest.

Deep breath, deep breath …

The toe bone's connected to the foot bone, the foot bone's connected to the ankle bone …

Her heartbeat slowed, not quite normal, but not quite heart-attack intensity either. The man was ridiculous, and he thought *she* was a danger?

She cleared her throat and glared. 'Seriously?'

He glared straight back. 'A precaution.'

'Right.' She resisted suggesting what he do with his "precaution" and thrust one of two torches into his hand. 'That won't help, but these will.' She flicked hers on.

'If it's all the same, I'll hold both.' He waved her forward. 'After you.'

Gun out in front, torch gripped awkwardly in his bad hand, he followed her inside. Impossible to fathom why she found the move so

Hollywood sexy. Given she was the reason for the gun. Given his distrust.

Writing detectives was messing with her head. *Mental note: make next hero a cowboy. Or better still, a sheikh.* Then again, alpha-men were as close to a turn-on as a splinter in her toe. *A cowboy, then.*

All that leather …

Teeth biting the inside of her cheek, she made her careful way down the stairs, flinching at the thump and subsequent trail of choice words behind her.

'Careful you don't shoot me with that thing.'

He grunted. 'I won't if I don't have to.'

Her torchlight wavered and she clenched her jaw. '*Comforting.*'

At the last step she flicked the switch. The flood of light into the room was immediate. She moved aside for Chase and scanned the area, trying to imagine the familiar space through his eyes.

The basement was an orderly clutter, everything she needed to make her books come to life.

The bar fridge hummed, brimming with her favourite non-alcoholic pear cider, and floral scents wafted, only just obscuring the must. She made a mental note to add more oil to the potpourri. Oh, and to change the bulb on the stairs. Although, maybe a call to an electrician would be more prudent, considering it was the fourth time this week the bulb had blown. Old house, old wiring. Time she organised those safety checks her agent recommended when she bought the place six months ago.

Her gaze roamed. Books – both research and pleasure – lined the left wall, while posters – anatomy, body language, even poisons and weapons – lined the right, along with the scrawled outline of her current book on a large interactive whiteboard.

To the side was her bragging corner – certificates and trophies, past and present awards that defined her decision to leave what could have been a successful career for the uncertainty of the written word.

Her desk and newly purchased massage chair sat in front, but it was what lay opposite that made her pause. What would Chase make of it?

Would he see it for what it was or imagine it was more? Winding a lock of hair round her finger, she tried to read his expression.

Easier to read Swahili.

It was impulse that made her bring Chase into her workspace. Would that same impulse be her undoing?

What was he supposed to look at first? Or think?

Chase lowered his gun and switched off the torch.

It wasn't just about the room; what looked like a stage bordered by thick, black drapes; books on murders and murderers and *65 Ways to Kill Your Victim;* or the dozen or so vacant eyes staring out at him from the far corner. Ten little dummies sitting in a row, waiting for what exactly? Death?

As a homicide detective, he'd seen his share of horrors. But something about this little dungeon gave him the creeps. The woman beside him appeared normal, a little ditsy, but hey, no law against that. She didn't seem anything like a killer, much as her basement raised more questions than it answered.

Miss Stacey Holland held a doctorate in Clinical Psychology. With honours. Who'd have thought? She had a brain and wrote romance. Hard to wrap his head around that. Could he add killer to that list? The more time he spent with her, the more he thought no. Then again, he'd never thought someone he trusted would turn against everything they believed to become a killer. More than eighteen months since it happened and the betrayal still stung. If he was wrong then …

A familiar shaft sliced the still-live portion of his heart.

He glanced across to find Stacey openly watching him. She blushed and dragged her gaze away.

'My victims.' She waved her hand toward the mannequins. 'I don't kill anything that has a pulse.'

'What's behind the curtain?'

'Whatever I want.' He lifted a brow and she shot him a brief smile, moving toward her desk. 'I'll show you.'

Remote control in hand, she aimed toward the stage and clicked. Whirring and creaking, the curtains opened. The lights dimmed, then a screen behind the stage jumped to life and he could have sworn he was in a multi-storey parking building. Another click and he could have been in any Melburnian suburban street. Then a carnival. Then the beach.

He watched the slow curve of her lips as she pushed up onto her toes. 'I'm a visual person, and seeing a scene helps me to write.'

The next vista looked too much like Dresden's paddock to be coincidence. Chase moved in and only then did he notice the bloody body sprawled flat against the wooden dais.

He raised his gun. 'Hit the lights!'

Chapter Five

'His name is Renaldo.' Stacey's voice quivered.

Chase was a pin-pull short of exploding. His head pounded, his arm throbbed like the devil and, instead of wallowing at home in a bubble of self-pity, he was with Psycho Snake Lady in her house of horrors.

She swallowed, her shoulders bobbing nervously beneath her top. He dragged his gaze away. Damn right she should be nervous.

He turned back toward the stage. Glassy blue eyes mocked him as he lowered his weapon. How the hell did he get duped by a hulking lump of plastic?

'You're a real nut-job, you know that?'

Her gaze narrowed 'You say nut-job, I say professional. I told you before, I'll do anything necessary to make my stories realistic. And before you get all excited and whip out your badge and handcuffs, that doesn't mean I kill real people. I use props.'

She unlocked and opened a cupboard left of the stage.

The pin standing between his temper and detonation edged closer to release. 'Are you serious?'

'Deadly.'

He'd consider the word a joke if not for the evidence. An arsenal of weapons of the likes he'd never seen before – firearms, knives, explosives, everything imaginable – methodically hung and ordered.

Waving her off with his gun, he couldn't help but notice the look she continually aimed his way, a look that harped "are you serious?". He shot a look back that snapped "hell, yeah – keep your distance or I'll shoot your ass", as he grabbed a long, curved knife, running his finger carefully over its saw-like serrations.

Not what he expected.

The pressure in his skull lessened. 'Plastic?'

'Polypropylene.' She had the audacity to puff up like a kookaburra on a wire fence. 'Each item is identical in size, length and weight to the original weapon, without the ability to cause serious injury.'

'I should arrest you, right now.'

'For what? Nothing I have here is illegal.'

He didn't know where to point first – the stage, the dummies, the deadly artillery. 'Yet, this entire set-up–'

'Shows I had no reason to kill your victim.'

'It proves nothing of the sort.' He didn't bother to curb the growl from his voice. 'The whole scenario, you, this room, smells fishy.'

'Back again with the jokes. I don't fish. That tackle I bought the other day was for a scene I'm working on.'

Chase sniffed, then centred on her weaponry collection. Not fishy so much as wet metal, like a pot left to rust in a river bed. With an element of sweetness, like burnt sugar. A smell too familiar to ignore. Disregarding the sarky roll of her eyes, he extracted a latex glove from his pocket and managed to pull it onto his good hand. No mean feat, but necessary.

'That may have been a joke,' his eyes scoured the contents of the cupboard until he found it, looping a gloved finger around the hilt before sliding it from its hook, 'but this is far from it.'

A fishing knife, cold and heavy and very, very real.

The blood coating the thin, double-edged blade was no more than a day or so old. It was dry, but not rancid. And he'd bet his badge it was human.

Which meant the weapon had a body to match.

'That's not mine.'

Stacey raised her shaky palms and backed away, as if negation and distance could separate her from the very real murder weapon and its implications.

Suddenly her head took up its throbbing again, and the scabs on both her knees began to burn. 'I'm being framed.'

Chase's brows arched like twin Matterhorn peaks. 'Does "pull the other" ring any bells for you?'

The man had a gall, throwing her words back at her. This was no time for comic relief.

He dragged an evidence bag from his jacket pocket and she watched the knife drop silently inside. Her mind whirled. Whoever planted the knife must have left something, a hair, DNA … If she could just take a look … She edged toward the cupboard.

Chase stepped in, gun and man staring her down.

She backed up and tried again. 'This is ridiculous! If I was guilty, why would I lead you right here?'

'I'm not sure I'm ready to delve into your mind and find out. From what I've seen, it's a pretty scary place.'

'Dammit, Chase! You're messing with my life. I didn't do this.'

His gaze travelled from head to toe, then leisurely back up. Her body quivered, as if his scrutiny had fingers; gentle, caressing fingers that made her want to swoon and melt.

Billowing heat rampaged over her pathetic, weak-bodied alter ego. Angry heat. Temptation to slap sense into him was only just outweighed by the fact that he still had a gun. And he'd promised to use it.

When he finished, his eyes found and held hers. 'Then you won't mind running through your movements the past forty-eight hours. Why not start with when you last opened your cupboard.'

She'd pictured him dragging her off in handcuffs, her writing cave torn apart by techies and forensics, her writing reputation ruined. Instead, he was giving her the chance to explain. There was still hope. She could still convince him to believe her. *She would.*

She peered over his shoulder and into the cupboard.

All she needed was to find the way.

God help him, he believed her.

Chase shrugged uncomfortably inside his sling.

That didn't mean he was ready to holster his gun. A killer had used Stacey's book as a manual for murder and he couldn't ignore that. She was steeped up to her stubborn porcelain neck in this mess. If he was right, unwittingly rather than by design. Either way, she had to know something. And it was his job to find out what.

Instead of following protocol and calling the knife in, he scanned the room for something to prove it was his gut and not his dick talking. To prove he wasn't mentally defending a killer because she made his body snap to attention and want things it shouldn't want.

'I think it was two days ago.'

A glance her way told him she looked as nervous as she sounded.

'Any way you can prove that?'

She arched a sculpted eyebrow his way. 'Any way you can prove when you last opened your closet?'

'You're not helping your case.'

'If I knew something that'd help, don't you think I'd share it?' Stiff fingers twisted the hem of her jacket. 'Maybe forensics will find something. The only prints down here will be mine. And now yours. If they find others …'

'What about friends or boyfriends?'

Golden curls bobbed about her shoulders. 'No one comes down here. It's private. A place I can lock out the real world and immerse myself in my book. It wouldn't be the same if it was open to all and sundry.'

'Yet you invited me in?'

Cat-green eyes narrowed. 'A necessity against your stalking.'

Ignoring words meant to get a rise, he moved toward her mannequin collection.

'When did you start *From Mishap to Murder*?'

'About eighteen months ago.'

The blood froze in his veins. 'Around the time of the Nine Knife Slasher's first murder.'

'Who says?' She strode toward him, stopping inches shy of touching distance, her eyes glued to his Smith & Wesson. 'You may be able to pick the moment he started emulating my character, but you can't say for certain when he began killing. I doubt William Huffey was his first victim.'

'William Huffey wasn't his first victim. Her name was Sara Cooper. She was twenty-nine, a secretary and mother to five-month-old baby Tom.'

Her mouth opened, then closed. No sound. Much like his old goldfish, Harvey. He almost expected bubbles to *pop-pop* out from between her lips.

'Recognise the victim?'

She nodded, then swallowed. 'The first victim in *Mishap*.' Her chin kicked up. 'I still say he's killed before. This isn't his first foray into murder.'

The idea wasn't foreign, and something he'd considered the moment he'd moved on from regarding Stacey as a suspect. *Maybe*.

Impressive that she'd reached the same conclusion.

Unless there's another reason she knows.

No.

He may laugh down Jayda's whole rhetoric on gut instinct. That didn't mean he didn't have instincts of his own.

'How'd you miss the similarities when the Nine Knife Slasher hit the news?'

'Uh, because I didn't see the news.'

Her tone was as smart as the comment. Instead of chewing her out, he let her continue. He needed the info more than he needed to rag her for the attitude. This was work, not personal.

'For the six to eight months it takes me to write a book, I'm a hermit. I write, eat and sleep my story, only coming up for air so friends don't call the coroner and start planning my eulogy.' She shot him a wry smile. 'Aliens could land and take over the world, and unless they made it into my writing cave, I wouldn't have a clue earth was in danger.'

'So, you hadn't heard of the NKS until now?'

'Heard about him, yes. Understood his MO and victimology with enough depth to suspect he was a carbon copy of the STS Killer, no.'

'STS?'

'Salute Then Slash.' She tilted her head and grinned. 'Sounds better as an acronym.'

'*Of course.*'

Her lips tightened. 'Your Nine Knife Slasher is meticulous, organised and displays an unusual amount of both patience and restraint. Much as he enjoys killing, it's the recognition he craves. And he may be done with the NKS-type murders, but that doesn't mean he's done killing.'

'You know your killers.'

'More, I know their minds. For example, how do I know Sara Cooper wasn't his first victim? Rarely will a serial murderer start on his sick path without displaying a sign that the kill is his first. The spectrum is broad, spanning from hesitation in execution, even an initial feeling of remorse, to a complete loss of control resulting in a disorganised crime and a scene left in chaos. They work up to it, experiment until they know exactly what gets their jollies on.'

He snorted. He couldn't help it.

Her chin jerked up. 'What?'

'Psychologist meets writer. It explains so much.'

'I'll take that as a compliment. Otherwise I'd have to slap you, something I'm loathe to do while you're still playing cowboy.'

Hand and gun dropped to his side. He turned, suppressing a shudder as his gaze roamed. Ten little dummies. A perfect mix of shapes, sizes, ethnicities. All bases covered. He inspected each vacuous stare until satisfied that none were real. Then he moved toward the stage.

The Huffey lookalike lay on his back, body rigid, Boy Scout pose complete with Boy Scout salute. A flawless replication of the real murder victim, down to the arbor knot in the thin wire that held hand and fingers in that salute.

His bloodstained abdomen was marked with the signature nine slashes. Circular. Meticulously placed. Something forensics stated was performed post-mortem in the real victims.

He waved his hand over the cuts. 'Real blood?'

'Of course not!' Again she gave him that "are you kidding?" look. 'I use a mixture of water, corn syrup and red food colouring. A drop of chocolate syrup gives a more venous tinge. At a distance, it's almost impossible to tell the difference, and the bonus is it's all edible.'

He lobbed an "are you kidding?" look right back. She didn't blink.

His left wrist spasmed, masking the now dull throb of his sprained arm. He winced, bracing against the sudden starburst in his vision.

Her gaze narrowed. 'Are you okay?'

'Bouncy as a border-collie in a ball-pit.' He drew in a long, steady draught of oxygen. Gotta love codeine. It just wore off too damn soon. 'Tell me about the STS Killer.'

'After you stop acting like some macho superhero and take something for the pain.'

A glance at his watch, then he waved the bloody knife and evidence bag. 'You know I have to call this in.'

The rose in her cheeks paled. Then her chin lifted. 'I know. I just hoped for more evidence on my side before you did.'

So had he.

He ignored the twinge in his conscience. Hackett would kill him. Hell, his boss had made a meal of his balls since that whole Night Terror debacle. Why should now be any different?

'Are the stairs the only way in and out of here?'

'Unless you're a mouse, yes.' She gestured toward the ceiling. 'The vents are way too small for anyone larger than pixie-size.'

He nodded, biting his lip against the brass band marching through his skull.

'I'll take you up on that ibuprofen.' Metal rasped against leather and his Smith & Wesson slid into its holster. He rubbed at the ache up his forearm. 'You can fill me in on your killer while you make us both coffee.'

Stacey's heart lamb-frolicked in her chest. 'You're not going to call?'

'Not yet.'

'Why?' She lurched back on her heels, biting her lip. Too late to drag the word back now. Last thing she needed was to push Chase so far he'd change his mind.

He flexed the fingers of his bad hand, considering her through narrowed eyes. 'Instead of looking a gift horse in the mouth, you *could* play along. Even show a little gratitude.'

'I *am* grateful. Thank you.' Pushing the hair from her eyes, her fingertips trembled against the damp of her brow. *Relief.* Although she wasn't anywhere near out of the hunter-filled woods yet. 'You're putting your job on the line for me?'

'This has nothing to do with you. I'm following a hunch. You just happen to be part of it.'

Why did his brusque denouncement sink her heart?

Her chin lifted. It didn't matter why he was doing what he was doing. Nothing mattered, past proving her innocence – the sole reason Chase was here.

'Of course. Contact between us was always about your hunch.' She knew, yet she couldn't stop from repeating the same mistake over …

She made for the stairs.

His rubber soles slapped over the wooden steps behind her, heat radiating between them before scampering up her spine.

When she shook her head it was to dislodge more than the hair from her face. 'How do you take your tea?'

'I don't. I'm a coffee man, through and through. And I'm particular.' He exhaled. 'Hot. Strong. *Sweet.*'

The headshake didn't work. Was his voice all low and lilty on purpose?

She stumbled. He caught her elbow and spice filled her nostrils.

His gaze burned, then his lips dipped with a chef's distaste of overcooked eggs. 'For the love of all sanity and safety, woman! Lose the ankle-breakers!'

She glanced down at the strappy leather criss-crossing her feet.

Shazz called them "sex on stilettos", swore they made male heads turn. Just not on her. What'd Chase say earlier? Stop trying to be something you're not?

She jerked her arm free. 'I'll have you know they're *Giaconetti.*'

'I don't care if they're Princess Leia's, can shoot death rays and will take out Darth Vader's Empire in a single swoop.' He shot her that look that made her feel ten inches tall. 'On you, they're a hazard to anyone within a five-kilometre radius. Wear something practical and less … treacherous, for god's sake.'

As if she needed his opinion. Or approval. She was done with that from any man.

Her ankle wobbled.

Dammit! Much as it galled, Chase was right. They were ridiculous excuses for footwear. Never again would she let Shazz vet her wardrobe.

All they did was test her balance and his patience and cause sexy detectives to view her with disdain. Chase had made it blatantly clear he hadn't an ounce of interest in her past his case. As if shoes would change that. Not that she wanted them to …

She had even less interest in him. Past ensuring she remained on the right side of inch thick iron bars, of course.

She held the door open. He followed her through, then closed it firmly behind them.

He held out his good hand. 'Key?'

She twisted it in the lock then clutched it to her chest. 'Why?'

'Because I need to secure what is now considered a crime scene.'

His attitude bugged her, but she got it. And that bugged her too.

She slapped the red stiletto key ring into his palm. He flinched.

Just desserts, buster.

'Trying to eliminate my other arm?'

Her gaze darted beyond his sling. 'Not intentionally.'

Before his scepticism wangled into her conscience, she whirled around, shucking her shoes en route to the kitchen.

If she'd written this moment, her detective would have done the same – namely doubt her and confiscate the key. Chase was a detective foremost, and just doing his job. Like he'd been doing from the moment he'd formed his suspicions and laid plans to trap her. Kiss and all.

Lucky she'd realised in time.

Lucky she lacked the interest to allow it to happen again.

Chapter Six

Coffee, hot and strong, filled Stacey's nostrils, drowning out the more subdued aroma of lemon and mint.

Curling her legs beneath her, she sagged into the black and white plush of her chaise lounge, hugging the blood red cushion to her chest, resisting the urge to burrow further into the back of her *chaise de relaxation* – a splurge and gift to herself after signing her first book contract.

This afternoon it was failing abysmally to live up to its name.

After locking her writing cave, she'd retreated to the bedroom, leaving Chase to clatter around her kitchen alone. More than a few calming breaths later, she'd tended her knees and traded her black pants for tracky-daks. The tattered outfit she'd tossed into the trash, wishing she could toss the entire situation along with it.

She shuffled to get comfortable, tugged her hot pink slipper socks up past her ankles. The dressing on her knees pulled at the tender skin, but at least it was clean and covered and in a position to heal. Unlike her nerves.

'Tell me about the STS Killer.'

Unfathomable blue eyes watched from across the jarrah slab coffee table. Waiting.

'His name is Travers Blake.'

Chase savoured a mouthful of caffeine as if it were god-sent. 'Sure you won't join me?' He waved the *Bug Me & I'll Write Your Sticky End* mug before savouring another draught.

Given the circumstances, she should have picked a different mug. One minus the visuals of a fly swat and squashed fly. Not that Chase had treated her to more than an arch of his brows when she handed it over. His look had since changed, and was now as close to a grin as she'd seen since their gruesome knife discovery.

She shook her head.

He closed his eyes and inhaled. 'It's good.'

'For high blood pressure and insomnia, yes.'

His eyes shot open and he frowned. 'You really don't drink coffee?'

'I did tell you.'

'You say a lot of things, doesn't mean you mean them. When you said you didn't do coffee, I thought–'

'–it wasn't about the coffee, it was about not having coffee with you?' All his games. Yet despite their situation, he was still playing. She clutched the cushion closer. 'I'll let you figure out which.'

'So, why keep coffee in your pantry if you don't drink it?'

'I may not drink the stuff, but I have friends who do.'

He rolled his shoulders and gritted his jaw, eyes darting sideways to Cuddles safely coiled around his favourite terrarium tree stump. 'You're sure that thing can't get out?'

'That thing has a name. And yes, I'm sure Cuddles can't get out. You watched me check his enclosure. Twice.'

He glanced sidelong at the terrarium again and she couldn't help but grin. 'Don't tell me the big bad cop's afraid of an itsy, bitsy snake?'

'There's nothing itsy and bitsy about that thing. And I absolutely refuse to call it that ridiculous name.'

'He's making you nervous.'

'Nerves have nothing to do with it. I happen to have a healthy dislike for anything slimy and slithery.' He checked his watch, his gaze narrowed and unimpressed. 'Describe Travers Blake.'

Slimy and slithery, my ass.

He'd probably never touched a snake in his life. Nice to know he checked his facts before spouting his views. Let's hope he approached work differently.

Withdrawing a notepad, he balanced it on the couch's arm, pen poised.

Back to business. Of course.

No time for bickering or setting him straight on snakes. Time was running out. Soon Chase would be forced to call his squad, and they needed a lead to the real killer before then. Unless she wanted to remain their prime suspect. No point deluding herself Chase could – or would – protect her otherwise.

The urge to leap up and race out of Chase's orbit, or better still, disappear from the face of the earth, was strong. Stronger, though, was her inclination toward survival and a life beyond this shit of a day.

'He's–'

'Oh, my god!' He jumped out of his seat just as a skinny black tail disappeared through her kitchen door. 'You have rats!'

Did the man know nothing about animals?

'You just scared the crap out of my cat.' She barely spared him a glare as she took off in search of her skittery, less than social baby.

He followed. 'No way was that a cat.'

'Keep your voice down, or you'll scare him all over again.'

'Seriously?' His breath fanned her neck.

She stopped, thrust her elbow backwards and couldn't help but smile when it contacted with taut muscle and dragged an air-filled *oof!* from his lungs.

'What the–'

'Shh!'

She headed for the fridge, and lifted Midnight out from behind it, glowering at Chase, daring him to say but a word. For once he kept silent.

Sensible man. This time.

Tense claws gripped her chest and she winced, cooing and stroking in an effort to settle the quivering body. Seems the big bad man liked cats as much as he liked snakes. More proof that he definitely wasn't the man for her.

Wherever the thought came from, she tossed it the hell back.

When that hot, fiery hole freezes over!

She had no use for men. Least of all the joking, control-freak kind. Lesson delivered compliments of her ex.

'How'd you know where he was?' At least he was whispering, although it didn't stop Midnight from trying to scramble up her shoulder toward safety.

'He likes the warmth and the hum of the motor. It probably reminds him of being in his mother's womb.'

'I'm not surprised he needs the warmth. Where's his fur?'

'He's a sphynx. They don't have fur.'

'Then what's the point?'

'That is the point. He's allergy-friendly.'

'That explains it.'

'Explains what?'

'The weird pets.'

Was he for real? 'Anything else? My pets are weird. My writing cave is fishy. My shoes are wrong. What about my furniture? My house? Or perhaps my hair? Is it too blonde? Is my skin too white? My ass too big? All of which are none of your damn business!'

Midnight's claws were drawing blood beneath her top. He needed away from the big bad man, and truth? So did she.

She left Chase standing there and headed for the back door. Outside was Midnight's enclosure, a mesh-enclosed area filled with runs, tunnels and hidey-holes all designed to keep a cat safe and entertained.

'A kingdom for a cat. Impressive.'

If he didn't stop with the comments, she'd deck him. Hell, even if he did, she still wanted to deck him.

'Isn't he allowed outside?'

She bit her lip and released Midnight, who zipped straight into his igloo.

'More judgements?'

'Call it curiosity.' His grin did not affect her knee ligaments. Or her heart. Not. One. Bit.

'I rescued him from a shelter just over a year ago. The workers there believe he was never allowed out as a kitten and has none of the skills necessary to survive outside. He may end up being able to cope, but I'm not willing to take the risk. Hence, this place.'

'That's dedication.'

'No. It's what you do when you care about something. It's called love.' She stepped out of the enclosure and waited for him to do the same before locking the door. 'Let's get back to Travers.'

She made for the living room, the brash heat across her back consequence of his closer-than-necessary presence every step of the way.

'Yes, let's. And just so you know,' his lazy drawl glazed over her skin with the warm slide of aromatic oil, 'your ass is perfect just as it is.'

Chapter Seven

'Travers Blake is twenty-four and the oldest of three children.' Stacey avoided the pair of twilight blue eyes and thoughts that their owner considered her ass perfect just as it is.

She swallowed. 'His brothers are twins, one's an architect, the other a business systems analyst. Travers never wanted to leave school. Much as he hated student-life, the thought of living in the real world was daunting. He started out as a secondary-school teacher and continued to study psychology part time until he qualified as a student councillor. He attempted, and got away with, his first homicide a year later. A vengeance killing, after his then girlfriend was attacked by her ex. One murder under his belt, he discovered he enjoyed it too much to want to stop.'

'You talk about him as if he's a real person.'

'He *is* real. In my head. In my book.'

'Sounds a lot like overkill.' He grinned. 'Pardon the pun.'

'That's why I'm the writer and you're the detective. Our visions of the world are artichokes and aardvarks.'

'Stacey-speak for chalk and cheese?'

'You could say that.' A familiar fire stoked her blood. 'You live in whatever reality the world hands you. I get to dream and plot and build my own.'

Her vision turned inward as she smiled. 'My characters are children of my imagination. They have lives, histories, good memories and bad. They scrape their knees as toddlers and as adults they bear the scars. Most of their lives will never make it onto a page but they tell me anyway, and I listen. Because every detail, every fall, is a part of who they are and what they will become. An interconnecting web that breathes life and sensation into what is more than just a two-dimensional character in a book. They are someone the reader will either love or hate, someone they'll cheer for or call to get the justice they deserve.'

'Writing's your passion.'

Air whooshed from her lungs. *Understanding.* He'd finally got it.

She met his gaze. 'It's the most important thing in my life.'

Awareness buzzed – the hot crackling of dry tinder under a fiery blaze. Her head felt fuzzy. Light. She sensed comprehension the likes of which she'd never expected to share with a man, least of all this surly detective.

Chase pushed up from the couch and strode toward the buffet. His eyes riveted on its contents, on the far wall, anywhere that wasn't her. 'I thought the deal about writing was you make it all up. Now you're saying you hear voices? Sounds decidedly cuckoo.'

For one magical moment she'd thought he got it. Got *her.*

Wrong. Proof first impressions were more trustworthy than second guesses. Chase was just a guy who thought being funny was a turn-on. Maybe true for some women, but not one who'd experienced the sad side of funny and survived.

'Why should I be surprised?' Her throat cracked. He turned and she ignored the unspoken question in his eyes.

Nothing to see here. Take your winning smile and witty comments and move along.

Deep breath. 'Once Travers started killing, nothing short of death or incarceration would stop him. A stance that cemented when the woman he'd killed to protect left him for another man.'

Chase seemed about to speak, then his gaze shifted and he moved back to the couch.

'And?' His brow arched until it disappeared beneath a sweep of nutty blonde.

'You read the book.'

'I did. But I want your take.'

'Because?'

'Because something in your killer attracted mine. I want to know what.'

She rolled her eyes, if only to mask the havoc his words had in her heart. Questions refusing to budge, like whether she was responsible. Whether all those deaths were on her. 'When you put it like that …'

'This isn't one of your stories, Stacey. It's my kind of real. That goes for the consequences. How much you cooperate now determines how much leniency you get when I call in my squad.'

Swallowing did nothing to dislodge the rock in her throat. She cleared it, then swallowed again.

If only she drank coffee. Addictive, blood pressure raising, insomniac properties aside, she needed something to relax. The usually effective lemon balm tea wasn't helping. And alcohol wasn't the answer when a mere sip sent her headway into the land of the lightheaded.

And a possible dependence on either scared the living crap out of her.

Chase appeared under the caffeine's effect. Or perhaps it was the ibuprofen. His shoulders spanned half her couch as he sank back into the cushions, legs crossed at the ankles. 'What else do I need to know?'

She inhaled the waft of his brew's rich aroma. Just the fragrance made the steel in her shoulders soften.

The steel in her chest remained.

'Everything about Travers is in my book. Your killer is a different matter.' She tugged at a curl, staring beyond Chase's shoulder at the Old Mother Hubbard teapot on the buffet.

'I've only scanned the details of Huffey's murder, and perhaps if I studied the others my profile would change. But from what I've seen, I'd say the killer is organized, aged somewhere between late twenties or early thirties, isn't particularly social but has learned to mask it, and lacks imagination and creativity. And most definitely, he's killed before.'

She dropped her hand into her lap. Her fingers curled around the cushion corner and tightened. 'One thing I know for sure. What he ultimately seeks is recognition. Which means that murder weapon in your evidence bag won't remain alone for long. There'll be plenty more where it came from unless this bastard is caught.'

Coffee dregs caught in Chase's throat.

A bout of coughing and one glass of water later, he unearthed his voice again. He sank back into what had to be the most comfortable couch in the Southern Hemisphere and stared at the woman scrunched up on a ridiculous monstrosity of a recliner that belonged more to Marilyn Monroe's boudoir than a wacky writer's living room.

Her gaze left her buffet and a line of ridiculous teapots, including one that looked too much like her rat-cat to be coincidence. Why wasn't he surprised? 'You got all that, how? Criminal Minds?'

There was that look again. As if *he* were the one with all manner of screws loose.

Imaginary people weren't whispering in *his* ear.

'I watch and love the show, but no. It's impossible to write a killer unless you understand a killer's mentality. My studies helped.'

'Psychology?'

'That, and a degree in criminology.'

Lucky his mug was empty so this time there was no splutter. '*You have a double degree?*'

'Almost.' Her eyes sparkled as she did that cocky, kookaburra thing again. 'I sit my final exam in two weeks.'

He felt his jaw slacken and snapped it shut.

One degree was a revelation, two was … what was it? *Outrageous? Impossible?* Stacey Holland was, quite simply, an airhead. A whirlwind on legs. Legs so delicious, he wondered how well they'd spread round his hips.

Where the hell did that hair-raiser come from? He palm-slapped his forehead. A spin-off from pain and painkillers. Had to be.

Did nothing in the world make sense anymore?

Yet … If he thought about it, her analysis of the killer was so close to his own it was as if she'd reached into his mind and yanked it out. Then there were her characters, regardless of whether they talked to her or not. They were so believable, so real, that some nut-job had decided to emulate one.

Her smile downturned. 'I get it. You can't believe I have a degree.'

Not just the degree. The intellect.

He chucked the thought. He needed her help, not hostility. And she didn't need the truth. 'We're off topic. How about you tell me who had access to your manuscript before it was published.'

Notepad and pen ready again, he waited.

She opened her mouth, then clamped it, moistening her lips. His gut tightened. That wasn't all. Denim had little give where it counted. He twisted his body as if to write more comfortably. A fiction. He was far from comfortable.

The distraction in her wide green eyes showed his weakness had gone unnoticed.

'I know what you're asking, and I know why, but I can't imagine that anyone I know would use my story to commit murder.' Her voice wavered, her shaking hands hugging a blood-red cushion to her chest.

'It's something we have to consider.'

The skin across her cheekbones tightened. 'I know. But it doesn't mean I have to like it.'

She sighed, shifted, winced as the loose fleece of her track pants chafed at her raw knees. Her thumb and forefinger arched across her temple, massaging the pressure points. Seems he wasn't the only one whose head resembled the rumble of a tram along its tracks.

She dropped her hand and trained her weary eyes his way. 'There's my agent, Rita Hayden. Anyone who worked on my submission at Thrasher Publishing. That includes my editor, Beth Samuels, my assistant editor, Des Whittaker, and their PA, Kelly Price. Oh, and the three judges who read my entry into the Heartstopping Moments Competition in the US.' She trailed her fingers along the edge of the cushion. 'That's about it, as far as I can remember.'

'It's a start.' His scrawl was barely legible. Then again, he didn't need a throbbing wrist for that. 'What about family? Friends? Boyfriends?'

'None of the above. I don't share my stories with my nearest and dearest until they're one hundred per cent ready for consumption.'

Was she being deliberately cagey? Not that he wanted to know for any reason other than for the case. 'Your boyfriend never pushed to read it? After all, I imagine there were parts of the book he inspired.'

Parts that inspired his thoughts even now as he watched a scarlet wave wash across her cheeks.

'Why should I be surprised?'

'Meaning?'

Strawberry curls bounded about her shoulders like irritated bilbies. 'I write fiction. That means the love scenes along with the characters *and* the murders ... They're. Not. Real.' Her voice was low, her words slow and punctuated as if speaking to a young child. Or someone a bit slow on the uptake.

Before he could rustle up a response, her lips pursed and she tilted her head. 'Is this your way of discovering whether I have a man in my life? Looking to become a contender, perhaps, *detective*?'

She had to be joking. 'I doubt I'd survive the experience.'

With the glare of a .30-30 Winchester, she lifted her chin. 'Some might say I'm worth the risk.'

'Well, they're either braver or more foolish than I.' He edged back into the couch. 'I'm not angling to be anyone's *anything*, so you can rest safe in your kooky, crazy, cat-lady world.'

The clamp of her lips was accompanied by a loud rap outside.

He pushed up and unsnapped his holster. 'Expecting anyone?'

She dropped the cushion she'd hugged like armour to her chest and unfolded from the recliner that very possibly was one, or even two, real live zebras in another life. Then she proceeded to pad past him in socks so pink they probably glowed in the dark. 'Don't you think you're overplaying this a little?'

'Perhaps. If we hadn't just found a very bloody murder weapon in your basement.'

Her hand froze mid-air, pique transforming to panic. 'Should I be worried?'

'I don't know. But it doesn't hurt to be wary. You're safe while I'm here.' He grinned. 'Although I doubt the reverse applies.' The joke was meant to calm her not ruffle her feathers.

He could just as easily have tossed another cat-cutting remark her way, for all the calm she displayed. 'That was supposed to make you smile.'

'Next time try something funny.'

He clamped his weapon over his heart. 'Boy, oh boy, woman. You don't mince words.'

Her shoulders squared and she seemed to gain two inches. 'Would you rather I lie?'

Magnetic pools of green dragged him in. He felt their pull, felt his body's response, making him the liar, because he did want to be somebody's something. For just a moment. Now. So that everything shit in his life could fade away beneath a sea of lust and her magnificent body.

The rap echoed louder the second time. '*Stacey Holland?*'

He jolted back to reality and whispered. 'Recognise the voice?'

She shook her head.

Her arm shuddered beneath his palm and he squeezed. 'Let's do this together.'

They moved in unison, he leading with his Smith and Wesson, her by his side, body rigid and trembling.

Just shy of the front door, he murmured instructions into her ear, the rich fragrance of honeysuckle almost overwhelming him. He tightened his grip around his weapon and reluctantly let her step forward.

'Who is it?'

Shoes shuffled over the weave of her smiling sun welcome mat and then stilled.

Nothing.

Then a loud throat clearing shattered the silence.

'Melbourne police, Ma'am. Please open the door.'

Chapter Eight

Chase dragged his gaze back from interrogation room one.

Despite the accusation in his partner's eyes, he couldn't erase the image of the slumped figure cradling her head in her arms.

'Who called it in?'

'Anonymous tip. And before you ask, we tried to trace the call but it bounced from so many towers, the trail looked like a pinball machine on speed.'

Other circumstances, the analogy would have made him smile.

'She didn't do it, Jayda.'

'You know this, how?'

'Instinct.'

She snorted.

He bristled. 'You're not the only detective in this squad with gut feelings.'

'I'm not sure it's your gut talking.' Her gaze volleyed toward Stacey. 'Pretty, isn't she?'

He resisted another look. 'I hadn't noticed. She is, however, a royal pain in my ass … and arm.' He waved his sling in the unlikely event she missed his meaning. 'But that doesn't change the fact we've got nothing to hold her on.'

'Which is why we have to let her go.'

'Good.'

'She can't go home until forensics have finished with the scene, and you know as well as I do that letting her go now is no clean bill of innocence. She's a person of interest in the Nine Knife Slasher murders, so regardless of whatever you've got going on, keep what's in your pants out of it.'

The geyser in his blood bubbled toward explode. He swallowed it back. He needed his partner onside more than he needed the vindication.

He forced a smile to his lips. 'Jealous much, Jayda?'

'Delusional much, Chase?'

It wasn't the first time he'd been accused of it. And this instance was less amusing than the last.

He grabbed his jacket. 'If there's nothing else–'

'Chase! Ass. Office. *Now.*' Hackett's bulbous face poked through the doorway, his glare as ominous from a distance as it was up close.

The day was racing from bad to unbearable. When a Detective Inspector ordered a subordinate into his office with even half that tone, rarely did it end well.

He downed a couple of painkillers, dry. Necessary to dull more than the pain in his arm. 'What's up his butt?'

'At a guess, he's pissed you're sleeping with a suspect. And when he sees your arm, he'll be pissed all over again.'

'Dammit! I'm not sleeping with her. The woman's danger on heels and, even if she were my type, mixing work with play is like pouring hot oil on a Grand Prix racing track – a fender-bender waiting to happen.'

Her look said she suspected otherwise. Of course, she couldn't conveniently forget their *almost* night together.

'That was a one off and a mistake. We both agreed.'

'*Detective!*'

Jayda raised two perfectly sculpted brows. '*Go.* No one keeps Hackett waiting and survives.' Her lip caught between her teeth as she tilted her head. 'I may not agree with what you're doing, but I've got your back. I know how much it sucks to be on the outer and, until the Night Terror, we've always been straight with each other. We can reach that place again. I trust you, Chase. I hope you know you can trust me too.'

With timing that mocked, tremors swept up his arm. Avoiding her gaze, he nodded, then turned toward his boss's office.

As if he didn't have reason enough to feel like a heel for lying, Jayda had gone and given him more.

Laughter was the Durant trademark, not bleeding hearts. And he'd spent a lifetime perfecting the act every time his heart threatened to make him *feel*.

He was so goddam tired.

Hackett had disappeared back into his corner office, and was no doubt crouched behind his desk, teeth bared and ready to pounce.

Air scalded his lungs when he dragged it in. He slipped into his "take no prisoners" saunter, plastered a smile to his lips and entered the lion's den.

Anywhere else, a round face and jolly demeanour were firm friends. Not here. Hackett never looked anything but a variation of pissed, spanning from "you'll keep" to "prepare to be hung, drawn and quartered". Today his expression clocked somewhere beyond the latter.

Chase pressed his lips into a grin. 'How about those Hawks last night?'

Reference to Hackett's beloved footy team and their all-out win didn't so much as dent his mood. A sign the exchange was not about to go well.

Hackett scowled. 'What's with the arm?'

'Sprain.'

His throat rumbled. 'Fan-fucking-tastic. Hathaway's off on some relationship retreat with the missus, half the squad's down with a frigging chicken flu virus-thing, and now you're off fieldwork because, what?'

'I tripped.'

'You *tripped*.' Fingers yellowed from years of nicotine abuse gripped the arms of his chair as he pushed out of it. 'Don't tell me it involved Little Miss Murder out there.'

'It–'

Hackett's palm shot up. 'I said, *don't* tell me. Just keep it in your pants, Durant. Last thing I need is the OPI stomping all over my nuts because one of my detectives couldn't keep his under control.' He scratched at five o'clock stubble that was fast approaching midnight. 'Where's your weapon?'

The second arm and pavement had connected, he'd known this moment was coming. Knowledge didn't make it any easier.

He could argue, but desk duty was better than no duty at all.

The holster refused to unsnap and with every second his boss's complexion deepened. Finally it gave beneath his shaky grip. Metal clanked against wood as he dropped the .38 onto the desk.

Hackett eyed it and nodded. 'Bring Thomasz up to speed on the NKS and glue yourself to that desk.' He inclined his head to the doorway. 'Light duties until you're cleared by a doc.'

Hackett's words sucked the breath from his lungs. 'Is that necessary?'

'Why? Gotta problem with getting cleared, Durant?'

His chest squeezed. Any tighter, his ribs would shatter. 'No, Sir.'

'Didn't think so.' Hackett flipped open a file, shuffling papers, adding to the collage littering his already littered desk. He glanced up. 'Why are you still here?'

Chase clenched his jaw against splurting something he and his career would regret. He turned heel and left the door to slam behind him.

Could the day get any frigging worse?

'They said I'm free to go.'

He braced to meet a flutter of dark lashes.

Seems so.

'Need a lift?'

Her Pollyanna smile was as innocent as a raincloud on a sunny day. It made him want to throw things – like the sling that had whipped his whirlwind into a tornado. But that wouldn't win kudos with Hackett; solving the case would.

That required information. And someone willing to act as chauffeur.

He met her smile with his own, and a nod.

'I need dinner and answers, in that order. Think you can manage it without adding to the body tally?'

Chapter Nine

He drew deeply on the heady mix of nicotine and tar.

Savoured.

Drew again, then snuffed the half-smoked butt into the ground before dispensing it into a plastic bag.

Nasty habit. A killer of one, in fact.

Should quit.

But why quit something that gave so much pleasure? And if such pleasures won him what he desired …

The wind picked up, salt and sea soaking his senses. He inhaled, relished the moment, the anticipation of what was to come.

Wide, terrified eyes followed his every move.

His mind flew to the words, and the woman who wrote them.

Once subdued, he fastened the mouth with fish hooks as one might fasten the seam of a dress before sewing. The victim was conscious when he began his gruesome task, feeling every prick, every puncture, until the pain became too much and, blissfully, he passed out.

Delicious.

What a glorious mind. Almost as glorious as her delectable body. Both of which would soon be his.

He licked his lips, tasting the terror; the adrenalin-fuelled panic that charged the air.

A grin spread across his mouth and he plucked the first hook from the bag at his feet, turning to the canvas before him.

He may not be the original artist, but this was a masterpiece all the same. So very different from the Nine Knife Slasher, but wasn't that why he was drawn to her? Her imagination. A compliment to his own.

At his feet, a fish swam circles in a lidded green bucket. Oblivious of its fate. Unlike the pathetic bugger cowering against his chains.

He pulled the upper lip taut from around the tight gag and stared into the brown bug-eyed stare.

'Now, now, just a little prick. You'll hardly feel a thing.'

Chapter Ten

Stacey glared across the glass dining table.

Chase swiped his mouth with the back of his hand and grabbed his last wedge of spicy meat-lover's pizza as though this were any ordinary evening; as though they were two friends sharing a meal and he wasn't sitting opposite someone who wished he'd choke on his next chunk of salami.

His ribbing about her links to the murders was wearing thin.

And now this. Banished from her home.

Chase had tapped his foot, glanced at his watch – *obsessively* – and scowled as she'd done the whole chicken-without-a-head thing, readying the place for her absence. She'd scowled back, determined not to allow his tough-guy attitude to rattle her. Her subsequent flustering further proof that merely thinking something didn't make it so.

She'd looked in on Cuddles – triple checked the terrarium clasps and front sliding doors. Midnight had refused to come out of his igloo, hackles raised at the sight of the impatient male behind her. Stacey didn't blame him. If she could've crawled into the cat's hideaway and escaped, she would have.

The kitty litter needed changing, food and water bowls filling. She'd left enough for a couple of days before securing the cat enclosure. No way would they lock her out of her home for longer.

With barely enough time to pack essentials into an overnight bag, she'd grabbed her laptop, notepad and props for her next scene. She was then hustled out of her home and into Chase's for a continuation of his interrogation. Where the hell did he get off? Despite his partner's stern "don't leave the city" warning, she was still a free citizen. She had rights.

'Careful the wind doesn't change.'

Her gaze bounded back to his. 'Huh?'

'You've been hurling daggers at me for the past ten minutes. Do you plan to continue or will I have to fight you for that mouth-watering veggie feast?' He reached for her pizza and before she could stop herself, she smacked his hand and slid the untouched box out of his reach.

One day she'd slap that infuriating amusement from his face just as easily – when she didn't need a cop in her corner, much as the "in her corner" part of that statement was a stretch.

He relaxed back into his chair, all sprawled and sexy. How was it possible to dislike a man your body wanted in every way imaginable?

She blinked the thought and every erotic, tempting image away.

'Sarcasm? I took you for smarter than that.' She made her gaze stroll slowly over his body. To make him squirm, not her. It didn't quite go as planned. She grabbed her water and knocked back more than half its contents, then swept her lips with the back of her hand. 'You could do with a diet cleanse. All that animal flesh is making you testy.'

His non-reply bugged her more than one of his less-than-witty comebacks. He cocked a brow, reached for his lager and took a swig.

The liquid moistened his lips; beer had never been so appealing. She dragged her gaze from his mouth and scooped up a slice of pizza, closing her eyes to give in to unadulterated pleasure. Her stomach rumbled, protesting at having waited so long.

'That's better. You need to eat.'

Her eyes pitched open as an explosion of tomato, basil and mozzarella rolled across her tongue. Swallowing, she jabbed at him with what remained of the slice.

'Don't pretend this is altruism. It'd be disastrous for your case if I collapsed from over-exhaustion or under-eating.'

'You don't think I can care, one human being to another?'

'I doubt you want to. Not when you're so stuck on using that humour of yours as a foil.'

His right eye twitched. Oh, yes. She'd hit one helluva nerve.

'Says the girl who doesn't date.' He pushed up from the table, all pounce-ready and predatorial. 'What are *you* hiding from, Stacey?'

Stilling her need to fidget, she rested back in her chair and breathed. *In. Out. In again.* Fingers tented, her inner psychologist regarded him. 'It bugs you, doesn't it? That I'm not interested.'

'Delude yourself all you like.'

He began stacking the plates and cutlery onto a tray. No mean feat one-handed. It was hard not to admire his determination, even while she resented his tenacity when it came to her and dating. Dog-and-bone syndrome. Stacey Holland wasn't anyone's bone.

'Unaccustomed to rejection, Chase?'

'This isn't rejection so much as denial. One day I'll demonstrate the extent of your lack of interest in me.'

The shiver up her spine was from cold. It was late. A wintry night. That's all.

'I should go.'

'We're not done yet.'

'You may not be, but I am. I've given you my insights. If you need anything else, we have that wonderful beast, email. No reason for us to meet again.'

A poor excuse for a brush-off. Clumsy at best. At worst? She'd leave tonight with no reason to return.

Chilli-salami protested in Chase's stomach.

He added her glass to the tray as she slipped into her jacket. Doubtful she was afraid of him, so it had to be her reaction to him that made her want to run.

Amusement was tempered with something more basic. 'Where will you stay? You can't go home.'

Her look questioned his intellect. Common sense made him do the same.

Damned if she didn't make him fumble, make him lose sight of himself, and he was at a loss. *Why her?*

'I'm going to a friend's.'

He yanked his mind back to reality and Stacey plucking an imaginary hair from her sleeve.

'Is she expecting you?'

A singular quirked brow said she'd seen through his question. Not that it mattered whether her friend was female or male.

'I'm always welcome, day or night.'

'Call first.'

'I'll call from the car.'

He touched her arm. 'Call so at least I know you're expected.'

'Such concern for my welfare.'

He was no less surprised than her. Then again, it made perfect sense – she had info relevant to his case. The case needed her.

Despite her gibe, she dug her mobile from her bag, the fervour of her actions dislodging his hand. She turned away, scrolling through her contacts.

He didn't make a pretext of clearing the table. Technical difficulties aside, he had no intention of pretending not to listen.

'Hey. It's me.' Mobile to her ear, she toyed absently with a lock of strawberry gold. 'It looks like rain outside.'

What the hell? It looked nothing of the sort. What was with the weather report?

Lowering her voice, she strolled toward the balcony doors and stared out at the sparkle of city lights.

From his end, the conversation made no sense. It didn't stop him from listening in and trying to change that.

'That's right. Just for a few days … *What?*' She glanced back at him, brows knitted. 'What kind of bugs? … Crap! … How long? … Aha … Really?'

The square in her shoulders dropped as a sigh escaped her lips. 'Sounds decadent. You're a lifesaver.' Her reflection grinned. 'Yeah, I'll add it to the list. I'll pick you up in an hour. Aha … The *what?*' Her green eyes found his in the glass reflection.

Her voice dropped. 'An uncategorical disaster I have no intention of repeating … Sure, when I see you. *Later.*'

She lowered the hand holding the mobile, her eyes still trained on the view.

He joined her. 'Problems?'

'Nothing an exterminator can't fix.'

He stepped back, hands raised. 'Should I be worried?'

She turned. The corner of her mouth quirked, glinting her eyes. 'Tempting as that thought is, the exterminator's for termites, not you.'

'That's a relief.'

'Mmm.' She glanced at a chunky blue watch that looked suspiciously like a kid's cartoon character. 'Time I was somewhere else.'

'Where?'

'Persistent, aren't you?'

'I know what I want.'

Her eyes met his, raspberry flush dusting her cheeks. She looked away. 'Albert Park.'

'That's ten minutes from here. I thought you had an hour.'

'Careful. Eavesdroppers seldom hear good things about themselves.'

'On the flip side, eavesdropping is a great source of information. Turns out we have more time than you thought.'

'Or less. I have stuff to do on the way.' She scoured the room and snatched the remains of her pizza before making for her bag and the front door. 'I'm sure you'll let me know if you need anything.'

The woman moved fast when she wanted to, or maybe it had something to do with her more practical choice of footwear. The fluoro orange runners may have screamed ridiculous, but they were less so than the killer stilettos that had been his downfall earlier.

Her fingers were already fumbling with the lock when he came to his senses.

'I still have questions.'

She thrust a business card in his hand. 'Email them.'

'I prefer face-to-face.'

'And I need to work. I've a book that won't write itself and an editor waiting for it. You catch the bad guys, I just write them. Remember?' Somehow she and her overnight bag made it over his front doorstep without mishap. She glanced back. 'Goodbye, Chase.'

She even made it down the front steps in one piece.

He let her go. Let her think she had her way.

Time enough to show her she hadn't.

Chapter Eleven

Twilight pinks, reds and oranges bathed Port Phillip Bay and the body tethered against the jetty's peeling green lamppost. Battered. Bruised.

Chase diverted his gaze back to the beauty of the skyline. 'Brings new meaning to the term "gone fishing", doesn't it?'

Medical examiner Rod Bearinger – or "Teddy", as he was called by his colleagues – peered over half-moon specs. His look said he didn't get the joke.

Hell, neither did Chase. But it was either lighten the mood or lose his breakfast.

He'd seen his share of death. It was part of the job. He hunted killers. Studied their victims' remains day in, day out. Repetition that should have bred immunity.

Stacey's printed pages caterwauled through his mind. A story yet to be finished and already it had made its way into the employ of the killer. One who'd followed her as she shopped in Hook, Line and Sinker two days ago, the very day he'd caught her purchasing wares identical to those used on the battered remains before him.

The wind riled, the once gentle lap of waves now an angry crash against the shoreline. Sea spray hissed through the wooden slats soaking his trouser leg and the legs of the dead man.

He looked up. Jayda ducked beneath the taped barricade and walked the long pier toward them.

Red hair whipped about her shoulders as she glanced his way. 'I thought you were relegated to desk duties.'

'I am. But no way am I dropping out midway through a case.'

She nodded, as he knew she would. Any detective worth anything would feel the same.

She turned toward the other man. 'What've we got, Teddy?'

The stern in Teddy's gaze softened as he returned her smile over his cane's brass T-handle. They connected. Two of a kind. Not a funny bone between them.

Sometimes a laugh was all that stood between sanity and losing your grip. A regimen he was too intimately familiar with not to follow.

Watching your mother die right before your eyes would do that to a person.

'Our victim is Dean Michaels. Age forty-five. Resident of Crow's Nest, approximately five kilometres north of Sydney, according to his New South Wales driver's license.' Teddy passed her a clear evidence bag containing an open black leather wallet.

Jayda glanced at it, then passed it to him.

Teddy gave a throat-clearing cough. 'I'd estimate he's been dead around thirteen hours. That'd make time of death around oh-five-hundred.'

Chase looked up from a photo very different to the bruised and bloody remains before him. 'Cause of death?'

'Asphyxia.' Teddy's gloved finger indicated dried blood on the side of the slumped head. 'Ante-mortem he received a blow to the right temporal lobe, not fatal, but strong enough to cause unconsciousness. Thick bruising around his ankles and wrists suggests he was bound with rope. I found a couple of nylon fibres on his sleeve which I'll send to the lab for analysis. His lips were sewn together with fish hooks. Given the lack of precision of the far left hook, I'd say it was inserted while he was still compos mentis. Mercifully, the poor soul lost consciousness soon after. Bruising on the nose and tearing around the mouth indicate someone pinched his nose while he struggled to open his mouth and breathe. A losing battle, I'm afraid. It didn't help that a Koi – a species of Carp often found in Japanese water gardens – was rammed down his throat while he was still alive. Within a minute he would have lost consciousness, after five or six his brain cells would have begun to necrotise.'

He lifted the victim's shirt, revealing deep purple bruising along the back. 'Lividity suggests he was untied post-mortem and left on his back for at least six or seven hours before he was moved here and rebound, this time with fishing wire.'

Much as his mind railed against the possibility, facts were facts. This murder was too prescriptive. Too identical to Stacey's manuscript to be coincidence. *Again that word.* Slim chance there were two psychos mimicking her books. He hated showing his hand, but he needed to know for sure.

'Anything to suggest this could be the NKS?'

Two sets of eyes spun in his direction.

'Other than both crimes being committed by some sick individual? No.' Teddy shuffled from one foot to the other, leaning heavily against his cane. 'The NKS sedated his victims and performed his cutting post-mortem. This killer doesn't appear to have cared whether his victim was awake or unconscious when he applied the fish hooks. The first death was ritualistic; the second, sadistic.'

'So the perpetrators are different?'

'I can't say for sure, but there's no evidence to support the theory of identical killers here.'

Jayda half-smiled. 'Thanks, Teddy. Let us know if you find anything.'

To anyone who didn't know better, she'd let Chase's question pass unchallenged.

She grabbed his arm and – *guide* wasn't quite the word – *carted* him away. 'What was all that about?'

'Just an idea.' He would've crossed his fingers, only she still gripped his arm. 'The NKS seems to have disappeared, and now another killer's come onto the scene? I guess it's wishful thinking that Melbourne is too small to produce two sickos in such a short space of time.'

Her hand dropped from his elbow but her stare held, as if trying to uncover the hole in his bucket of lies.

Guilt niggled. They were partners. That meant sharing theories, whether tested or not. Only, this was more than just a theory. It was another shovelful of dirt burying Stacey deeper into the footprints of a murderer. He knew she was innocent. Unlikely that Jayda or the rest of homicide would share his point of view. Which meant holding back on key evidence and theories until he had something more to go on. Which meant not sharing with Jayda until he had more definitive proof. How much more definitive than Stacey's written words he wasn't willing to stipulate.

Of one thing he was certain – the killer wasn't finished just because he'd finished re-enacting Stacey's first book. Now her work in progress was fair game.

And when he was done there, what next?

'Chai?' Shazz's head poked around the bedroom door.

Stacey raised her right index finger and nodded, the fingers on her left hand continuing their symphonic trail over the keys. Her groove was back, inspiration driving the scene from her mind onto the page. She didn't choose the time, it chose her. And she knew well enough to make sure she listened when it did.

Lucky for her, Shazz knew it, too.

The *click clack* of her keyboard, like a clock marking the seconds, melded with the hum of traffic five stories below. Horns blared and tyres squealed. Then came the sirens, her subconscious failing to register whether they were linked to fire, police or paramedics.

Blood pumping, she dropped her hands to her lap and stared at the screen. Satisfied was an understatement. *In the Throes of Murder* promised to be her best book yet.

She flexed her shoulders, rubbing the pull of muscle at the back of her neck. It was true, a writer could write anywhere; but ergonomics meant the difference between pleasure and a proverbial pain from her head to her butt. The apartment may have been plush, but its furnishings were chosen without a writer's needs in mind.

'One hot drink sans caffeine!' Shazz burst into the room brandishing a small tea tray and spice that taunted Stacey's nostrils. 'Thought I'd wait until the typing stopped before I poured.'

Stacey blinked. Dusk had cloaked the sun, darkening the room. The luminous green numbers beside the bed showed it was three hours since she'd sat down and flexed her imagination. The pass of time was a blur; the result, gold.

She wrapped her hands around the warm ceramic, eyeing the pile of choc dipped cookies on the tray next to Shazz's espresso. 'You're a lifesaver.'

'Yeah, I've heard that.'

'And about as modest as a red lace teddy from Victoria's Secret.'

Brows plucked and painted beyond all recognition waggled. 'I do my best.'

Stacey chuckled, hot liquid filling her nose, setting off a round of splutters. She daubed her face with a wad of tissues and they shared a grin.

'Oh, by the way, I found this on the living room floor.' Shazz dropped the envelope Stacey had collected from her PO Box that afternoon onto the desk. In the drama that was today, she'd forgotten all about it.

Giddy lightness filled her chest. Something nice in a day full of not so. Perfect timing, as if he knew she needed it.

She slipped the thick yellow paper under her keyboard to read and savour later.

'Any news from the exterminators?'

Shazz offloaded the tray before snagging her mug and a cookie. 'Landlord says a couple more days and he should get the all-clear. Mind you, I'm not complaining if Jagger allows us to continue staying here. Who knew he owned such a swish place?' Her gaze circled the white-washed walls and Mediterranean-style prints. She popped the entire cookie into her mouth. 'Wha' 'bou 'oo?'

Years of practise helped with translation. 'Who knows?' Her eyes closed briefly as she sipped and swallowed. *Bliss.* 'When is a crime scene no longer a crime scene?'

Brows raised, Shazz dropped onto the bed.

Stacey sipped again. 'When it's not.'

Shazz groaned. 'If you're thinking of branching from novels into comedy, don't.'

'Not good?'

Her friend shook her head. 'So bad it's funny, but not in a good way.'

Stacey grinned, selected the smallest cookie on the plate and nibbled. Heat zinged across her tongue. 'Aunt Milly's Dark Chilli Choco-Sensations?'

'Of course. Is there any other?' Shazz grabbed a second helping of the best choc-chip cookies in Australia, perhaps even the world, and contemplated. 'What's the latest with your hunky hero?'

'He's about to realise the case isn't the only thing drawing him and Brianna together.'

Shazz tut-tutted, rolling eyes the same shade as the chocolate in her mouth. 'Not the book's hero. *Yours.*'

She frowned. 'I don't have a hero.'

'What about your dishy detective? Didn't he save you from time in the slammer?'

She barely acknowledged the cliché and its ridiculousness.

'Firstly, he's not *my* anything. Secondly, I'd say innocence played a pretty big part in my being cleared.' She glowered through the steam in her mug. 'And stop with the "OMG, really?" expression.'

Shazz snorted. 'Is there really such a thing?'

Stacey chomped the remainder of her cookie, her mouth determinedly closed.

'Well, have you at least called him?'

The crumbly, sticky, decadent mess clogged in her throat. She downed it with a swig of chai and mopped the tears from her eyes. 'Why would I?'

'Oh, I don't know. To see how the case is going, how his arm is healing or, just putting it out there, whether he'd be in for another bout of research, this time of the personal kind.'

'I'm not interested.'

'Could've fooled me.'

'I don't date, Shazz.'

'It was three years ago, Stace. Don't let the actions of that dickless turd rule another three years.'

Stacey pushed at images that threatened to undermine how far she'd come. She would not be controlled; she was not that person anymore.

'I rule my decisions and what my future yields. I want to write, entertain my readers, be the next big New York Times bestseller. There's no room for anything else, least of all a man who's too busy joking his way through life.'

'So, if he didn't joke?'

'I'd still kill this conversation.'

The silence roared across her eardrums.

Shazz took a long sip of her drink, then speared her with a look that left her nowhere to run. 'Life's not like one of your characters, Stace. You can't just hit the "kill" button when things get tough. And you shouldn't. Because the good stuff tends to follow the bad.' She scooched over and rested her palm on Stacey's knee. 'I'd hate for you to miss the good stuff. Not all men are going to be like Brad.'

Stacey dragged steel into her lungs. This had nothing to do with her life and the men who'd thrown stones at it. Brad. Her father.

This time when she inhaled, her breath wobbled. 'And not all women need a man. Simple.' She raised her palm as Shazz's mouth opened for more unsolicited wisdom. Much as her words came from love, understanding even, she just didn't get that Stacey was happy. She didn't need a man for that. 'Two days ago I told Chase to email if he has questions. He hasn't. End of story.' It was. Along with the hole that yawned in her stomach.

James Bond's theme pealed from her bedside table. *Thank you, universe!* Welcome interruption.

Shazz glanced at the mobile's caller ID then up at her. 'Chase isn't important but he's in your contacts? With his own ring tone? Interesting.'

Sudden warmth invaded. Warmth she neither wanted nor needed. 'Not interesting. He was research. And there are others who have the same ring tone.'

Shazz's eyes found hers. 'You going to answer it?'

'Nope. I told him to email.'

The look she got this time shrieked "seriously?" Shazz snatched the phone up before she could think to react and answered on speaker.

'Stacey Holland's phone. Who may I say is calling?'

'Detective Durant.' Impossible to stave off the slither of heat at the sound of his voice. And oh, she tried. 'Is she around?'

With a definitive head shake, Stacey sliced her hand across her throat.

Shazz blinked, innocent as a feather-covered feline in a chicken coop. 'What's it regarding?'

'Confidential police business.'

'Of course it is. One moment.'

She grinned as she passed the phone. 'Detective Durant for you. He says it's important and *private*.' She winked.

Stacey mouthed the words, *You are dead to me! Dead!*

With little other choice, she accepted the phone. 'Detective?'

His chuckle was richer and warmer than the dark chocolate on her tongue. 'Come now, Stacey. After that kiss, don't you think we've reached first name basis?'

She waved her hand and glared at Shazz. *Go!*

Her friend had the audacity to laugh. *I knew it!* she mouthed back.

'*Stacey?*' The word was breathless, hot. Any possible answer caught somewhere between the back of her throat and the heat between her thighs.

He found his voice again. 'The silent treatment? I didn't know our relationship had progressed so far.' Again he chuckled, and the deep rumble was like a stroke over her stomach, and lower. 'Or is it just wishful thinking on your part?'

Chapter Twelve

Stacey's teeth ground like white chalk over a blackboard.

Oh, to drag Chase down a peg or five! If she hadn't vowed never to see him again, she'd storm right over and demonstrate her thoughts on sharing anything with him, least of all a relationship.

'Am I still on speaker? I'd hate to say something meant for your ears only.' Laughter oozed from his voice, like lava from a volcano.

Shazz grinned, winked, then – after Stacey all but gnashed her teeth at her – she finally left the room. Stacey glared at the mobile screen and jabbed the speaker to off. Too late. The damage was done.

Realisation hit. 'You *planned* that?'

'Despite your ever-absent sense of humour, I'm sure your friend was amused.' He sounded positively early-bird-catches-the-worm chirpy. Damn him!

'Oh, she'll be more than that. You can be the one to fend her off when she starts co-joining diaries, booking up weekends and holidays, planning double and triple dates.'

'But you don't date.'

'Not for the want of her trying.'

'Don't tell me. She's the friend with the fancy shoe collection.' His voice was one big smirk. 'Seems I'm not the only one who thinks it's a waste.'

'What's a waste?'

'You out of the dating scene.'

Her eyes rolled over every point of the compass. 'Because a woman can't possibly be happy without a man?'

'Because your company is too good not to be shared.'

The way he said it – the way he didn't pause but just blurted it out – she could almost believe it. If she wasn't already *au fait* with male manipulations.

'Why are you calling, Chase?'

'I need to see you.'

Again a tremor rippled through her. She focussed on the past. 'I can't.'

'Can't or won't?'

Damn, it was almost as if he knew.

'I have a deadline.'

'So do I. It's called "catch a killer before he strikes again".'

'You don't need my help for that.'

'But that's where you're wrong.' Papers rustled, and before she could protest, he continued. 'With your books, what comes first, writing or acting out your murders?'

The question was so left field, it took a moment to shake the remnants of their earlier conversation. Oxygen helped.

'I write them, act them, then edit. Why?'

'Do you know the dates you wrote each one?'

'Not off-hand. I'd have to check my archived files. *Why?*'

'Just a hunch.'

'Care to share?'

'Meet me and I'll explain.'

'I told you, I can't.'

'And I'm telling you, you don't have a choice.' Exasperation doused the customary oozed-amusement. 'Dammit, Stacey. Don't you get it? My squad doesn't believe you're innocent. The evidence is packed against you and the only reason you're still free is they don't have enough on you to make an arrest. Not yet. But I'm sure if they keep digging they'll find something.'

Air was suddenly scarce. 'I'm not a killer.'

'Circumstantial evidence says otherwise. And before you knot your knickers into a macramé wall hanging I'll tell you that I think it's deliberate. He's been targeting your stories. Yours and no one else's.' Something slammed in the background. A book? A fist? 'Aren't you curious why?'

'I–'

'Push aside whatever reasons you have for wanting to avoid me. If you're as innocent as you profess, prove it.'

The VW Beetle shuddered into the curb. Chase cringed. Hubcaps ground against concrete until Stacey jammed on the brake and they both jerked against their seatbelts. The cringe transformed to a wince. Her skills on wheels weren't much better than her skills on heels.

A quick scan of the street yielded no familiar faces. It was still early morning – not yet nine. His shoulders relaxed as he unclipped his seatbelt. It was safe to get out of the car.

He snorted. *Car.* A subjective description that failed to capture the ridiculousness of "Sidney". Yep, her ride had a name. And a fluffy pink steering wheel. This was not the vehicle she'd used the day she tripped into him. It was like one of those hippie campervans, only kiddie size. Psychedelic. Floral. Dictating sunnies and a bottle or two of beer before your eyes were ready to take it all in.

'Why are we here?'

She was already out, tapping runner-clad toes on the pavement, glaring at him through the open window as if he'd just burst the balloon that was her day. The handle dug into his palm as he wound up the glass, dragging his attention from the mould of denim over her thighs. He shoved at the car door until it gave, then joined her on the street, clenching and unclenching the fingers of his bad hand. 'I thought it'd be fun to reminisce over one of our many encounters.' He grinned.

The humour was lost on her. Again. One day he'd make her laugh.

He shook his head, glanced up at the blue and black banner for Hook, Line and Sinker. That's where his focus should be. A case. A killer. A life in the force or … not. A diagnosis that could set his path either way. Matters of far greater importance to expend energy and time over. What did it matter if one romance writer found him funny or not?

'A body was discovered last night at St Kilda pier. His hands were bound with fishing nylon, his lips skewered shut with a row of three fish hooks, and a fish was thrust halfway down his throat. Sound familiar?'

She gasped, swayed. He grabbed her arm and she leaned into him. His grip tightened.

'*How could he know?*' Her lashes fluttered so wide it was a wonder her eyes didn't pop out of their sockets. 'How did *you* know?'

'There was a printout of your chapters in the basement. It was evidence.'

She stiffened. 'Don't you need a warrant or something?'

'You're worried about privacy?'

Her eyes clouded. 'I don't know what I'm worried about.' She swallowed. 'He knows what I'm writing. As I'm writing. That scene is less than a week old.'

'Understand why I need you now?' His fingers unwrapped from her shaking arm and he stepped away. 'To help me find this guy.'

The breath she took was a visible bracer. She nodded toward the store. 'How do we do that here?'

'My team already has copies of the store's security and I've spoken to the attendant who served you that day. All that's left is for you to walk me through your movements.' He led her in the front entrance and paused just inside. 'Which way?'

'If you have the security footage, why do you need me?'

'To follow more than your footsteps. To understand why you chose that particular method of murder. To get into your mind and figure out why the killer wants to do the exact same thing.'

She considered him for seconds that seemed longer; then, mouth set, she turned. 'This way.'

Of its own accord, his gaze rested on the soft swell filling the back of her jeans.

He dragged his eyes northwards. 'Why the fishing reference?'

'Alex's father fished.'

'Alex, being?'

She stopped so suddenly he had to grab her shoulders to avoid bowling into her. 'This is a spoiler for *In the Throes of Murder*, so whatever I tell you remains between us, right?'

'I can't promise that, Stacey. A murder investigation trumps keeping your plot secret.'

Her look said she blamed him for the violation, for dragging her out of her safe, oddball life and into the "throes" of a murder investigation. She blamed *him*, not the bastard littering bodies across

Melbourne.

He let it go.

She huffed. 'Alex White is my antagonist. His mother disappeared when he was five. We're never told, but the underlying belief is that his father killed her and disposed of her flesh as fish-bait.'

'Anyone ever tell you, you have a sick mind?'

'Readers want reality and I deliver. I won't apologise if it offends your sensibilities.'

They stopped in aisle five, fishing tackle.

The moment he thought he had Stacey Holland picked, she yanked the rug out and confounded the crap out of him.

No need to work her out, Einstein. You just need info. His gaze ambled over row after row of fishing reels, the haphazardly stacked rods in the corner ... anywhere but on those accusing green eyes and impatient-pressed lips. 'I'm guessing there's more to Alex's story than pleasant days spent fishing with dad?'

Her gaze followed his. 'I have no idea why his father took him. Perhaps it was a show of control, or perhaps he thought leaving the boy alone could only lead to mischief. Either way, Alex would sit a small distance from his father, silent and still. One slip and he'd get a clip round the ear, *if he was lucky*. If not, his father would bind him to a tree with fishing nylon, sometimes until the day's end. Other times, if he was particularly drunk or angry, he'd gag him and leave him there overnight.'

'Nice guy.'

'*Not.*' She grimaced. 'In terms of victimology, Alex targeted men, mid to late forties, receding black hair, brown eyes, on the podgy side, beer gut and all.'

He quirked a brow. 'His father?'

She nodded. 'That leads us to methodology. Alex restrained and silenced his victims, binding their wrists with fishing line, fastening their lips with fish hooks. He was enacting revenge on his father over and over. Regaining control of his life.'

'You've created a sicko.'

'A *fictional* sicko, no different to any other you'll find on the net if you type in "serial killer".'

She was indignant. Cute. A little wacky. But her appearance didn't match the horror that had to fill her mind. He was intrigued. And despite every instinct warning him against it, he wanted to know more.

'You're different.'

Her expression was wry. 'To what?'

'How I imagined you.'

'I can't help the way you see me. And I won't pretend to be something I'm not.'

With a mulish chin lift, she glared as if he'd asked her to do just that.

Spunky and sexy. A bucketload. Add to that magnetism. She drew him in. Made him want to feel her lips beneath his again. He swayed in.

'Need any help?'

The male voice scratched through Chase's reverie. He jerked back. Stacey did the same. The stacked fishing rods wobbled at her back, then scattered to the ground.

Daydream over, the klutz was back. The woman needed a licence to breathe, let alone move.

Stubby fingers caught a rod mid-fall. Burt Walters. The over-eager shop assistant. A Cheshire Cat smile puffed out between his cheeks. 'H'lo again, dee-tective.'

His squat, round face and guileless expression towered above Chase, making him at least six feet plus tall. His breadth was a fair match for his height. The man was too helpful. Too interested. And required more digging than a standard background check just to see what he was hiding.

Everyone was hiding something.

Rods clattered back into their stand and Stacey rubbed her palms up and down her thighs.

Burt's eyes glinted, tracing their movement.

'We're done here.' Chase inserted himself between them. 'Time to go.' He slapped a business card into the other man's palm. 'If you see or remember anything unusual, you know where to reach me.'

'Sure thing, dee'tective.'

Yep. Way too obliging, shrewd eyes a mismatch for that happy-go-lucky demeanour.

With a hand on Stacey's waist, he propelled her out of the man's line of sight and onto the street.

She shook free. 'Now that we're done–'

'Uh, uh, wishful thinking.' He raised sling and arm. 'I need a driver and you're the reason. So, congratulations, Stacey. You've got the job.'

'Never heard of a taxi?'

'Never heard of staying on the good side of the law?'

She arched a brow. 'Dabbling in blackmail now, are we?'

'More like mutual incentive. I get out from behind that damned desk and you get to help clear your name.'

'I thought that was your job.'

Stacey glared at Chase.

All she wanted was to slap the confounded smugness from his face. 'Why do I feel more manipulated than mollified?'

'Molli-*what?*'

The low buzz of a mobile escaped from his pocket.

'Going to get that?' She didn't wait for an answer. Rummaging through her bag, she headed for the car, a million indignations clambering across her tongue. She looked up. *What the–?*

'Hey!'

A helmeted head popped up from behind Sidney's psychedelic frame.

Keys clattering in her hand, she leapt forward. 'What are you doing?'

The figure froze, then sprinted to a nearby motorcycle, slinging a leg over as the engine roared to life.

'Stacey!' Chase's voice faded to nothing as she sprinted toward the leather-clad figure who'd been breaking into her car.

Up close, Sidney appeared to have sustained no obvious damage. Not that she could see amidst the paint's vivid swirls and strokes. The motorbike – was it a Harley? – screeched out of the parking lot and onto the road.

She scrambled into her seat. Chase yanked his door open. 'Stacey!'

'Get in!'

He leaned across and grabbed her arm. 'Stop! Don't insert that key!'

Only then did the wheels in her brain kick into sync with her thudding heart. She'd written a scene just like this. In the still unfinished manuscript Chase had read as evidence.

Metal scraped against the ignition and her hand fell into her lap.

Air around her seemed suddenly sucked of oxygen as she fought for breath.

'Car bomb?'

Chapter Thirteen

The hissed words froze on Stacey's lips.

Chase battled his expression. 'I doubt it, but let's check anyway.'

The reassurance in his smile failed. She could see how much it cost him. Her eyes flitted as far as peripheral vision allowed. Not far without moving her neck. She wouldn't, just in case …

He was wrong. Had to be. This was an overreaction and she'd slap him for it when it was past. Her heartbeat faltered.

Just for now, she'd do as he said.

Chase circled the car, then ducked from view. She heard a grunt, a scrape of gravel. Needles pricked her back, the muscles so taut it seemed they'd snap if she had to hold still for much longer. Her head began to spin. His face popped into the rearview mirror. She tried to gauge his expression, tried to work out whether the nausea in her throat was warranted. *Impossible.* The man was a poker whizz.

He moved away, mobile in hand. The conversation was short. Expression grim, he approached her window and slowly opened the door.

'How're you doing?'

'Is it safe?'

'A couple of checks inside then we'll be sure.'

His mobile trilled and he glanced at the screen before turning it off and slipping it into his pocket. Dropping to his haunches, he leaned in, his hand brushing her ankle. Her leg twitched.

'Try not to get too excited. Save it for later.' His brows waggled, but the accompanying smile lacked his normal cheek. She could have kissed him for wanting to set her at ease. Only her lips were dry and she wouldn't – couldn't – move.

He ducked and next thing she knew his head wedged between her ankles. The heat was immediate and inappropriate. Before she could steel the heady rush of blood, he'd checked under her seat and was up again, checking the ashtray, the glove compartment, the CD player. Then his hand was on hers.

'You can get out now.'

She tried to move. Failed. Lead weighted her legs and whatever messages flowed from her brain were lost en route to her limbs.

'I can't.'

She'd never thought to see understanding in his eyes. Or to need it so much. He squeezed her shaking hand. 'Much as I love the role of hero and saviour, carrying you one-handed isn't going to happen.' Supporting her feet, he encouraged her to turn and face him. 'Let's do this together, okay?'

She'd barely nodded before his hand scaled her thigh, rounding her hip, sliding beneath her butt, pulling her forward and up. Her feet struck the ground and she lurched into him.

'Gotcha!'

Warmth flowed into her trembling limbs. His free hand wrapped around her waist, holding her tight. She didn't try to break away, didn't want to. Despite knowing she should.

The sound of screeching tyres achieved what her willpower couldn't. A car door slammed and she pulled back.

'*What the hell, Chase?*'

His redhead partner. What was her name? Jaya? No, *Jayda*.

Colour crept across Chase's cheeks. He stepped back, releasing her as though she were the very bomb they'd feared.

'Bomb squad's on the way and you're necking a suspect?' She grabbed them both and dragged them clear of the car.

Two marked vehicles pulled up and Jayda barked orders at the emerging officers, instructing them to clear the area and set up a five-hundred metre perimeter until the experts arrived. Which they did as soon as the words left her lips.

Bomb squad's white, unmarked van parked just shy of the blue and white taped perimeter where a small crowd had begun to gather. Three men piled out of the back, followed by a black robot the likes of which would fit seamlessly into any sci-fi flick. As it rolled toward her car, a mini tank readied for combat, reality set in, along with a shaking she had no power to stay.

What've you got yourself into, girl? Writing was supposed to be the safe option, a place where havoc existed through words alone. There was safety behind her keyboard, no need for limelight or fanfare until the likes of Ellen or David Letterman wanted her as a guest on their show. What didn't exist in all that was a madman intent on bringing her books to life, or worse, intent on blowing her and everyone within a five-hundred-metre radius to smithereens.

Hugging her now shivering body, she worked at stamping warmth into her frozen toes. Whatever sun had been out was now swallowed in a billow of thunderous cloud. The car park was empty, eerily so, as if in prelude to some disaster. An omen in any writer's mind.

Please, don't make it so.

Chase's expression was as thunderous as the sky and she couldn't bring herself to move closer and turn all that barely suppressed wrath her way. She bit her lip and prayed for the heavens and her car not to explode.

Chase didn't even glance her way as he headed toward the men beside the van. He avoided Jayda, or perhaps it was the other way round. Impossible to read what was going on, though it was clear that something was. When he returned, he maintained his distance, unwilling still to break the silence. Or look her way. She followed suit. Their distance was best. For the case. For her.

A lifetime of palpitations battered her heart until the robot rolled and dipped its way back to the van. The all-clear was given and within minutes it was as if nothing untoward had taken place. The tape came down and the crowd dispersed until only she and Chase and the officers remained.

Jayda stalked toward them.

Chase watched her approach, *affected*. As if his partner meant more than work. As if she'd caught him, pants down, cheating. Her eyes were the green of rainforests; her lips the kind of raspberry that tempted a man to lose himself. She'd seen it, written it, too many times before. Bet *she* looked and acted sexy in heels. *Where the hell did that thought come from?* And jealousy? Over a man she didn't like, let alone want?

He couldn't even bring himself to make eye contact, only had eyes for *her*.

'What the hell kind of game are you playing, Chase?'

He jammed his good fist into his pocket. 'She was scared. I was comforting. No crime in that.'

'There is if she's got your dick on a lead.' Jayda said the words softly, calmly, as if Stacey weren't even there.

Had she looked? If she had, she'd see Stacey was far from a femme-fatale, far from able to lead any man's dick *anywhere*.

Everything in Chase's demeanour said he agreed.

Through narrowed lids, steel invaded the blue of his irises. 'My dick's capable of thinking for itself, thank you. And it's nowhere near this case or the *witness*. Innocent until proven guilty, right Jayda?'

'I'm saying this not only as your partner, but also as your friend. You're treading a wire-thin fault-line, Chase.'

'Concern appreciated, but unwarranted.' His hand was out of his pocket now, clenched at his side, his shoulders and back ramrod taut, uncompromising. Subtext: back off. 'What's the deal with the car?'

She glanced toward Stacey's psychedelic beast, brows raised. 'Someone tried to jimmy the bonnet open but it looks like you disturbed them before they could do whatever it was they were planning to do.'

Chase dragged his hand down his face. 'Prints?'

'They were wearing gloves.' Stacey didn't realise she'd spoken until both sets of eyes hit her —one accusing, one lacking the warmth they had, was it only ten minutes earlier?

She swallowed. 'They wore a helmet, leather biking gear and gloves.'

'Any idea who'd want to harm you?' Jayda's gaze bored into her, as if Stacey should know. As if she considered Stacey were behind the incident. Behind everything.

'Until recently, I'd say no one. But now …' The trembling started again, and this time it brought along tears. 'I–'

Chase's expression softened, as if he cared she'd just lost everything in her life that was safe, that was certain. His hand curled around hers and she hated that it made a difference. That she couldn't pull away.

Jayda didn't even pretend not to notice. She glared at their coupled hands, then at Chase. 'I hope to hell you know what you're doing.'

'She's the victim in this. Our killer, or whoever that guy was, is still out there.'

'You're too close, Chase.'

'If you're suggesting my judgement's compromised, think again.

My judgement's just fine.'

'I'm not saying anything that Hackett won't when he hears.'

'From Hackett, I get it. From you? I thought you knew me better than that. Guess the whole trust bullshit you dished out Monday avo was just that. Bullshit.'

Jayda flinched. As if his words struck with the precision of a boxer's blow.

Then she pulled the blinds on her expression. 'Trust is a two-way street, Chase. Remember that next time you decide to keep things from me.'

Her lips pursed. 'Stevens has witness descriptions of the offender and the bike's partial numberplate. I'm sure he'll pass them onto you. We've got everything we need from the car so it won't need to go into evidence. Meantime, you might want to consider the definition of light-duties and focus on mending that arm, not flirting with pretty murder suspects.'

He watched his partner storm off, avoiding what would surely be more daggers aimed his way from the woman beside him. Feisty had always been his weakness. Another reason he'd thought himself interested in Jayda all those months ago. Not so now.

That dig about trust. Did *she know?* His hand trembled, as if in warning.

He ditched the thought. Not possible. She would have said. She was just fishing, nothing more. She knew something was up but wasn't sure what. As long as she didn't start digging …

He didn't check if Stacey was still beside him; he sensed her presence, and didn't stop to ask why or how she had that power.

'We should go.'

Pain slammed his right bicep. 'Ouch!' He turned to the woman who'd delivered the punch. 'What was that for?'

'You and your overactive imagination almost gave me a heart attack!'

Was she for real?

'I just saved your life.'

'From an imaginary bomb threat? I don't think so.'

'I was looking out for your safety. A little thank-you wouldn't hurt.'

'If you hadn't dragged me here under the pretext of investigating, there would have been no bomb, real or otherwise, to *save* me from.'

'You don't think this psycho could have planted something at your place? Your friend's? He wanted under your car's bonnet for some reason. Whether to tamper with the mechanics or plant an explosive, I don't know. What I do know is the threat was very real.'

As was the scene in her book. A bomb rigged to explode the minute the key turned in the ignition. An image that clutched at his throat and squeezed.

The rose drained from her cheeks. Then the hue in her eyes darkened to deep sea green.

'You're freaking me out again. Stop it!'

The quiver in her voice said she wasn't as tough as she'd like him to think.

Her chin jerked upward. 'I'm done here. I have to get back to my book.'

'Do you think that's wise?'

'No wiser than sticking with you!'

She turned toward the car. He grabbed her arm, felt the shaking she was trying so hard to hide. 'Stacey, slow down. *Stop.*'

She didn't pull away. She didn't face him either.

He loosened his grip, more a caress now than a clasp. 'If you begin writing and a body turns up, how are you going to feel?'

'I can't stop writing because some sicko thinks it's fun to kill like I do in my books.'

'And you can't keep writing when you know it'll mean the end of someone's life.'

'It's not fair.'

'Life rarely is.'

She turned to him then, her eyes wide and moist. She was scared. He got that. What he didn't get was why he felt the need to hold her until the fear left her eyes and they filled with other more rampant emotions.

He dropped her arm. 'I'm on your side, you know. Much as you may not believe it, I don't want to see you hurt.' He searched her expression, watching the angst slowly seep away. 'Are we okay now?'

There was only minor hesitation before she nodded.

He swallowed, then nodded back.

'Wait here a sec. I need to speak to Stevens before we go.'

It didn't take long to get the info he needed. The partial plate rang bells. Either that or he was a convert to the ideology of coincidence.

As if the universe disputed the fact, his mobile rang. Her third call in the past hour.

'Gracie. What's up?'

'Why have a phone if you never answer the stupid thing?' His sister's voice shrilled like a hungry cockatoo pecking at an empty birdfeeder. The way she always sounded when they'd gone longer than she liked between calls.

'I was kinda busy when you rang. But I'm not now.' He glanced at Stacey leaning against her car. Not so much a lie as a stretch of the truth.

Gracie sniffed.

His focus snapped back to her wavering voice. 'Are you okay?'

'*No.*' Another sniff. Then the rustle of tissues and a loud, nose-clearing blow.

'Hey, sis. What's wrong?'

'Jagger.'

Just the name and pressure ballooned in his chest. 'What'd the bastard do this time?'

'He wants money.'

'No way!'

'He's JJ's father.'

'If we're talking labels, you forgot to include scum and lowlife.'

'He may be a crap husband but he's always been a good dad. He said they'll kill him if they don't get their money.'

'Who's they?'

'I don't know. Some loan shark or bookie, I guess.'

'He'll never learn if you keep bailing him out, Gracie. He's made his own bed. Let him get goddam comfortable in it.'

Sniff. 'What do I tell JJ when he asks why I did nothing to stop his dad getting hurt, or worse, killed?'

'That his father would sell him if it meant another bet on the horses.'

'I won't be that person. I won't turn son against father, no matter what his crimes.' Her voice caught like burs on his skin. Chafing. Wearing at his resistance the way she knew it would. 'Please help him, Chase.'

'As a brother-in-law or officer of the law?'

'Both. If not for me, do it so JJ has a dad.'

He loved that Gracie rooted for the underdog, that she was all about saving the bird with flu, the cat with the crazies, the dog with a tail that wouldn't wag. Anyone and anything was fine with him, except her scum-of-the-earth ex-husband.

'Please, Chase.' Damn! That wheedly voice always got him. Like a needle excavating for just the right nerve. And she knew it.

'Fine. I'll see him. I can't promise any more than that.'

'You're the best brother. *Ever.*'

'And the biggest pushover.'

He could hear her wobbly grin all the way through the line.

'Thank you. I may not want to be with Jagger, but that doesn't mean I want him dead.'

He wasn't about to admit he felt the same. A life was a life, no matter how low, and it was his job to preserve all manner of life, at all costs. Regardless. *Uphold the good.* Australia's equivalent of the LAPD's *protect and serve.* He meant to follow both mottos.

His gaze roamed to the hippie-Beetle the moment Stacey looked up, eyes wide, raw. Something shifted in his chest, nabbing his breath, squeezing. She pushed away from the car and his legs moved of their own accord, bringing them closer.

Focus. On anything but her face. That expression, the vulnerability.

He inhaled, deep, heard Gracie do the same at her end. 'Happen to know if Jagger still has that old motorbike?'

'I guess. Why?'

'Remember the licence plate?'

'JAG457.' Gracie's tone sharpened like the cutting edge of fresh paper. 'Why do you want to know?'

'Curiosity.' The memory of Stacey's comment last time he'd used the foil almost made him smile. Only this time he wasn't the cat.

He stopped just short of Stacey, avoiding the question in her gaze – and was that need? – a realm of possibilities.

He switched his mind back to his sister's words and ended the call.

Seems Jagger had more to explain than his re-emerged gambling and debt problems.

'Remind me why we're here.'

Stacey flicked the right indicator, turning into the first free parking space. There weren't many. The cream and red-brick building rose up on their left, blazoned with the giant white letters above the entrance. ZOO.

'I don't believe I told you.'

She cut the ignition. 'Then maybe you'd like to enlighten your chauffeur.'

'Or maybe not.' He reached for the door and pushed it open. 'Wait in the car.'

'Or maybe not.' She jumped out and made for the entrance, locking Sidney, leaving man and car behind.

It was an age since she'd visited Melbourne Zoo – *too long* – and thoughts of remedying the oversight hit with nostalgia and a welcome wave of relief.

He caught up with her at the front barriers. 'Dammit woman, you're stubborn.'

'Pot and kettles and all that.'

'Inspired, Stacey.' His voice was as derisive as a blatant eye-roll.

She dug in her heels and whirled to face him. 'Want me around? Well, you've got me. Take it or leave it, Chase.'

She saw the moment his mood changed. The heat in his gaze zinged to her mouth, making blood pump there, and other less noticeable places. He moved in, filling her senses with spice and fire, his right hand sliding round her waist, pulling her close.

Her knees buckled and she collapsed into him. He braced, seemed ready for her. Should she pull back? She thought about it, even tried sending a message from brain to feet, but she couldn't find the strength.

He lowered his head, a whisper's touch to her mouth. *'I take it.'*

Then his lips met hers and thoughts of anything but enjoying them fled.

The people, the car park, the world, faded. Chase surrounded her. Taut muscle pressing into her from the front, his hand pulling her into him from behind. And his mouth possessing her like a demon. *Hot. Unleashed.* He tasted of coffee, freshly ground. She liked it. Opened her mouth, mentally begging him for more.

She'd written kisses like this. Hungry, equilibrium-rocking kisses that tilted the earth's axis and made you forget everything but losing yourself in mindlessness and ecstasy. Now she knew how they felt.

Writing them would never be the same.

A wolf-whistle carved through the buzz in her ears.

Chase pulled back.

Oh, god.

Did her hands scrabble to keep him there? She unfurled her fingers, released fisted handfuls of his shirt, managed to find her feet again to step away.

'Why'd you do that?' She scrubbed her lips with the back of her hand, trying to look any direction but his.

In her peripheral vision he appeared as thrown as she. At least she wasn't alone in the losing-it-to-a-moment-of-insanity department.

He managed to rein himself in far quicker though. Those dangerous lips kicked upward and the need to connect with them again arrowed through her.

The glint in his eye said he knew it. 'You gave me two options and I picked.'

'I don't remember telling you to jump me.'

'Yeah, 'cos my shirt unbuttoned all by itself.'

Her fingers flexed, as if letting go all over again.

She dragged her gaze from his gaping neckline and more chest than her libido needed to see right now. 'You were telling me why we're here.'

He quirked a brow. 'You were heading back to the car.'

'Not happening.'

'Then we're at an impasse.'

'Or not. You were in an awful hurry to get here. Funny how the hurry's suddenly disappeared. Well, I have nowhere else to be and all afternoon to be there.' She shot him a wide smile, subtext *bite me!*

And just so he had no illusions on how unrattled she was, she reached across and fastened one of his buttons, patting his chest as if the sight and feel of that muscle didn't send her heart racing or her knees to the consistency of jelly. *Again.* 'Seems your impasse may have been somewhat premature.'

He all but growled. 'I could just cuff you to the car.'

'And I could leave you here minus a ride home.'

He glared at her and she glared right back. He'd asked her – no, that wasn't right, he'd *ordered* her – to ferry him around. No choice, no regard for what she wanted. Well, he could darn-well deal with the consequences, whether he liked it or not. He was stuck with her, for better or worse, until they solved the case and it was safe to go back to her normal, centred, dependable life again.

His teeth ground, as if to bite back words he'd regret. 'Fine! Stay close and don't say a word.'

'I wouldn't dare.'

He glared again.

She grinned. 'Wow, you play the bad part of "good cop, bad cop" *so* well.'

'It's not too late for me to cuff you.'

'I'd love to see you try.'

Chase clenched his jaw.

Damned impossible woman.

He stalked toward the gate, sensing her presence behind him, tamping the urge to call her bluff and cuff her regardless. She might just enjoy it. Hell! He'd enjoy it. Having her helpless and at his mercy wasn't an entirely unpleasant prospect. And for that reason he was ending this discussion. Now. It wasn't the prospect that worried him. It was the aftermath.

A couple of zookeepers blocked the entrance. He craned his neck and saw others directing a small crowd through the exit near the gift shop.

He flashed his badge.

'What's happening?'

'A situation in the reptile enclosure. But our Emergency Response Team is dealing with it, detective.'

'Is Jagger Nelson involved?'

The woman's gaze sharpened. 'He's assisting.'

'I need to see him.'

'You'll have to wait until we have the all-clear.'

He waved his badge, just in case she missed it the first time. 'This can't wait.'

'How do you feel about coming face-to-face with an Eastern Green Mamba?'

'Is it poisonous?'

'Only if you eat it. It is, however, highly venomous. One bite and thirty minutes later we'll have a real need for your squad's services, detective.' He could have sworn she smirked. 'Still don't want to wait?'

He steeled his shoulders, made sure the shivers inside didn't escape and make him appear a damn fool. Two encounters with two snakes in one week.

No thanks.

The woman narrowed her gaze, smirk still firmly in place.

What the hell was it with women today? If he didn't know better, he'd yell conspiracy. Not that Mary – or so her name tag said – was far wrong. Slimy and slithery, he could do without.

'I'll wait.'

Mary shot him an I've-got-your-number-and-I'm-dialling-that-bastard expression.

Stacey's wasn't much different. Combined, they were rising mercury on his blood pressure.

'The big bad detective, scared of snakes. Who'd have thought?' Stacey shook her head, eyes gleaming with what he could only describe as relish with all the trimmings.

'Snakes do *not* scare me. You, however, are another matter.'

'Nice deflection, detective. I saw the way you looked at Cuddles. Shoot first, talk later, with life-or-death horror scrawled all over your face.'

'Your overactive writer imagination is meddling with your marbles, Stacey. This is nothing past valuing my safety more than cuddling up to some type of lizard.' He suppressed the shudder that accompanied the denial.

'Snakes aren't lizards. Although they both fall under the class Reptilia.'

'Swallow an encyclopaedia?'

'Forget to swallow your happy pill?'

'Touché.' He grunted. 'Snake or lizard – or whatever label you use – won't make me dislike them less.'

'I think we need to delve deeper into this phobia of yours. What it is you're really scared of?'

His gut clenched. 'I'm not one of your characters to prick and prod with all your mumbo-jumbo psychobabble. Once upon a time, I don't like snakes. The end.'

'Perhaps an up-close-and-personal encounter with Cuddles would cure that.'

'Or perhaps not.'

Her mouth opened but he didn't wait to hear what she planned to say. He left her mid-pout and approached zookeeper number two this time. Max. A male. Someone more likely to see reason and sense.

'What's taking so long?'

Max the zookeeper squinted. 'Why do you need to see Jagger so urgently?'

'Why do you ask?'

The man measured him before lifting his gaze past his right shoulder. He turned in time to see a couple of uniforms get out of a marked car. 'I guess it's no secret now. At first we thought one of the keepers had failed to secure *Kabibi Chausiki's* enclosure properly and that she'd merely escaped ...'

'But?'

'But there's no sign of her anywhere near the reptile house, and on closer examination the lock to her enclosure appears jimmied open.' Max puffed his cheeks then let out a long, slow breath. 'It appears someone has just broken in and stolen a snake capable of killing several humans with just one bite.'

Chapter Fourteen

Everything about Jagger Nelson made Chase's blood boil. His swagger, his devil-don't-give-a-fuck grin, and nowhere near least of all the way he'd hurt and was still hurting his big sister.

He reclenched his right hand. All he wanted was to smash the arrogance clean from the bastard's face. 'What the hell trouble have you got yourself into this time?'

A baby-bottom smooth chin jerked up and white the likes of toothpaste commercials shone out from a mocha-chocolate face. 'Nothing I can't handle.'

'That's not what I hear.'

'Gracie should never'of told you.'

'What? That you're guilting hard-earned money out of her yet again?' Firestorm blazed through his gut and he wanted nothing more than to unleash the flames onto Jagger. 'Who do you owe this time? How much?'

'This ain't your trouble, Chase.'

'Gracie's trouble *is always* my trouble. And anything with your name on it is ten times worse. Stay away from her, Jagger, or so help me god, I promise–'

'What?' Attitude oozed through his voice like oil-grease through a leaky valve.

Well, Chase's gasket was past leaking and ready to kick Jagger's smarmy ass. 'You'll damn well regret it, you son of a bitch.'

'Ooh, pretty cop is turning Dirty Harry. Playing like a big boy now, are we?'

He clenched his fist, raised it …

Cocky bastard just grinned. 'Go ahead, tough guy. Do it. A car park of cops make the best witnesses, don't you think?'

His gaze skirted the buzz of activity just metres away – uniforms questioning a group of zoo visitors found in and around the reptile house.

And then there was Stacey, chatting animatedly with Mary. Although the odd side-glance indicated she wasn't as oblivious of his little *tête-à-tête* with Jagger as he'd like.

He unfurled and furled his fist, hand shaking – from nerve degeneration or anger, impossible to tell.

Jagger Nelson would keep. Pond scum was fodder for all manner of beasts. And this pond scum would be his, minus an entire car park of witnesses.

Meantime, he had a job to do – something he was damned good at.

Ten minutes. That's all the time he had before handing Jagger over for questioning. Best he use it wisely rather than following instinct and decking the self-serving son-of-a-bitch.

'Still have that old motorbike of yours?'

Jagger's brown, almost black gaze sharpened, even while his body still leached that world-owes-me-a-break attitude. 'Nah. Was stolen last week. Why?'

'See this?' He waved his badge in front of a face any mother would find too easy to love. Shame what lurked below the surface wasn't as endearing. 'It means I get to ask all the questions and you get to answer, nice and polite-like.' He slipped the leather wallet back into his jacket pocket. 'Did you report it?'

'Yeah. But the pigs did jack-shit in getting' it back. Surprise, surprise. Prob'ly stripped for parts 'n dumped in the Yarra, for all anyone could care.'

'My heart bleeds for you.' Shame the bastard hadn't been dumped with the bike. 'Convenient though, don't you think?'

'Convenient for what?'

'Where were you earlier today, let's say between eleven-thirty and one-thirty?' He took a notepad and pen out from his pocket.

'Here.'

'For the entire two hours?'

'Well, yeah. I have lunch between twelve 'n one. Before 'n after I was preparin' enclosures for relocatin' some of the residents.'

'Residents?'

'A frilled-neck lizard 'n some blue-tongues. Why?'

He patted his jacket pocket. 'Remember?' Tapping pen to paper, he watched for any sign of guilt. 'Can anyone vouch for your movements?'

'I guess. Steve McEwin was wiv me in the Reptile House.'

'And is Steve here now to confirm that?'

'Uh, he left early. Not sure why. You'll have to ask the head reptile handler.'

Chase made a note. 'And after that?'

'I went to the staffroom. Anyone would'of seen me grab a coffee at lunch.'

'You remained in the staffroom until your break ended?'

'Well, not quite.' The bugger's eyes shifted.

Gotcha!

Aaand there was the lie.

'Define "not quite".'

'It means I went for a walk.' Jagger's gaze narrowed. 'Do I need a lawyer?'

'Don't know, Jagger. Do you?'

'I ain't done nothin'.'

'Meaning you've done something. I'm just trying to figure out what.' It was time to change tack. 'Heard of the fishing superstore Hook, Line and Sinker?'

'Might'of.'

'Yes or no will suffice.'

'Am I bein' arrested or somethin'?'

'Just some routine questions. That's all.'

'Well, I know my rights 'n I plead the fifth.'

'You've gotta stop watching all those US cop shows. The fifth amendment doesn't apply in Australia.'

'What about freedom of choice? I have a right to stop talkin'. And to a lawyer.'

'Looks mighty suspicious, Jagger.'

'Mighty smart, more like.' His lips clamped.

'Are you involved in the missing snake scenario?'

Nothing.

'Did you visit Hook, Line and Sinker today?' His left eye twitched. But that was the extent of his reaction. A crowbar couldn't have pried those lips apart.

Then they spread into a sneer. 'Unless you have a reason to

question me, I don't have a reason to stay.' The swagger was back, as well as that arrogant, kick-in-the-nuts grin.

Clear as a spring September morning, the bastard was hiding something. What wasn't clear was what it involved – Gracie, the snake, or the failed car-tampering?

Something didn't read right. Jagger was a low-life, but he wasn't a killer. He'd never tinkered with bombs or car-tampering in the past. Not that scum wouldn't rise up and move ponds if it had the chance. Money talked. Louder than any other damned incentive he knew.

And then there was the mamba. An exotic snake someone smuggled into Australia over a year ago, confiscated by quarantine and given to the zoo. A snake worth a lot of money to the right black-market buyer.

Was Jagger the culprit? Or was the still MIA Steve McEwin? Zoo staff and the police were searching for the missing reptile handler. When found, he'd be facing a shitload of charges – federal, customs, quarantine, along with breaches of the Environment Protection and Biodiversity Conservation Act. In short, jail-time was pretty much a given. *If* he was found guilty.

Steve's disappearance was suspect, but not conclusive. Nothing fit. Jagger had neither the means, brains, nor nous to pull anything off other than petty thievery or any number of botched misdemeanours. A snake from a high security enclosure? It was a stretch.

Yet, something in his demeanour, aside from the ass-wipe arrogance, said he was holding something back. What was he hiding? Whatever it was, better to let him think he'd got away than to push too far. For now, at least. When video surveillance came back from outside the fishing superstore, then he'd be all over his ex-bastard-in-law's lying, conniving ass. Meantime, Jagger would need watching.

He made a call. Chris Collins said he'd be there within the hour. An ex-cop turned PI with more time on his hands than he liked, and an itch to get back in the game. Something he'd done for Chase on and off since divorcing his wife and leaving the force a few years back.

He looked up. Stacey had moved away from Mary and was leaning against the zoo's brick wall, simmering, no pretence at trying to hide how pissed she was that he'd told her to stay while he left to do what he had to do.

Jagger approached her and – *hell!* Was that a hug?

He stalked over. Fast. 'I had no idea you two knew each other.'

'There are a great many things you don't know about me, detective.' Her lips were pursed and inviting and too damned fine to throw away on that oily waste of space.

Jagger's palm caressed her elbow and he wanted to deck the guy. For no other reason than it galled being in his space way longer than was palatable. Then the bastard grinned, as if a woman getting the better of Chase had just made his entire smarmy-assed millennium.

'I have to get goin'.' Again he gave her a hug, and *kiss*. On the cheek. The only reason he remained unscathed. 'Say *hey* to Shazz.'

With a mocking tip of his head, he winked. 'Great catchin' up, Chase, my man.'

He only just held back until the bastard was out of earshot. 'How do you know Jagger?'

'He's a friend of a friend.'

'He's bad news. Stay away from him, Stacey.'

Her brows jumped in that "are-you-on-uppers?" way of theirs.

'Don't assume this thing,' she swung her hand between them, her phone almost wiping out his eye in the process, 'us working together on the case, gives you any say over me or my actions. This is *not* a dictatorship. I'm my own person, with my own life, my own friends, whether you like them or not. Grin and bear, Chase. There are some things in life that you just can't control. I'm one of them.'

'He has a motorbike.'

From her five foot plus height she somehow managed to peer down at him through bronze-tipped lashes. As if he were the one a-fuse-short-of-a-lightbulb in this discussion. 'And that makes him undesirable?'

'No. That makes him a suspect for your bomb scare this morning.'

Her cheeks puffed and she burst into what could only be termed as gales of laughter. Whole hurricanes of it. Not the response he'd expected. What did he have to do for her to appreciate the seriousness of the situation?

'This isn't a damn joke, Stacey!'

She spluttered. 'That'd be a first.'

He tried again. 'His bike matches the partial license plate.'

'Along with how many other Victorian's?' Thankfully, she managed to hold back further amusement. Just. 'Jagger's a softie. He couldn't hurt a fly, let alone Sidney or me.'

'He's a lowlife who used to be married to my sister.'

'Yeah, he mentioned that. He also mentioned you two never saw eye to eye. I guess this over-protective brother thing got in the way of you becoming pals.'

Pals! He almost chucked his lunch. 'His out-of-control gambling problem did that all by itself. He nearly cost Gracie everything, our family home included.'

'So you guys have history. That shouldn't affect my relationship with him.'

'*Relationship?*'

'Jealous, Chase?' She bowled on. 'You don't need to like him. On the flip side, you don't need to pin every bad thing that happens onto him, either. Jagger would never hurt me.'

'You're impossible!'

'And you're out of line.'

Her heels must have dug ten feet into the ground. He bit back another retort – just more water flowing off her infuriating, obstinate back. Her eyes flashed as she glanced at her phone, then her happy hippie-mobile in the distance.

'If you're done here, I have a life to get back to. *After* my taxi duties are dispensed with, that is.' And with that she stormed off, the angry sway of her butt causing his temperature to climb even more.

If not for his appointment in – he checked his watch – just under two hours, he'd have something to say about her calling the day quits on him. As it was, her tenacity rankled.

With a growling gnash of teeth, he stalked after. Snake thieves and Jagger bloody Nelson were the least of his problems right now.

Chapter Fifteen

He shook out a cigarette, twirled it between his fingers, then jammed it back into the pack. High time he kicked the habit. What he needed was a substitute. A fucking ripper to replace the hit and buzz of nicotine.

Already the blood hurtled thick and fast through his veins. *Anticipation.* The hunt. The sacrifice. The final possession.

He tossed the pack into his bag. Turned to the far wall.

Fetid damp laced the air. His throat.

His fingers twitched. *Ready.*

Wide eyes gaped at him across the wide space, sweat running rivulets down over-red cheeks and into a quivering red gag-ball.

Green algae slimed the stone surrounds and running water echoed through one of the nearby tunnels. He turned to the man splayed against the wall by rope and chain. Bullies were an inferior class of filth who didn't deserve to live. And if killing that bully served his purpose, served to prove a point? Even better.

The man whimpered. Not so tough now he was on the other side. Then again, bullies never were. Soon his whimpers would slide into shrieks. Well-earned pleadings that would fall on deaf ears. Mercy wasn't afforded to the undeserving. And even the deserving missed out sometimes.

He clamped his jaw. Time was at his disposal and he had no fear of discovery. Stone and thick earth made sure of that. Nature's natural sound-proofer.

Grit and wet crunched beneath his feet as he approached the simpering coward. He squealed. A paschal lamb ready for slaughter. A double-crossing lamb who should have stuck within the boundaries he'd been given. He couldn't afford mistakes. Mistakes were for fools. And he wouldn't be made a fool.

Never again.

Wide liquid brown stared back. Fear. Horror. How long till the fucker peed his pants? He smirked, sliding the knife out from its cover and inspecting the long thin blade in the dim blue light. Little lamb let loose a guttural moan and ammonia filled the air.

Not long, it seemed.

He grinned.

Time to throw him a party he'd never forget.

Chapter Sixteen

There has to be a link.

Chase tossed his pen onto the desk and scratched his good-for-nothing left arm. He'd tried removing the sling after his less-than-gracious "taxi driver" dropped him home, but the momentary relief wasn't worth the resulting pain and – much like the woman who'd slam-dunked him into this darned predicament – it wasn't worth the trouble either.

A glance at his watch indicated two hours had passed since another missed appointment. He couldn't fathom why he kept putting it off. Wouldn't *knowing* be better than this confounded uncertainty?

Cement clagged in his gut.

Apparently not.

He stared down at the jumble of papers. Better to focus on what he could control rather than what he couldn't. First the Nine Knife Slasher copied Stacey's Salute Then Slash Killer, and now he'd copied her Fatal Fisherman. What the hell kind of sick ideas did she have going on in her head? They were so gruesome he'd be wary of the woman if she wasn't so damned ridiculous.

He pushed aside thoughts of other attributes that didn't help his case and shuffled a paper to the top – a Venn diagram of sorts, comparing her killers to his. What linked the two different MOs other than a bothersome romance writer? The NKS stabbed his victims nine times in a precise, circular pattern; he undressed them, and then posed them in a salute, fingers tied with wire to hold them in place. Imposing humiliation and compliance.

Similar could be said for the Fatal Fisherman. Victims were bound using fishing line, a fish carcass rammed down their throat, fish hooks locking their lips together. Forcing them to swallow their happiness and freedom, if you take the symbolism of the fish and its placement literally. Again compliance, only this time a rejection of all that is good.

Did the killer relate to this, to his fictional "mentors", or was it something else that drew him to emulate them?

What?

Which lead to his next question. What was with the straying from MO?

In the case of the NKS, the bodies may have been dealt a beating, but the death had been merciful. *If* you could call death by murder merciful. The victims must have been unconscious when stabbed – wound placement was too precise, too surgical, with the absence of any form of defensive wounds.

So how did he make his victims remain still long enough to stab them until they died? The tox screen had come back negative. That along with the absence of puncture marks on the body suggested no anaesthetic, unless it was something untraceable through standard forensic testing.

Which lead to the next question. Why veer from the fictional STS Killer's MO by this *mercifulness?* The NKS had trussed his victims then stabbed them while conscious. Was Stacey wrong and was this his first foray into murder? Unlikely, but not impossible. Or was the killer squeamish? Perhaps he'd have considered this if not for the next round of victims.

The Fatal Fisherman – a very different kettle of fish, pardon the pun. He sutured his victim's lips while they were still compos mentis. Brutal. Cruel. Violent. Difficult to believe the same man was responsible for both deaths. Even more difficult to believe that there were two madmen imitating Stacey's books.

And there he came, full circle. *Why?* The answer had to lie with Stacey. She was the link. And whether she liked it or not, somewhere in that scary, scatty mind of hers, she held the key to the killer.

Which meant he needed to see her. About the case.

He grabbed his phone and began to dial.

Chapter Seventeen

'**W**hat makes you such a bad-assed mother fucker?'

He smoothed the thin blade across the trembling cheek, then dipped the edge, laughing at the pansy squeal as his toy jolted back from the cutting edge. He let him. Minor victories now would smell all the sweeter later, when the hope they promised were snatched from the double-crossing coward's grasp.

'Because you hurt on girls?'

His fingers twitched.

Tough guy didn't look so mother-fucker tough now. All trussed and tied up. A delectable lamb to slaughter. His lamb. And this time, his slaughter. *His style.* The man's legs splayed, thick rope binding each one to a metal ring riveted into the mould-covered brick. Two more rings fixed his arms tight above his head.

Black-brown eyes followed his every move. The man tried to speak past the gag-ball. Couldn't.

He dipped his head. Considered. *Why the hell not?*

He ripped it out.

Through hacking coughs, his little lamb licked his cracked lips. Shame there was no saliva to wet them. Thirst could be a killer.

He snorted. Grabbed a bottled water from the table, unscrewed the lid and took a deep swig. He dragged the back of his hand across his mouth and sighed, grinning, slurping his lips Hannibal-style, just 'cos he could. '*Nice*. Like liver with a dash of Chianti. So *satisfying*, don't you think?'

Little lamb's eyes jolted wide, quivering. Didn't matter that he abhorred every kind of bean, fava included. Would never sink to bringing any part of this man's flesh to his lips. The hint was taken and goddam if the pussy hadn't just peed his pants. Again.

'I d-don't hurt girls.'

'You don't?' He stepped back – didn't give a fuck who the man had or hadn't hurt – and continued the game. Surprise was the mask he wore now, leading into worry. A paw tap to his prey, minus the claws. 'Oh, my. Seems we have a problem then.'

The man nodded frantically. 'A mistake. You have the wrong man. Let me go and no one will ever know.'

Relax.

His cock hardened, his claws readied. He smiled, feigned relief. 'How considerate. What do we do now?'

Contrite. Concern, even.

Idiot player didn't get when he was being played. 'Cut me free?'

'Of course.'

A simple task. He moved first to the man's right hand. 'Hold steady, I'd hate to nick you by mistake.'

He nodded with relief, relaxed even.

Palm pressing hard against palm, he sliced. The man screamed. He moved fast, ramming the ball-gag past his teeth and against his tongue, easing it back as he gagged, then securing the strap. No sense ending business before the fun began.

Blood dripped from the wound and he inhaled, licking his lips, savouring the tang of wet metal against his tongue.

Then he continued.

Skin skidded apart, blood beading and spurting out against the metal edge. The man screamed again, a silent terror-filled scream, gagging and gasping against the red rubber. Hope died a quick death at the first cut of the knife. The light in his eyes would take much, much longer.

He applied pressure, drove his throbbing cock hard against the trembling body. Flesh squelched, cartilage snapped. The blade hit pay dirt and hacked into the bricks beneath. The digit dropped to the ground. He left it in its bloody pool, bringing the knife to the fucker's pretty-boy face.

His cheeks were wet, quivering.

Weak. They were all weak. And fickle. Said one thing, meant something else. Well, he'd learned to play the game. Promised hope, delivered despair. Acted like he cared, then fucked them hard up the ass. Broke them the way they'd break him given the chance.

No mercy.

The only path to survival in this fucker-kill-fucker world.

Chapter Eighteen

Bliss on the lips, cellulite on the hips. Lots of it.

Damn!

Crumbs of triple choc and buttery cookie melted over Stacey's tongue as she sunk her teeth into pure decadence, then washed it down with a swig of warm milk. Stretching out, she flexed her toes, wrapped the plush blue of her dressing gown around her ankles and sank back into the cushioned black and white of the chaise lounge. She took a couple of seconds and savoured, eyes closed, mind in a place where cookies were god.

That should be everywhere. Including here, where she belonged. *Home.* Impossible to describe the relief at watching the police leave, her writing cave no longer an active crime scene, even if their leaving was amidst a storm of gritty, black fingerprint powder and accusatory, mistrusting looks.

That they thought she was guilty couldn't have been clearer – no other prints but hers had been recovered from her writing cave. Angst whirled like a sandstorm through her belly and she drowned it in another bite of bliss. Exquisite cookie crumbs and mind-melting chocolate.

Closing her mind to unchocolatey thoughts, she munched. Lost herself for a few moments more. *Heaven.* A land of cookies with no calories and weight shedding the more you consumed. Then reality hit. Her eyes shot open. A splat of spindly limbs thumped onto her thighs, courtesy of the silky bundle making her lap his home. 'Midnight!'

Paws padded against her chest as he plopped onto his stomach and stared at her through wide, emerald eyes. His satisfied purr vibrated all the way down to her fleece-covered toes. Cookies, cats and Cuddles. The path to happiness. She grinned at the scrawny black face, stroking his ears, watching his wide eyes become hooded and his head droop in ecstasy.

What more could you want?

Fans.

A four-letter word she loved almost as much as she loved Aunt Milly and her entire range of cookie sensations. With a stretch, the tips of her fingers snagged the thick yellow paper from the coffee table.

Love this book.
Inspired.
So real it gave me shivers.
Next NYT bestseller.
Your Biggest Fan.

Typed words – an entire page of them – fuelling her to keep doing what she did best. Creating kick-ass romantic suspense. She slipped the letter into the folder with the others. Words of encouragement and congratulations from people who loved her stories. Who spurred her to keep on keeping on.

Stretching for the table once again, she nabbed her *Writers Rock!* notepad and flipped the cover. Just because she was banned from the computer, didn't mean she should stop writing altogether. She clicked her pen. Once. Twice. Waited for the words to come.

Another bite of choc chip, more guilt, crumbs, and … *nothing.*

A series of long, therapeutic strokes over Midnight's back. One more. Another pen click. *Nope.*

The pad skittered across the table, and Midnight braced, digging cutlass claws into her skin. She yelped, Midnight jumped. The pad barely missed her half-empty glass, then smacked onto the floor. The pen followed. Midnight shot her a less-than-impressed glare then flopped back down.

He'd blocked her. Three days ago words had flowed onto the page, now they'd dammed up so tight, there was no way in hell they were breaking through.

Soft, silky skin rumbled once again beneath her fingertips. None of the usual easing filled her chest.

It was like someone had tied her up in ropes and was slowly, unrelentingly drawing them tight. She had a story that needed finishing, exams in less than two weeks preceded by a crap-load of study, and some madman on the loose using her words as his bible. And every cell of her brain was stuck on a confounded detective who thought she was a certified idiot.

Proof she *was* an idiot, if all she could do was think about *him*.

He was a detective. Not much different to a cop. She didn't date cops. *If* she dated at all, that is. Caffeine buzzed through a cop's blood, only second to booze. They were unreliable. Inaccessible. *Emotionally detached.* Hid their problems in a bottle and their hurts behind an outpouring of humour. Had days when they didn't care who they hurt or how they'd missed their daughter's birthday. *Birthdays.* Ages five through to twelve.

More cookie. An entire round this time. Filling her mouth. A swig of milk and orders to whatever part of her brain had allowed the old hurts to surface, to send them back from whence they came.

And damn the man for dragging them out.

Arrgh! She needed to get back into her groove. Reignite her writing mojo. Forget a past she'd left well enough behind.

Time for a shower. Nothing loosened the kinks in her muscles and kicked her brain into gear like a wash of steamy, hot water. Guaranteed relaxation that had never failed before. No reason for it to fail now.

She pushed up from the cushions, reinstating a disgruntled Midnight back into their midst. He arched, kneaded the crap out of the fabric and plopped back down. If he could have talked, he would have claimed the chaise as his. She knew better than to argue.

She closed the back door, opened the kitty flap leading out to his enclosure and padded into her en suite bathroom. It didn't take long for the water to heat and steam to rise. Shedding her robe and PJs, she stepped into the stall. Gave herself over to heat and heaven.

Was that ringing? She paused and cocked her head. Not that it mattered. If the call was important, they'd leave a message, and if not, shower therapy trumped idle chit-chat.

She tilted her face toward the spray, cleared her mind. Pushed at every thought until she was one with the water and its roar across her eardrums. Her fingers combed the hair back from her face, following the cascade, over her shoulders, her breasts, experiencing the bump of every rib, her tummy, *lower*. She moaned.

Lips brushed hers. *Chase's.* Followed by hands, making her needy and ready and so freaking hot. She opened her mouth to his kiss, craved it more than she craved her next cookie …

… and spluttered.

Her eyes shot open. Her body slammed back to earth. To an empty stall and humiliation.

Damn! Second time damn!

She'd wanted to wash him from her mind, instead he'd followed her into the shower. Followed her everywhere, making her want him like *they* were the sum product of her rampant imagination. That was for her characters. Fiction. Not here, now, real life.

She shook back her hair and twisted the hot water tap. Cold hit her with the clarity of the morning after.

This whole killer thing was screwing with reality, melding fiction and fact until she couldn't tell the difference. Her life was *not* a book. This was *not* a romance. She did *not* want Detective Chase Durant. She cut the water and grabbed a towel from the heated rail. He'd ruined writing for her, and now he'd done the same to showers.

Solve this case and get him the hell out of your slopping, bedraggled hair. Because then, he'd get the hell out of her life. *Her thoughts.*

Rubbing the crap out of her body didn't help. When it should have rubbed him from her mind, all it did was send her nerve endings into a Chase-craving frenzy. And she wanted him more.

Then she heard his voice and knew she was losing her mind. She nudged her toes into her slippers, shoved her arms into her robe and yanked the belt tight.

A door slammed. She froze. That wasn't her mind. Someone was in her home.

Before she could freak out and cower in the shower like some poor re-enactment of Psycho, she scanned the room for a weapon. Not something she'd ever thought to stock in her overloaded bathroom cabinets.

Her fingers wrapped around her *50% MORE!* hairspray can and tested its weight. Large, wieldy, solid. *Perfect.* An arsenal of household self-defence weapons resided in her head, and she'd practised using every one of them – in the name of research, of course. She discarded the lid and shook the can. Ensuring the nozzle faced outward, she made for the door, ignoring the hefty *thud thud* of her heart against her eardrums.

Surprise was her most valuable asset. That, and a can whose contents would render her intruder both blind and disoriented while she walloped them over the head with it.

She was ready for this. Any longer and she'd talk herself out of it. *Breathe. In. Out. In.*

She wrenched the door open.

He had his back to her, scanning her dressing table, no doubt for jewellery or something equally as valuable to steal. Then he turned and she launched at him, spraying into his eyes, the *thud thud* of her heart nosediving as she came face to face with the man she'd just fantasised sharing her shower.

Chase whipped round just as a blue, fluffy monster leapt out of the bathroom and sprayed burning liquid into his eyes. His right arm shot up as a can hurtled toward his head. One-armed and blind, he stumbled forward, pushing back until they both tumbled onto what he assumed but couldn't see was her bed. Even with one arm and a sling he managed to pin her there. Pain factor – minimum.

He cracked his eyes open to see Stacey's panicked expression through a haze before he was forced to slam them closed again.

'What the hell, Stacey!'

'My question, exactly. What the hell?'

She punched him in the chest, as if she hadn't done enough damage already.

He pulled her up, eyes still clammed shut. 'I need to wash this crap out before I'm blinded for good. Which way is the bathroom?'

Her hand wrapped around his wrist, less-than-gently "guiding" him. 'It's not *permanent*.'

'Let's hope for your sake, you're right.'

'Don't be an ass, Chase.'

She tugged and his toe snagged on something, pitching him forward. Only her grasp and his shoulder colliding with the door prevented him from falling head over ass.

He wasn't proud of the language flying from his mouth. But, *hell!* She acted like this was his fault.

'How am *I* the ass here?'

Running water splattered against porcelain, then a wet cloth slapped him square in the face. He dropped it and ducked, splashing handfuls of cool, cleansing liquid over his eyes.

Bliss!

'You're the cop. "B and E" mean anything to you?'

He blinked, then rinsed some more. The burning lessened. Now opening his eyes wasn't so much raging fire as a sandpaper rasp against his eyelids.

'Your back door was unlocked. I called and you didn't answer. I was worried.'

'My back door was closed. I checked it myself. And in case you haven't noticed, I'm perfectly capable of taking care of myself. I've been tying my own shoelaces since first grade. Remember?'

He looked down. No shoelaces. *Big, furry monster feet.* He looked up. *To go with a big furry monster robe.*

'Take a picture, why don't you. It lasts longer than a perve.'

'Real cute, Stacey.'

'So I'm told. What are you doing here, *detective?*'

'I'm a masochist and it was time for my daily dose of pain.'

She scrunched her nose and managed to glare down it at him, despite being half a head shorter. 'Funny.'

'It's either that or I haul your ass to the precinct and book you.'

'For?'

'Assaulting an officer.'

'Who didn't identify himself.'

'Assault with a deadly substance.'

'Yeah. Hairspray's a real killer.'

He clenched his jaw. 'Pissing me off.'

'Haven't heard that one before.'

'It's new. I'm sure I could find something to make it stick.'

'Lucky for me you've got that rocking sense of humour then, isn't it?'

Damn, but she made his blood boil. So much so, he wanted … *what?* To push her back onto that bed and peel away every ridiculous furry blue layer until he reached the soft, luscious curves he'd felt beneath him before. Just after she'd tried to super-spray and style him, that is.

Yep. He was fucked. Well and truly.

He ducked and sluiced water over his eyes again. Not that they didn't need the wash. But the action gave sense the time to return. He grabbed a towel, dried his face and took another, clearer look. Head to toe.

'You're dressed like *that* and I have a sense of humour?'

Arms crossed, she glared; fluffy, blue and ridiculous. 'What are you doing here, Chase?'

At least he was no longer "detective", though her tone was as sharp as her gaze and no warmer than it had been the moment they first crossed paths. Even the purse of her lips was the same. Along with his reaction to it.

She pulled the robe tighter, which only accentuated what it hid. His entire body tightened.

Aha. *Fucked.*

'I came to discuss the case.'

'Ever heard of email?'

'Not conducive to discussion.'

'Telephone, then.'

'I tried. You didn't answer.'

'I wonder why?' She tapped her bottom lip, then clicked her fingers. 'Oh, that's right. *I was in the shower.*'

He tried to stem the torrent of thoughts over that visual. Hot sudsy water trailing every inch of her naked body. His blood heated and forged southward. He coughed and refocussed on her crabby expression. Because *she* had every reason to be crabby right now.

'Can we move past this and onto the case?'

'At ...' She glanced at her wrist and a monster watch that – scarily – was a perfect match to her get-up. 'Ten at night? I don't think so.'

'I'm already here.'

'And I'm all ready for bed.'

Silence.

Her hand fluttered to her chest. Red bloomed across her cheeks and she stalked out of the bathroom.

He grabbed the wet towel and caught up with her in the living room, biting back a grin. 'Is that an invitation?'

'In your dreams!'

'Nightmares, more like.'

'If I'm so difficult to be around, why do you bother?' Impossible to miss the quiver in her bottom lip.

When she acted all strong and independent, it was too easy to forget how soft and vulnerable she was inside. Like now. He pressed the towel against his eyes, a heaviness descending on his chest. Lately, all he seemed to do was flit from one fight to the next. Jagger. Stacey. His squad. The world. He never used to be so *angry*. Although anger trumped fear. And for once, the humour wasn't helping. God only knew what could.

Stacey's arms folded tight across her chest. *Armour*. He was all-too familiar with that. Her chin raised, waiting for him to strike. Hurt clenched in his gut, deep and low. Was he that predictably callous?

A sigh escaped before he could stop it. 'Damned if I know.'

Her eyes widened. 'Meaning?'

'Don't know that either.'

'Then what do you know?'

He swallowed and didn't pause to think or filter. 'That despite the risk when you're around, being with you makes me forget.'

Chapter Nineteen

Stacey's heart bunny-hopped.

At first she thought he was serious. That he no longer considered her an airhead and clumsy and giraffe-in-Givenchy-heels ridiculous.

That maybe a man of substance hid behind the jokes.

She stepped forward, unsure why, only sure she needed the connection. Thought perhaps he needed that too. She even allowed honesty to push aside denial. She'd wanted Chase to want her the moment his gaze met hers across the precinct eighteen months ago. Now it appeared he wanted the same.

His jaw dropped, as if his words surprised him as much as they'd surprised her. Then his mouth snapped shut. He blinked, and his lips slipped into that goofy, devil-does-Dallas grin, freezing the soles of her feet to her over-worn cream carpet.

'No doubt the memory loss hit when you slugged me one with your arsenal of hair products.'

His grin slipped, but it didn't stop her from wanting to slug him all over again. This time, hard. How could she be so stupid as to think…? Obviously no thinking was involved. Lessons were there to be learned. To stop her from opening up to hurt all over again. Chase was no more reliable than her father. And no more deserving of her trust. He was a cop. And cops kept the world safe, at a cost. They were never reliable. Never home. Never there for their families. Their daughters.

She backed away, checked her belt, made sure it was extra tight and secure.

'You bastard.' She swallowed. Blinked hard. 'Don't play me with your mind manipulations. I'm not interested. In you. Your games. Anything to do with you. I'd rather eat Huhu bug stew than let you into my life.'

'This isn't a game. There's a killer–'

'And you know as well as I do this has nothing to do with that.

Whatever the hell problem you have in that mashed-up mind of yours, keep me out of it. I have enough complication in my life without you piling on more.' She tugged her belt again, just in case. 'Time you left, Chase.'

'I didn't mean–'

'Don't worry, I know exactly what you meant. You told me to stop being something I'm not. Well, this is it.' She raised her hands, pirouetted awkwardly in her robe and slippers. Made sure he received the full Cookie Monster experience. 'Bet you think I shouldn't have ditched those stilettos now.'

If nothing else, her interlude with Chase achieved what the shower failed. The feisty return of her mojo. Cookie in one hand, pen in the other, this time when ink hit the paper, words flowed.

Brianna wouldn't rest until she discovered the Fatal Fisherman's identity. And more, she planned to do it alone. Sebastian didn't believe she had the skills or the smarts. Said so, categorically, rejecting every suggestion she offered up regarding the case. Regardless her criminal psych degree that said she knew better. She was a nuisance, he said, trailing danger and disaster behind her. So much so that he felt obliged to protect her, 24/7. It wasn't as if she could keep herself safe.

She was about to prove him wrong. Setting a trap for the killer and catching him when everyone else had failed would do just that.

C is for cookie, that's good enough for me.

Her pen paused.

The mobile ringtone didn't just fracture the silence, it fractured her flow. She blocked the noise and stared at the page. Where was she?

Brianna's trap.

C is for cookie …

Damn.

She glanced at caller ID and sighed. Not a call she should ignore, much as temptation prodded her to turn the phone to silent and flip it onto its face.

'Des.'

'Stacey.' He gave a throat-clearing cough. 'What's up with my super-star author? You've been unusually silent lately. Everything okay?'

Another sigh, this time as she dropped her chin onto her palm. 'Are you asking as my assistant editor or friend?'

'A bit of both.'

Her sigh wasn't entirely unwarranted. She could hear the frazzle in Des's voice, knew this call was more about appeasing his stress than hers. His next words cemented it.

'Your deadline's in a week and it's not like you to be anything but finished by now.'

'I've had a couple of setbacks, nothing major,' she crossed her fingers, 'but I might need another week or so to fix up some of the final scenes.'

'We don't have a couple of weeks.' His voice spiralled like it always did under stress. Like a dentist's drill seconds before it hits. She tilted the phone from her ear, not quick enough to stop the reactionary twinge in her teeth.

And Des's spiral was nowhere near over. '*In the Throes of Murder* needs to be on every shelf, virtual and otherwise, by Christmas. The schedule's tighter than a virgin's chastity belt and there's no moving that sucker. You need to be on this, Stacey.'

She rubbed circles into her temple, but if anything the pressure grew. So much for delaying until the killer was caught. But she had a contract. And contracts wait for no man, woman or psychopath.

She stopped rubbing and jabbed the pressure point beside her right eye. 'It'll be on your desk before the week is up.'

'I don't doubt it.'

She heard the familiar rustling, pictured his over-played slam and dunk, the scrunched-up wrapper missing the trash – by a mile – as he popped his favourite mint into his mouth. Stress unburdened, he'd moved on. She had no such luxury. How would she test those scenes without pissing off Chase and invoking the killer?

Damn.

'I should get going.'

'There's another reason for my call.'

More than Des's version of a friendly editorial nudge?

'Stacey. You there?'

Again the spiral.

She winced. Hell, she'd be anywhere if he'd just cut the caterwauling. 'I'm here.'

'We have a problem, at least I think it's a problem.' *Pause.* For effect, maybe. Or perhaps another mint? 'Any chance you changed the dropbox passcode?'

'No. I'd have told you if I had. Why?'

'I just tried to check the edits on your last instalment of *The Suspense Will Kill You* series and it says the code's changed.'

'Can't have.' She was already pushing up from the couch. 'Let me check.' She ran-walked to the study, listening to Des's barely restrained huffing all the way. Patience was not a Des strong-suit, or any suit at all, for that matter. 'Just give me a sec to log on.'

'You're not already logged in?'

'Wow, Des. Much as it may surprise you, I do have life interests outside writing.'

'Not when you have a deadline.'

'You should be pleased. Life interests enrich my writing.'

'Oh, like your hunky fireman?'

She ignored the irk in his voice.

Her heart fluttered. A gentle, teasing quiver of anticipation. 'Ethan? He's a friend – who *you* introduced me to – and research.'

'Ah. But research for what?'

Dull throbbing rumbled against her temple. Again with the irk. When they'd been through this. She didn't mix work and well, the other. Too messy. Too much like burying bodies in your playground. And Des, well, he was Des. Her assistant editor. Nothing more. No flutters or heart racing or holding your breath. Just Des.

Much as he'd hinted he'd like to be more.

The throbbing increased, a bass drum beating just shy of her left eye this time. 'Stop stirring the pot when it's empty.'

'You forget, I saw you at the awards' dinner.'

And then Chase showed up. Her heart flutterings leapt into overdrive.

The dropbox login popped onto the screen.

Thank god.

She typed *BonnieAndClyde20* – Des's choice, not hers – and hit enter.

No go.

She tried again.

Nothing.

'It's not working.'

'Not news to me. Did you allow anyone else access to our files?'

'Not a chance. You?'

'Only the usual suspects, Beth, Kelly, myself.' Another rustle and some serious chomping. 'I'll get Tech onto it. If our dropbox is compromised, who knows what else they've managed to access. Damned hackers and pirates.' He grumbled the last words through a mouthful of mint.

It was like a door opened and cold wind licked up her spine. First her computer, now dropbox. Why? What were they after?

More killer moves?

The thought wasn't even close to being funny.

'Is your malware protection up-do-date? When did you last run a virus scan?' The barrage continued, nothing out of the ordinary.

With Des in a tizz, you had to let him run his course, much like a virus. So she did what she always did – automatically inserted a response between each pause so he didn't up and start again, this time with her "undivided attention".

She listened, agreed, pressed one hand to the churn in her stomach while the other rifled through her desk until she found an external hard-drive still in its original packing. The one she'd bought in an attempt to be organised and backed-up in case of a computer emergency.

This was so much more than that.

Aha-ing and nodding, she freed the little black box from cardboard and plastic, then held her breath, connected it and laptop, and began transferring every file, every word she'd ever written, onto its whirring innards.

The bulb above her desk flickered. Reminder she'd neglected to call the electrician. Again. Not without reason. Visions of workmen traipsing noise through her writing peace and productivity had kept her holding her breath, hoping the extent of her wiring problems was only the odd blown bulb in her writing cave. Now that the problem had scaled the stairs, seemed her blind eye was demanding glasses.

'I'll let you know when we can access dropbox again.'

She nodded – not that Des could see – and ended the call,

watching file after file transfer onto her drive.

Breathing was shallow, laboured. She doubted the tightness in her chest would lessen until every last file had moved from her computer. Her throat caught. She'd get another drive. Back-up her back-up. Store that one with Shazz. Then she'd print out every work-in-progress, every research file, every plotting table, just in case.

Even then, would the easiness return? The kind she'd known once upon a time when her most meddlesome dilemma was what curve-balls to throw at her characters before allowing them their happy ever after.

Now someone was throwing the same wily balls her way.
And when he finished?
She shivered.
What then?

'External hard drives are with data storage. Aisle seven, just round to your right.'

Stacey nodded thanks to the woman dressed in store colours of red and grey, and skirted the line of laptops, veering into aisle seven, which did indeed house a large range of "data storage". By the time Ethan joined her she was scanning row-upon-row of boxes boasting specs in what may just as well have been Klingon.

Her pocket beeped, then broke into James Bond's theme. She slipped out her phone, double-checked caller ID, then slipped it back in unanswered for the fourth time that afternoon.

'Sure you don't want to get that? Sounds like someone really wants to get hold of you.'

Too much truth in that statement.

Her body warmed. 'The feeling isn't mutual.'

Ethan moved closer and she focussed on that, his scent, something foreign and exotic, making her think of balmy nights and basking under an Oriental sky. She inhaled, savouring, committing his scent to memory, filing it away.

The corners of her mouth kicked up. Whoever said writing was a drug couldn't have been more accurate if they'd said a cat's whiskers helped them to "see" in the dark. Once you caught the writing bug, it was near impossible to shake. Life was research, every moment an inspiration for her next scene, her next chapter, her next book.

Chills crawled across her skin and the grin faded. Where the thought had once yielded pleasure, now a killer's touch had slaughtered it of any enjoyment.

Ethan's fingers whispered across the tips of hers and the chills warmed.

She met his gaze. 'I know how busy you are, so thanks for the lift.'

'Your car battery dying wasn't all bad. I got to see you, and I don't mind playing chauffeur.' Perfect white teeth grinned back, fluttering her heart. 'Anything for my favourite author.'

Somehow he managed to make cheesy appealing. Needles pricked at her conscience. The whole car battery pretext wasn't *entirely* true. More pricking needles. So, it wasn't even remotely true. But wouldn't he think her ridiculous if she told him the truth? That she'd almost sat behind the wheel until memories of a leather-clad bikie had made her freeze. Panic, even.

Ethan seemed oblivious to her nerves. Better he remained that way. He strolled a little way down the aisle, inspecting the overflowing shelves.

'How many gig do you need?'

The reason she was here.

Again her gaze skimmed Klingon looking for sense. How much was a gig? One book. Two. Ten? She scrunched her nose. 'A lot.'

He laughed, and her toes curled. A warm and fuzzy toe-curling that funnelled up into her tummy.

'This should do it.' He waved a box identical to the one she'd opened last night.

'Maybe I should get two.'

'You're better off with a second back-up on dropbox, or emailing yourself the file.'

She swiped her hand through the air. 'No internet. I want everything off-line.'

'Then get one of these.' He dropped a pink heart USB into her palm.

'Cute.'

'Yes it is.' Only he wasn't looking at her hand or its contents.

Someone must have ramped up the heating and aimed it her way. Her fingers closed around the plastic and she met his gaze. He made to lean in. The pitter-patter of little kitty feet in her heart kicked into a full cat front-line chorus.

Oh, god!

She turned, slammed into a wall of boxes waiting to be shelved. They wobbled, but she managed to steady them, then turned back and bowled straight into the man she was trying to avoid.

Again her phone rang. This time she didn't take it out and check it. Her gaze found a black mark on her right sneaker, then switched to a toe trying its darnedest to peek through her left. *When did that happen?*

One palm curved her bicep, holding her still. The other lifted her chin. 'Hey.'

She blinked, her heart doing its darnedest to beat right out of her chest. 'Sorry.'

'Relax, Stacey.' His thumb brushed the skin just above her elbow, making it tingle. The other dropped from her chin to her throat where he couldn't miss the racing gallop of her blood.

She shivered. 'I wish it was that easy, Ethan.'

'It can be. Want to talk about it?'

Yes. No. Maybe.

Or maybe not. The more she rehashed, the more mess merged into reality. It should have stayed in her books, this chaos. Instead it was out there, driving her to act like an idiot at every opportunity.

Whirling her up into a tornado of madness.

Take a breath. Another. Slow …

Fiction was so much easier to handle than this.

His hand dropped and he stepped back, disappointed. She was too. She wanted this, right? Only how could she and Ethan start something with Chase still in the picture. And he *was* in the picture, much as she'd tried her darnedest to rub him out. They were so unsuited. Aardvarks and avocados. A bad fit in every which way. Unlike Ethan. Ethan was pizza and cheese.

She clutched the hard-drive to her chest. 'I should get back.'

'No time for tea?'

It was so cute that he never used the term "coffee". Always remembered her aversion to the term. The beverage. And yet his thoughtfulness didn't affect her heart rate nearly as much as a certain detective storming into her bedroom and stating her company helped him to forget.

Forget what?

Ethan cupped her elbow. 'There's a cute little café not far from here.'

The numbers on her watch were a blur, but the movement dislodged his hand, winning her precious seconds in which to catch some sense.

She shook her head. 'I've got a deadline.'

'Any research I can help with?'

Almost black eyes bored into hers. She knew what he asked, and with that knew he wouldn't get the answer he wanted. Too much crazy filled her life right now. How could she add any more? Perhaps when everything was resolved …

'*In the Throes of Murder* has no firemen.'

'We both know that's not what I meant.'

She swallowed, thought her knees would fold. His hand shot out and tightened around her arm, staving her crumple to the ground.

'Am I wasting my time, Stacey?'

He drew her in, the way he'd drawn her in when his firefighting buddies laughingly offered him to her as research – *nudge-nudge, wink-wink*. He'd taken her seriously, bought her lunch, advised on her scenes, asked intelligent, interested questions about her work, despite the fact he was a male and she wrote romance.

Ethan was *kowabunga hot* – Shazz's words – with qualities she admired. Frank, not funny. The kind of man who rescued cats from trees, helped old ladies cross the road and thought she looked sexy in stilettos. The kind of man she wrote into the heroes in her books. The kind of man she should date, if she were to start dating again.

If fear and idiocy could for one second stop confusing her and pushing her into Chase's arms, she'd be kissing Ethan right now. Enjoying it. How did she feel about being with Ethan? Not closed to the idea. Not ready, either. Now just wasn't right. But now wouldn't last forever.

'You're not wasting your time.'

His smile deepened, with pleasure. *Hope.* She should have felt that flutter again.

She shifted her gaze and met a pair of keen brown eyes seconds before they turned away. That gaze, the fleshy pink face, looked suspiciously familiar. No doubt because they were.

Burt. Hook, Line and Sinker's over-inquisitive sales assistant. Seemed she wasn't the only one looking for additional data storage.

Acknowledge or not to acknowledge?

Before she could decide, he grabbed a box and disappeared into the next aisle.

'So I have a chance?' She returned her attention to Ethan and opened her mouth. He pressed his finger to her lips. '*Shh.* Don't answer now. We have something, Stacey. And I know we'll be amazing together. So, let's take this slow, as slow as you like. I'm willing to wait until you're ready, now I know I'm not wasting my time.'

She nodded. Smiled. Looked into his eyes and saw joking blue, not black, framed by sandy hair and a crooked, devil-may-care grin.

Chapter Twenty

Things were hotting up, like a cauldron simmering over a temperate flame, waiting patiently for the kindle it needed to blaze.

His blood pounded.

She was ripe, ready. *Primed.* Almost set for him to make his move.

Cool metal dug into his palm as he gripped the shelf, watching her waltz through the checkout as if she owned the goddam store. Grateful is as grateful does. And she wasn't nearly grateful enough for all he'd done. Perhaps it was time for another lesson.

He watched her eyes light, her lips smile and knew she was lying. Was any sap dumb enough to lap up her drivel? His gaze shifted. It seemed so. And not just one. Plenty, fawning around her, when she should have had eyes for him.

She was blinded by lust. And lust would be her downfall.

He would make it so.

But first he had to build her up. Make her stand tall. So that when she cut and bled at the knees, the fall would be her complete destruction.

Chapter Twenty-One

'**M**ore champagne?'

Stacey dragged her gaze from food she lacked the stomach to eat to her agent and editor sharing a stilted tête-à-tête across the table.

Why not? Isn't that what Saturday nights were for? Partying.

She nodded, and Des sloshed golden liquid into her glass before replacing the dripping bottle back into the almost-melted ice. Wasn't as if life would get any worse tipsy. And maybe, just maybe, it'd look better. Rose-coloured, alcohol-distorted glasses and all.

'Bonnie wrote poetry since school, but her work didn't rise to fame until she teamed up with Clyde. He must have been her muse.'

She nodded. Raised her brows. Looked as if Bonnie and Clyde's story was as riveting as last week's Game of Thrones. It certainly was to Des. Just as well, since he was in the middle of editing their biography. At least his fascination kept him from exploring other topics. Like her.

'"Let's take 'em for a lark" were Bonnie's words before a kidnapping, proving she was as committed to their crimes as she was to Clyde, despite what others say to the contrary.' He barely paused, barely replaced lost oxygen before burning up more. 'Her second poem likens their gang to Jesse James before she predicts their mutual deaths, her only solace that they'd go down together.' He grinned. 'A modern-day Romeo and Juliette.'

Not even close. Not that she was *au fait* on anything Bonnie and Clyde past the fact they were outlaws who robbed and killed. The plot may be Shakespearean, but there was nothing Romeo and Juliette about it.

She glanced at her watch and bit back a sigh. Too early to call it a night – at least another hour of listening to Des bending her ear toward boredom and pasting a happy smile to her expression before she could even contemplate saying her goodbyes.

Their waitress stopped, snapped the serviette from Stacey's lap, refolded and reset it back in place, then moved onto Des, who paused his monologue long enough to enjoy the interaction way more than he should. After she was gone, he slapped a red-brown flop of hair back from his forehead, then straightened his already impeccable pink shirt and tie.

She grabbed her glass. Sipped. Tried not to sigh.

Something had changed in their relationship. Nothing concrete, just an airy-fairy undefined *something*. Nothing to do with the missing dropbox password mystery. Tech had solved that almost immediately. Some computer glitch way beyond her comprehension. No. The tension between her and Des stemmed from a different source. If only she had an idea *what*.

She scrunched her nose while rescrunching the fabric bristling her knees. Opulent efficiency didn't make for comfort. It just added zeros to the bill, and meant your water was sparkling and your cutlery so shiny it reflected with blinding accuracy off the chandeliers. A Maxy's falafel and chips would have gone down much easier. As would an evening at home with a good book. Or even a bad one.

She wasn't fool enough to believe tonight was solely about launching Thrasher's new Suspense Bites line with her novella *A Minute Past Murder*. Both editor and agent were too circumspect. The air too thick for celebration. The covert glances and questioning looks too obviously lacking in festivity.

'So, how's the book coming along?'

And there it was. The dreaded question.

Her fingers wrapped round the fine crystal flute and she raised it to her lips, eyes anywhere but on Des. 'It's coming.'

'Much like a eunuch's erection.'

Wine spluttered out from her mouth across the table. A quick succession of inhales to catch her breath and she grabbed a serviette, daubing the mess, croaking apologies to the wide-eyed Rita and Morticia opposite. Des's words shouldn't have surprised. His way and comments had been inappropriate from the moment they'd met. Why should that change two and a half years into their working relationship?

Regardless, her feathers ruffled. 'Is that supposed to mean something?'

His hand hovered over the antipasto platter, then dive-bombed a Kalamata olive. 'Yeah.'

He popped it into his mouth and chewed as if he hadn't just insulted the crap out of her. Copper-brown moustache bobbing ridiculously, he grabbed another olive and added it to the first, chomping and talking with his usual epitome of etiquette.

'Your work's always flawless. It flows like a well-oiled Maserati, even first draft.' He spat the stones onto his plate in rapid-fire, replacing the finished olives with two more. 'Your latest scenes are different. They're forced and unnatural, as if you're trying to do something you can't. And we both know that's bollocks.'

His squint was so pointed she could almost feel its sharp jab. Was this an interrogation?

'Something or someone's stolen your focus. At first I thought it might be the fireman, but now I'm not so sure.' Talking and chewing, he barely paused for a breath. 'Is it that detective you have the hots for?'

She arched a brow, worked at acting offended, not guilty. Even lifted her fork to grab an artichoke from the platter.

'I don't have the hots for Chase.'

'Beth says otherwise.'

Her fork clattered, empty, onto her plate and she dropped her hands into her lap, ignoring her subconscious which wondered – not for the first time – why Des never used her editor's nickname. 'Since when is my private life topic for discussion at Thrasher Publication?'

'Hold onto your hosiery. This isn't an attack. It's concern. For you. You're part of the Thrasher family and that means we look out for each other. I worry about Beth's long hours, she worries about my lack of sleep and we both worry about you and your writing. Or lack, thereof.'

Her fisted serviette would give any passing waitress palpitations. She inhaled, long, slow, so she didn't lash out and hit Des square in his olive-chomping jaw.

Personal touches. The close family camaraderie. These were the benefits of working at a small publishing house. Reasons she'd stayed on, regardless of her mother's insistence she leave for somewhere more prestigious. Thrasher had taken a chance on her when no one else would. They'd seen her rise from a nobody in publishing to someone.

Leaving was akin to leaving family. Turns out staying meant relinquishing all privacy. Her mother was right, once again. Warm and fuzzy was no reason to stay. And friendship only spanned as far as your next bestseller.

'I've never let you down before.'

Something in Des's expression made her squirm. As if his mind had suddenly moved on from her writing.

This time when she went for the artichoke, she stabbed it hard and took a chunk into her mouth. Not as refined as her surroundings, but she wasn't up to pretending she was something she wasn't. The strappy *Givenchy* sandals cutting into her ankles didn't count. And damn said hot detective for planting the thought in her mind.

'You've never had a boyfriend before.'

He said it as if her love-life was the company's business. His business, even.

She sipped her champagne, swallowing resentment and cool liquid in one large gulp. 'I still don't.'

Her eyes met the brown pair contemplating her more deeply than professionally acceptable. His interest wasn't news. That whole elephant in the room thing that he'd never hidden, that she'd never acknowledged. A comfortable, happy medium that was apparently no more. His gaze shivered across her skin, making her wish for more cover. A trench-coat, something more than her scoop-necked blouse and knee-length skirt.

'Why not?'

First he was anti-boyfriend, now he wasn't?

He waggled his fingers over the table's hors d'oeuvres, as if they and nothing else were important. Least of all her answer, which would only ruin a perfectly functional working relationship. The only relationship they would ever share.

'I'm focussing on a career that a lot of men won't take seriously, and I won't settle for less.'

'I take you seriously.'

Option toss-up. Gulp back another swig of champagne or pass him the entire platter of olives so he could turn his focus anywhere but on her? She went for option three, the yellow option. *Evasion.*

'Of course you do. Like any fabulous assistant editor would.'

She smiled, flourishing the words with a champagne swig. The light in his expression turned to dark.

'And I wouldn't be an AE worth his salt if I didn't get to the heart of what's stopping you, so you can move forward and finish and do the best goddam job you can.'

He and Morticia had done that – helped her move from good writer to great. Encouraged her search for authenticity. Even assisted with the design of her writing cave. But that didn't give them rights to fish into her personal life and doubt her when she'd never let them down before.

Chair legs squawked their protest as she pushed her chair back from the table and stood.

'I won't waste conversation on something that's moot. The book will be finished, and it'll be brilliant.' She dropped her scrunched serviette to the side of her plate.

It was difficult to walk and not run across the floor. Once the Ladies' lime green door swished closed behind her, she planted both hands on the counter and dropped her head.

Doubts. A truckload. When she'd believed she'd dealt with them, won the Ruby Award and moved on. Obviously she was wrong. No matter her outrage at Des, the facts didn't change. She wasn't focussed, wasn't working on all four cylinders. Her Maserati had turned Mini.

All over a man she didn't have the hots for.

Calm breaths. Relax.

The lime green walls didn't help. Her stomach swirled as if caught portside in an ocean squall.

The door behind her opened. Pushing up, she stuck her hands under the automatic tap and for once the stream of cold water was instantaneous.

Beth – *Morticia* – shot a smile at her in the mirror, then proceeded to straighten jet black hair ruthlessly ironed into submission.

She leaned in, brushing an imaginary eyeliner smudge with her pinkie. 'You okay?'

''Course.'

One sharp, black eyebrow arched.

Did that sound defensive? It was, but dammit, she didn't need her dirty undies airing for everyone to ogle.

'So, what's the deal with Mr Hot Shot Homicide Detective?'

First assistant editor, now editor. Like a record on repeat.

She gritted her teeth. 'No deal.'

'Really?'

'Yeah, really.'

'And you're okay?'

'Why does everyone think I'm not?'

Morticia turned, eyes so black they made her pale skin almost translucent. 'For one, your hands have been under that water for the past five minutes like you're trying to make as if nothing's bugging you. And two, you're struggling to write, and what you're writing isn't the Stacey Holland awesomeness you've wowed me with before.'

Her hands froze. The water stopped. Beth yanked at the towel dispenser a couple of times and passed a wad of paper across.

In automaton mode, she took it and began to dry. 'There's some stuff going on right now, but I'm on it. And the scene I'm working on is going to rock your black lace stockings off.'

'Good.' Morticia's gaze moved back to the mirror. 'Miss this deadline and we miss entering the Rita next year. You've won Australia's most prestigious romance author's award. It's time you won America's too.'

A jitterbug started deep in her stomach.

A good – *holy shit!* more sleepless nights – jitterbug.

'I'll make the deadline.' She tossed the paper into the rubbish.

'I know you will.' Morticia's angular hand curved cold against her bicep. 'I'm happy for you. He's hot and from all appearances at award's night, he couldn't peel his eyes off you for a second. Enjoy the fun, but don't forget, there's more than just your dreams at stake here.'

It wasn't until she heard the swish of the door that she realised she was alone again. The jitterbug was now a sack of potatoes. It wasn't the words, it was her tone. The underlying message that if Stacey stuffed up, the least of her worries would be a late release date.

Shoulder muscles bunched and ground as she braced against the counter. She needed a massage. Or a tropical island getaway with only her computer and an endless stream of silly-named cocktails topped with equally silly multi-coloured umbrellas.

What she didn't need was *this*.

Head-spin.

Chase making her suspicious and jumpy and weak-kneed with his theories of conspiracy and stalker killers. Her writing was suffering, and now, it seemed, her reputation with her publisher was too.

Uncertain how things could get much worse.

Her purse vibrated.

One glance at caller ID showed the universe knew exactly how and, yep, things could get worse.

The door flung open. A shock of purple hair and fluro-orange chiffon stalked in, glared at the ringing phone in her hand and entered a toilet stall. Derision from every avenue.

No sense delaying the inevitable.

'Mum. Hi.'

'Hit "send" yet?'

A sigh escaped before she could bite it back. 'Nearly.'

'What are you waiting for?'

The thigh bone's connected …

Breathe.

'It's not finished.'

A toilet seat clattered, followed by a flush.

'*Where* are you?'

'The Royale Brasserie's bathroom.'

'Shouldn't you be writing?'

No acknowledgement of her location past the fact she wasn't in front of her computer.

Colour clasher woman left the bathroom the same way she came in. Glaring, stalking, without washing her hands. *Ick!*

'You have a deadline. You have exams in two weeks. You can't afford to slack off now.'

Her legs moved, carrying her to the end stall before pivoting her back the way she'd come. As if she could ever forget, without her entire cheering squad plus one to remind her.

'I'm allowed to go out once in a while, Mum. It recharges me.'

'Have a Red Bull. Plenty of time for socialising after you hit New York Times' bestseller list.'

She turned. Stalked. Turned. Stalked. This had to be how tigers in captivity felt. 'Tonight isn't social, it's work. I'm with Des, Beth and Rita.'

The huff was only marginally tempered by the knowledge of who she was out with.

'Bestsellers don't come to those who wait, Stacey. You need to get out there and make it happen. Each new release has to leave the previous for dead.'

Her mother's words funnelled through the phone like evil-green smoke, sucking any residual oxygen from her lungs. *In the Throes of Murder* was more than leaving her first book for dead. Bad pun aside, her mother didn't know that, and she didn't need to know.

Another inane answer, a flurried goodbye and she ended the call as the door swung inward again.

Rita.

'What's this I hear about your hot detective distracting you from your deadline?'

Chapter Twenty-Two

Scents of salt and wet seaweed clung to Stacey's nostrils, hair whipping about her face, chilling and burning her skin all at once. Again she cursed the scrunchie still sitting on her dressing table. She tucked another clump of hair behind her ear only to have it slap against her cheek two seconds later.

Give it up, Stacey!

A gull's distant caw speared the silence, then dulled until all that filled her ears was the sound of the wind and the waves and her own shallow, laboured breathing.

Fingers all thumbs, she fumbled with the nylon fishing line, tugging it tight around metal and fibreglass alike. The pole shuddered, the line slipped through her fingers. A fibreglass arm sprung out and slapped hard against her hip.

She flinched.

Oww-ch!

Although, really, what was one more bruise?

Renaldo had never behaved so badly. Or was it the oncoming storm?

The lamppost light flickered.

She grabbed the mannequin's hand, rewinding the line around his wrist, huffing at the hair plastered over her forehead and eyes.

Black clouds growled across a churning sea, dusk having long-since tumbled into dark. The air grumbled, fierce, furious, like a wild boar barrelling toward its prey. No sane person would be out. Which meant no one was around, perhaps for miles. Exactly what she needed to enact this one, final scene so she could finish her book.

Again she fumbled. Tying knots with gloves wasn't easy. And bare hands wouldn't do. The Fatal Fisherman was too clever for that. No DNA or fingerprints allowed. Which meant she should have brought a beanie and surgical gloves. A mistake she wouldn't have made if she wasn't frazzled moments before leaving the house.

One guess why.

Or should she say, one guess *who?*

No matter how much she determined to avoid him, her stalker detective seemed just as determined to thrust himself into her life. Which meant he'd pitched up a tent in her brain and was hunkering down for the indeterminate future. Her only hope of keeping her sanity intact and embarrassment at bay was to stay away as much as possible.

Today being day one.

Her hand slipped. The fingernail inside her glove bent to an angle no nail should bend to.

'Ouch!'

Her voice echoed unnaturally loud, unnaturally out of place. She shivered, not merely from cold now. Since when did she get nervy?

Since her ghoulish plots had one by one sprung to life.

Her grip on the line slipped again. She yanked off the glove, squeezing her finger either side of the nail, watching the line of white slowly turn to blue.

A plastic bag skidded across the sand, the wind giving it wings and the twirling grace of a dancer. Sand eddied and swirled, and she squinted against the onslaught.

Renaldo stared up at her, his blank, dispassionate gaze suddenly mocking. Menacing.

Newspaper wrapped around her leg, whipping angrily. She kicked, wriggled, stamped, but it wouldn't budge. Breath constricted in her chest. She let go of the line and clawed at her calf. The paper caught and clung to her wet skin until it wrenched free, flying from her fingers and into the dark beyond the lamppost.

Her heart thundered.

The wind howled.

Again she shivered, unable to stop.

Time to go. She'd wing the rest.

You don't wing it. You never "wing" it. That's why you win awards. Why you'll win the Dagger to the Heart Award, the Rita, become the next romantic suspense NYT bestseller. Because your books are real.

Her head whipped back.

Too real.

She scooped up the fishing gear and heaped it into her duffel bag. Untying Renaldo wasn't as easy. Fingers became thumbs, and sticky red flowed from her knuckle.

Damn. That's all I need.

Real blood was so much harder to wash out than the edible kind. Now she owed Renaldo a new shirt.

Thunder ripped from the heavens, talons of light snatching across the blue-black sky.

Blood and stained mannequins were the least of her worries. She hiked Renaldo under her arm and turned toward the car. Salt-soaked air stung the back of her throat. Her pulse raced. Her free hand hunted her keys out, wedging the largest between her middle and forefinger, raising it like a sword before her body.

Something clattered to her right. She whipped round and her grip on Renaldo slipped. She froze, waiting, straining to see beyond the beam of yellow from above. Nothing changed.

Idiot!

She hitched Renaldo back under her arm and made for the car park, her legs not moving nearly fast enough. Numb and cold dulled sensation in her fingers. Her keys slipped from her hand. She bent to pick them up, ears booming, and stiffened.

She swung round. Could have sworn she heard a noise.

Nothing.

A lot of nothing that added to one big roar. The wind. The waves. Her imagination.

She shouldn't have come. She shouldn't have ignored every one of Chase's calls and she definitely shouldn't have ignored his orders to hold off on the writing and research until they'd caught the killer. Regardless of the underlying message from her publisher and agent at dinner last night.

What if *he* was out there now, watching? Waiting.

Killing his next victim.

She dumped everything into the back of the car, Renaldo included, slammed it shut, then fought the wind to reach her door. Trees bowed and swayed like seaweed, dust and debris swirling in great rolling mists along the bay. The door almost wrenched from her grasp and she pitched into her seat, slamming it behind her, dulling the howl outside to a shrill whistle.

Nothing close to what was in store. Time to be gone.

Keys in the ignition, her shaky hands clutched the wheel, the bones of her knuckles jutting starkly from beneath her skin. Drying blood crusted her fingers and smeared over Sidney's steering wheel.

Deep breath.

Just a bit of weather. A little wind. More than a gentle breeze, less than a tornado. Nothing dictating a dose of Prozac. A hot drink would fix her nerves, a sticking plaster her finger. She just needed to get home and all would be well.

She reached for the ignition. Froze. Squinted.

Something flapped from under one of the wipers. She switched on the car's full beams, not that she expected to see anyone. Who'd be crazy enough to brave the coast on a night like this? Who other than her, that is.

The car park was empty.

Why would someone leave promotional bin fodder on her windscreen in this weather? Either way, an answer to that question didn't rid her of the problem. Or stop the feeling that somewhere out there, evil eyes were watching. Fanciful notions of an overimaginative suspense author.

Shake that thought, you goof-ball!

She switched on the wipers. The black rubber shuddered, strained, churning the mechanical *whir* slowly into a squeal. She flicked them off before poor Sidney lost a limb, rolled down her window and reached around. Her fingertips didn't even come close. She pushed up with her legs and edged her shoulder out. *Nope.* No avoiding it. She couldn't do this from inside. Whatever it was obstructed too much of her view to leave it on the windscreen for the drive home. It had to come off.

Again she looked around, squinted through the wind and the murk. Delay tactics.

Grow a pair and toughen up, Stacey! It'll only take a few seconds.

Before she could second-guess herself, she lurched outside and skirted the open door. The envelope – not promotional flyer – was taped to the windscreen, wedged firmly under the wiper. No wonder it hadn't budged.

Her few seconds stretched to minutes, bracing against the wind, squinting as the first fat drops of rain splashed onto her hand and face and trickled down her neck. She wrenched the tape free and leapt back inside the car seconds before thunder cracked and the heavens opened. She dropped the splattered, yellow packet onto the seat beside her. Now wasn't the time to ponder the whats, whys and wherefores around her mysterious package.

Leaning forward, she edged out of the car park and onto the street. Twenty minutes until she'd be home, and that was on a good day. The windscreen wipers raced the raindrops, not nearly fast enough to make vision anything more than adequate.

Thirty-five minutes later she pulled into her driveway, pressed the garage door control and got nothing but a pitiful shudder from the rollers. She pressed again. Not even a shudder this time. Some fatalistic part of her wanted to bang her head against the steering wheel and scream. The practical side wanted out of the storm and into the safety of her own home.

Keys in her hand, she let practicality win, grabbing her handbag and the envelope and bracing before opening the car door. Sleet burned her hands and face as she battled a sheet of blinding hail with a ridiculous run-walk, too aware that the gods weren't even close to being on her side right now. The last thing she needed was to slip on her path or halfway up the stairs to her front door. It wasn't as if she could get any colder. Or wetter.

The key scratched against the lock until her numb fingers managed to insert it and turn.

Her first easy breath came as the door slammed closed behind her. Only seconds in the rain and the chill already seeped through her blood and into her bones. Shucking her shoes at the front door, she made for the kitchen. Best to attack the cold from the inside. A hot cup of lemon and ginger tea was just the thing.

She dumped everything onto the breakfast bar and flicked the switch for the jug. What she needed was a change of clothes, a hot shower, maybe even a shot of something medicinal in her tea. A rummage through the pantry showed she was out of brandy. Just tea then. Merely the thought eased her body's chill a little.

Her finger had stopped bleeding. A quick wash and a sticky plaster and she was fixed. *Perfect.* Her scene worked and she was home safe. *Stick that in your wazoo and smoke it, detective.* Her breathing slowed, along with her heartbeat.

She turned. Her gaze skimmed the countertop and whatever

breath she'd found caught in her throat.

The chill returned.

Red seeped through the yellow of the envelope. Chillingly familiar. Chillingly real. The red of blood other than her own.

'What the blazes were you thinking?'

Stacey tried to stand tall – to glare, lift her shoulders, her chin, show that Chase's onslaught had no effect, that she was nowhere near about to fall apart – but her shivering body wouldn't quit. Tears pricked her eyes and all she wanted was to slap that disdain from his face.

The sound was like the crack of bone china against her kitchen's ceramic tiles.

She yanked back her hand. He staggered, eyes wide, rubbing his reddening cheek, as if, well, as if she'd just slapped him. She stared down at her burning palm, almost as red as his face.

'What the hell was that for?'

This time her shoulders squared just fine. 'For being a dick.'

His nostrils flared, bringing to mind a dragon about to spit fire.

'Let me get this straight. You avoid me, ignore my calls all day, wait until a category two storm is brewing, leave the house and act out a murder scene for your book, *despite my advice to the contrary*, putting yourself in the line of danger so that the killer not only watches you, probably even copies you, then leaves you a message. And *I'm* a dick?'

Answers came thick and fast and she bit every one of those gems back. Last thing she needed was more of his yelling. The pound in her head had long surpassed jackhammer status and massaging her temple did nothing to lessen it.

The dragon tempered its fire. 'Don't you get it, Stacey? You could have been hurt, or worse.'

His expression softened, as if he cared.

Of course he does, you idiot. It's his job.

Her shoulders slumped like thick, wet clay. 'Can you go now? And take *that*,' she swallowed, 'that thing with you.'

The envelope taunted her from the kitchen table. And a finger.

Severed. Bloodied. *Real.* Tied up with white ribbon in a perfect bow. A gift from some psycho-killer nut-job.

The table had to go. Doubtful she'd ever look at it without seeing the blood. Such a lot of blood for one small piece of flesh. Nausea funnelled up her oesophagus and into her throat. She battled it back, closed her eyes, turned away from what once belonged to a person. A real, living, breathing person. Were they still? Alive, that is. Or had he killed them, too? And why leave the finger for her?

She clutched the back of a chair.

Was he like a cat? Killing his prey, bringing its still warm body as an offering, a gift. Was he seeking her approval? Her gratitude?

Oh, god!

'I think I'm going–' She dashed for the bathroom.

Dropping to her knees, she leaned over the bowl and dry retched. Saliva ran riot in her mouth, but nothing came out. Her stomach churned.

'Shit!' Chase dropped down next to her, combing her hair from her face, bunching it up, holding it back. If she was in any mind to think, she'd wonder if it meant anything. Only she wasn't. And it didn't.

Someone was out there, killing for *her*. All those dead bodies, that finger – all gifts, *for her.*

'I can't do this. It's too …'

'Real?'

'Frightening.'

'You've written worse.'

'But none of it was real. That–' She gestured to the door, the kitchen, and swallowed. 'That is.'

His palm circled her back, rubbing, warming. Comforting. 'You need to be more careful.'

She nodded. What else could she do? Chase was right. She couldn't act as if nothing was wrong. As if her life was normal and safe and everything would be okay. It was none of that and everything she poured into her books.

Murder.

Chase felt the instant fight seeped from Stacey's body.

Her shoulders hunched, her body slackened, and now the threat of vomit was gone, he pulled her toward him and into his arms.

He didn't bother to tell her that everything was going to be okay. That *she'd* be okay. No sense in that. They'd both know he was lying. He didn't know shit. That included the identity of the sick bastard who'd targeted Stacey and left his gruesome gift on her windscreen.

His squad would arrive any moment. But before they did, he needed to know Stacey was okay. That her spirit was back and she was ready to fight this. That she was ready to fight this, together.

There was no surprise with the thought. No panic, even.

He wanted to be there for this crazy, snake-loving danger-wielding woman. And more, he wanted to keep her safe.

Stroking her hair, he inhaled the fresh scent of honeysuckle and wet sand. 'You can do this.'

With a shake of her head she buried her face deeper into his shoulder. His heartbeat spiked. It was a long time since someone had leaned on him, needed him, like this. His working arm tightened around her, as if it had a mind of its own, as if it'd never let her go.

No time to ponder that puzzle.

He eased her back until he stared into deep liquid green. 'Stacey Holland, you are smart and strong and brave, and you *can* do this.'

Those oceans of green widened, then she licked lips that trembled, spiking more than his heart.

'You forgot clumsy and ridiculous.' She pushed herself up and away from the toilet. Him.

He followed. Framed his hands round her face so she'd see nothing but the truth in his eyes. 'No, I didn't.'

Her lips parted. If he'd retained any manner of brain he would have declared this the wrong time, the wrong place, the wrong everything.

If …

That useless organ had abandoned him at least five minutes ago, maybe more. Instead, it emptied, like a slot machine on a winning streak, leaving him with only one thought – how much he wanted to taste her right now. And how she looked like she wanted that too.

With his brain batteries fried, there was nothing else left for him to do.

He dropped his lips to hers.

Chapter Twenty-Three

He's going to kiss me!

Stacey's gaze darted toward the door.

Pull back. Move away. Tell him to stop.

She wedged her hands between them, palms flat against his chest and his racing, beating heart. Spice, the kind that warmed, that felt safe, surrounded her.

Her fingers lost themselves in the shirt cotton and male heat. She held her breath, closed her eyes and leaned in.

Lips met lips with barely a touch. Soft. Tentative. Teasing.

Her eyelids scrunched closed and all those wonderful visuals she injected with comprehensive insight into scenes just like this, evaded her. The world didn't stop spinning. Stars didn't burst like New Year's Eve pyrotechnics. The planets didn't collide.

What happened was surreal. A silence born of wonder. The world melted, like chocolate coating from its biscuit centre, and she sank into Chase, sliding her hands out from between them to clutch his hips, pulling him in.

There.

The kiss deepened.

Regardless of anything else, what he thought about her, felt about her, his body wanted her. And that was more than enough. Losing herself in this moment, this madness, meant leaving the madness of the world behind. And never had that been a more appealing prospect than now.

Her heart jackhammered against her ribs. Where his body hardened, hers softened. Where he pushed, she yielded. Awareness narrowed, the walls caving until all that remained was him and her and one magical, immeasurable kiss. *Aunt Milly's Choco-Sensations.* Like the cookie of all cookies, this was the kiss of all kisses.

Then someone tossed in the chilli. Senses heightened. Need

sharpened, his lips harder, his hands more urgent. Her midriff scorched with the brush of his palm as he eased under her top. Her eyes opened. If she wanted to stop, now was the time. A kiss was one thing, going further was …

Her fingers trembled across the scrunched white cotton of his shirt.

The first button took some manoeuvring. She licked her lips, persisted. It suddenly slipped free. She released a second. A third. No turning back now. No sense resisting the irresistible.

The edges of his shirt fell away, revealing …

Her breath hitched, her hands roaming his chest, lower. Hot skin. Smooth. Alive. She fumbled with his belt. He groaned, his palm cupping the underside of her breast, reaching up, squeezing, kneading her toward ecstasy.

Her head fell back, her eyes fluttering closed. She moaned.

'Stacey?'

'Aha.'

His hand stopped. Her eyes flew open, finding need in his. Raw. Untamed. Uncensored.

'You're okay with this, right?' The question rasped from his throat, restraint beading his brow.

Only one answer existed, one she sensed he craved as much as she.

'I–'

A round of knocks echoed from her front door. Another.

She froze as chickens burst into frenzied clucking. Add disconnecting her ridiculous door chime to the electrician's growing fix-it list. When she finally got round to calling him, that is.

The rise of Chase's brows didn't come close to masking his frustration. Hell, it was a perfect match for hers.

'Chickens?'

'They had a special on. It was either that or Jingle Bells.'

And there was that look again, questioning her sanity. His.

'My squad's here.' He pulled back, hand dropping, cold air replacing the warmth of his touch. His gaze darted toward the door, his body language conveying more than his words could – he didn't want his team knowing they'd been making out. She nearly snorted at the schoolgirl phrase.

He straightened the spikes from his hair.

Of course. Not *them.* Jayda. Bombshell. The partner he'd told Stacey was a pain in his ass.

She backed away. 'You called them?'

'You have evidence relevant to their case. I had to call them.'

'Of course.' She tugged her t-shirt back into place. 'You might want to make yourself presentable before we open the door.'

Watching him fumble with his buttons one-and-a-half handed made the tension in her shoulders double. She bit back a *for goodness sake!* – fuelled with a stern eye-roll at his buttoning-efforts and a kick to her ass for letting things go so far – and slapped his hands away. Her fingers were almost as useless as his, but with more than the usual concentration she soon had the finicky buggers fastened.

'Thanks, Mum.'

'I am not your mother!'

'Oh, I know *that*.'

Already flaming cheeks flamed redder. Her reaction just now had been anything *but* motherly. It was flagrant. Positively outrageous. *Wrong.* Hadn't she just declared she wanted Ethan? Nice, dependable, understanding *Ethan*. Not Chase. A man who made her lose her temper, her mind, all sense of herself. Who thought he could sweet talk and joke a path through her defences to get his way.

Movements awkward, jerky, he attempted to tuck his shirt into his trousers. No way was she helping with *that*. Then he stepped so close she could almost feel him against her again. His hand beneath her top, his hardness between her legs.

Sheesh!

She stumbled backwards, unable to drag her gaze from his.

'Hey.' His palm curved over her bicep. Hot. Vital. Electrifying. 'Are we good?'

'Of course.' Again she moved and his hand dropped. Any more and she'd end up in the shower stall. An image she so did not need with Chase around.

Skirting him, she made for the door just as another round of knocking and clucking began.

He snagged her hand. 'Are you okay to do this?'

She shook it off, glaring at him and his stupid idiot question. 'If I say "no" will it all go away?'

Again that look. ''Course not.'

'Then I've no choice but to be okay. But, hey, thanks for your diversion back there.' She nodded toward the bathroom. 'Perfect for taking my mind off everything until the cavalry arrived.'

Chase's head jerked as if she'd slapped him.

She guessed in a way she had. Kind of like when he pulled back and she realised she'd just been hors d'oeuvres to Jayda's main and dessert.

If the past had taught her one thing, it was that trusting her instincts was a mistake. And so were those last few moments with Chase.

Diversion?

She thought their kiss was a *diversion?*

Stacey pushed past and the shock of her words, her disdain, glued his feet to the floor and his tongue to the roof of his mouth. Until he saw her unlatch the door without checking who was out there first.

He shoved her out of the way and levelled his gun before the door fully opened. Just as well. It wasn't Jayda. Or "the cavalry".

Black-rimmed eyes gaped at his weapon, whiter-than-white hands dropping a water-logged, out-turned umbrella to slowly move above her head. The umbrella clattered onto the welcome mat – a dancing, smiling sun almost as ridiculous as its owner – and rolled over onto a worn pair of black army boots.

The Addams family show tune tripped through his mind. What was the mother's name?

'Morticia!'

That was it.

Stacey elbowed past, again, glaring and muttering beneath her breath. 'Put that thing away before you hurt someone.'

How did a woman with two university degrees – almost – who studied and understood the most basic natures known to man, manage to get everything so incredibly wrong? Didn't she get he was trying to protect her?

She half-closed the door, doing everything she could to block him out.

Not a chicken-chirping chance.

He edged over, moved so close he felt the heat radiating between them. The blush on her cheeks said she felt it too.

Giving an unhampered view of her stiff get-the-hell-away-from-me shoulder, she focused on the woman at the door. 'What are you doing here?'

'I was worried after last night, so I thought I'd stop by and check on you.' Risen-from-the-dead eyes looked him up and down. 'Seems things are more serious than I thought.'

Stacey tossed her head. 'Nothing I can't handle.'

'What on earth do you have to handle that needs a guy with a gun?'

He stepped in then, forcing Stacey to widen the door to prevent being squeezed out of the conversation. 'Guy with a gun has a name.'

Stacey looked anything but happy at being cornered into introducing them, so he took the initiative and offered his hand. 'Chase Durant.'

"Morticia" rubbed her wet palm over wet trousers and launched into a bout of enthusiastic hand shaking, her bony palm as cold as her over-white skin tone suggested.

How the hell did all that black paint stay in place? Given the heavens had unleashed like waters escaping the gates of a canal. Just as well the porch provided protection, otherwise they'd have another reason to argue, given there was no way Goth Woman was coming inside before Jayda arrived. Before his squad had secured the evidence.

'Chase Durant? *The* Chase Durant?'

She continued shaking, her face filled with what he could only describe as an *a-ha!* expression. He couldn't help but smile. So Stacey had mentioned him? First to one friend – was it Shazz? – now to another. She may tell herself he was a diversion, but you don't tell everyone you know about diversions. You do, however, tell the people in your life about a person of interest.

Was he a person of interest to Stacey? And if so, what was with the whole diversion thing back there? Something he'd get out of her, later.

For now ...

He turned back to Goth Woman. 'And you are?'

'Beth Samuels, Stacey's editor.'

A car door slammed. Multiple footsteps splished and splattered over the gravel path, indicating more than one visitor. He managed to save his hand and peered past Beth. No false alarm this time – his squad had arrived.

Jayda and Sam braced wind and rain to join them at the front door. The proverbial house party, although the set of Jayda's mouth was anything but jovial. And it had nothing to do with the dripping strands of her hair. The way she eyed first Beth then Stacey made it more than clear she was still pissed at what she saw as his fraternising with a suspect. Probably thought he'd added another – Beth – to the mix.

This had to be her version of the-shoe-on-the-other-foot treatment. Less than a year ago she'd been on the outer, hunting the Night Terror with her reporter boyfriend while on enforced leave. Now was his turn for a taste.

Only Stacey wasn't his girlfriend. She was intrinsic to the case, not as a suspect but as a vital source of insight into the killer's mind. And because of that, and whatever other link she had to the psychopath, she was in danger. He just wanted her safe. In his care, his bed.

WTF!

He would have staggered backwards if he hadn't been gripping the doorjamb. Where the hell did *that* come from? Residual of five minutes ago? It was the only plausible explanation.

'Chase. Stacey.' Jayda turned her glittering green glare to the woman beside her.

Curiosity filled Beth's expression as her gaze moved across Jayda and Sam, to him, then back to Jayda before she made her own introduction. 'Beth. Stacey's editor.' She tilted her head, not unlike a magpie contemplating a juicy worm for breakfast. 'And you are?'

'Interested in why you're here.'

Eyebrows tweaked within an inch of disappearing arched above an over-sharp gaze. 'I'm visiting Stacey.'

'Why today?'

'Why is that relevant?'

Jayda's badge answered that question.

Black painted lips formed a perfect O. 'I was worried.'

'About?'

'Her.'

Jayda's gaze narrowed. 'What about her?'

Beth bent, dragged her umbrella up from the smiling sun and

shook. Jayda and Sam stepped back, less than amused. Not that a few more drops made a difference. Wet was wet. There was no such thing as wetter.

'I'm not sure what you're asking.' Beth shrugged painfully bony shoulders. 'I'm Stacey's editor *and* friend. I was worried. I came. There's no cloak and daggers here.'

Jayda looked as if she thought otherwise. Without comment, she turned to Sam. 'Stay here.' Unspoken meaning, *watch them.*

Stacey still clutched the door, as if at any moment she'd slam it shut.

Jayda put pay to that. 'Let's move this party in from the cold.' She stamped her boots on the happy mat and stepped inside, forcing Stacey back. The others followed, crowding in the entranceway.

Then she turned to Chase. 'Show me what you've got.'

Another pointed look to Sam and she strode down the hall.

The temperature in the house must have been minimum twenty-five degrees centigrade, about as cold as a party pie fresh from the oven. Any frost in the air was all her.

Deflection time.

He shot her a grin. 'How's my ole buddy, Seth?'

She didn't appear amused. Or fooled.

She huffed. 'Now I know you're as guilty as all sin. Are you sleeping with her?'

He couldn't stop the heat from finding his face and only hoped she'd pick it as rage. 'Of course not!'

Not an all-out lie. Trying didn't count.

'There's no "of course not" about it.' Her gaze raked his less-than-perfectly tucked shirt.

If Stacey had helped with it like she'd helped with his buttons, Jayda wouldn't have reason to doubt him. Then again, if Stacey's hands had wandered anywhere near his waistband, Jayda would still be standing on the doorstep and he'd be inside … well, just that. *Inside.*

His reaction to that thought didn't help.

He turned and made for the kitchen. 'It's been a long day, that's all. Just because your top's less than perfectly buttoned, doesn't mean you've enjoyed a quickie before driving over.'

When he looked back, the expression on her face made him bark with laughter. 'Or maybe it does. Well, well, wonders never cease.'

She stopped, unsuccessfully hiding her recovery, a kind of floundering like a recruit's first reach for his weapon. 'This has nothing to do with me or Seth.'

'Actually, it has everything to do with you. Just because you worked a case and banged the help, doesn't mean I'll do the same.' He raised his hand when it seemed she'd argue, and barrelled on. 'Stacey has insight into a killer and for some reason he feels connected to her. This message proves it. It wasn't that long ago you were left a message. Or have you forgotten?'

He'd wandered into asshole territory, felt the transition with every pain-filled cut on Jayda's face. The knowledge curdled his stomach, but there was no turning back. Not if he was to protect Stacey and prove her innocence.

Granite carved through the hurt in Jayda's expression. 'No, Chase. I haven't forgotten.' She shook her head, sighed. 'If you're so certain she's in danger, request a security detail.'

He slapped his forehead. 'Why didn't I think of that? Hackett's sure to jump at the idea.' Dragging his palm down his face, he forced his temper to retreat. 'I'm staying here until we catch the killer.'

Her expression was all too knowing.

He shook off his own misgivings. It was his job to – what his counterparts in the US put so succinctly – serve and protect. That's exactly what he was doing.

His first priority.

Not that he'd quibble if anything happened between them in the interim.

'It's a big house, and there's more than one bedroom.' At least, he thought there was.

Her lips clamped, then she nodded. 'If anything turns up, keep me in the loop.'

'Like now?'

'Yeah.' She barely blinked. 'How's your arm? Any chance of passing that medical and getting back on the job?'

His heartbeat stumbled.

He rubbed his wrist. 'It's getting there.'

'You're not stalling, are you?' Her gaze pricked his skin like a steel-tipped lance.

He stabbed right back. 'Why would you think that?'

'Just a feeling.'

'Your gut? Might just be it's an hour past dinner.'

She sighed. Yet another female who didn't appreciate wit.

Her gaze shifted to his left shoulder and he stiffened. The action was a sure-fire sign she was about to spout something he wouldn't like.

She pushed sopping hair back from her face. 'Rather than hear this from someone else, I thought I should tell you in person.' She drew in a deep breath. 'I've requested a transfer.'

His stomach pitched.

He wasn't wrong. He didn't like it one bit.

'Why?'

This time her gaze jumped to her right. A stretching the truth kind of "tell".

'Seth and I are moving interstate. He's landed a spot at the Sydney Tribune and I need a change.'

'From me?'

'Everything. Melbourne's not the same since ...' Her voice wavered.

He nodded. She didn't need to finish the sentence, and neither did he. They both knew.

'Where will you go?'

'Northern suburbs.'

'When?'

'After the wedding.' *A month.* 'Hopefully by then this whole copycat serial killer fiasco will be wrapped up.'

'So, I'm up for a new partner.'

Her brows raised.

He shot her a grin meant to mask how much her news affected him. 'Hope she's hot.'

''Course you do.'

'There has to be a cost–benefit to losing a damned fine partner.'

Her eyes glazed, her smile a ghost of smiles past. Then it was gone and her shoulders squared. 'Labs came back on the knife.'

His mind ran to keep up with the swerve in conversation. 'And?'

'The blood was porcine. No human DNA or fingerprints. Nothing to identify who owned the knife or who put it in your girlfriend's cellar.'

He didn't react. Didn't need to give her a reason to stop talking.

Her raised brows said she knew it. 'Every and any store, actual or online, stocks that brand. We'd have more luck tracing a coffee bean to its tree than determining where that knife was purchased.' Lips pursed, she raised her chin. 'So, we have a solid reason why the knife was chosen. Shame we can't say the same for your girlfriend.'

Each dig was a waft of live fish-bait under his nose. He wasn't biting. 'The evidence is in the kitchen. This way.'

He crossed the living room, she followed. 'I'll need to question her.'

'I know.'

'You realise this makes her appear more guilty, not less.'

If he didn't know better, he'd guess she wanted Stacey to be guilty.

'She's being targeted.'

'So *you* say.'

They stopped beside the small, square kitchen table to stare at the envelope and its bloodied contents.

'*I* say this situation's great publicity – for her and her publisher. Don't you find it interesting that her editor showed up, today of all days? I've a few pointed questions for our Goth wannabe. If links between these crimes and Stacey's books get out, sales will skyrocket. Good for Stacey, good for her editor, good for everyone with something to gain, financial or otherwise.'

He met her gaze. 'But they haven't. So what does that tell you?'

'She's distracted.' He barely blinked at the word, much as it robbed the dry from his mouth. Lucky his partner – soon-to-be ex-partner – didn't notice. 'But if I'm right, it won't take long for her to make a move.' Jayda's glare was the pointy end of a very sharp spear. 'I believe it's a matter of *when* and not *if* she'll begin exploiting the murders as her own personal marketing strategy.'

Chapter Twenty-Four

'**N**o sense locking up. We're going out.'

The slumps in Stacey's shoulders slumped some more. Now Chase's squad was gone, all she wanted was to collapse into bed with a hot water bottle and thaw the cold that had drilled deep into her bones.

She let her hand fall from the deadbolt and turned to face Chase. 'We?'

He nodded. 'You're taking me home to pack.'

Some of the slumps straightened. 'Going on holiday?'

'If you call moving in here a holiday, then yes.'

Stress, exhaustion, they were making her hear things. Like Chase saying he was moving in.

She shook her head and focussed real hard on his lips, to make sure she got it right this time. 'Moving where?'

'Keep up with the program. I take it you've got a spare room?'

'Yes. No. You can't stay.'

'Which is it? Yes or no. And, actually, I can. Unless you'd prefer moving into my place.'

'No one's moving into anyone's place. You have yours, I have mine, and never, ever shall the little parallel pointy lines meet.'

'That'd work fine if a killer wasn't following you. But since he is, I'm not leaving your side.'

'Then I'll make it easy for you. I'm leaving yours.'

Chase bit back a grin until he realised Stacey was serious. Before he could stop her, she'd opened the front door and was bounding down the stairs. She'd obviously forgotten about the weather – Melbourne in all its glory. Branches lashed about the treetops, rain splintering out from the billowing storm clouds above. It didn't escape him that she'd chosen a raging storm over his company.

With a growl he followed her out, leaning into the thrashing wind and rain. 'You can't leave. We're in the middle of a category two storm.'

She forged on, her hair whipping about her face, her thin layer of clothing already sodden and clinging to her trembling body like a second skin. 'I can do whatever I want.'

Howling the likes of hungry dingos filled the air, wind gusts snatching and tossing leaves and debris into an angry swirl.

He ripped a leaf from his cheek and grabbed her arm. 'Don't be ridiculous, Stacey. It's not safe out here.'

She whirled round, wrenching from his grasp, hand waving back at the door and dry shelter they'd left behind. 'And it's not safe in there either.'

Her pale lips clamped after the words left them. As if they slipped through without her consent. He couldn't hear but he'd swear her teeth were chattering.

'Safe from what, Stacey?'

She backed up, hands carving the air. 'I'm not doing this with you.'

He swiped the wet from his face. '*What* aren't you doing with me?' He tried to look innocent. Figured he must have failed when she harrumphed and marched off again.

She aimed her keys at her car and pressed. She reached out for the door.

'*Don't!*'

She froze.

Then she spun round and glared, shoving back clumps of sopping hair from her face. 'Stop trying to manipulate me with your conspiracies and kisses.' Again her lips clamped. Another slip. Her face turned beet red beneath the streaming rain.

She wasn't fooling anyone. Their "diversion" before had her thrown. And he'd bet box seats at the MCG she wanted a rerun. If he had any box seats to bet, that is.

Her hand dropped, her keys dangling at her side. 'There's no car bomb.'

'Are you willing to bet your life on it?'

That threw her. She hesitated, shifted her gaze from him to the car and then back again.

'Fine! I'll walk.'

'To where?'

'I don't care. Somewhere where you're not.'

'This is ridiculous.'

'Great. Now I'm ridiculous.'

'It's cold and it's wet.'

'Then go inside. I didn't ask you to follow me.'

He shoved back the urge to grab her and shake the stubborn from every ramrod bone in her body. '*You* called me. Remember?'

'To help. Not jump my bones!'

'I didn't jump anything back there. The leap was mutual, and you know it.'

She spun round. 'Maybe it was mutual, or maybe I was so shit-scared I just wanted to forget.'

He ignored the cut of her words. And the fact that they shouldn't have cut, that he shouldn't have cared. What did it matter why she'd reacted to him? She had, and that was good enough for now. For what they both wanted. What better way to keep her safe than to keep her in his arms?

'Let's forget together.'

'What do *you* have to forget?'

He clenched his left hand as far as the numbness would allow and readjusted the sopping sling with his right. The pain from the fall had lessened. The other, not so. But what did he expect? Can't fix something when you don't know how it broke. Tests would help. So simple. All he had to do was call and book and show up.

There isn't time.

But there would be when the case was over. He ignored the whine in his head that he was stalling. Avoiding the inevitable. Something he'd perfected since watching his mother slowly wither and die.

He swiped the wet from his face and pitched it to the kerb, mentally pitching his thoughts with it. Stacey needed someone to keep her safe. And there was a killer that needed catching. All actions which took precedence over a diagnosis that – tests or no tests – wouldn't change anything but the *knowing*.

He shrugged. 'Everyone has something.'

'That doesn't answer my question.'

His nose twitched, begging for a sneeze. Sniffing it back, he dragged his plastered top from his skin. 'Can we at least go inside and discuss this?'

She shook her head and he was close enough this time to hear her teeth chatter. 'Here is just fine.'

He may be altruistic – some might say with a dash of horny on the side – but he wasn't stupid. Tell just one person, and that secret was suddenly a ticking time bomb.

And if that one person happened to be a woman who'd do anything to wash him from her spun caramel locks … he wasn't going there. Even in those weak moments when he wished he could.

He sighed. 'I get it, Stacey. More than you know.' His shoulder rolled against the wet dig of the sling. 'You feel like you're losing control, like your life's swerved off the rails and when you try to get it back, the steering wheel snaps off in your hands. You're frustrated. Scared. Don't want to give in, but you're at a loss how to fight. I can help. We can work the case, find this bastard, steal back your control. You won't need to be alone, and you won't need to be scared. All we need to do is stop fighting each other and focus on the real enemy.'

Deep, devouring green stared up at him, delving all too closely, as if she were able to read between the lines and *know* just how much he got how she felt. He shifted, as if breaking her gaze could break her link into his brain. His shoes squelched.

Injecting swagger into his stance, he cocked a brow. 'I'm not leaving while there's a chance he might hurt you. That means I need to pick up a change of clothes, my toothbrush and some PJs. But if you'd prefer not to take me home, I'm happy to sleep naked.' He grinned at her then. 'The choice is yours.'

'Not much of a choice.'

'Depends on your preference.'

She huffed, but he could sense her caving.

Time to ease her over the edge. 'This isn't about us or the fact that I want you.'

Her already flaming cheeks intensified.

'This is about keeping you safe, so you're not my next crime scene. So it's not your finger next time, wrapped in ribbons and placed on someone's windscreen. And you don't become another notch on this sick son of a bitch's scalpel.' He dragged in a breath, dialled back his irritation. 'Safety or digging your heels in? What'll it be?'

Another huff, this time for effect. Then her gaze gripped his. 'It's my house, so what I say goes. You sleep in the spare room.'

She acted as if she'd found a spider in her shoe. Then the expression changed, as if she'd looked closer and discovered spider-babies too. 'And there's no naked sleeping under my roof. It's PJs or you're out!'

Chase ended the call, Gracie's distress still ringing in his ears. Mad didn't come close to describing the burn in his gut. It took every shred of restraint not to slam his fist into the car door. If that door had been a particular asshole's face, holding back might not have been so easy.

He glanced at Stacey, perched behind a pink fluffy steering wheel that looked like a poodle sporting a bad rinse, then at the road ahead.

'Turn right here.'

She spared him a look. Again with the glare. Although she did listen. He braced as the car swerved round the corner. Add a huff or several to that glare and the temperature in the car rose toward mercurial. Just as well. It was still bloody freezing outside, and in his bones, regardless of the fact his clothes had seen the inside of Stacey's tumble dryer for the past hour. Now they'd finally hit the road and she looked less impressed than if she'd just swallowed a fly.

He grinned. 'Better hope the wind doesn't change.'

'You're not the slightest bit funny.'

'Wasn't trying to be.' He squinted out at the road signs. 'Take the next left.'

'Your place is right.'

'We're taking a detour.'

She scrunched her cute, disapproving nose. 'Not another down-memory-lane trip? Our last one at Hook, Line and Sinker ended in disaster.'

'Could have been worse.' He didn't bother to grin this time. The quip was neither meant to be a joke nor funny. 'We're visiting.'

'The girl you were just talking to? Gracie, right?'

'Yeah.'

'She's in some kind of trouble?'

'Some kind.'

Her bottom lip plumped. 'Who knew you were a knight in shining armour to so many damsels?'

The set of strawberry gloss between her teeth sent certain parts of his body into unwanted action. She looked anything but happy. As if …

'You wouldn't be jealous, would you?'

Her snort was about as ladylike as a brawny scratch of the proverbials. 'You fancy yourself a little too much.'

He chuckled. 'I'm not the only one.'

Lips pressed firmly together, this time she grunted.

They passed the old community centre, paint peeling, lawn just short of overgrown. Then the park where as a teenager he and his mates played footy, checking out the local girls who gathered to gossip and check them out right back.

'Next left, then it's the yellow weatherboard on the right. Number fifty-two.'

She turned the pink circle of fluff like it was the steering wheel of a Lotus GTE in the Bathurst 1000. Her hippie-mobile swerved and this time bracing didn't prevent the *thwack* of his elbow against the car door. Her almost-smile was a dead giveaway. Yep, as green as the rampant sea in her eyes.

With twinges shooting up his arm, he should've been pissed. Instead he grinned. Risking life and limb had become the daily norm when Stacey was around. And if nothing else, she made all the mess around him disappear, red-hot temper and all. Not so shabby, even if it was only for a moment.

The car skidded into the curb outside the sunny bungalow which had once been pale green, his mother's favourite colour.

'Stay here.'

'Am I supposed to bow and say "Yes, Master" to each of your dictates?'

How could anyone not love that fire?

Shit!

Shove that thought away. Far, far away. Vault it, then forget the combination. 'Your place, your rules. My world, my rules. And the rules right now are, stay in the car.'

She scowled. Huffed. Harrumphed. Nothing like the woman who'd just melted into him, made him melt everywhere but where it counted. She gripped the wheel like she wanted to grip hold of his neck.

He manoeuvred out of the car and turned. 'Don't go anywhere.'

'I know the drill. Don't talk to strangers and don't move without telling you.' Daggers glared up at him. 'Ten minutes. That's all you get. Any longer and you'll walk home, with or without your damn PJs.'

He didn't bother to fight the twitch of his lips. 'Ah, and here we come to the crux. Deep down, you want me without PJs.'

Her glare was like ice. 'Delusional much?' The ice dropped to that ridiculous blue monster on her wrist. 'Nine and a half minutes. *Tick, tock.*'

He slammed the door. She wouldn't dare …

A short, unpainted nail tapped the watch face, her mouth a flat, uncompromising line.

He moved slower than his usual amble, regardless of the storm that had at least eased a little, crunching and squelching along the gravel until he left the path and climbed the steps leading up to Gracie's front door.

One glance to the eyesore at the curb confirmed Stacey on her phone now, animated, smiling. Even at a distance he could tell the smile reached her eyes. In his mind they sparkled, her mouth curving upward, deepening the bow in her lips. A bow he'd touched and tasted, wanted to taste again.

He frowned. Miss Stacey Holland was filling his thoughts too entirely. Not to mention the ache much, much lower. *Only one way out, old boy. Satisfy your curiosity then move on.*

He adjusted his belt, turned back to the peeling pineapple door. Whatever his sister wanted, it'd be a well-needed drag of his mind back to reality and his body back to sense. She may have been older, but that fact had no bearing on his need to protect her. A need that stemmed from way back, and a lifetime of habit.

He knocked.

Nothing.

He knocked again.

This time he heard movement beyond the thick oak.

Key scraped against lock and the door inched open only as far as the safety chain allowed. Eyes – weary, red-rimmed – peeked through the gap.

Recognition filled the chocolate brown. The door closed, the chain jangled, then it opened just wide enough for him to edge through. With a hasty click it snapped shut beneath Gracie's whitening fingers.

The pallor and pull of her skin across her cheekbones clenched the muscles around his heart. Before the question could leave his lips, a blue blur hurtled up the hall and slammed into his thighs.

'Unc' Chase!'

He brushed a fringe of bouncing afro-curls back from the most angelic two-year-old face on the planet.

Him, biased? Never.

That same angel snatched his trouser-leg too close to moving bits for comfort, and tugged. ''tory, 'tory, 'tory.' He glanced at his mother, then back again. '*Pease.*'

Warmth like none other billowed in his heart.

Another tug of his jeans and wide eyes as deep brown as his father's stared out from baby-soft olive skin. 'Hairy 'clary?'

Chase dropped to his haunches, receiving a mammoth-sized hug for his efforts. 'Sure, bud.'

'Jag, why don't you fetch your book for Uncle Chase?' The voice's waver made him look up in time to see his sister's attempted smile. 'See if you can find the new one, too.'

A sharp band of colour slashed her cheeks, her eyes bright but tear spent – testament to how badly he'd failed in his oath to protect her.

His chest constricted. He hadn't seen that expression since Mum …

Too close to home.

He straightened and moved in, arms open wide. She stepped back, bit her trembling lip, her shoulders making a valiant attempt to square.

He pulled up short, vowing to tear Jagger apart, piece by slimy piece when he saw him again. 'You look like crap.'

'Words every girl longs to hear.' She turned the key and deadlock, refastening the safety chain.

The clamber of toddler feet and waddle of nappy clad jeans disappeared down the hall.

'Stay out of the living room, JJ.'

Without a word, the little man did just that, veering left toward the bedrooms.

'What's up, Sis?'

'This.' With a deep sigh, she led him toward the off-limits living room and swung the door open.

'Holy shit!'

If he thought his sister looked bad, her living room looked much, much worse. Splintered buffet drawers and their contents lay strewn across the floor. Side tables were upended and clouds of stuffing puffed out from cushions, their couches slashed beyond repair.

He plucked a shard of glass from the carpet that once belonged to the print above the couch. The picture had been ripped from the frame.

'What the hell were they looking for?'

Her expression masked. 'It's just a random break-in.'

Not a great liar, his sister. Even when they were kids, he'd managed to get at the truth by guilting her into it. Time and age had changed that, although the tells of falsehood were still there. She tugged at her top lip with her fingers and tried to mask their tremble.

'When did it happen?'

'This morning. When we were at Stef's.'

Crazy cat-lady. Didn't every neighbourhood have one? Only this nutter had a shock of blue-rinsed hair, a houseful of furry felines and no green Houdini snakes. Even in crisis, Stacey shoved uninvited into his thoughts. He shoved back.

Blue-green glass cracked under his shoes. Remnants of Gracie's op-shopping obsession – some retro peacock lamp that had offended his eyes from the moment he was coaxed into assembling it. Even the fact he'd never have to see the monstrosity again couldn't placate him.

Thank heavens she and Jagger Junior were out during the break-in. If they'd been home … the alternative didn't bear thinking about.

'You can't keep covering for that bastard, sis.'

Her gaze darted, even as her jaw tightened. 'I'm not covering for anyone.'

His jaw followed suit. 'What'd the cops say?'

'I didn't call them.'

'You …?' He clenched his teeth against words he'd only regret later and pulled out his mobile.

Her head jerked. 'What are you doing?'

'What you should have done.'

She snatched at his arm. 'No!'

The shake in her voice, the fear in her eyes, made him return the phone to his pocket. 'Godammit, Grace! Stop protecting him!'

'Mum-eee!' The sing-song voice bounded down the hall toward

the living room.

She moved to the door. 'It's not *him* I'm protecting.'

Fingers wrapped tight around the handle, she spared him a look – that old-time look when she'd turned twelve and he stated there was no way she'd have anything to do with Bobby Dean, irrespective of their father's distracted consent. She'd not listened then, wasn't listening still. Without a backward glance, she stalked from the room.

Blood pounding, he scoured the chaos. Every broken bit reeked of his scum ex-bastard-in-law's stench. He'd been warned. Ignored and acted regardless. Didn't matter whether this was Jagger's doing or any one of his cronies, there'd be no free pass this time. The age of hiding behind Gracie's skirts had ended. Time to make good of his promise.

But first he had a scene to search, a nephew to read to, and a woman in a ridiculous excuse for a car who wouldn't wait forever. He made for the window and peered through the lace curtain. A measly eleven minutes and the hippie-mobile was gone.

His gaze moved to the a mound of shredded paper, once JJ's Mother's Day card from kinder, now good for nothing but the trash. A boil like none other bubbled up inside. Stacey could wait.

No one threatened his family. His loved-ones.

This fight, he could win.

First he called in a favour that would see a uniformed officer watching Stacey until he arrived. With her safety ensured, he called Chris to check on Jagger's movements. The call clicked straight to voicemail. He left a less-than-cordial message requesting a less-than-tardy call back.

His focus returned to the room, dirt spilling over the windowsill and onto the floor. He snapped a couple of pics on his phone. Then, pulling on a pair of rubber gloves from his pocket, he scooped a sample into a specimen bag, labelled it and set it aside. A closer look, a dust for fingerprints; then he moved to the couch, making quick work of his inspection. Each inch of the room was scrutinised. No cushion stuffing or broken picture frame unturned.

Not calling the cops didn't stop the investigation. And Gracie should have known better than to expect it would. Whoever had trashed the place was looking for something. And that something was linked to his weasel of an in-law.

A weasel of an in-law who'd never get the chance to hurt his sister again.

Chapter Twenty-Five

Damn old houses and ancient electrical wiring!

Stacey flipped the light switch. Up. Down. Then up, down again. Not even a flicker.

While you're at it, damn detectives with their drown-worthy eyes, sexy smiles and less-than-amusing wit! They've no place outside my books. Or in my mind.

She let the door between house and garage slam. The open roller door – opened manually – allowed enough light for her to edge along the wall without severing a limb or worse from any one of the hanging gardening tools. Then she skirted Sidney's bumper to the other side. If she'd arrived earlier, instead of avoiding home and the possibility of Chase waiting for her, sunlight would have made the process easier. As it was, twilight red slashed the sky, soaking the white-washed walls as if they dripped blood.

Melodramatic? Yeah, well she was a writer. She lived for melodrama.

On the damned page.

Her heart *thrumped* so hard, she tasted the fear in her throat. She swallowed. At least the storm had abated. Something to be thankful for. Her fingers fumbled with the meter box, and then the master switch. *Flip.* No go. *Flip, flip.* And there ended her electrical expertise.

She froze. Poised her mobile. Strained to hear.

A bang. A clatter.

There it was again.

The wind?

She switched her phone to flashlight, bathing the room in a soft white. The beam wavered, dimmed then frittered to nothing. She mouthed a few choice words.

Great timing to need a charge.

Her hand reached for the closest potential weapon she could find. It skipped over a rubber cactus she'd picked up at a garage sale but had yet to install in Midnight's enclosure; a stack of still to be used hula hoops; a yoga mat she'd overenthusiastically bought after a single lesson; a punching bag still in its original wrapping; her mum's old rust-bucket exercise bike. Spoilt for choice. No gardening tools on this side.

The cactus it was.

She swung her gaze left, then right. Couldn't see a damn thing.

The noise came again.

Outside.

Her heart charged like a wild rhino battering against her ribs.

Wind howled. Of course it frigging did! All she needed was the sound of footsteps and heavy breathing in her ear and the setting would be the perfect cliché. Oh, and perhaps a bar or two of Psycho music. She shivered. Blessed as an overactive imagination was when writing, other times it was an infernal curse.

Difficult, now, to hear anything over the ringing in her ears. No manner of pressing could drag the phone back from the dead. She stuffed it in her pocket, held her breath and edged closer to the driveway.

You should go inside and call Chase.

No!

It was probably nothing.

Bang. Clatter.

She jumped.

Of course, it's nothing!

Still, shouldn't she call someone? Dial triple zero? Just in case.

And if it's nothing, I'll look like a fool. Not news to Chase, but still …

She straightened, braced the cactus in front with both hands and moved slowly toward the roller-door exit. What she wouldn't do for a *50% more* can of hairspray right now. Or a sexy detective … If she was in a book, readers would accuse her of being too stupid to live. Hell, she'd never even consider writing this scene.

She stopped. Inhaled. Listened. *Nothing.*

If she'd been thinking clearly, she would have used Sidney's tail lights. *To go back, or not to go back?* Ah, that was the question.

She shrugged at her silliness, leaned forward, peeked out. Left. Right.

The side gate swung slowly outward, then slammed back against its hinges.

See? Nothing.

Idiot.

Beyond the gate, down the side of the house, nothing moved but the old lilac bush rippling in the wind. She wedged the cactus under her arm and fastened the latch. Hands trembling. Heart thumping.

Then she heard it. The footsteps she'd jokingly taunted herself with earlier.

Her fingers tightened around her weapon.

Don't think. React.

She swung. Hard.

A breathless *oomph* told her she'd hit target. Barely taking a breath, she swung again.

'Fuck!'

Shit!

And she'd worried calling the cops would make her look foolish.

'What the hell, Stacey!' Strong hands yanked the cactus from her grip, probably in case she was tempted to swing it again.

Smart move. She was more than tempted.

'What the hell, Chase?' she mimicked. Her hands found her hips. 'Why are you here?'

'To protect you.'

No way should she feel even slightly guilty that he was rubbing his slinged arm.

'Unnecessary.'

His brow quirked in a way that should have been arrogant and unappealing. Something was up with her douche-bag radar, because since when were scathing eyebrows sexy?

He grinned. 'We've already hashed out this argument, and I won. Remember?'

'Finished your knight in shining armour duties with your girlfriend, then?'

Damn the pique in her voice, and how it had to give the wrong idea. Her heart was still pounding against her ribs, her nerves jumping like a bunny on an electric wire. He'd just scared the living bejesus out of her. The dig was her way – albeit childish – of dealing. That's all.

His mouth tightened. Ah, she'd hit a nerve.

'Gracie's not my girlfriend, and she's fine, thank you.'

Red raced up his neck. Not just one nerve. Seems she'd hit an entire, hot-firing bundle.

'You, however, are far from fine, or safe. What the hell were you trying, back there? Death by cactus? Do you really think this,' he shook the limp hunk of rubber, '*thing* would stop someone from harming you, or worse?'

'Lucky for you I didn't grab a shovel.'

'Lucky for you, you didn't need it.'

She returned his glare with one equally as cutting. At least, she hoped it was.

'Are you planning to spear me with that look all evening, or can we take this inside?' He lifted a backpack from the ground. 'I brought PJs.'

Damn if that grin didn't send a troupe of dancing butterflies through her tummy.

You're pathetic, Stacey!

With all the cats and butterflies under his spell, her stomach lining would be a disaster before long.

He unzipped and opened the bag. 'And I brought cookies.'

She recognised the box all too well. With Pavlov precision, her mouth watered. Hopefully her overzealous cactus-beating hadn't pounded them to crumbs. No guilt there either. She couldn't help the way her mind worked.

'Triple choc?'

He nodded, eyes sparkling. 'With chilli.'

She had a tough time keeping her tongue from rolling out red-carpet-style from her mouth.

How did he know?

It didn't matter. He had Aunt Milly's Choco-Sensations in his hand, and that meant he'd earned entry into her house. *Just the house.*

But first …

'Can I borrow your phone? I need to make a call and mine's dead.'

He unlocked the screen and handed it over. Their fingers brushed for that clichéic contact, and damn if her response wasn't just as clichéic. This was sending her own level of pathetic beyond normal.

She avoided his gaze and entered one of the only phone numbers she remembered while heading back toward the garage. A warm buzz prickled up over her back. Forgivable if it had only stopped there. She squirmed, tried to act as if she wasn't completely affected by his close proximity. Since when had she *felt* the presence of any guy who just happened into her bubble? Since when before *him*, that is.

Stretching up, she yanked at a red rope, cursing every inch of her house's fritzed power supply. As the roller door eased down, warmth pressed into her back, a large hand enclosing over hers and the rope. She froze, but there was nothing cold about the molten heat flooding every inch of her body. Hard muscle enveloped her as the door shuddered to the ground.

She dragged breath and sense into her lungs, let go of the rope and stepped away.

'Sexual fantasy emporium. Pain or pleasure?'

Somehow she'd missed the disappearance of the ring tone. Shazz never did things by halves. Her voice bounded out from the phone and one look at Chase's devilish grin confirmed he'd heard every word. If she moved fast enough, she might just lose him, or at least rack up enough distance so every one of Shazz's words didn't bombard his sense of warped humour.

'One day someone's going to take you up on your offer.'

'One day I hope someone does!' The roll of her friend's laughter massaged the knots below her neck.

She rotated her shoulders and glared at the useless roller-door power switch. Whatever electrical nightmare killed the house lights had now spread to the garage. Damned inconvenient considering the man at her heels.

Once inside, Chase closed the door, pitching them into shadowed darkness. She edged toward the buffet, the room silent but for Shazz giving one final laugh–cough. Seems Chase was sensible enough to stay put until she'd rummaged through the drawer and located a torch. She flipped it on.

Blue eyes and wide, kissable lips sprung into focus. She screamed and stumbled backwards. The torch slipped from her fingers and hit her big toe.

'Oww!'

A firm hand grabbed her arm, preventing her from tripping over the wavering light at her feet. He pulled her close. Her breath hitched, tumbling her through a delicious wave of heat and spice.

'Hey, Stace? You okay?' Shazz. Her saviour.

She tried to push Chase away and he wasn't having any of it. Her breath wasn't quite her own, her heart trying its damnedest to escape her chest cavity. Everywhere she turned he was there, in her space, in her mind, driving her bat-shit crazy.

She swallowed, tried to sound as if she wasn't thoroughly turned on. 'I'm fine. Just stubbed my toe.'

Shazz snorted. 'Full armour is the only solution.'

Her skin burned. 'Haha, very funny.'

Impossible to edge right or left. The man was everywhere. She twisted and tried butting him with her shoulder. Steel-enforced muscle.

'What's up with the phone? This isn't your number.'

'Mine's dead so I'm borrowing a friend's.'

'Anyone I know?' The teasing nudge-nudge, wink-wink of Shazz's tone didn't help the rise of heat on her skin.

'No one important.' She didn't wait for further inquisition. With Shazz, distraction was the best strategy. 'I need to call your electrician.'

'You and the entire female population. The man's a walking circuit overload.'

She rolled her eyes. 'It's my house that needs rewiring, not me, you idiot. Can you text his details to this number?'

'Sure. Mention my name and he'll give you a package deal.'

She snorted. 'Why does everything you say sound sexual?'

'Because it is. Lighten up, hon. Sex is food for the soul and good for the health. It's a known fact that women who are sexually active are fitter and live longer than those who aren't. You might want to put that in one of your books.'

At least the dark hid the heat still burning over her face and down her neck. 'Yeah. Good to know. I should call him now. Speak soon?'

'Did I tell you he thought you were cute?'

The snort was automatic and unstoppable. 'Oh, a hundred times.'

'Play your cards right and you might get more than an electrical certificate of compliance.'

'Hanging up now!'

'Love you!'

The low rumble of Chase's chuckle did nothing for her mood. Something that had fast moved from peeved to all-out pissed off.

'Do you have no sense of personal space?'

She elbowed his abdomen, giving him no option but to move after a deep *oomph!* Lucky. Her next strike would have been much, much lower. She ducked and grabbed the torch, holding it up in time to see him wince and rub his stomach.

His lips dipped with humour. 'Just helping you stay healthy.'

'Hold back on the bright ideas, buddy. My health's just fine, it's yours you should be worried about. And take note, you're more than able to ensure my safety from a distance.'

'Not as much fun, though.'

'Matter of opinion, I'd say. Here.' She dumped the torch in his good hand. 'Make yourself useful and check what switches are working, if any. There's a heap of candles and matches in the bottom drawer in the kitchen.'

'Trying to clear the way for your conversation with your circuit breaker?'

If she didn't know better, she'd say this dig was laced with jealousy. But that would be ridiculous.

'Yeah. Thought I'd have a quick bout of phone sex before he pops over for some up close and personal to check out my wires.'

'Ah, she does have a sense of humour.'

'Who said I was joking?' She glared across at two sparkling baby blues. When that didn't work, she waved him off. 'What are you waiting for? Go!'

She almost thought he wouldn't. Then he mumbled something unintelligible about short circuits and finicky women before torch and man bobbed toward her kitchen. Even with him gone, her heart barely slowed from hundred-metre sprint pace.

The phone pinged and she clicked on Jasen's number, ignoring the winking emoticon Shazz had sent along with it. A brash Aussie accent dropped to a husky drawl as the answer to all her electrical problems realised who was on the other end of the line. Unfortunately his more than obvious interest wasn't strong enough to make him available earlier than noon tomorrow, even with her offer of a bonus over and above his late call-out fee.

And although Jasen's regret sounded genuine, she wasn't even remotely amused with his teasing mention of candles and romantic dinners ... given the man making himself comfortable in her house, clattering his way through her kitchen cupboards and drawers, and into her thoughts.

The room held no logic.

Chase slammed closed a cupboard and opened a drawer. Pots were stored where one normally stored dishes, glasses where there should have been pots. And don't get him started on the state of the cutlery drawers.

And the stuff she had in the pantry …

'I see you found everything, then.'

She hovered uncertainly in the doorway, just beyond the halo of candlelight surrounding the island bench. The shadows masked her expression. Her voice, however, communicated perfectly her feelings on his presence. She wouldn't admit to herself that she wanted him here. Wanted him more than her friend's lady-killer electrician.

'Eventually.'

'So, you worked out my system.'

'You have a system?'

'Sure.' She plunked her elbows on the bench and he gleaned the faint hint of a smile. 'It's alphabetical.'

'Alphabetical?'

'Yeah, you know, A, B, C–'

'I know what alphabetical is. It just doesn't make sense in a kitchen.'

'Of course it does. Haven't you ever searched like crazy for something because you have no idea where the hell you put it when you used it last? I never have that problem.'

She grinned, as if he should be impressed because she'd done something equally as brilliant as finding a cure for cancer.

'That's why your grater's with your glasses.'

'And my garlic press.'

'But your bowls are with your plates.'

'That comes under dinner.'

'So what do you use for lunch?'

The eye-roll was unnecessary. As was the overexaggerated patience in her voice. 'The categories are flexible. Just because plates are stored under dinner, doesn't mean they can't be used for another meal.'

She spoke as if what she said made sense. As if she were logical and sane, and every other living person who organised their kitchen conventionally wasn't. No sense trying to wrap his head around the enigma that was Stacey Holland. He'd tried and discovered what a mind-bender it was, how it did nothing but cause that same head to swim.

'So, where do you keep your takeaway menus? Under T?'

She reared up. 'I don't do takeaway.'

'Like you don't do coffee or dates?'

'Precisely.'

'But everyone does takeaway.'

'Not me.'

He nodded toward her hand. 'I need my phone.'

'Why?' She passed it over the counter.

'Because I need pizza, and your freezer and cupboard contents don't extend that far into the edible.'

'Everything in my kitchen is *very* edible.' She frowned. 'With the exception of Cuddles's rats in the freezer. And perhaps Midnight's cat food and snacks.'

Dead rats, *what?* Lying between the frozen peas and fish fingers? He couldn't prevent the shudder as he opened her pantry.

'Then tell me, exactly what is ...' he grabbed out a large plastic bag and read, 'kwin-oh-a?'

'Quinoa – pronounced keen-wa, by the way – is a superfood.' She nodded, as if that said it all.

'Like superspud or batsquash?'

She whipped the bag from his hand and stomped to the pantry. 'So not funny.' Dumping it back on the shelf, she slammed the door in case he missed the message that her pantry was off limits to him now. Not that he saw that as a bad thing.

She filled the kettle and set it on the stove. Gas. Just as well. Then she reached for the only item in the room that fit *his* definition of a "food" that was "super" – some rich aunty's choc-chip cookies he'd bought as appeasement.

'A superfood is nutrient-rich and beneficial for health and well-being.'

'Oh, like those?'

Her hand barely paused as she flipped the lid and plucked a cookie from the box. She hitched her hip against the bench and arched a brow with a look that said slapping him would have felt a whole lot better. Instead she took a slow bite of cookie and chocolate. 'This is for my soul.'

'Your body doesn't benefit?'

Her gaze dropped to her stomach. 'Sometimes more than it should. But we all have our vices.' Her mouth flattened, as if she didn't like what she saw.

His gaze followed hers, enjoying curves that begged further exploration. He had no interest in stick insects who hadn't eaten a decent meal since, well, never. No stick insect was Stacey Holland.

One of the things he liked about her.

She devoured the cookie as if her life depended on it, licked the crumbs from her lips as if every one was ambrosia. Then in a waft of honeysuckle, she reached past him for another. He liked that about her too – no pretence. Now she was done with her ridiculous footwear fad, that is.

Reluctantly, she slid the box toward him – an offering, an appeasement of sorts. It was obvious how much she loved them. That she was willing to share, albeit grudgingly, meant something. He selected one and took a bite. His eyes almost rolled back in his head, his tastebuds tumbling halfway to heaven. Just the right amount of crunch and crumble and butter. Chewy, but not too much. Chocolate added to perfection. And a hint of something he couldn't quite pick.

'Amazing, right?' Her cheeks were flushed, her lips crumb-laden until with a flick of her tongue the crumbs were gone.

Need jolted low in his abdomen. She seemed to understand his inability to speak. Thought it stemmed from savouring the moment, the cookie. Not her. Heat, thick and fast, surged his blood. Dammit, he wanted her. And she stood there, licking her lips, oblivious, surrounded by her cookies and alphabetised kitchen cupboards.

'The chilli-choc half-dips are even better.'

She opened a large drawer that at a guess encompassed E to G, given its contents included an egg beater, frying pans, and all those G items, including the two glasses she grabbed out and filled with cold milk. She slid one along the bench with a smile that sent all four chambers of his heart into spasms.

'Milk and cookies. They just *go*, don't you think? Kinda like sun and sand. Scooby Doo and Shaggy. Fred Astaire and Ginger Rogers.'

He nodded, because anything he said would make him sound a fool, or put a scowl back into her expression, when her smile and the warmth in her eyes right now was a full-on wrench to his common sense.

Even her backhanded logic was a turn-on. And her babbling. They were growing on him. He could go as far as to say he *liked* them. *Her.*

I want her to like me.

A crumb caught at the back of his throat. He knocked it back with a generous serving of milk, even though he wasn't a huge fan of the stuff.

The idea took root. Grew.

The kettle whistled. She cut the gas, staring at the hiss of steam, her fingers still on the knob. She startled. Turned away from the stove and grabbed a cookie as if it were as vital as the breath she'd just robbed from his lungs.

Suddenly, it was important Stacey liked more than just his kisses. It was important she liked *him.*

He waved his hand through the air. 'Turkish delight.'

The cookie wavered over her lips, teasing, then dropped away. 'Huh?'

He shook his thoughts from her mouth and focussed on the cookie instead. 'You were talking vices. Mine's Turkish delight. Only, not the regular kind. This one's made with apricots and pistachios from Malatya, and is better than, well, practically anything.'

'Sounds divine.'

'And difficult to find. Only a few places in Melbourne stock it, and only occasionally.'

She gulped down some milk. Finished the last of her cookie, licking every one of her fingers until they were clean.

He tried to look away. *Tried.*

Something caught in his throat. Possibly his tongue. More than probably his brain.

He coughed. 'I don't get to indulge nearly enough.'

'Perhaps you should find a different vice.' Soft moss eyes fluttered up to meet his.

They drew him in, wrapped him up, spun him every which way

until he couldn't think straight. Could barely talk straight. But he tried. 'We don't choose our vices, they choose us.'

'Poetic.' She held his gaze.

He could barely breathe. 'Truth, actually.'

'I never considered you for a black-and-white guy.'

Two steps separated them. He breeched the distance until the heady aroma of honeysuckle and chocolate surrounded him.

'Consider me now then.'

He hadn't meant to say the words, hadn't realised they'd sprung to mind until they sprang from his mouth. But now they were out, he didn't regret them. Her cheeks were baby beet red, her laboured breathing stretching the patience of her black tee. Stacey was not what he'd ever considered his type, yet she was everything he wanted right now.

Her head tilted, her eyes wide, the green all but swallowed by fathomless black. She licked her lips and he wanted to do the same. For a second it seemed as if she swayed toward him. As if she beckoned. Wanted him as much as he wanted her.

He dipped his head, held his breath and braced for a delicacy to surpass all the chocolate and cookies and Turkish delight imaginable.

Chapter Twenty-Six

*O*migod-omigod-omigod-omigod!

He was going to kiss her.

Crap!

She wanted him to kiss her.

She didn't. *Crap*. That was a lie.

Thoughts as straight as a fluted cookie cutter bamboozled her brain. One of those confounded thoughts wouldn't quit – each time they kissed, it was a kiss of convenience. *She* was a convenience. Because if Chase didn't feel obligated to watch over her, he'd be somewhere else, with someone else, kissing them. Never in his right mind would he *choose* her.

She swayed, tempted, felt the decadent brush of his lips against hers. Tasted Chase. Chocolate.

He groaned, increasing pressure, his fingertips digging into the flesh of her upper arms.

No!

Her eyes shot open. *They were closed?*

Dragging apart, she swiped her sleeve across her mouth and kicked a shitload of sense into her butt. His breathing was laboured, heavy. A quivering lick of her lips and she could still taste him. Her chest felt sucker punched. His expression said he felt the same. No idea why. It wasn't as if he'd been interested in her *before* they'd been thrust into this situation together.

Convenience.

She backed up, squared her shoulders, slammed the kitchen counter, then spun round until she could reach the kettle. She lit the gas again and sighed when a deep whistle indicated the water had begun boiling instantaneously. Hands shaking, she pulled out her drawer of cups, colanders and cutting boards. The cups clattered against the saucers as she set them on the bench. 'How about some tea?'

Chase looked about to explode. She couldn't think about that right now. It was too … *tempting*.

And wrong.

She looked away, busied herself with rifling through her tea collection. 'I've a really yum choc-mint black tea. Some orange blossom oolong.' She risked a peek at him over the box. 'There's even popcorn, if you're interested. It's good for the stomach.'

'Tea's the absolute last thing I want right now.'

Her chin jutted into a position that had to be anything but attractive. She didn't care. Spared him a look to tell him so, even as heat spilled out over her skin. Tea was the last thing she wanted, too. But the best thing for the moment. So soothing. *So normal*. Normal was good. Normal was necessary. Normal was needed to stop her grabbing the front of his shirt and yanking both of them into a whole lot of trouble.

He glowered. 'You know what I want, and it's not oolong or choc-mint.'

'Well, it's all you're getting.' She grabbed the packet of tea beneath her fingers and ripped it open, before plunking the bag in her cup.

'We'll see about that.' He turned his back and began tapping his mobile.

She poured her water in silence.

'*Antonio's Pizzeria*? Tara, is that you?' His voice softened, teasing. He moved away and out of the circle of candlelight. 'I was beginning to think we'd lost you to the Mediterranean sun and sand.' The deep rumble of his chuckle skittered through her body, every nerve ending screaming over her slam-foot-down obstinacy to keep her distance.

His voice was smooth velvet, rich chocolate. *Flirtatious*. 'How was Amalfi?'

One hand clamped round the cup while the other dunked the bag. Once. Twice.

'You don't say? Well, I'm glad you're back. I've missed our weekly chats.'

Cranberry and pomegranate wafted through her nostrils. She dunked again, more for distraction than need. Tea, no matter how enticing the aroma, had lost its appeal.

'I'd love to hear more, but I'm in need of pizza and coffee, not necessarily in that order. What's your delivery time to Windsor?' Another chuckle. 'You're a doll!'

She dropped the string, grabbed the torch and headed for the back door. It was time for Midnight's feed, anyway. And if she stayed any longer she'd either throw up or toss her tea, cup and all, at his head. Neither option was a sock-rocking choice.

She whistled. Listened for the patter of paws. Got no response.

Strange that Midnight hadn't come running before now. Unlocking his tunnel and cat door, allowing him access to the house, were among the first things she did after walking in the front door. At the very least he should have popped his head inside to mew "hello". Then again, he had a sixth sense for detecting "company". And avoiding it. This was one instance when she didn't blame him.

She grabbed the food on her way through the laundry and hip-nudged the back door.

'Miiidnight!'

Whistling her usual cat-call, she rattled the container and reached out to unlock the cage. The gate swung open at her touch. Her heart catapulted into her throat.

She whistled again. *Nothing.* Swung the torch left, right, everywhere – into every nook, every cranny, every hidey-hole – for a sign her little black baby was just hiding and not *gone.* Her arm ached but she refused to stop, kept shaking the food, her body cold, heavy. He always came when he heard dinner was near.

There was no meow. No lithe warm body wrapping around her ankles, head butting against her calf.

'Midnight!'

She left the cage and fled into the back garden, only stopping when pitch black enveloped her and her measly torch beam. No electricity meant no light other than the one in her hand, and finding a black cat in the dark was the proverbial needle in a sewing factory.

She needed help.

'Chase!'

She listened for some indication he'd finished his flirting and heard her call. Perhaps he wouldn't come. Worst case, he was pissed she'd led him on, then left him cold. He wouldn't get that she'd left herself colder.

She made for the house. *'Chase!'*

The back door slammed open, a thin beam of light blinding her momentarily. She squinted.

Phone spotlight in one hand, gun in the other, Chase did that whole cop swing left and right, scan the area thing. She didn't even wonder that he was using both hands. Or where he'd got the gun when his service weapon had to be back at the station. He'd come out to help her.

She dropped the food as she rushed to him and grabbed the sleeve of his shirt.

'Midnight's gone.'

His look was a mixture of many things. Understanding wasn't one of them.

He grizzly-bear growled. 'Damn, Stacey. What the hell? I thought something bad happened.'

'It has. Midnight's gone. We need to find him before he's hurt.'

He holstered his gun and scanned the area. 'He's a cat. He'll come back when he's hungry.'

'He won't. He's an inside cat with no road sense, no idea of the dangers out there.' She waved her arm into the dark. An eerie openness that swallowed everything in its path.

Oh, god!

'He'll be lost and lonely.' Again she tugged his arm, uncaring if she seemed pathetic and helpless. Right now, that's exactly what she was.

The old grizzly moved from his voice to his expression. He glared, growled, grumbled. Looked as if he'd like nothing better than to sharpen his claws and tear her to shreds. Then something in his face softened, like it suddenly clicked how much this meant to her.

Or maybe it was the tear she rubbed hastily from her eye.

He sighed. 'What do you suggest?' He shook his head, whether over her pleading or his giving in, she didn't know. Or care.

'We get more torches, search the backyard, then if we don't find him …' She bit her lip, blinked, hard.

Not finding Midnight wasn't an option.

She drew in a breath. 'We widen the search to the street and neighbours' backyards.' She made for the back door, relieved to hear Chase's footsteps close behind her.

'Oh, and I'll need to borrow your phone again.'

He handed it over.

She opened the call keypad and stared at the numbers, trawling her memory for inspiration. Impossible when she speed-dialled everyone she knew.

With a sigh she gave up and Google searched St Kilda Fire station.

'Hi, it's Stacey Holland. I need to locate firefighter Ethan Miklem. Is he there?'

If he'd guessed why she wanted his mobile, he wouldn't have passed it over so readily. As it was, he fought the urge to snatch it back. It irked him that she wanted Muscle Man when *he* was right there. Irked him that she'd broken their kiss instead of admitting she wanted him just as frigging much as he wanted her.

He holstered the .38 he'd picked up from his place when he picked up his PJs. Much as carrying a concealed weapon was against Federal law, the danger of not carrying it far outweighed the danger of getting caught.

'You'll send him a message? That's great. Thank you! Ask him to call this number ...' Deep sea green stared his way, waiting. He gave her the number, slow so she could repeat it for whoever was on the other end. Another round of exuberant thank yous and she hung up.

'Why'd you call *him*?'

Her look said she picked the green in his voice and it failed to impress. 'Because Ethan's a firefighter and he has access to resources we don't.'

'You couldn't ask anyone else at the stationhouse?'

'I ... uh ... No.'

She turned toward the house.

He grabbed her arm, little more than a feeling stopping him from allowing her obvious fluster go unbroached. 'What does that mean?'

'Nothing.' A mumble that told him this wasn't even close to "nothing".

'Doesn't sound like nothing.'

She wrenched out of his grasp. 'It means they think I'm just as much of a joke as you do. Satisfied?'

One last glare, then she stormed through the back door, just as the first splatterings of rain hit his face. Considering she had both the torch and his phone, he had no choice but to chase after her, if he didn't want to lose her or be left out cold in the dark. Pun definitely intended.

He found her in the kitchen, rifling through her pantry cupboard.

'Hey.' He dropped his palm to her shoulder, felt the muscles stiffen beneath it. 'I don't think you're a joke.'

Fingers clutching the handle of a large Dolphin torch, she straightened, dislodging his touch. She sniffed, swiping at her eyes with the back of her hand.

'You do, and it's not a big deal. Just help me find my cat, okay?'

He slid a finger beneath her chin and lifted until he stared into bright liquid green. 'We'll find Midnight, I promise.' His thumb swiped at a tear. 'And just so you know, I find you to be many things – exasperating, exciting, intriguing, dangerous, *sexy* – but never a joke.'

Before she could react, he swept his lips across hers, the barest of touches that sent his heart into fibrillations. He pulled back before he couldn't and eased the Dolphin from her hand. 'Let's start in the backyard.'

Stacey's body was wet cement. A big, hefty lump of it.

Her shoulders slumped and she couldn't for the life of her straighten them. If only the cement meant she couldn't feel pain.

She shivered. Debated collapsing onto the couch, but doubted she'd be able to drag herself up again.

Warmth sidled up behind her, the soft touch of a palm on her shoulder setting off another round of shivers.

'Go dry and change before you catch cold.'

Even Chase's hot breath against her neck, the concern in his voice, didn't cut through the chill. The thick candle on her coffee table flickered, throwing out light and warm vanilla scents that didn't quite mask the aroma of Chase's cold, untouched pizza.

She stared down at her dripping clothes and the growing puddle at her feet. Melbourne weather had unleashed all its glory just over an hour ago, three hours into their fruitless search. Not that it mattered. She wasn't stopping until Midnight was safe.

She shook her head and sopping mess of hair, and waved her dying torch. 'I need new batteries and I need to be out looking for my cat. No point getting changed if I'll only get wet again.'

She rubbed her neck, stopping only a handful of raindrops from trailing under her top. The escapees added to the damp on her skin and made her squirm – like Incy-Wincy crawling down her back. 'I'm fine.' Of course her body chose that moment to make her teeth chatter.

'Dammit Stacey. You're not fine! Change, warm up, have some oolong or whatever, and I'll go back out and look for Midnight.'

'You're just as wet as I am.' She thrust out her chin and tried to ignore the goose-bumps shivering up and down her arms. 'I can't ask you to do that.'

She sneezed. Twice.

'You didn't ask. I'm offering.'

'Why?'

That threw him. Although he recovered conveniently fast. She, on the other hand, wasn't doing so well, considering her brain cells were pretty much frozen into inaction from cold and wet. Men had less body fat yet they felt cold less. Go figure.

'Why am I offering?' He clenched and unclenched his left hand, which had to ache, despite him having ditched the sling when he'd rushed outside to her rescue hours earlier. 'Someone needs to keep you safe.'

'That's not your job.'

'It is if I want it to be.'

Hard to make sense of that statement. Although she could read between the lines and insert a crapload of meanings that would be more fantasy than reality.

He gripped her shoulders and walked her out toward the hall. She dug in her heels and stopped.

Inflexible abs ploughed into her back.

Warm.

She gritted her teeth. 'Where are you taking me?'

'Your bedroom.'

More wishful thinking. Damn the brain freeze that had frozen every shred of sense she'd clung to since their kiss.

She whirled round. 'You are *not* taking me to my bedroom!'

Deep, dark blue sparkled with amusement. Anger she could have handled better.

'I *am* if you won't go alone. I'll even warm you up myself if you don't change.' His grin went partway to breaching the chill. She didn't doubt he'd be successful in banishing the rest.

'Here.' He dumped an unlit candle and box of matches in her free hand, and pried the torch from her other. 'Have a bath, defrost, try and relax.' He handed her the smaller torch. 'I'll change the batteries in this and continue searching where we left off. I'll even call Fireman Sam and see where he's at.' His gaze razed her resistance. 'Deal?'

Rough fingers skittered over her shoulder and down her goose-bumpy flesh. He cupped her elbow, his thumb circling the underside of the joint, and she bit her lip to prevent swaying into him. To stop from fisting his shirt and pulling him down for another mind-numbing kiss.

Dear god, she shouldn't be so terminally tempted. Like a damned disease, she couldn't fight him. His clothes clung in a way she wanted to cling, and it was near impossible not to notice every muscle-plane over that beautiful, hard body.

He leaned in as if to meet her halfway. She pulled back, wrapping her fingers tighter around the torch, still warm from his touch.

'Promise you'll keep looking?'

'I make a habit of always keeping my promises.'

Hadn't he promised they'd end up in bed sooner or later?

Why the hell did that have to pop into her brain now?

'OK. But keep me informed.'

He nodded. 'How much charge does your mobile have now?'

Thank god for car chargers and the little time they'd spent driving round on their search for Midnight.

She checked. 'Forty per cent.'

'Should be enough. Just keep it with you and don't make any unnecessary calls.'

He winked, gave her a quick peck on the nose for what seemed no other reason than to trap her further under his spell, and headed for the kitchen. She heard drawers open, batteries being extracted …

She shed her sopping shoes and socks and padded toward the bedroom. Thoughts she'd successfully pushed aside while busy began clamouring in now she wasn't.

Had she left the gate open?

She was certain she'd locked it this morning before leaving the house, but her mind was so fixed on Chase and his effect on her, she couldn't be sure of anything but the buzz in her blood saying it wished he'd stayed and made good of his promise.

Shake that!

Impossible to shake the guilt. Ever since Chase, she'd neglected her babies – first Cuddles, now Midnight.

If they didn't find him …

They'd find him. Between Chase and Ethan, he wouldn't stay lost for long. For once, her positive affirmations were going to work. She leaned the torch on the side of the bath only long enough to light the candle and place it next to the sink. Raspberry and chocolate. Conducive to decadence and relaxation.

Much as the idea of a bath sounded heavenly, it wasn't right. Not while Midnight was still missing. She leaned into the shower, turned on first the cold then hot taps. Peeled each layer of sopping material from her skin, one by one.

Doubtful that sleep would come. She was too tightly wound. Worried. Wanting Chase. Knowing he was the last thing she should be focused on with a killer at large and her baby out wandering lost in the cold.

Impossible to stem the thoughts, let alone the urges they dragged along with them.

Every time she thought she had Chase figured – thought she'd found sense and a reason to stay away – he slashed her resolve by doing something so extraordinary that it made her question why she couldn't let herself go. Why she couldn't trust him and the feelings she didn't want. Extraordinary things. Like braving the rains to find a cat he didn't even like. Like looking out for her, over and above the call of duty and the case. Staying when she dished out more than enough reason – and angst – for him to leave.

Yet he didn't leave.

Was that why she pushed? To see if he would? To see how much like her father he really was?

Steam eddied through the cool air and she stepped into the stall, tilting her face up to catch the full brunt of the spray. Washing away inadequacies her psych training dictated were only in her mind. In the scheme of things, what did it matter how Chase viewed her? Their arrangement was based on practicality and nothing more. He was a cop. Impossible to move beyond that. The profession dictated it.

A dollop of shampoo in her palm quickly transformed to a flurry of honeysuckle-soaked suds. She dug her fingertips into her skull. Maybe she'd dig some sense in there while she was at it.

You couldn't take the cop out of the man. Her mother tried for years until her will snapped and she couldn't try any more. It was all too hard. Too much pain. Too predictable – to think things could be different for her. The job would drain every ounce of emotion until he had no more left to give. She wouldn't enter a relationship with anything less than her partner's all.

If she considered entering a relationship.

If she found someone who could see past the dull, commonplace author who lived vicariously through her characters. Yep. Her real-life hero would have to be one hell of a contender. Worth the risk. Freedom was too precious to be bargained on a smattering of empty promises and dreams.

Shame on her if she trudged down that road again.

The steaming water washed at the soap until her hair was silky and clean beneath her fingers.

She wouldn't allow Chase to sweet talk – or act – his way under her skin, into her bed. She wouldn't be that vulnerable again. She could be grateful, gracious even, for his help. But there'd be a distance between them. If for nothing else but her sanity. She was a romantic, after all. Believed in love and happy ever afters. Wrote them every single day.

But this wasn't her book. And Chase wasn't her hero. Important to be clear on that, much as he was out right now, searching for Midnight in the cold and the rain. She knew herself all too well. Lose her head, and her heart would follow.

She turned off the taps and stepped out of the shower. Dragged the large pink towel across her body and shivered, the delicious slide all too reminiscent of a man she needed to forget. Her body softened. Warmed. Yearned.

More than anything, she wanted not to want Chase Durant in her life. Yet she couldn't stop feeling happy that he was there, all the same.

Chapter Twenty-Seven

'**H**oney, I'm home!'

Chase scanned the hallway, listening for signs of movement. His knock had gone unheeded, and now his greeting. Not quite the welcome he'd expected.

Stamping off the excess rain, he relocked the front door and slipped Stacey's spare key into his pocket. *The key from under her front doormat.* The mind boggled. How did a supposedly intelligent woman think that leaving the means to enter her house in such an obvious hiding place was smart? Or – heaven help him – *safe*. Doormats, plant pots, fake rocks – there was a whole list of commonly used places, each one a sure-fire precursor for a break-in. Bad decisions even if a killer *wasn't* gunning for you. Seems he and Miss Holland were overdue for a serious discussion around safety.

'Stacey?' This time he made the call more a loudish whisper. Perhaps she was sleeping, although he'd been sure she'd be waiting up and worrying.

Happy to see him. Although not so happy with his news.

He shed his jacket, the lined leather not nearly thick enough to protect against the wet outside. His shirt clung to his skin as if he'd swum fully clothed in the sea. His jeans hugged and chafed in places better left alone. He raked sopping hair back from his forehead and with no other place to wipe, rubbed his palm up and down his thigh.

The house was dark, quiet. An eerie desertedness clung to the walls and ceiling.

Heat sliced through the chill in his bones. She'd better be asleep and not out searching alone in the hail and wind. Not after he'd waged war with those very same elements and gone a round – nice and pleasant-like – with Muscle Man, just for her.

He stalked toward the living room and tossed his jacket over the back of an empty armchair. The candle on the coffee table was minutes from burning out and the cool air smelled of vanilla ice cream. He shivered and snuffled back a sneeze.

Her bedroom door was open, her bed unmussed and still made from the morning. Her en suite bathroom was dark and empty. Damn, he'd better find her safe and unharmed! And when he did find her, he'd kick her ass from here to Hobart for causing his already pounding skull to implode.

He'd spent the past two hours freezing his nuts off, searching for her rat-cat who was in all probability safe and dry, hiding, somewhere close by and out of the rain. Because what creature would be stupid enough to venture out in this wild-assed weather?

Fool that he was.

Her tears had him wanting to do anything just to make them stop.

So, after hearing the running water of her shower, steeling himself from joining her, he'd checked the doors and windows before stepping out into dark-wet-frigging-icicle weather typical to the tail end of a Melbourne winter.

He'd stayed out for as long as humanly possible, but now it was too late, too dark, too impossible to continue. He'd come home empty-handed and as if that wasn't bad enough, he had news worse than the fact that her cat was still missing. Which he'd share, only after he railed her for putting herself in the line of danger. Again.

He made for the kitchen. Even checked her walk-in pantry. Not that he had reason to believe she'd hide in there. Her almost dead-as-a-doornail mobile still sat on the bench. No way of calling her. And after he'd told her to keep it close by. Just one more instruction she'd ignored.

How to find her?

There was always Fireman Sam. The man had acted so damn smug when they'd met, he wouldn't put it past him to hide the fact that Stacey had gone back out in the weather again. Perhaps they were out there, together, right now.

She made him so frigging mad, he wanted to …

Don't go there.

The chill on his skin was starting to sink inward. This time he sneezed for real.

With shaking fingers he worked at pulling his mobile from his wet jeans' pocket, then he scrolled down to the last entry under recent calls. Made to press the number. Froze.

What the …?

There it was again. Like a bear grunt. Half snort, half snore. Coming from the living room.

This time he walked round to the front of her zebra-crossing couch, and the reason he'd missed her before became apparent. Not only did she have a zebra couch, but she had a zebra throwover rug. The woman was camouflaged into her furniture, a pink nose and shock of strawberry curls the only signs she lay snuggled beneath the striped black and white. His gaze dropped. Not entirely true. Now he knew her socks to be of the glow in the dark variety. A fluorescent pink toe twitched, then disappeared underneath the covers.

She snorted again. A snuffle, almost. Like she was one sniff short of a cold. Her lips parted, slowly curved upward, a soft-as-a-breeze sigh escaping through them.

Difficult to stop from staring. She looked so peaceful. *Harmless.*

Hah! The truth couldn't have been further afield. She threatened everything he thought he knew and wanted. And she didn't have a clue.

Best things stayed that way.

One last look and he dragged himself off for a final check of the windows and doors before he gave in and joined her under that fluffy, tempting rug. A quick look in the cat enclosure confirmed Midnight hadn't returned while he'd been gone.

Another sneeze. This time more insistent. He searched for, then grabbed, a handful of tissues from a box in the kitchen. He needed out of his clothes and into a hot shower before he caught the chill he'd threatened Stacey would catch.

A pink fluffy towel set waited for him on the end of the bed in the guest bedroom. She'd even added a mini-soap and some of those little shampoos you get in a hotel. The gesture didn't mean anything, was probably something she did for all her guests. He smiled, just the same.

The steamy water did wonders for his body. He hadn't realised how cold he was, until he wasn't. Even his wrist wasn't protesting more than a muted grumble at being out of the sling. He was ready to return to work. If it wasn't for the doctor's certificate Hackett seemed hell-bent on getting first. How to get around that?

Unless he didn't.

Bite the bullet and take the tests.
Coward.

Only it wasn't so much cowardice, but wishing the whole wretched possibility would go away if he avoided it long enough. Genetics sucked.

And tests wouldn't make one ounce of difference past confirming his best – or worst – fears.

He ripped open the soap. Scents of honeysuckle filled the stall, and soon his body was drenched in the same heady aroma, as if Stacey's body were there now, plastered against him. His gaze dropped to lower, suddenly active extremities. Even thoughts of his uncertain future couldn't compete with the mere suggestion of her. She had his dick on a string.

Why the hell did the woman need to complicate everything? He wanted her. She sure as hell wanted him. Enough said. Her obvious desire, and even more obvious refusal to give in to it, was driving his mind and body to distraction. Hence, his sudden anatomical discomfort.

His hand dropped. One palm braced against the condensation-ridden glass, the other wrapped and dragged in an effort to ease the discomfort. His breath hitched.

His blood surged. His heartbeat thundered inside his eardrums.
Bang!
Cold air sluiced across his skin.

His eyes shot open.

Sleepy-green eyes stared back at him from inside the open bathroom doorway. Or not quite back. *Down.*

He dropped his hand and felt every falter of her widening gaze as it wandered upward.

No hiding her interest now. He grinned. Opened the shower door and let her take a good, hard look. 'Something you wanted?'

'I … uh …'

Her hands seemed awfully busy wrestling with each other in front of her body, her cheeks turning pinker by the second. She backed away, bumped into the door and stumbled as it slammed closed behind her.

'I didn't realise you were …' Again she seemed lost for words.

'Naked?'

She cleared her throat. 'In the shower.'

'And now you know?'

She turned and reached for the door. 'I'll leave you to it.'

'Sure you don't want to join me?'

'I- uh-' She fumbled with the doorknob and he knew she wanted to. He also knew she was fighting it like a samurai. She braced, gaze flitting any direction but his. 'I just wanted to know if you found Midnight.'

He shook his head, hating that the gesture sapped the hope from her eyes.

'We'll go out again first thing in the morning.'

She nodded. Turned the knob. 'I should go.'

'You could stay.'

She hesitated, mere seconds. He held his breath. Then the door yanked open and that blast of fresh air hit him anew.

'I'll see you outside.' She paused, didn't turn, just stared out at the hallway, her shoulders square and unyielding. 'And don't forget your PJs.'

Something stronger than tea would have been a godsend.

But Stacey'd never had a need like this before. As a result, her cupboards yielded zip relief. Desperate times and all that, she'd even considered the semi-crystallised vanilla essence in the pantry. She should've replaced the old medicinal brandy last time she went to use it and found it empty. Would alcohol fumes from the bottle help?

Not rock bottom, but she was close.

Her fingers flew to her throat, fluttering over the racing pulse that proved mind had little control over matter.

She'd wanted to stay.

Oh god!

Not because she was drowsy or dreaming or in need of comfort. She'd wanted to stay because the sight of Chase touching himself dragged at desires she'd buried so deep she'd forgotten they even existed. She'd wanted to do everything he was doing, and oh, so much more.

Knees wrapped tight under her rug, she sank deeper into the plush back of the chaise lounge, and grimaced.

She'd considered it.

He'd been cocky – hell, pardon the pun! – and teasing, and even when he asked her to stay, humour filled his expression. She was still a joke, no matter how much he continued to deny it. And if they came together – yet another unfortunate pun – she didn't want to be merely a moment's entertainment. She wanted to be …

She wouldn't say it. Because if she did, it meant she'd crossed over to the dark side, and she wasn't going there again. Not for anything. Or anyone. Sexy blue eyes, be damned.

'You missed a great shower.'

She jumped.

Shit!

Warm liquid sloshed over the side of her cup. She dumped it onto the coffee table, focussing anywhere but on the sight of a towel-clad Chase still wet and fresh out of the shower. Just as well she'd been nursing the drink for his entire ten-minute wash. Not that she'd been keeping time.

The tea's lack of heat didn't stop her from rushing to the kitchen and sticking her hand under a stream of cold water. If only her head fit under too, then perhaps her body would return to its normal, pre-naked-Chase temperature.

Hot palms rested on her shoulders, their heat simmering down the entire length of her back. Nowhere near the level of distance she'd intended maintaining.

Her heart thudded.

Warm breath stroked her hair. 'Are you okay?'

His concern seemed genuine. But hell, what did she know? Every ounce of intuition previous to his influx into her life had gone AWOL. And what worried her more? If his hands were on her shoulders, what was holding up that damned towel?

A flurry of honeysuckle and soap and sexy man stole her quota of oxygen.

She clenched her jaw. 'Forget something?'

'Oh …' He leaned in closer – was that possible? – and his breath fanned her neck. 'Like this?' An immediate burn the likes of more than just tea scalded her skin. His lips brushed the base of her neck, just above where his fingers caressed her shoulders. And dammit, she leaned back into him. Even sighed. At least, she heard a sigh, and it wasn't him. He was too busy kissing her into submission.

No!

She slapped the tap off and shrugged out of his grasp.

'I meant clothes. We had a deal.' She tried to look anywhere but at her pink towel, which should have looked ridiculous, but instead looked way too inadequate. It wrapped low on his hips, a happy trail of blonde hair dragging her gaze downward to delights she'd seen only minutes ago.

Oh, god!

She needed help. A lobotomy. *Something.*

'I heard a noise and wanted to check you were okay.'

His excuse for walking around half naked was almost as lame as her attempts not to notice how hot he looked. Patting the wet on her hand with a tea towel, she masked any trace of interest and tried for scathing.

'I will be when you cover up.'

'Why, Stacey? Tempted?'

This time the scathing was genuine. 'You really should rein in those delusions of yours. They make you seem needy.'

The words flicked a switch. His easy grin faltered then twisted into a scowl. 'I am *not* needy.'

Bullseye! Nerve central. The distance she needed. Even the flicker of guilt at her goading, after he'd been there for her, after he'd searched for Midnight in the pouring rain, couldn't stop her.

She squared up, managed a glare, eye level. 'Really? Then why's it so important that I want you?'

'That has nothing to do with importance and everything to do with you being honest about how you feel.'

'I'm honest.'

'And I'm Hugh Jackman.'

She snorted. 'If only.'

Chase ignored the dig. Stacey was stressed, worried. Hitting out. He knew that.

He also knew she wouldn't jump Hugh if he rocked up right now and offered himself on a platter with some of those cookies she loved so much. Just as she wouldn't *jump* him. She had issues, *didn't date*. That meant anybody. Chase Durant didn't own exclusive rights to that Stacey Holland groove-train.

Every male instinct said she was at war with her desires. The question was why.

He focussed on the crystal-green of her eyes. 'One minute you kiss me, the next you push me away. You're a mass of yo-yo signals – how honest is that?'

She pushed back from the kitchen bench, lines on her forehead creasing to deep, angry chasms.

'You want honest? Try this. I won't be controlled and I won't be manipulated. *If* I decide I want a man, he won't be some lightweight who thinks everything in life is one big laugh-fest. Or a cop whose emotions are so far gone, he couldn't touch them even if he had the nerve to try. I've been there, done that. The t-shirt's in tatters and I won't wear that disaster again. My life is my own. And so is my body.' Her eyes flashed, flinted emerald.

She was like a steam train, all heat and fire and full throttle ahead. And he'd just been slammed. He watched her steadily reddening face while clutching the front of his towel. Last thing he needed right now was wardrobe failure.

She'd been bitten before. Interesting, but not surprising. And he'd bet he knew the culprit's identity.

The slam of her palm in his vision forestalled his move forward and questions begging for answers.

'Those yo-yo signals you're reading? They're the "I haven't had sex in three years" signals. And if I had any plan to remedy the situation, it wouldn't include a rash jump in the sack with any Tom, Dick or detective.'

He couldn't help it. Of her entire diatribe, one thing leapt out. *'Three years?'*

Her gaze narrowed, furrows channelling her brow. 'Of course that's what you'd hear.'

'I heard the rest.'

'And ...?'

'I'm sure I read something on the net that said otherwise.'

'You Googled me?'

Damn. He'd stuck his foot in a place he'd hoped never to tread. Too late now to deny it.

'You were a person of interest in a murder investigation. It came up.'

She scowled and snapped a few choice words, then glared down at his towel and the tent even this conversation couldn't quash.

'Seems that's something you experience a lot.' Her tone was drier than his throat. 'If those trashy articles are the reason for your interest, you'll be sorely disappointed. I don't play – or for that matter, sleep – around.'

'Rest assured, the reason for my interest is all you. Although the line of men in your life interests me, considering your so-called disinterest in dating.'

'You might like to remember that not everything you read is real. Stories can be planted. It's called promotion.'

Jayda's accusations leaped through his mind. 'And you planted them?'

'Not me.' Her lips clamped. He doubted even a crowbar could open them again.

'I get it. Truth doesn't sell books. Sensationalism does.'

Her gaze narrowed. 'What would you know about truth?'

Perhaps not a crowbar, then.

Eyes sparking fiery amber, her arms waved as if tying a large ribbon. 'You wrap honesty into a shroud of humour. Bet you couldn't be honest and open if your life depended on it. Least of all if a relationship depended on it.'

A ten tonne cannonball slammed the air from his chest.

What he'd give for that luxury. But revealing what lay behind the jokes was tantamount to madness. It meant trusting Stacey with his past, and more, his future. His career. Nothing in their association gave him reason to trust her a little, never mind that much.

Circumstances had thrown them together, and granted, the idea of being "together" with Stacey wasn't wholly unpalatable, but it didn't mean they were buddies or pen-pals or anything more than together for now. They were two people attracted like hell to each other. That was it.

Now all he had to do was get himself out of the hole he'd dug himself into. No truth, but no lies either. A diversion then. With a brief waggle of his eyebrows for effect. 'Depends. Does that would-be relationship come with benefits?'

'And *there's* my point.' Her frown deepened.

His gaze shifted from her disapproval to the pineapple print beside the door. Its pair, a large watermelon, hung on the other side. Even the ridiculousness of her art choices couldn't stave off the burn in his gut. The fruit had legs, and more, they were dancing.

He was a jerk, no question. But being a jerk was better than being kicked where it hurt – off the force and out of a job – due to a hard-on and a bout of misplaced trust. The crudity sat badly. But so did life's uncertainty. Rock and hard place hurt like bloody hell.

The room's temperature seemed to dip while pressure in the air and his head spiked. He rubbed his brow and it felt clammy beneath his palm. 'I guess that's a "no".'

Stacey's full lips slackened. As if she'd expected something more. The cut behind her expression gutted. But better this than promises he couldn't keep.

'Why am I even surprised?' Taut fingers tapped against her thigh, her face stone-set. 'Not everything in life is a joke. I get you think I'm amusing. A lightweight, even. Yet, this conversation is neither. If you had any idea at all, any respect for me at all, you'd take me seriously and meet me halfway here.'

Her words filtered through his mind, meandering and hazy.

The tapping stopped. In its place her fingers flexed and fisted jerkily at her side. As if she wanted to sock the words into his brain until they stuck. He didn't doubt he deserved it.

Her voice wobbled. 'I don't want a joker, or someone who won't consider what *I* want when it comes to what's best for me. I want someone who doesn't feel they have to mould me into something I'm not. Someone who likes me, ridiculousness and all. Just as I am. Someone like Ethan.' Her hand flew to her mouth and she took a step back. Swallowed. Blinked.

Then her chin jerked up, her eyes still flinted and firing. 'Honest enough?'

One point for Fireman Sam. And if honesty was catchphrase of the day, Stacey's fireman was the better fit. Could promise her everything she wanted, and deliver. What did Chase really have to offer? Other than the obvious, that is. The thought wrenched at his gut in a way he never imagined it would.

His bare feet shuffled on the kitchen tiles. 'Just because I joke, doesn't mean I don't take things seriously.'

'What it means is you're hiding from something you don't want to face.'

Never argue with a psychologist. A losing battle from the start.

She tilted her head. 'And I get that. I just don't need to get dragged into it.'

'I'm not dragging much while dressed in this get-up.' He winced at the knee-jerk reaction. Hated it. The situation. His conditioning. The fact that Stacey was right.

Shit!

Like a thunderbolt, it hit him. Much as he desired – *hungered for* – her body, that wasn't the extent of his need. He wanted more. Her approval. For her to like him, past their attraction and the sex she so obviously craved but wouldn't admit to.

Crazy, when he didn't particularly like himself right now.

Winning her over meant change. *An impossible task.*

His head buzzed and he squinted, the candles on the bench glinting unnaturally bright. He blinked, chills flitting over his skin as the mother of a sneeze hit. He grabbed a fistful of tissues, blew and started up a tom-tom right between his eyes.

He pushed an unsteady grin to his lips and won barely a flicker of her death mask. A mere glimpse of disappointment before she blinked it and any residual softness away.

Too much honesty. While he stood there, freezing his nuts off in a pink fluffy nightmare. The towel was meant to tease. Turns out all it did was throw her off-side and make him wish he was fully clothed and could drop the pretence for once.

But what did she want him to say? That he'd cut the jokes and get straight to the chase. The man behind the humour. He wasn't even sure who that man was anymore. Cut the humour and would there be anything worthwhile left?

Cold shivered up through the soles of his feet.

Overthrowing a lifetime of habit was like shifting a mountain of rock. To make a difference, he needed to make a start. No need to tell her everything – he couldn't – but he could offer something. Move the mountain, one rock at a time.

She was watching him, softening her expression as he tossed the tissues into her trash.

'I don't want to change you.'

Soft turned to stone. 'Much.'

'At all.'

She tut-tutted, shook her head, then tapped each finger in turn. 'Aside from the shoes and the clothes and the two left feet.'

'Those are your hang-ups, not mine.'

'You say hang-ups, I say character traits. They make me *me*. And wanting to change any one of them means you don't accept me as I am.'

A bass drum joined the tom-tom in his skull. He tilted his head. Maybe that'd dislodge the pound. Squinting sure as hell didn't. 'You know we're not talking a lifetime commitment here?'

'We're not talking anything 'cos we're done.' She sliced her hand through the air, her glance straying to the blue monster on her wrist. 'I'm off to bed. Go put some clothes on 'cos all you're gonna get dressed like that is a cold.'

Chapter Twenty-Eight

The tom-toms wouldn't let up. And what was worse, an entire percussion section had joined in.

Even if Chase could have lifted his head from the pillow, his body would have refused to follow. It was leaden. Cold. Damp beneath blankets that weren't nearly warm enough. He peeled his eyelids open, one at a time. The room was bright. Daytime bright.

He rolled over. Groaned. Squinted at the bedside clock. Groaned some more.

Pixilated red melded into sharp digital lines.

Shit!

He threw back the covers and immediately lost too many degrees of warmth, while the room did a great impression of a spinning top. He closed his eyes and counted until the rotations slowed to bearable. He reached twenty. Ignoring the shivers, he pushed up and steeled against the fog in his head. He should have been out looking for Midnight over two hours ago. He'd promised. Reneging so soon after their less-than-amicable exchange wasn't something he was willing to contemplate.

Chase Durant didn't renege on promises.

He swung his legs over the side of the bed and a wave of uncontrollable shivers hit. Another groan escaped. His skull felt like a damned walnut jammed between the jaws of a nutcracker. His hands fisted into the duvet, bracing, so he didn't fall flat on his face.

There was a soft knock at the door.

'Chase?'

An answer formulated in his head, but the words wandered off course somewhere en route to his mouth. His brain was a wad of fuzz, his body a sweat-slathered, shivering mess.

Another knock. 'Chase? I'm coming in. You'd better be decent.'

He lacked the energy to laugh.

The door edged open. Fully clothed and bright-eyed, Stacey gawked for a full ten seconds before she seemed to realise and wrench her gaze away.

'You're naked. Again.'

He was wearing clothes. At least, he was where it counted. And now, the black cotton boxers should have been more than enough to prevent offending her overactive sensibilities. Much like the towel he'd worn last night, just to tease her.

He leaned forward, ready to tell her so.

Bad move.

Once the lean started, he couldn't for the life of him stop. The ground rose up to meet him and he anticipated the crunch before it hit.

Funny that this time round, the joke was on him.

One minute she was spellbound by a shitload of glistening skin – tight abs and oh-so-amazing pecs – the next she was pissed Chase had ditched his pyjamas, *again.* And then none of that mattered as his face turned powder-pale, and he swayed and toppled toward the ground.

In a move worthy of the Olympic arena, she leapt, reaching out to grab his arms as he fell toward her. She didn't think past that moment. He'd been there for her, and now she would do the same in return. She wouldn't let him fall.

Dead weight slammed against her chest. She wobbled backwards, and would have been fine if not for his shoes and clothing, strewn across the floor as if dropped striptease style. She faltered, lost her balance and butt-crashed onto the floor.

It didn't get any less painful the more it happened. Or less humiliating. She shuffled and yanked out a shoe from underneath her butt. The weight on top was another story. Chase's almost naked body lay between her legs, his head smack-bang between her breasts. He groaned, but didn't move. Seemed happy to remain exactly where he was. Even sighed as his hand flopped up and landed back down on an uber-sensitive nipple.

Hot flush. Of the non-menopausal variety.

She edged his hand away – her head saying *no*, her body screeching *yes please!* – and pushed against his shoulders. Her palms burned. His skin was sweltering, clammy. And he was shivering.

'Chase?' She brushed a mat of sopping blonde hair from his face. 'Are you okay?'

Stupid question, when she could clearly see – and feel – that he wasn't.

Words muffled into her chest. She shifted. Squirmed. Shouldn't have enjoyed his breath on her body so much. He stirred and, eyes closed, mumbled something that sounded a lot like 'bull in a bullring'.

He was delirious.

She pushed against his shoulders again. Nothing happened.

He snuggled deeper into her and sighed.

'You can't stay here.' She tried pushing him to the side. He barely budged. Was super-glue stuck. 'Chase? You have to move.'

'*Don't.*'

Fingers curved around her breast and tightened, making her squirm again. She bit back a moan and removed them, eliciting a deep, discontented sigh from the man attached to the offending hand. She would have thought the whole I'm-stuck-to-you saga a ruse if not for the sweating and shaking and laboured breathing.

That didn't mean he was staying put.

Only one thing for it. Hands braced either side of her thighs, she edged backwards and out from under him. His head bounded over her ribcage. *Bump, bump.* Down her stomach. *Bump.* Into her pelvis. *Bump.* Over her thighs. *Bump.*

Ridiculous to be turned-on by a feverish man who'd no doubt remember nothing post-recovery.

His head dropped to the floor. He mumbled. Dragged the clothing out from underneath and tried to lay it partway over his back. All the while shivering like crazy.

As if she wasn't guilty enough over her outburst last night, she dropped head first into an entire vat of it now. He'd spent the better part of yesterday's storm in the middle of it, traipsing the streets, looking for Midnight, and now he had an all-out fever and god knows what else. It didn't help that he'd felt the need to swan around in only a towel after his shower. That wasn't the point. He'd helped her out, and then she'd ripped into him all because he found her attractive and wanted her.

And she wanted that, but didn't.

She didn't date anyone, least of all cops. Yet he made her want to break every rule that was meant to keep her safe and free. Made her wish he didn't resemble everything in her past that hurt and stopped her from taking a chance and allowing a man into her life.

If anyone was a psychological study in contradictions, not to mention lunacy, she was it.

He mumbled again. Shivered.

She scrambled toward him. First things first, he needed warmth. Which meant moving him back into bed. She leaned across and grabbed his shoulder, using all her weight to roll him over. About as easy as shifting granite rock.

'Come on, Chase. Help me out here. Roll over.'

She tried pushing him up and over. No go. Even when she leaned back against him and used the bed leg at her feet for leverage, he barely moved.

He'd been compos mentis when she first knocked on his door, but now he was a feverish mess.

Think! You can't just leave him on the floor.

He had to move himself.

She raced out to the bathroom and returned armed. 'I apologise in advance, but you need to wake up and this is the only way I can think of achieving that.'

She tipped the cup of cold water over his head. The stream ran down the side of his face. He gasped. His eyes shot open and he tried to lift his head.

'Chase.' She dumped the cup and slapped his cheek until his gaze focused her way. 'Roll over.'

He moaned, but when she pushed his shoulder up he did the rest. Now he was on his back she could see how pale his face was.

Crap!

She leaned over and grabbed his shoulders. 'Let's get you into bed.'

A ghost of his former smile slid across his lips. 'Thought you'd never ask.'

Vice-like limbs snaked around her waist and tightened. Her arms splayed outwards and she collapsed. *Splat.* Onto him. Breath shuddered into her lungs. Spice laced with all-male sweat. Lack of sleep and worry was making her vulnerable. Recognising that was half the battle. Finding the strength to push away was the other.

He's sick, for god's sake! Doesn't know what he's doing.

She hated that last part. And hated more that she wished it weren't true. She steeled against snuggling in and kissing every unwanted degree of his fever away. Instead, she pushed up.

His palms slid over her hips and onto her ass. Cupping. Pulling her down.

Unbelievable. The man was delirious and still horny.

She wriggled out of his clutch and grabbed his hands. Pulled.

This whole process was getting old. Time for a different tack.

'Chase, if you want to go to bed, you need to get up.'

With incentive came strength. He rolled over and together they sat, then pushed up into a stand. Arm heavy about her shoulders, he staggered the few steps to the bed. No awkward moments. None past her unintentional grope of his groin as he tripped. And Chase grabbing her boob instead of her arm as he lost balance. Just your average encounter with a randy, fever-afflicted detective.

He fell back into the sheets and sighed as she covered him. Ashen fingers clutched the duvet, his breath shallow, and he seemed to forget all about getting her to join him. It made checking his temperature easier. The thermometer in his ear *beeped* and she stared at the screen: 39.5°C.

Hell!

A medic she was not, but she knew enough to know anything above 37°C was bad. At or close to forty? Well, that was too close to critical to be considered anything but serious.

Incredible how well-oiled the medical system could run, at times. All it took was one three-minute phone conversation and the on-call doctor arrived on her doorstep within the hour. Diagnosis: a high-grade fever. Treatment: keep the patient comfortable and hydrated, and his temperature below forty.

Twenty-four/seven care.

She dragged her old lazy-boy recliner into the room, and a small table complete with water jug, water bowl and fresh facecloths. It took her the better part of fifteen minutes, but once done, she curled up and called as many animal shelters and local vets as she could.

It passed the time, but more, it averted her from Chase-watching and made her feel at least partway useful in the search for Midnight. Not that anything came of the calls.

No news was good news. Right?

Ethan phoned in with nothing to report. That whole "good news" scenario again. And better than the alternatives. He promised to pin up "LOST" posters. She thanked him profusely, all the while watching the unsteady rise and fall of Chase's chest beneath the blankets.

In between calls, she worked at keeping his body warm and comfortable through the chills, cooling him with a wet cloth through the sweats. Every hour the beep on her phone prompted her to prop him up, hold a cup of water to his lips and encourage him to drink. Every four she topped up his ibuprofen.

He still drifted in and out of a feverish delirium. The temperature running its course, so the doctor warned. That didn't make it any less frightening. To see eyes sunken in a face so pale it was almost blue. It made her more determined to nurse him back to his old self.

Shazz's hunky electrician arrived at noon. Jasen. Toolbox in hand, with denim ripped in all the right places and a t-shirt stating "Electricians Spark Best". She didn't doubt it. The man was hot. The fact he knew it and worked it relentlessly made him less than attractive. Plus, the sick man in her spare bedroom needed her.

Leaving Jasen to her wires, she returned to Chase's side. She hunkered in and made herself comfortable with her notebook and pen to work on the last chapters of her latest, very neglected book. Or *tried*. The normal thought flow that transposed into scenes was blocked. It didn't help that her laptop was off-limits. It was like the killer had plugged the link from her brain to her hand, preventing anything of substance from breaking its way through.

And with Chase out of the loop, who knew what was happening with the case. Presumably his team was still working it. Presumably still in the dark.

At least no more bodies or body parts had surfaced. A small mercy, but a mercy nevertheless.

From one hopeless task to another, she opened her criminology casefiles. Ten days until her exam and over one hundred pages still to read. Retaining anything was like wading through golden syrup, then wading through a fast running stream. Nothing stuck.

The order and control she'd sustained for so long was slowly slipping through her fingers.

Jasen popped his head through the doorway. She jumped up and pulled the door to behind her. His gaze roved as he informed her that he'd fixed the problem, temporarily – something more than a blow out and less than an all-out electrical disaster. A possum had chomped through the wires. Hero that he was, he'd removed the dead animal and repaired the offending circuit.

Electricity restored, he promised to return at the end of the week to completely rewire the house. He looked forward to seeing her then. *Wink, wink.*

Eye-roll.

Just one more complication to add to the already growing mountain. An overcharged electrician and wires that either blew a fuse or a possum.

A deep sigh cut into her thoughts.

She looked up from her notes as Chase sighed again and chucked the covers, sprawling onto his back, one arm flung above his head, the other hand resting low on his stomach. His breathing seemed easier. Something the back of her mind registered, as the front, very conscious part soaked up the unhindered view of bare chest and abs. Taut muscle. Tanned. Tempting. Her gaze pinned to the broad expanse of shoulders, the taper to narrow hips, the runway of hair that disappeared beneath the waistband of his boxers, along with the tips of his fingers. Scenery that should have inspired writing. Instead it inspired in other, not wholly unpleasant ways.

He snorted and flopped onto his side. View change.

Biceps. Back. Buttocks. *Breath-robbing.*

As her inner writer alliterated, her inner woman swooned. Divorce didn't equate to dead. Dormant maybe, but the advent of Chase into her life, her home, meant dormancy had transformed to desire.

Disaster waiting to happen.

Chapter Twenty-Nine

Chase's hand inched further downward and whatever breath Stacey still retained, fled.

Critical didn't begin to describe her temperature. Or the fact she was drooling over a sick man. Didn't that make her a different kind of sick? A lurch and a scramble had her out of her chair, but not out of the realms of temptation. Cookie Monster indicated it was way past lunch.

Feed one hunger, won't the other disappear?

Eyes averted – the small crack in the plaster just above the bed had never held so much fascination – she pulled the covers up to his chin, cursing once again his lack of PJs and her overactive libido.

Three and a half years without a man hadn't seemed long before. Closer to four years if you were talking sex. More if you were talking good sex. Her entire sexual history if you were talking hot. All courtesy of a control-freak husband who viewed life as one big laugh-fest. That included his wife and any aspirations she might entertain outside their relationship and home. Writing being the biggie. *No wife of mine's gonna write that bodice ripper shit.* Life was a joke, not Bradley Collins.

Easy fix – a twelve-month separation and one divorce. She was her own woman, living her own life. Answering to no man.

In or out of bed.

Her stomach hadn't been staunch enough to go that road again. Three years since she'd been with a man. And suddenly she wanted what she'd vowed would never control her again. A man in her bed. In her body. In her life.

Shit!

She grabbed the thermometer.

A hacking cough, one heavy breath, then dangerous waters – that no-go zone, half-naked man she should avoid at all costs – rolled over and slipped into slower, steadier, rhythmic breaths. She glanced at the little rectangular screen. Temperature 38.5°C. Better. But not low enough to be considered out of danger. She ran the back of her hand across his clammy brow, faltered as he whispered something that sounded a lot like her name, then sped from the room for the first time in hours.

Fresh air would clear the cobwebs, and more, obliterate her cravings for the wrong man. Seems she had a proclivity for comedians with control issues. And while short-term she had no doubt Chase would be oh, so much better than good, long term he'd bring nothing but disappointment and another trek down heartache lane. A threat to her hard-earned freedom, the key to which she'd never surrender again. Least of all to a clown. Even a cute clown.

The rain had stopped and a cool, post-storm freshness clung to the air outside. A tang from the neighbour's lemon tree skirted the boundary fence while a temperate breeze ruffled the leaves overhead.

The door to Midnight's enclosure was ajar, just as she'd left it. The fresh bowl of his favourite tuna snacks still full, still untouched. His favourite hidey-hole in the igloo, still empty. Any hopes that her baby would find his way home were dwindling. For a cat without street-smarts, the longer he remained lost, the higher the chance he might never be found.

Each thought wrenched her heart. How could she have saved him from death once, only to have him face it again?

Stop it!

Why was she assuming the worst? Ethan was looking. He'd do anything to find Midnight. He'd done it before. He'd do it again.

One final scour of the area, and she turned to leave.

Froze. Her hand flew to her throat where breath clogged like damp clay.

Blood.

Not much. More a smear than a trickle. But it was enough.

No!

Moisture scuffled at her eyelids, her chest crushed between the giant jaws of an iron vice. She gasped for breath.

The toe bone's connected to the foot bone, the foot bone's connected to the ankle bone …

Another gulp for oxygen.

The blood was nothing. Didn't mean that her baby was hurt. This was an overreaction. Her writer's imagination. Finding fingers on your windscreen did that to a person.

Oh god!

Another thought. Only this time, too dreadful. Too wrong.

Could the killer have Midnight?

'*No!*'

Stacey's head jerked up and away from the bloodied stain.

Chase.

She dashed up the stairs and into his bedroom.

Short, agitated breaths burst through his dry lips as his head lashed to the side. '*I'll be good. I promise.*'

She brushed hair back from his brow, clammy heat blazing beneath her fingers. With a damp facecloth, she daubed the burning skin. His lips continued to move, this time wordlessly. His head twisted again.

'Shhh.' She curved her palm down the side of his face. Checked his temperature – 38°C. The fever was breaking, but the delirium seemed to be getting worse. Or was that a sign he was getting better? She hadn't a clue.

She turned to re-dip the facecloth in the water bowl.

He grabbed her wrist, eyes wide and wild as he strained to lift his head.

'*Please! Don't go!*'

'I'm not going anywhere.'

'*I don't want to die.*'

Her heart twisted.

Easing him back down, she gripped his hand in hers. 'You're going to be fine, Chase.'

She said the words as much for herself as for him. Because hearing them helped her believe it. Quivering, sweating, he gripped her hand as if it were a lifeline. A Chase nothing like the man who'd teased and provoked and tempted her to break every vow she'd made the day she signed papers that would mark the end to her three year marriage.

What if he wasn't going to be okay? What if he – *gulp* – died? Like

Annabelle. Sure, she was a character. With a fictional 40°C plus fever. That didn't matter. Her research was meticulous, and Annabelle's death was based on fact.

She shook her head and the craziness; the line between fact and fiction was becoming blurred.

Chase Durant was her protector. There to keep her safe, catch a killer. Drive her to distraction. He was going to be okay. Had to be. And within no time he'd be back to his old self, doing all of the above, and more. Until they were at loggerheads again, and she was cursing him and wondering how the hell she could have wished for the old Chase back.

She smoothed his brow, leaned over, and with no idea why, kissed the damp skin. Something fluttered into her heart. It had no name, no label, but it filled her up and made her feel empty all at once. What was that supposed to mean? *Nonsense.* A psychological study that once again showed she was losing it.

She tugged the chair closer. Chase seemed calmer when her hand was grasped in his. And it was her job to make him calmer. Better. Her cloth was already damp, but it was cool, so she wiped his brow and kidded herself that her heart flinching at every laboured breath was nothing.

A *patter-patter* on her window told her the rain had started up again. And Midnight was out in it. Was he cold? Scared? In danger? The latter didn't bear thinking about.

Her stomach growled. Still empty, despite the lunch hour having been and gone. She had no fortitude for food. And her heart? Not empty now, so much as brimming with guilt. She'd brought this on Midnight. Brought pain and suffering on every person who'd fallen prey to a killer obsessed with her stories.

Stories. Written words which should never have transcended the paper – virtual or not – they were written on. Fiction. Entertainment. Worlds created for readers to lose themselves in, safe in the knowledge that no matter how terrifying the narrative, they were still *safe.*

It took a moment, but oxygen finally reached her lungs.

She'd created a monster, albeit in fantasy, and now he was real. How to catch a killer based on her stories? Perhaps the answer could be found where the problem originated.

It was an idea. Rough and flimsy at best. But it was more than they had before. *They*. Her and Chase. A team, of sorts. The concept didn't bug nearly as much as it had.

Just as well.

She'd need his help if her plan was to work. And, more, she'd need to trust him. With her life.

Chapter Thirty

The keys *tap-tapped* beneath his fingertips, echoing through the eaves and *rat-a-tat-tat* of rain against the roof tiles.

He scowled at the blank screen.

The cursor flickered. Taunting.

She thought she was so fucking clever, stopping her story to stop his next move. As if she *knew* the real man behind the murders. As if she had half a clue how her story would end.

As if the story were hers to control.

He flexed his fingers, scowl slowly sliding toward a smirk. She may not know him yet, but she would. The clock was ticking, the time drawing near.

Adrenalin charged his veins. Wild. Heady. Impatient.

His cock swelled.

Anticipation made his possession all the sweeter. She needed him. Wanted him. She just didn't know it yet.

He stood. Adjusted the fly cutting into his engorged flesh. He needed release – hot, wet heat to pound and possess and ease the pressure so he could focus once again on the prize. On what came next.

It didn't matter that she'd written nothing since that last delicious scene. He didn't need to wait for her inspiration. He had plenty of his own.

But first, one indulgence before he lost himself in the other. He cupped his cock. Squeezed. Found pleasure in the pain. Pictured pink-painted lips sucking and sliding until he spilled every last seed deep down her greedy, grasping throat.

He knew enough to know the need wouldn't abate with his hands alone.

He grabbed his mobile.

There was no shortage of pussy if you made the right promises, whispered the right words, made the right gestures. Women were easy, believed what they wanted to believe. Craved love and lust until it made them blind and stupid and desperate.

Just as well.

Fuck the one you can until you get the one you want. He had every intention of doing just that. He swiped the screen and began to dial.

Chapter Thirty-One

*F**loating. Down, down …*

Stacey's body jerked upright and her eyes slammed open. She shook the dregs of sleep from her mind – the spare room, the spare bed, *the man in it* gradually falling into focus.

Her fingers slowly unfurled from the chair arms. No real chance of falling, but it still felt pretty real. Somehow a sleepless night agonising about Midnight and fantasising about half-naked homicide detectives meant she'd slept at her post.

Orange twilight snuck through the blinds, stretching into long shadows over the walls and ceiling. Three or four hours at least since she'd "rested" her eyes for just a minute. She glanced at her watch the moment Cookie Monster's eyes began to flash. Ibuprofen top-up time.

Chase's breathing had settled to a low murmur, his lips curved in the faintest of smiles. Tension leeched from her shoulders and her lips matched his for the first time since he'd collapsed onto her, was it over twenty-four hours ago?

She leaned forward and rested the back of her hand against his brow, his skin less like wet paste now, a little closer to the healthy bronze she'd grown accustomed to. Her hand slid down his cheek to stubble that made her heart trip a little more than facial hair should.

In fact, everything about Chase did something to her body it shouldn't. From cliché to catastrophic, her body was no longer her own. He drew her. Had from day dot when she'd tottered into his precinct on Shazz's disaster heels, and asked if a detective would be willing to assist with her book. He'd turned, his gaze raking a slow – excruciating – amble from head to curling toes, then toes to burning cheeks back up again, before his lips slid into his killer grin and he'd declared it would be his pleasure. The roll of his tongue over that last word had shivered its way throughout her body.

Reflexes had taken over and her mind had melted, but not before one thought. *No, it'd be mine.*

No, that wasn't true. There were other thoughts, all X-rated, and all better left in her books, not her bed, or against the wall, or sprawled on top of his desk …

Arghh!

Brain drain from that moment. And it'd weakened her resolve ever since. To the point where she questioned how bad a one-night stand, or even two, with Chase could be. How wrong it would be to kiss him now. Start at his lips, move down over hard, sculpted pecs, and keep going until she drew him into her mouth before edging up and straddling him, taking him inside once again. Only this time he'd fill her where she'd throbbed – off and on, like her fickle on-the-fritz lightbulbs – since the moment he cast his baby-blues her way.

The fact that he was feverish, wouldn't remember a single moment, didn't seem to factor. She was losing the plot, her sense of right. His sickness, his vulnerability, seemed to be chipping away at hers. Did that mean she was a bad person? Because it was wrong, the whole doing anything with Chase. What good could come of it?

Relief, for one.

His eyes fluttered open, hazy, disoriented. Then the clouds disappeared to reveal clear, lucid blue.

'Stacey?'

Her fingers had somehow slipped beneath the covers and his nipple budded into her palm.

Holy crap! She snatched back her hand. Swallowed. Tried to look as if she hadn't been sprung groping an unconscious male body. 'I'm here.'

He nodded, closed his eyes once again.

Then she remembered, with the miniscule part of her brain still attached to reasonable thought. 'Chase, you're due for more ibuprofen. Can you sit up?'

She wrapped her arm around his shoulder and supported him as he washed down a glass of water and two white pills. Then she lowered him back onto the bed.

His fingers curled around her wrist, his gaze latched to hers. 'I don't want to change you.'

His head hovered inches from the bed, his breathing shallow and laboured. His grasp unrelenting. 'You're perfect. And ridiculous. And I love ridiculous.'

Then he collapsed back into the pillow, eyes closed.

Hands shaking, she wiped his brow again with the wet cloth.

He was delirious. No sense attaching importance to the blatherings of a man who swung in and out of sensibility so fast it made her head spin like a potter's wheel at full tilt. That included his much earlier distress, which sounded more like a child than Chase. Whether dream or real, it was none of her business.

That didn't stop her inner psychologist from wondering what caused his fear of desertion. And whether it was a driving force to his almost obsessive need to joke about everything that threatened to make him feel.

For the first time in Chase didn't know how long, his head wasn't one thud shy of exploding.

He risked a peek and discovered the room was dark enough not to drive the tom-toms back into his skull. Only then did he open his eyes fully. First thing he noticed was the strawberry blonde head propped against the side of a large recliner. Slow breaths escaped from pink, barely parted lips. In sleep she looked so vulnerable, so approachable. He didn't doubt her bite would return when she woke. That didn't mean he couldn't enjoy the view before then, while his mind tried to work out how long he'd been out of it, over a frigging cold, no less.

Last thing he remembered, he'd been about to deliver a ripper of a reply to Stacey's "are you decent?" when the ground had rushed up toward him. He'd braced for the *thud*, and experienced an almost pleasant slide into soft, warm, womanly curves.

The rest must have been dreams.

That included memories of his ten-year-old self peeking through his parents' bedroom door moments before his mother's eyes had closed for the very last time.

He shivered, cold but for the warmth in one hand. His gaze shifted, and the reason Stacey's body sat awkwardly became clear. Her hand was wrapped around his.

His chest squeezed.

Piecemeal, other bits came back. Stacey putting him to bed, tucking him in. Sponging him down. Encouraging him to drink. Kissing his brow. Despite her harsh words and not wanting him around, she'd nursed him. He strained to remember and couldn't pick a time when his eyes had opened, however briefly, and she hadn't been there.

Then he remembered other things. Ramblings. What did he say? More to the point, what did she hear? *That* remained hazy. He didn't remember talking about his fears, the sickness, but that was no guarantee he hadn't.

His gaze moved from their joined hands back to her face.

Another squeeze. This time to his heart.

What was it about her that made him want to trust? To open up and let a tide of emotions flood out. She confounded him. Threatened his safety, his peace of mind. Yet knowing that, he still wanted her. Still wanted to share with her.

No idea what scared him more.

The curve of her lips deepened and his eyes latched there as her tongue flicked moisture along their length.

And there went every ounce of sanity he had left.

Burnt brown lashes fluttered, then opened. Within a heartbeat, the clouds in her eyes turned to cognisance.

Her hand snatched back and she clambered into a sit. 'You're awake.'

Within seconds something cold – a thermometer, he soon discovered – pressed into his ear and she was all efficiency and distance. His very own Florence Nightingale.

'How d'you feel?'

'Like I've been dragged through a ditch backwards.' His awkward grin earned none in return.

She glanced at the thermometer's LCD. Nodded. Let out a small sigh. 'Your temperature's pretty much back to normal.'

'Have you found Midnight yet?' He pushed up.

The sigh caught in her throat and the pink in her cheeks deepened. 'Uh, no. Ethan's still out looking.'

Good for Ethan. Bet *he* never got sick.

Her gaze edged sideways, as if the sight of his bare chest disturbed her. As if by not looking she wouldn't feel something or wouldn't let on that she felt something. The ploy wouldn't work for her any better than it'd work for him were the roles reversed.

He straightened and shucked the covers.

She almost toppled out of her seat. 'W-what are you doing?'

'Getting up. I promised I'd help look.'

'Oh, no you're not.' Her palm contacted his chest and the skin burned. Hers too from the way she snatched it back. 'You're recovering from a high-grade fever. It's bed for you for the next twenty-four hours, at least.' She pulled the covers up, dropping them in a way that meant she didn't touch him again.

He fought back a grin. Ethan's fine health didn't seem so bad in light of her reaction. Yeah, he enjoyed her discomfort, more than he should after she'd cared for him. But hey, he was human, and a man.

Her gaze never once met his. 'Do you want a hot drink or something to eat?'

'Coffee?'

'I have Chai. It's kind of the same.'

The woman had obviously never tasted real coffee.

'Pass.' He shuffled to get comfortable and his stomach rumbled. 'I'd kill for bacon and eggs.' Saliva hiked a party on his tastebuds at the mere thought.

She glanced at her watch, refrained from commenting on the hour being more dinner than breakfast, then latched onto a spot on the wall just shy of his left shoulder. 'Nix on the bacon, but I'll see what I can do.'

Then she tripped out of the room. *Tripped*, because maybe the carpet had a kink in the doorway? Not that he could see one, but hell, if one existed, Stacey'd sure as hell find it.

He dropped his head back into the pillow, and couldn't help it – his mind drifted backwards. Maybe it was the virus still tug'o'warring with his body, or maybe it was the way Stacey had nursed him. The way his father had nursed his mother. Fears he'd battened deep down were somehow freed and battering through his mind. Helpless wasn't a state he enjoyed, no matter the perks of having Stacey as his nurse.

Parkinson's wasn't a cold. You didn't recover after a twenty-four hour stint of ibuprofen and care. No happy ending waited at the end of a positive diagnosis.

He wasn't foolish enough to believe that ignorance would make the problem disappear. And life was getting more complicated not knowing. If he didn't have a future, then he couldn't have a present, with anyone. It wasn't fair on either party.

Least of all Stacey.

He startled.

Unexpected.

Then again, so was Stacey. She was fresh air in a life that had become interminably stale. He wanted freshness. Wanted fun. *Craved* them. And most of all – his heart kicked – he craved Stacey.

Which meant sooner, rather than later, he had some blood tests to take.

Chapter Thirty-Two

*C*reak.

Stacey's head jerked up. *Breathe.* Treacle-thick air caught in her throat. Her trembling fingers gripped the edge of her desk, her gaze juddering over an area that never seemed lacking in light before.

Her sanctuary. Her writing cave. The basement Beth and Des had helped shape and design.

The space had always creaked and whistled, yet it had brought her solace and a storm of ideas. Now it set her shoulder blades so tight, she'd surely need a vice to pry them loose.

The stage curtains fluttered. Drafts always entered through the ceiling vents, randomly moving the ruffled green velvet. It had never freaked her out before. The stage hidden behind the curtains had never freaked her out before.

She'd never longed to be somewhere else. Or have someone else here with her.

Her head dropped to her palm. Would the room ever feel the same again? Would she?

The papers before her blurred.

She swallowed. Stared at the little blue collar on her desk. The time for looking had well past. Three days, and still no news of Midnight. No trace but his collar snagged on the bushes in her back garden. That and the blood …

She blinked.

Nothing left for her to do but wait and hope and move on with other priorities.

The scrawled words in her notebook drifted into focus. A draft of which she'd type into her computer – when Chase gave the okay. When she drummed up the courage to tell him and put herself in the path of a psychopath.

'I thought we agreed you'd postpone writing until we caught the killer.' Chase left the bottom step and stopped less than a metre from her desk.

The skip of her heartbeat, the release in her shoulders, should never have been over a man like him. Like her father. She swallowed. Weird, but even his bossiness didn't irk half as much as it had.

'Why are you out of bed?'

'Because I've no good reason to stay there.' An eyebrow quirk should never have been so sexy. 'Unless you're offering one?'

Heat scampered across her cheeks. So, she'd been overhasty. He still irked, playing up with that whole "everything's a joke" mentality. Well, about time the roles were reversed.

'Of course.' She stood. Slipped out from behind the desk. Stepped closer. 'My bed or yours?'

The overpowering pound of her heart was worth every bit of his reaction. Teeth clattered as he yanked his bottom jaw up from floor. The double-take. The heat in his gaze.

'What are you waiting for, Chase? Isn't this what you want?' Her fingers wavered over the top button of her blouse.

He watched, measured her every move. Heating her body, freezing her fingers. Preventing her taking that next step and slipping the button free. There was only so far she was willing to go for a joke. And the way his gaze devoured her, she wasn't sure whether the joke was still on him.

His gaze sharpened, his lips curving into that killer grin. Dear god, if her legs gave out now, she'd be a molten mess on the floor.

'Who needs a bed when we have a perfectly good desk right here?'

He swept her papers aside and they fluttered to the floor. 'Top or bottom?'

She blinked. Tilted her head. Heard wrong. *Right?*

'W-what?'

'Which do you prefer?' He stalked toward her. 'I'm partial to both, so I'll let you choose.'

He had no qualms about unfastening his shirt, releasing the last button, so close static electricity crackled from his skin to hers.

Suddenly her idea to irk back wasn't such a good idea after all. 'I was joking.'

'Ah, but you don't joke.'

'I learn fast.'

'I'm counting on it.' One step brought his thighs in contact with hers.

Urgent fingers dug into her hips and she swayed. He tugged. Her body sighed, sank into him and savoured.

Traitor!

Her palms planted flat against his chest, experiencing every racing beat of his heart. Every clench and release of muscle.

Dear god!

No! Her mind was unequivocal.

Her body, not so much.

Joke and punch line were lost somewhere between the burn beneath her palm and lips slowly ducking for her throat. Heat seared her skin, slow, melting kisses that buckled her knees. Her back bumped the edge of her desk and he eased her up, skimmed his palms down her thighs, encouraging them to open as he moved inside. She squirmed, the hard press of his erection shuddering against parts of her that hadn't been this close to a man for so long she'd forgotten how good it could feel. How right.

He groaned, stole her lips, swallowed her sigh, any and all coherent thought.

Sex with Chase. On her desk. In her writing cave. In the middle of the afternoon.

It was about to happen. And that was okay. More than okay. It was wondrous. Overdue. Not fast enough.

Her hand slipped down his chest, over every bump of his ribs, his stomach, his waistband, and she didn't stop. Couldn't. Wouldn't.

She cupped his hard, hungry flesh, stroked, squeezed, opened her mouth and kissed him back with a need that cried out for completion. Throbbing between her thighs had her giddy and greedy and wetter than she ever remembered. Drought did that to a person.

Her fingers fumbled with his fly, slipped inside, felt him tremble and harden further against her palm.

In mirror action, he tugged the tie on her slacks, slipped his fingers beneath her waistband and pressed against wet lace. She wriggled closer, opened her legs wider, quivered as he strummed her like the strings of a harp.

Distant music filtered into her ears.

Hell, he was so good, he created a symphony.

His fingers breached the lace and sunk deep into her flesh. She clutched, panted, rolled her hips and ground against them.

The music persisted.

The symphony between her legs stopped.

Chase wrenched back. Breath shuddered through his lips and his eyes clenched for mere seconds before his gaze latched to hers.

The music was louder now, only not music. Her mobile.

He eased her hands from their delicious exploration, his chest heaving as if he'd been running.

'You should get that.'

Was he serious?

'It can wait.'

She tried to free her hands but he held them firm.

'What are you doing?'

'Stopping this while I can.'

'I'd rather you didn't. If I don't have sex right now, I think I might die.' No understatement. Her flesh throbbed. Hungry, empty. Oh, so needy.

Didn't he feel the same?

She freed a hand and slid it back into the warmth of his jocks. His breath hitched, but it didn't stop him from removing her hold one more time.

Damn! Had the fever scorched his brain?

She froze. Or had he taken her joke and made it his? Was that kiss, that … other stuff, all just fun until things heated up and he realised he was no longer interested? Had never really been interested.

You're not woman enough to interest any man.

Why did Brad's words have to slam her brain now?

No. That wasn't it. Couldn't be. She'd held his interest in her fingers only seconds ago, until he'd snatched them away.

'I thought you wanted this.'

'I did. *Do.*' He shook his head. Seemed to be battling more than her braced hands. 'There's something I need to tell you.'

Was he kidding? Now?

'Like a *chat?*'

'Like a confession.'

Shit!

'You have an STD?'

'No.'

'You're gay?'

'No.'

'Is everything down there,' she nodded toward his still very alert crotch, 'in working order?'

His expression was a mix of exasperation and amusement. 'Of course.'

'Then it can wait.'

She tried to drag his hands back between her legs, to finish what he'd started, but he was so much stronger. And determined.

'You started this.'

'I know. And you've no frigging clue how hard it is for me to stop.'

She had a fair idea.

'Then don't stop. *Please.*'

She was pleading Chase for sex. No pride. No restraint. So not the Stacey Holland she'd cultivated the past three years. And she was powerless to stop. Couldn't think past getting his hands back on her body and his mouth back on her lips. Or her skin. Anywhere, really. She wasn't fussy so much as desperate.

His grip tightened. 'The conversation concerns where this – us – *we* are going.'

She searched his face and found no humour, just sincerity. The last time he'd worn that expression was amidst delirium and declarations that she wasn't a joke.

Yep. Fever-fried brain.

After all their argy-bargying the past months, weeks, she was finally ready the moment his marbles had gone walkabout. Gotta love Murphy and every one of his bloody smart-assed laws.

Her mobile broke into Cookie Monster chorus again.

'You should get that.'

He stepped away, adjusted his jocks, rezipped his fly, sending her heart into a free-fall way beyond disappointment. What was this whole phone fascination thing? He even plucked it from her desk, frowned, then passed it across.

She didn't bother to check the screen. Just tapped *yes*. Blanked her mind. Tried to forget how she'd just melted, moaned, begged him not to stop.

And hoped her body would follow suit.

Are you out of your frigging mind?

Yeah.

Chase skirted the desk, placing valuable distance between him and the woman he wanted to make love to more than anything. She turned away, continuing her whispered conversation, allowing him time to catch his breath. His senses.

Remnants of their near miss stained her cheeks, leaving her shirt's neckline askew, the strings of her trousers hanging loose and uneven from the waistband.

His cock was so goddam hard he could barely stand straight.

She'd been willing. Ready. Begging him not to stop. And what had he done?

Stopped. Told her he wanted to talk. *Talk.*

A god-awful moment to develop a conscience. To want to give her all the facts before they took that next step. A step toward something more than just sex.

Stacey made him want to feel and hope and look to the future. But what future? He had no idea what awaited him; what he could promise her, and what he couldn't. One thing he did know, he wouldn't put her through the hell he'd watched his father endure, when it was still early enough for them both to walk away, emotions intact. He'd done the right thing. He knew it was right.

But it felt so fucking wrong.

'That was Ethan.'

On hands and knees, she scooped the papers up from the floor, then stood, eyes focused on her trousers as she brushed them off with her free hand and headed for the stairs.

'He's found Midnight.'

Good news. It had to be. She was too upbeat for it to be bad.

'Is he—'

'He's at a vet's in Mt Waverley. I'm meeting Ethan there now.'

Great. The cat was safe.

His chest tightened. He'd wanted to be the one who found it. That whole hero complex – the reason he'd trekked through the rain and insisted she stay behind. Because he'd seen the blood on the cage and wanted to protect Stacey from discovering the worst. He may have been wrong, but his intentions were right. Still were.

'I'll come.'

Foot braced on the bottom step, she paused. Her look said she picked the irony of his words and wasn't impressed.

'That's not necessary.'

'I'm not doing it because it's necessary.'

She sighed, hugged the papers to her chest. 'Stay here, hold the fort, twiddle your thumbs if you like, because you're not coming. *I don't want you to come.*'

He didn't miss the double-entendre. Didn't doubt it was deliberate. Something twisted in his heart. The part that smiled when she smiled. He wanted to follow, but to say what? I won't make love to you because after it happens we may want more and I don't know if that's something I can do?

She climbed the stairs without a backward glance, swallowed by dark as she breached the boundary of light. The bulb had gone again. And Stacey's lady-killer electrician was due in a couple of days to fix it and the rest of the house's wiring.

He'd be there to see that was all he fixed.

As for the rest? She may not want him around, but she still needed him. If for nothing else but protection. And – with a kick to the gut – he realised, he wanted to be around too. If not for Stacey, for someone.

Which meant a phone call to his doctor this afternoon, and a multitude of tests to show whether the future he wanted was a possibility or merely wishful thinking.

Chapter Thirty-Three

Chase's mind reeled, and even the burning throb inside both his elbows couldn't lessen the effect.

The Doc had said rest. He'd been pricked and prodded, had given enough blood to keep an entire army of mosquitos happy for a month. The results should be back in ten to fourteen days.

Then he got the call.

What to think? Not that he was surprised, but the news raised more questions than it answered and was enough to get him back behind the wheel of his car.

Amid a squeal of tyres, he stopped outside the shiny white block of apartments. He had no idea how Jagger had managed to wangle that – to live in some swanky unit while he, supposedly, owed a shitload of money. The man had accomplished a score of things in his lifetime, not least of all his final coup – a fatal stab through the heart.

Something Chris had failed to prevent, his vigil cut short with a blow to the temple. Lucky that was all he'd sustained. An overnight hospital stay and a generous dose of ibuprofen and he was on the road to recovery. It could have been much worse. He could have shared Jagger's fate.

Jayda met him halfway up the path.

'I told you not to come.'

'Did you expect me to listen?'

She sighed. Shook her head.

'I want to see him.'

'You know I can't do that, Chase. You're too close to this case.'

'I'm a homicide detective. Of course I'm close.'

'He's your brother-in-law.'

'*Ex.*'

'Who you've shown ongoing hostility toward.'

He clamped his jaw against further revealing the extent of that ongoing hostility, despite Jagger's demise.

Jayda barely blinked. 'What's this I hear about you threatening Jagger at his place of work last week?'

'How'd you hear about that?'

'You've worked this job long enough to know that type of shit always rises.'

True. But not so great when it was your shit.

'The bastard was fleecing Gracie for money. I told him to back off.'

'Actually, you told him he'd regret it. What'd you mean by that?'

'Exactly what I said. Hell, Jayda. The man made enemies in his sleep. He was in debt up to his beady eyeballs, had just received one of probably a string of death threats if he didn't make good. Perhaps that's where you should be looking, not here.'

'And we will. But there are other considerations.'

'Such as?'

Her gaze narrowed, as if measuring the impact of her words. 'Jagger's missing a finger.'

Fuck!

He tried to stay calm, tried not to think the worst, whatever that was.

Jayda tilted her head, still scrutinising, still measuring. 'Why would someone leave Jagger's finger on your girlfriend's windscreen?'

'You know as well as I do, two plus two doesn't always make four. It may not be his finger.'

'How many fingerless Cubans do you think are wandering around Melbourne?'

Just his thought.

'Jagger is – *was* – a friend of a friend of Stacey's.'

'What was their relationship?'

'Friendly. They don't get together for coffee and catch-ups, if that's what you want to know.'

'I want to know everything. Like why he was caught on video tampering with your girlfriend's car outside Hook, Line and Sinker.'

The information battered round his brain, along with the knowledge that he'd never be able to cross-examine the bastard as to why.

His jaw clenched. 'Well, that's all I know. Other than the man was a scumbag and I'm glad he's out of JJ and Gracie's lives for good.'

'Be careful who you say that kind of thing to, Chase.'

'You know I didn't do this. You know me better than that.'

'I do.' Air puffed through her lips and she straightened, as if to match his six feet plus with her inflexible five-and-a-half. 'Just not the same as I used to. Ever since the Night Terror, something's changed. *You've* changed. I almost miss all those lame jokes you tortured me with.'

'I'm still funny.'

'You were never funny. Just trying. And now you're not even that. You're distant, and something's going on that you aren't telling me.'

The green in her eyes was liquid. He'd hurt her, was hurting everyone around him. Just another fucking side-effect of his "maybe condition". Again, that urge to share when he'd never felt it before. He bit it back, knew it would pass, and moved on before he did something he'd regret.

Like commit career-suicide.

'What's news on the Michael's murder out at Port Phillip Bay?'

Another sigh. But she let it go.

'Same dead-end as the previous murders. No prints. No DNA. No witnesses. No leads.' Her eyes flashed. 'None, that is, but your girlfriend.'

This time he wouldn't let the dig slide. 'Dammit, Jayda. She's *not* my girlfriend.' Considering their non-event earlier, the words couldn't have held more truth.

'Whatever she is or isn't, she's a suspect. I need her to come into the station and answer a few pointed questions.'

'About?'

'Jagger. The string of serial murders that match the murders in her book.'

'She's told you everything she knows.'

'And she can tell me again. Forwards, backwards, sidewards, every-which-way until I'm satisfied I know everything she does. You know how this goes, and if you weren't dick deep into this woman, you'd be thinking with the head that counts.'

She shook her head. Almost looked sorry for her outburst. *Almost.*

Her voice softened. 'Don't get involved any more than you are, Chase. This is career making or breaking stuff here. If she's guilty, you'll be answering your own storm of questions. And before you ask, this crime scene and every one subsequent, are off-limits until I get the okay from Hackett.'

Before he could blast her one more time about where his dick had and hadn't been, and take her to task about cutting him off from the case, Jayda was storming back toward the building's entrance.

He turned toward his car to find another parked so close it was a damn-well ass-kiss. No surprise when he saw who slinked out from behind the wheel.

Hackles rose upon hackles as the snake approached. 'Seth.'

'Chase.'

Their customary Mexican stand-off. The reason reporters didn't make a showing anywhere near Chase's Christmas card list. If ever he were to "do" Christmas, that is.

'What are you doing here?'

'My job.' Of course. Big-wig reporters for The Melbourne Telegraph broke big-wig stories. Jayda's stick-your-nose-into-other-people's-dirt hound dog fiancé. He'd slept his way into the Night Terror case, and now he was marrying into a diamond-mine of more headlines. Why stop when you're on a good thing?

He ignored the unease stemming from his thoughts. He had every right to be pissed.

'Don't let me stop you.'

'Why are you here, Chase? Thought you were on leave.' Seth stared pointedly at his wrist and he resisted the urge to clutch it with his other hand. Or use it to flatten his pretty-boy perfect nose.

'Not your business, Seth.'

'Actually, that's where you're wrong.' Seth glanced at Jayda through the glass entrance double doors, set his lips in a smile as if they were enjoying some macho-friendly chat, then turned back to him. 'While you're partnering my fiancé, anything you do near or around her is very much my business. Her life is in your hands, and from what we both know, those hands don't always operate as well as they should.'

'You bastard.'

'I'm not the bad guy here. Just looking out for the woman I love. I'm sure you'd do the same in my shoes.'

What he hated more than a smart-ass reporter was a smart-ass reporter who was right. Didn't make Seth's knowledge of his condition any easier to chew. Seth had muscled in on his rescue op, won him a dressing down by Hackett, and was sticking his nose where it should never be stuck.

'I'm looking out for her, too. And I've been doing that a darn-sight longer than you.'

'Why do you think I've kept quiet? The fact you care about Jayda is your saving grace. Call me whatever you like, it won't stop me doing anything to ensure her safety. And if that means outing you, so be it. If your boss hadn't benched you, this conversation would have come a lot sooner. Get yourself checked and get yourself fixed. Because, right now, you're putting everyone around you at risk, and that includes yourself.'

With another theatre-worthy grin, a slap on the back and a smart-ass man-to-man wink, he nodded before heading toward the building and Jayda.

Chase was hard-pressed to join in the whole buddy-buddy routine. Only not doing so made him the bad guy. Seth was trying, he wasn't. The world according to Jayda. Any thoughts of returning to the job before the test results came back were moot. Stuck somewhere between Hackett's orders for a full physical and Seth's threats that he'd no longer keep his reporter mouth shut.

All problems that would have to take back-row seats. Jagger was dead. And the killer had gifted his finger to Stacey. Neither action featured in her book. The killer was acting off-script.

Which meant his days of predictability were over and the danger to Stacey had just jumped to critical.

Chapter Thirty-Four

Home-cooked aromas scarpered through the front door as Stacey stepped inside. Italian, tomato-based, mouth-watering.

Her tummy rumbled. She'd skipped breakfast, hadn't the stomach for lunch, and now that it was way past dinner her body berated her negligence with a sharp pound in her head and lethargy in every limb. One thing stopped her from rushing into the kitchen and indulging her tastebuds – the man responsible for producing the reaction in the first place. The same man responsible for her hunger.

She'd successfully avoided him all day. Hadn't seen or heard from Chase since she'd taken Ethan's call yesterday and left to see Midnight, palm slapping her head the entire drive for letting go with him and breaching every one of her rules post-Brad.

Then other matters pushed her slip in good sense to the back of her mind.

Midnight was alive, albeit battered, bruised and broken. An altercation with a car, the vet said. Thankfully, Ethan had found him by the roadside before he'd frozen and starved to death. It didn't bear thinking about. He needed an operation to reset and hopefully save his back leg. But first they needed to fight the infection sucking the life from his weak, emaciated body. Thoughts of losing him after he'd been miraculously found squeezed at her heart as she'd signed the paperwork, given him one final stroke and kiss, and thanked Ethan profusely for his part in finding her baby.

Then, needing something she couldn't quite define, she'd declined his offer of a drink and headed home, hoping not to see Chase, yet hoping she would. Palm-slapping her head once again for her stupidity. An empty house had awaited her, along with two officers in a parked car out front, requesting she "accompany them to the station for questioning". Questioning about what, they wouldn't share. It wasn't until halfway through her "interview" they gave her the answer.

Jagger was dead – *murdered* – and missing a finger.

The tone of their interrogation was clear. They believed she knew more than she was telling. And that Chase was somehow involved. She may have her reservations about the man, but whatever his flaws, he wasn't a murderer. And she told both good cop and bad cop as much, earning two pairs of raised brows and more than a few knowing looks. That they thought she and Chase were sleeping together was obvious.

Funny. Their being wrong wasn't half as grating as wishing they were right.

A pot clattered and those aromas assailed again. Her tummy rumbled, more rigorous than before.

Deep breath. Now or never.

She dropped her bag and keys on the coffee table and made for the kitchen. Tried not to think about what they'd been doing last time she saw him. What he'd stopped them doing. And why.

She still didn't know why.

And didn't want to know. Any thoughts of developing their relationship were gone after he'd made it clear he wanted to talk more than … that other stuff. Who was she kidding? His rejection hurt. She'd opened up and he'd turned away. Cementing Brad's vile words and accusations in her mind – that she could never hold a man's interest. Hell, she'd even failed during a bout of passion. How could she ever recover from that?

Distance was the only way forward. Both physical and emotional. She wouldn't make that same mistake again.

'You're home.' His gaze searched hers. For what? Signs of residual lust?

Not happening.

She blanked her expression. *No interest here.*

Her nose twitched.

He lifted a spoon, tasted, added a couple of twists of freshly-ground rock salt and a dash of some freshly chopped herb, no doubt basil from the aroma. Then he stirred and tasted again.

The twitch in her nose turned to an itch. She scratched, focussed on the stirring and the bubbling pot, not the lips licking the sauce from the spoon, or jeans moulded to perfection around parts she'd been up close and personal with only yesterday.

Her body warmed. So much for not thinking about *that*.

'Yeah, I'm home. No thanks to your buddies at the station.'

'I called to warn you, but you didn't pick up.'

How was she to know his messages weren't more blows of embarrassment?

'The phone was on silent.'

He nodded as if he believed her. She half-smiled as if everything was okay between them.

The air crackled with proof it wasn't.

'Did they tell you …?'

'About Jagger?' She rubbed her eyes. 'He's dead. They think you're involved.'

He didn't look surprised. Or particularly worried.

An overwhelming need to sneeze hit. She grabbed a tissue, blew and blinked. Water flooded her eyes.

She scanned the kitchen bench, looking for the culprit of her attack.

Chase added a sprinkling more of herb. 'They'll get over it. There was a line of people who wanted Jagger dead, most of whom had a helluva lot more to gain than me.'

She returned her gaze to him. 'And the fact that his finger turned up on my windscreen?'

'Could be for any number of reasons.'

'I'm not stupid. It wasn't just anyone who killed Jagger. It was *him*. The Copycat Killer.'

'He has a name now?'

'Yeah. It fits. At least it did until he murdered Jagger.'

'We don't know that for sure.'

She snuffled. Grabbed another tissue. *What the hell!*

'Either you're a shithouse detective or a shithouse liar. I'm trying to figure out which.'

'Okay, so I want to protect you. Is that a crime?'

'Only if you get caught.'

He snorted. 'And here I thought jokes were off limits.'

'Only if they're not funny.'

Before they got stuck in a roundabout conversation that would make her like him again, she nodded toward the simmering sauce.

'I hope you made enough to share?'

'More than. Hungry?'

'Enough to eat an entire veggie patch.'

'Ah, the vegetarian equivalent of a horse?' He grinned.

She couldn't help it. She grinned back. 'Yeah.'

Her tummy flip-flopped, ignoring every one of her orders to stop.

She moved closer and peered into the pot once again. 'What is it?'

'Just a quick tomato sauce with olive oil and a dash of chilli. To be served with gnocchi and garlic bread.'

Again her tummy reminded of her neglect. Loudly.

He held out the spoon. 'Want to try?'

She almost did, then didn't. Wasn't getting that close again.

She stepped back. 'I'll set the table.'

'Done.'

It was. Complete with wine glasses, serviettes and the reason for her snuffles – a big box-display of tiger lilies. No wonder her head was a balloon one breath short of exploding.

Atchoo! More tissues. 'Those flowers have to go.'

She sniffed, blew, sniffed again. It didn't stop that eye-itch thing she hated.

'I bought them for you.'

'I don't do flowers.'

'You– *what?*' His look said "aliens have invaded my kitchen".

Not his kitchen. Mine.

'Don't most women *do* flowers?'

'I'm not most women.' She sniffed. '*Hay fever*, Chase. The reason I don't have a dog. The reason my cat is a Sphynx. Fur and flowers are the worst triggers.' Another sneeze, the eye-itch thing running into a waterfall. 'Take them away, *please*, before this turns into an all-out attack.'

He did as she asked. Swiftly disposed of the offenders outside, pollen and all. Diabolical that of all flowers, he'd chosen the worst for her condition. To ward off further sneeze fests, she downed a couple of anti-histamine and tossed the tablecloth into the wash.

'You never told me you had hay fever.'

'There are a lot of things you don't know about me. Like I don't know every little thing about you.'

Something – the way his expression shuttered, the way he turned and stirred the sauce when she doubted it needed more stirring – made her wonder what he was thinking. What he was hiding that made him close off so suddenly and so completely.

The reason he'd told her they can "forget together'?

What did Chase want to forget?

'I'm ready to dish up.'

She let it go. The less they knew about each other, the better. Entanglements didn't make for easy goodbyes. Something that would happen when the Copycat Killer was caught.

It wasn't as if they were friends, or anything.

'Parmesan?'

'Love it.'

Two bowls lined the bench. First he added the gnocchi, then the sauce, a sprinkle of chilli flakes and finally a fresh grating of cheese. Two twists of the pepper grinder and her mouth was watering again.

'What can I do?'

'Grab the wine from the fridge.'

She crossed the kitchen and opened the fridge. *Her* fridge. Filled with food she didn't recognise.

'You went shopping.'

'I can't cook with stuff I can't pronounce.'

A tub of coffee commandeered an entire corner of the top shelf. The other corner brimmed with stacked bottles of beer.

He'd moved into her house, her fridge.

She grabbed the bottle and closed the door, closing her thoughts along with it. 'The wine's red.'

'Rosé.'

'I don't drink red.'

'This isn't red. It's light and sweet and bubbly. You'll like it.'

Bossy. Always bossy.

A bowl in each hand, he headed for the dining table.

'Live dangerously, Stacey.'

Was he serious?

'Tried that. Got a dead man's finger on my car and a detective living in my house for my troubles.' She dumped the bottle next to his glass. 'I'll leave the danger to my books and go with water.'

'I don't drink Rosé. I got it for you.'

'Why?' She waved her hand. 'No. Don't answer that.'

He'd said it as if it meant something. As if the gesture was more than an "I'm sorry for being a dick".

Apology not accepted.

Memories of how he'd made her feel seconds before he pulled

away stormed her mind.

'It's time we clarified exactly what's happening here. We're not living together. We're co-existing. I have no choice but to share my house with you, that doesn't extend to my bed. I need your protection, not your body. So any and all conversation from now on will be about the case, and only the case.'

She dragged in a breath and barrelled on before she lost the nerve. 'And while the elephants are out and running wild, this afternoon was a mistake. I don't want to talk about it. It never happened. Will never happen again.'

She stared longingly at the food and ignored the hungry growl from her stomach. 'I seem to have lost my appetite.'

She snagged an end of garlic bread, a glass of water and turned so she didn't have to see whatever look her words had dragged into Chase's expression. 'I'm going to bed.'

Chase watched Stacey walk away. *Again.*

It seemed all he did lately was watch her walk away.

Hurt. Angry. Scared.

While he'd been so wrapped up in "the world according to Chase" he hadn't considered she'd view his peace offering as anything other than welcome. He hadn't even asked about Midnight.

Selfish bastard.

He should ask her to stay. Tell her … what? The reason he'd stopped wasn't because he didn't want her, but because he wanted her too much? That made a shitload of sense. About as much sense as his life right now.

Nothing gelled.

Like the Copycat Killer targeting Jagger.

Thank god Gracie was okay. He'd broken the news in person. Much as Jagger was a scumball, he was her scumball, and the father of her son. She'd been sad, but stoic. It cut him to see his sister cry, he'd dried too many of her tears in past years when their mother was too sick and their father too busy caring for her to notice his kids needed care too.

He'd insisted on staying, she'd insisted he leave. She was okay.

Regardless, he called Chris – recovered and raring to thwart the bastard who'd decked him – and asked him to keep vigil outside her house. Doubtful Jagger's death had any connection to her, but he wasn't taking any risks after that break-in. The evidence of which had led to yet another dead end.

Much as he'd cursed the living bastard to hell, that didn't mean he wanted him dead.

So, who did?

The Copycat? Why?

He sat at the table and stared at the empty seat opposite. Lifted a fork, speared a gnocchi coated with tomato and cheese, then dropped it down again. Up till now, their copycat had copied different MOs by different killers with different motivations for their murders. Now, suddenly, he'd broken that trend and gone solo. Again, why? Jagger's murder was more personal. What other reason was there? It, the timing, had to reveal something about the killer that his copycat killings didn't. Jagger had tampered with Stacey's car. Why? And was that incident connected somehow to his death?

So far, the killer seemed to be celebrating Stacey. Mimicking her books, bringing them to life, but to what end? For fame? Was it someone she knew, someone else who benefited from her success? Investigation into Thrasher Publishing showed a small but growing publishing company that seemed legit and marginally successful. Stacey was their biggest, most lucrative author and seemed largely responsible for their climb toward success.

Was someone in the company trying to fast-track that rise?

Background checks on employees, especially those closely associated with Stacey like Des Whittaker and Beth Samuels, came up clean. That indicated nothing other than they had no priors or hadn't been caught yet. Her agent, Rita Hayden was also clean. Everyone around her, squeaky Palmolive liquid-detergent clean. Again, that didn't mean shit. It just made it harder for him to find who was responsible.

He needed to look into Jagger's last week. His associates. Who he owed money to. Who he'd pissed off lately. He needed to look deeper into Stacey's life, and the lives of the people around her. And most important of all, he needed to make damned certain he didn't leave her side until the sick son of a bitch was caught and behind bars.

Chapter Thirty-Five

A*rrgh!*

Stacey tossed the covers aside and sat up.

Damn! Blast! Drat, and double damn!

Even with her fist pressed against her stomach the rumbles continued. Only now the rumbles were louder, angrier and they actually *hurt*.

No avoiding it. She needed food and she needed it now. The clock said it was five past midnight. With any luck, Chase would be sound asleep – submerged deep enough in la-la land not to be woken by her need for a midnight forage.

Wind whipped against the windows. The eucalyptus seemed to creak more rigorously than usual in the front garden, its branches rapping against the side of the house like a stranger pleading entrance from the cold.

Donning her gown and slippers, she eased the bedroom door open and listened. No sound. A good sign. On blue fur-lined tiptoes, she made her way toward the kitchen. It was dark. Empty. Another good sign. For the first time that evening her shoulders relaxed.

A bowl of gnocchi had been left in the fridge, securely glad-wrapped, next to a large jar of pickles. Was there anything the man hadn't bought? Two minutes in the microwave and her insides were fighting to gnaw their way out. Stir, then another minute and she thought she might die from anticipation. Aromas of tomato, herbs and cheese filled the room so that nothing existed but the food and her hunger.

Fork in one hand, bowl in the other, she collapsed at the breakfast bar and dove in. There was no one around to watch and even if there had been, she was way past caring how she looked as she stuffed her face with possibly the best gnocchi and sauce ever. Rich tomato. Garlic. Sweet and tang. And a hint of heat. *Heaven.* Nothing this good came out of a bottle. Each and every flavour smacked against her tongue, blitzing her tastebuds. Mouthful followed mouthful. After the forth she managed to slow.

By the seventh she was searching the fridge for something to drink. Chase's wine taunted her from where it sat unopened on a shelf inside the door. She considered, then didn't. It was a guilt gesture and she wasn't having it. That the gnocchi was part of the same gesture didn't count. The food she needed, the wine she could do without.

She poured herself a glass of water. Sat back down, then raised the fork to her mouth.

'Couldn't sleep either, ha?'

She looked up. *Chase.* Her heart thumped. She looked down. Sighed. Relief, of course.

'So you own pyjamas after all.'

No fair that his grin made her melt and yearn until she couldn't think straight. She stuffed the fork into her mouth and chewed more vigorously than perfectly prepared gnocchi required.

He rubbed the back of his neck, PJ top parting from PJ bottoms. She fought the drag of her gaze to that spot of taut, bronzed skin. Heat slathered her veins.

She chewed some more.

'Yeah. Last time I went without them didn't work out so well for me.'

She glared. Ignored the drag of heat deeper. Lower.

He dropped his hand. Gave a sheepish grin. 'The fever.'

Oh, that.

He grabbed a beer from the fridge. Unscrewed the top. Elbows on the white granite, he leaned in, all-discerning blue eyes watching her across the benchtop.

'So, the blue monster was hungry?'

His gaze ran over as much of her dressing gown as the breakfast bar allowed. She pulled the two sides tighter across her chest.

'Cookie Monster.'

'Who?'

'Don't tell me you've never heard of Cookie Monster. You know? Sesame Street? One of the longest running children's shows in around one hundred and fifty countries worldwide.'

The light in his eyes flickered, then fizzled. 'I never watched much

TV as a kid.' He swigged his beer and shifted his gaze to her bowl. 'How's the gnocchi?'

'Good.' Guilt made her tag on more. 'Thanks.'

'Just good?' He twirled the beer bottle. 'Your expression before said it was much more than that.'

'You made it from scratch?'

'Yeah.' The dark in his eyes faded, replace by a twinkle. Old Chase was back. 'An ancient family recipe.'

'Really?'

He knocked back a mouthful of beer. Grinned. 'Nah. It's from *Pane Vino e Peperoncino*.'

'Good book.'

'Good recipe.'

The fork scraped the bottom of the bowl as she scooped up the last of the sauce and licked every bit of it clean. *Better than good.* If he wasn't around she would've licked the plate too.

'Don't hold back on account of me. I know you want to.'

Again that grin. If she wasn't sitting, her rubber legs would have folded. As it was, the burn of her skin must have turned her face as red as the sauce. Hopefully he'd think it the chilli and not the suggestion in his words.

'H-hold back?'

'From licking the plate.' He cocked his head. 'Why? What'd you think I meant?'

She didn't lick the plate. Didn't even contemplate answering. Avoided that mind-melting grin as she dumped her dishes in the sink and made for the door.

His voice followed her. 'First thing tomorrow we work on the Copycat profile.'

She turned. Gripped the doorframe. 'I agree.'

'You do?'

'Don't sound so surprised. I can see reason, when it exists.'

His lips quirked. 'Glad to hear it.'

She turned away, hesitated, then turned back.

'He broke MO.' Chills coasted along her spine. '*If* he was the one who killed Jagger.'

'It was him.'

She knew, but hearing her suspicions confirmed made it all too close, too real.

Too terrifying.

'I think so too.' She suppressed a shiver, pulled her dressing gown tighter. The cold didn't lessen. 'So, what now?'

'We work out why he's obsessed with you.'

She could have argued. What was the point when Chase was right? The Copycat Killer was obsessed with her. He'd mimicked her books. Left her trinkets. At a guess, to let her know he was killing for her.

All that wonderful gnocchi lurched in her stomach.

They had to catch him, and to do that, they had to uncover whatever connection they shared. Too many years of study, too many late-night cop shows, made it impossible not to join the dots. This was someone she knew. Or at least, someone who knew her. Who wanted her attention.

Only two questions remained. Why? And how far was he willing to go to get it?

Bang!

Chase peeled his eyelids open as yet another round of pounding hit the inside of his skull.

What the …!

Then came the drilling. Not in his head. Just outside the room. Or was it above? It took another few moments to wade through the lingering fog of sleep and then it hit – Stacey's sexy electrician. *Hell!* Was that today? He'd planned to be up and around when the man arrived. Didn't trust the smarmy bastard with Stacey as far as he could toss him.

He stared at the ceiling. He was so goddam tired all the time. What was with that? His hand wasn't any worse than it was, say, a week ago. Still, with a condition that affected each one of its victims differently, that didn't mean shit. He almost wished for the results now. Just to know. One week and he would.

His stomach rumbled.

In less than fifteen minutes he was in the kitchen, yawning over a mug of steaming coffee, wondering where the hell the woman in question was. Surely not up in the roof with the tool, and his tools? A distant tinkle of laughter, then a door slammed. Seconds later he made himself busy with the toaster as she entered the kitchen.

'Good morning.'

Her cheeks were flushed, her greeting as chirpy as the whistling going on somewhere above them.

''Morning.' He tried not to sound pissed.

The arch of her brow indicated he'd failed.

His drink was the perfect foil for his frown. 'You're particularly cheery this morning.'

'And you're not.'

She dumped a mug in the sink and he spied dregs in the bottom.

'Don't tell me you've succumbed to the dark side?'

When she gave him her "what the heck are you on about?" look, he waved toward the sink.

'Coffee? Oh, that's Jasen's.'

Her voice wrapped around the man's name. All flirty. Breathy.

A mouthful of hot brew and the subsequent burning of his tongue prevented his scathing thoughts from leaving his mouth and becoming another point of contention between them. Last thing he needed was to add what she'd incorrectly perceive as jealously. Chick-magnet man wouldn't be around long enough to be a problem.

'He says the job will take three days all up.' She grinned. Rinsed the cup and set it to dry on the rack. 'That means he'll be back again Monday and Tuesday next week.'

It shouldn't have sounded like the best news she'd had all day. Time to refit the lid on that can of worms and redeploy her focus elsewhere.

'I've been thinking about how Jagger fits into the case and have a couple of ideas around finding the Copycat. Thought we might nut them out together.'

With a nod she busied herself at the bench. 'I've a few ideas of my own.'

He sipped again. Considered.

Something was up. Her shoulders had suddenly squared so tight she'd fit perfectly into a box, and it took two tries before the lid of her teabag tin clattered open.

Her palm flattened against it as if willing it not to run. 'Let me make a hot cuppa and then I'll join you in the living room.'

He hitched a hip against the counter, watching her fill the jug and set it to boil. She opened a cupboard and hunted out a black cat teapot.

So Stacey.

'I can wait here.'

Her fingers paused on the cupboard handle. 'I'm sure there must be more interesting ways to wait than watching me rattle around the kitchen.'

'Can't think of any right now.'

Her jaw clenched. 'Another joke?'

'Wasn't meant to be.' He watched her deliberately avoid his gaze. Roundabout never worked with Stacey, so this time he'd try direct. 'What just happened?'

'What? Nothing.' Her mug clunked onto the bench. 'Why'd you think something happened?'

'Because one minute you were all chirpy and oh-what-a-beautiful-morning happy, and the next minute you … just weren't.'

She sighed. Turned. Seemed to brace herself before meeting his gaze.

Her mouth opened, then snapped shut.

'I won't be managed.'

What the—

'I'm not managing.'

'You're there every time I turn around. Watching me. Wanting to know what I'm doing. What I'm thinking. I need space.'

'Space, meaning?'

'You in your place, me in mine.'

'The killer's still out there, Stacey.'

'Believe me, I know.'

'I'm staying until that changes.'

She raised her brows. *'Managing.'*

'It's a helluva lot better than being murdered.'

Colour ebbed from her face. 'That's low, Chase.'

'And not far from the truth. You need to be careful Stacey. This guy is watching, and he seems happy with that *for now.*'

He scrubbed his hand over his chin and watched his words shudder through her.

'No telling how long that will last.'

Chapter Thirty-Six

'**P**ossums don't drink Coke and eat Doritos.' Stacey clutched her pen and tried to stop the travelator in her brain from taking off toward speculations bordering ludicrous.

Instead she focused on Jasen draped against her doorway. Her hunky electrician who wanted to date her and check out more than her wires, who'd just informed her that someone had broken into her home, tapped into her electricity and hacked into her Wi-Fi.

The killer?

Her head spun with freakish Exorcist speed.

The toe bone's connected to the foot bone, the foot bone's connected to the ankle bone …

Crap!

The familiar chant didn't make a fig of difference. Neither did the deep, slow breathing that usually helped oust the panic from squeezing her chest and every bit of oxygen from her body. Short of screaming and yelling and sobbing uncontrollably, she slammed fist and pen into her desk. Sharp pain shot up her wrist, the pen's nib dinting the varnished oak. Again she wanted to scream. The mark in the wood just one more thing to thank the psycho-bastard Copycat Killer for.

Jasen shuffled his feet, the sprawl in his fabulous physique stiffening so that his body was rather less comfortably trailing against her doorjamb.

Take a chill pill, Stacey.

It wasn't Jasen's fault someone other than possums had camped out in her roof. That someone had been … watching her?

Don't freak out. Don't freak out.

Nope. Not one iota of difference.

Breathe. Deep, deep breath.

Her heartbeat boomed so loud, how could Jasen not hear? Poor guy must think she was a fruit-loop. A whole box of fruit-loops. Well, he could get in line with half the Aussie male population. One seriously annoying detective, included.

It's okay. Everything's okay. This is just a little hiccup. Some less-than-healthy paranoia, but to be expected under the circumstances. People don't camp out in other people's ceilings. They just don't. That's for the movies, and books. Not real life suburban Melbourne.

Just because you have snacks in your roof, doesn't mean anyone's been living there.

Still her brain whirled on the travelator, unable to get off. Didn't matter what mantra she tried, it still felt like someone had rammed a straw in her lungs and was slowly, deliberately sucking.

Frigging breathe, for god's sake!

Positive affirmations were for suckers. They sure as hell never worked for her. So why should they work now, *with a serial killer out to get her?*

Breathe.

Jasen scrubbed his unshaven jaw and blinked eyes that had to captivate and mesmerise women on a daily basis. 'Are you okay, Stacey? You look kind of pale.'

He pushed up from the doorframe and crossed the room. She swivelled her chair and watched him perch on the edge of her desk, his legs dangling precariously close to hers. Pale had to be an understatement, given her shaking hand and the lack of staunch in her legs. She couldn't have stood, even if she wanted to. She gripped onto the desk and tried for calm. She didn't need to dump her crazy theories onto her poor flirty but well-meaning electrician. What she did need was a visual of what he'd found. Something to get her into the mind of the killer.

'Can you describe exactly what was up there.'

'Of course.'

His hand rested on his thigh as he spoke of cut wires and patches and other such terms that meant crap-all to her. Described the litter of empty cans and packaging that made up her intruder's snackfest while he – *what?* Waited? Watched? Listened? Planned his next kill?

She shuddered.

Jasen leaned closer, his gaze stroking her body as if he'd like nothing better than for his hands to follow suit. Oblivious to the pound in her head or her lack of interest in him past solving her electrical problems. He smelled every bit as manly as Chase. Maybe more so, with his sweaty tee and pheromone-filled denim. He just wasn't her type. And this wasn't the time. And she wasn't interested in revoking her hard-won independence.

And he's not Chase.

Damn! As if that should make an ounce of difference. The thought could go right back into whatever hidey-hole it scampered out from.

Time to switch off the libido and switch on her inner detective. She knew enough to know how this should go.

'I'd say they've been there a while.' Jasen shifted and his boot brushed her calf as she pulled her gaze up from his hand to his sunburned face. 'Probably left from the last time someone worked on the place.'

Of course he'd think that. Because how many Aussies lived in a world where a serial killer was so fascinated by them, they wanted to live under the same roof.

Kill and cut off fingers, then wrap them in ribbon as a gift.

Creepy.

She shoved away the thought, and the subsequent shudders. 'Did you leave it all up there?'

He shook his head, clearly affronted, as if she'd accused him of dumping the stuff himself. 'I cleaned it up for you. Any old food or food smells will attract mice and rats, and they just love to chew on wires.' He shot her a grin that once upon a time might have made her heart flutter. 'I'd love you to call me again, but not for solving your electrical problems.'

Her brain glazed over the flirting to the hard-boiled fact. In any other situation, clearing away the mess would have been the right thing to do. Just not here, because now all the evidence was gone.

'Did you take any photos?'

He stared at her as if her wires were as loose as her house's. 'Uh, no.'

'Oh, well.' Not much she could do about it now. And if she pressed the point, he'd only consider her more neurotic than he already did. 'Thanks, Jasen.'

Again his gaze did the whole slow-skate up and down her body thing. 'My pleasure, Stacey.'

It didn't make sense. That the killer would camp inside her house when with all that modern technology afforded, he could have watched her and stalked her more safely from afar.

So why break in?

Because he wanted her to find the signs he'd been watching her? Because he wanted her to be freaked? Well, give the psycho a gold star, he'd succeeded. She was well and truly freaked.

Chase would crack it when she told him. Not about someone stalking her, but about the evidence being cleared. It was just one more reason for him to resent Jasen. That he already resented his presence was obvious. All those macho caveman instincts would be leaping to the forefront. Not jealousy so much as a dog pissing on turf he was just passing through. Not because he wanted it, but because he sure as hell didn't want any other dog to claim it.

'I'll see you after the weekend.' Resting an elbow on his knee, he leaned in. 'Unless you agree to dinner tonight.'

Dinner with a hot electrician who was – very obviously – very good with his hands. It should have been tempting.

'I – I can't.'

'You're so tense.'

He swivelled her chair, and her open mouth clamped shut as two very strong hands clamped onto her shoulders.

'You need to go out more, Stacey. Have fun and let go. Nothing's so bad that it should put a frown on your face.'

She'd heard worse pick-up lines. She'd also written better. And what did it matter? Jasen would be fun. That was a given. But that fun wouldn't come without a price. He wasn't asking her out as a friend, and she wasn't interested in being more. To anyone.

A familiar quirky grin sprang into her mind.

Why'd she have to think about Chase now? He didn't want her. He'd made that perfectly clear with his earlier rejection. But that wouldn't stop him from having a thing or five to share about her going out with Jasen. And really, she was too old to play games. Too jaded to believe that seeing another guy would make Chase realise what had been staring him in the face all this time. That he wanted her.

That was book fodder. Not real life fodder.

Only the crap from her books came true. The murder and mayhem.

The romance was fiction through and through.

And through and through, she was stuck in this saga – with a detective who escalated her heart rate and raised her temperature. Stuck until they caught the killer and they could both walk away to continue their respective – very separate – lives, as they'd done so many times before.

'Tell me you didn't leak this.'

Chase, all red-faced and steam-train seething, waved his mobile between Stacey and her scrawled profile notes. Dropping her pen, she grabbed the hunk of plastic from his hand – shuffled further against the arm of the couch as he dropped down beside her – and stared at the screen.

Her heart screeched to a halt.

No surprise he was one breath short of exploding. She wasn't exactly thrilled either.

Online media. Saturday morning's ground-breaking news. *Author's Fictional Murders Come to Life.*

The headline wasn't the worst of it.

Romantic suspense author, Stacey Holland has landed deep in the midst of murder. Ms Holland and her award-winning book, From Mishap to Murder, have become "items of interest" in an ongoing homicide investigation as similarities between the author's fictional murders and Melbourne's Nine Knife Slasher murders have come to light.

The Nine Knife Slasher claimed three lives mid last year, the serial killer's name reflecting the ritualistic circle of nine stab-marks left on each of his victims' chests.

After months of investigation, Melbourne's homicide squad have reopened the case and are actively investigating links between Ms Holland's book and the murders.

Ms Holland was unavailable for comment, but sources from Thrasher Publishing – responsible for printing Ms Holland's award-winning novel – revealed the author is devastated and doing everything she can to assist the police catch the Copycat Killer. Work on the second book in her Murder Madness trilogy has been put on hold until the case is solved.

'It's the only responsible thing to do,' stated our source within the small publishing house. 'This senseless killing must stop, and until it does, Stacey won't continue to write when her words might then be used for more sinister purposes than enjoyment. She refuses to be responsible for the loss of more lives. Her books are meant for entertainment, not re-enactment. She renounces these murders vehemently and asks that the killer refrains from taking any further victims.'

In an interesting twist, a series of fan letters have come to light which suggest these murders are more personally linked to the author than first believed.

Homicide Detective Inspector, Terry Hackett stated …

Grrr!

If not for the repercussions and another dose of Chase's anger, she would've flung his phone at the far wall. He was already peeved about the ceiling squatter debacle. Forensics had been through the entire area and found nothing. Not a fingerprint or hair or any form of evidence to suggest who had been up there and why.

And now this …

That whole "unavailable to comment" cop-out was bullshit. Not once was she contacted by anyone other than the police regarding the case. And she'd been more than available for them.

And a fan letter? Correction. *Letters.* No one at Thrasher had ever mentioned a series of letters. She was unaware any correspondence existed – threatening or otherwise – other than the letters she'd personally received. Yet, suddenly they surface, just in time for headline news. Incredible they'd been kept from her, and worse, from the police, until now.

Seemed that someone within Thrasher was speaking on her behalf. Tailoring the story, for what? Promotion? Who was it? The paper's so-called "source". Beth? Des? Or someone outside her editorial circle in the company? Someone callous enough to use the murders to further book sales. Someone she knew, trusted.

Her gut gave an answer and she pushed it back.

Surely not.

This had to be paranoia whispering in her ear. No one she knew would do that to her. Feed her to the dingoes. Make her suffer more than she already was. Chances are the answer was none of the above and the reporter uncovered the story via other means.

Her gaze dropped to the bottom of the screen, and her heart dropped along with it. She scrolled down and stared. *Melbourne Telegraph*'s headline wasn't the only one she'd scored.

At the onset of her writing career, she'd chased a dream. Worldwide exposure and notoriety. A wealth of followers. Not personal, but for her stories. Maybe even a movie deal. *Fame.* Only not like this. Reality had a habit of swindling the stuffing from her dreams.

Author Writes Murders for Real.
Murder, She Wrote. From Literature to Life.

And then there were other headlines less gracious.

Stacey Holland: Writer or Wreaker?
Author or Assassin?
A Murderer's Marketing Strategy.

The career she'd worked so hard to forge was crumbling. Just as the taste of success settled on the tip of her tongue, it was ripped from her mouth. Her books would be forever associated with death. The real kind.

'Well?'

Chase was still glaring. Still pissed.

So was she.

'What do you think?'

He shook his head, the glare softened, but not totally gone. 'I know what I'd like to think.'

'You may imagine this is a career maker for me, but as far as I'm concerned it's a career breaker. I don't want to sell my books at the expense of innocent lives.'

'What about these letters?'

'I have no idea what they're referring to. I've never received threatening or death-related letters. If I had, I would have notified the police immediately.'

'So, who hid these letters from you and leaked the story?'

'If the two people are one and the same, that is.' She tapped the notes in her lap. 'I've been wracking my brains trying to figure out who. Do you think,' her voice wavered, 'do you think whoever leaked this *is* the killer?'

He squinted, softened some more. 'I doubt it. I'd guess this is more opportunism than narcissism. Although, saying that, I don't doubt our killer is a narcissist.'

'He wants attention.' Her lips quivered. 'Particularly mine.'

He swayed toward her, seemed to realise his mistake and jerked back.

He peeled the mobile from her hand and scrolled the screen. 'It's that same question we keep revisiting. Why you?'

'It's not as if I'm special or particularly interesting.'

He stopped scrolling and met her gaze head-on. 'You are to me.'

Shit!

Stacey pureed his mind and made him blurt out whatever crazy thought entered it. To think it was one thing, but to voice it? After he'd resolved to wait.

Her eyes widened, as if his words slammed her like a car's headlights, high beam. As if it was he who had her scared, not her crazy psycho stalker.

She jumped up from the couch and crossed the living room to the window. 'Stop playing with me, Chase.'

His chest tightened. He stood, closed the distance. Stopped just short of where she stood, frowning out at the street. 'That's not what this is.'

'What is it then?' She turned, eyes liquid and unblinking. 'One minute you kiss me, the next you accuse me of the unthinkable. You want me, then you don't. You tell me I'm special, then call me impossible. What's that, if it's not cat and mouse?'

A mother of a hole you've dug for yourself, man.

He sighed. 'Confusion.'

'For me, yes.'

'And for me.'

What are you doing?

Somehow he'd boarded a steam train. The coal was burning hot with no chance of slowing any time soon. Something inside didn't want to slow. *Selfish?* Maybe. But there was a part of him that didn't want to be misunderstood. Not any longer. Not by Stacey.

Her hands clenched at her sides. 'You keep throwing half-baked suggestions out there like a damned carrot, hoping for god knows what. I'm not your donkey, Chase. Or your plaything. And I don't appreciate being treated like either.'

'That's not my intention, Stacey.'

'Then what is your intention?' Air puffed out of her mouth, fluffing her fringe only to have it fall further down over her eyes. Unsteady fingers shoved it back, tucking it tight behind her ear. 'You ask me to trust you, yet you give me little reason to see you as more than a comedian hankering for his next big laugh. I know it's a cover, and most times, it's a pretty damn good one. Then it slips, and the day before yesterday happens. Why?'

'Why the day before yesterday? As in why did I start or why did I stop?'

She blinked. Swallowed. Breathed in deep and slow. 'A blanket "why". Whatever answer will make sense.'

His shoulders tightened so much they hurt. 'The day before yesterday happened because I wanted it, and I stopped because I wanted it to be the start of something more.'

'I said *make sense*, Chase. That makes no sense at all.'

Words weren't his forte. Opening up ran a pretty close second when it involved talking about a weakness. And somewhere at the head of it all was Stacey. Yet, if he didn't do this now, the door might close forever and she might never give him another chance.

So this was it. No hiding behind a laugh. The moment of truth.

As unfamiliar as the feelings poking through his chest and into his heart.

Chapter Thirty-Seven

'I like you.'

Head bang! What the hell kind of declaration was that? *I like you.* A pimple-faced teen could concoct better.

'A lot.' *Yeah. Great improvement, Romeo.*

No surprise, his revelation didn't dent Stacey's less-than-enthralled disposition.

Her green eyes were cold. Unimpressed. Accusing.

'So you kissed me. Did …' her hand spiralled through the air, 'all that other stuff, and then stopped because you,' two sets of two fingers bobbed eye-level, '*like me.*'

'You're the wordster. I'm just a homicide detective who makes light of crap so he doesn't have to cope.'

And there was the jaw-drop. *Expected.*

What he hadn't expected was the speed with which the jaw snapped back into place.

'Crap, like …?'

He opened his mouth, almost couldn't, then stopped thinking and spoke before he lost the nerve. 'My mother dying when I was ten.'

The glacial cut of her gaze softened. *'Chase.'*

His heart hammered as a myriad of expressions flitted across her face.

'I'm so sorry.' She opened her mouth, clamped it, shook her head and opened her mouth again. 'I can't imagine how hard that must have been for you.'

And so it began.

No sense opening the box if he didn't spill the contents right there and then for her to see.

'No harder than her decision to give me life while knowing it would cut hers short.'

Stacey blinked.

Chase's words tugged at her heart, while the crack in his voice, the raw pain in his expression, they wrenched and dragged tears to her eyes. Big. Strong. Tough to crack. Descriptions that summed Chase to a tee. They scrambled hand-in-hand with infuriating, bossy and all-out sexy. She'd guessed at something lurking just below the surface of his humour. None of her surmises had come close to the truth.

He looked so lost, hands hanging slack at his sides, bearing his soul, something wholly unfamiliar to him. Warmth funnelled out from her mind and into her heart. He'd navigated that unfamiliar territory with her. She didn't think about why or what had changed for him now. Enough that he'd made the journey, and she wouldn't be the one to thwart it.

Going to him, she took both his hands and led him to the couch. This time when they sat, she didn't shrink away. She tucked one leg beneath the other and turned to him, the closeness of his thigh making her blood warm, her heart racing as if this instant was more momentous than a man unloading what must have weighed on his chest for years.

Silly, when that's all this was.

'Tell me.'

'It was Parkinson's.'

She steeled her expression to one of support and listening.

He shuffled, and she knew instinctively it wasn't the couch which made him uncomfortable. She waited. He'd opened the conversation. How far he'd run with it had to be his choice, not hers.

'She was diagnosed at the age of thirty-five. Early onset. Rare, but I guess she was one of the lucky ones.' With a scathing twist of his lips, his fingers tapped erratically against his knee. 'Medication helped keep her symptoms at bay. That, exercise and a healthy diet. Then she fell pregnant.'

The tapping quickened. 'An accident. One her doctor had warned against. He also warned her against going off her meds and taking the pregnancy to full-term. Mum wasn't one for taking advice, good or otherwise.'

His fingers stilled, but for a tremor. Difficult not to see how deeply the memories still affected him. 'Not much is known about Parkinson's and pregnancy, but in Mum's case the stress of carrying a baby for nine months without meds accelerated the onset. After I was born, the symptoms didn't lessen. The progression was slow, but it was always downward. And it lasted for ten years until her body couldn't take anymore.'

Until now his gaze had latched to the far wall. For the first time since he began talking, he faced her.

'Growing up in our house, there wasn't a lot to laugh about.' The corner of his mouth quirked in an almost-smile. 'But sombre wasn't allowed. Mum would always look for humour in things and Dad wanted nothing more than to make her happy. At first, it was a game. To help Mum forget the pain. Then she died, and it helped us forget ours.' He rubbed the stubble on his chin. 'It became a part of life. Still is.'

'Your mother sounds like an amazing person.'

'She was.'

It didn't bear thinking. Her mother may criticise and drive her crazy and never believe she was good enough, but she was still her mother. She wanted her to succeed, to be something. *Someone.* And what she did, she did out of love.

She covered his hand. Squeezed. 'Losing someone at any age is tough. But at ten … I can't imagine what your family must have gone through.'

Inane sentiments. Writing was simpler than thinking on her feet. The glibbest of comments could take hours to perfect, yet seem natural and spontaneous on the page. Real life wasn't so easy.

'My memories of her are mixed.' He turned his hand and squeezed back. 'Earlier, she was pretty much like any Mum, just weaker. In the later stages, she rarely left the bedroom. The hardest days were the ones when she didn't recognise us. Days when Dad marched us out of the way because she was having a bad turn. Those days, I used laughter to shield Gracie and hide how scared I was.'

He stared at their joined hands. 'And, now I'm using it to hide that you're more than a person of interest in an investigation. You've become a person of interest, to me.'

At first, his words wafted like a pale mist overhead. Then their meaning hit, a thunderbolt straight to her heart.

'You're *interested?* In *me?*' Was that squeaky voice hers?

'Yes, Stacey Holland.' That earlier whisper of a smile bloomed into one of his knee-quaking grins. 'Interested and intrigued. I want to date and have coffee. Talk and get to know each other. All the things you don't *do* and I've never done, I want us to do them now, with each other.'

What was she supposed to think? Do?

She'd thought about a moment like this more than once in the past weeks. Wondered how it would play out. How it would feel. Then she'd shaken the insanity, remembered his harsh words and scathing tone telling her to stop acting like something she wasn't. Remembered that guys like Chase didn't fall for women like her.

Now, it seemed they could.

'What do you say, Stacey?'

Thoughts tumbled around her mind.

If the killer hadn't forced them together, would this moment have come? And when there was no killer forcing them together, what then? Would his "interest" remain or would he realise his feelings were incidental to the situation and not her?

And did it really matter either way?

It wasn't as if he were proposing marriage. Just dating. And sex. Somewhere in this all lurked sex. That large, hulking elephant that had stalked them, hounded them, trumpeted loudly every time they were in close proximity. And sometimes when they weren't, those moments Chase wheedled into her thoughts, taunting her body with hedonistic promises of how it would be if the elephant were to win. Something she'd been tempted to allow. Hell, she *had* allowed it. Had spread her legs and begged him not to stop as his fingers strummed life into a body that had been sexually sober for too long. Then he'd pulled away, leaving her feeling dirty. Used.

Now it seems his change of mind was his way of setting things right between them so the sex wouldn't be just sex. It'd be … *what?* Love? Not that. But something more than like. Something akin to respect.

Blue eyes watched her, no hint of humour there now. Just sincerity. Uncertainty. And something else. He'd shared some of his past with her, and that made a difference to what bandied between them. It may not be rockets and blasters, but it was a start.

And it meant something.

She met his gaze, struggled for inspiration, something to seal the moment and let him know she was interested too. A wide, blank canvas stared mockingly back. His hands clenched at his sides. The longer she waited, the thicker the air grew between them until it'd surely paralyse them both. No time for composition, so she went with first instincts.

'Thank you.'

Thank you?

Chase stared. What did she mean by thank you? Thank you for sharing? Thank you for your interest? Thank you, but no thank you?

'Thank you for being honest.'

Ah, that. He battened down the doubts.

Not an answer, but her uncertainty shaved the edge off the disappointment. And at least it acknowledged he was headed in the right direction.

'I thought it was a good place to start if we're getting to know each other.'

'It was. *Is.*'

He watched her take a deep breath. Consider. Breathe again.

'It's a good start.' She pushed up from the couch.

'And?'

'Let's wait and see what happens next.'

'You're serious?'

'Very.'

She seemed to be waiting. For a joke, no doubt. He didn't have one.

'I want you, Stacey.

'I know.'

'You want me too.'

'I know.'

'It's simple arithmetic. One plus one makes a perfect pair.'

'Perhaps. But there's more at stake here than mutual need and a moment's honesty.' She ruched her hair back from her face. 'Trust. And that only comes with time.'

A couple of steps and she'd reached the door.

'Where are you going?'

'It's dinner-time for Cuddles.' She paused in the doorway, then turned. 'I really do appreciate your honesty. It means something. A lot, actually.'

Her lips twitched, then spread into a wide, roguish smile. 'And as for trust, well that's a door that swings both ways. So, how about we start with your first lesson in snake handling?'

Trust was a door that swung both ways.

True.

Doubtful, though, that it extended to pythons. All one and a half metres and two or so kilograms of him. Heavy, hefting muscle that if it tightened, well, let's just say pretzel wasn't a position that had ever appealed.

'If you're going to tense up just looking at him, what are you going to do when you hold him?' Stacey's look was half amused, half exasperated and a whole lot of sexy.

Didn't change that she wanted to wrap him in a lethal weapon. Other than herself, that is.

'Have a coronary?'

'You big baby. He won't hurt you.'

'Because a snake's never eaten a human before.'

Said animal wrapped firmly around her arm and began inching up to her shoulder.

'A green tree python?' She snorted.

Something he would have found cute if a rally of nerves weren't partying up in his brain.

She readjusted her grip so the beast didn't wrap his constricting body round her neck. 'His staples don't go beyond rodents and birds.'

'There's always a first time.'

'Stop stalling and come here.'

It almost sounded sexy. If not for the bulky green lump in her arms.

'I thought the plan was to feed it, not play with it.'

'We can do both. I'll feed him after you've had a hold. It's not good for a snake to be handled after eating.'

'Can't be good to hold a snake before eating, either. Isn't he hungry?'

She arched a brow. 'Seriously?'

'Deadly.' The word was supposed to be funny. Only when spoken out loud, it didn't sound remotely amusing. So, okay, he was being a baby. He had a thing about snakes. Had a thing since *Australian Geographic* featured that big South American bugger eating a whole crocodile. *Whole.* What was it? "A" something.

Ana-friggin-conda.

'Stand like I showed you.'

Because he was a patsy as well as a damned baby, he stuck his arms out robot-like and felt the muscles in his neck and shoulders scrunch.

'*Relax.* If Cuddles senses your nerves he's going to get nervous too.'

'And we don't want a nervous snake.'

'No, we don't.' Her eyes latched to his. 'Ready?'

'If I say "no" does that mean I don't have to do this?'

'You don't *have* to do anything. But a relationship with me means having a relationship with my animals.'

He grinned. 'Are we having a relationship then?'

'Right now we're holding a snake and sharing a moment.' She blushed. That smooth, perfect skin a barometer, but for attraction. Emotion, too.

Reading her was getting easier by the day.

She lifted the body up, dropping the front half of Cuddles into his hand. Cool. Smooth. Not at all slimy. Sweat beaded his armpits. His body tensed, the GTI race of his heart making him regret agreeing to this madness.

And madness it was. Snakes killed.

'Relax.' Stacey touched her free hand to his chest. She had to feel the craziness of his heartbeat. Had to know he was shit scared over the emerald green lump in his arms. 'I'm here Chase. You're fine.'

Her gaze found his, her voice soft, lulling, while the sashay of her hand over his chest gave his heart a whole lot of other reasons to race.

'Holding a snake is about mutual trust. Provide stable support that'll make him feel safe and he'll move over you gently and almost lovingly.'

She relinquished the tail end to his other hand. Their fingers brushed. He barely registered the snake for the feather of her touch along the inner flesh of his arm.

'Think of the snake's length in thirds. One hand should support the lower third and one the upper.' Her palm skimmed up to his bicep, where she readjusted Cuddles from moving up further. Her breast pressed against his elbow. Was she trying to turn him on? Because, dammit, she'd succeeded. While holding a reptile, no less.

'He's a constrictor, so he'll feel safer if his tail has something to wrap around. Your arm, for instance.' Again she guided the head down from wrapping once more around his shoulder. 'Try and keep him in front of your body, where you can better control his movement. He'll go in the direction his head points, so adjust your upper hold to manoeuvre him where you want him to go. Your hand movement should be slow and fluid, matching the motion of the snake, keeping those thirds in mind as you continue to support him.'

It was almost cathartic, Stacey's low murmur, her hands on his body, the slide of cool snake in his arms, his movements matching the rhythmic coil and glide while sensing the animal's acceptance.

Who knew holding a snake could be sexy?

'How do you feel?'

Doubtful that "hot" was the appropriate answer, or the one she was waiting for, so he went for the obvious.

'Better than I thought.'

She nodded, cupped her palm around the back of his hand. 'Loosen your grip just a little. That's it. Let him feel safe without feeling restricted or trapped.' She grinned. 'You're doing okay. Not bad for a big baby.'

He wasn't quite ready to rave about the experience, but, surprisingly, it wasn't the worst thing he'd ever done. With a little persuasion, he might even consider doing it again. If Stacey was around to talk him through it.

'Ready to give him up?'

The snake yes, her touch, no. Unfortunately both went hand-in-hand.

Weight left his shoulders and he dropped his arms. Cuddles curled his tail round Stacey's wrist, his upper body almost lovingly curving against her other arm. She headed for the cage, giving Chase time to call his libido into question.

Stacey wrapped in a snake was *not* sexy. Even if she were wrapped *only* in a snake. Naked, but for the snake.

The visuals shunted his mind.

Hell!

He turned, adjusted his jeans.

He was losing it. Whatever the hell *it* was. And she was the cause.

'Dinnertime, gorgeous.'

'Thanks, honey.' He grinned, spun back to catch her attractometer on high. Hand still gripping the lock on the cage, her cheeks bloomed rosy red.

'Oh, you meant Cuddles?'

'Who else would I mean?'

His lips twitched. 'A guy can hope.'

'Haha. I thought we'd dispensed with the jokes.'

'Only for stuff that matters.'

Her gaze riveted to his, seconds that made him want to speed up, not slow down. He stepped toward her. She dragged her eyes from his and headed for the kitchen. The moment was gone, but not his amusement. He chuckled. Refused to apologise for enjoying tugging Stacey's strings.

He stared at the snake now back inside its cage. There was something mesmerising about the slow slide and coil of Cuddles around his branch. Tropical fish in a tank had nothing on this. Not that he was warming to the animal. A dead snake was still the best kind of snake.

Perhaps just not this one.

'Here we go.'

Stacey edged past, a pair of long metal tongs clasped in one hand. It wasn't until the other blue-gloved hand opened that he realised what had changed in the room. The smell. Like wet mice. Or rats.

Dinner was being served.

Gross.

Call it what you like – morbid curiosity came to mind – he couldn't look away. Five minutes. That's all it took between Stacey dangling the prey over Cuddles's wavering head to the snake swallowing its entire meal, whole.

Anaconda came to mind again.

Just as well he'd held the thing before watching it eat.

Whatever hunger he may have had for dinner was swallowed along with that dead, white rodent. Not that Stacey was squeamish. No surprise. A snake feeding was nothing compared to the murders she wrote. Or the murderers.

Food for thought if he wanted to entangle himself with her more than he already had.

Chapter Thirty-Eight

'**W**hy, Beth?'

No tiptoeing through the tulips. Lies and manipulation were a bitch Stacey wouldn't let bite her in the butt again. She'd waited all weekend to make the call. Stewed and simmered until her watch hit nine and she knew her editor would be in.

She edged her feet out from where they curled underneath her and stretched, flexing her pinpricked toes toward the far end of the couch.

That she'd used her editor's real name for the first time since she signed with the Thrasher team wouldn't have been missed. Neither would its intent. Silence bloomed at the other end of the phone line. The hurt, indignant kind. Well, those sentiments swung both ways, and she had first dibs.

'If we're not friends, I thought we shared at least a semblance of mutual respect.'

'We are. And do.' Beth coughed a little throat-clearing, divertive kind of cough. 'I didn't leak the story to the press.'

'So you say.'

'So I promise.'

She didn't have to see her editor to know her reaction; blood-red lips clamped thinly, her angular frame stiff and upright in her high-backed office chair. Her desk would be OCD organised, her gaze fixed to the framed diploma on the far wall. Black-tipped nails would wrap deliberately around ironed strands of raven blue while she listened to her uncharacteristically out-of-line author step more out of line as her temper escalated.

'And the letters? How did I not know they existed?'

'We thought it best you didn't know.'

'We?'

Silence.

'Who's *we*, Beth?'

She sighed. 'Des didn't want to scare you.'

Des presumed way too much.

'They were *my* letters. Don't you think it should have been *my* choice?'

'Maybe now. But back then you'd just won the RuBY, you were on a roll. We didn't want to ruin it for you. And they were only letters.'

Her stomach clenched. That's how it started. Being managed. Manipulated. It's only a dinner. Only a dress. Only a silly book. How *could* they? Knowing how fast she'd run from being handled in the past. How she'd vowed never to be handled again.

Her breath came in short, shallow gasps, her chest so tight her lungs hurt. She swung her still needle-pricked soles to the ground and rested her elbows on her knees, dragging in gulp after gulp of air until her head no longer floated drunkenly above her shoulders. Her mind roared.

How dare they?

She pushed up and strode the breadth of the living room, then whirled round and strode back again.

'*Only letters* – meant for *me, my eyes* – which now seem to have been written by a killer.'

'There was no way we could know that.'

More pacing. More trying to keep her temper in check.

'At the time we thought it was the right thing to do.'

'Keep telling yourself that every time there's another murder.'

'This isn't on me.' Beth's voice wobbled in a way Stacey never thought she'd hear.

Well, she should be affected. She'd done wrong, and she needed to know how much.

'That's a damn cop-out, Beth, and you know it. You don't think giving the police those letters twelve months ago would have made a difference?'

She heard a sniff, a nose-blow. 'There's no way either of us could know that. And then when we realised there was a killer copying the STS ...'

A siren blared inside her brain.

'You *realised?* When?'

More silence. More sniffing.

Lucky there was a phone line between them or Beth would be on the receiving end of more than an angry voice.

'When Beth?'

'The day you were nominated for the RuBY.' Her hesitancy, the barely there quality of her voice, both indicators she was aware of her guilt. That didn't stop the denials from keeping on keeping on. 'Not so much a realisation as a hunch. There were similarities, but we couldn't be sure–'

'Are you frigging kidding? They weren't similar. They were the goddam same!'

'Des said–'

'There's an awful lot of "Des said" going on here.' The hand clutching the phone to her ear ached. It didn't help that the metal dug into her palms, hampering circulation. She ordered her grip to loosen. 'So, tell me about this source mentioned across the media? Was that Des too?'

Silence again. The loaded kind.

'Beth?'

'No!'

Weird. And a little too vehement to be empty.

She spun round and flung her hand through the air. 'For god's sake, stop covering for him.'

'I'm not.' Papers shuffled, then a pen dropped. Another sniffle. 'Your mother came into the office the day after I visited you.'

Her toe caught on the rug, she stumbled, righted. Dragged in a deep breath. It didn't counter the whirlwind change in topic. Her mother was a regular visitor at the Thrasher offices, so why bring it up now? The possibilities would have made her squirm in her seat if she'd still been sitting. Instead she focussed on breathing. Tried not to let her imagination gallop ahead of reason.

Breathe. 'For her fortnightly visit? What was it this time? Pumpkin pie?'

'Pecan.' Beth gave a little half-cough. The kind she used when she needed time to think. 'She asked how you were going.'

Realisation slammed head-on.

'So, you told her.'

'I didn't think there'd be any harm.'

Of course she didn't. She wasn't to know that where her mother was concerned, there was always harm.

'You mentioned the letters?'

'Not me.' The implication was clear.

Des.

Of course. Men wrapped around her mother's finger like strands of ribbon around a present. Loving. Thoughtful. Caring. Supportive. Faces that endeared Candace Holland to the outside world. Shame those sentiments didn't extend further than skin deep. And never in the direction of her only child.

Nothing but better-than-your-best was tolerable. Nothing less than reaching the top ever allowed. And once you reached that pinnacle, you were never *there.* Or *enough.* There was always a higher peak to scale, an accolade more significant than the last to realise. A success mere inches from her fingertips to bring her one step closer to becoming someone worthwhile. Not a joke or a nobody trying to make it in a world where she didn't belong.

A world her mother craved more than anything. Her daughter's happiness included.

No need for Beth to say more. The situation took on the clarity of crystal.

Her mother leaked the story.

Fame's not a boxed-up commodity, Stacey.

Candace Holland had categorically proved her point again; stepped outside that box and dropped her daughter firmly into the spotlight. Only this time the press had more than a glorified childhood – or was a better word "fabricated'? – and accounts of sexual prowess surpassing her characters. They had a stalker killer and hints of … what? Collusion?

Would her mother really steep so low?

She didn't want to answer that, as much as the answer hollered vehemently inside her brain.

A couple more choice words to Beth – she still wasn't off the colossal hook created by her lies and deceit – then she hung up.

More of her mother's pearls addled her mind as she took up pacing again. She couldn't stop. Not if she didn't want to lose it – her temper, her sanity. The one shred of comfort she'd clung to growing up. Her mother loved her. Through all the picking and prodding and relentless pressure, it was all done out of love. Right?

Celebrity reputations aren't like laundry, Stacey. Grubby is good and much harder to forget. Mud on your shoes leaves footprints the media can't ignore. Everything has a price, and it's only those willing to pay who hit pay dirt.

She slumped into the couch, her weary feet unwilling – unable – to pace any longer. She'd thought Candace Holland had a limit. A thick black line never to be passed at the expense of her daughter.

Now she wasn't so sure.

'How could you, Mum?'

Stacey slumped deeper into her once-comforting massage chair and stared blankly at the dark, empty stage, the absence of props reflecting the absence of ideas that had once elbowed eagerly into her mind.

Just another dreaded phone call she'd finally drummed up the courage to make. Beth's had been a whole truckload of double-choc cake compared to this one. Her chest muscles were so tight, any minute now her organs would be crushed from existence. She barely dragged in enough breath to fuel her next words as her hand clutched the mobile to her ear. 'This time you've gone too far.'

'Pah!'

No different to her mother's reaction the last time she leaked information to the press.

Why was Stacey surprised? No matter that the deaths weren't a consequence of her actions, it was still wrong. Of course, her mother's black and white logic wouldn't allow her to see it that way.

'Do you love me?'

White noise filled her ears. Her mother's silence. Difficult to know what answer it conveyed.

'What a silly question.'

'It's not Mum. All this publicity. This scrabbling to get to the top. It's actually hurting me.'

'Stop being so sensitive. I'm doing this for you.'

The words held conviction, but lacked the persuasion of the past. Or maybe with a killer after her, Stacey's views had changed.

'If that's true, you had to know this isn't what I want.'

'You're young. You don't know what you want. That's why you

have a mother, so I can handle all of that for you.'

This was getting her nowhere but headache central.

And glutton for punishment or not, she still had to know. 'Why did you do it? You had to know I'd look guilty.'

'Guilty, schmilty. Since the story hit, sales for *From Mishap to Murder* have skyrocketed. There's a whole new audience out there, waiting for the next Stacey Holland hit.'

'What about the threatening fan letters? Did you write those?'

'How could you even ask? Of course not!'

Her outrage was laughable. Her limits equally so.

Stacey inhaled, long and slow. 'I've stopped writing *In the Throes of Murder*.'

'Of course you have. It looks bad if you don't.'

'I'm not doing it because of how it looks or because it'll get me more sales. *People have died*.'

'Yes. And that's terrible.' Her mother's voice held as much compassion as a thug debt collector on payday. 'But the situation is what it is, and if your career can benefit ...'

'I don't want to benefit from murder.'

'That's a little naïve, don't you think? Do you think the media make money from pictures of fluffy cats and cheeky ice-cream-covered toddlers? No. Murder means mega-bucks, and why shouldn't we be allowed to cash in on it too?'

'I'm not the media, and I don't want fame at the expense of someone's life. It's called having respect for the dead.'

'And what use does a corpse have for respect?' The exasperated sigh was no less than Stacey had heard too many times before. It was filled with sentiments that started with "my daughter the disappointment" and only got better from there. 'Be sensible, Stacey. They're six-feet under and beyond hurt. But it helps us, so, why not make the most of it?'

Once again that question of how far would her mother go for fame was answered.

She dropped her head in her palm, her fingertips digging into the pressure points at each temple. She should have realised her mother's skin was too thick for compassion to burrow inside and find her heart.

'And what about their families?'

Another rendition of her mother's large, long suffering sighs echoed down the line. 'Do you want success or not?'

'This has nothing to do with success.'

'It has *everything* to do with it. If you're not willing to put yourself out there, you'll never be found.'

Another of her mother's pearls.

'You're exploiting their loss. It's wrong. On so many levels, just … *wrong.*'

'You're upset. Why don't you book another session with Anthony? He's a first-rate psychologist. I'm sure he can fix whatever's wrong.'

That thick, iron wall was impenetrable.

She'd long-since left behind the black post-divorce insecurities. Yes, Anthony had helped, but she'd moved on from the need for soul-searching analysis. She was stronger. Self-reliant. Knew right from wrong, no matter how much her mother's manipulations tried to muddy her convictions.

Tense fingers massaged the spiralling tension in her forehead. 'This isn't a take-a-pill-and-get-better scenario. Someone is killing people, using my books as their guide. If I benefit from their deaths, how much better am I than the man who murdered them?'

'You don't get to pick and choose your opportunities. You just have to grab them when they show up on your doorstep.'

Nothing, not even murder, could put a dent in Candace Holland's purpose.

The drill inside her skull was just shy of unbearable. Twenty-seven years and she couldn't do it anymore.

'It's over, Mum.'

'What's over?'

'Our working together – this partnership, my writing, you managing. We want different things for different reasons.'

'You're upset, darling. Don't make rash decisions you'll later regret.'

'This isn't rash. It's something I've been considering for a while now.'

This time her sigh was anything but suffering. 'You can't just fire me. *I'm your mother.*'

'I'm not firing you. I'm moving on. I want to make it in writing on my terms, in my way. I appreciate all you've done, but now it's time I took responsibility for my own life and my own direction. I need to grow up sometime.' She tried to keep the pleading from her voice. She wasn't asking permission. She was telling.

So, why didn't it feel like it? 'This is me growing up, Mum.'

'You're overwrought. Take a deep breath and let's talk about this in the morning when you're calm and rational.'

'You're right. I'm overwrought. But this decision isn't rash. It's what's best for both of us. I get to concentrate on writing and you get to find out what makes you happy. This is your chance to do something for yourself. Live life the way you want to live it. I'm going to be okay, Mum. And I know you will be too.'

Silence.

So much louder than the backlash she'd expected.

'Mum?'

'Take a good, hard look at what you're doing here, Stacey. When all this is over, I'm sure you'll see things more clearly.'

Her mouth opened but the words met the empty buzz of the dial tone.

Blood roared through every vein, an endless pound inside her brain.

Dammit.

Going in, she'd known her mother wouldn't take well to being cut from her writing career. But she'd expected anger. Shouting. Railing resentment.

Not dead-calm refusal to accept it was time their professional lives parted ways.

Perhaps she needed time to get used to the idea. Time to appreciate their split as an opportunity, as a gift, not a slight.

A thought born of the wishful part of her brain. The part that ignored Candice Holland's bull-headed obstinacy and her determination to get her own way, no matter what the cost.

Stacey tunnelled her vision on the taxicab's fare counter.

28.48 slowly clicked over to 28.49. If she stared hard enough, waited long enough, the bottle-green Audi parked impatiently in her driveway might give up and go away.

Fat chance.

After escaping Chase for a night out with "the girls" – namely Shazz and a few of her friends – she'd almost begun to feel normal again. *Almost.*

Almost kidded herself she still retained some shred of control over her life.

The pleasant roll of alcohol through her system, teamed with the low rumble of the taxi's idling engine, could have been soothing. Any other time but now. The driver turned and stared at her expectantly. Still, she didn't move. Still, the numbers continued to click over.

He shifted in his seat. 'This is the address, yes?'

She dragged her attention from the mounting fare to meet his cappuccino gaze. Nodded. Sighed. Rummaged through her purse before handing him a ten and twenty dollar bill. 'Yep. Home sweet home.'

Sitting in the confines of the cab wouldn't make the rest of the world go away. It would still be there, still stifling, when she opened the door and stumbled on out. Something she should do before Hasid's mix of amusement and concern turned to irritation.

'Thanks.' She waved at the coins in his hand. 'Keep the change.'

Another sigh, and she dragged herself out of the backseat.

The Audi door opened, and the reason she wanted to leap back into the taxi and drive away – somewhere, anywhere but here – stalked toward her in two inch *Givenchy* heels.

Perfect!

It's not too late to run. She'll never catch me in those shoes.

Except the ramifications from that cowardly move would last a helluva lot longer than the few moments of angst she was about to endure.

Pushing a smile to her lips, she crossed the front yard to the driveway. 'Mum.' She kissed an impeccably made-up cheek, careful not to disturb the hairstyle.

Her mother checked anyway. 'Don't crowd, Stacey. It's not seemly.'

It shouldn't still hurt, that her mother viewed hugs as nothing other than perfunctory.

She sighed. May as well get the crap over and done with.

'Why are you here, Mum?'

'Aren't you going to ask me in?'

No. Because then I can't walk away when it gets too much.

She bit back the words and tried for something less … Pearl Harbour.

'I'm tired, Mum. Can't this wait until tomorrow?'

'No, it can't wait. You've dodged my calls for two days now, so you can stop dodging and face up to me in person.' She gave a theatrical swirl of her hand. 'And I won't discuss business with my daughter in the middle of the street, either.'

'We don't have any business to discuss.'

'I say otherwise.'

'I won't change my mind.'

'And I'm not discussing this out here.'

They glared at each other, and for once, Stacey didn't back down. She was over backing down.

Her mother growled, no doubt unaccustomed to her daughter's newfound backbone.

Get used to it, Mum. There's a lot more spine where this came from.

The keys jerked angrily in her mother's perfectly manicured hand. Subconsciously, she noted the design choice this week was butterflies. Consciously, she wondered what she'd done in a previous life to have this one screwed with so much.

'Stacey Marigold Holland! If nothing else, I've taught you sufficient manners not to make your mother stand out in the dark, in the cold!'

Between her porch light and the streetlamps, it wasn't anywhere near "dark". And the evening held a spring glow that hinted of summer nights not too far in the distant future.

This was just another rant to guilt Stacey into giving in. As she'd always done in the past.

Something clattered.

They both spun round.

Her front door swung open and a large, hunky shadow stepped out onto her porch. 'Stacey?'

The other reason she hadn't invited her mother inside jogged down the stairs and headed toward them.

Just one more conversation she'd like to have avoided.

Her mother's lips thinned, her expression as warm as ice freshly chipped from a glacier. 'So this is why you didn't ask me in?'

The subtext was flashing-neon clear. *Yet another distraction and you're living with him? No wonder you never finished your book.*

Chase joined their delightful tête-à-tête and cupped her elbow. 'Is everything okay?'

Giddy warmth frittered up her arm. She dragged her gaze away from two blue pools that gobbled every inch of her emerald silk dress and heels he wouldn't approve of. They finally landed on her face, taking in the heat that had to translate to a roaring red flush.

Candace Holland never missed a trick, particularly when it involved her one and only daughter.

Eyes almost an identical green to hers narrowed. That they'd taken in every bit of Chase's admiration and Stacey's reaction was a given.

She jerked her arm from Chase's touch, not even trying to keep the scathe from her voice. 'Just peachy.'

Two sets of eyes fastened on her, waiting …

Her mother tut-tutted. 'Aren't you going to introduce your *friend*, Stacey?'

She sighed. Impossible to avoid it now. 'Mum, this is Chase Durant. Chase, this is my mother, Candace Holland.'

Now to wait for the aftershocks.

Chase grinned as he offered his hand. 'Nice to meet you, Candace.'

'Ms Holland.' Her mother didn't even attempt to smile back. Instead she stared at his hand as if he were offering her cow dung. 'Your name sounds decidedly familiar. Where would I have heard it before?'

He withdrew his hand and rubbed it against his denim-clad thighs. 'Perhaps in relation to the recent Copycat Killer murders. I'm one of the investigating detectives.'

Her mother's gaze swung back to her. 'You're dating a *detective?*'

'We're not dating. He's just staying with me until things settle down.'

'In the spare room?'

She tried, really tried not to roll her eyes. The heat on her cheeks she was powerless to prevent. 'Of course, Mum.' Along with the cut in her voice. 'Do you want to check?'

'Don't be silly, dear. I'm sure the detective understands.' She gave

Chase one of her megawatt smiles. A movie star, red carpet smile, the kind not really aimed anywhere but just for show, the kind that never quite reaches the eyes. 'A mother can't be too careful when it comes to looking out for her daughter.'

'Of course.' Chase cupped her elbow again, brushing his thumb back and forth over the sensitive skin just inside, making her want things that were anything but appropriate when your mother was present. 'We both want what's best for Stacey. And rest assured, Ms Holland, your daughter couldn't be in safer hands.'

His grin melted her body, while his insinuation boiled her blood.

Not that her mother was much better.

This was tug'o'war and Stacey was the rope.

She clutched her bag to her chest, rather than tossing it at either one of their smug, false-smiling faces. Let them play their petty games. She didn't need to stick around and be a part of it.

'I'm going to bed.' She leaned in, pecked her mother on the cheek, this time making sure her hand snagged the hair. 'Good night, Mum.'

She turned to Chase. 'Don't forget to lock up before you turn in.'

Her shaky hand scrummaged through her bag as she walked toward the front door.

That her mother hadn't "discussed" her business meant that was a gem waiting for their next encounter. Normally the thought would fill her with dread, but she was too bone-tired, too emotionally worn to care.

Tomorrow was another day.

All she could hope is that it'd be an improvement on the one she'd just had.

Chapter Thirty-Nine

The passionflower tea was an abject failure.

Grass with a hint of citrus rolled across her tongue and slipped easily down her throat. She waited for calm to infuse her body, as the sleeve promised it would. As it had every other time in the past. Half a cup gone and her muscles remained locked, the pound against her skull just as harsh.

Scrawled notes stared up at her from the kitchen table. Forensic psychology. A favourite subject, yet not a word of the open pages had perforated the blockade in her brain. Time was hurtling by and she was nowhere near ready to sit her exam. Deferring seemed her only option. It was either that or a big fat "F".

Either way felt like failure. Along with letting a psychopathic scumbag steal just another facet of what was once her life. She couldn't write. Couldn't study. Couldn't open a newspaper or scan online media without being bombarded about her more than tenuous – and questionable – links to a killer. The cup clattered onto the saucer. She shoved the papers back and dropped her head into her arms. Her only solace – a few hours of peace while Chase was out doing whatever it was that detectives did.

He hadn't asked her to accompany him – or chauffeur – and she hadn't asked why. Had welcomed the time alone. It was so long since she'd had the house to herself – her own space. Solitude that was once a balm to her nerves. Now the silence brimmed with noise – wily threads of panic that said she'd created a monster who couldn't be stopped.

Which meant her "plan" was becoming more pressing by the minute.

The thought increased the pound against her skull. Because that meant presenting her plan to Chase.

More pounding.

She raised her head.

Only not in her skull. This time it was the front door.

Tempting to just drop her head back into her arms and wait for whoever to give up and leave. Her mind continued to race. The guilt – all those deaths – so much a part of her now she barely remembered a time when it wasn't.

Even more tempting was a distraction from her thoughts. She pushed up and made for the door. Checked the security peephole – Chase's nagging reminder ringing in her ears – and stared out at the overblown face staring back. Her stomach roiled. She should have stuck with first instincts and stayed put.

She jerked back, her trembling fingers suddenly ice cold.

Where she'd changed every facet of herself possible in the past two years, her ex-husband remained chillingly unchanged. Close cropped hair smoothed back with way too much product, eyes close-set, the left slightly smaller than the right. Thin lips flattened into a cursory curl.

'Open up, Stacey. No sense hiding behind the door. I know you're there.'

Her body jolted, her gaze darting left then right. The peephole was one-way, the door solid wood.

How'd he *know?*

A lucky guess, no doubt, and the fact that after two years of failed marriage he still knew her failings better than he should.

If only she could turn away and ignore the barbed taunts, but wouldn't that mean he still held power over her? The thought was even more unbearable than coming face-to-face with a past that seemed determined never to leave.

She unlatched and opened the door.

'Ah, Stacey, nice of you to come out from your cowering.'

She steeled her expression to neutral, her grip tightening on the handle. Acknowledging his taunt would only give him power she'd vowed never to give him again.

'What do you want, Brad?'

'To see your Mona Lisa face. Oh, and to give you these.'

He thrust a bunch of gerberas into her hands – an entire hayfever fest. And the look in his eyes said he knew it.

'Congratulations on your success.' His termite-ridden gaze raked her from head to toe until her body crawled. 'Killing people to sell books. Who'd have thought you had the balls?'

She clamped her jaw against every biting response that leapt to her tongue.

Her nose twitched but she ignored it. Wouldn't give the sanctimonious bastard the satisfaction. 'It's so sad you haven't moved on. You need to get a life outside the disaster we shared.'

His gaze turned granite. 'I've moved on, plenty. I'm senior partner now.' He perked up like some pompous, prancing peacock.

Bully for you.

She stared him down rather than comment. The bastard didn't deserve any accolades, least of all from her. Her eyes itched like crazy but she wouldn't blink. Wouldn't let him know his "gift" was having its desired effect.

His chest puffed out even further. 'And I'm engaged to Senator McAvoy's daughter.'

No surprise at the name-dropping. Brad always was and always would be about the appearances.

She raised her chin. 'My commiserations. Does your slave-to-be know you're still obsessed with your former wife?'

His gaze narrowed, stubby fingers clenching and unclenching at his side. She edged backwards. That he'd never struck her before didn't preclude him from starting now. Perhaps she'd walked out before he'd had the chance.

'Thanks for the visit, but don't bother dropping by again.' She inched the door closed. 'I'm sure the bottom of my garbage bin will be more than appreciative at receiving your "gift".'

She stifled a sneeze as a steel-capped boot wedged between doorjamb and door.

'I hear you're fucking some cop.'

Her gaze darted up to meet the raw anger in his. 'Then you hear wrong.'

'The flush on your cheeks says otherwise. I'm guessing you've learned a thing or two since our marriage if he's sticking around. Or maybe there's another reason? Convenience, perhaps?'

It took all her effort not to flinch. 'Remove your foot before I slam it in two.'

A sneer oozed across his lips. 'Hit a raw nerve, did we?'

'Not so much as I'm bored with this conversation. As I was bored with our eternity of a marriage.' She glared at his foot, then his blazing face. 'Don't bother calling again because next time I'll call the cops.'

He snorted. 'Good idea. High-profile attorney versus smut-author connected with murder. Wonder who they'll believe?'

She rammed the door against his foot. Hard. Then pulled back to do it again.

Scowling curses, he withdrew just in time for it to slam shut.

With trembling fingers she double-locked the door, secured the security chain, then dropped her forehead and palm against the cool, hard wood.

'Leaving you was the best fucking decision I ever made.' The jeer filtered through two inches of solid oak and any residual calm.

Always the last word.

That she'd left him seemed to have conveniently slipped his mind. Along with the fact that he'd never really "left" her. The flowers. The random contact, like today.

'If only that were true, but like a bad smell, you keep turning up. Perhaps your wife-to-be might like to know about your little visits. And the flowers. I'm sure she and her father will find them most interesting.'

'You bitch!' The door jerked then shuddered. No doubt he'd put the steel caps of his boots to use. 'You'll regret even considering it.'

'Is that a threat?'

'You bet your fat ass it's a threat. And just know, it's nowhere near empty.'

'Then I suggest you get your tight-attorney butt off my front doorstep and get lost. Because there's something you need to know about the person I am now. I don't threaten easy.'

She pushed away from the door and stalked into the kitchen before he could cut her further with his reply.

Her tea was cold. Useless.

She tossed the dregs into the sink, clutching the stainless steel edge, staring at her wavering reflection, fighting the drag of helplessness. How did he do it? Still. After she'd wiped her life of him. Made a name for herself regardless of his aspersions. Tried so damned hard to leave that old Stacey behind.

His words swilled like acid around her stomach.

Convenience.

Not true.

She was more than that. Had so much more to offer than Brad had ever given her credit for. His insults were aimed to bring her down, a penance for leaving him, putting pay to the promise that he'd never let her forget. She knew all this. And more, she knew Brad's penchant for making those around him feel small so he could feel big. Nothing had changed.

That included the crack in her confidence allowing old insecurities to burrow their way in.

Chapter Forty

Stacey trudged up the double flight of stairs as if approaching her own funeral.

Thrasher Publishing sat on the second floor of Colonial House in Port Melbourne. A dignified old building, located directly above the State Government's embarrassing first and failed attempt at planning a Melbourne Rail Link underground. They'd passed the planning stages, even started excavation, then realised digging was too close to Melbourne's main sewer. The mistake had cost the taxpayer millions of dollars and the government the next election.

But it meant that the beautiful old building, and those surrounding it, remained unscathed. And the deserted tunnels had provided a great basis for her underground finale in *From Mishap to Murder*. Beth had more than willingly offered to be her guide.

Stacey clutched the handrail at the top of the first flight and inhaled, deep, even though she wasn't remotely out of breath. Then with a sigh, she continued her climb.

Memories goaded her mind around the first time she'd scaled these stairs. The elation. The feeling she could spread her wings and fly anywhere. Do anything, be anything. Back then, that wondrous day had marked the beginning of the rest of her life.

Now every step closer to the offices she'd once loved made her heart ache.

Even writing had lost its shine.

The career that once saved her seemed destined to destroy her.

Palm pressed flat against the frosted glass, she drew in a double mouthful of oxygen and pushed. The door swished closed behind her as she approached the large, tan reception desk.

'Hey, Kelly.'

The young girl looked up from her computer screen, brushing sleek blonde hair from her eyes, her face breaking into her customary wide smile. 'Stacey. How's it going?'

Her gut tightened. 'If I said "good" would you believe me?'

'A real life serial killer copying your book? Probably not. Difficult to know whether you should feel honoured they chose you or shit-scared.'

She grimaced. 'I'll go with the latter.' Her gaze darted to the far, right office. 'Is Beth in?'

'Morticia? She's on a call. I've got the documents here if you'd like another look while you wait.'

'Sure.'

Kelly slid a thin wad of papers toward her.

'And Rita rang. She's stuck in traffic, so she's running a little late, but said she shouldn't be too far off.' Another megawatt smile. 'Take a seat. Morticia won't be long.'

Stacey glanced at her watch. 'I could only find a half-hour park. Do you think we'll be done in time?'

'Shouldn't be a problem. Worst case, if it is, one of us can go down and move the car.'

Stacey forced a curve into her lips. 'Thanks.'

She grabbed the contract and walked to a set of cream couches and small round table all clustered together against the far wall.

The prospect of being in Thrasher's offices any longer than necessary clamped every muscle in her neck and back, fuelling the growing throb in her temple and right between her eyes. She blinked, trying and failing to focus on the papers in her lap.

She hadn't spoken to her editor since their last, less-than-amicable conversation three days ago. Hopes she'd be able to avoid any face-to-face contact had nosedived when her agent called with the news Thrasher wanted her to go into their offices and sign the revised contract for *In the Throes of Murder*. Why she had to do it in person, she hadn't a clue. And neither did Rita. She'd bypassed her agent and called Des direct, asking him to post the paperwork. He'd said *no*, and she lacked the energy to argue.

She glanced at her watch. Fifteen minutes remained on her parking meter. Of course she'd be late. Murphy's Law was a fixture superglued to her life these days. Everything from untimely phone calls to a late agent and traffic conspiring to make her uncomfortable and grouchy while she waited for a meeting that would only serve to make her more uncomfortable and grouchy.

A shadow darkened the unread papers in her hand. She looked up to find Kelly out from behind her desk, immaculate as always in what she could now see was an orange and black shift dress topped with two inch heels. Seemed everyone could wear the buggers with grace but her.

Steam curled up from the black mug clasped in the PA's orange-tipped fingers. 'I thought you might like a cup of your usual.' She passed Stacey the mug and crisp peppermint scents filled her nostrils. 'And Morticia's off the phone, so you can go in now.'

'Thanks.'

She hiked her bag strap up onto her shoulder, clasped the mug and papers, and crossed the office floor.

The door to the corner office was open, so she walked straight in to find Beth standing at the window. Wall-to-wall glass overlooked the magnificence that was Port Melbourne. The Spirit of Tasmania moored proudly alongside Station Pier. Sparkling blue water mirrored a cloudless sky, while a few die-hard fitness fanatics jogged along the beach, making the most of the waning sun's rays. Winter's chill still clung to spring, but the cold in Stacey's blood had nothing to do with the seasons.

Beth turned, so slowly it was as if the view had tethered her gaze to the pier and the hulking red and white ferry. Her half-smile was spiked with uncertainty. 'Thanks for coming at such short notice.'

'It wasn't as if I had a choice.'

The blood-red lips tightened, hurt shadowing her gaze.

Stacey's back stiffened. She wouldn't feel guilty. Beth deserved her wrath, and more. She squared her shoulders and resolved not to care so much. It was her downfall. *Caring.* It made her weak. Made her believe people gave a rats when all they wanted was their own grubby gain.

Her editor seemed intent on ignoring her pique. Instead, she made her way to her desk, resting black-tipped fingers and slender palms against the tidy surface before lowering into her large ergonomic chair.

Stacey's gaze couldn't help but stray to the array of award-winning book covers that filled half the wall behind.

From Mishap to Murder hung dead-centre, pride of place.

She clutched the burning mug of tea to her chest.

Memories stormed. Two and a half years ago she'd entered this office and seen that wall. Then and there she'd sworn to earn pride of place on it someday. Now the thought made her want to puke.

'How are you, Stacey?'

She shifted her gaze from the wall to her editor, sitting behind her desk, as she'd always done, as if nothing had happened. As if she hadn't just lied and betrayed and made a mockery of their relationship, both work and personal.

One hand clenched the soft leather of her handbag strap as she blew over her still steaming mug. 'Showering me with fake concern won't change things, Beth. I'm still mad. And I'm also late. The moment Rita arrives, we'll sign the contract minus the civilities and then we can all go our separate ways.'

She sipped her tea and burned her tongue in the process. Of course she did.

She transferred her gaze to the small frame perched on the corner of Beth's desk – her, Des and Beth the day she won the RuBY. Des owned a partner to that photo, as did she – pride of place in her writing cave bragging corner.

How had she arrived at a place where that photo afforded nothing but pain?

'None of this was meant to hurt you, Stacey. Fan mail, hate mail. It's like good reviews and bad reviews. Better you focus on the positives and ignore the negatives. It doesn't serve any purpose other than to bring you down.'

'That may well be, Beth. But it wasn't your choice to make. I signed my book over to Thrasher, not my life.' She raised her hand when it looked as if Beth would argue the point. 'There isn't anything you can say that will change things. So let's concentrate on business, because there's nothing else between us.'

She leaned forward, dropped papers and mug onto Beth's desk. Trained her gaze on the blurry black print and not the woman she'd trusted with more than just her career.

Beth gave a half-cough. 'This arrived yesterday. I wanted to give it to you in person.'

She reached into her desk and produced a guilded frame containing a certificate and logo that Stacey well recognised. That and her name, printed in bold black script.

Her heart performed a leap and pirouette, despite her anger. 'I finalled?'

'Yep. One of six finalists in the People and Publisher's Choice Awards. You wrote a damn good book, Stacey. Even without the publicity around this Copycat Killer, you'd make waves. You'd win competitions and kick literary butt on your own merit, not his. Congratulations.'

Head-to-toe delight nudged back the gloom. *This* was the reason she wrote. Because people enjoyed reading her stories. Enough people to make a difference.

The certificate in her hands proved it.

A knock on the frosted glass cut through her thoughts. The door inched open and Des poked his head in. 'Sorry to interrupt, but Rita's on her way up.'

Beth nodded. 'Thanks Des.'

He checked his tie and the sharp-ironed cuffs of his pink shirt – did he not know Gucci made other colours? – his gaze sliding from his boss to Stacey. 'Kelly mentioned you were in a half-hour park. If you don't want a ticket, you should move your car in the next five or so minutes. Unless you want me to do it?'

The door swung open and a blur of red burst in. Dressed in a shade that perfectly matched her hair, Rita coloured the room with both presence and musky perfume.

Stacey stood up and they hugged.

'It's good to see you, Stace.'

'You too.'

Rita sashayed deliberately toward Beth. They shook hands, chocolate brown eyes coolly assessing Beth's almost black. The air was stilted. Tense. About as awkward as any one of their past encounters. Reassuring to know there were still things Stacey could rely on.

Her agent dropped into a chair and crossed her black, stocking-clad legs. 'Let's get stuck into this. I have,' she glanced at the filigree gold watch circling her wrist, 'twenty-seven minutes before I need to move my car.'

Beth coughed. One of those little coughs she made when nerves threatened her composure. 'That shouldn't be a problem. Now you're here, signing won't take more than a few minutes.' She glanced at Des, still propping up the doorway. 'No need to move Stacey's car. We'll be finished in less than fifteen minutes.'

Rita leaned forward and dropped a bundle of papers onto Beth's desk. 'I doubt it. I read over my copy again last night. There were a couple of typos I'd like fixed, along with a couple of minor amendments.'

Beth bit back a sigh, and words Stacey could read without them leaving her editor's lips. Rita had received the contract two weeks ago. Why wait until now to bring this up?

Beth's nod was sharp and snappy, a match for her tone. 'Des, bring it up on my computer and check the changes, will you?' She turned to Stacey and held out her palm. 'I'll move your car, if you like.'

How many occasions had she offered to do just that, and Stacey had thought nothing of it?

Not so now.

'Thanks, but I'll do it.'

Beth dropped her hand and blinked. 'Of course.'

Stacey headed for the door. 'I'll be back in five.'

Rita glanced up from the mass of papers. 'Actually, I'd like your input, Stace. Can you stay?'

She shuffled the keys in her hand. Met Rita's gaze. Sighed. 'Sure.'

Beth extended her hand again.

She dropped Sidney's keys into her palm. 'It's three doors down on the corner, just outside The London tavern.' Then, she added, 'Thanks'. Because it didn't seem right not to.

'No problem.' Beth's dark-rimmed gaze searched hers for mere seconds before Stacey turned away. She'd find no forgiveness there.

What's done was done, and there was no undoing the past.

Beth sighed and, in typical Beth style, sailed through the door as if her black combat boots had wings. 'I won't be long.'

Nobody said a word as she left.

Des made himself comfortable at Beth's desk, performing his two-fingered tap-dance across the keys. He paused and looked up. 'Where to first?'

Rita flipped through her post-it-note-covered copy. 'Page seven. Main provisions …'

Stacey pushed out of her chair and moved toward the window. She should be listening. Should be a darn sight more interested in a contract she'd surrendered blood, sweat and tears to win. Thrasher Publishing had embraced *From Mishap to Murder* and turned it into a sensation. They'd taken a chance, contracted an unknown wannabe writer and moulded her into something special. Both Beth and Des had worked their butts off to make her once-raw manuscript shine. And for that, for every additional, generous inch they'd given, she'd always be grateful.

But business was business, and loyalty only spanned as far as the next lie.

'Stace?' Rita's short, squat nail tapped the page open in front of her. 'Last chance. Are you sure you want to delete this clause.'

Without looking at the page or the point of Rita's finger, she knew exactly what her question referred to. *Page 22, point 4.4. Options.*

'Positive.'

In the Throes of Murder would be her last book with Thrasher. High-time she moved on.

The irony in finally doing what her mother had ragged on her to do since *Mishap* hit New York Times bestseller status wasn't lost. The difference now was she had no choice and a healthy conscience. Her motivations were sound.

Staring out at the blue expanse of sky over the bay helped slow her heartbeat near to normal. Even the pound against her temple lessened. She'd always loved this part of Melbourne. She'd signed her first contract here; had stared out this very same window and vowed to buy a place with a view after she cut her first million-dollar royalty cheque. But with publication had come reality – by the time that cheque arrived, she'd be hard-pressed to afford a balcony, let alone even half a one-bedroom unit.

Light flashed.

Her gaze darted to the street below. Another flash – this time blinding – and a rumbling roll much like thunder. The impact slammed her eardrums.

She winced.

The building shook.

Her heart leapt to her throat and battered, beast-like, trying to break free.

Des and Rita rushed to the window.

'Shit!'

'Was that a car crash?'

'An earthquake?'

'An explosion?'

'Someone should call the fire brigade.'

Lead filled her limbs. Her brain. Her heart the only living, moving thing in her body. Everything else froze.

Impossible.

No …

'I'm calling it in.' Des grabbed his mobile and began to dial.

Her mind reeled, rejecting every possible upshot of the blast.

It wasn't a bomb. Or deliberate. Or her car.

Jagger was dead, so the failed bomb attempt died with him.

It must have.

Her legs found life. Without a word or another single, untenable thought, she bolted out past reception and pushed through the exit. Down two flights of stairs and out onto the crazy, burning, fear-ridden street – gasping, panting, mentally fighting possibilities that clutched her chest and robbed every new breath.

Her shoes slapped against the pavement as her lungs squeezed and threatened to implode. Smoke scoured her throat; grit scraped her eyes until they burned.

And all she could think as she raced toward Beth and the flames and the spot where she'd left Sidney just over half an hour ago was *I didn't get to tell her goodbye.*

Chapter Forty-One

Dense smoke and ash clung to the air, clawing at Chase's throat, drenching his clothes.

Uniforms guarded the periphery of the scene while firies worked on the flames, calming the blaze to just a few sodden sparks. Too late for Beth Samuels. Doubtful she'd survived past that first fatal blast, detonated the moment she'd turned on the ignition.

Sidney was now little more than a wretched pile of metal and plastic.

First Jagger, now Beth. Only Beth wasn't the intended victim.

Fists dug into his thighs as he fought the need to punch something. *Someone.* Preferably the son of a bitch who'd killed Stacey's editor along with her beloved car.

He'd vowed to keep Stacey safe, and he'd dang-near failed. If she'd started the engine instead of Beth …

But she hadn't, and this latest, fucked-up attempt on her life made him even more determined not to leave her side.

He glanced across at the huddle just outside the cordon – Stacey, her agent, her assistant editor. *Now editor?* Could a possible promotion be motive enough for Des Whittaker to engineer his boss's death? His gaze slid to the agent, Rita Hayden. Word around was that she and Beth didn't get along. Could a personality clash drive one woman to kill another?

Was this and the previous fumbled incident outside Hook, Line and Sinker related?

Were they connected to the Copycat Killer, or were there two distinct motives at play here? Two distinct killers?

His head reeled with the barrage of possibilities, but his heart held steadfast against every battering ram. Of one thing he was clear – the bastard wouldn't get this close to his crazy cat lady again. He wouldn't allow it.

Jayda and Sam were talking to someone he didn't recognise from forensics. The new guy, Sebastian something or another, an import from their sunshine state of Queensland, was questioning the head firie.

Doubtful either would have anything to add. The Copycat didn't leave clues. He didn't leave anything he didn't want them to find. Like severed fingers and the charred remains of a dead woman.

They needed a lead. Soon. Needed to profile the bastard and catch him before whatever sick-assed end he sought became reality. It involved Stacey. That much was clear. What wasn't clear was how. And Chase wasn't twiddling his goddam thumbs until the answer decided to make itself known.

He scoured the area, looking for someone conspicuous. Someone who seemed out of place. Someone who looked more enthralled than horrified at the burned remains in the car.

No one stood out. But perhaps forensics' video feed would reveal what his roving gaze missed. Didn't these sick bastards get off from watching the aftermath? Chances are this son of a bitch was the same. And if so, he was out there somewhere, watching. The way he'd watched Stacey for the past year and a half.

He clenched his jaw and stalked his way toward Jayda to see what, if anything, she'd discovered.

I'll get you, you sick fucker.

I'll get you before you get her.

No progress.

Chase shuffled the pages of a file that grew daily. Larger. More perplexing.

More deadly.

How to make sense of it?

Jagger was dead. Beth, too. Add to that the trail of copycat deaths, and it was as if each step moved them further from identifying the killer.

Over a week of working the case, of questioning Jagger's friends and family, neighbours and acquaintances. Even the slimy bastard who still wanted his money. Chase had put pay to that notion quicker than a flea aiming for a dog's butt.

His team had worked the bomb scene, sifting for clues, looking for witnesses, suspects. Something – anything – that would move them one step closer to solving the case.

Nothing.

Then he'd called Chris and asked him to take Gracie and Jag Junior somewhere safe.

And he'd called Jayda, asked her to email forensics' report, along with copies of the so-called "fan letters". Two days studying and restudying them. The killer profile. Examining Stacey's characters, her murders, then weighing them against what they knew of the Copycat.

Jack shit.

With Stacey no longer writing, the copycat murders had ceased. Was that the reason he'd strayed from MO and killed Jagger or was there more to it? How did Stacey factor into it all? Was the bomb an attempt on her life or had he somehow known she wouldn't be the next one to drive her car?

Doubtful the last option was the most rational, but the idea that now Stacey was a target was unconscionable and setting his gut to the consistency of cement.

In his peripheral vision, he watched her, curled into the couch, the tips of her screaming pink socks poking out from beneath her bottom.

Nose scrunched, hair spiking out at all angles, she ran her fingers through again. 'We can't catch this bastard if he's killing willy-nilly.'

The grin was instantaneous. 'Willy-nilly?'

'He copied my books until I stopped writing. Now there's nothing to copy, he's strayed off on a tangent.'

Her lips trembled and he knew why. She was thinking about her editor. Guilt eating her up inside over her death.

'This isn't on you, Stacey.'

'How is this *not* on me. Beth died moving my car. In a bomb blast meant for me.'

'You aren't responsible for what this sick bastard does. That's all on him.'

'Tell that to Beth and her family. I'm sure it'll make a heap of difference when they're scattering her ashes over the Shrine of Remembrance.' She swallowed, blinked back a litany of other thoughts that had to be cutting her up inside. 'All this time, I thought my books had spurred him on. That he identified with them in some warped way and that's what started his whole sick-assed spiral into serial killing. If that's the case, logic says that if you remove the cause, the action loses its fuel. In light of that theory, this whole tangent away from copycatting makes no sense.'

He scrubbed his jaw, watching for her reaction. 'Is it, though?'

'What do you mean?'

'Is this a tangent or is this our real killer?'

The top of her pen played peek-a-boo with her lips.

Hot. In fact, everything she did ranked in degrees of heat. This was seven. Even those ridiculous socks factored on the scale. A three.

Images barraged his brain. Stacey writhing beneath him, naked but for her glow-in-the-dark pink foot coverings.

Three wasn't nearly high enough.

'Chase?'

His mind dragged back, kicking and screaming, his gaze deserting her socks for her face. Brows arched, she stared at him, a little bemused, more than a little irritated.

'Uh, sorry. What was that?'

'I said, that makes a lot of sense. But it doesn't help predict what he's going to do next.' Again with the pen, this time tapping against the pouty flesh of her bottom lip. 'Let's look at this in sequence. Why Jagger? Was his death personal?'

'That'd make sense if your connection with Jagger was more solid. Like if you were dating or had dated in the past.'

He tried not to sound as if he were digging for any other reason but the case.

The pen stopped its tapping and her eyes darted to his. 'I have never shared any romantic involvement with Jagger.'

'Good.'

Her lips quirked. *Dammit!*

Of course she'd misread his meaning.

He bowled on. 'If we rule out jealousy, what then?'

'Either Jagger discovered something about the killer, was already connected to him or did something to royally piss him off.'

'Enough for him to sever body parts, while his victim was still alive. That's pretty damn brutal. And personal.'

She visibly shuddered. 'What if this is about that whole original car bomb incident?'

'I've been wondering about that. Either Jagger was working for the killer or the killer discovered he tried to hurt you and retaliated.'

'Yet three days ago Sidney blew up.' Her lips wobbled.

It was as if she'd lost two friends in that blast, not one.

Air shuddered through her lips and into her lungs. 'So what does that mean? I'm the Copycat's plaything and no one else's? Either he means to kill me or protect me, depending on how he feels at the time. I'm not sure which makes me feel more … ick.'

'Ick?'

'Can you think of a better word?'

He chuckled. 'No. But I'm not the writer.'

One not overly plucked brow arched. 'It's a fallacy that writers can instantaneously find all the right words for the right occasions. Crafting a perfect piece of dialogue takes me hours. Speech requires seconds. Hence, *ick*.'

Her logic was impeccable, even if her mind was a wily labyrinth he had not a hope of navigating.

He mentally reviewed his case notes. 'We need to figure out his angle.'

'If he *really* wanted me dead, I'd be dead already.'

'He'd have to barge through me first.'

'Of course.' She rolled her eyes, nicely divulging how highly she viewed his protection skills. 'More and more, I wonder if that bomb was his perverted version of Russian roulette. Or his way of demonstrating how well he knows me. As far as we know, he's been studying me for at least eighteen months.' He saw her shudder. Couldn't begin to imagine how the knowledge of being stalked by a serial killer must make her feel.

She rubbed her hands up and down her thighs, creating warmth, as if to make out her reaction stemmed from cold, not fear. 'He must know that more often than not, either Des or Beth move my car when I visit their offices. Was he banking on that happening? Was I never his intended target? Did he know how angry I was with them both, and was this his way of protecting me once again?'

'So, once more this case leads full-circle to you.' He slapped his notebook against his knee. 'There are other authors out there. Other serial killers. Why you? Why your characters? Your acquaintances and friends?'

'To make a statement? Get my attention?'

'Why? And when he does, then what?'

She winced. 'That's what scares me. He's got my attention. What next?'

'At a guess, he moves on to the real reason for the murders.' He waved his notebook at her. 'Any ideas Madame Psychologist?'

'Not yet. But I'm working on it.'

'Let's think this through. What are the main reasons a killer craves attention?'

'The thrill. Power. Lust. Reward.' She stared at the far wall but he doubted she was admiring the Van Gogh knock-off of a grumpy-looking cat as white as Midnight was black.

The pen twirled between her fingers. 'I'd say the Copycat enjoys the thrill. Power and notoriety come a close second. Given his letters.' She swallowed. 'Lust? I haven't seen any evidence. And reward? That's normally in the form of money. More commonly a female motive than male.'

'Lust doesn't necessarily have to relate to the victims. It could be something he seeks. Perhaps even the reason he craves your attention.'

Colour drained from her face, and she grabbed her water from the table, clutching it to her chest. 'You think he fancies me?'

'It's a possibility. And, let's face it, completely understandable.' His look was pointed. Like an arrow straight from Eros's bow. 'Any unrequited or jilted lovers in your past?'

She squinted at him over the top of her glass. 'Are you sure this line of questioning is case related?'

'Why else would I want to know?'

She snorted.

He wasn't going there. Not yet. 'The clue has to lie in those letters.'

'*If* he wrote them.'

'You think it's possible he didn't?'

'I don't think we can rule out the likelihood. Although the thought of two psychos out there, one advocating what the other one is actually doing …' She shook her head, as if shaking off the thought. 'I think we need to look at both sides and see where it leads us.'

He shook the three photocopied letters in his hand before dropping them onto the wood slab coffee table. 'That means profiling this guy to see if there's an overlap with the Copycat.'

'I have an idea about that.'

'Already?'

'It's not like I have much else to do, considering both writing and study are impossibilities right now.' She spread the letters across the high-polished jarrah surface. 'The sooner we solve this case, the sooner I get my life back and we both return to some semblance of normal.'

No telling what she meant by normal. Like whether it excluded him or the two of them together. Something he'd have to work on if there was a chance of finishing what they'd started down in her dungeon of doom. Hard didn't come close to what he experienced when he thought about that.

Then there was his hankering for more than just a one-time thing.

Her fingers played across the pages before plucking up the first.

If she'd meant for him to keep his mind on the job and off the two of them together, she should have worn something other than the ass-hugging jeans and black-and-white scoop-neck top. And lace the colour of watermelon pushing her breasts up and out so that every time she leaned forward it was a miracle they remained covered.

She met his gaze, then cocked her head and smiled. As if she guessed his thoughts, even encouraged them.

Minx.

Then her lips pursed and her eyes returned to the paper in her hands.

Voice deadpan, she read. '*Clap. Clap. Clap. Bravo Stacey Holland. You've crafted a fictional masterpiece worthy of death row.*' Colour seeped from her skin, regardless that she'd read each letter countless times already. '*But I wonder, will your courage match Cindy's when you meet the genius of your making face-to-face?*'

She looked up. 'Cindy's my heroine from *From Mishap to Murder*.'

A fact he knew already, after reading every chilling and erotic word, unsure whether to be more fearful or turned on by the end of it.

He dragged his mind back to the letter. Each word was meaningful and deliberately crafted.

Not *if* they were to meet, but *when*. Stacey's hesitation over the word said she'd picked it too.

The paper crinkled and scrunched in her palm. '*I wait, baited breath, to witness the calibre of your worth outside the pages of your book. As artists, it's only natural we pit our skills against one another. And may the greatest mastermind win.*'

Her breath wobbled, then caught, and he watched her battle to calm her nerves. Recognised the moment she won.

She looked up. Eyes, no longer haunted, filled with determination. Steel.

'It's a challenge.' She swallowed, a tiny crack in the veneer of her courage. 'He means for us to face-off, in some kind of warped contest. A match of our minds.'

Another swallow, this time followed by a shudder. 'To the death.'

Chapter Forty-Two

Chase watched Stacey's shoulders square, as if she were ready to take on the bastard killer.

God, he loved that about her.

He pushed the slip of that thought away, back into whatever crazy box it came from. It was just an expression, the sum of which didn't add to the value of the individual words.

"Love" was an emotion he had no rights to. Not without the backup of a future behind it.

All he knew was Stacey wouldn't face the bastard. And if he couldn't control that, he'd ensure the one thing he could control – she wouldn't face him alone.

'He's baiting you. It's the kind of thing these sick bastards do.'

She dropped back into the couch, her shoulders slumped again, even as she still clutched the letter in her white-knuckled hand. 'I've met him, haven't I?'

'More than likely.'

'I hate this.' The words were so soft, they could have been thoughts. Hers.

His.

Because he hated it too. Hated that she was scared. Hated that he felt powerless to take it all away. A detective's badge and gun meant shit when he couldn't get a handle on the son of a bitch psycho.

'I can't believe your idiot publisher thought it was a good idea to keep these letters a secret.'

Before his eyes she seemed to shrink even further into the couch.

'What is it, Stacey?'

She lifted her head, her gaze miles away. 'I spoke to Beth about it before …' She swallowed, waving her hand rather than voicing words too painful. Too real.

He noticed she no longer called the other woman Morticia. Hadn't for a while now, even leading up to her death.

'What did she have to say?'

'That Des was behind keeping those letters secret. And that he guessed the killer was copying my book as early as June last year.'

Fuck!

He grabbed his phone from the table. 'He's a fucking idiot!'

'He kept it quiet for me. To protect my book.'

His finger pulled back from dialling Jayda's number.

'And you think that warrants the lives lost since then?' He couldn't prevent the scathing in his voice. Saw it slap Stacey as sure as a palm-slap across her face.

She leapt up from the couch and glared at him across the table. 'Of course I don't. I didn't want this! I never asked anyone to protect me or push me or make me famous. Not like this.'

Her chest heaved, her eyes wild, trapped, like an animal the moment it realised there was nowhere to flee. 'All I wanted was to write. To have people read my books. Now it's as if everyone around me has taken my dream and run with it until it's not even mine anymore.'

Large tears slid down her cheeks, unchecked, her body shaking so hard he thought she might shatter with the slightest touch.

'Dammit, Stacey.' He skirted the table. Turned his anger inward.

You idiot.

Stacey wasn't to blame. She was just as pissed – probably more so – at discovering the truth. He pulled her into his arms and held her trembling body tight until she softened against him.

Resting his chin in her hair, he inhaled. *Honeysuckle.* 'This isn't on you.'

He rubbed slow circles over her back, sighing when he felt the gradual ease in her breathing. 'I promise, we'll drag the entire Thrasher Publishing staff over burning coals until we get answers. Every single guilty bastard will be held accountable for those deaths. And first up on that list is Des.'

She shuddered, and her eyes clenched closed against his chest as she held her breath. 'Do you think it's him?'

The idea wasn't foreign. It had entered his mind more than once during the investigation, but until now there'd been nothing but gut instinct to go on. Nothing to provide his unit with the probable cause needed to haul Des in for questioning. At least now, with the bomb blast outside their offices, he'd been handed his reason.

'I don't know if it's him.' He allowed his arms to tighten, didn't want to let her go.

Only he had a call to make.

'But I'll do my darnedest to find out.' He pulled back, hands still resting at her waist. 'I need to call Jayda and fill her in. Will you be okay?'

She nodded. Looked up at him with such trusting, he wanted to be worthy of it. All of it. That meant keeping her safe. He'd do anything, risk anything.

Three days ago he could have lost her.

The world around him shifted as two orbs of liquid green swallowed him whole. Life gained meaning in a way it never had before.

His hands gripped her hips as his mouth opened, to say something, anything, to tell her what he felt.

She leaned back. 'How did you make the connection?'

His mind fumbled. 'The connection?'

'Between my book and the NKS.'

How did he?

'It was obvious once I read *From Mishap to Murder*.'

'But why did you? You're not my target audience. I'd have thought women's genre fiction would hold little, if any interest for you.'

'Perhaps. But the author held enough interest to make up for it.'

She pushed her palm against his chest. 'Be serious, Chase. I want to know. Why did you read it?'

He thought back to the moment he downloaded her book. 'It was something someone said to me.'

'Who?'

'I don't know. Does it matter? They're not related to the case.'

'How do you know?'

'Because it was probably someone at the precinct or–' Air sucked from his lungs.

'Or what?'

'Shit!' His hands dropped from her body and he staggered back against the couch cushions. How the hell had he not thought about that until now?

'Tell me, Chase.'

'He joked about it, way back. Said most women would kill for attention from a man like me. The comment was snide. Nasty. Just the kind of dig he'd made countless times before. I didn't think anything of it.'

It all rushed back to him now. The look on the smug bastard's face. The way his lips twisted as he mentioned Stacey, her book, how she wanted more than just research from him. How Chase should give her what she wanted before she took her attention-seeking efforts one step further.

'He didn't mention your name, but he dropped enough hints to get me wondering. So I read your book.'

Her eyes were wide, filled with an idea fact dictated couldn't be true.

'Oh my god! He could be the killer. Or know who the killer is.'

'There's no doubt he knew the killer.'

'Stop it with the roundabout cop-speak. Who is it?'

If he could have slammed his fist through the wall without scaring the crap out of Stacey, he would have done it.

The biggest lead and he'd figured it out too late. Damn, he hated that douchebag-Seth was right. The mix of preoccupation and denial over his condition had made him sloppy, dangerous to those around him. And the continued reign of the Copycat was on him.

Beth's death was on him.

'Chase! Who the hell was it?'

He spoke past the thick wall, building brick-by-brick in his throat.

'Jagger.'

Chapter Forty-Three

Metal.

Cold. Hard. Heavy.

The rounded grip cut into his palm. His fingers tightened – squeezed – sliding blade effortlessly against blade.

Well-oiled. Razor-sharp.

He looked up into dark, wide eyes, so very much like his own.

Passive. Fearless. How long until they changed? How long until they slipped aboard the ride from hopelessness into terror. Despair. Resignation.

How long until he peed his pants like a shit-scared little kid?

He grabbed the foot and yanked it up onto his knee. Not yet trembling. Not yet braced.

Looked up again. Still no fear.

His lips spread thin across a smile designed to intimidate.

Something flickered in his expression. A glimmer. Weakness. The foot in his hand tensed.

Again his fingers squeezed.

Screams shattered his eardrums, blood splattering to the floor at his feet.

He let the blood-soaked foot drop.

Guttural sobs replaced the screams. The severed toe rolled back and forth in the sink until it caught in the strainer.

He wrapped the dripping foot in a towel, sobs sliding into racking breaths. Then silence.

He focused on his plan. What was still to be done.

Raised his head and stared at the tear-stained face before him.

Not long now …

Chapter Forty-Four

'**D**es is missing.' Chase dropped his mobile onto the kitchen bench and flicked the switch for the kettle.

Stacey's head jerked back as if the slap of his words was real.

She swivelled on her breakfast barstool to face him more fully. 'What do you mean, "Des is missing"?'

'He was supposed to front up for more questioning this morning and didn't show. No one's seen him at Thrasher Publishing, he's not answering his mobile and his flat in Elwood is empty.'

All colour fled Stacey's face. 'Do you think the Copycat Killer got to him?'

'Or he is the killer.'

'Damn, I hate this!' She dragged a fist across her tired eyes and glared at him across the counter. 'How am I supposed to know who's a friend and who's out to kill me or destroy me or protect me in some warped crazy-assed way?'

'I can't answer that. But we can't rule out anyone. Not if you're to stay safe and alive.'

Which is why he'd called Seth for a favour the moment he left the bomb scene five days ago.

That he was already in deficit as far as favours went with Jayda's fiancé didn't stop him. Stacey's safety was at risk, and he'd deal with the devil himself if it meant thwarting the danger that hovered above her head these days.

There'd been provisos – of course there had. He wouldn't have expected any less, and he'd agreed to every single one of them. In return, Seth agreed to get his "sources" to take a closer look at Des and Thrasher Publishing, as well as Rita, Ethan, Jagger and even Stacey's sexy-shoe friend, Shazz. Chase didn't question who or where Seth's sources came from – his job was worth more to him than finding out. Anyone close to Stacey was a possible Copycat contender. And he wasn't taking any chances by assuming their killer was male. On the off chance they'd got the sex wrong, they needed to consider all avenues.

'So I can't trust any of my friends. Any of my colleagues. I have to live in a bubble, and what? Trust only you?'

'Pretty much.'

'That sucks.'

'Dealing with a serial killer will do that.'

'Humour is not appreciated right now.'

'What would you prefer I do?'

'Tell me everything's going to be okay. Tell me no one else will die because this psycho has some crazy obsession with me. Tell me I'm going to be safe. That we'll both be safe.'

'You want me to lie?'

'No. I want all of those things to be true.'

'Me too, Stacey. But they're not. None of them.' He leaned back against the counter, and tried to act as if every one of his words wasn't stealing whatever hope she had left. He wanted to take her in his arms, vow he'd die before he let any harm come to her. That he would do anything to keep her safe, because he wouldn't survive if he was forced to live a life without her in it.

But she wasn't ready to hear the words, and he wasn't ready to say them out loud. Not when they were so new. So raw. So unnerving.

Instead he crossed his arms and traded feeling for fact. 'We have to be realistic. Until we figure out who this guy is, no one is safe. That means you're stuck with me, kid.'

His best Humphrey Bogart impression and it missed by miles, if the look on her face was anything to go by.

'The police are looking for Des. They'll find him. It's only a matter of time. Meanwhile, I'm making tea and we're going over the day of the bombing and what you remember one more time. Perhaps we'll come up with something that'll help us figure out who the killer intended as the real victim.'

Her sharp intake of breath cut him to the core. Then she shook her head. 'Before we do that, there's something we need to discuss. Something that can't wait.' Her hand shook as she clamped it at her side. 'I've got a proposition for you.'

His heart bucked rodeo-style. Then it stopped.

Nothing in Stacey's expression indicated this was the kind of proposition his body had in mind.

Now she'd got those six words out she didn't seem in any rush to enlighten him. Her fingers cupped a mug that was almost empty, and almost certainly cold.

His patience only stretched so far.

He grabbed himself a mug from the cupboard, dropped it onto the bench and flexed his hand. 'And what might that be?'

'I've figured out how we can catch the killer.'

Every ounce of his attention riveted to her.

She pushed at hair already curled behind her ear, her gaze darting anywhere but his direction. 'I want to write another chapter online.'

Overbright eyes swerved and sucker punched him right in the gut.

'And I want to use me as bait.'

'No way!'

He pushed up from the bench and stalked to the far side of the kitchen, the charge of his heart more than double the speed of his soles slapping against the white floor tiles. Shy of the fridge, he swivelled and stalked right back again. No matter which direction he faced, the level of harebrained in her scheme didn't drop. *No absolute fucking way.*

'I haven't told you my idea yet. Can't you at least consider it before you shoot me down?'

'You did. I did. The answer is still "no".'

He stalked again. It was either that or shake her so hard that sense couldn't help but sink into her brain.

'I could just as easy do it without you.'

He grabbed her shoulders. Didn't care that his grip probably hurt like hell. *Don't you fucking dare.*

'Everything alright in here?'

A cocky Aussie accent. Mr Super-Fix electrician who wouldn't leave. Something to do with the aerial and internet, or so Stacey said. Doubtful that's why the swaggering bastard was still sniffing around. The red in Chase's vision transformed to a raging bushfire.

What Stacey contemplated was suicide.

Nothing was alright.

Chase dropped his hands. Stepped back. Caught the terror in Stacey's eyes. Wouldn't allow himself to feel guilty. That expression was nothing to what the killer could put there given half a chance. He didn't stop to question the ferocity of his reaction. Playing with a snake was one thing, playing with a serial killer was something else entirely. At best it spelt disaster, at worst … well, death wasn't the worst that could happen. Not with a sick psychopath who played with fish hooks while playing with his victims.

None of which was getting within an inch of Stacey.

The killer bastard may have issued a challenge. Didn't mean she had to take him up on it.

'Stacey?' In overalls too tight to be practical, her sexy electrician hovered just inside the doorway. Untimely and unwelcome.

'We're fine.' Fingers clenched and unclenched at Chase's side. 'Shouldn't you be off fiddling with wires or something?'

'I heard shouting.' He turned his back to Chase. 'You okay, Stacey?'

Chase positioned himself between the two. Ignored the poison-tipped daggers in her expression. He had a few of his own.

'Stacey's okay. I'm okay too, if you're interested.' He let rip his most intimidating interrogation stare. 'We're all okay, and we're having a discussion. A very private discussion, get my drift?'

Jasen side-stepped and caught her gaze. 'Stacey?'

The man had balls, he'd give him that. Wonder if he'd still have them staring down the barrel of a .38.

He inhaled.

Step it back, man. Mr Electric may be a nuisance but he's not the problem.

Stacey's crazy-assed proposal, however, was.

'I'm fine, Jasen.' Rosy lips twisted into what was supposed to be a smile.

The other man would no doubt take it as such, but Chase knew better.

'Thanks for checking on me.' Her chin kicked up. 'Our discussion became a little more heated than it should have.'

He didn't miss the sting as she shot him another look.

Mr Electric nodded, obviously unsure, but not willing to push the matter with Stacey's reassurance and Chase's presence staring him down.

'Then, as long as you're okay …' He glanced at his watch. 'I'll be done in about fifteen minutes, so if you need me, holler.'

He shot her a grin so blatantly seduction-packed that Chase wanted to vomit. And deck him. Lucky he sauntered out before need turned to action. Only after firing *him* a warning look.

Stacey jumped up from her seat and all but slammed her hands against her hips, barely waiting for the door to close behind her wannabe hero. 'What the hell was that?'

Her tone may have been low, but the edge to her voice was anything but soft.

Well, "edgy" he could do right back. 'You are *not* playing snake and mouse with a killer. Because that's exactly the way it'll play out.'

'I have to.'

'Bullshit!'

'Don't you get it?' Her voice tumbled out over quivering lips. 'I'm the reason he's out there. The reason he's targeting who he's targeting, killing the way he's killing.'

'If we're pointing fingers, if I'd figured out Jagger's involvement sooner, we might have caught the Copycat by now.'

'If I hadn't written a serial-killer suspense, he wouldn't have a prescription to kill.'

'He would have found another way.'

Her hand sliced through the air, even as she shook her head, disbelieving. Discounting his words. 'He must be stopped.'

'And he will be. Just not by you.'

'Why?'

'Because I won't have you hurt.'

'That's not your choice.'

'As an officer of the law, I'm making it my choice.'

She glared. He glared. This was one time he wouldn't back down.

Nostrils flaring, chin jutted skyward, she was of the same mind. All that remained of her dragon-obstinacy was fire.

She puffed out a breath brim-packed with exasperation and rage, but thankfully, no flames. 'Tell me how *you* plan to catch him then.'

'I'm working on it.'

'And while you "work on it" people are dying.' Palms facing the sky, her eyes wheeled their gut-wrenching way through his defences.

'If only for the next victim's sake, at least hear what I have to say.'

No frigging way!

Nothing would sway him.

But how to sway her?

Make her think she has a chance.

Yes!

Seem to consider her idea, then shoot it down.

'Sure.' He made for the fridge. Caffeine wasn't nearly strong enough to get him through the next hour. Beer in hand, he opened the B drawer and grabbed a bottle opener. 'On one condition.'

She topped up her mug from the teapot. 'Which is?'

'After I hear you out, I'll assess your idea and decide. And that decision will be final.'

'On my condition.' Her eyes flashed emerald. 'You don't get to reject it outright. I expect an acceptable, sound reason if you're to convince me not to go ahead.'

What the hell was he getting himself into?

Not that he wouldn't find a flaw in her plan. One that came to mind almost immediately was foolhardy. Then there was idiocy. Oh, and insanity. Should he go on?

'Agreed?' There was no give in her expression.

That was fine. He wasn't prepared to yield either.

'Agreed.'

And may the sane man win.

'We both agree the Copycat Killer is obsessed with – or at the very least connected to – me. Correct?'

Stacey didn't allow her gaze to stray from Chase, sprawled all cocky and confident in the armchair opposite.

He nodded, enjoying his beer, not taking her in the least bit seriously. 'Correct.'

She wanted to grab the bottle from his hands and pour every drop of the frothy liquid over his stubborn skull. That he intended to humour her and then reject her idea outright was so obvious she'd have to be an idiot not to have figured it out. Seemed he still considered her a lightweight.

It also seemed he'd forgotten she wasn't a roll-over-and-scratch-me-senseless kind of girl. That panty-warming grin only charmed so far. And it wouldn't come close to preventing the fight he'd have on his hands if he couldn't provide something more concrete than a "me Tarzan, you Jane" opposition to her plan.

'We've also established that he's organised, and until now, patient and restrained. But I believe that's changing.'

She hunkered deeper into the cushions and hugged her cooling mug to her chest.

'I've been considering the concept of murder mentors. Heard of them?'

She didn't wait for more than a nod before continuing. 'As you probably know, there are some killers who look to more established killers as their "mentor". They study their methods, believing they can avoid making the same mistakes and hence continue their spree unhampered. Obvious cases are Michael Madison and Anthony Sowell, Israel Keyes and Ted Bundy.'

'All good points.'

If they were so good, why the dubious look? At a guess, he was still humouring her. Or he wasn't sure where she was headed.

He'd soon catch on.

'I believe the Copycat sees me as his mentor. He copied my murders, but now he's adding his own spin. Venturing out, while still maintaining his link to me by choosing victims I know or by leaving mementos of his killings for me to find.'

Eyes of fathomless blue bored into hers. She shuffled, curled her feet beneath her body. Wished for the luxury of escaping his scrutiny.

'So far you're not telling me anything I don't know.'

Legs crossed at the ankles, beer bottle pressed to his lips, he was the epitome of relaxed. And if he was trying to rattle her, he was doing a damn fine job. Regardless, he wouldn't find weakness in her expression. She wouldn't let him.

Her heart hammered.

'The key lies in my writing. If my books are his murderous guide, it makes sense to use those same books to anticipate his next move, placing him somewhere of our choosing, in a position of our choosing, using his ego and obsession to trap him.'

With barely a breath, she continued before she lost her nerve.

'He knows the Nine Knife Slasher was caught in my first book. He knows the Fatal Fisherman will be caught in my second. Yet, so far, he remains free. That's his weakness – he's cocky and self-righteous. And he'll take up any challenge we set for him, because he believes he's invincible.'

One breath and she bowled on.

'I propose we write a scene, a blatant challenge he won't be able to resist, and set a trap.'

The casual spill of his body over the armchair tightened. Like the coils of a spring, he was wired, readying for the rebuttal.

Not easy to remain calm when the idea scared the living bejesus out of her. What she proposed was equivalent to an invitation that shrieked "pick me" to a psychopathic murderer. She knew what was at stake. She'd thought and mulled, tossed and re-tossed over her options. There weren't many, but one thing she knew for sure – she couldn't continue to sit and wait while lives were being lost.

Add to that another certainty. She needed Chase on her side if she was to have any chance of coming out the other side of this alive.

Chapter Forty-Five

'**R**un through that scene for me.'

It wasn't easy to make out like he was considering her proposal, but that was exactly what he did. He leaned forward, met her gaze, nodded for her to continue.

Stretching her right leg forward and her body back, she inched something out from her trouser pocket. 'I can do one better.' She slid a crumpled piece of paper across the coffee table. 'You can read it for yourself.'

'You wrote it already?'

'On paper. I'll type it into the computer when we're ready to go ahead.'

He didn't rise to the bait of her words, much as they made his jaw clench. Her assumption this whole saga was going ahead was as warped as her thinking he'd consider letting it happen.

He dropped his bottle onto a coaster, slid the paper closer and unfolded it. Scanned the precise print looking for flaws.

'It's rough, I know. But we can nut out the details together. After all, I'll be counting on you to back me up.'

'You need an entire unit.'

'Lovely as that would be, I doubt they'd willingly agree.'

'Because this is ludicrous.'

'You say ludicrous, I say lucrative. Whatever the label, it's the only way to stop him, fast.'

Some wayward portion of his mind nodded, had the audacity to agree, even while the Stacey-struck part wanted to wrap her in his arms until the world around them was safe. A fallacy. Working homicide had taught him that much.

Safety was never a guarantee. But eradicating the Copycat upped the odds. As did not letting Stacey out of his sight until the bastard was caught. Something he doubted he'd want to give up once this saga was over.

When did that happen?

When had common sense absconded only to see him fall for the most unlikely woman and more, want a future when he couldn't guarantee that he'd be there to share it with her?

He was past railing against the unfairness of the universe. Watching the slow death of his mother had consumed every last vestige of that useless activity. And he knew well enough it achieved jack-shit.

Forever may not be a guarantee, but now was. And that meant ensuring Stacey's safety while he still had the capacity to do so, no matter the cost.

He waved the paper at her. 'This has so many holes, it smells of Swiss cheese.'

She dropped her feet to the floor and sat up. Leaned toward him. 'Then help me fix it.'

'You could get hurt.' Or die. He didn't say the words. Could see in her eyes she'd already considered the possibility.

She clamped her lips and lifted her chin. 'I'll have you to see I don't.'

His chest tightened.

He pushed up out of the chair. Stared out the window. Turned back to face her. 'We can't rush into this. I need time to think about it.'

Her gaze widened. As if she'd never expected the concession.

Neither had he.

His gaze strayed back to the window and the heavy sway of the old tree in her front yard.

Call it weakness. Or testament to her confidence, placing her life in his hands. His fist clenched – not nearly as tight as it had a year ago – testing the wisdom of her faith.

If he thought an all-out *no* would end her foolishness, he'd have uttered the word here and now. But Stacey hadn't been one for listening in the past. No reason to believe she'd begin now. And he wouldn't give her cause to go solo.

Better to show her how irreparable the holes in her plan were. How ill-equipped she was pitting herself against a killer.

'Where're you off to?'

Stacey whipped round and tried not to look as guilty as she felt. Chase filled the kitchen doorway, mug in one hand, slice of buttered toast in the other.

Her stealthy tiptoe to the front door obviously hadn't been stealthy enough. 'The vet's.' The rental car keys jangled against her palm. 'Midnight's coming home today.'

'Of course.' He downed the remains of his coffee and chomped a generous bite of his breakfast. 'Give me five and I'll come too.'

When had breathing become so cumbersome?

No one had the right to look that good at eight-thirty on a Wednesday morning. Not when every sleepless hour from last night was carved so clearly onto her face. Ten hours of tossing and turning between visions of being sliced and seduced – the curse of a writer's imagination.

That the sexy part of the reel was still rolling was the curse of a writer's hormones. And it had been way too long since she'd allowed them free reign. Outside of fantasy and waking dreams in the morning's early hours, that is.

The reality of perfectly filled denim had fire scorching her blood, evoking memories of what she'd found when she delved beneath it. Waking up hungry and horny wasn't the greatest way to start the day. Not when she had a plan to perfect and a killer to catch.

She needed to regain her sense of balance.

Hence her attempted escape this morning.

Failed attempt.

'I can drive, if you like.' He grinned, drawing her gaze to his lips and her memory to what he'd done with them in her dreams.

Her heart stuttered. 'You don't need to come.'

Oh god! Even their conversation was a turn-on. Was this her brain's way of coping with the fear? Focus on sex instead?

The burn on her cheeks was so hot, pancake mix would have bubbled up in seconds.

'I know. But I need a change of scene, and if I drive it means you can keep an eye on Midnight.'

He turned toward the kitchen, and she didn't notice the mould of fabric over his butt, even though that's where her gaze fell. It all sounded so reasonable. So thoughtful, even.

His actions weren't controlling, they were caring.

Not so easy to tell the difference.

'Let's go.'

He was back. She should have told him no.

Instead, she hitched her bag higher onto her shoulder and passed him her keys. Followed him out her garage door.

'Can you pop the boot?'

The immediate *click* indicated he heard and complied. She dropped the cat box inside the little blue hatchback and edged her way to the passenger door, inching it open before squeezing through and sidling onto her seat. With a click her seatbelt locked into place.

She opened the console and pressed the garage door control. One of the first things she'd asked Jasen to fix.

It creaked and whirred and opened, letting in the fresh morning sunlight.

Sunshine after the storm. If only the same could be said for her life.

They backed out of her driveway and she watched the roller-door shudder to a close. News blared out from the radio: the Nasdaq had fallen another two basis points; a gunman had shot two dead and wounded a cop at a local shopping centre; the Eastern Green Mamba was still missing from Melbourne Zoo.

She leaned forward and changed the channel to something musical. Less depressing.

'You're awfully quiet this morning.'

His voice sliced through her effort to submerge into the mundane.

Not that it was working. When her focus should have been on the mess her life had become, all she could think about was the man beside her. And how if he accepted her plan, he'd be the only thing standing between her and death. How if things had been different, they may have stood a chance. That the heat and conflict of their first meetings could have led to heat and conflict between the sheets.

That was the way these stories played out in fiction. But she couldn't write her own reality – catch killer and hero in one fell swoop, and land a happy ever after worthy of another RuBY Award.

That kind of reality would mean Chase wanting her, past these moments of enforced babysitting, despite her battiness and bad history and earlier bad choice in footwear.

'I was married, you know.'

Perfect way to bring those thoughts into action. *Not.* Too late to shove the words back from wherever the hell they came.

Chase's gaze darted her way before returning to the road. 'I know.'

Her gut instinctively clenched.

'You do?'

'You forget. I thought you were a crazy killer-author before I discovered the killer part wasn't true.' This time his side-glance was accompanied by a sheepish grin. 'It came up in your background check.'

'You never said anything.'

'If circumstances had been different, I wouldn't have known unless you wanted me to.' Green traffic lights turned from orange to red and the muscles in his thigh tautened as he stepped on the brake. 'I figured you'd tell me when you were ready.'

'Ready for what?' Another case of her mouth motoring without the backup of her brain. Her fingers twitched. She dragged her gaze upward and away from temptation.

'For sharing.' He turned to her. 'Your marriage is your past. It's personal and none of my business. Unless you want it to be.'

Was that a question?

Or did she want it to be because that meant he wanted it to be his business too? Because he wanted *her* to be his business?

Cyclic madness that would turn her into a crazy woman if she let it.

'His name was Brad. But you probably already know that.'

He eased onto the accelerator. 'Let's say I don't.'

Yeah. Easier that way.

It was a long time since she'd felt the need to share the failure of her marriage with anyone. Least of all a man. And who'd have thought the first man would be Chase?

Why?

Easy to kid herself it wasn't the "who" so much as the "what". The opportunity to purge an entire crockpot of emotions churning up her insides.

Easy to deny this wasn't a test. That revealing the sordid details of her marriage wasn't a lesson on the type of man who could never – would never – be a part of her life again. To see if Chase was willing to fit that bill.

Crazy woman status wasn't sounding so crazy after all.

'He was a lawyer and the son of one of Mum's friends.' Highly suitable, highly successful. Her mother's words.

'I was in the middle of my psych degree, and he was a couple of years older, already well on his way to making partner of Duncan, Henderson and Associates.'

He whistled. 'Big name.'

The largest up-and-coming law firm in Australia? She nodded. 'Big everything.'

Back then she'd seen it as a positive. She'd also been young, naïve and gullible, traits her marriage and ensuing separation had successfully snuffed out.

She swallowed. 'Our romance followed a nice, smooth path. We dated, had fun and fell in love. Brad proposed, I fell in love a little more and said yes.' Her lips twisted in perfect synchronicity with her stomach. 'My mother was ecstatic.'

'Sounds perfect.'

'Ever seen the movie *Sleeping with the Enemy*? Perfection is like the mirror-glass surface of a lake. All serenity and calm, with no clue as to what lurks below until you take the plunge and dive in.'

She rubbed her wrist, wincing at a memory that still clutched her chest so tight it was difficult to breathe.

Chase gripped the steering wheel until his knuckles turned white. 'He hit you?'

'No. *No.* Nothing so obvious. And nothing until after the whole "I do" hoo-ha.' She dragged her palms over her thighs and stared at the damp lines of dark blue left in their wake. 'The honeymoon was over well before the honeymoon was over. If that makes sense.'

He didn't comment and she didn't wait to see if he would.

'You see, Brad was funny and smart. And going places.' That last one was for her mother. 'He accepted me as I was. Didn't push me or seem to want to mould me into someone I wasn't.' Another one for good ol' mum.

'Before Brad it was just mum and me at home. Marriage meant a different direction. The freedom to be who and what I wanted to be.'

Oxygen dragged into her lungs. 'At first, I thought his suggestions were thoughtfulness. Relax, he said. Take time from your studies, ease into married life. Focus on our relationship. Our home.' Another breath. 'I finished my Masters and he said there was no hurry to find a job. I looked anyway, but every time something I liked came up, it fell through.'

Rays of gold sunlight glared through the windscreen, making her wish she'd remembered her sunnies. She lowered the sun visor and tried not add to the already generous web of crow's feet bordering her eyes. 'Then from out of nowhere came the digs. The house wasn't clean enough. My cooking wasn't tasty enough. I wasn't employable. I had no dress sense. Nothing I did or said was right.'

Chase scowled. His fingers flexed around the steering wheel. 'Why didn't you leave then?'

'Because leaving would be failing, and Holland women don't fail.' She raised her hand. 'And before you lecture and go all righteous on how leaving is a show of strength, not weakness, those words aren't mine. They're part of a whole string of pearls belonging to my mother, and I grew up clinging to the lot of them.'

He quirked a brow. 'Amazing you turned out so normal.'

The snort burst through her lips before she could stop it. 'Since when would you even consider calling me normal?'

He grinned. 'Everything's relative. Ski on Mt Hotham, you'll think it's high until you try the Swiss Alps.'

'So what you're saying is there's a scale and I'm somewhere on the normal side of crazy.'

It was his turn to snort. 'Couldn't have put it better myself.'

'Really? Maybe I should consider a career in writing or something.'

'Or something.'

Her knee ligaments were defenceless against that grin. Lucky she was sitting or "normal" would mean sprawled all over the floor at his feet.

'What did it?'

Her brain was still swamped in a land where those lips were meant for more than just talking. She shook every one of those thoughts to the road outside.

'What did what?'

'Made you leave? You were married how long?'

'Two years.'

He whistled. 'You stayed, then … what? Something changed?'

She shook her head, staring down at the tangle of veins popping up over the backs of her clenched hands.

'That's where you're wrong. Nothing changed. Not as far as Brad, that is.' She shifted in her seat. It did nothing to lessen the discomfort. 'I had two choices – go insane or escape into my imagination. The latter was so much more appealing.' She grimaced. 'And my way out from under all the criticism. I found writing, and with that, I found solace. Once I started, I couldn't stop.'

Her heart did that erratic hurdle thing it always did when she let herself remember. 'I guess you could say writing saved me. It was my first real love. The one part of me Brad couldn't break.'

The skin drew taut across Chase's jaw and the erratic beat of his pulse.

She moved her gaze to a blue SUV through the windscreen. 'I joined an online writing group. Even dredged up the courage to enter a writing competition. I didn't expect anything past feedback on where I'd gone wrong. Turns out, I did better. More right than wrong. I won.'

The smile was automatic, along with the familiar glow that filled and fluttered inside her chest. The feeling never got old. Never wore out or waned.

Never say never.

Weight dragged her lips downward.

Would the taint of that madman's mania ever wash out? A pivotal moment in her career – her life. Once filled with pride and accomplishment. Now it was mud.

She blanked her thoughts. *Don't stop now.* Not until it was all out there. It was only fair that Chase have all the facts before deciding if what he felt for her was more than a mindless flirtation.

Convenience.

She shoved Brad's words and his last visit from her mind. They had nothing to do with her and Chase.

She inhaled as they stopped at a set of lights and Chase turned his gaze to her. 'With the writing came more digs. More cuts. More dragging me down. Then my competition win transformed into a contract offer, and Brad's scathing turned to fully-fledged anger.'

Every word snatched at the knots in her stomach. 'Writing smut wasn't a career befitting of his wife. And definitely not the wife of a partner in Duncan, Henderson and Associates. I had to stop.'

A car horn blared and Chase returned his gaze to the now green light and the road.

She shoved at the curl fallen across her eye and noticed her hand was shaking. 'That moment, the realisation, it was like being struck by a thunderbolt. Our marriage was a circus and I was Brad's show-pony wife – smart, okay looking, a perfect homemaker who didn't cause ripples. That included not spreading shame over him and his beloved law firm.'

She focused on her breathing. Focused on getting through to the end. 'But I couldn't let go. Writing was the one thing keeping me sane. And the one thing that gave me the strength to leave him and never look back.'

'How did he take it?'

'Not well. Partners don't divorce. My leaving was an embarrassment, regardless of the spin he put on it. He did everything he could to get me to stay until he realised nothing would work. Then he stopped. But not before he vowed that choosing writing over our marriage would one day destroy everything that mattered to me.'

Chase's gaze spun toward her, piercing, before it returned to the road. 'Where is he now?'

'Brad? Still in Melbourne. Still at Duncan, Henderson and Associates. He's just been promoted to senior partner.'

'And you know that, how?'

'He visited.'

'When?'

When? Days seemed to meld seamlessly into one another lately, but for some events that set them apart.

'The day before Beth ...' She still couldn't say it.

'I need a conversation with your ex.'

'You think Brad has something to do with this?' A ripper knot twisted her gut, making her head whirl. 'He may be a control freak, but he's not a killer.'

'I could name a handful of psychopaths whose nearest and dearest have said the same.'

She could have named more. But she'd lived with Brad for two years. Shared his bed, his home. Regardless of how miserable he'd made their time together, to profile him and the Copycat, meld them together to make one … she couldn't.

It didn't fit.

Then again. If she looked at the situation from Chase's point of view, from the outside looking in, her ex-husband had one hell of a motive.

Chapter Forty-Six

Wafts of rubbing alcohol and wet animal assailed Chase as the glass door closed at his back.

His rubber soles slapped against the Pine O Cleen polished tiles, the aqua walls and reception desk projecting a coolness despite the burgeoning heat of the almost summer-like day outside.

He slipped his mobile into his back pocket.

Jayda had promised to look into Brad, although she hadn't promised to call if they brought him in for questioning. He'd just have to call her again and press the point. Otherwise he'd be forced into locating the bastard himself. An exchange that wouldn't be pretty.

That the bastard had to answer questions around the case was one thing, but his mistreatment of Stacey was something else entirely. Someone needed to "point out" the error of his ways. And how any further contact would no longer go unchecked.

His gut twisted. What she must have gone through – enduring his taunts for the years of marriage, drawing up the courage to finally leave. She needed a medal at the very least. She'd already earned his respect.

He followed her ramrod back, dodging jowls dripping saliva, a caged pair of chirping budgies and a large ball of fluff in a box – a *real* cat with fur enough to compensate for Midnight's lack.

A golden retriever plopped its head onto a teenager's lap and watched as he passed. Eyes of liquid brown snatched at his heart. He swallowed, but couldn't rid the feeling of loss, the possibility of one more dream over before it had a chance to start.

Stacey dropped Midnight's cage at her feet and rested both arms on the L-shaped reception desk.

He dragged his eyes from the now tail-wagging canine and focussed on the epitome of efficiency in white lab coat behind the counter. The vet, whose nametag identified her as "Cheryl", pushed back a wisp of brown hair escaped from her ponytail.

'He had a good night and gobbled up every last drop of food in his bowl this morning. He's a little miracle, that one.'

A sigh eased the taut in Stacey's expression, lowering her shoulders like the slow release of a balloon. 'You're sure he's okay to come home?'

Cheryl smiled. 'Absolutely.' She glanced down at a computer screen then back at Stacey. 'Come through and see for yourself.'

The consultation room was lime green and small, smaller still for Stacey's close proximity and complete avoidance of conversation. She checked her phone, the far wall, a line of animal anatomy posters, the open door that had swallowed Cheryl seconds after she'd shown them into the room.

The whole on-off mood thing was growing thin. What the hell was up with her now? Was it memories of her ex, something he'd said, something he'd done or just plain something about him?

'Stacey?'

She dragged her gaze from the clock on the wall.

'Here he is!' Cheryl ambled in and lowered Midnight's cage onto the examination table.

Stacey turned toward the other woman, not even trying to stifle her sigh. One step forward, an entire mountain trek backwards.

The vet eased the cat out of the cage. Chase swallowed back the hoot of inappropriate laughter. Midnight looked ridiculous. *Amendment* – more ridiculous. Three skinny black legs and one fat stumpy white one protruding from a scrawny excuse for a body. More than ever, he resembled rat more than cat.

Stacey leaned over the animal, stroking non-existent fur and murmuring as if he were a child. Her gaze softened. Warmed. Watching Midnight in a way he wanted her to watch him.

Stupid. To be jealous of a scraggy lump of skin and bones.

'The stitches will need to come out in a week.' Cheryl gently turned Midnight and he shook free of his ridiculous notions.

His gaze fell to the tips of the vet's fingers and a wound that ran almost the length of Midnight's side. No disputing the cat had been through the ringer. He had to be a feisty little bugger to have come out alive. A fighter, like his owner.

'The biggest threat to this little guy's recovery right now is infection so keep him indoors and make sure the wound stays dry. I'd like to see him in a couple of days to check for fever and that the infection is still under control. Let's say Friday. By the time we take the stitches out the worst should be over and it'll just be a matter of his leg healing.'

She held up a clear bag of white pills. 'You'll need to give him one antibiotic tablet twice a day with a pill gun. Ever used one?'

When Stacey shook her head, Cheryl proceeded to demonstrate how the syringe-like contraption worked. Midnight barely resisted, allowing her to push the dispenser down his throat. If the cat wasn't still dosed up on drugs he doubted the process would run as smoothly.

So much easier if Midnight were a dog. Wrap the tablet in cheese and he'd more than likely gobble it up of his own accord.

'Gently rub up and down his neck to encourage him to swallow. Not too bad, is it?'

Stacey looked as if she disagreed. 'What if he doesn't swallow?'

'Follow these steps and you'll be fine. But if you have any problems, bring him in and one of the nurses will show you again.'

Stacey didn't appear convinced. Mind you, neither was he. Just as well he wouldn't be playing nursemaid to the rat. *Cat.*

'He'll also need something to relieve the pain and inflammation over the next few days, so give him one of these daily, after food.' She held up a second bag.

'And lastly, spray his stitches and cast twice a day with this.' She shook a green and yellow bottle and sprayed.

Midnight barely acknowledged the action beyond an uninterested sniff as the smell of green under-ripe apples wafted through the room.

'The bitter taste will keep him from biting the cast or stitches if they become itchy. Just keep an eye out, because if he begins to bite anyway, we may need to put an e-collar around his neck.'

Cheryl gave what was meant to be a reassuring grin. From the look of Stacey, it failed.

'We'll take the cast off in four to six weeks. By then he should be back to his old self.' Another grin. 'Any questions?'

Stacey's eyes were wide as she scratched Midnight's head and tried not to show how swamped she was with information overload. The set of her mouth, her shoulders, her erratic breathing, all gave her away.

She buried her nose between his ears and kissed him, then

continued to stroke what part of him wasn't covered in cast and stitches. 'Why do I need to see you again on Friday? Does that mean Midnight's still at risk?'

'With infection there's always a risk.' The reassurance in Cheryl's smile was lost once again. 'Midnight's fine and healing well, so try not to worry. I'd just like to double-check he continues to respond to the antibiotics and that the stress of going home doesn't affect his recovery.'

Another smile as she eased Midnight back into his cage. This time Stacey managed a brief one back before her gaze returned to the black nose pressed against the metal criss-crossed bars.

'Well, then. Let's go to reception and make those follow-up appointments.' Cheryl handed her the two bags of tablets and spray bottle, which she stuffed into her already overstuffed bag. Who knew what inessentials she had tucked away in there?

Midnight's cage in one hand, Cheryl opened the door with the other and led them toward reception.

'I can't tell you how much I appreciate everything you've done for Midnight.'

Cheryl slowed for Stacey to catch up. 'I'm just glad he came to us in time. Left out in the rain any longer with those wounds, it might have been too late.'

Stacey skirted the front desk and he followed as Cheryl sidled up to a young girl topped with hair one shade short of a carrot. A brief volley of medical-speak directives and the receptionist's fingers bounced over the keyboard. The printer whirred and spat out paper, presumably the bill.

The receptionist passed it across the counter, then stared at the computer screen. 'We need two follow-up appointments, the second to remove stitches. Let's see.' A couple of mouse clicks then she raised her gaze to Stacey. 'That's Friday twelfth and Wednesday seventeenth. Do you prefer morning or afternoon?'

The rush of traffic filtered into the waiting area as the front door opened then whooshed slowly closed. Cheryl's gaze shifted, as did the receptionist's, both mouths curving into large, appreciative grins.

Cheryl ran her palms down the lapels of her white coat. 'Here's the man you need to thank for saving Midnight.'

Hackles rose across Chase's back even before he turned.

Ethan strode across the waiting area as if he owned the place – a cheesy model grin pasted to his face and full takeaway coffee holder balanced in one hand.

'Ethan.' More hackles at the way Stacey's skin flushed as she turned. 'What are you doing here?'

The vet did everything but purr as Ethan handed her a coffee. 'He's checked on Midnight every day since he brought him in.' Her flush matched Stacey's. What did Fireman Sam have that he didn't? He swallowed a growl that would get him nowhere but into either or both women's bad books.

Ethan passed carrot-top a cup, 'vanilla soy chai latte, *Madamoiselle*', and Cheryl the remaining tray, 'yours is the one on the left. I asked for an extra shot of coffee, just the way you like it'. He grinned at both women before turning to Stacey. Chase might have been invisible but for the brief, tepid nod his way.

'I knew you were picking Midnight up today and this is my cunning way of seeing you.'

'I'm sorry I didn't call, I've–'

'Been busy. I know.' His grin softened, and Chase watched both women swoon. Any time now he'd lose his breakfast if the whole mutual appreciation and flirtation rigmarole continued. Not that either of the other women's reactions bothered him. Only Stacey's.

She turned back to the receptionist. 'Morning or afternoon is fine.'

Ethan chatted easily to Cheryl as Stacey booked her appointments and Chase felt about as useful as a ruptured appendix.

Something about Ethan made every sense, second and otherwise, sit up and take note. Chase's decision to dig made perfect sense. With both Jagger and Beth dead, he had justification enough. No stone unturned, and all that.

Stacey's safety was paramount.

And if he uncovered dirt, bonus. Anything to make her re-evaluate Mr Hero's hero status. Anything to remove him from the running.

He'd never proclaim to be a saint, especially when it came to something he cared about. The time for bullshitting himself was over.

He cared about Stacey. His chest tightened, not unpleasant, more of a yearn than an ache. The thought of her with another guy – especially if that guy was Ethan – added a sharp stab to the mix.

His gaze shifted. Somehow Stacey was done, shoving the

appointment card into her pocket.

Cheryl checked her computer and called for her next client, the receptionist answered the phone and Stacey moved closer to Ethan, far enough for only snippets of conversation to filter back to him. And he was stuck carrying the cat box out to the car. He really should have paid better attention.

'I know you're busy clearing your reputation and solving the case. Let me help.'

Stacey's response was too soft for him to hear. He lengthened his stride, past the tail-wagging retriever who lifted his head, eyes begging for a pat.

'Hey, boy.' His fingers sunk into warm, golden fur and something inside clicked. The feeling of rightness. Of home. Another yearn socked him one right in the solar plexus.

The day he turned ten was the day he'd vowed to get a dog, just like this one.

One day. When he was old enough. When he could make his own decisions. When he could control his own life. Yeah, he'd promised himself a dog. The dog that circumstances had robbed from him growing up. When he left home, when he completed his training, when he found a job, when he moved house, when he was more settled. That "when" had continually moved a bar that never fell within reach. He was still waiting for the perfect time.

Now the rose-coloured glasses of youth had dimmed, his vision was clearer than ever before. He hadn't been waiting for that perfect moment, he'd been waiting for imperfection – the disease that took his mother's life, the same one that could very well take his.

Why plan a life – why live it – when everything you plan and enjoy could disappear with an indiscriminate roll of the genetic dice? He'd waved away his entire existence waiting for disaster to strike. He'd been so wrapped up in the possibility of dying, he'd forgotten to live.

Stacey's connection to Midnight. Even her connection to that burly lump of muscle she called Cuddles. Nothing could rob her of that. *Unconditional, undying love.*

He wanted a piece of it.

A grin to the boy and one last scratch behind the dog's ear, then he headed for the door.

He wasn't impetuous enough to think it didn't matter which way the results fell. Of course it mattered. Who didn't want a happy ending? But whatever the ending, it didn't mean the lead-up couldn't be enjoyed. *Lived.*

He wanted to live.

That meant no more waiting for the perfect moment. The perfect moment was now.

Chapter Forty-Seven

'If I could read your mind I'd know what to apologise for now.' Chase shot Stacey a look before returning attention to the road.

A deep sigh escaped her lips, her hands twisting relentlessly in her lap. 'You don't need to apologise for anything. You're just doing your job.'

One stab, straight to the feeling, caring part of him. That she still thought that, now, after all he'd said and done. How much clearer did he need to be?

'Yes. I'm doing my job. I'm also where I want to be.'

She swallowed. Seemed to find unwavering interest in the drab line of weatherboard houses out her side window.

Late morning sun spilled in through the windscreen and he lowered the sun visor and pushed his sunnies higher up the bridge of his nose. The air outside was fresh and crisp, post-storm. A great day for new beginnings.

'You're right. My job is catching the Copycat, and that's exactly what I intend to do. But spending this time with you, making sure that you stay safe, is because you're more than just a case to me.'

She hugged Midnight's cage close to her chest and shot him a side-glance. 'Is that why you're still here instead of back at the precinct?'

His heart clattered its way to the car floor.

A decision to start living every day without waiting for an axe to fall was one thing. Lumbering Stacey with more worries – like his possible non-future – when the Copycat had given her enough already was quite something else. Plus, full disclosure wasn't a place he was ready to go. Not yet. After years of living with his head buried in the sand, he needed time to wrap that same head around his new stance before he let anyone else in. Even the woman who'd facilitated the change.

'Partly. That and I need a full physical to step out from the desk your heels stuck me behind.' He shot her a wry grin. 'Hours best spent finding our killer.'

'He's acted out two very distinct murders off-script only days apart. Do you think he's escalating?'

'I don't know. I was wondering the same thing.'

'I've been wracking my brains to figure out what connected the killer to my characters. Why emulate them compared to any other fictional killers out there?' Her fingers poked through the cage door, stroking Midnight's wrinkly, black skin.

Slowly the square of her shoulders softened, as if the action soothed her. 'Much as their lives and MOs are different, there are some similarities between the NKS and the FF. Both had weak or absent mothers. Both had angry, heavy-handed fathers. A bully was their first victim – the violent ex-boyfriend of a girl the NKS was interested in and a drug-dealer intent on bullying the FF.'

'I don't see how that helps us with profiling the Copycat. The people he killed – all except Jagger, that is – are innocent and not a threat to anyone.'

'I know.' Her gaze narrowed and she glared out at the horizon through the windscreen. 'Damn! This is impossible!'

'I don't think the answer lies with your fictional killers. This isn't about him finding some sick similarity with them. There's one thing that links both them and their victims.' He slanted her a sideways look, then returned his attention to the road. 'You.'

Colour drained from her cheeks as the finger stroking Midnight shook.

He clutched the wheel, when all he wanted to do is pull over and pull her into his arms. 'So we come back to the question you so skilfully avoided earlier – are there any jilted boyfriends or pining men in your life who could be resentful enough to commit murder.'

She shook her head. 'I'm not the kind of woman who inspires men in that way.'

She had no idea how wrong she was. But perhaps that was part of her charm.

'The alternative is that the killer is obsessed with you and believes murder will win your attention, and ultimately, your love.'

'And if he doesn't get it, what then?'

Her expression said she already knew the answer. 'He'll kill me, won't he?'

She shoved a strawberry lock from her face and swallowed. 'We have to catch this bastard before that happens. That means going ahead with my plan and putting me in his path as bait. Because whether I do or don't, I'm dead, anyway.'

If someone attached ten-kilo weights to each of Stacey's shoulders, she would've felt little different.

She wiped her feet on the welcome mat, stepped over the threshold and entered the only place she truly felt safe right now. Strange, considering someone – *the killer* – had hidden in her roof, eating corn chips, watching, waiting, while she wrote his next murder …

Heart pounding, she locked and double-bolted the front door after Chase, then placed the cat box on the living room floor and released the catch.

Midnight gave a little sniff, but didn't seem inclined to do more. He backed further into his box.

Seems they both had ideas on where was safe and where wasn't.

She left him to his hideaway and pottered. Kept her hands so busy that her mind had no opportunity to stray.

First task was to set up a comfy corner for her convalescing baby. Furniture had to be moved so that cat and Cuddles could enjoy their own very distinct, very separate spaces. Swapping couches and armchairs around revealed the carpet underneath needed cleaning.

No time like the present.

She dragged the vacuum cleaner out and threw every ounce of energy into the task. *Why stop there?* She moved into the hall, the bedrooms. That's when the shocking state of her furniture hit her. With wood polish and a duster, she attacked every surface. Then she dragged the vacuum cleaner out again, because shouldn't you vacuum *after* dusting, not before?

For whatever reason, Chase stayed out from underfoot, refraining from comment, which must have almost killed him. Perhaps he sensed her mood and his lack of action stemmed from self-preservation. Or perhaps he needed the space to think, or not think, like her.

Either way, he made himself at home in her kitchen, and once again, diet-defeating aromas made her mouth water and her hips shudder with both anticipation and despair. Not that she'd been watching her intake for an age now. Certainly not since she had other things to focus on. Like serial killers and sexy detectives. One infinitely more pleasing than the other.

Throughout Stacey's spring-cleaning mania, Midnight alternately glowered at her and ignored her from his new pride of place. One thing that didn't change was how clearly unimpressed he remained throughout.

But now her house was clean, and she'd barely given a thought to the storm-cloud hanging over her head.

She moved Midnight's food and water bowls nearer to his bed, and grabbed his food from the laundry. His ears twitched and he lifted his head, wide emerald eyes watching as she approached, shaking the container.

'Hungry, boy?'

She crouched down, scratching his ears and over the back of his head. He leaned into her fingers, his contented purring pretty much the best sound in the entire world. The starch in her shoulders softened.

'Let's get some food into you, hey? Make you all healthy and strong again.'

She cooed and scratched some more.

'So good to have you home, my gorgeous boy.'

She ducked, rubbed her nose in his neck and sniffed the reassuring cat smells, along with residual disinfectant from the vet's. Not long until that would fade. Not so the scars. Without fur to cover it, the white incision that spanned the length of his body would be a constant reminder of how close she'd come to losing him.

She thrust the thought aside. He was home now. And safe. She wouldn't be letting him out of her sight any time soon.

One last reassuring rub beneath his ear, then she flipped the container lid, and poured, a shower of pellets clinking loudly against the ceramic.

Midnight sniffed.

He pushed up, stretched, made his wobbly way toward his bowl.

Her hand jerked, raining brown pellets over her newly vacuumed carpet fibres. The room dipped, swayed, lost focus. Her heart thumped so hard, copper coated the back of her tongue.

She stared. Swallowed. *Screamed.*

It's fresh. Perhaps a day old, definitely no more than two.

Random, drifting voices – Chase, Jayda, other members of Chase's squad – their words nudging and grasping along the periphery of Stacey's mind.

Thoughts stabbed through the cottonwool in her brain.

Another body out there somewhere, waiting to be discovered. Another body part left for her to find.

The killer in her home.

Nowhere is safe.

If anything had remained in her stomach, she'd be hunched over the toilet, puking her guts out. Only she'd done that on and off for the past half hour, leaving a hollow, gnawing chasm where her stomach used to be. The bitter tang still coated her tongue.

She wrapped the blanket tighter around her shoulders and tried not to think about it. A toe. In Midnight's food. In his bowl. The cat gnawing at the flesh, teeth scraping and sliding against bone. The catatonic wail that turned out to be hers.

Chase tearing into the room, weapon drawn, only to find her slumped on the floor, staring at what remained of someone's toe.

Oh, god!

She raced for the bathroom and dry gagged. Saliva drenched her mouth, bile scalding its way up her throat making her gag some more. She spat into the bowl, but the bitterness remained.

Hand shaking, she flushed and stared at the blue swirling water, seeing nothing but that bloody, bitten toe. She scrunched her eyes closed. The toe didn't go away.

'Stacey. Are you alright?'

Her eyes flew open.

Chase crouched down beside her, hand warm and steadying on her shoulder. Her breath slewed fast and shallow through her trembling lips.

Stupid question. No, she wasn't alright. Would never be alright.

Once again reality had slammed its big, ugly mug in her face. Had poked out its tongue and taunted her with its temerity. This nightmare would never end until the bastard Copycat was caught. The police seemed clueless as to how to do that.

She wasn't.

And the thought dragged a fresh torrent of bile up her throat.

'Hey, I'm here.' His palm drew wide, reassuring circles over her back. 'You're safe, Stacey. No one's going to harm you. I won't let them. I promise.'

His words were soft, soothing. And they were as full of shit as the sewerage pipes in the ground beneath their feet.

She pushed up and grabbed a towel, dragging it across her mouth before wrapping her fingers around the edge of the sink and staring at the pale, petrified reflection before her. 'You shouldn't make promises you can't keep.'

He stood, mere inches separating them, and met her gaze in the mirror. 'As far as promises go, I have every intention of keeping this one.'

She swallowed. 'Wh—whose toe is it?'

He shook his head. 'We don't know yet.'

'Des is missing.'

'I know.'

'Do you think …?'

She couldn't say it. Couldn't think it. Not without a mountain of guilt raining down over her conscience. First Beth, now Des. She'd accused them of the unthinkable, and it seems she couldn't have been more wrong. They were innocent.

And dead.

And she was the link.

She stared down at the sparkling white porcelain. It offered no answers. Or relief.

'Stop beating yourself up over this.

'Easy for you to say. You didn't create this monster.'

'Neither did you.'

Her head jerked up and she glared at his double in the mirror. 'Read my book lately?'

'That's fiction, Stacey. This is real. And your book didn't create this sick bastard. He did that all by himself.'

'It doesn't matter how many times you tell me, in however many different ways, I still feel responsible.'

'This guy is a psychopath. He's cruel, cold-blooded and unpredictable. He enjoys what he does, and if he hadn't copied your story, he would have found another way to kill.' He scrubbed the back of his neck. 'Can you see now why your plan is a disaster waiting to happen? This guy isn't playing around. He's dead serious. *Deadly serious.* You put yourself in his path, you land yourself in the thick of his sick-assed mind.'

'He won't stop until we stop him.'

'Not "we". This is a job for the police.'

'In any other instance, I'd agree with you. But they have no way of drawing him out. I do.' Her hands dropped from the sink to clench at her sides. 'Didn't someone once say that tolerating evil leads only to more evil? That when good people stand by and do nothing, wickedness reigns?' She stepped forward until his heat became hers. Her heart hammered with thoughts of what she was about to say. What she was about to do. But there was really no other way forward.

Do or die.

She lifted her gaze, gripped the sink behind her as she drew in a deep, soul-steadying breath. Chase didn't move, watching her with eyes so blue she wanted to dive in and never come out.

Only that was fantasy. The stuff of her books.

And this moment, these next few days, weren't the stuff of dreams. They were nightmares. They were real. And they wouldn't stop without someone stepping in and doing something.

That was her.

'I can't do this alone, Chase. But I can't not do it either.' Her hands left the cold porcelain to rest flat against warm, alive male. 'We need to stop this monster. *We. Us* as a team. Because it's the right thing to do. And because my conscience won't let me be if we don't.'

Chapter Forty-Eight

'I'm not letting you out there without the skills to protect yourself.'

Chase stared down from one-and-a-half-plus metres, and much as his words were rough, she could see his mood had softened. He was coming around.

Surprising.

Or maybe not so after recent events. After the killer invaded her home, her life. Her misguided sense of security.

She shivered. Sunlight spilling in through the window wasn't nearly warm enough to soften the memory of that toe. She tossed that thought and the stream of weakness that accompanied it. She wasn't weak, wasn't powerless. And she wouldn't allow some faceless beast to make her so.

She glanced up at Chase. Tried to guess what he was thinking beneath that expression – half detective, half rogue. Wholly unreadable.

Either way, she hadn't expected to get half this far without a fight – gloves off, fist-to-face, down and dirty. A confrontation much worse than their heated exchange when she first proposed her plan.

This was a victory, of sorts, and she allowed the satisfaction of the almost-win to warm her. It played along her nerves with a deep-seated tremor that wished he'd been able to replace her idea with a better one. She didn't want to die, and she wasn't naïve enough to discount the likelihood of death as an outcome to her plan. That didn't mean she was willing to sit and wait for the Copycat to destroy everything and everyone she cared about before coming for her.

Chase dropped the paper onto the table. 'Other than your uncanny habit of bringing a man to his knees, with or without your friend's killer footwear, how can you defend yourself?'

An almost smile wavered across his lips.

It didn't stop her irritation at the return of his less-than-amusing sense of humour, or the intimidation from his height. She stood and moved round the table to face him.

'I'm an ace shot with a .22 and a .38.'

'God forbid! You and a firearm are not getting up-close and personal. Not on my watch. I'm talking basic self-defence.'

'You forget I got one up on you when you broke into my house.'

She nabbed her cup of *berry buzz* tea from the table. Sipped. Smiled. Liked that she'd dug a little under his skin.

His brows furrowed deep into the bridge of his nose. 'Firstly, I didn't break in. You left your door open. And secondly, you only got one up because I didn't want to hurt you.'

The snort erupted before she could swallow, spraying tea out onto his chest. 'Tell that to yourself enough and you might believe it.'

He stared down at the mess on his shirt, then at her as if she were the one kidding herself. He daubed the wet with a handful of tissues from the table, then stepped in. 'If you're so expert at defending yourself, defend this.'

He grabbed her arm. Before his hold set, she gripped his wrist from below and pushed up, twisting her hand, snapping it out of his hold.

His eyes widened.

Gotcha!

'Not so shabby, hah?'

He was still cocky, but the bravado dropped a notch. 'Lucky first try. What about this?'

He fastened on both wrists.

With a twist and snap she was free again.

'Not so lightweight now, Mr Hotshot.'

He grabbed the front of her t-shirt. A grip across the knuckles, a twist, turn and pressure on the underside of his wrist and she had his entire arm under her control. He wasn't going anywhere in a hurry.

'Damn!'

Still gripping his arm, she increased pressure, forcing him down at an angle she knew to be awkward and uncomfortable. To say nothing of embarrassing. 'Yield.'

'You're frigging kidding me.'

'Not in the least. Say it.'

'Dammit Stacey!'

She leaned into his arm.

He hunched over, tried to push back, but she had the upper hand. Oh, so gloriously *literally*.

He grunted, huffed more than a little, then growled. 'Yield.'

She let go and he stepped away, supporting his arm.

She tried not to grin too widely. 'Maybe I should be the one giving the lessons.'

He rubbed his wrist. 'This isn't a joke, you know.'

'Words I never expected to hear from your lips.' She grinned. 'So, I might have done a class or two in self-defence.'

'Really? Who'd have guessed?'

'Wanna show me a few more moves, detective?'

'You enjoyed that way too much.'

She didn't even try to hold back her glee. 'I'm only human.'

He clenched his fist. 'If you've put me back into a sling ...' He examined his arm.

She did the same, small grains of guilt trickling in. She'd meant to prove a point, not hurt him. In all their interactions, she'd never meant to hurt him, much as there were times he believed she had. And there were times she wished she could.

She touched his arm, leaned in closer.

Fingers wrapped around her biceps and the earth disappeared from under her feet with a single swipe of his leg. Her back thudded onto the floor.

Chase straddled her hips, his hands pressing hers back into the carpet either side of her head.

Her breath quickened. From the surprise of it all, nothing more.

She struggled, bent one knee and tried to force him over. Nothing had any effect other than to widen his grin.

'Lesson number one. Never lower your guard.'

What she'd do to wipe that smirk off his face.

She made her body go limp. A tactic. Let him believe he held the upper hand then steal it away when he relaxed. Easy peasy.

Not.

Her heart thrummed.

Each shuddery breath filled her nostrils with spice and man. *Heady. Intoxicating.*

With the fight gone, her mind snapped into realisation. Her body beneath. His body above. Every point of contact burned. Yearned. Turned her on so profusely that she enjoyed his strength, his touch, wanted more.

Her only regret, the clothing separating them. And his hold, so clinical, when she craved personal. *Intimate. Skin on skin.*

She squirmed. *Throbbed.*

His expression heated. As if he guessed her thoughts.

She needed distance before she did something stupid. Like ask him to kiss her. And not even ask. Order. *Beg.*

She tried to free her hands. Couldn't.

'You won't get loose until I let you.' He grinned. 'Yield?'

She stopped struggling, glared up into eyes filled with more amusement than the situation dictated.

Fire blazed her cheeks. 'You're enjoying this way too much.'

'I'm only human.'

She kicked up her legs. *Nothing.* 'Chase!'

'Just one little word and you'll be free. Unless you're enjoying this way too much as well.'

The heat was back. In his gaze. Her blood.

This – their *discussion*, the whole self-defence rigmarole – was to get Chase to agree to her plan, not get her into his bed. Not that the idea was unpleasant – just ill advised. *Wrong.* They were together to prevent more bloodshed. Not get it on.

Even if she wanted it. *Needed it.*

She needed Chase's support of her plan more. They'd catch the Copycat, then she'd get a semblance of her life back. One without a bossy, overbearing, *heavy* man in it.

Numbness inched down her right leg. Threads of it eddied into her chest. She wanted him off. Wanted him to stay. To and fro madness that made her head spin. Reasons against were losing traction. Even his recent rejection held less sway. If she were about to bait a killer, who knew if she'd escape the situation alive?

That meant leaving no regrets.

Which meant she should banish reason, raise her head, keep going until her lips met and melded with his.

Which meant trusting that he wouldn't turn away and leave her humiliated this time around.

Stacey's lips trembling against his sent a thunderbolt straight to Chase's groin.

Surprise was swiftly overtaken by primal instinct. Her tongue demanded entrance and he wasn't fool enough to refuse. She tasted fresh. Sweet. Of ripe berries and honey. He drank greedily, letting go of her hands to spear his fingers up through her hair, holding her head just so.

She moaned. Dropped her freed hand to his chest.

His heart gunned.

Arching against him, her fingers splayed downward, tugging at his belt, then moving lower still, cupping and squeezing until he thought he'd burst.

Her tongue darted into his mouth, giving, taking, sucking every last breath from his body. His cock was so frigging full it hurt. Any more and there'd be no stopping. Possible it was already too late.

He dragged his lips back, the first wrench of oxygen searing his lungs.

Her eyes were dark, the green almost wholly swallowed by black. She licked her lips and, god, he wanted to do the same.

She made him want so much. Need so much. The world around and everything in it no longer mattered.

He panted. 'If we keep going I won't want to stop.'

Her lips curved upward, bruised from his kiss, red and plump and tempting as hell. Then they parted, robbing his will not to take them again before she gave the okay.

Dammit all!

He ducked, devoured. Didn't give a damn he'd intended to take it slow.

Beaded nipples thrust against his chest. His hand found one ripe, round mound and squeezed. She moaned. Bucked her hips, wrapped him into her legs, opening herself. He was so close, but so damned far – so much clothing and baggage standing between them.

Life was too short to keep holding back. If they didn't take their chances now, who knew whether they'd get the chance again?

His lips slid along the angle of her jaw, to her throat, to the throbbing pulse below her ear. Her moans fell into whimpers – needy cat-like mewls that stopped his heart and fuelled the throb in his groin.

Honeysuckle filled his head and he muttered into her skin. 'I can't stop wanting you.'

Her breath hitched. 'Then don't.'

Insanity. Pure and simple, that's where she dragged him. And he didn't care. Gave over to every crazy, irrational need this woman drew out of him.

He nipped her ear, sucked it in. Feasted. Her legs tightened, ankles digging into the backs of his calves, hips undulating, mimicking his need with her own.

Knowing how much she wanted him made him want her all the more.

He rolled over, pulled her on top, tugged her top loose and smoothed his palms under and over her skin. Wanted her clothing gone. His too. Till no barrier existed between them.

One by glorious one, her fingers slipped his shirt buttons free, then moved down to his belt buckle.

The tab of her jeans unsnapped, then came the slow rip of the zip as he dragged it down. Her gaze locked with his.

His buckle loosened, and she took to his jeans. Couldn't seem to open them fast enough. Then she stopped.

Eyes wild, strawberry blonde locks streaming riotously about her face, she leaned forward, hands braced either side of his head, her lips almost touching his, the tips of her breasts tantalising his chest.

'One request before we continue.' Her tongue dragged against his bottom lip, dragging a groan out from deep in the back of his throat.

Then she grinned, eyes like emeralds flashing sin and seduction. 'Take me to bed, detective.'

Chapter Forty-Nine

Stacey's words slammed Chase with the force of a ten-tonne cannonball.

She moved from licking his bottom lip to sucking it hard into her mouth, her tongue performing wonders he couldn't help but imagine over other areas of throbbing, needy flesh.

His cock thrust so hard against his fly, his jeans should have split open already. He wished to hell they would. One less barrier between him and heaven.

He ravaged Stacey's mouth, drew on every shred of her essence until his head swam with intoxication. Gripping her hips, he pulled her further into him, losing his mind in the buck and grind of her body against his. A fully clothed body that needed to be naked. Now.

He reached for her top.

She pulled back. God help him if she wanted to stop. Trying would be the death of him.

Red, kiss-swollen lips curved slowly upward and his brick-hard body hardened beyond a point he'd believed physically possible.

Now wasn't the time for talking, a lesson he learned last time he tried. But that didn't mean she couldn't know how much this moment meant. 'I want you more than I've wanted any other woman.'

The curve of her lips faltered. His heart dipped. She recovered well before he did, even if her smile wasn't as full as it was seconds before. He was a full-blown idiot. He hadn't had nearly enough time to convince her, and more, had no right until he knew he could give her what she deserved. A future.

And anyway, since when did talking trump sex?

Since his emotions kept getting the better of him, that's when.

She slipped her hand between his legs tearing a growl from his throat. 'Then what are you waiting for, detective?'

He grabbed her wrist.

'Stacey, I want you, *this*, but I also want more. For me, this isn't just sex.'

Her expression – the word that came to mind – was haunted.

Then she masked it again, and stood – scrabbling, almost rendering him inactive with a knee just right of his groin. Two feet firmly, and safely, on the ground, her fingers edged the hem of her top upward.

His breath caught.

She paused, seconds that spanned millenniums, then whipped the top over her head, tossing the flimsy material onto his chest.

This time the lace taming her breasts was lavender. Her fingers played over the scalloped edge and his gaze followed every mouth-drying move. She brought her finger to her lips, rolled her tongue over the tip, then dropped it to her lace-covered nipple, rubbing back and forth until it was so swollen it should have pushed clean through the material.

Somewhere between shedding her top and now, he forgot to breathe.

His head swam. Inebriated with the thought of her. With the thought of the two of them together.

She slid her hands over her hips and beneath her jeans, easing them down, bending forward, her lace-clad breasts swaying as she manoeuvred the denim past her knees and over each foot until it was released. Then she straightened, turned, providing an eye-full of her delicious derrière wrapped in a wedge of satin that matched the colour covering her breasts.

Links from head to body severed. He couldn't have spoken even if breath had remained in his lungs.

She arched a brow. 'Right now, let's worry about the sex. We can discuss the "more" later.'

Then with a cock-tugging sway of her hips, she left him lying there and made her way slowly toward the open bedroom door.

Keep walking.

Stacey's heart hammered. Could Chase hear it?

How could he not? The *boom thrash boom* against her ribcage was enough to cross oceans, continents, even ice caps all the way to the North Pole.

The burn of his gaze rolled over her back, settling blissfully, hedonistically, between her thighs. She'd seen that look as she straddled his body, stoked it as she tossed her top and invitation at him before making her exit on two sticks of wobbling jelly.

She daren't turn. One slip of concentration could well end with a slip onto her butt, putting pay to an erotic summons worthy of her books. Hell, it *was* one of her books. Or at least, a scene she'd cut from a book draft. It may not have worked in her story, but it sure seemed to work now.

As long as she kept walking and didn't think.

She gripped the door frame and heard him scramble up behind her.

Don't look back.

The nerve that had brought her here – half naked to her bedroom door, sexy detective at her heels – would flee. And then maybe he'd see through the siren façade to a writer of romance who didn't have a clue how to live it. Who didn't have a clue how to hold a man's interest past the "batted eyelashes and sexy sway of her hips" seduction.

Hard warmth pressed against her back, sure palms sliding around her waist and fanning up over her tummy toward her breasts. Her breath hitched. She'd dreamt of this. Before knowing the real Chase she'd wanted him. And now she knew him, nothing had changed.

Not true.

Gentle fingers swept her hair aside, wild kisses fanning the back of her neck. She shivered.

Now's not the time.

She shook her head but the thoughts stuck.

Chase wanted more. And funny – not the "haha" kind – she wanted that too.

Impossible dreams.

Nothing past this moment was certain. Nothing she could depend on, that is.

He cupped her breasts. Plucked her nipples. Squeezed. Wildfire blazed her blood, nerve-endings zipping the length of her skin with awareness and need.

She moaned. Leaned back into him. Revelled in the contact.

Soon she'd face-off with a killer; every moment until then was a gift. Rare. Perhaps even her last. Which meant now was for making memories, not regrets. It was for making each second count, not for wondering why he was with her, or how far his interest spanned. Or whether it would hold once the real Stacey came to light.

Now was for now.

She turned, skimmed her hands over his chest, edging her fingers beneath his open shirt, pushing it back and over his shoulders. He shrugged and it fell to the ground.

Then she cupped the back of his head and pulled him down toward her lips.

No regrets.

"More" could come after her face-off, when she knew "more" was possible. But the sex? They could have it all, right now. Lose themselves until the world around them and all its cuts and bruises disappeared.

The wind howled, the eucalyptus's branches rapping at the window. A noise once filled with comfort, now edged with menace.

She pulled back. Shivered.

He cupped her face. 'What's wrong?'

Her lip wobbled, uncontrollable. She couldn't get it to stop. 'I don't want to be scared anymore.'

Pools of limitless blue dragged her into their depths. 'I won't let anyone harm you, Stacey.'

'You say that like you have a choice.'

'I do. I'm not leaving your side until he's caught.'

And after …?

She couldn't say it. When the danger and threat was gone, when she could run her life again, make choices, be strong, would he still want "more"? Would he accept crazy, collision course Stacey? Or would he need to change her, control her, make her into something she wasn't, much the same as everyone else had done her whole life?

Because who she was without change would never be enough.

Chase clasped Stacey's hand and tugged her into him.

The small crinkle in her brow indicated she'd started thinking again. A dangerous preoccupation. She needed to feel, lose herself in the moment. Realise how good they could be together.

The gunning of his heart in his chest intensified.

His palms traced the dip and flare at her waist and cupped her buttocks to pull her closer. He pressed her into the wall, urging her thighs open with his knee. She complied, grinding her hips into his leg, grabbing his head as she'd done before to pull him down for a kiss.

His blood surged, his mind well beyond restraint. As his lips plundered hers, his hands sought her breasts, freeing them of the lace so they thrust up, plump and full, their nipples tight and hard, begging for attention. Cupping, squeezing, urging them higher still, he swallowed Stacey's moan before leaving her lips to taste the ripe, rosy flesh spilling out against his palm.

He licked and swirled and licked and sucked, drawing her deep into his mouth, his teeth grazing and tugging the taut buds until her hands raked through his hair, her body grinding against his in a way he'd imagined since first setting eyes on her in the station all those months ago. She moaned and gasped and mewled with every draw, then her hands scrabbled to the open tab on his jeans and down over his jocks.

He swelled into her palm. Felt so goddam hard he thought he might split in two with the slightest provocation. He needed out of his clothes and into Stacey before he lost himself to her hand running over his cock and her lips sliding across his shoulder to his neck.

He lifted his head, captivated for a moment in turbulent green. It was all there. Desire. Passion. Need.

Before thoughts could invade, he dropped his hands to her thighs and lifted her legs up around his hips. Her thigh muscles clenched, her arms wrapping around his neck, bringing those wondrous breasts back into contact with his chest.

Striding through the door, he made for the bed and let go. She toppled onto the mattress, her eyes widened, her lips and cheeks as ruby red as her kiss-swollen nipples.

As she lay tumbled and gasping on the rumpled covers, hair wild about her face, he shucked his jeans and jocks in one sweep. She edged backwards until her shoulders hit the pillows, her fire-flecked eyes watching his every movement. Burning every inch of his flesh.

He rifled through his wallet then tossed it, dropping two foil packets onto the bedside table. First thing in the morning he was hitting the shops. Two would get him through the night, but it wasn't nearly enough for what he had planned. His vow to start living.

And that vow started now, here, with Stacey.

His gaze roved every luscious, bared inch. 'Dammit, you're beautiful.'

The flush in her cheeks deepened, but the sparkle in her eyes, the curve of her lips, was immediate. 'And impatient. I'm not some piece of art to be admired from a distance. This is a hands-on experience, *detective.*'

She licked her lips, her hands fluttering over her tummy, then achingly, slowly upward.

He forgot how to breathe. Again.

Palms cupped the ripe flesh, squeezing, taunting, drawing up raspberry buds that called out to him. Begging.

His mouth dried. *Watch or join in?* Both options with merit, but the itch in his fingers, and lower, swung the vote.

He dropped hands and knees onto the bed, crawling upwards, running his fingers over her ankles, her calves, her knees, heading toward the miniscule scrap of lace still resting between her legs. She smelled of spring flowers and dewy meadows. And deep, potent musk.

Heady. Intoxicating.

He blew and she shivered. Skimming his hands up her thighs, his fingers slipped beneath the elastic and she moaned, raising her hips. An opportunity not to be wasted. Lowering his head, he dropped his mouth and drank her, lavender lace panties and all.

She gasped, bucked, opened up for him.

Damn, she was so ready, so responsive. He tugged the lace aside and licked, sliding his finger into wet heat and swollen, hungry flesh.

Air hissed out from her mouth. *'Chase.'*

Her hands in his hair, his name on her lips ... *Fucking amazing.*

He sucked and she screamed.

Who knew she was a screamer, and more, that he'd like it. With each slip of control, her head thrashed side to side, her cries more urgent. Insistent. Demanding.

He nipped and sucked again, just to hear how much she wanted him. As necessary as drawing his next breath.

'*Chase, please.*'

Her fumbling hands urged him up. One last taste and he complied.

Straddling her hips, he grabbed a condom. She snatched it from his hand and ripped it open with her teeth. So goddam hot. His cock jerked, the thought of that mouth taking him in, swallowing every last inch until he was so deep inside he forgot himself.

'Swap.'

He stared into eyes so dilated they appeared black. Blood-starvation meant a second passed before his brain caught on. She wanted on top. No problem with that. He let her free to scramble over him, luckily with no irreparable damage. Doubtful the knee to his kidneys would affect past the immediate discomfort.

The view from below was spectacular and worth the fleeting pain. Full breasts spilling over the support of her bra, wet heat perched just shy of his cock, so perfect, so ready.

Breath caught deep in his throat as she settled the rubber against his tip and slowly rolled it upward. He bit back a groan, fisted the sheets so he didn't flip her back over and dive deep and hard into her right there and then.

She reached his base. Squeezed.

Hell! There was a real possibility he might die before he made it inside.

'I've wanted to touch you like this since I saw you in the shower.'

As if his heart wasn't beating fast enough, it kicked up a notch. Dry didn't begin to describe the desert invading his throat.

So this is how it feels to be alive.

She raised her hips and touched his tip to her folds. Throwing back her head, she cupped her breasts, stroking and squeezing, then with excruciating slowness, she lowered her hips and took him inside.

Chapter Fifty

Nerve-endings fired like wires caught in an electrical storm.

With each edge downward, Chase slowly, deliciously, filled her. She'd imagined this moment more times than she could count, written scenes such as this in each of her books, but neither memory nor prose came even close to the sensation of Chase between her legs and the slide of his hard muscle deep into her body.

Decadence. He made her that way. Made her feel desired and sexy, without all those trappings she'd considered necessary to entice and interest a man. So much so that she closed her eyes, her hands moving without conscious thought to her breasts, imagining that he played and massaged as he lodged deeper into her life, into her.

Slipping down one inch more, her clit rubbed at his base. She shivered, opened her eyes.

Deep tropical blue watched her through hooded lids. 'Damn, you're hot, woman!'

She grinned. Not so clumsy now.

'Not so bad yourself, detective.'

With a knee-melting grin, his hands covered hers, his fingers plying and plucking her nipples until she cried out.

She tilted her hips, felt the press of him intensify. She lifted, then slid slowly down again, teasing that spot just inside that made her squirm and shudder and cry out his name.

He groaned, tweaked the already over-sensitised buds. Pleasure bordered pain.

She dropped forward, bracing her hands either side of his head, and he tugged a nipple into his mouth. Drew on it, feasted, like she was some mouth-watering treat.

Hot damn! Each pull dragged so deep, her sex quivered. *Begged for more.*

She raised her hips, lowered, raised her hips and lowered again.

His teeth grazed across her nipple as he met her thrust for thrust.

His breathing came faster, matching hers, his hands skimming down her side to cup and squeeze her bottom with each upward drive.

Awareness splintered, from flesh experiencing the slide of his cock, to each and every firing cell in her body. Her heart thundered, her body soaring so high she never wanted to come down.

Sensation swirled, lightening her body, spiralling her out of cognizance and into oblivion.

As she raised her hips, his hand slipped between them to the tight bud of nerves tottering on the brink of release. He strummed and the room blazed in white incandescent light.

Her orgasm hit in waves, rolling, all-encompassing, white-tipped breakers that crashed against any dwindling misgivings, toppling her over the edge of reason and restraint.

And Chase was right there with her.

He tensed, his fingers grasping her butt so tight, it was as if he never intended to let her go. One final thrust and he shuddered into her pulsing flesh, the glaze of his lips over her shoulder making her quiver all over again.

Her body buzzed, her blood roared.

He caught her mouth, moved his hands up to cup her face, kissing her as if his life depended on it. As if she were his next vital breath.

She collapsed against him, warmth filtering from his body to hers. Never so comfortable. Experiencing the lull and rise of his laboured breathing, the brush and caress of his hands as they drew circles across her back and buttocks.

If only they could stay that way forever. A place where the outside world no longer existed. Where they were happy and satisfied and safely cocooned. Where nothing and no one could break through and rob their happiness. Their peace.

She gripped his shoulders and her mind floated on the heady scent of spice and sex.

Wind howled about the eaves outside. Not another storm, surely? Even the eucalyptus seemed to agree, its creaking trunk discernible from the other end of the house.

She shivered.

Shouldn't she move?

Not that she wanted to. No. But lying with some hulking woman on top couldn't continue to feel comfortable. Or sexy, even.

Her palms pressed against the crumpled sheets to push herself up. Impossible. An iron-grip held her down.

'Don't move.'

'I'm squashing you.'

'Not a wholly unpleasant feeling.' He grinned and her body tingled all the way to her heart. 'But you must be cold.' He reached over and pulled the covers across her back.

She dropped her head onto his chest, the race of his heart pounding against her ear.

Drumming in sync to hers.

So many things drumming in sync.

If only the timing wasn't as crappy as the needling reminders that all wasn't well in the world. That the promise of this moment and how it spanned into the future was in the hands of a sick psychopath who thought it fun to kill and maim and mimic her characters.

And perhaps at some stage, her.

Stacey snuggled seamlessly into his side, like the wrap of his favourite sweater. Comfortable. Warm. A perfect fit.

Like she'd always been there. And always would.

Burying his nose into her hair, he let the sweet aroma of honeysuckle and her surround him.

Her delicious peaches and cream ass filled his palm and he eased his hand upward, walking his fingers up the small of her back. She trembled, pushed further into him. Wiggled and wrapped her legs even tighter around his, making him hard and hungry, yet again.

'Chase!'

Her hair tickled his chin, her delicious body quivering as his fingers continued their stroll over her waist and down over her tummy.

'You called?'

She squirmed. 'Stop it!'

'And who knew the serious Stacey Holland was ticklish?'

'I'm not ticklish.'

'These fingers,' he twirled round her belly button, 'say you are.'

'I'm– Ahhh!'

His fingers had a mind of their own. He dropped onto one elbow and proceeded to enjoy her belly. What would have been her panty line, had she been wearing any.

'You're–'

'H-*hot*?' She squealed.

'So responsive.'

He straddled her legs and found the spot, the smooth skin where her hip and leg joined. She writhed beneath him, naked, beautiful. *His.*

Her body shook.

'Chase!'

Scrabbling at his wrist, she tried to stop him. He grabbed her hands and pulled them up, pressing them into the sheets above her head with one hand while his other continued his onslaught. 'You want more?'

'No!' She gasped. Half giggled, half screamed. Wholly took his breath away.

Her body twisted, turned, flushed pink, glistening, radiant. Taut nipples grazed his chest, slick skin sliding and bucking against his.

His fingers worked between them, over her waist, her stomach.

'Please!'

She was breathless. Breathtaking.

He propped up on his hand, watching as she caught her breath. Wild strawberry curls fanned about flushed cheeks and lips. Rose-tipped breasts rising and falling with every breath.

'Your grasp of the English language is phenomenal. You should try writing or something.'

Indignation flashed across her face. The kind laced with amusement.

'Smartass.' She rolled him over. He let her.

Straddling his hips, hands either side of his head, she lowered her body until her the tips of her nipples touched his chest. 'With that attitude, you should try being a cop or something.'

The snort escaped unchecked. 'I'll take that under advisement.'

'Such big words.'

'You have no idea.' He grabbed her ass, pulled her into the part of him that grew bigger by the minute.

Black almost swallowed the green of her irises, the grind of her hips showing she was nowhere near immune, despite her cocky – pardon the pun – attitude.

Then her hands inched around his waist. Feather-light fingertips scuttled across the sway of his back and lower, and he nearly bucked clear off the bed.

Her grin widened, eyes sparkling fun and laughter. 'Who's ticklish now, detective?'

'Tell me something.' Chase shuffled onto the edge of Stacey's pillow.

Resting his head on the back of one hand, he took his fill of glorious flushed cheeks and wild, passion-filled eyes. That he'd made them so was all-the-more breathtaking.

Her lips quirked. 'What kind of something?'

'Oh, I don't know. Anything. Something interesting.' It was a wonder to see the cogs in her mind work – the little furrows nudging just between her eyebrows, the purse of her delectable tongue between her teeth.

Within seconds, the quirk lurched into the semblance of a smile. 'A male praying mantis has two brains so that when the female devours his head during sex, he can still seal the deal.'

He would have snorted, if that was his thing.

Instead he edged away, just a little, back onto his own pillow. Not because he thought she'd turn all praying mantis on him or anything, but because his focus was better from a distance.

'O-kay. Perhaps not just *anything*.' He dug his hands beneath his pillow and tried again. 'Something you've never told anyone else before. Something happy.'

Again the furrows, the bite. He could forever lose himself in every aspect of her face, study every nuance and micro-expression until he knew them all. And he'd never grow tired.

This was the epitome of living. Being with Stacey. Sharing his life.

'I was six.' Her gaze softened. Warmed. The hint of a smile tugging at her lips. 'Dad came home from work early that day. He wasn't drunk. He wasn't angry. He was …' She blinked. Smiled a little more. Sighed. 'Happy. Funny. *Fun.*'

She closed her eyes, for just a second, as if reliving that moment, that feeling. Then her eyelids fluttered open and her bright, green gaze stalled his heart.

'For the first time in forever, he didn't do that whole "grab a beer and slump in front of the TV" thing he did most other nights. Instead, he hunted out my favourite game, Uno – the one with a machine that spits cards out at you when you press a button – and set it up on the kitchen table. With the music on loud, we spent the evening playing and laughing and devouring two entire bowls of salty, buttery popcorn.'

She sighed. A happy kind of sigh, full of sweetness and sugar-coated memories. 'Then Dad's favourite band came on, AC/DC. *Highway to Hell.* God, he loved that song! He grabbed Mum's hand and twirled her round the kitchen. Then he grabbed mine, lifting me up, whirling me round and round until the entire world was a blur and I was so giddy I couldn't stand up straight.' Moisture battled her eyelids. 'I don't remember laughing so hard or feeling so happy ever again. It's one of my only memories of us as a family – no fighting, no angst. Just bliss.'

He reached over and tucked a curl back from her face. 'It's a beautiful memory.'

She snagged his hand and brushed her lips across his knuckles.

Heat coursed through his blood, a direct hit to his groin. He groaned, leaned in.

Her gaze widened.

She let go. As if she hadn't meant to act so instinctively. So *lovingly*. As if she immediately regretted giving in to impulse.

A long breath escaped her lips and she blinked. 'Tell me something. Something to make me smile.'

He stemmed his disappointment.

New beginnings meant focusing on what he had, not on what he hadn't. Or what could or couldn't be. *Live in the now.* It was a good mantra. One he needed to adopt, no matter what his prognosis for the future.

What to say to make her smile?

His mind raced, then gave a mental finger snap. 'The longest movie ever made runs for 85 hours. Want to guess its name?' He didn't wait for an answer because he couldn't wait to see her smile again. '*The Cure for Insomnia.*'

Her eyes widened, sparkling, fun-filled. 'No way!'

'Yes, way.' He soaked up the spreading warmth that came from making Stacey smile, returning her smile with one of his own. 'Very possibly one of the worst movies ever released. But its one claim to fame is making the Guinness Book of Records some time round the late 1980s.'

'I can't believe you even know that.'

'Less scary than cannibalistic insects though. Right?' He wiggled his brows and won a bout of tinkling laughter.

'I'm a suspense author. My middle names are "mayhem" and "murder".' The smile slipped just as quickly as it had appeared.

Two words, once representing fiction without consequence outside her story, now a gruesome reality.

He was well-acquainted with both words. Had been for the six-plus years since joining the force. But never before had they affected him the way they did now.

Solving crimes – helping the living, the hurt, to find closure – had always been cathartic. A way of healing the pain that death and loss trawled through the lives of others. But now those two threats cut so close to his heart, he felt the knife's blade as if it carved his tenuous existence anew.

He hated that Stacey hurt. And more, he hated that he lacked the power to make the hurt go away.

What he could do is make her forget, even if just for a while.

'Did you know the longest recorded flight of a chicken is thirteen seconds?'

She snorted – the cute snort that always accompanied a short spate of laughter. 'Someone actually timed that?'

He nodded. 'A chicken-lover, no doubt. Probably the same one who designed your doorbell.'

She snorted again. Louder.

And something, her reaction, the joy in seeing her smile, made him shuffle closer and cover that snort with a kiss.

He combed his fingers through the curls tumbling her flushed cheeks, cupped the back of her head and drank every delicious drop her mouth had to offer.

She kissed him back. Taking and giving with such abandon, his heart clenched, even as muscles much lower stirred and tightened. Then she peeled her mouth from his, nipped and sucked his lower lip.

And everything below the waist hardened. Unbearably.

She smiled. Licked her lips. 'That was nice.'

What he felt went way beyond anything as tame as "nice". Circumstances, with more than a sprinkling of physiology, meant he lacked the wherewithal to debate it. Not when every lick of her lips tugged his cock further into wakefulness.

'Your turn now.'

He searched what little matter of his brain remained. His turn for what? Possibilities scarpered through his imagination, but her tone indicated she was somewhere else entirely.

Her smile widened, as if she read every one of his triple-X-rated thoughts.

She reached for his hand, wrapping it in hers. Not an ounce of regret this time. 'Tell me something real. Something that makes you smile.'

It took a few moments, a few deep but surreptitious breaths, and then he was able to wrack his brain. To think of something he'd never shared with anyone else before now.

'There's not a moment of my childhood that I don't remember my mother being sick.' He inhaled. Let the breath out slow and long. Then inhaled again. 'But earlier on, before the Parkinson's took its toll, she had days that were better than others. Days I'd return from school to find her sitting in an old recliner Dad bought, just for her. She'd smile, pat her lap and I'd climb up armed with a pile of my favourite books. Then she'd read to me. Just me.'

He couldn't help but smile. 'She was an amazing storyteller. Mimicked all the voices, made every single character come to life. I'd snuggle into her, feel her heart beating against my ear, curl her hair around my finger and breathe in the lavender from her clothes.'

He closed his eyes momentarily, reliving the sweet, soothing fragrance and the warmth that accompanied it. 'There was a lavender bush out the front of our house. I'd pick the flowers and we'd dry them together, then put them into little bags. Whenever I smell lavender, I think of her. I think of the times she used to read to me and make me feel like our life could be normal and happy after all.'

Stacey cupped his cheek in her hand. He nuzzled into it and

breathed in her scent, turning his head to kiss her palm.

For the first time in forever, it was as if happy were within reach.

'Great memory.' She smiled. 'All kids should read books. I would have tried my hand at children's stories if I wasn't so hung up on murder.' She frowned. 'That didn't come out right.'

'I know what you meant.'

The frown seemed determined to stay. He was equally determined to see it gone. He searched for something …

'Sooo …'

Got it!

He grinned. 'Did you know there's a world record for seeing how many times you can attempt a world record?'

Her lips twitched as she slapped his chest. 'Now you're just making that up.'

'Nope. True story. Although for the life of me, I can't remember the details.'

'Just when you had my attention too.'

'Well, let's see if we can get a better hold on that attention, shall we?'

His hand found her breast, warm, soft, responsive. He ran his thumb across the nipple and felt it tighten. He did it again, harder, and her breath hitched.

Much as he could have played there all night, there were other wonders waiting for his exploration.

He pushed up on one elbow and shed the covers, his gaze eating every delicious inch as he experienced an overwhelming desire to witness her body's reaction to him. Her nipples were rosy and taut, the rise and fall of her breasts sharp and erratic, reactionary to every brush, every stroke of his fingertips.

He skimmed lower, feathering out over her ribs, circling her belly button, watching the quivers, the shudders, the slow dilation of her pupils, the plump of her parted lips as each short, needy breath escaped.

Walking his fingers downward, he encountered the band of silken skin only inches from heaven. Her breaths were shallower, shriller, sharper. Every ragged release tugging at his diminishing control.

Damn, but he wanted her. In every way imaginable, hard and heated, soft and savouring. On the bed, in the shower, splayed out over the kitchen bench like the most delectable of desserts.

His fingers continued their exploration, his ambling taking him beyond the thatch of curls that previous endeavours revealed were a surprising match to her strawberry blonde hair, and then further still.

'Oh, *Chase*. You're–'

He slipped two fingers between her folds. She gasped.

'Hot?'

He found that taut bundle of nerves and circled. She mewled.

'Happy?'

He flicked. She bucked.

'Horny?'

He delved deeper, the pull of tight, sultry flesh fuelling the burning hunger in his groin.

She shuddered. *'Hankering.'*

He paused his fingers. 'For?'

'This.'

In seconds she'd pushed him back and, sheathed, ready, his tip nudged into her slick, wet heat.

Then leisurely, lusciously she took him inside.

And nothing else mattered but her and how much she meant to him.

Chapter Fifty-One

Stacey's eyes shot open.

She stiffened, ears straining for whatever had dragged her from dreams so X-rated, she could create a whole new alphabet.

She squinted. Not that it made a difference. Dark shadows filled the room, the sense of space familiar, yet not so.

She wasn't alone.

Memory of the night's activities slammed her further into wakefulness. Hard male heat cocooned her from behind, muscular arms wrapping her up in front. Silence roared against her eardrums.

Then …

A crack. Like dry wood in a campfire.

Another. This time resounding. Ear-splitting.

Then a string of them. The air trembled. The house shuddered.

Boom!

Chase jerked up. 'What the fuck was that!'

Her feet were already dropping to the shuddering floor. 'An earthquake?'

'In Melbourne?'

Surely not another explosion?

She ran to the window. Contrary to every bit of earthquake safety advice she'd been exposed to. Which wasn't much.

Melbourne wasn't an earthquake zone. Then again, that's what they thought about Christchurch, until 2011.

She strained to see. Difficult in the waning dark, but she saw enough.

Her heart pounded so hard it struck the back of her throat. 'A tree collapsed onto the house.'

Wood splintered, a dry crackling. Empty. Echoing.

Fissures snaked across her en suite wall and a large eucalyptus branch stabbed the plaster just above the bedroom door.

She dragged on a t-shirt and pants, then tried to open the window. It stuck fast.

'We have to get out, Chase. The house is collapsing.'

She turned to see he was already in his jeans and shirt.

'Out of the way!'

A sheet wrapped around one hand, he punched the glass. It shattered, and with the second punch, large fragments fell onto the grass below.

'Put something on your feet!' He cleared the large shards still stuck to the base then draped the sheet over the rest. 'You first.'

She clambered up onto the bedside table.

Chase offered his hand. 'Careful of the glass when you hit the ground.'

She nodded, barely hesitated as she eased through the gap, flinching at the sharp burn on her elbow as it found possibly the only remaining sliver in the frame.

Cold pricked her bare arms, wind whipping her hair about her face, slicing through her scant tee.

Racing heartbeats blared against her eardrums, but through the uproar she heard shouts, a dog barking, sirens wailing, their warning growing louder by the second.

She shivered, wrapped her arms around her body as if she could wrap out dawn's cold and the sight of her home – her guest bedroom – obliterated by the hulking eucalyptus. Shivers erupted into all-out shakes. If Chase had been inside …

No!

Warmth wrapped around her arm and tugged. 'Let's get clear in case the whole framework gives way.'

She pulled back, her blue fluffy heels digging into wet grass. 'I can't. Cuddles and Midnight are still in there.'

Her voice shook, her vision blurred with the threat of tears. She turned toward her beautiful house, now snapped and broken like a pile of matchsticks.

Chase tightened his grip. 'Go somewhere safe. I'll find them.'

Her head jerked up. 'This isn't the time for bossy machismo. I'm coming.'

His blue gaze assessed hers, mere seconds that made her heart race with images of her babies trapped. Or worse. Then he nodded. 'Wait here. I need to cut the electricity.'

In seconds he was back, his stern, unsmiling face so unlike the Chase she'd first met. He barely blinked. 'Stay close. And if I say get out, you go, no matter what. Deal?'

She nodded. No sense arguing when it'd only cause further delay. That didn't make her compliant. Or the pushover she'd been in the past. No matter that Chase's actions were well-intentioned, she made her own decisions. Took her own risks. Would save Cuddles and Midnight without heeding some man's dictates.

Even the man she'd just made mad, crazy, mind-blowing love to.

A touch of warmth frittered away the cold. The promise of sex with Chase had nothing on reality. But that didn't mean her synapses were singed. That her brain was so sex-scrambled, normal function had ceased. She was still her own woman.

Any feelings she might or might not have wouldn't change that.

He turned, she followed, eyes scouring the splintered wood-slats and cracked roof-tiles. The enormous tree trunk blocked their path – had sliced through the wooden boards of the house's façade – forcing them to retreat to the footpath before they could skirt the giant roots, then what remained of her guest bedroom. Through the punctured outer wall, she could barely make out the fractured mess of the closet, the dressing table. The bed Chase would have slept in had he not shared hers.

She shivered, despite the dying wind.

The sirens were in the street now, and any moment firies and police would arrive and take control. Tell her she couldn't risk her life for a couple of kooky animals.

She rushed past Chase, who wasn't rushing enough. She wouldn't give them the chance.

'Whoa! Hold on, Stacey.'

She jerked free. 'Midnight!' She whistled, called again.

Chase sighed, then joined in, calling, whistling, sticking close by her side.

The rear of the house wasn't so bad. The front – her guest bedroom – had taken the brunt of the fall, the tree slicing the wood as if it were a knife and the house a block a cheese. It would have fared better if it were brick. Her mother's voice, her warnings, piercing her eardrums, even in thought.

Regardless, her beautiful home was a thing of the past.

She reached the place that was once her living room and peered through a now shattered window. Cuddles's terrarium had toppled over, the door splayed open.

No sign of the snake.

She had to get in closer.

Chase grasped her wrist. 'No, you don't.'

'I need to get in there.'

'Not until the firies arrive.'

'That could be too late. Do you know how fast snakes move? Or how easy it is for them to just disappear?'

'Believe me, much as a snake on the loose ranks up there with charging rhinos and raging lions, I'm more concerned right now with whether the house will collapse further, especially while we're inside.'

'Then you stay here.'

'Do you think it's me I'm worried about?'

Her heart stopped. But she couldn't think about his words, or how they made her feel. Not now.

'Then stay close. And if I say go, you go no matter what. Got it?' She grinned, then didn't wait for a response. Began looking for a way into the mess.

Doubtful humour-boy would see the humour in her words. Not that the situation was even slightly funny. It was far from.

But it was either that or cry.

Her home had been her sanctuary. Her writing cave, her haven. Where would she go now?

Her mother's? She'd barely escaped the suffocation of her teens. Life with Brad had saved her, until it became its own form of torture. Then after their breakup, she'd bitten her tongue and clutched her sanity, only just making it out intact when she found this place.

Now it was gone, she might have no choice but to return to her mother's. How could she? Knowing what she knew.

Impossible.

She was about to slip through when Chase stepped in front. 'I'll go first.'

She let him go. After all, he was letting her follow, when he could have gone all overbearing detective, flashed his badge and "officially" ordered her away.

They moved slowly through rubble, floor and ceiling now close neighbours. Lightbulbs smashed, wires exposed, plaster crumbling and broken where branches had punctured their way through.

Close-up she confirmed what she'd seen from a distance. The terrarium was empty.

Dammit!

'Stacey.'

She turned. Spotted what Chase had spotted. Her beautiful boy wrapped around his favourite hat stand, now lying on its side.

'Thank god!'

Within seconds he'd wrapped around her shoulders and they were looking for Midnight. That he'd only recently escaped death kicked and pawed at her thoughts. How many of his nine lives did her little man have left?

'Midnight!'

'Miss?' A man in firie yellow popped his head through the window. 'Come out of the premises, please.'

'I'm looking for my cat.'

'Is he black with a leg-cast?'

Her heart hammered. 'Yes.'

'Then we have him. I need you to come out. This structure is unsafe and could collapse any minute.'

They squeezed out, back the way they came, to more than a few eyebrow raises and smart comments. Seems the greater public had never seen a woman with a snake escape a collapsing building before.

Chase flashed his badge at a firie who looked to be in charge. 'Any idea how the tree fell?'

'We're waiting on an arborist, so we'll know more once he arrives.' The man flicked his gaze her way, then back to Chase, not even bothering to lower his voice. 'Meantime, you might want to find a safer place for that snake.'

Chase seemed almost as unimpressed as she at the comment, which made her feel marginally better. Although nothing could stem the feeling of loss every time she looked at her shattered home.

Her gut wrenched.

How the hell had this happened? The tree wasn't particularly old, or dying even. Yes, she hadn't tended her garden much lately, but trees needed little tending. And lack of annual pruning shouldn't have resulted in *this*.

She stepped onto the front lawn and scoured for Midnight, warmth seeping up her back from the press of Chase's palm.

His presence, his support, were the only things keeping her sane right now. Difficult to imagine how she could have coped this last week without him.

And if not for last night …

Impossible for him to have survived the tree and crumbled ceiling that was now crushing what would have been his bed.

'Stacey!'

The voice filtered through the raucous of chatter and panic and firies and police securing the area.

She turned. Her heart skipped a beat.

Pulling away from Chase, she raced toward the path. 'Ethan!'

Chapter Fifty-Two

Shit's stench never left your shoes, even after you scrubbed the living crap out of them. Seems Stacey's fireman was much the same.

And jealousy wasn't something Chase should feel. Not after the night they'd shared. Not when he had the girl.

Had. Past tense being the gut-kicker here.

Her face was all lit up at macho man who had, once again, donned his tights and cape. Because, of course, snuggled in his arms was none other than Midnight, the magically appearing cat.

That he'd saved the cat once was opportune. Twice? Well, that was just confounded, and yet damned interesting. Previous delvings into Mr Ethan Miklem had come up empty. Yet there was something squeaky about the man. And it wasn't Pine O Clean cleanness.

He just had to dig deeper. Isn't that where the shit irrefutably settled?

'Chase!'

He turned. Cringed. 'Jayda. What are you doing here?'

'I was just passing.'

'Really? Through Windsor? Bit out of your way, isn't it?'

She shrugged. 'A call came out for your girlfriend's address. Thought I'd check it out.'

Funny how the girlfriend reference didn't rankle nearly as much as it had in the past.

'A tree collapsed.'

'So I see.' Her gaze sharpened. 'Think it means anything?'

'Before the car bomb and recent body-part incidents, I'd have said no. But now …' There was no sense in holding back on his suspicions. Not this time. 'It's a warning. Or another goddam failed murder attempt.'

'Way outside his normal MO.'

'So was Jagger, Beth and our toeless John Doe.'

She nodded. Didn't bother arguing. Which rang more bells than a Swiss dairy farm. Her next words cemented his suspicions that there was more to her surprise visit.

'Update on Jagger – he was connected to three of the Copycat victims.'

His interest sat up, ears perked. 'And the others?'

'Nothing obvious, but we're still looking.'

'It doesn't make sense that Jagger's the killer. But maybe he knew who was.'

'My thoughts too. We're looking into acquaintances, business or otherwise. And we'll need to speak to Gracie at some stage.'

'She's on vacation.' *Hiding, with a PI I've hired to ensure her safety.* Yeah, not details he could share without revealing the break-in and the fact it was never reported. The fact he'd been withholding info from his team.

Whichever way he turned, he walked a wavering tightrope.

'Let me know when you want the interview and I'll get a message to her.'

'Thanks.' She bit her lip in that way of hers that said what she was about to say wasn't something he wanted to hear. 'There's another reason for my visit.'

At least they'd moved on from the "I was just passing by" bullshit.

'News on the bomb?'

'Nope. Forensics and bomb squad are still sifting through the rubble they collected from the scene.' Air puffed out through her lips – a sign he was going to hate whatever she was about to say even more than he first thought. 'Hackett's booked a check-up for you next Friday. He wants you cleared and back at work.'

Some instincts were never wrong.

"Back at work" meant leaving Stacey unprotected. A clay pigeon, primed and defenceless against the Copycat Killer's sick form of target practise.

'What if I take leave?'

She didn't look surprised. If he didn't know any better, he'd say she'd read his mind. Not a great prospect.

'What's stopping you from taking that physical?'

'This isn't about the physical. I can't leave Stacey alone. Not after this.' He waved toward the mess that was once her home.

'Well, I doubt he'll go for the leave. And he'd want a solid reason to approve it. More than a desire to babysit your girlfriend.'

Nothing less than he'd expected from Jayda. She invariably had something to say, and wasn't averse to spilling it, volcano-style.

And she wasn't finished.

'Is there anything I should know, any other reason, stopping your return to work at the end of next week?' Her gaze strayed to his wrist and the marked absence of a bandage.

So, she believed more than Stacey was keeping him from the job he loved. And once upon a time, she would have been right. That whole "being discovered" scenario no longer worried him. Funny how his hand had barely twinged the past few days. More pressing worries had hijacked his attention.

Like Stacey being the next possible victim to a serial killer whose obsession was closing in.

When he thought about last night and what could have happened had he been in his bed, beneath that tree … His elimination would clear a path for the killer and any chance of protecting Stacey would be gone.

The bastard had to be caught before he struck again.

Stacey's plan might be crazy, but it was the only plan they had. Much as he hated it, much as he wanted to wrap her up and keep her safe and out of harm's way, today's events demonstrated how efforts in that direction were futile.

And now, where they'd thought they had more time, it seems they had less.

One entire week until Friday. His blood test results would be in by then. If they came back positive, he'd be stripped of his weapon. Relegated to desk duty, this time for good.

Unarmed and out of the field wasn't something he contemplated while hunting a serial killer. He needed every resource available. That included the possible backup of his team.

'Chase?' Jayda. He'd almost forgotten she was there.

She released a short, sharp breath. 'There *is* something, isn't there?'

'Nothing.' He steeled his expression. Whatever madness marauded his brain, it didn't need to be written all over his face. 'I'm just concerned for the life of a witness.'

Again with the lip biting. Then a barely perceptible smile. 'I'm happy for you, Chase.'

His head snapped back. It was seconds before his mind wrapped around her words. 'Why?'

She dipped her head, considering him. Like he was some damned shop window display. 'You're different. I don't know what it is exactly, but it suits you.'

Doubtful she referred to his current commando state. As unliberating and uncomfortable as it was.

Her side-glance toward Stacey cemented his suspicion.

He dragged his attention back from the woman surrounded by her menagerie and fireman. 'You were dead-set against it not so long ago.'

'When I thought you were just dicking around. Now I sense this is more.'

He didn't confirm or deny it. Didn't need to. She'd already made up her mind. And what the hell, she was right.

'For what it's worth, I think she feels the same way.'

He tossed playing cool and blasé to the curb, and glanced toward Stacey to find her watching him back. Her cheeks flushed and she returned attention to macho-man. Nodded at something he said.

Difficult to know whether her perceived interest was wishful thinking on his part or kick-to-the-heart real.

He turned back to Jayda. Amusement etched every line of her expression. That she was enjoying his uncertainty was clear. That he didn't much care was a surprise. 'What makes you say that?'

'That she likes you?' A sparkle lit her expression. 'It might be the way she's aware of you, no matter where you are. The way she stares at you when she thinks you're not looking. The way she's glaring at me right now, as if she'd jab a stick in my eye given half the chance.' They turned in unison, in time to catch Stacey's frown before she dragged her gaze away.

Jayda grinned. 'That girl has it bad. Almost as bad as you.'

For once her dig didn't grate. In fact, he couldn't help it. He grinned back.

'Finally a woman to make Chase give up the chase.' That she was there in semi-professional capacity must have been the only thing stopping Jayda from falling about the ground with laughter. *Hell.* She'd ragged about his humour more times than he'd watched Dirty Harry reruns. Now she was slapping him with hers, and it missed being funny by a mile.

'If you want to bring a plus-one for the wedding, let me know.' She winked. *Winked,* for god's sake. 'We could always find space for one more.'

'Your bed's just in here.' Chase swung the door open and stood aside.

Stacey edged past, her elbow brushing his chest. His muscles contracted hungrily.

The way her eyes kept darting back to his, the expression on her face, it was clear she felt responsible for endangering his life. Didn't she get she was equally responsible for saving it? He was living. Breathing. More than merely existing.

An active participant in life once again.

And it was all Stacey. A crazy cat-lady, complete with snake and killer heels. A woman who created death and havoc in the pages of her books, but who was funny and sexy, and endearingly ridiculous, who devoured a plate of vegies with the same relish as he devoured a steak, who made him want her with every ounce of his being.

She spun full-circle, her green gaze roving, absorbing every last detail. 'Interesting.'

He turned from thoughts of her, to the real, larger-than-life woman before him.

'Revisiting your second childhood?'

He chuckled. 'I never finished my first.'

His gaze followed hers, over the Thomas the Tank Engine quilt, over a bookshelf brimming with all his old childhood favourites, plus a few new ones; The Wiggles, Teletubbies, Hairy Maclary. And in the corner, on a low wooden table, stood the proud beginnings of a Lego pirate ship he and Jagger Junior had built together his last visit.

'Mmm, finally something we both agree on.'

She carefully placed the cat carrier containing Midnight onto the bed.

Cuddles was already secured in a replacement terrarium they'd picked up on the way. That he had a reptile in his living room – a damned snake to boot – was more than a little incomprehensible. Then again, the fact he'd willingly invited a woman, and her scraggly rat-cat, into his life, was a first.

And somehow, at some stage, he'd warmed to the scaly devil. As much as one could warm to a cold-blooded, constricting lump of muscle, that is. That Stacey loved him, made him lovable. It was as simple as that.

'You don't have a secret love-child hiding under the bed or in the closet, do you?'

Her voice may have been light, but the undercurrents were anything but. He may be dense at times, but he got that her question was more than an attempt at humour.

She needed to know for more than feeding casual curiosity.

'My nephew sleeps over sometimes. This is his room.'

Again her gaze wandered. 'Nice.'

'He thinks so.'

'Although I've always been more of a Hi-5 kinda girl.'

He chuckled. 'Don't let Jagger hear you say that. He'll be scandalised. Well, as much as a two year old can be scandalised, that is.'

'Jagger?'

His mouth tightened. 'Jagger and Gracie had a son. Jagger Junior.'

She nodded. 'And you're the doting uncle.' Her eyes sparkled, her perfect lips twitching. *Tempting*. 'Doesn't quite fit with my impression of you.'

His gaze riveted to her thirst-quenching mouth. 'Must everything fit into a nice, tidy box?'

Her fingers toyed with the blue cat-box handle. 'Personally, I've always liked "untidy". A little unexpected goes a long way to crafting a good story.'

He moved closer. So close, honeysuckle thrummed a heady path across his senses. 'And what if it's not just a story, Stacey?'

She swayed toward him, her fingers still fixed on the shaking blue plastic. He had no such anchor, nothing to hold him in check. He reached out and gripped her hips.

Her breath hitched. 'All the better. Life should never be tidy.'

'You're right. What I feel for you is anything but tidy.' He cupped her jaw, his thumb brushing her cheek, his heart racing like a V8 supercar gunning for the finish line. 'You're never what I expect. And when I think I've got you all worked out, you throw me again like some wild boomerang.'

'Boomerangs never stay thrown. They always come back.'

His eyes locked with hers and he moved in. 'I know.'

Wide, shimmering emerald stared up at him, the racing pulse at her neck begging his mouth for repletion.

She licked her lips and he bit back the growl thrumming deep in his chest.

'What do you feel, Chase?'

'Too much, and yet, not nearly enough.' Even a gulp couldn't dislodge the clog in his throat. Or the drain in his brain. He was making no sense, floundering, when he should have been used to her effect on him by now.

Impossible to get past the irrefutable truth.

He nearly lost Stacey, before he'd really *had* her. Had her to hold and love and cherish. All those old-world things he'd never contemplated until she toppled – literally, bad heels first – into his life. If he hadn't kissed her last night. If she hadn't let him. If they'd held back instead of giving in to whatever spell bound the two of them together …

Life was too short, even without the fear of his mother's condition wavering over the hazy threads of his future. Anything could take them, any time. And a serial killer on their heels made the possibility so many times worse.

There was no reason to wait and every reason to tell her now, how he felt. To tell her his feelings weren't a joke. For the first time in his life, he wasn't interested in hiding behind hollow laughter. This was love. And he wouldn't back away, no matter how the prospect scared the living hell out of him.

Hand still cupped to her cheek, he brushed at the frown lines about her mouth, his heart kicking against his ribs as she leaned into him, turning her head, brushing her lips to his palm.

Wild heat stirred his groin.

He groaned. Pulled her hips flush with his own. 'It's like my life was suspended until you hit the release button and set me free. I've been waiting for something or someone to live for, and now I've found it. *You.*'

Red bloomed across her cheeks and down her neck. Down beneath the taut neckline of her top.

Her eyelids fluttered, then shot back open, wide, her gaze dragging him deeper under whatever crazy spell she wove.

'I feel the same.'

His head jerked back. 'You do?'

She nodded. Her lips trembling, pink and provocative, and glistening wet under the attention of her tongue. 'After Brad, I vowed I'd never let a man into my heart again. You changed that.'

'I'm in your heart?'

'You stormed right in. Like you stormed into my thoughts. I couldn't stop you.'

'Did you want to?' His breath snatched in his lungs, waiting, hoping it wouldn't all go away. That she wouldn't second guess, wouldn't think and change her mind before giving them a chance.

'With every fibre of my self-preserving being.' She covered his hand with hers. 'And then I discovered that strong and self-opinionated wasn't such a bad thing. Especially when it's wrapped in a package of warmth and compassion and second-rate humour.' *Grin.* 'And it doesn't hurt that you cook a mean veggie pasta.'

'So, you're saying you like my package?'

'Really? That's all you got from that whole spiel?'

'Hey, what can I say? Opportunities like that are too good to pass up.'

'Well, what about this?'

She removed his hand from her cheek and brought it to her mouth.

Lips the make of his fantasies, his dreams, slowly wrapped round his finger.

Fuck!

His cock bucked against his fly with jealous hunger, his mouth dry, panting almost, as soft and supple lips ran along the finger's length, sucking, drawing, deeper, harder, her tongue twirling, making him so goddam crazy he could barely see straight.

Her eyes never left his, even as she drew him back out, licked her lips and cat-got-the-milk smiled.

'What you gonna do about that opportunity, detective?'

Chapter Fifty-Three

Sleepy love-drugged haze enveloped Stacey's brain, while strong arms and a warm body enveloped her in an entirely different, all-too-delicious way.

It seemed that Chase-filled nights came with unexpected pleasures. At the top of her list – spooning. Such an innocuous word.

Such a sensual concept.

Skin on skin. Beating hearts in sync. His breath fanning her neck. Her hands clutching his close to her chest. Legs tangled. Sweat mingling.

Perfection.

Who knew love and romance, topped with mind-melting sex, existed outside the pages of her books? She'd never looked for any of it. In the world of Stacey Holland, a relationship meant relinquishing control. It rendered her soul battered and bruised, her heart broken, all under the guise of "love". And left her flailing in a world where she'd always come out lacking.

Her mother. Brad. And of course, her mind. There lay the worst offender. Because she could see now how she'd enabled the rest to happen.

Thinking about then – the version of herself before now – the acerbic churn in her gut was less, still lingering, but not gut-wrenching debilitating. A vagrant reminder of roads never to be travelled again.

Acknowledging the failure of her marriage had been the first in three steps to getting her life back. Drumming up the courage to leave Brad had been devastating, but life changing. She'd launched her career, soothed her wounded soul by submerging into a fictional world where shit happened, but there was always a happy ending. Her heroines always found love, in the form of some hunky, beta-type hero, and she'd resolved that was enough for her. She'd closed her mind – and her heart – to finding her own happy ever after. For some people, tumultuous happiness just wasn't meant to be. And she'd accepted she was one of them.

Writing was her first and only love. She'd remained faithful, and her muse had responded in kind. She was an award-winning novelist. Carving a career. Following her passion. Each subsequent achievement adding one more notch to her belt of, albeit blinkered, satisfaction.

Until a hunky homicide detective peppered new meaning into the word "satisfaction". Now she had a taste, her formerly unseasoned life held no allure.

Writing was still her passion, but it wasn't alone. The moment was a lifetime coming, but she was happy to have her cake and eat it, too. For however long it lasted.

Life was never a guarantee, less so when a psychopathic killer viewed your writing as some kind of sick mentorship. And now she was laying a trap. Although she trusted Chase would do everything he could to keep her safe, she wasn't naïve enough to discount the risks. Much as every element of their plan had been examined, re-examined, then examined again, there was always a risk.

Which meant their days could be numbered.

Chills crept across her skin, despite the delicious warmth wrapped tightly around her.

Difficult to reconcile that the moment everything was going right in her life, it could all go so terribly wrong with just a metaphorical click of a pen.

But she wouldn't let those thoughts rob her of this special moment. Or the next. She'd cherish every second as if it were her last.

No regrets. No time wasted.

No holding back or waiting. The right time was now.

'Ouch! Son of a motherf–'

Stacey looked up from the computer screen in time to see Chase grip his hand and grit his teeth. That didn't stop the parade of profanities from toppling out of his mouth.

'What?'

Jaw still tightly clenched, he squeezed out one word. 'Nothing.'

His desperate cling to machoism, despite his obvious pain, well-deserved her eye-roll, not to mention the disbelieving snort. 'Yeah. Because every day there's at least one person cracking their nut over "nothing".'

He glared. 'It's just a scratch.'

She hit "save", only too glad to take a break from "the scene". There was none of the pleasure of the past. The joy of a story unfolding, her characters moving stoically toward their finale. Where once she'd drawn pleasure from writing, now the knots in her stomach tightened like a fist seconds before a sucker punch.

Another thirty or so minutes and she'd be done, each typewritten word marching them one step closer to an end from where there'd be no going back.

To draw the killer out of hiding and into their net.

Maudlin or not, the next twenty-four hours were all she could depend upon. After that, her plan would switch from the hypothetical, her only certainty being one of two outcomes – the killer would be caught or she would be dead.

She left computer and menacing thoughts behind and headed for the now indignant Chase. Any distraction at this point was welcome. Even a spitting-at-the-bit sexy detective.

'I'm fine.'

She grabbed his hand. 'Let me see, poor baby.'

It wasn't too difficult to unfurl his fist. He barely had the strength to hold it closed.

Her temperature spiked. 'Hell, Chase. When did you do this?'

'Yesterday. I think I cut it on the window.'

'You think? I'd say you did, and more.'

If the idiot wasn't already in a crapload of pain, she would have slapped him.

What the heck.

He flinched. 'Oww! What was that for?'

'For being a douche.' She ignored his growl, examining what had obviously festered into a large red welt over the past twenty-four hours. 'There's still glass in here.'

She squeezed and he flinched. 'Son of a bitch!' He snatched his hand away.

'You need to see a doctor.'

'No way. It'll be fine.'

'Stop being such a stubborn ass. It's infected. Leave it and who knows what'll happen to your hand.'

Colour ran kicking and screaming from his face. He had to realise the implications of a wound on his right hand, but she pointed them out all the same. 'Can you even grip a gun?'

When he spoke this time, his voice was thick but determined. 'I'm *not* going to a doctor.'

'Fine! I'll get the damn thing out myself. I need a needle, a pair of tweezers and some antiseptic.'

'No way am I letting you armed with a needle anywhere near this.'

'Suits me.' She snagged her mobile from beside her computer and began to dial. 'I'm sure my doctor will be able to fit you in.'

His pounce was reminiscent of Midnight attacking a troublesome fly. He snatched her phone and huffed. Funny that she found it kind of cute instead of infuriating. Just two weeks ago her reaction would have been very different.

'Fine.' Another huff. 'Only because I'll never hear the end of it.'

Yeah, because this wasn't about the pain.

Mules had nothing on Chase when he dug his heels in and she wasn't giving him the chance to change his mind. With a needle from her travel sewing kit and tweezers from her toiletry bag, she ordered him to *sit!* on the edge of the largest ensuite spa bath in the history of mankind.

He braced himself as if she were about to stab him with a one-inch spike.

Seriously? The man faced bullets and bad guys every day and a little needle scared him? Or, more to the point, her with a little needle. She didn't know whether to be insulted or amused.

With a half-grin she settled for a happy medium of both.

She rinsed his palm with hot water and peered at the wound.

'Stop wriggling for god's sake. You're worse than a little kid.' Right down to the grumpy expression. She resisted a fully-fledged grin in case he thought she was enjoying this as much as she was.

She eased the skin apart to look inside.

'Damn Stacey! You'll be the death of me.'

'No. You have that market cornered all by yourself. Why the hell did you leave it so long?'

'Because it was just a cut.'

'With a glass splinter inside.'

'How was I supposed to know that?'

'Oh, I don't know. Perhaps if you stopped being such a guy for one moment and became a man.'

Damn!

A storm unleashed in her brain, a whirling, pounding maelstrom her conscious mind recognised as a mega-reaction to something that should never have bugged her. Certainly not *that* much. That it did, that Chase had ignored his hand and acted as if everything was fine, that nothing bad was happening, cut too close to wounds of the past.

As she ignored the shock in his expression and tilted his hand this way and that, looking for the shard that had aggravated a scrape into a crippling sore – and her nerves into a whorl of anger – every male who'd swanned through her life and made light of what really mattered pummelled her patience. She'd imagined Chase had moved past that need. He'd opened up about his mother, admitted his jokes were just a front to hide the hurt and loss he'd suffered as a child.

She'd understood, he'd said he wanted to be different. For *them* to be different.

They'd talked. Formed a bond. Which led her to believe they'd moved past the point where Chase denied his feelings and hid behind a happy-go-lucky façade of ambivalence.

Apparently not.

Despite what she'd seen as their developing closeness, he hadn't shared something as simple as a cut palm. If he couldn't share the small stuff, how would he share the hurts that really mattered? And if he didn't share, how could they ever get close enough to make their relationship work?

He hadn't learned. Hadn't changed. Nothing that happened between them made a difference. He was still hiding his pain.

What was it that relegated common sense from the male brain?

He flinched, and she unclenched the fingers that held his hand tighter than necessary.

'Hell, Stacey. Don't build this up into more than it is.' He winced as her tweezers hovered just shy of the now exposed splinter. 'It's just a cut.'

The raging storm roiled from her head and rolled out over her tongue.

No matter that he'd consider her off her rocker. Again. This wasn't about a mere cut. This was about her life, her future. And whether she could share it with a man who wasn't willing to share his back with her.

'It's not "just a cut" Chase. This is about you dealing with stuff instead of burying your head, and hand, in the sand. Hiding from the truth doesn't make the problem go away. It festers, and all you get at the end of the day is half a frigging beach in your mouth and a situation so blown out of proportion that you're miles beyond any realm of finding your way back again.'

The pain in his hand had nothing on the tearing wrench in his heart.

It was almost as if she *knew*. She'd summed up his entire life in that one, throw away statement. Over a stupid scrape, of all things.

What cut most? She was right. Life hadn't been simpler because he'd avoided facing the big stuff. It hadn't been easier to blithely carry on and leave the uncertainty to fate. He hadn't enjoyed life more. Or lived it more. Or carved a path that would light up even a little corner of the world after he was gone. Sure, Gracie would miss him. Jag Junior too, until with each passing year memories of Unc' Chase would fade.

Not so much a legacy as a smattering of opportunities missed.

And all of that assumed he had "the gene".

If he didn't?

Well, it didn't sit any better knowing he'd wasted half his life waiting for something that was never going to happen.

A couple more days and he'd know. But, regardless of the outcome, Stacey deserved the truth. When they'd ousted the killer from her life, she should know why he'd acted as he had in the past. And how she'd made a difference to his future. No matter the blood test outcome, she'd given him the courage to reclaim his life back, and whatever her decision, whether she stayed or moved on, his world was forever changed.

She needed to know all that, and somehow, through his bumbling, he needed to tell her.

'There's a possibility I have Parkinson's.'

She blinked. Her hand jerked.

A red-hot poker stabbed up through his palm. *'Fuck!'*

Stacey looked triumphant and all too pleased with herself as she waved her tweezers and the mother of all splinters in front of his swimming eyes. 'Got it!'

No wonder his hand had throbbed like the devil.

She dropped tweezers and glass offender onto a paper towel and grabbed his squeezy bottle of iodine antiseptic.

'Hand?' Her voice brooked no argument. If he hesitated, it was for no other reason than the take-no-prisoners grit in her expression. 'This might sting, but we need to kill any bacteria planning to make your hand their home.'

'I doubt it'll hurt more than – *Holy mother –!'*

Fire ripped through his palm.

This time her grip prevented him pulling his hand away. That she was enjoying this a little too much was more than obvious.

And that she hadn't acknowledged his blurted confession didn't escape him. Even through the distraction of his palm burning like all frigging hell.

'That's it.' A quick daub with some gauze, then she popped a couple of new squares over the now dry but brown stained skin and stuck them down with a criss-cross of fabric tape.

She tilted her head and inspected her work as if it were some inspired adaptation of Monet or Matisse. 'Keep it dry and clean, and if it still hurts in the morning, I'm dragging your sorry ass to the doctor, no matter how hard you kick and scream.'

She stood up from the edge of his still-virgin spa bath, turned her back and busied herself at the sink.

He tried to clench his fist and clenched his teeth instead. Holy shit! Between his head-in-the-sand survival skills and her digging for frigging gold, they'd made a right balls-up of his palm.

Stacey was right. How the fuck was he going to hold his weapon if their plan came to fruition?

She added soap to her palm and turned on the tap. 'Surely you know.'

He stared at the rigid lines of her back, his silence no doubt revealing his confusion.

She sighed, then spelled it out. '*The Parkinson's*. You must know. There are tests that'll confirm whether you're at risk. Right?'

The words came out of nowhere. When he'd wondered if she'd heard his blurted statement at all.

He dropped his still smarting hand to his side and watched as she busied herself drying her hands, packing stuff away, looking anywhere but his direction.

'Yeah. There are tests. I just never took them.'

Her hand stilled, her shoulders rising slowly as she zipped up her enormous, black cat-shaped toiletry bag.

Then she turned to face him, her liquid gaze piercing every barricade he should have erected before the onset of this conversation. 'Why?'

'What difference would it have made? I'd still have the disease. And my life would still end horribly.' He winced.

It was the first time he'd spoken the words aloud, and the muscle-wasting, dignity-robbing reality slammed his hard-won composure sideways. The reality sucked. And scared the living shit out of him. But he couldn't stop now.

His reality was already set the day a random sperm knocked on a random egg and begged to be let in. Nothing he did herewith would change that. But how he lived his life until that equally random gene seized its control, was something he could change. That journey began here. With letting Stacey into his mind, and as a result, his life.

'When you look at things from the outside, taking those tests seems the most logical action. But for me, not knowing meant there was always the chance I didn't have the gene. A little thread of hope that would die the moment the results came in and I *knew*.'

'And you say I'm certifiable.'

'Yeah, well we all have our measures of crazy.'

'So, instead you ignore the whole thing. The master of denial.'

'It's how I cope. How I've always coped.' He scrubbed his chin with the fingers of his non-throbbing hand. 'Growing up, Dad taught me about that whole crying and spilt milk thing. At the end of the day, the floor's still a mess, and that milk ain't gonna clean itself up. His words, not mine.'

His smile was wry, and there was no way that sucker reached his eyes. 'So you just deal with it. Deal and move on. Don't think about what could happen, because it'll happen regardless. Why waste precious time worrying about the inevitable?'

'Funny.' Her smile was as dry as his. 'My childhood was the complete opposite. Mum was constantly telling me to quit hiding and face the truth. Because when you bury your head in the sand, there's always someone who'll sneak up and kick you in the butt when you least expect it.'

'What if you knew you'd get kicked anyway? Then what would you choose?'

He hated the pity in her eyes. Of all the emotions he'd hoped to evoke in Stacey, pity was his least favoured.

'Honest?' The whisper of that word sashayed across his senses. 'I don't have a clue.'

He nodded. Swallowed. Coughed to clear his throat. 'Before today I never had a reason to find out.'

Now he had her wide-eyed and lip-pursed attention. 'Before today? What does that mean?'

'It means I never imagined I'd find someone to share my future with, so there was no point finding out whether I had one or not.' He sucked in a breath. 'Things are different now.'

'Because of me?' The words squeaked out through trembling lips.

He nodded. 'I took the blood tests just over a week ago. Results are due back any day now. By this Friday, at the latest.'

'This Friday? As in, five-days'-time Friday?'

'The one and the same.'

Her lashes fluttered, then her eyes shot open, some manner of emotion filling her expression that he couldn't define. Every muscle in his body locked. So much uncertainty had peppered his life before now, yet the uncertainty of Stacey's response twisted his gut into more knots than it had seen in a lifetime. That she was fundamental to his change, to his views of a future, was unequivocal. If she rejected him now, would his leap into cognisance have been for nothing?

No. Whichever direction his life took from hereon in, it was his choice.

He'd hiked the dark road for so long. That gloomy space wedged between living and loss. Whatever Stacey's answer, whatever she decided, it was better this way. His life would be better this way. And if nothing else, he'd always be grateful to her for leading him toward life's sunnier path.

He dragged in a mouthful of much-needed oxygen. Making the decision didn't make the wait any easier. Or lessen those stomach-clenching knots.

'Why didn't you tell me sooner?'

'I tried.'

'When?' He saw the moment she got it. 'Oh!'

Her cheeks flushed.

He couldn't help but remember too. Her body splayed out over her desk, the chill of her writing room's air on his back, the heat of her body beneath him. Then the confounded arrival of his conscience and his need to tell her before they made that irreversible transition to lovers. Because in some subconscious part of his brain, he'd craved the emotion as well as the physical.

Damn if he didn't sound like a romance writer.

'Your timing was …'

'Questionable?'

Her lips twitched. 'That's one word I might use.'

Along with inconvenient. Insane. Damned uncomfortable. He agreed with them all.

'I wanted to tell you before things got out of control.'

She snorted. 'And how did that work out for you?'

He couldn't stem the snort in his reply. 'Yeah, well control seems in short supply when I'm around you.'

'Finally. Something we have in common.'

Much as he welcomed her admission, it wasn't headline news. Their mutual physical attraction had cut – welcomely – into his sleep the past few nights. He was well aware of how she reacted to his body.

No, this conversation was about something deeper than sex. More than burying himself in her body. He wanted to burrow into her heart.

She turned away again, this time opening his mirror cabinet, rearranging the shelves to tidy away the antiseptic and gauze.

If the disease didn't get him, sure as hell the suspense would. Bad joke? Perhaps. But wasn't she supposed to smile in that gut-wrenching way of hers and tell him the Parkinson's didn't make an iota of difference? That she wanted to be with him, no matter what.

'Taking that step, taking those tests, was incredibly brave, Chase. Knowledge is power.' The cabinet clicked shut and she turned back around, hands clutching the black cat bag to her stomach, her gaze darting toward the door. As if she'd rather be anywhere but where she was now. 'I can't remember who said it, but it's true. Now you'll know what you're dealing with, and be able to, well, deal with it.'

She nodded, her tone, her expression, an indication their conversation had entered its final stretch.

Was he already losing her? Not that he'd had her in any but the physical sense. And the knowledge was a deep fucker of a knife to his chest.

Yet, how could he blame her? Every day he relived the memories, his father enduring the living hell that was watching the woman he loved slowly wilt before his eyes. Every day he'd vowed never to force that life onto another. He wouldn't start now. Especially not with the woman he loved.

Yeah. Idiot that he was, despite trying his darnedest not to, he'd fallen in love.

Perhaps he should have waited to tell her. And maybe if he had, there would have been nothing to tell. All that perfect-world hoo-ha and the happy ever afters that Stacey wrote in her books.

Well, you couldn't write real life.

He'd done the right thing. Stacey should know what signing up for a relationship with him meant, before it was too late for her as well. Before her emotions were as involved as his and the thought of loss cut deep and hard into her very soul.

Yeah, he'd done the right thing.

Even though in his gut it felt so very wrong.

Chapter Fifty-Four

The irony would have made Stacey laugh out loud, if she hadn't wanted to curl up in the closest corner and bawl the living crap out of her soul.

Instead she collapsed onto the bed and closed her eyes to the swirling ceiling above. A million thoughts darted around her mind, like moths bewitched by a flickering flame. She couldn't think straight. Even slightly curved. Nothing.

Connection between brain and tongue had severed the moment Chase shared his pain with her. She'd frozen. Struggled with how to react. So she just … didn't.

He had to feel like shit right now.

Life sucked.

No, that wasn't true. Just her life. Today.

Did she sound egocentric? Perhaps. But with so much promise ahead – another award-winning novel almost finished and an amazing man who thought she made a difference, who loved her enough to change everything about his life so he could draw her into it – all that, and a farm-load of shit was about to hit the fan.

Thinking straight was the least of her problems.

Hell.

Thorny ropes wrapped around her chest and squeezed. Her shaky fingers clutched at the rumpled duvet.

Breathe.

She might die tomorrow.

Breathe.

Chase might die soon after.

Her hands clenched so tight, sharp pain spasmed out from her palms and up her wrist. But not enough to distract from the hurt in her heart.

Hollywood couldn't have written it better. Even *she* wasn't this cruel to her characters. Sure, life was never a certainty, but their certainty had been snatched away with the roll of some freakish dice.

Whichever way she turned, any future with Chase was doomed.

Not that the Parkinson's mattered. Well, it did – it sucked, along with every other sucky thing in their lives. But it didn't make a difference to her wanting to be with Chase. *For better or worse, right?* That was just the "for worse" part. And there'd sure as hell be a lot of the better before the worse hit.

If only she could see past tomorrow. See past her plan and catching a killer no one else had been able to catch.

Were they kidding themselves? This wasn't a Richard Castle form of reality. Novelists didn't team up with detectives to catch the bad guys. That privilege was a thing of the movies. Not real life. And certainly not hers.

She didn't get happy endings.

New starts, yes. But not the really good stuff she gave to her characters after putting them through hell. Was she about to go through hell only to enter another hell at the end of it all?

Spiralling. That's what she was doing.

Positive thinking had fled. In fact, last time she saw it, she was chucking her guts down a toilet bowl after realising Chase believed her to be a murderer.

Life hadn't improved much since then.

Gahhh!

She slammed her fists onto the bed, opened her eyes and pushed herself up. Cracking the sads and sorrys wouldn't save her from this mess. Finishing that scene and taunting the killer would.

Should she go to Chase first? Tell him the Parkinson's wasn't the issue? That her fears were about tomorrow and not being able to think past facing up with a killer.

Only, what good would that do?

Better to get through tomorrow and start afresh.

Because he loved her.

Sure, he hadn't said it. But to say she made the difference, that she was the reason he wanted to have a future, that had to mean he loved her.

And she loved him too. Which meant starting afresh with Chase.

She let her heart flutter, let it sing. Let the heat zip through her body to warm and soothe her soul.

Chase wanted to be with her.

She strode to the door, fingers wrapping around the cold of the door handle.

And she wanted to be with him too.

All the more reason to get back in front of her computer. To make sure they succeeded and survived their plan tomorrow, to live another day.

Chapter Fifty-Five

S*hit!*

Chase didn't stop there. Every F- and B- and S-word he could think up volleyed through his mind. If he could slam his fist through the computer screen and still view the documents in his inbox, he would.

He'd asked Seth for information on a hunch, and that hunch had paid off, with interest.

He grabbed his mobile and hit speed-dial. He needed to know what Jayda was doing now she had a more-than-possible suspect. That she was aware of her fiancé's intel was a given. Had she already arrested the Copycat's sorry ass?

Silence permeated his study, punctuated only by the dull drone of the mobile in his ear.

Stacey was holed up in her room, no doubt finishing the scene designed to catch the man whose face now filled his computer screen. A job that might now be moot.

Not that anything was certain until the suspect was apprehended and his guilt confirmed. Suspicions and rhetoric did not a killer make. But everything on Chase's screen pointed to it. The troubled childhood. The feeling of abandonment. The shunting from foster home to foster home. The need to be noticed. Accepted. Respected. The willingness to go to any lengths to win all three.

The weight pressing against Chase's chest lightened, but it wouldn't lift altogether. That would happen when his hunch paid dividends. When his future was more certain.

Part of him wanted to rush into Stacey's room and tell her the news. Tell her that once the suspect was arrested, she'd be safe again. Free. The other part dreaded the fallout. The hurt when she realised her hero in smarmy armour was a killer.

And there was the other part. The little niggle in the far corner of his brain that wondered if her interest would fade once the threat to her safety was removed.

That was the part he pushed to the side.

This is the voicemail of Detective Jayda Thomasz …

He directed his mind back to the job, to the dispassionate cadence of his partner's voice. The phone beeped and he told her to return his call. Never once did his gaze waver from the deep brown, almost black eyes staring back at him from the screen. He pressed *end* and dropped the mobile onto his desk.

He shouldn't be floored. Every classic sign in existence had been there all along, but still …

He'd considered Ethan a nuisance. Much like a crab that nipped at your toes under the sandy, white-tipped surf at the beach. Never once had he pictured a deep-sea angler fish and its welcoming incandescent glow snaring prey into rows of sharp, jagged teeth.

Had Ethan cat-napped Midnight only to rescue him a few days later so he could play hero with Stacey? Had he performed similar such acts previously? It wasn't unusual for his type of personality – the recognition-seeking kind – to create life or death situations only to leap in last minute and fix them. Something psychologists labelled "hero syndrome".

With firefighters it usually manifested itself with arson. But who was to say it couldn't span more than one type of crime. Like murder.

Stacey had to be familiar with the term. Now she was familiar in more than just name.

Blood thundered through his brain, his clenched fists ramming hard against the wood veneer of his desk.

The bastard better hope the taskforce found him first.

He glared at his mobile willing it to ring. It did nothing but glare blankly back. With a growl he scooped it up and jabbed redial on the screen.

One ring and it clicked.

'Chase.'

He dragged his attention from the computer screen to the voice in his ear, and the job he'd determined to do, no matter what the cost.

'Jayda. Have you found him?'

'Hold on.' Background noises faded and he listened to her even breathing, then the snap of a door as it closed. 'I assume you're talking about Ethan Miklem? Not yet.' Her voice echoed, as if bouncing from blank wall to blank wall. 'His flat in Fitzroy was empty and he hasn't checked in with friends or family for the past three days.'

'And St Kilda fire station where he's stationed?'

'The same. Looks like he caught a whiff of our suspicions and did a runner.'

'I'm not sure how. The info only hit my inbox a couple of hours ago. When did you raid his flat?'

'About the same time.'

Another volley of words spanning A to Z bandied his brain. 'He has no alibi for the last three murders. We can't let this bastard escape.'

'He won't get far now we know who he is.' She cleared her throat. 'We've issued a warrant Statewide, and every media outlet in Australia is airing his picture as we speak. If he so much as buys a stick of gum, we'll get him.'

'How the hell did his past not come up before? Petty misdemeanours, a couple of minor assaults, all before the age of ten. God knows what he did after that never came to light.'

'What can I say? In the name of child protection, his juvenile records were sealed.'

'Which protected him, not his victims.'

'*If* he's our guy.' Her tone was laced with caution.

'Do you have any doubts?'

'Not many. But I'd like to get face-to-face with him just to make sure.'

He couldn't argue with that sentiment.

His screen disappeared beneath a flurry of bubbles. He clicked the mouse and stared at the man he'd been chasing the past two years. The man who'd tossed everything he cared about into a sea of jeopardy.

'There's something else.'

His gut clenched at her tone.

'Bradley Collins didn't show up for questioning yesterday. And he was MIA from his office today. Something he's never been for the past five or so years he's worked there.'

'Shit! Any evidence that Ethan's involved in his disappearance?'

'Nothing.' Papers rustled through the line. 'Your girlfriend find any missing body parts the past couple of days?'

Fuck it all. That was all she needed.

'Nope.' His hand clenched into a fist he wished he could ram through the smarmy killer's jaw. 'I need to be there when you catch this bastard. I want back on the task force.'

He could almost hear Jayda shake her head through the bristling silence.

'Not until you pass that physical. Hackett was adamant.'

'Fuck Hackett. That medical's in less than three days. You're gonna catch this son of a bitch before then.' At least, he hoped to hell that was the case.

'There's nothing I can do, Chase. I'll keep you posted, but Hackett will have my ass too if he so much as hears I'm feeding you info while you're off the case.'

'Which I do appreciate.' He couldn't stop himself. 'Although, I know you're only using it as an excuse 'cos you miss me.'

Her snorted laughter didn't even slightly shift the impact that one, tiny medical exam held over his life. Rock and a hard place had never seemed more crushing. If he took a physical, chances are he'd be off the team for good. And if he didn't, he'd be off the team when they caught the Copycat. Either way, the situation was lose-lose.

Kind of like telling Stacey the man she admired was a serial killer. Being both the deliverer of the news, and male, didn't bode well for Chase. Impossible to miss the pattern of men in her life, their habit of letting her down. Brad. Ethan. Her father. Yeah, he was a scumbag who'd dug up her past and uncovered one Senior Constable Geoffrey Holland. Cop. Alcoholic. Cad. The term may be archaic, but it fit the man to a tee.

That two out of three of those labels fit Chase also, even superficially, was a kick to the guts. And it made him wonder why she'd gone against every instinct to be with him at all.

One more thought for him to push aside.

That a man could walk out on his kid … What would drive him to do it?

Leaving Candace, he could understand. But there'd been no application for custody, no visitation. He'd left his five year old daughter and never looked back. Then a hit and run robbed him of the chance for a turnaround. They'd never found the driver and

Stacey lost the opportunity to front up and ask the questions that must be burning her up inside. That made her look at him as if he'd do the very same thing, given half the chance.

'So tell me how loverboy managed to unseal sealed records?'

She sighed. 'Let's just say that I have no idea how and where Seth gets his information from, and it's better it stays that way. Suffice it to say, it was touch and go with getting a warrant.' Papers rustled in his ear as she cleared her throat. 'Did you know Miklem helped your girlfriend with research for her first book? That the character was a fireman and he ended up being in cohorts with the killer?'

'Yeah, I did know. But nothing indicated a connection that was more than fiction.' Or more than a simple case of caveman-derived jealousy.

He listened while Jayda outlined a shitload of evidence that indicated why Ethan was more than likely the killer. And his mind couldn't help but thrash to and fro. How had he missed it? Had he swayed too far against targeting Ethan in case his suspicions were labelled as the green-eyed monster rather than insightful detecting?

Or had overprotectiveness and angst over Stacey's ex blinded him to Fireman Sam's suitability?

Too late now to figure that one out. Whatever the case, they were where they were. And if Ethan had gone underground, perhaps it would take Stacey's ploy to coax him back out again.

'Thanks for the update. And keep me posted, okay?'

'As long as you do the same.'

He relaxed his fingers long enough to cross them. 'Of course.'

Chapter Fifty-Six

The muted *ping* lured him to his computer, like a cat drawn to the swishing tail of a juicy, fat rat.

He grinned. Savoured the accelerated thrum of blood through his veins.

A click of the mouse and the screen refreshed to catch a stream of words scampering across the page.

So her hiatus from writing was over. *Interesting.*

Had she succumbed to his challenge or had her need to write overridden her fear of repercussions? Was she finally embracing his work, his offerings?

Or were her actions more suspect?

His gaze followed the flow of words, the staccato beat of his heart thrumming against his ribs.

Whatever her motives, the moment he'd awaited had finally arrived.

The patience, the planning, they all led to this one instant.

His story was about to unfold.

Chapter Fifty-Seven

Coffee grounds bounced and rolled across the gleaming countertop. The deep breath didn't still Stacey's hand, but she managed to fill the machine and switch it on all the same.

All those reasons she didn't drink the stuff seemed pointless now. And she needed something with legs. Something to get her through the next six or so hours.

D-Day had arrived.

Dreaded. Danger. Disaster. *Death.*

Such were the joys of a suspense writer. A litany of D-words to evoke a sense of doom. See? Another goodie.

Where were the D-words for success?

Fresh beans tantalised her nostrils, mocking her for resisting their pull for so long.

As the milk warmed, she picked up her mobile and hit "buy" on the link that would see a mega box of Malatyan Turkish delight delivered to Shazz in the next week. If nothing else, picturing the surprise on Chase's face when she presented them to him put the ghost of a smile on hers.

And planning for a future beyond the next couple of days fuelled her hope and lightened her heart in a way nothing else could.

She poured the heated milk into the brew, added sugar and inhaled. Somehow the aroma boosted her spirits. Funny how coffee had a power that tea was sadly lacking.

Closing her eyes, she sipped deeply and sighed.

Now all she needed was a tub of Aunt Milly's Choco-Sensations and she'd be in heaven. A transient place, but a type of heaven all the same.

Eyes still closed, she savoured. Imagined a place with sandy beaches, lulling waves and no diseases or serial killers or bullies determined to make her into something she wasn't.

'Stacey Holland partaking of forbidden fruit? What *is* the world coming to?'

She spun around and hot liquid sloshed over the edge of the mug. It only just missed her hand, splattering onto the floor at her feet. Chase lounged in the doorway, looking hotter and more flavoursome than anything she could pour into a cup.

She dumped her remaining drink onto the bench and snagged a couple of paper towels, squatting to mop up the mess. And subdue her rampant heartbeat. 'It felt like a coffee kind of day.'

One brow jumped so high it almost leapt clear from his forehead. Such was the extent of his surprise. A little of the clamp in her shoulders relaxed. Last thing she needed was a discussion on why she was drinking something she hadn't touched the past three years.

He nodded. 'I was thinking something stronger, like whiskey. But I get your drift.'

She straightened, tossed the towels and retrieved her mug. Only then did her gaze drop to his hand. Or rather, what was in it.

Any calming effect from the coffee evaporated.

'These just arrived for you.' He waved the flowers ever so slightly and her nose began to twitch.

The bouquet was oversized and garish, and the sickly sweet fragrance made her want to puke all over it. Already her eyes were watering and her nose began to itch. Her stomach knotted so tight, she wondered if it would ever unravel. How did Brad know she was here? Unless he was the reason.

Shit! Was he responsible for the tree? For more?

Her head swirled and she gripped the bench at her back with her free hand. 'Chuck them.'

'You don't know who sent them.'

'I do and they belong in the bottom of the trash.'

Chase eyed the extravagant display of wealth and power. *Control.* 'Who are they from?'

'Brad.'

His gaze narrowed. 'Did you know he hasn't shown up to work since Monday?'

Something in his expression sent shivers deep into her bones. 'You think the Copycat hurt him?'

'That was the assumption, until these showed up.'

'They don't change things. He has a standing order with the florist.'

'Yet they came here. How would he know?'

She had no answer to that one. Nothing that didn't make her stomach curl.

'Doesn't he know you're allergic?'

'Very well.'

'And he still sends them. Nice guy.'

'Yeah. The best.'

'Does he do this often?'

'Enough.' She didn't need to tell him how often. Her ex's fortnightly reminder that he was still out there, still watching. Still believing she was nothing.

'Have you thought of getting a restraining order?'

'Yeah. Because they're always ultra-effective.'

The flowers hovered before her, as if waiting for her to take them. Just the thought and the skin on her fingertips burned. They were hateful and toxic and everything that she'd left behind in a relationship that had almost killed her. That he'd found her and sent them, today of all days, couldn't be coincidence. Brad wasn't a coincidence kind of guy. He was deliberate and ruthless and inflicted pain any way he could.

And it was working.

'In case you were wondering, I checked for bugs. There were none.'

Of course not. Subtle wasn't Brad's forte either. If he wanted to snoop, he'd be less restrained. Like the time he placed a spy watch on their bedroom dressing table to check she didn't cheat on him when he was out.

The memory shivered up her spine. 'The only creepy crawly that needs checking is the bastard who sent them.'

'I wasn't talking that type of bug.'

'I don't care, Chase. Get rid of them. *Please.*'

At last, he didn't argue. Just left the room and tossed them, same as he'd done with the bouquet he'd bought her all those days ago.

She stared into her almost empty mug, but the coffee dregs didn't help. Her stomach swirled.

Something stank.

Not flowers.

The whole scenario. The killer seeking her out. The attempts to muddy her career, her reputation. Brad's final words moments after their solicitors declared them legally divorced. The acerbic tone still burned every time she remembered. Yet she shivered as if caught in a blizzard.

She'd lingered inside her solicitor's sixth floor offices until way after he'd left. When she'd finally crept through the exit, certain she was safe, he'd been waiting outside. Before she could turn back, he'd grabbed her wrist.

The resulting purple-blue band had taken two weeks to fade to a jaundiced yellow.

You think you're free now, bitch? Think again. He'd waved at the papers in her hand, spitting each word through thin, twisted lips. *That paper means fuck all. And for the rest of your pathetic, piss-poor life you're going to regret this.*

You're nothing. You'll always be nothing. A boring, empty, worthless excuse for a woman. And some namby-pamby book deal won't change that.

Every heartbeat stabbed against her ribcage, memories rising, real, tangible, searing the back of her throat. His face, ugly and intimidating, was as clear in her mind as it had been that day. The reek of his garlic and ginger lunch still thick on his breath.

One day everything in your life will turn to shit, and I want you to know it all started today. This moment. With this action.

He'd yanked her toward him. Slapped his lips hard over hers. Stole every bit of freedom she'd believed she'd won by signing the papers and severing their relationship.

Struggling had been fruitless, his strength far outweighing hers. Only when he was ready did he thrust her aside. Her back had slammed against the building's brick façade and he'd sneered down at her as if she were less than a bug beneath the heel of his shoe.

You're mine, Stacey. And I don't give up what's mine without a fight.

Dark, dispassionate eyes had flicked over her body before he'd left her there, trembling, trying her damnedest not to cry.

Then she'd stumbled her way home and worked her butt off to make a life, to forget the psychological hold he had on her and be free.

The fortnightly flowers had been distasteful but a relief – she'd believed them to be the extent of his "fight". Until now.

Had she been wrong?

Would Brad use murder to make a statement? To make her regret leaving him for freedom, and for her career? To control her once again?

Her breath faltered.

'I could go a coffee too.'

The words pulled her back to the kitchen and the lukewarm mug in her hands. And the man opposite, who poured himself a coffee and topped up hers, all the while watching her with an intensity that frayed her nerves like a loose thread frayed a sweater.

She sipped, willing bitter and sweet to wash away memories that no matter how hard she tried, just wouldn't let go.

Chase brushed past and heat sizzled up her arm. In fact, she was hard pressed to find any part of her body that wasn't aware of him.

He bustled around his kitchen as if he felt comfortable in it. Well, his cooking prowess, as far as Italian cuisine went, proved that.

White cotton strained across his shoulders, every flex and release burning her vision, her body, her mind, to the point it was impossible to think of anything else.

'So, there's something I need to tell you.'

She dragged her eyes back to his, her mind back to the fact that in a few hours they'd be further setting her plan in motion. One that could bring her face-to-face with a murderous monster.

Perhaps Brad.

She knocked back a mouthful of bile with a swig of hot brew, burning her mouth and tongue in the process. Distraction, at least, from thoughts better not contemplated.

Deep breath. 'I think the killer might be Brad.'

Chase froze, surprise cutting his features as if she'd announced his jokes were the most hysterical thing she'd ever heard.

'Why do you think that?'

'I think he's obsessed with me.' Heat scalded her cheeks.

Saying the words aloud made them sound even more ridiculous than they'd sounded in her mind. But now she'd started, she had to keep going.

'Since the day our divorce came through, I've received a flower delivery every second Friday. It was a tradition Brad started when we were married, because he thought making our own traditions would be cute, and doesn't every normal woman like flowers?'

Chase's disgust mirrored her own. 'But with your allergy they would have made you sick.'

'Yep.' Another swig of coffee, but the rock lodged in her throat wouldn't budge. 'He told me to take a pill and get over it. To stop being a princess and act like a proper wife for a change.'

'The bastard!'

'In both character and birth. His mother never told him who his father was. I'm not even sure she knew. But I think the taint in his past made him even more determined to be "normal". To live a normal life. Do what everyone else did to fit in and make a name for himself, despite his dubious beginnings.'

'He laid his insecurities onto you. Tried to make you small so that he felt bigger.'

She nodded. 'Classic small-dog syndrome. Not a technical term, but it fits.' She shot him a wry smile. 'I thought his threats to control me related to the flowers. But what if it's more?'

'He threatened you?'

'The day our divorce was finalised. And every once in a while when he decides to visit, like last week. But what if he's been watching me? Killing people to get my attention?'

'You need a restraining order and we need to find the son of a bitch.'

Her breath caught sticky and syrupy at the back of her throat. 'So you think he could be the Copycat?'

Instead of looking as if they'd solved the case, he looked away. Knocked back what must have been half his mug of strong and steaming coffee.

'Your ex may be an asshole, but I don't think he's the killer.'

'He's perfect for it. Why–' Something clicked in her brain. 'You wanted to tell me something before. Was it about the case?'

'We think we've identified the Copycat.' His shoulders squared, as if bracing for an attack.

From her?

Her heartbeat stepped up its stampede. 'And?'

His gaze locked with hers, and he hesitated in a look that said his news was bad. Worse than bad. Unbearable.

'Who, Chase? I'm not so fragile that I'll fall apart with a name.'

She blinked, appearing just as fragile as she professed not to be. Then she dragged in a deep breath. 'Nothing can be worse than thinking my ex-husband is a serial killer.'

That was debatable. Regardless, he nodded.

Decision made.

'It's Ethan.'

It didn't make sense.

Stacey's hand froze on a pair of black pants hanging in her closet, her mind as thick as a batch of triple-choc cookie batter.

A decision on what outfit to wear to a sting was trifling when measured against real-life dramas.

Ethan was a cold-blooded killer.

Her hand dropped and she collapsed back against the doorjamb.

Every sense screamed against the idea. He'd helped her out more times than she could count. Saved her. Saved Midnight. Insight stabbed her brain. How many times had he appeared when she was in trouble? When something bad happened. He'd taken charge, turned it around and made it good.

She'd been so relieved. So grateful.

So incredibly stupid.

He'd kissed her.

She kissed him back.

She scrubbed her fist across her mouth, swallowing thick sawdust down her throat.

All those people. Dead. Dismembered. To get her attention? For what? So she'd turn to him? Fall in love with him?

Something that may well have become reality if not for Chase.

Any food in her stomach and she would have chucked. But somewhere between luring a killer and finding out he was a friend, her appetite had fled. Just as well, or she'd be staring at the bottom of a toilet bowl. Something she'd been doing an awful lot of lately.

If not for Chase, she might have fallen for Ethan. He was everything Brad wasn't. And he'd seemed genuine, seemed to really care for both her and her pets. He'd given her Cuddles, for god's sake.

Respected her allergies and hadn't told her to "man up". Spent hours teaching her about caring for snakes, handling them.

Her heart argued it had to be wrong, but her head with its inner psychologist said it was a distinct possibility. There was his history. His lack of alibi for recent murders.

They'd found her missing polypropylene knife in his apartment.

Why would it be there if he wasn't the one who swapped it for its real, blood-soaked counterpart?

Add to that the fact that he was now missing …

All through this hellish nightmare, somewhere in the back of her mind, she'd believed knowing the killer's identity would make a difference. Would make her feel safe. All she felt right now was sick. And about as far from safe as she'd feel inside the jaws of a shark.

The rack of clothes before her blended into a meandering mish-mash of colour.

She lifted her chin and pushed her back away from the hard wood.

The only way to change all that was to catch the bastard. That meant carrying out her plan and luring him out of whatever hole he'd scuttled into.

What to wear?

What you always wore to a battle.

Armour.

'Team Leader one, this is Team Leader two. Come in.'

Chase's earpiece crackled, but not so much that he couldn't pick the waver in Stacey's voice. 'I'm here, Stacey, reading you, loud and clear.'

He dragged his gaze from the sway of Stacey's ass to the wavering Hook, Line and Sinker sign on his iPad, courtesy of the camera hidden in Stacey's cap. The scene panned left, then right, delivering a full view of the surrounding car park. He shifted behind the steering wheel, popped a couple of sticks of gum in his mouth and stretched his legs to prevent the looming attack of pins and needles.

That's a "check" on the camera and mic. If only he could do the same for the entire wacko plan.

They were taunting a sick son of a bitch without the backup of his unit. He needed his head examined.

Only the bastard had gone into hiding, and how else to tempt him back out but by using the woman with whom he was obsessed? In theory, the idea made sense. But in the harsh reality of a tightrope walk, there were so many things that could go wrong. Yeah, he may have agreed to the whole "trap a killer" scenario, but that didn't mean he had to like it. Or that he believed it was the best option. He just didn't have an alternative or the time to formulate one.

At least now *they* were running the show, not the psycho bastard playing out his sick power games.

And if Ethan was out there, which he didn't doubt, this was the moment they'd lure him into a false sense of security. Into thinking he was still the one calling the shots.

The superstore's sign bobbed at the top of the iPad screen, growing larger with every one of Stacey's shaky steps. Spearmint burst across his tastebuds as he raised his gaze to the windscreen and watched her superfine body recede between the regimented lines of parked vehicles.

Peripheral vision took in the surrounding area – the movement of cars, customers, a dog tied up just shy of the entrance. But always his eyes returned to Stacey. A magnet to his thoughts, his emotions.

He swallowed, dragged his gaze back to the iPad screen. 'Eyes and ears are a check. Looking good, Stacey.'

'You better not be checking out my ass.'

With a hoot of laughter, he nearly spat his gum clear out of his mouth. 'And here I thought you wanted me to check it out. Isn't that why you wore that tiny impersonation of a skirt?'

'You think I wore this skirt for you?'

'A man can hope, can't he?'

Silence.

He heard her unsteady breathing. Imagined her nervously nibbling at her bottom lip. And just when he wondered if he'd taken their banter too far, she swallowed. 'The skirt wasn't for you, but the black lace G-string underneath it is.'

This time he damn near swallowed his gum.

That she had the power to turn him into a blithering idiot with just a few words was testament to how far he'd fallen. He swallowed. This wasn't the time for getting so hard he couldn't think straight, or losing his wits so he was unable to keep her safe. Plenty of time for that later.

'Why the silence, detective? You don't like my choice in underwear?'

Was she kidding? He – and all his moving, reacting body parts – liked it just fine. Even better if they were somewhere to enjoy every inch of that lace, and the delights that lay beneath it.

He swallowed. 'I'll show you just how much I like your underwear choice, later. Right now, we're working. That means cutting the chatter, otherwise someone's going to think you're either looney or speaking into a mic.'

'Or talking on my mobile.' She waved the blue rectangular monster across his view.

'Clever girl.'

'Did you ever doubt it?'

'If I say "yes" does that mean tonight's off?'

She snorted. 'Depends how you behave between now and then.'

His thoughts were anything but good. Behaving bad with Stacey was a pull he couldn't resist. He just had to resist it for now.

'Put your phone away and concentrate on what you're supposed to be doing.'

'That's a big ten-four, Team Leader.' She dropped her phone into her purse and looked around. 'All clear in the perimeter, boss. I'm going in.' He almost expected the Bond theme to follow.

He shook his head, unsure whether to laugh or growl. He let loose a mix of both, lips twitching, voice gruff and low. 'Knock it off, Stacey. *Focus.*'

The jokey two-way radio chit-chat was her way of forgetting how shit-scared she was, of coping, of checking he was still watching her back. He got that. But the situation was far from funny, and his sense of humour had left the moment she'd become a killer's target.

And she should have known by now that he'd do anything to keep her safe.

The sign disappeared and the large glass entrance filled the screen before he got his first view of the superstore's interior since last week.

'Okay, I'm in.'

He scrubbed his chin. 'I can see that.'

Too many TV cop shows had her ten-fouring like she was right in the middle of one.

'I see what you see, remember?' If he was an eye-roller, that's exactly what he'd be doing now. 'Just make your way through the store, get what you need, and keep looking around so I get a bird's-eye view of the place. Let me know if you even catch a glimpse of someone that resembles you-know-who.' He squinted at the screen. 'And quit with the talking.'

'Damn, you're bossier than a bull-rider.'

He snorted. 'And you just worked that out?'

'Nah. Knew it the moment I met you.'

'Stacey?'

'Yeah?'

'Stop. Talking.'

She *hrumphed*. Only, not with the exasperation of the past.

Rows of camping furniture and tents flashed by. Tackle boxes, flies, rods. The basket in her hand slowly filled, and as she scanned the area, he scanned it with her, looking for some indication that the bastard was watching.

His gaze skipped over the rotund father and his equally rotund son; the old-timer with the white shock of hair and red plaid shirt; the family of four; the two teenagers, one dark-haired, one light.

No one stood out. After all, if Ethan showed, he'd have to show in disguise.

Not that he had to be in the store to be watching.

'Look up at the ceiling.'

'Oh, so *you're* allowed to talk?' She looked, even as she whispered her sass.

He counted three cameras in her vicinity. One above, one right and one left.

'Turn around and do the same.'

'Bossy!' At least she muttered it through clenched teeth, and from the sound, without moving her lips.

With everything going on, she still had spirit. What he admired about her. *Loved*.

His grip on the iPad tightened. Every time the thought speared his mind, it threw him anew.

Yep, give the man half a dozen Havanas. He was in love with this wacky blue monster, snake-loving, danger-wielding, cookie-craving cat-woman.

Emotion rolled over him, minus the panic. The fear. The desire to run and hide and dodge as he would have in the past.

Wonder made his head spin and his body believe it could soar.

It still blew his mind to think that when this bloody mess was stuffed back into its box and they were free to do whatever the hell they liked, he was going to start the rest of his life with Stacey. With Midnight and Cuddles and a dog. *Buddy*. He'd always wanted a dog named Buddy. Nothing stopping him from getting one now. They'd just have to work around her allergies. Or get a Midnight version of a dog. Something.

But they'd work it out, together.

Rows of hooks and flies and sinkers and lures filled his vision. Then she turned to the fishing line.

'H'lo. It's Stacey, isn't it?'

She whirled back around, and all Chase could see was a broad chest and pinned nametag. *Burt*. Mr Cheerful and over-helpful. Stacey's gaze lifted and a blotchy pink face came into view. The man grinned ear-to-ear and Chase's gut tightened.

'You have a good memory for customers.'

Ogling brown eyes gobbled her up. 'Only ones worth remembering.'

Stacey chuckled, but Chase caught the nervous wobble in her voice. 'I bet you say that to all the girls.'

Burt's grin widened and he nodded toward her basket. 'Need any help?'

She glanced at its contents, then shook her head. 'I'm done.'

'Let me carry that for you.' He coaxed the basket from her hand. 'So, you like fishing? You and your husband must go out an awful lot.'

'I'm not married.'

'Boyfriend, then.'

'I don't have a boyfriend.'

Chase's jaw clenched as he watched the cash registers bob slowly closer.

'How is that possible?'

'I just never met the right guy.'

The man dumped her basket on the counter. If his grin spread any wider it'd span the entire Southern Hemisphere.

Chase wanted to arrest the bastard on the spot. Neither reasonable nor logical, as far as reactions go – but where Stacey was concerned, both sentiments had well and truly left the building.

That Burt had the hots for Stacey didn't make him a suspect. His interest didn't make him anything other than a normal red-blooded male attracted to a very attractive woman. Which in turn made him a pain in Chase's ass.

Stacey's joking refusal when he asked for her number was the man's only saving grace. And the fact that she was mindful enough of their mission to look up and around every few minutes. Obviously not as taken with Burt as he was with her.

As her gaze – and hence the camera – wandered, he spotted nothing out of the ordinary. That didn't mean Ethan wasn't around somewhere, watching, waiting. He almost certainly was.

And Chase wanted more than anything for him to take the bait now.

Because if he didn't, that meant enacting part two of Stacey's plan. The part where they'd both come face-to-face with the killer.

Chase unlocked the front door and drew his gun, scanning the entrance before striding inside. 'What's your ETA?'

'Ooh, I love it when you talk all professional and detectivey.'

The thick heat in Stacey's voice sizzled up through his earpiece, burning his brain. What it did to brain number two wasn't much different.

'ETA five minutes. Any reason for your hurry, detective?'

Nothing other than he was so fricking hard, he could have split wood. 'We have unfinished business to discuss. Namely, your choice in underwear.'

Her sharp intake of breath was gratifying, but not nearly as gratifying as her in his bedroom right now, in those panties and nothing else. Damn, he was pathetic. And he didn't give a shit.

'Why Chase, are you saying you don't approve?'

'Won't know until I've made a full and thorough inspection.'

'I like the sound of that.'

He did too.

Weapon still drawn, he made a quick sweep of the house, inside and out. Taking care of business so he'd be free to take care of pleasure when she walked through the front door. Part one of their plan was over. Part two was set for tomorrow. Until then, he had a whole lot of hours free and nothing but Stacey to fill them with.

He adjusted the shrinking crotch of his jeans and re-entered the living room.

And froze.

The hairs on his neck prickled.

Something wasn't right.

Weapon drawn, he circled, scrutinising every familiar item, every surface, only to stop before the snake enclosure.

One hand flew to his earpiece. 'Cuddles is out of his cage.' He stared at the open door, then scoured the room. Cuddles was nowhere to be seen.

Was the animal some freakish Houdini reincarnation?

'Damn!'

His thoughts exactly.

Worry replaced every ounce of tease in her voice. 'Can you see him?'

Again his gaze combed the area. There were no hat stands for wayward snakes to curl around and make his search easier. Nothing that looked enticing enough for a snake to wrap onto.

'Nope. I'm searching now.'

'I'm only a couple of minutes away. Why don't you wait?'

His heart slammed against his ribs. 'And waste all those snake-handling lessons? Not a chance.'

You can do this.

It was almost as if the snake were testing him. Or maybe it was the universe.

What did Stacey say? *A relationship with me means having a relationship with my animals?* A kind of "love me, love my pets" type of thing. Well, he was just about to show her how frigging much.

Crawling on all fours, he searched under couches, the TV cabinet, anywhere one and a half metres of reptile could curl up and hide.

'He's not in the living room. I'll take a look in the kitchen and bedrooms.'

'Be careful, Chase. Remember not to spook him. Let him know you're there, and try not to reach across his head.'

'Don't say you're worried about me.'

'Not you. Cuddles. He's sensitive.'

'You sure know how to wound a guy.'

Her laughter was deep and throaty, and made him want things now that had to be on hold until a certain reptile was back in his cage.

'Find my snake and I'll make it up to you.'

This time the accelerated beat of his heart wasn't reptile-related. 'You have a deal.'

Slowly, cautiously, he cleared the kitchen and moved down the hall toward the bedroom.

He dropped to his knees and missed a breath. 'He's under the bed.'

'Can you move it without spooking him?'

'Sure thing.'

Fingers wrapped tight around the bedpost, he pulled, sliding and bumping the bed over the carpet fibres until he met a beady yellow gaze.

You can do this.

He'd held Cuddles almost half a dozen times. Picking him up and putting him back in his cage shouldn't be that difficult.

He bent forward.

Only …

He froze. 'What colour are Cuddles's eyes?'

'Green. Why?'

'Shit!'

He straightened, watching the snake leisurely uncoil, its long length hugging the wall, heading his way.

'What is it, Chase?'

'This snake has yellow eyes.'

'Are you sure?'

'Yeah.' He backed up, slowly. 'I think I found the zoo's missing Mamba.'

'Chase, you need to get out of there.'

The panic in Stacey's voice matched the panic beating the crap out of his heart. He inhaled. Blinked.

Told himself he had too much to live for to be bitten by a snake today and die.

The large green lump slithered toward the bed, then disappeared. And much as looking into those cold, beady eyes freaked him out, not being able to look into them freaked him more.

Fuck!

All the reasons he hated snakes rushed to the forefront of his mind. Like the fact that Australian snakes were among the deadliest in the world.

Only this snake wasn't an Aussie. It was a Mamba, lethal, brought here to kill him. Work of the Copycat Killer. It had to be.

He breathed in. Out. Edged slowly backwards to avoid spooking the creature now somewhere under the bed. That *he* was spooked was incidental.

'Chase, what's happening?'

Speech was impossible past his Arctic throat. Cold. Dry. Barren.

He was almost at the doorway.

He reached back to steady himself. All he had to do was back through and then close the door.

Piece of pie.

One more step to safety.

His chest constricted, as if one of the suckers had wrapped around his lungs and was slowly squeezing. He stepped back. So close.

The door swung slowly toward the frame. Closing.

His heart beat wild. Erratic.

A flash of green darted out from under the bed.

The long body looped back over itself in a figure eight and slithered across his toes. His foot jerked.

Fire stabbed his ankle through his jeans.

He whirled round, but the snake was gone.

And so was he, it seemed.

'Chase!'

His head throbbed.

'Stacey!' *Damn.* 'The snake escaped.' He yelled into the mic, because maybe yelling would make her listen to sense. 'He's either in the hall or the living room. Stay where you are.'

The front door squealed open on its hinges, then it clicked to a close. Of course she'd ignored him. The woman was as stubborn as all hell.

He slumped against the wall, head resting in his hand. 'You need to stay away.'

His ankle throbbed, warmth flushing up through his calf from two little puncture marks and venom that, even now, was stealing through his system. The room swayed like a car at the top of a Ferris wheel.

'Too late.' She appeared in the doorway, all flushed cheeks, windblown hair and mega-attitude.

One look at him and she had her mobile in her hand. In clipped tones she gave the emergency call centre his details, then she brushed past and into the en suite. Cupboards banged, things clanked and then she was back. 'Where'd he get you?'

'My ankle.'

'Sit!' As if he was a dog.

His lungs burned, each breath a shallow, wrenching drag from his chest. Before his knees buckled and he lost the benefit of choice, he allowed himself to slowly sink to the floor. 'The mamba could come back any second.'

The words sounded distant, as if they'd emanated from someone else's body, someone else's mouth.

Stacey closed the door between the bedroom and the rest of the house.

He felt pressure on his shoulder. 'Lie down and let me worry about that. I've already called the zoo. A handler's on his way. Another is bringing some antivenom. He'll meet the ambulance on the way to the hospital.' She dropped down beside him, dropping a pile of stuff into her lap before removing his boot. Then with a large pair of scissors, she hacked at his trouser leg right up to his thigh. 'I hope you're not too attached to these.'

He didn't give a flying fuck about his jeans.

There was a deadly snake on the loose, ready to attack the moment they opened the bedroom door.

Untamed curls and red-ripe lips rippled and swirled before him.

He swallowed. Tried not to lose focus and give in to the toxic thrum of poison overpowering his bloodstream. 'I don't want to lose you, Stacey.'

Amber-flecked emerald met his gaze. 'Then we're on the same page. You are not going to die, Chase Durant. Not today. Not under my watch.'

Beneath the denim, the skin surrounding the double puncture marks was blue, and so goddam swollen, no surprise if it split open like a banana peel. The entire leg throbbed like fucking buggery.

'I need you to stay still and calm, Chase. Can you do that?'

He didn't have a clue, but he nodded anyway, and the room swam a little more.

Stacey grabbed a bandage, and with shaky hands began to wrap from just above his toes. As she covered the bite, she grabbed a pen and drew an X. He would have asked her why, but the words wouldn't line up and form more than a jumble of nonsense.

'You're lucky I renewed my St John's first aid qualifications last summer.' She shot him a wobbly grin but her fingers didn't once pause with their task. 'Because of an unusually high spate of snakebites, we spent a couple of hours on the topic. I got an A in wrapping, but I guess the proof will be in the packaging.' Another grin, then she returned her gaze to his leg.

Funny. Of all the ways he'd imagined leaving this earth, this was never one of them.

The staccato of his beating heart reverberated through his chest.

'When I pictured you flat on your back, this wasn't quite what I was after. You sure know how to throw a girl off her guard, detective.'

Stacey's voice flowed like the silky slide of water over his skin. She kept talking. To keep him occupied. To stop him thinking of what would happen if his body succumbed to the poison battering about his system.

He didn't want to die. Not when he'd finally found a reason to live.

Some distant portion of his brain registered he couldn't feel his leg. Couldn't feel Stacey's touch or the pressure of the bandage, which, if he edged his head to the side and looked down, he could see had just passed his knee. It was as if he'd been chopped in half at the hip and everything below ceased to exist.

Stacey floated above him, her wavering outline steadfastly wrapping his leg while she continued to talk in soft, soothing tones.

He couldn't remember a time he'd been happier. Ludicrous when you considered the crap in his life – serial killers, a possible deadly diagnosis and even deadlier dose of venom racing through his system.

Only a few minutes since the toxin had entered his bloodstream and already his senses were fading. If his heart beat any faster, it might damn well burst *Alien*-style from his chest.

'Chase? Are you still with me?'

Cool hands brushed his brow, his cheek. Her warm gaze burning up his vision, his heart.

He wasn't planning on dying, but if he lost any say in the matter, he needed her to know the truth.

'If I don't make it out of this–' The words left his tongue, fuzzy, thick, unsteady.

'Don't say that. You have to fight it, Chase.'

'I will. Am. But if I don't–' He swallowed against what felt like a thick coating of cottonwool and grit, pushing his words out on a weedy rasp. 'I love you, Stacey.'

She nodded, as if he hadn't just offered up his soul, his life, and her lips twitched into a wondrous half-smile. 'Want to know something funny?'

The answer jammed in his throat, a wracking cough ripping out from his chest, burning up the back of his gullet.

His vision swam. Greedy, grasping claws scrabbled out from the murk blanketing his mind, dragging him toward a fathomless black hole that tottered just beyond the brink of consciousness. He fought it, focusing solely on the swimming green of her gaze.

She blinked, and even through the haze, he could see the moisture in her eyes. 'I love you too.'

Despite her orders for calm, his heart hammered.

Then the world turned black and disappeared.

Pacing had never been her thing. What was the point? All that back and forth, wearing the floorboards, carpet or tiles out for no real gain.

It made no sense.

Stacey spun on her heel and tracked back the way she'd just come.

Yet here she was. *Pacing.*

Engaging in that useless activity. Why? Because it made her feel as if she were doing *something*. And she needed to feel that now. Needed it with every storming, battering, racing beat of her heart.

How had she moved from cursing Chase with insect infestation to considering the impossibility of facing a life without him?

She whirled around and almost slammed straight into a wall of starched white and blue. She pulled up short of the blonde, blue-eyed nurse she'd accosted for information every half hour for the past six or more hours. 'Stacey Holland?'

Her smile was stiff, while her heart charged full throttle in her chest. The woman was probably a year or two younger than her, yet her demeanour made her seem years older.

'Mister Durant has been transferred to ICU in the Eastern wing. He won't be allowed visitors until tomorrow.'

'Can I at least see him?'

'Not until he's stabilised, no.'

'Can you at least tell me if he's going to be okay?'

'That information's limited to family members. I've already told you more than I should.' Which was pretty much zilch.

Stacey inhaled, her heart barely skipping a beat as she took in the name on the woman's uniform. 'Well, Sally, does a fiancé fit into that category?'

Chapter Fifty-Eight

*C**rap! Did she really say she was Chase's fiancé?*

And why didn't she want to run, hide and vomit at the thought? Not being freaked at the idea of being linked to Chase freaked her even more. Chase was right in his first impressions of her – she was a complete and utter nutcase.

Nurse Sally looked pointedly at her bare left ring finger.

She pressed her palm hard against her side to stop its shaking. 'We don't believe in rings.' The words rushed out before the woman could comment. 'It's the vows that hold us together, not a loop of metal and stones.'

One thing about being a writer, the imagination never wanted for stories. And this was a ripper. A story, nothing more. But if it secured the information she needed …

'Fair enough.' Sally's narrowed gaze accompanied a sharp nod.

At least she wasn't debating the point.

'Chase's body took a beating, but luckily the envenomation wasn't severe. Whether the snake was a juvenile or it didn't get a good grip when it bit, I don't know. But your fiancé's responding to the antivenom, and whoever bound his leg at the scene restricted the spread of venom considerably.'

'That was me.'

Brows a few shades darker than her hair arched upward. 'Well, you did a good job. I know the ER doctors commented that your mark over the location of the bite enabled them to cut open the bandage without completely removing it.'

'St John's first aid.'

'Just as well you paid attention.'

She'd thought the exact same thing as she'd bound his leg and prayed he'd make it.

'Will he be okay?' She held her breath.

'We'll know more in twelve to twenty-four hours. We're monitoring for symptoms of envenomation as well as adverse reactions to the antivenom.' For the first time, her severe features softened. 'You should go home and get some rest.'

Home.

The word gouged a large, gaping hole through her chest.

Where was that? Her house lay crumbled under a tree and Chase's place seemed less welcoming and safe without him. 'I'll stay here.'

'We close this ward to visitors after eight. You'll need to wait elsewhere. Here.' She handed over a small square of paper. 'This is his new room number. Show up any time after 9am and if he's stabilised you might be able to see him.'

And that was it.

There was nothing more for her to do.

She handed Sally a card with her mobile number. 'Please call me if anything in his condition changes.'

'His next of kin's been notified. She's interstate and won't make it here till the morning.'

'Is that his sister, Gracie?'

The woman didn't answer.

St Andrews was smaller than its larger, city-based counterparts and well known for its friendly family-infused ambiance. Seems that Sally had missed the memo.

Although, to be fair, the nurse had given out more information than she probably should. Stacey had to be grateful for at least that. She wandered downstairs, wandered into a café and ordered coffee. Two in two days. The habit, the need for something other than life to pick her up, was returning. And she lacked the energy and inclination to stop it.

A corner table freed and she snapped it up, dropping her weary body into hard unforgiving plastic and turning her gaze to the window, away from the pristine white walls and floors that reminded her of where she was and why she was there.

The hospital car park sprawled beneath an expanse of royal blue. In the distance, fiery streaks of reds, oranges and yellows banked the horizon, but they were fading fast. With dusk came darkness. Grasping black fingers stealing the light from the earth as surely as a killer was stealing the light from her heart.

She squeezed her eyes closed only to open them again in an effort to drive away the dark. As if that were possible.

What was his plan?

The snake hadn't been meant for her, of that she was sure. Cuddles was as familiar as the slide of her laptop keys beneath her fingertips. From a distance she would have picked the exchange immediately.

That left one explanation.

The killer – she still found it near impossible to think of him as Ethan – had been aware of their movements. He knew Chase would arrive home first. Counted on him looking for Cuddles. And he'd counted on him not recognising the difference until it was too late.

It had almost been too late.

She blinked. Weary eyelids warred with the growing moisture beneath them.

If she hadn't been so keen to get back. Hadn't raced every orange light and pushed the speed limit as far as she had, she would have been minutes later. Valuable minutes equating to a greater spread of poison through his body. As it was … The Eastern Green Mamba was one of the top venomous snakes in the world. A beautiful creature, but deadly.

She concentrated on breathing past the catch in her throat.

Just hopefully not today.

She focused on the fading light outside. The slow spill of cars exiting the hospital grounds as visiting hours came to a close. Anything but the aching tear in her heart.

Icy fingers wrapped tight around the warm ceramic mug as she sipped. Savoured. Allowed the caffeine to work its magic.

When things had reached their worst with Brad, when life had been unbearable and she'd seen no way out, she'd turned to outside means for boosting herself back up. Not drugs, although there were times she'd berated her level-headed self, times she'd wished she could let go and drown herself in some pill-popping or joint-smoking high. If her writing hadn't offered her avenue for escape, who knows what would have happened? But it did, and the day she left Brad was the day she vowed to stay clear of a rollercoaster that could very well suck her in and never let her go.

She'd felt the pull back then. Was feeling the pull right now. A desperate, debilitating need that threatened all vestiges of her control.

Only, this was just coffee. Just to settle nerves that wouldn't settle themselves.

Where once writing had filled that role – provided a sanctuary from everything that had gone wrong in her life – now it offered nothing but pain.

People had died with the wave of her hypothetical pen.

Regardless of intent, she was somehow responsible.

And now Chase had fallen under the killer's bloody radar, all because of her. Because he cared about her and because he wanted to keep her safe.

Her shaking hand knocked back a mouthful of nothing from her cup.

The large coffee machine beckoned from across the room. She dragged her gaze away and toward the display of cakes beside it. Not quite Aunt Milly's but beggars couldn't be choosers.

She wove her way through the haphazard tables to the counter.

She should call someone – anyone – so she didn't have to go through this alone. But was he watching, even now?

Her head whipped side-to-side.

The room was nearly empty. A lone nurse sitting by the far wall, a couple of weary visitors no doubt performing the same all-night vigil as she. No, he wasn't in the café, but that didn't mean he wasn't watching.

Would her call for company pinpoint his next target? Was he even now plotting his next move? Questions she couldn't answer, just as she couldn't guarantee the safety of anyone she called.

Which meant she couldn't call anyone.

She couldn't even check-in with Chase's sister. Didn't have her number to let her know Chase wasn't alone.

Scrubbing her eyes, she scanned the gleaming glass display, picked out a crusty looking choc and raspberry muffin, and two cookies that looked as weary as she felt.

The night loomed.

She made her way back to her table, dropped into her seat and settled in for the night.

With a blur of blue numerals, eight fifty-nine clicked over to nine-hundred and the time that had seemed swallowed by the interminable night finally arrived.

Stacey unscrunched her sleeve, tugged it down over her watch and dropped her arm. One deep breath and she strode toward the counter with purpose and as much of an air of no-nonsense as she could muster after twenty-four hours without sleep.

Splashing water over her face and neck in the hospital bathroom had done nothing to wash away the ingrained grit or fatigue. Every muscle complained with the persistence of an angry rhino yet she couldn't have closed her eyes and slept even if there'd been a bed to fall into.

Another deep breath and she was at the counter, diving straight into speech before the nurse behind it could knock her back. Jackie – or so her nametag said – was sympathetic but firm. She needed to check with the doctor before any visitors were allowed in. She pointed to a trio of chairs nearby and suggested Stacey wait until ten when the doctor was due in the ward. Instead of yelling and stamping and slamming her fist against the shiny white countertop, Stacey blinked back a fresh flow of tears and retreated into a chair.

Life sucks!

It'd been a while since she'd allowed herself to drown in a pity party for one. With a will of their own, the list of "life sucks-isms" rolled like film credits through her mind.

A killer was stalking her. That was the biggie.

Even bigger. *He was her friend.* And if their theory was right, *he killed Jagger, injured Midnight, earned her trust and then stamped all over it with his hulking great boots.*

Her mother valued fame more than her own daughter's happiness. Not necessarily news, but the realisation still hurt.

Her home was a pile of rubble.

Cuddles was missing.

The man she loved was in hospital.

Her heart twisted, fresh force driving a lone tear from her eye. She slapped it away and gulped in a fresh bout of disinfectant-infused air.

Thank god it was Friday.

'Ms Holland?'

Another scrub to her eyes and she turned toward the voice.

Jackie.

'The doctor's given the okay for visitors.' The nurse motioned for her to follow.

Stacey pushed up out of her chair, pitching forward as her handbag strap wrapped round her ankle.

The nurse's hands shot out, preventing her fall. 'Hey, are you okay?'

Stacey nodded, certain if she spoke the tears would flow afresh.

Jackie's clear blue gaze softened. 'You should go home and get some sleep.'

Sally's words from the night before. Did these women not get that she *couldn't?* That every time she closed her eyes, Ethan's face flashed before her, gruesome, grinning. Vampirish teeth dipped in blood as if he'd feasted on human flesh.

She pulled back and shoved the guilty handbag strap over her shoulder. Her heart smacked against her ribcage, last night's cookie and muffin-fest rising up her oesophagus. She swallowed, focused on the soft slap of Sally's sneakers on the pristine tiles, the white-painted walls and the beaming sunlight streaming through the thin strip of windows overhead. The fact that Chase was well enough to receive visitors.

'He was asking to see you. Seemed surprised when he had a fiancé and she was waiting outside.' She shot Stacey a sympathetic grin. 'Must be pretty new, right?'

She managed a clearing cough to the throat. 'A week.'

'I thought so.' Another smile, then it was gone. 'He's still quite weak, but the antivenom seems to be working. I'd just ask you keep him as calm and quiet as possible. Anything that raises his heart rate at this point will only set back his recovery.'

'So, he's going to be okay?'

'He should be ready to walk down the aisle in no time at all.'

Stacey followed her into a small, private room to the right, cringing as Jackie's words echoed off each one of its four walls.

'I'll leave you and come back in fifteen minutes. After that, he'll need to rest.'

Stacey turned to the starched, white bed to her left. All the reasons she'd amassed for holding back, for taking things slow, for waiting until life returned to some semblance of normal, fled in a rush of emotion.

'Chase!'

Before she could think or second-guess her reaction, she was at his side, kissing his lips, his face, breathing in his scent. His very alive, male scent.

Even though he lay flat and motionless, his face almost as pale as his pillow, he managed to rustle up a grin. 'Ah, my hero.' The words ruffled her hair, sending shivers all the way down to her toes.

She wrapped her hand around his, mindful of the peg-like sensor monitoring the pulse on his finger and the three sets of tubes and monitors she'd somehow negotiated without incident.

Now that she was close, he appeared less pale, more green. As if suffering from seasickness rather than a deadly toxin.

He nudged further into her neck and inhaled. 'Damn you smell good.'

She shivered, enjoying the sensation all too much. 'I bet you say that to all the girls.'

'Only the ones who save me from certain death.'

She winced. Some jokes cut too close to the bone to be considered humour.

Like …

'So, I hear we're getting married.'

That.

Heat scarpered up her neck and over her face. 'It was the only way to get the nurses to tell me how you were going.'

'And here I thought it was a sign you wanted me for more than my body.' His grin was incorrigible, but his meaning was clear.

And she wasn't ready for any of it. Thinking it was one thing. Saying it out loud? That made it all too real, to terrifying.

Scenes of a crazy *While You Were Sleeping* woman tracked through her mind. She wouldn't be *her*, the woman who won her man because he was grateful.

She didn't want grateful, she wanted …

This wasn't the time to go into what she wanted.

Protection mode leapt in just in time with a comeback. 'You didn't seem to mind the other night.'

His gaze heated, even while his smile wavered. She got that he wanted more. He'd already told her as much. She was pretty sure she wanted more too. But marriage? It hadn't been mentioned, and hell! Was she even ready to contemplate that downward-spiral again?

Cloudy blue eyes pierced right through her, as if reading every convoluted twist of her turmoil.

Her gaze dropped to the warm hand in hers. 'How are you feeling?'

She heard his sigh, but kept her gaze lowered. Safe. 'Like I've been bitten by an Eastern Green Mamba.' His fingers tightened about hers. 'What about you?'

She swallowed. 'Relieved.'

'I'll go with that sentiment.'

'So, what's the prognosis?'

'I'll live. Although I feel as if I've just come off a month long bender. The word "seedy" pretty much sums it up.'

'You do look a bit green.'

'Feel it too.' He drew in a deep breath. 'Did they find the snake?'

'He's safe and sound back in his cage at the zoo.'

'And Cuddles?'

She shook her head, heart twisting. 'I can't believe Ethan would hurt Cuddles.' The thought of him being caught up in a fight that wasn't his slumped at the base of her stomach. Her animals were innocent. They didn't deserve any of this. 'Then again, I never believed Ethan would do half the things he's done. Or at least, seems to have done.'

'That's why most serial killers are so difficult to find. They imitate behaviours that blend them seamlessly into society.'

'I've studied every psychopath and sociopath I could find. Reading or writing about them is one thing. Coming face-to-face in real life is something altogether different.'

'About that. Where are you staying tonight?'

'I haven't thought about it.' She blinked. 'Here.'

'Not for a second night. Not looking like you do. Like you haven't had a decent sleep in weeks.'

He wasn't far wrong. Doubtful that would change anytime soon, though.

'You need to go somewhere safe, have a shower, rest. But not alone. What about shoe-lady?'

'Shazz?'

'Yeah. Call her and get her to pick you up from here. I don't want you alone until I get out of this place.'

'You must be feeling better. You're all bossy and overhanded again.'

The heat in his gaze held hers as if it'd never let go. 'I want you safe, Stacey.'

'I know.' She nodded, inhaled, the depth of that gaze pulling every heartstring she owned. Oxygen shuddered into her lungs.

Chase needed to stay calm and she wasn't ready to go back to his place. Not without him. 'Midnight's already there. As soon as they caught the mamba, I found him hiding on top of the fridge. Seems he likes the warmth and the hum of the motor.'

'Good. Then there's no reason for you to go back.'

'Except for clothes.'

'Borrow Shazz's.'

'Her clothes are like her shoes.'

'Then any chance of keeping my heart rate steady during your next visit will be zilch to none.'

Her heart rate was anything *but* steady. Heat crawled mercilessly across her cheeks. It wasn't news that Chase found her sexy. He'd demonstrated the fact more than a few occasions the past week. But hearing him say it was really something else. Being wanted, appreciated. It wasn't something she'd ever contemplated. Brad had killed that little darling long ago and she never considered the possibility after that.

It was the reason she didn't "date" – until Chase gave her no choice.

Dating meant opening up to heartache. Or relinquishing control she'd fought hard – and was still fighting hard – to hold onto.

Not gonna happen.

'I love it when you blush.'

Damn if his words didn't make her blush more!

'Was there someone you wanted me to call?' She didn't wait for an answer, just bowled onward with barely a breath. 'Like your sister? Your squad? Or someone else? I didn't call before because I didn't have their numbers. Or know if you'd want me to. But I can call someone now. If you like.'

She bit her lip. What the hell kind of babble just erupted from her mouth? Ridiculous to feel nervous when there was no reason for it.

Lips far too distracting slid into a smile that arrowed straight to her knee ligaments. Then for the first time since she'd entered the room, Chase tried to push up.

She pressed against his chest, her palm flexing against hard, warm muscle. 'Hey, stop that. You need to stay flat.'

He grunted and dropped back down. 'Damn! This isn't what I'd planned.'

Her heart catapulted. 'Planned for what?'

Slowly his hand reached for hers. She felt the warmth of his fingers wrap around hers, the warmth of anticipation wrapping around her heart.

Her pounding, juddering heart.

'When you have a near-death experience, life suddenly springs into focus. Things, once fuzzy, become suddenly, solidly clear. Your doubts fade. Fears too, surprisingly. And second-guessing becomes a thing of the past.'

His breath shuddered in through his too-pale lips. 'Maybe this is the worst time to say this, then again, maybe it's the best.' His grasp on her hand tightened, even as it trembled. 'Stacey Holland, I want to be a part of your life in whatever capacity you'll have me. Boyfriend, lover, partner, and maybe someday when you're ready, *husband*. I don't want to waste another moment of however long I have left in this life, whether it be years, months, or mere days. I've wasted too much time already. I want to fill every second I have with what makes me happy. And what makes me happy is you.'

Those crazy nerves danced like a troupe of butterflies across her stomach. But where once those dancing feet would have trembled with fear, now they jumped with joy.

She was a grown woman, with grown-woman feelings. Time she grabbed those reins and rode that horse till it dropped. She was allowed to change her mind. Allowed to change her views on coffee and dating and relationships.

Allowed to love Chase if it made her happy.

And with everything else in the universe working against that emotion, all the more reason to go for it. Her eyes locked with his deep blue ones.

His lips trembled into a smile. 'Tell me you feel the same way too.'

Any doubts that might have lingered, crumbled.

She leaned in, the clinical odour of hospital linen not nearly strong enough to obscure the familiar maleness she'd come to love.

Her lips found his, and everything in the world righted again. She felt whole. Safe. Real. He obliterated her fears. The self-doubts. Filled her with hope that the past didn't wield any control over the future.

She pulled back, just a little, and lost herself once again in that gaze.

'I do.'

Chapter Fifty-Nine

Chase sank into the cracked vinyl of the visitor's chair. Elbows digging into his thighs, he hunched forward, aware of every muscle, every aching bone and tendon and inch of flesh as he tried to catch his breath.

Two days in a hospital bed was two days too many.

It was time to return to real life outside the four white-painted walls that had been driving him crazy the past forty-eight hours. Time to catch a killer.

'Chase.'

His head jerked back and his mind froze. 'Doc Griffiths.'

Two white-cloaked figures melded into one as he forced his eyes into sync. The resulting blur was better than a room of doubles. A lingering by-product of the mamba's venom.

Approaching six foot, sturdy build, mid-tanned, bushy salt and pepper hair, his specialist brooked a commanding presence. He clasped a tan file in one hand, a pen in the other. That he might hold the answer to Chase's future in the metaphorical palm of his hand was a distinct possibility.

The relative calm of his heartbeat was over. With the Doc's appearance came a leap into hyperdrive.

He unhooked Chase's chart from the end of the bed. 'I was hoping I'd catch you before you checked out.'

'How'd you know I was here?'

'When admin logged into your file, my office was notified that you'd been admitted. Talk about rotten luck. A snakebite. Who'd have thought?'

Luck had nothing to do with it.

He bit back the anger. 'Yeah. Who'd have thought?'

A quick scan of his chart, then the Doc hooked it back up. 'I won't ask how you happened to come face-to-face with a snake. You detectives seem to live in the throes of danger.'

'It comes with the badge.'

'I'm sure it does. Although I'd have thought a bullet more likely than a snake attack.'

Chase couldn't manage more than a wry grin.

'I've got your test results.' He waved the file in his hand. 'Save you coming back in, I thought I'd pass them on now. If you're okay with that?'

Was he okay with that? He lacked the energy to decide either way.

The chair's armrests cut into his palm, his grip so tight he could feel the metal frame beneath the cracked vinyl-covered foam.

'Sure. Now's as good a time as any.'

His cloudy gaze slid past the white-clad figure to the doorway. Hopefully Stacey was more than a few minutes away. Last thing she needed was to see a grown man cry.

The thought, a sorry attempt at humour, fell short. Somewhere in the three-feet under category.

Griffiths nodded toward the bed beside Chase. 'Mind if I sit?'

He waved his hand, swallowed the morbidity and nodded back. 'Sure.'

That the Doc wanted to sit wasn't good. Or was that if he'd asked Chase to sit? Moot point since he was already sitting.

His entire life hinging on one diagnosis, and his brain was a frigging merry-go-round with one central focus – Stacey.

The Doc was about to announce a verdict that meant the difference between a lifetime with the woman he loved or sharing a few good years before they slowly turned bad. Either way he couldn't imagine a future without Stacey, but was he greedy to want more than just a little?

He pushed forward in his chair. Mulling over what would or wouldn't be didn't make a damn bit of difference. Genetics had decided his fate long before today. Now at least the uncertainty would be gone. He'd know either way.

He looked at the man waiting patiently for his thoughts to settle. It was a dire day when your doctor knew you that well.

He wrapped his lips around a grin and pushed indifference into his voice. 'So, they have you making house calls now, Doc?'

'Ha! Only for a select few.'

'Not sure whether to take that as good or bad.'

The smile in the other man's expression died. And with it died the beat of Chase's heart. He inhaled, deep. Then let the air out long and slow until he was ready.

'Hit me with it. No sense beating around the mulberry bush and all that nursery nonsense.'

The older man stroked his greying moustache before consulting the file. That he knew the diagnosis without looking, Chase had no doubts. But the Doc always liked to be one hundred and ten per cent ready before he spoke.

'The results came back from your blood work.' He looked up, the staunch in his expression softening. 'I won't overload you with all that medical jargon I know you love, and I'll come right to the point.'

Chase's mouth was so goddam dry, like he'd swallowed the entire length of Nine Mile Beach. He would have reached for the water beside him, but for the trembling in his hands. His legs weren't much better. He could have blamed the venom or the antivenom. Or the fact he'd had fuck-all sleep the past two nights.

That the shaking returned the moment his fate was about to be dealt couldn't be coincidence. Much as, unlike Stacey, he believed in the buggers. Much as he wanted to believe in it in this instance.

His heart slowed. He could almost believe it stopped. Breath caught and held in his throat.

One more glance at the file, then eyes the colour of Chase's gun bored into his. 'You don't have Parkinson's.'

Air whooshed from his lungs.

He slumped forward.

You don't have Parkinson's.

Elbows braced on his thighs, he gasped for breath, head spinning so fast he couldn't see shit.

Somewhere in the back of his mind, the Doc's voice continued. Words floating, random. *Hyperthyroidism. Treatable. Medication. Recover.*

Yet his conscious mind had but one train of thought.

You don't have Parkinson's.

Words tripped over words.

You're going to live. Love. Have a life.

The all-Aussie dream — Stacey, a menagerie of whacky pets and a white picket fence.

Everything he'd ever wanted, and so much more.

As long as he didn't die in the next forty-eight hours trying to catch a killer.

'How many fingers?' Stacey raised her hand and held her breath.

Chase didn't even bother to look up from his gun, in pieces and laid out on a black cloth on the living room table. 'Don't be ridiculous.'

'There's nothing ridiculous about it. We need to wait.'

He looked at her then. 'Why?'

'Because you were just bitten by a mamba and have no idea how many fingers I'm holding up.' She wiggled them, just to make her point.

He quirked a brow. 'I was bitten five days ago and that makes the timing perfect. The Copycat won't expect us to act so anything we do now will catch him off guard.' He dipped a tiny brush into some liquid and picked up the gun. 'And the answer was three.'

She dropped her hand. 'Three what?'

'Fingers.'

He proceeded to clean the barrel as if that was that. As if he'd made his point and the discussion was over.

He should have known better.

'You can't just dismiss my opinion as if it doesn't count.'

'That's not what I'm doing.'

'Then what are you doing, Chase?'

He dropped the gun, wrapping a ball of cotton wool around the brush. 'I'm preparing to catch a killer before he comes at us again.'

'You need to be ready.'

'So we can give him more time to prepare? I don't think so.' He spared her a brief glance and set about cleaning the cylinder. 'I wouldn't do this if I didn't think I could. You need to trust me.'

'Just as you need to trust me. And respect my point of view.'

'I respect you.'

She slammed her hand over the gun. 'Then you need to stop what you're doing and listen.'

He raised his hands and leaned back in his chair. 'Fine. I'm listening.'

Why did it always feel like he wasn't taking her seriously?

Her gut churned.

'A day or two won't make a difference to the killer, but it'll make a difference to you. The venom and antivenom are still wreaking havoc on your system. You're still shaky and not at full strength. And your vision's not one hundred per cent returned. You may have been well enough to leave the hospital, but you're not well enough to face a killer.'

'I'm fine.'

'This isn't a splinter, Chase. You can't fix it with tweezers and a band aid.'

'And you can't catch a killer by sitting back and writing a scene. This is my job, Stacey, and I know when I'm ready to go out there and do it.'

She crossed her arms and hated that the gesture looked defensive rather than offensive. His obstinacy was royally pissing her off. 'I want to wait a couple of days.'

He shook his head. 'It's too risky.'

'So, I get no say in the matter?'

'Sure you do.'

Her gut twisted. Just when she thought things would be different, they turned out to be exactly the same.

She got a say, but it didn't count.

Chase was determined to go ahead, to put himself in danger, to go against every instinct she had that said they needed to wait.

She got that the Copycat would expect him to be recovering at home still. In fact they'd set things up over the past couple of days so he'd think just that. They wanted him to feel safe. Cocky. To believe he had a clear path to continue his sick plan – but she wasn't convinced.

Funny how swiftly their roles had reversed.

Stacey crossed the room and stared out the window. The sun had reached its highest point in a cloudless blue sky and soon it would begin its downward descent. Time filed a death march toward sunset, and the advent of their plan.

And what then?

Could she really stay with a man who refused to take her and her opinions seriously? Was she being unreasonable to expect more, when he'd given her so much already? No one should go into a relationship expecting to change the other person. She'd been on that receiving end, and she'd vowed never to go there again. Her heart twisted. It didn't mean she loved Chase any less. Or needed him any less. But she needed to love and respect herself at least as much. And she owed it to herself not to settle.

Warmth cloaked her back seconds before arms wrapped around her and he buried his face in her hair.

'When all this is over, what say we go somewhere? Just the two of us. Sun. Sand. Sex.' His breath feathered across her neck. 'Not necessarily in that order.'

His palms rode a delicious path up her belly to her breasts. Her body rebelled her brain, her nipples hardening even before he reached them.

Manipulation, pure and simple. He was using her body's weakness to sway her mind.

She stiffened.

His fingers stalled and he lifted his head. 'I know you're worried about me, and I love that you are, but I'm ready for this.'

She wanted to let it go. To sink into his arms and allow his warmth to envelop her. To trust that all would be fine. That they'd be fine.

But she couldn't. She'd come too far only to let him drag her backwards.

She pulled away. 'I don't think I am.'

'What? Ready for phase two?'

'Yes.' She turned to face him.

His expression froze. 'What do you mean?'

'We should wait before making plans.'

'O-kay.' His gaze narrowed. 'Why?'

'This isn't the time to get stuck into discussions on where we are or aren't going in the future.'

His hands fell to his sides. '*Aren't going?* What does *that* mean?'

Damn! She hadn't meant it to come out like that. Not now. Not while their focus should be on catching the Copycat.

This was the worst time for this conversation.

'Forget it.'

'I don't think I can. What are you trying really badly not to say?'

'Can't we do this later?'

'I think we should do it now.'

'And what you want counts more than what I want, right?'

'Where's this coming from, Stacey?'

'From past mistakes I don't intend to make in the future.' She clamped her lips. That sounded way worse spoken than it had in her head.

'By mistakes you mean what? Me?'

Now she'd started, there was no turning back. She crossed her arms and fought not to crumple over what she was about to say. 'Not you. *Us.*'

His head jerked as if she'd slammed it with her fist instead of her words. *'We're a mistake?'*

She shook her head. 'That's not what I meant. You're putting words into my mouth.'

'That's only because you're not doing it. Are you breaking up with me? Now?'

Crap. All she'd wanted was to postpone their plan and instead she'd pulled the pin on a grenade.

How had she gone from wanting to protect him to wanting to end things between them?

She didn't want to lose Chase. Then again, she didn't want to lose herself either. Where the hell did that leave her?

Up shit creek without a frigging canoe, let alone a paddle.

'Stacey, the least you can do is be honest here. What are you saying?'

She let out a breath. He'd backed her into a corner and left her with no other way out.

Her chest squeezed even as she forced the words through her lips. 'We're not on the same page, Chase. Circumstances threw us together, and in the heat of the moment I thought we could make things work.'

She swallowed against the rasp of sandpaper in her throat. 'I'm sorry. But I was wrong.'

'Dammit Stacey! You're not going out there.' Chase grasped the doorjamb as if it were his life source, as if he couldn't stand without it.

The sunglasses shielding his eyes from the sun's glare also masked his quick scan of the area. The street was deserted, but that didn't mean they weren't being watched. He glared at the woman glaring straight back at him from the front path. 'We had a deal – no more writing and no more research.'

Stacey blinked, the keys in her hand jingling with nerves she tried so hard to hide.

She was easily the most stubborn woman he knew. Which made her stance all the more convincing. And when all he wanted to do was run down the stairs and wrap her into his arms, he tightened his grip on the wood and set his expression to grim.

She gritted her teeth. 'That deal is killing my career.'

'Better it kills a career than another victim. You go out there and do this, you may as well wield the knife yourself.'

She blinked. Impossible to tell whether the tears brimming eyes were part of the act or real. 'That's not fair, Chase.'

Her lips were anything but steady.

He was an all-out jerk. Even though they both knew the accusations were empty and he didn't mean a word of them. Things said in the heat of the moment were often that way. But he knew Stacey well enough to know they cut. To know she'd thought the same more than once, even though it wasn't close to being true.

But he had to rip into her. Hard. Outraged. As if he would do and say anything to make her listen. As if they were at odds and she was about to head off in a tiff, on her own personal crusade.

That they *were* at odds – that she'd all but told him they were *a mistake* – only served to make his anger all the more real.

He growled. 'I tell you what's not fair. You reneging on our deal, especially when I'm still recovering and can't guarantee your safety.'

Her head whipped back. 'I'm perfectly capable of guaranteeing my own safety.'

'Don't do this, Stacey.'

'You've no right to ask that. I'm not breaking any laws.'

'You are if you take my car.'

'Too late.' She pressed the key and the Hilux's central locking system clicked. 'What are you going to do? Report me?'

He scrubbed at three full days of facial hair. 'Can you even drive a ute?'

She rolled her eyes, set her expression to stone. 'Once again, doubting my capabilities. I'm not as useless as you think.'

He sighed. 'I never said you were useless. I just want to keep you safe.'

'Well, that's not your job.' She yanked the driver's door open and slid in behind the wheel. 'You're a detective working a case and a source of research for my writing. Don't kid yourself that you're more.'

The slam of the car door shuddered through every muscle, every bone. He winced, watching his car skid out of the driveway and accelerate down the road. Stacey slowed at the intersection, indicated right and disappeared from sight.

Her words slumped, large, hulking boulders in his chest. Throwaways spoken in the heat of the moment shouldn't carry so much weight. But how could they not? When his greatest fear in all this mess was losing Stacey. Losing the life he'd finally discovered he'd be able to live.

He backed into the house and closed the door. Adjusted the mic in his ear and prepared to listen to Stacey's final shopping spree before they embarked on the last chapter of their plan.

The finale.

The moment he'd catch the bastard and make him pay for every terror and hurt he'd made her suffer.

Chapter Sixty

In Hot Water's anchor slipped into the ocean with an almost silent *plop!*

Stacey gripped the handrail and stared out from the bow into the yawning night.

Normally once a boat left St Kilda marina for the bay, the wind would howl over the top deck like a pack of coyotes. The boat would rock, waves rolling and smacking against the large fibreglass hull, the motion lulling, relaxing, cloaking her in a sense of peace and serenity.

Not so tonight.

The air was still, the ocean deadly quiet.

Deadly.

God, she hated that word, the connotations and images it evoked.

She unfurled her fingers from the handrail and glanced at her watch. Quarter past midnight. *Ahead of schedule.*

Sneaking out of the house and breaking into the marina had been surprisingly easy. Even easier was hotwiring the boat she'd selected earlier before easing it silently, stealthily out into the bay. No witnesses.

No witnesses, that is, bar one.

He was out there. She *felt* him. Like a splinter wheedling through her skin and deep into her flesh. Watching. Waiting. Eyes piercing her back. Presence chilling her blood.

She rubbed her ice-tipped hands, blew white puffs of warm air into her palms. To no avail. Her fingers were so frosty cold they hurt. She should have brought her gloves. Should have remembered something that simple.

Right now she couldn't remember what she had for breakfast. No doubt nothing. The hollow echo growling through her stomach reminded her she'd had very little for lunch either.

Did coffee count?

Seems she'd done what she vowed never to do. Fall into addiction.

She could do with a steaming mug of the stuff now. Craved it more than she craved her next breath.

The only craving it didn't come close to was Chase.

The deck creaked. She spun around, her eyes wracking the fathomless dark. Impossible to see a thing. The slivered moon was no help. Another creak and her ears strained. For a sign. The slosh of water, the clatter of a man dragging himself up and over the side.

Nothing.

It had to be the fibreglass contracting with the cold night air. Sounds she'd heard countless times in the past. Never once had they set her heart to race. Her blood to curdle. Her mind to conjure up a trail of possibilities, all equally terrifying.

If her heart beat any faster there was a distinct possibility it would burst free of her chest and take flight.

The need to hear Chase's voice was overpowering. But they'd agreed no contact once on the boat. Nothing to alert the killer to his presence. Now was not the time for nerves, or doubts about whether she could do this.

She had to.

Another glance at her watch and one into the black expanse beyond the bay. A buoy bobbed just metres to her right. Nothing else moved. Nothing to indicate where he was hiding. She just knew he was. Knew it with every rampant beat of her heart.

The beats skipped.

It's time.

To do what she'd come for. To move their plan one step closer toward ending this thing, once and for all.

She clapped her hands in an attempt to warm them, and tried to look as if she were enjoying this as much as she had that night all those months ago in Dresden's paddock.

Back then she'd been oblivious to any threat. Had no concerns past perfecting the scene.

If only she could wind back time.

If you did, would you still have Chase?

Chills shivered up her spine. That something so good could come from something so bad …

Not that she still had Chase, not in the real sense of the word. Her earlier theatrics had put pay to that. She was still questioning her decision. And sanity.

One more clap and a shake of her head dislodged the thought.

'Okay, Renaldo, up and atom!' If her voice shook, she could only hope the Copycat would attribute it to the frosty night air.

With Renaldo's hands clasped in hers, she dragged him up, the familiar texture of fibreglass cold and damp against her palm.

Her heart weighed a tonne, the sense of loss so sharp, so surprising, it stole her breath. She was losing a friend. Warped as it may sound, Renaldo had been with her since her split with Brad. A silent companion who'd watched her grow and strengthen the past three years. He'd suffered her rantings, her tears, her every whim when it came to crafting a scene. And he'd helped her forge a career in a field she loved.

The last thing she wanted was to lose the only mannequin she'd salvaged from her shattered home. She grasped Renaldo's hand, and swallowed back an overwhelming desire to hug him. What he represented, a symbol of how far she'd come, would soon be lolling at the bottom of the bay.

Just one more reason to hate Ethan from here to hell.

She'd see him spend the rest of his days rotting in a cold, dark cell. Nothing less would suffice. And only then would sacrificing Renaldo be worth it.

Instead of the hug, she squeezed his hands, closed her eyes for just one moment before opening them and staring into his guileless blue gaze.

Goodbye Renaldo.

The whisper melded with the ice in the air and dissipated the moment it left her lips. With fingers she wished were steadier and warmer, she checked the fishing line around his wrists, the three-strand rope attaching weights to his waist.

The fishhooks were already in place.

She braced her back, bent her knees, and slowly, carefully, lowered him over the side.

Chase tried to flex his foot and failed.

The dark wasn't the worst part. Or the confined space, his body bent so tight he felt like a damned pretzel. It wasn't even the numb in his left leg or that his left arm resembled the pin-pricked stuffing of a pin cushion.

None of that.

No. The worst part was the silence – resonant, booming quiet that flooded his eardrums and made it near impossible to hear. Much like the rush of the ocean when you pressed a shell against your ear.

Scents of salt and seawater mingled with the odour of fresh rubber, swamping his nostrils until he could barely breathe. That they'd found a boat in the marina with a dingy already inflated was a blessing. That the dingy was more functional than comfortable was just tough.

He blinked, eyes still not quite in sync. But an hour at the shooting range had recalibrated his aim. When Copycat and gun barrel came face-to-face, he wouldn't miss. Plus, he had the element of surprise.

His right hand tightened around his semi – with barely a twinge from the cut that once housed a glass splinter – and he held his breath. Listened. Couldn't hear shit over the damned waves in his ears.

Then he could. A loud splash, something heavy dropping overboard.

Renaldo.

He steadied his breathing, cleared his mind. Focused on the gun in his hand and what was to come.

It was nearly time.

Soon Stacey would be free and clear, and their plan would turn to him. He'd have one shot. One shot was all he needed.

Metal scraped against metal. Then another splash as Stacey eased the weights over the side.

One. Two. Yet another.

An odour, sweet, acidic, filled his nostrils.

Cold-wet slithered across his ankle.

Before he could panic about snakes and other biting, venomous possibilities, rough bristles cut through his socks and into his skin. Some kind of rope?

He shot up. Tried to break free of the canvas covering the dingy. It stuck fast.

His fingers fumbled at his ankles. The rope yanked. His leg jerked. Once. Twice.

Wood hammered against his spine as he was dragged out from the canvas, over the side of the dingy, onto the back of the boat.

Fuck!

His heart pitched into the back of his throat. He gagged.

Thoughts swirled, wading thick and slow through a treacle-filled mind.

He holstered his gun, reached again for the rope. The knot was too tight, his fingers too awkward. His head too fuzzy.

He scrabbled for a handhold.

The sea inched closer, the air grew denser, plunging his mind deeper into confusion.

Thoughts scrambled through thick mist, but for one – the killer knew their plan. And he was retaliating with a plan of his own – no waiting as he'd done in the past. He'd started copying now, with Chase. Which meant if he succeeded, Stacey would be next.

Rubber and canvas slipped through his grasp. His palms burned. His lungs were liquid fire. Silence roared, the crush of his ribs squeezing breath out through his mouth.

He tried to call out, tried to warn Stacey, but nothing more than garbled noise coursed up his throat.

He fumbled in his pocket. His other. Slammed his head against the fibreglass hull as cold air cut across his skin.

He gulped, dragged in three sharp breaths and slapped hard against water so cold it burned.

Sinking.

Down. Down.

No stopping.

He clawed at the water, his dwindling cognizance, but the rope, the weights, dragged him down.

He fought to slow his breath, slow his panic, reached into his pocket one last time. Frosty fingertips found metal, wrapped around it and slowly withdrew.

Lungs burning, bursting, he prayed he could stay conscious long enough to stay alive.

The moment Renaldo's body hit the water, the wind picked up.

Stacey dropped the fourth and last weight over the side and the first fat drop of rain hit her forehead, then slid down her nose. She rubbed it away and stopped a second before it had time to make it past her eyebrows.

Her head jerked back and she froze. She held her breath and strained to hear.

Wind howled across the bow and waves slapped lazily against the hull. Her ears were playing crazy-assed games with her mind. She could have sworn she heard a splash stern-side. Now there was no sound but for the ringing in ears straining too hard to hear. She glanced toward the stern. Tempting as it was, she couldn't go back and check on Chase. It was too risky. They were too close to ending this thing for her to wreck it because of nerves.

She stared down into the black glistening water, inhaled a lungful of salty sea air, and said one final goodbye to Renaldo.

Then making her way back to the bridge, she rejoined the two severed wires, fired up the engine, and carved a course back toward the marina.

Chase's chest scalded like the devil, every gasp razing like a wildfire down his throat and into his lungs. Still, he kept swimming, kept counting.

Three strokes, one breath. Three strokes, one breath.

Linked his mind to the mantra. *Three strokes, one breath.*

If it strayed, his thoughts went to Stacey, and he couldn't go there. Not when he was still an age from the marina and she was alone back there with *him*. His pocketknife had saved his life; now he needed to reach land in time to save hers.

The shivers wouldn't stop – scorching from the inside, freezing from the outside. The water pricked like a thousand tiny porcupines rolling across his skin.

He raised his head, gasped, and choked on the spill of sea and salt into his mouth. A black tower rose up before him and he reared back. Too late.

Bone and metal collided. His head spun, the thrash of his heart against his ribs so painful each smack stabbed like a knife.

Paddling, fighting to stay afloat, he stared up at the looming buoy. Numb fingers wrapped around the weather-bitten rope about its middle. He fought for breath. Fought to stop the spiral of his head from dragging him under.

His weary muscles trembled, taunting him to let go.

He tightened his grip.

Squinting toward the lights of the marina, he tried to pull his two wayward eyes into focus. How much further did he have to go? Between the dark and his fucked-up vision, he hadn't a hope in hell of figuring it out. He just needed to keep on swimming, keep on counting, keep on fighting, until he reached Stacey.

Had she realised he was no longer on board?

If she hadn't, did that mean she was safe?

Damn but it was the one thought he clung to. The bastard seemed more interested in eliminating the people around her. For how long? Until he had a clear line to her?

The thought pierced his chest as if real, fortified steel.

Not while he had breath still left in his lungs.

Just a few more drags of oxygen and he'd be right to continue.

He clung to the rope, bracing against the pull of the current beneath the surface. Now the counting was gone, other thoughts crowded his mind. Freezing his nuts off while stalking a serial killer was the least of his problems. Sharks were known to venture into the bay. Not often, but all it took was that one instance – being in the wrong place at the wrong time. The way his luck was running, he wouldn't put it past one of the buggers to slip in and take a bite or more out of one of his legs.

Every slide, every touch beneath the surface dredged up visions of *Jaws* and his body a bloody, flesh-mangled mess. He braced. Blanked his mind, inhaled and loosened his hold on the rope. Threw himself back into the water and began to count.

This time he sensed it before he hit – another dark mass rising up out the ocean. He pulled up, stopping just shy of the looming black hulk. A dull beam filtered out from a skylight and it took a moment to realise he stared straight at the hull of *In Hot Water*.

He didn't have to find the killer. The killer had found him. Only he didn't know it yet.

Swallowing every ragged breath, he edged portside, steering clear of the rudder. He didn't plan on being shark bait with the sudden start-up of the engine. He blinked, listening for an indication of the bastard's whereabouts. Not that he expected it to be that easy.

Of course it wasn't.

That left him no choice. He edged slowly toward the stern, and a short rope attached to a metal fitting just above the hull. He grabbed the rope, braced, and with shaky arms, began to drag himself out of the water. Hand climbing up over hand, he pulled, wrapped one arm over the side and reached up with the other.

Pain exploded through his temple.

Awareness receded in a blaze of bright lights and agony. Firm hands wrapped around his wrists and heaved.

The world flickered. Another crack rammed against his skull and all went black.

But not before he stared into the deadened gaze of the Copycat Killer.

Chapter Sixty-One

*D*on't freak out!

She wouldn't. *Couldn't.*

Where are you, Chase?

Stacey wrung her hands, dragged her gaze away from his front door and glared at her mobile.

He should have called by now.

That he hadn't …

Oh, god!

Bloody severed fingers burned her retina.

No!

That would not be him.

He's alive.

She had to tell herself that. Had to believe it.

She'd told him she loved him, then taken it back. Still wasn't convinced they could work. That she could take a chance and fall deeper into love only to lose him when he came to his senses.

But none of that mattered.

Regardless whether their futures were destined to be joined or otherwise, she couldn't lose him. Couldn't bear to see him hurt, or worse.

Her head spun.

Stop it!

He's alive dammit!

She stared at her watch, but staring didn't change the fact that Chase was over an hour late checking in. And no matter how many times she told herself he was okay, the churn in her gut indicated otherwise.

The killer must have seen through their ruse. *Her* ruse. And instead of being caught, he'd slapped their plan sideways and done the capturing.

She had to call his partner. Had to tell her what they'd planned.

Had to tell her she was to blame for throwing Chase in the path of a killer.

Fuck!

A poker stabbed at Chase's skull just above his left eye, every jab drawing bile up his throat and into his mouth. Chilling damp seeped from his wet clothes, drilling through his skin and deep into his bones.

He shivered. Dragged in as much oxygen as his burning lungs would allow.

And slowly forced his eyes to open.

A dull blur slowly merged into semi-focus and with the help of a muted blue glow – the source of which he couldn't see – he took in his surroundings. Stark concrete smeared with black and mould-green. Perhaps some tunnel or an old abandoned building basement.

Either way, the reek of dirt, dank and decay said he was underground. Deep underground.

Far from discovery.

He tried to move. Thin rope tethered his ankles to the iron legs of a chair. More rope bound his wrists tight behind the backrest. He yanked his hands and sharp bristles chafed his skin.

Raw anger made his body jerk. He slammed his feet against the concrete ground, rocking the chair so it almost toppled into the wall behind him.

Pain arced up his leg, jarring his lower back. He winced.

You stupid, bloody fool!

He'd grown soft. Smug. Let his heart rule his mind, giving his dick free reign to take over sense and make him lose control. His love, his complete and crazy obsession for Stacey, had put him here.

The hands of fate had swallowed him whole. Or more specifically, the hands of a psycho-bastard who'd think nothing of slicing him into pieces before sewing them back together with fishhooks and nylon just to fulfil some sick-assed blood-lust-driven appetite.

He slammed his head back and contacted with unforgiving cement. The poker jabbing inside his skull fragmented and a million spikes stabbed his brain.

In his fumbled attempt to keep Stacey safe, he'd ignored the signs. Hadn't fully grasped that *he* was the intended victim of the bomb, the snake. Their sting. Their plan had played right into the killer's hands, providing the perfect opportunity to remove Chase from Stacey's orbit. Now here he was, trussed up like some witless beast, all set for slaughter. That the Copycat meant to kill him was evident. That had been his plan all along – to create a clear path to Stacey.

And Chase had opened the door, rolled out the red carpet and welcomed the bastard in with the promise of coffee and cupcakes.

Denial roared through his chest.

Stacey would not be a murderer's frigging cupcake.

His fingers fumbled over the knot.

He wasn't dead yet. He had a future worth fighting for and no fucked up psycho-killer would steal that away.

The numb in his fingertips morphed into needles. He growled, straining against the ropes, gaining nothing but a scalding burn at his wrists.

Ohhhh.

He froze. *Was that …?*

The noise came again. Faint, but close.

Human. And barely alive.

He turned his head. The moaning drifted out through the arched opening behind him.

Was it Stacey? Had the bastard captured her too?

His heart twisted so tight it almost split in half.

He pressed his feet into the ground and jerked his body forward. The chair juddered against slime and stone, but it moved. A centimetre. Maybe more. He jerked again. Again. Several times more until he'd cleared the lip of what turned out to be a fork to two tunnels. Now all he had to do was manoeuvre around it. He levered the ground with his right foot and, centimetre by centimetre, turned his chair toward the left.

The ropes chafed his ankles, his wrists. His head pounded. His back stabbed a protest with every jolt, every judder.

His gaze jerked left, right, then left again, scouring the area.

Where is he?

The man who'd caught him. The man who planned to kill him.

Surely not far. Doubtful he could resist the lure of fresh meat for long.

A shuddering thought, one that fuelled his efforts to reach the other captive. He needed to find her, break free and get both of them the hell out of there, fast.

Was *he* watching?

He strained to see beyond the blue glow, but his eyes refused to cooperate. As far as his fucked-up vision went, there seemed no evidence of video cameras. That didn't mean there were none. Just none that were obvious.

He continued his "plant foot, jerk body" motion until a silhouette came into view.

Another chair, another tethered body.

From the clothing, from what he could see of shoulder-length hair through caked dirt and blood, his assumption had been right. It was a woman. That was the extent of his examination. Whoever she was, she faced away, her body slumped awkwardly to the side. If not for the spasmodic moans, he would have presumed her to be dead, or pretty near it. His gaze swept the figure, head to toe, his breath lodged like ice at the back of his throat.

He latched onto her tethered hands and air whooshed from his lungs.

Thank god!

It was her nails, painted leopard-print, once perfect, now chipped and torn.

That was the first thing he noticed. The first thing to lessen the pound in his head, the dread and fear drilling away at his heart. Stacey's nails were clear of colour. And she'd never worn them that long – too impractical for typing.

From what he could see, the woman's clothes were expensive. *Gianni* something or other, or some such designer. Jayda could have filled him in if she were here.

That heaved the pound back into his skull.

That she wasn't here was probably his dumbest mistake out of an entire trail of mistakes he'd made when it came to the case and keeping Stacey safe. He should have drawn his partner into his plans. She'd given him no reason not to.

Unlike his piss-poor attitude last year with the Night Terror. He'd given her plenty of reason to leave trust at the front door. She should have wiped her feet of him after that – after he'd shut her out and doubted her – but she hadn't. And in return, he'd kept secret vital information on the Copycat, personally and professionally held her at arm's length, all over a diagnosis that was now moot.

Fool that he was, he'd believed he could protect Stacey single-handed. Even catch the killer. As if with his new diagnosis came new strength, and the chance to prove himself. A hero complex that may just be the death of him if he didn't find a way to get out of his bindings and then out of these tunnels.

Despite the sharp aches – every muscle, every bone, every time he moved – he manoeuvred the chair until he came face-to-face with the last person he'd expected to see trussed and tied up beside him.

Straight brown hair with flecks of red. Clear skin, but for smudges of blood across her right cheek and forehead. Green eyes. Lips once red, now dry and cracked and bruise-swollen.

The confidence had sagged from her shoulders. The belligerence leached from her gaze. She may have been imposing once, but now Candace Holland was a slumped bundle of ragged designer silk and grime.

'Ms Holland?'

She moaned and raised her head. 'The *detective*.'

Eyes so much like Stacey's, but colder, emptier, glared back. He could have been shit on her stiletto for all her tone.

Her gaze narrowed.

Thin lips pursed, bared teeth biting through words that resonated as clear as crystal barbs. 'Why the hell are you here instead of protecting my daughter?'

Stacey collapsed into a chair, staring across the uncluttered desk. Jayda's narrowed green gaze stared back, sympathetic, *pitying*.

No.

The grubby walls of the precinct crowded inward, squeezing every fighting breath from her lungs.

Bitter screams crowded her brain.

It's not true.

Her voice croaked. 'Are you sure it's him?'

Jayda gave a sharp nod. 'There's no doubt.'

There it was.

Damn!

Bile swamped the back of her throat.

She swallowed. Fought the rush of guilt over yet another death.

It's not your fault, Stacey.

Only it was. It was all her fault.

They've got it wrong. He's not dead.

The ramifications of them being right …

She gripped the chair's armrests as if they might give her some grounding, some sense of stability, and stared through the near empty precinct to the double glass doors and the street beyond. Cracked vinyl scratched her palms and her gut churned.

Pushing through those double doors wouldn't mean escaping this nightmare. She was up to her frizzy blonde locks in this mess. And now, so was Chase. What's more, she'd tarnished the memory of a man who'd shown her nothing but kindness. Who her heart had insisted wasn't a killer, despite overwhelming evidence to the contrary.

She should have listened to her heart.

Now it was too late.

Ethan's dead and it's your fault.

She shook her head, shook the thought. Tried to think past the pound in her head. 'There must be some mistake.'

Jayda twirled a pen in her fingers, then tapped the file on her desk. 'We received the toe in an envelope two days ago. DNA matches hair provided by Ethan Miklem's sister.'

'Ethan has a sister?'

'And a half-brother, it seems.' How did she not know?

They were supposed to have been friends. Not that she'd call herself that now. The "friend" label was one that had to be earned. Valued. Respected. She'd done none of that.

She was a self-centred bitch who'd believed a good man to be a killer. And now he was dead.

Jayda tapped once more.

Stacey stared at the rise and fall of the pen. 'So, what now?'

'Now?' The sympathetic pity-party had come to an end. Jayda's gaze hardened. 'I'll organise a uniform to escort you home. We'll take it from here.'

'I'm not leaving.'

'You can't possibly believe I'll let you help with the investigation?'

'You have little choice.' If Jayda's gaze was rock, Stacey's was clear-cut diamond. She would *not* be dismissed like some disobedient schoolgirl. 'Firstly, I can't "go home",' her fingers bobbed in the air around those two last words, 'because my home is lying under a hundred plus feet of eucalyptus. Secondly, for some sick reason, the killer is doing this because of me. So, either I help solve the case from within, or you send me home and I go off and look for Chase on my own. Those are your two options.'

Jayda's lips gave the merest of twitches. 'You must drive Chase to absolute distraction.'

Her lips did the same. 'You have no idea.'

Something shifted. As if somewhere between the lines they'd discovered understanding.

Stacey's gaze riveted to Jayda's and it was like staring back into herself. Even though the other woman acted all hard-assed and cool, she was anything but. Jayda wanted to find Chase just as much as she did.

'Did you contact Ethan's half-brother?'

'Not yet. We're having difficulty finding him.'

'What do you know about him?'

One more scrutinising look, then Jayda slid a folder across the desk toward her. 'This.'

Stacey dragged her chair closer, leaned forward and opened the file.

The detective flipped open a small notepad. 'Robert Miklem, aged 35, last known address five years ago was in Penrith, just outside of Sydney. Nobody's seen or heard of him since.'

Stacey blinked. Stared. Blinked again. Nothing changed, least of all the face staring coldly back.

So familiar, yet not so.

Her breath caught. Would there ever be a moment in this case she didn't want to chuck her guts?

'There's a picture in there.' Jayda's voice echoed distantly through thick fog.

So many thoughts, blasting her brain. So many lies and mistruths. For what reason? Why would brothers keep their connection a secret unless it was bad?

Seemingly oblivious, Jayda leaned in and stared at the photo. 'It's more than ten years old, but I've got tech running it through a facial aging simulation to see what he'd look like today.'

Stacey's brain slammed into lock-down.

She didn't believe in coincidences. Never had, never would.

No coincidence meant this was the lead they were looking for. If only she could read between the lines, discover the truth behind what she now knew.

That tech was wasting their time.

'You don't need tech to work out what Robert Miklem looks like today.' She clicked her mobile, scrolled through the photos until she found the one she was after.

She stared down at the screen, at the picture taken less than a month earlier. Such a short time ago. How could things have sunk so bad, so fast?

She wouldn't collapse into a heap and crawl into the corner. She wouldn't bawl her eyes out until there was no more bawl left inside.

She'd step up and find Chase, if it was the last thing she ever did.

Do or die.

The last time those words flitted through her mind, she'd told Chase they were a team, that they were in this together. Nothing had changed.

Correction.

Nothing bar one thing.

She was ready to take a chance on the man who'd taken a chance on her. Ready to give her all, her life, to save him. Because she'd fallen in love. And regardless of where that revelation left her – *them* – she wouldn't leave Chase out there alone with a killer of her making.

'What aren't you telling me, Stacey?'

Jayda was no longer tapping. The pen wielded in her hand as if it were a sword. If Stacey wasn't still reeling from shock, she might have been intimidated. All she could feel right now was dread. And a large shaft in the place where her heart used to be.

Everything slipped seamlessly into puzzle-perfect sense. How the killer knew her. Her writing. How he'd second-guessed her at times she struggled to second-guess herself.

'I know exactly who Robert Miklem is. And I know where he's been hiding these past five years.'

She swallowed and fought the pound that spread from her heart and now throbbed between her eyes. Sliding her mobile across the desk, she forced herself to meet Jayda's gaze. 'He changed his name, his hair's a little darker, his build a little heavier.' She dragged a mouthful of oxygen, kicking and screaming, into her lungs. 'But if I'm right, he's been living in Melbourne for the past three years or more, right under our noses.'

Chapter Sixty-Two

'**S**o, how do you plan on getting us out of this mess, *detective?*'

Cold, cutting words, spoken as if he were to blame for their predicament. Even bound and dirty, Candace Holland acted like a prima donna to whom the world owed everything.

Their chairs sat back-to-back, thanks to a shitload of manoeuvring on his part, and even more complaining from *her*. With his fingers straining to free the knots at her wrists, he couldn't see her face, but he could sure as hell hear the derision that had to cut deep into every line of her expression.

Snarky, bitter, about as far from the fun-loving, sassy daughter he'd fallen in love with as Earth was to some outer planet starved of the sun's rays. And much as he wanted to tell *Mrs Holland* what she could do with every one of her aspersions, she was still Stacey's mother. Still a life that didn't deserve to die. The sooner they escaped, the sooner he could take leave of her charming company. Until then, he needed her just as much as she needed him.

His fingers fumbled over her ropes.

'After I've freed you, you untie me, then we find a way out and call for back-up.'

'You make it sound so simple.' She shrugged.

His fingers slipped, the rope he'd been working free falling back into place.

Yeah. With anyone else but Madame Moaner, it would be.

'Hold still!'

He puffed out a breath, gritting his teeth to prevent swearing bloody murder at the woman fidgeting behind him. His fingers fumbled with the knots around her wrists, and every swear word in existence reeled through his mind as she jerked her hand.

'Ouch! That hurt!'

Didn't she get it'd hurt a helluva lot more if the killer returned to find them still there?

The woman was a grade A pain in his ass. 'Then stop your damn fidgeting.'

'Perhaps if you weren't such a Neanderthal I'd be able to.'

His teeth ground. But rather than grounding her out, which'd serve no purpose but to spike his already shooting temperature, perhaps he needed a different tack.

He'd loosened the first knot. Now all he had to do was ease the rope through the loop then begin working on the second.

'So, having a daughter who's an award-winning novelist – you must be pretty proud of Stacey's achievements.'

Her *hah* insinuated he didn't know shit.

'An author's only as good as her latest book.'

He could picture the flare of her nostrils, the fire and smoke shooting from her lips.

'It's all well and good to say she's making inroads, *detective*, but success isn't about looking back at where she's been. It's about looking to the future and where she's going. And there's no room for anything other than her writing if she's to reach the next peak in her career.'

He may just be a redneck detective – her insinuation, not his – but he knew a back-off speech when he heard one. You'd think she'd be happy someone was looking out for her daughter. Instead she acted as if *he* were the criminal here.

He gritted teeth that wanted nothing more than to bite back. 'Stacey's got guts and determination. She'll get what she wants and she won't let anything – or anyone – stand in her way.'

Subtle yet incisive.

He released the first knot and began work on the second. At least the hands beneath his were relatively still. Possibly because they were clenched so tight. His dig may have been petty, but it felt whopper-with-cheese satisfying. And it didn't hurt for her to be forewarned. When they got out, when the killer was caught, he'd be a permanent fixture in Stacey's life, whether her mother liked it or not.

So while it'd be that much easier, and pleasant, if Candace Holland liked him, it didn't make a difference. He wouldn't be bullied into losing the best thing that'd ever happened to him. All he had to do was convince Stacey. Something he'd spend the rest of his life doing until she came around to the only truth that made sense – they were meant for each other.

He didn't kid himself it would be easy pitting himself against Candace. She'd be anything but a pushover when it came to what she thought best for her daughter. She'd already proved as much with leaking the killer's link to Stacey to the media. Without any regard for Stacey's well-being or feelings.

'It may surprise you, *detective*, but what we want and what's best aren't always in sync. That's where a mother must do what she believes is right. No matter what the consequences.'

Difficult to know what she meant. Was she referring to him or hooking the interest of a killer? Damn, he hoped for Stacey's sake it was the first. If she had anything to do with steering the killer into her daughter's life …

The thought was too preposterous. Too … *insane*.

No mother could be that merciless. Regardless how strong the lure of fame.

Still, it did beg the question. Why was she here?

'So …'

His fingers ached, his shoulders, back and neck burned as if caught in a vice. And his entire focus was escaping this hellhole just to find Stacey and know she was okay.

That was after he'd ensured the Copycat Killer would never kill again.

He flexed then fisted his hand before reaching once again for the rope. Still no sign of their captor. He was past questioning his luck and just thankful it was turning his way. The second knot was almost free. Just one more minute and she'd untie him and they'd both get the hell out and call for back-up.

'So, how'd you manage to get dragged into this mess?'

Her hand jerked, bending his thumb back and wrenching the rope from his grip.

'Son of a–!'

Thumb and nail throbbed. But that wasn't anything on the pound in his skull.

'I have no idea why I've been targeted.' Her voice was sharp, no doubt a match to the razor he'd have seen in her eyes had they been face-to-face instead of back-to-back. 'And I don't appreciate your insinuation that I do.'

What the fuck!

He hadn't insinuated crap. But her reaction begged questioning. Like why she was so defensive? No smoke without fire, even if the source were as small as a piece of glass locking the rays of the sun.

'Don't you think you should focus your energies on getting us out of here, rather than idle chit-chat and trying to woo the mother of the woman you're fucking?'

This time it was his hand that jerked.

A real piece of work, was Candace Holland. He'd never been more tempted to leave someone, regardless of their fate. Only, that broke every code he'd ever believed in, and he wouldn't compromise his ethics, even for a first-rate bitch like the one behind him.

And she was Stacey's mother, after all.

He jerked the rope, didn't bat so much as an eyelid when she yelped.

'Do you want to get out of here or not?'

'Of course I do.'

'Then keep the fuck still and don't move until I tell you to.'

Where niceties had proved useless, his harsh words seemed to work. She huffed, but she kept still.

He slid the last knot free, relief like a rolling massage over his aching shoulders.

'How's that?'

'Well done, detective.' He twisted around, watching as her no doubt numb fingers worked over the knots at one ankle, then the other.

When she was done, she stood, stretched, ropes still clutched in her hands, then squinted toward the forked tunnels.

'Time to untie me.'

She turned. 'Or not.'

Chills racked up his spine. 'What do you mean?'

Her ski-ramp nose hiked up two notches, icy green eyes glowering down its length toward him. 'It doesn't suit me to do so.'

He wrenched his hands. Achieved nothing but cutting blisters on his already burning wrists. 'You're not fucking leaving me here!'

'That's where you're wrong.' Her lips thinned, her nostrils flared. 'Remember those things that a mother must do to protect her child? Well, this is one of them.'

The words constricted his heart as if she'd wrapped her clawed talons around it and squeezed. 'You think leaving the man she loves to die is protecting her?'

'Precisely.' She tossed the ropes at his feet. 'Men very rarely live up to their promises in anything but fiction. You may profess to love my daughter now, but when times get tough, you'll cut and run. Or make her life a living hell.' Her icicle-ridden gaze narrowed. 'One round of pain is fodder for her writing. Two will break her.'

So many thoughts caterwauled through his mind. That she considered Brad's treatment of Stacey, their whole fucked-up relationship, beneficial was outrageous.

'You don't get to make that decision for her, Candace.'

The use of her first name dragged disdain to her lips, but she held herself in check. 'You might want to review your situation, detective. That's exactly what I get to do.'

'And if I escape, what then?'

'Oh, I doubt very much that you'll escape. He's very meticulous in that way.'

'If you know him that well, you'll know that leaving here won't mean you're safe. Both you and your daughter are in danger.'

'Oh, I do know him. More than you think. And I have too much dirt for him to risk hurting either of us.'

Was she delusional?

She'd just been tied up, for god's sake. And knocked around, if the blood and bruises on her face were anything to go by. Yet, she thought she was untouchable. That she had something on the killer he and his unit didn't. Something that would keep her from harm.

The penny may have taken a frigging age to hit the ground, but once it dropped, it hit pay dirt, sure and fast. 'You've been working with him?'

A perfect, blood-soaked eyebrow arched upward. 'I wouldn't put it exactly like that.'

'Then how would you put it? Considering your actions put Stacey at risk?'

She strode forward, then stalled. As if she thought better of getting too close. It didn't stop her from towering above him. 'Stacey was *never* at risk. Not for one moment would I have agreed to that. Everything I did was for her. Has always been for her.'

'What? Destroying her car? Her house? Brutally murdering the people around her? How is that beneficial?'

'Life isn't always kind. You of all people should know that. Sometimes the best lessons are the ones that hurt the most. I gave up everything, my career, my independence, to make a good family life, and her father still left us. Like my father left my mother. We all need those lessons, and Brad was Stacey's.'

She swallowed and licked her lips. 'We made a winning team, she and I. Growing up she learned that a woman doesn't need a man to succeed. She can be strong and self-sufficient all by herself. All the men in our lives do is hold us back. And after Brad, she couldn't help but agree. Had sworn off men and relationships. Until you.'

Again her sneer shot chills through his blood. 'You're my Achilles heel, detective. But now I've found the cure.' She brushed at the dirt on her ripped top, an action that seemed more symbolic than effectual. 'Don't worry about Stacey wasting her life and mourning over you. She'll move on pretty quick once she realises the true calibre of the man she thought she loved. The same as she did for her waste of space father.'

A punch to the gut would have had the same effect.

His head jerked back. 'You lied about her father. And you're going to lie to her again.'

'Not really. What I did before doesn't concern you. And you may not have done any of it yet, but you will, given the chance. They always do, you see.' She considered the tunnels before moving toward the left and lighter of the two.

At the entrance, she turned, eyes so similar yet so different from her daughter's stared dispassionately back at him. 'Goodbye, detective.'

Acid hit the back of his throat.

He watched her disappear, hazy blue swallowing her up until the only reminder of her presence was the click of her heels against the stony ground and the ropes she tossed at his feet.

Then her footsteps stopped. Not faded – *stopped*. And as fast as they'd receded, they grew louder.

As if she'd had second thoughts.

As if she weren't all bad, after all.

The lock of his shoulders loosened, and he raised his head, peering into the murky blue. He'd be a fool to think everyone had some good in them. The job taught him that much. The Copycat, for instance. Psychopaths and sociopaths. They were irredeemable.

But Stacey's mother was neither.

With all his years on the force, he had to believe in the good of man – and woman – otherwise what the hell was he fighting for?

A shadow moved into the tunnel. Candace Holland. Backing up. Hands raised.

Another shadow followed.

He recognised the face. Recognised *his* gun in the bastard killer's hand.

The sneer was new. As was the cold and calculating in the brown of his eyes as he hobbled closer.

'Ahh, I'm so glad you've both become acquainted.' He waved the gun, forcing Candace toward her only recently vacated chair. 'It's nice to know who you'll share your last few moments with before you die, don't you think?'

His arm swung. The gun slammed against Candace's skull and she crumpled to the ground. Then he stalked toward Chase, arm raised once more.

'So, forensics came back on the toe.'

Stacey met Jayda's gaze and tried not to gag at the memory. The sound of cat's teeth gnawing against bone …

She swallowed, nodded, steeled her features against the memory.

The detective glanced at the open file on her desk, then back up at Stacey. 'DNA matches Desmond Whittaker. Your assistant editor.'

Rock slammed into her chest, stealing her breath.

It didn't make sense. Was she wrong?

Her chest squeezed.

Des was dead.

Ethan was dead.

What did that mean for Chase?

Moisture battled against her eyelids and she blinked it back.

He would not be dead.

They *would* find him. And she'd never doubt happy endings again.

But she couldn't linger on those thoughts now. She had a job to do and a man to save.

Think, Stacey.

If neither Des nor Ethan was the killer, who was? And where had he taken his victims?

Was she wrong about the photo? About the man who'd lied to her for the past three years?

'Did they find any trace evidence?'

'Good question.' Jayda nodded, looking impressed. 'They found a mixture of,' she lifted the file and squinted, '*Stachybotrys chartarum, Cladosporium sphaerospermum and Nigrospora*. All species of surface black moulds, as well as some *Aspergillus* species. An airborne mould.'

'So we're looking for an old building.'

'Impressive. Sure you're not a cop?'

'Yeah. I leave all that excitement for my stories.'

'Perhaps I should read your book sometime.'

'Perhaps you should.'

The unuttered words trailed through her thoughts. *When this is over.*

Jayda returned her gaze to the file. Her lips thinned. 'So, we're looking for any one of thousands of old buildings in Melbourne.' She slammed the file back onto the desk.

A bulb flickered in Stacey's brain. Dim, but a light all the same. 'Maybe. Maybe not.'

'What do you know?'

'I don't *know* anything, but let's think of this through the eyes of the killer. The central focus around his murders is me.' She winced. 'So, with that in mind, the building has to be something associated with me.'

'Your house.'

'What's left of it. Although, I doubt you'd find much of any of those moulds in my basement, given that the Mould Medics treated the entire area before I moved in.'

'So, if not there, where?'

'Thrasher Publishing? Maybe in all of this, both the publishing house and I are the targets. Given that both my editor and assistant editors have been murdered.' Again she winced. 'There's a whole labyrinth of underground tunnels in Port Melbourne, including a set underneath Thrasher.' Another wince. If the wind changed, she was in deep shit. 'It'd be a perfect place for murder.'

'And you know this, how?'

'Because I contemplated that exact scenario in *From Mishap to Murder*. I decided against it though. Thought it was too cliché.'

'Well, let's hope the killer doesn't agree.' Jayda was already standing, already heading toward her boss's office, a man whose face was red and round and looked constantly pissed off. That Chief Inspector Hackett wasn't a happy man was an understatement. That he scared the living crap out of Stacey, while in the same instant fascinating her, was yet another understatement. The perfect inspiration for a character.

And if she'd had either the inclination or the time, she'd probably profile him.

As it was, she was struggling to profile the man that counted right now. Figuring out the Copycat Killer was impossible. What the hell use were all her studies if when put to the test, they failed? Abysmally.

'We're getting a team together, leaving here in five minutes.' Jayda checked her holster, grabbed her keys.

Stacey stood and grabbed her bag. 'Great.'

'You're staying here.'

'No way. The killer's made this whole thing about me. So, I'm the only one who can stop him. You have to take me with you.'

She watched Jayda waver. Watched her grudgingly reach her decision.

'You stay in the car.'

'Fine.' It wasn't. But she wasn't arguing, when arguing wouldn't get her out of the precinct and nearer to Chase.

She'd figure out how to sway Jayda when she got there.

And then she'd have to figure out how to outsmart a killer who'd outsmarted her and the entire police force every bloodstained step of his way.

Chapter Sixty-Three

Sharp pain burst across Chase's cheek. And again.

He peeled his eyes open to find the bastard who'd rammed his gun against his skull bending over him.

His face split into a grin and he slapped him once more. 'Welcome back, detective.'

Then he stepped back and surveyed the area. 'We are gathered here today …' He smacked his forehead. 'Oops, wrong ceremony.'

His grin was demented.

A man who was supposed to be dead.

A man very much alive.

Regardless, his limp suggested he was less one toe. That he'd do that, butcher himself to fake his own death, demonstrated how much of a fucked-up fucker he was.

He blithely hummed a few bars of the Funeral March as the straps of a backpack slid down his arm and the bag dropped to the ground. He squatted, dragged open the zip and began rifling through its contents.

Extracted a pack of cigarettes and lit up.

Chase took stock of his surroundings for the first time since he'd been slapped toward consciousness. The tunnel had been replaced with a room or chamber. And worse, he recognised the set-up – the stage on which his chair sat, like a prop in some freak show; the cupboard no doubt containing an arsenal of weapons; and the slump of dummies lined up against the far wall.

He squinted and his blood froze. *Not dummies.*

He recognised one face, guessed the other.

Ethan and Stacey's now dead stalker-ex. There was one conversation he'd no longer need to have. And beside them, another man whose face matched that of the zoo's missing reptile handler.

He glanced back at the man responsible, still crouched on the ground, still humming Chopin past the cigarette dangling loosely from his mouth. The bastard chose that moment to look up. He met his gaze and the hack of his laughter chilled Chase's blood.

Held captive by a dead man. How ridiculous was that? And worse, he'd been working with Stacey's mother. How much, he wasn't sure. But guilty is as guilty does. Candace Holland was just as culpable in every single murder as the man lording over them.

A friend and a mother. Two people Stacey had trusted. Bloody ironic really.

He shot a venomous glance toward the "mother", once again trussed to her chair. If she'd released him as planned, their situation would have been very different right now.

He could see by her face she knew it.

He hoped the bitch stewed on the thought.

The death march morphed into a Whistle While You Work whistle, as contents were extracted from the bag and positioned in a perfect line at the killer's feet. First a spool of fishing line. Next a bag of hooks, some sinkers. A pair of pliers.

As each item joined the last, Candace's eyes widened, her skin paling until he wondered if she might disappear completely. A pair of bolt cutters hit the ground and she whimpered.

Chase lifted his shoulders and blanked his expression. Refused to give the bastard the satisfaction of knowing he had him freaked. Regardless, his fingers flexed at the thought of bolt cutter blades pressed against them. For a man who'd coldly amputated his toe in order to fake his own death, nothing was beyond the sick realms of possibility.

One deep breath and Chase narrowed his gaze on the double crown, like two beady eyes staring him down. 'What is it you want?'

He looked up from the bag. 'Oh, so many things.'

One slow drag on his cigarette and the bastard stalked closer.

Chase glared right back at the fucker.

His chuckle was devoid of humour. 'We could start by seeing what's so special about Detective Chase Durant.' With a flash of metal, shirt buttons skidded over the concrete floor. Then the thin knife blade flicked the edges of Chase's shirt open.

He flinched. Hated that he'd shown weakness.

The cold gaze crawled down his now exposed abdomen. 'Such a

wonderful specimen. So perfect. Flawless, even.' He withdrew the cigarette from his lips and glanced down at the curling smoke. 'A disgusting habit. I keep telling myself I should quit.'

It dangled between his fingers. He leaned in on a waft of peppermint and stale ash. 'So bad for one's health.'

Sharp heat singed Chase's chest and he jerked against his restraints.

'Mother fucker–!'

The bastard stubbed the cigarette more than once, twisting – like a hot poker piercing into his flesh – until the glow dimmed.

Charred skin filled his nostrils.

He grinned. 'Not so perfect now, are we, detective?'

'What the fuck do you want?'

He dropped the crushed cigarette into a bag and then into his pocket. From another pocket he extracted a mint which he proceeded to unwrap and pop into his mouth, before slam-dunking the wrapping into a bin. 'Don't tell me a hotshot detective like you hasn't figured it out yet.'

He had a hunch, but he'd give anything to be wrong.

His grin was gruesome and greedy all at once. 'I want Stacey.'

Candace gasped.

His lips thinned across bared teeth as he glanced her way. 'Poor, poor Candace. Just when you thought you'd found someone who really gave a crap, the mean old world delivers a blow right to your achin' breakin' heart. You were a means to an end, my lovely, nothing more.' He lifted the bolt cutters, snapped them open and shut, taking pleasure in her fearful shudders before placing them back down.

Chase's mind raced. The killer and Candace?

So much made sense now.

Her assertions of having dirt on the killer. His insights on Stacey.

Chase yanked his hands. Stretched his fingers, reaching for the knots. *Impossible.* His gaze scoured the area, looking for something – anything – that would help him escape, even as he searched for something distracting to say.

'Stacey will never willingly be with you. Even less if you hurt people she cares about.'

'I don't need her willing, I just need her alive. The rest she'll learn, in time.'

The words carved through his soul.

Over my dead body.

That the vow might turn out to be true he wouldn't consider.

His gaze slid over walls slathered with green and black algae. Over a set of shiny metal wrist and ankle restraints bolted to the wall, just to his right. The kind you'd find in old prison movies. Only these were new, but not unused. Red caked to their surface and to the wall told him as much. Had Ethan fallen prey to them? Had Jagger? He may not have liked either man, but neither deserved the fate they'd been served.

Neither did he. The only fate he'd accept was freedom, and reuniting with Stacey.

At his back was what looked to be an iron door, heavily bolted. Were they still in the tunnels? Possibly. He doubted the bastard could have dragged him far in his chair. And it didn't feel as if he'd been untied while he was unconscious.

'It's only a matter of time until my team figures out you faked your death.'

'You really believe they're that clever? When they haven't even uncovered my true identity?'

What the hell did he mean by that?

He zipped up the backpack, stood, and set it aside. 'If we're knocking about scenarios, here's another one for you. A famous romantic suspense author disappears and all they find is a finger. Or maybe a toe. We'll cross that digit when we come to it.' He grinned. Ghoulish. Chilling.

He hobbled closer, favouring his right foot. 'So, editor and author are dead, the last known murders of the man police call the Copycat Killer. There are no real leads. Interest in the case wanes. It turns cold and as time passes, life continues on its own merry path. The media move onto more pressing matters, and the story of Stacey Holland and her novel that came to life will soon be a blip in the past. The cops will focus their resources onto other more imperative cases, leaving me free to live my life with the woman I love.'

'You've been editing fiction so long, you can't tell what's real and what's not.'

'We make our own reality, detective.'

'Some things you can't control. Like Stacey. She'll never love you back.'

He snorted. 'It's almost tempting to let you live long enough to realise your error.' His gaze narrowed to two black slits. 'The Stockholm syndrome has been known to kick in as early as a few days after capture. Give me a few weeks and Stacey'll never want to leave.'

Fire blistered his veins. 'You sick bastard.'

'I won't apologise for knowing what I want and making it happen. If that's sick, so be it.'

'My daughter is going to kick your butt, you asshole.'

Chase started. Candace leaned forward, eyes blazing like a dragon on the verge of attack.

He'd almost forgotten she was there.

Words spat like flames from her lips. 'She has more balls than you'll ever have.'

The bastard laughed, his loathing gaze crawling from what remained of her strawberry blonde coiffure to the grubby-scuffed tips of her designer stilettos. 'Wait until she discovers just how far her mother was willing to go for a few measly book sales. For a slice of fame, even if it's enjoyed from one degree of separation. When she sees how the people she trusted betrayed her, she'll have little choice but to trust the man who is there for her now.'

'Why kill to get her attention? Why not just ask her out?'

'So I could butt heads with her cock and bull idea about not dating?'

Chase grunted. *At least she didn't lie about that.*

The killer leaned in. 'What's that?'

Damn! Did he mutter the words under his breath?

'It wasn't a lie. She told me the same thing.'

His leer was cold. Cruel. 'Strike out, did we detective?'

Better he believed he had. 'So, it seems.'

'Yet, I know you've been fuck-buddies since the night I let that dimwit find her skanky cat. Since I killed Jagger for letting himself get caught tampering with her car.'

The words sucked up every drop of moisture from Chase's mouth.

'Jagger was working for you?'

'He owed me money, and that very fact gave him little choice in the matter. Although, when I told him you were the intended victim, well, I reckon he'd have done it all for free.'

'Why Stacey's car? She could have been hurt. Killed. Yet you profess to love her.'

'What's love without a little uncertainty?' He cocked his maniacal head. 'That she survived everything I flung her way is the universe saying we're meant to be. Just as the universe will send her to me when the time is right. It's our destiny.'

'You're demented.'

'You say demented, I say determined. It's all semantics, detective.'

What was he to say to that?

If he could knock every pearly tooth out of his mouth, every filthy word from his head, he would.

Only, he was a fucking prisoner.

He clamped his lips and waited.

If only he'd leave them both again. He could undo the knots, and this time Candace would have no choice but to set him free. Surely she wouldn't be so dumb-ass as to make the same mistake twice?

The bastard glanced at his watch, cocked his head, then considered them both with eyes of cold, calculating black.

'Riveting as this conversation is, it's time we moved on.' He crouched, hand wavering over the pliers, not stopping until it rested on the bolt cutters. He straightened, weighed them in his palm, then ambled slowly toward them.

His fingers wrapped around the red rubber grips as he leisurely tested their measure. Then his gaze skipped over Candace toward him.

'This is just too delicious. Mother and lover.' Another snap of sharp metal jaws. 'Which one do you think should go first?'

'The area's secure. We're ready to go in.'

With a burst of static, Jayda returned her two-way to her belt.

Stacey glowered at her from beside the stony-faced uniform and the wrong side of the blue and white taped barricade. To no avail. Seems scowling brandished a blanket "no effect" on detectives with guns.

Not that it mattered. She had her own agenda, and it didn't involve playing the good girl with her designated babysitter.

Jayda's expression had already transformed into the kick-ass cop mode each one of her counterparts wore as armour. They were ready to face a killer.

And she should have been part of their plan.

Tight fists clenched at her side.

Jayda's cat-green eyes narrowed. 'Remember our deal and stay put.'

She didn't bother to answer. But she didn't nod or smile agreement either. The moment Jayda was gone, she'd initiate her plan.

'You'll be safer here. And Chase'll be safer too. We need to rescue him without worrying about your safety. Got it?'

She nodded then. But it indicated anything but compliance.

'O-kay then.'

With a stern look to Mr Stony-face – or Officer Taylor, so she'd been told – Jayda joined four other detectives entering the front of the building. Another group had already circled round the back and were no doubt entering the tunnels through the manhole Beth and Des had shown her oh, so many months ago.

So much had changed since that day. All she'd sought back then was authenticity and an award-winning story. She'd won both, plus the validation Brad had made her so hungry to find with his constant battering of her confidence.

Chase had given her that. And more. He'd given her his heart. All she wanted now was a chance to give him the gift of hers in return.

'So, Officer Taylor, how long have you been a cop?'

'Long enough, Ma'am.'

Her lips twitched. 'Long enough for what?'

'To know you have no intention of remaining here with me. I, however, must inform you, I've no intention of letting you out of my sight.'

The twitch stopped, overtaken by a full-on frown. 'You know the man I love is inside?'

'So I hear.'

'What would you do if it was the woman you love? What then?'

'I'd do anything and everything I could to set her free.'

'So, you get it.'

'Just because I get where you're coming from, doesn't mean I'll risk the raid over sentimentality. You're staying put until I'm instructed otherwise.'

Okay. So her plan was defunct. Time to develop another.

'Damn, I wish I hadn't drunk that last mug of coffee. Don't suppose there are any loos around here?'

'Ones with back windows to climb through while I wait outside?'

'No, the kind that'll stop me peeing my pants.'

He didn't look the least bit amused. Or fooled. 'You'll just have to hold on.'

'How long.'

'As long as it takes.'

'That sounds like a helluva long time.'

He narrowed his gaze, his big hand resting against the gun at his hip. 'I know Detective Durant. Did you know that?'

Her head snapped back. 'No, I didn't.'

'He's a good bloke. Funny. Dedicated. A credit to his job. I want to see him saved just as much as you do.'

'Good. Then we're on the same page.' She scrubbed her forehead, damp and clammy despite the air's underlying chill. 'You should let me go.'

'I told you that so you understand why I can't.'

'The sole reason the Copycat is killing is to get to me. He's obsessed with me. Wants to impress me. Taking that into consideration, who do you think he's more likely to listen to? A gun-wielding detective or the woman he's prepared to kill for?'

'You approaching the killer puts the detective in more danger, not less.'

'How'd you figure that?'

'Once he has you, there's no reason to keep Detective Durant alive.'

'There's no reason now. Don't you see, I'm the only one who can stop him?'

He shook his thick, numbskull head. 'That's our job. Yours is to stay here and let us do it.'

How could he not see it? The Copycat wasn't keeping Chase alive to get to her. More, he was killing him for that same end. And if she got to him before he hurt Chase, perhaps there was a way to convince him of letting Chase live. Even if it meant trading places.

She'd do that. Trade places if it meant Chase got out alive.

She had no doubt Chase would turn around and save her right back.

First, she needed to escape Dick Tracy's staunch protection … *Shazz*. One mention of the weather and she'd know something was up. Their code had never failed in the past.

'Can I call a friend or must I ask permission to do that too?'

'Sure you can call. But put your phone on speaker.'

There goes that idea.

Trying her darnedest not to huff, she crossed her arms. And huffed. 'You really are one of the most suspicious people I've met.'

'I've probably watched as many cop shows as you have. Maybe more. If there's a trick, I've seen it. Bananas in exhaust pipes and sugar in the engine only work in Hollywood. This is the real world. Cops aren't that gullible. The danger is real, and death isn't something you can rewrite if it doesn't work the first time.'

'You sound a lot like Chase.'

'I'll take that as a compliment.'

She glanced at her watch. Five whole minutes since Jayda had gone in.

Static burst from the two-way strapped to Stony-face's belt.

'Can we at least wait in a car?' She waved her hand at the line of marked and unmarked vehicles behind them. 'My feet are killing me and I'm bushed.'

'If you want.'

He followed her to a nearby unmarked sedan. She reached for the front door and he slapped his hand on the window. 'In the back.' She gave him "the look" which he returned with a "nice try" expression. Her heart dropped and splattered onto the cracked concrete beneath her feet. The ruse would have worked if she'd written it. Why couldn't life be more like a book?

Her fingers froze on the handle. The Copycat's victims, her scenes, *his*, slammed her mind. They were here because her story *had* leached into life. There were still other things he hadn't copied. Best to be thankful for that and not wish for more.

She slipped into the back seat, her gaze scanning the interior. Did unmarked police cars have the same internal locking system as marked cars? Was her plan over before it started?

The stern Officer Taylor stood outside, watching.

She lay down across the backseat and waited. A shadow fell over the door as he peered at her through the window. She held her breath. He straightened. Turned. Didn't retreat as she'd hoped.

Damn!

She kicked the door and flinched. *Oww!*

Tears sprung to her eyes.

Now what?

She was running out of options. *Running out of time.*

Think.

She couldn't. Her brain was frozen and all she could think about was Chase. His precious finger left on the windscreen of her car.

Bile coursed up her throat. She swallowed it back, shoved at the images.

No!

There had to be a way out of the car without her sentry noticing. She could call Shazz now.

She glanced at the window, and the beady brown eyes staring back.

Not without being noticed.

Scrunching her eyes closed, she willed her breathing to slow. Losing it wasn't an option. She still had to try. Still had to save Chase.

Static shrilled just beyond the window.

She peeked through one eye.

Her bodyguard raised the two-way and answered. She felt his gaze on her, then heard his receding voice as he stepped away from the car.

Her cue! She wouldn't get another.

She inched toward the far door. Prayed, then sighed in relief as it opened. The click was marginal, but she still lay there a few seconds, heart galloping, in case he heard.

No shadow. No accusing glare.

She eased the door open, slowly, carefully, praying for no giveaway squeak, and then she slipped outside before easing it together once again. Holding her breath, heart still racing, eyes darting left, right and centre, she crept around the line of vehicles before circling back toward the building. She had one more trick up her sleeve.

Slipping through the entrance of the Old England Pub, another glorious white building adjacent to Colonial House, she made her way across the foyer and turned left down a narrow corridor. The grey door toward the end was marked "private" but she turned the handle anyway. She glanced over her shoulder and then pushed. It was unlocked, as it was the last time. As she'd been assured it always was.

One last check that she was alone, then she slipped inside. The door clicked closed and she slumped against it, the painted metal icy and unforgiving at her back. Her breath caught. Dark, damp and disinfectant shrouded her, sucking the oxygen from her lungs.

Shaky fingers fumbled in her handbag. Seconds ticked into minutes. Her heartbeat pounded so loud it crowded all thought from her mind. Her fingertips contacted plastic. *Her torch.* She snapped it on and a mess of buckets, mops and old rags sprang into view. On shaky legs, she battled her way through, wishing she were headed toward Narnia and not a killer.

Past experience proved wishing didn't create alternate realities, but it didn't stop her wishing that wasn't the case. Seemed she was a fool who still believed good would always trump evil. She had to if she was to get through what lay ahead without losing her nerve.

Her head spun. Her breathing too fast, too shallow. She dragged the back of her hand over her forehead before sweat dripped into her eyes.

Her vision blurred.

She blinked. Tried to slow her breathing. Her head continued to whirl and she gulped in a sharp mouthful of air.

The flashlight beam wobbled as she located the large metal shelf. It was already angled away from the wall.

Every heartbeat pushed bile into the back of her throat. Sweat laced her palms, her neck. Beads of it snaked between her breasts, and a bucket-load more soaked her armpits and ran rivers down her back.

The small room was big enough to move around in, yet the four walls crowded her. As if they moved slowly inwards, crushing her mind, every sense of space she owned.

And the sensation was about to get worse.

She peeked around the shelves. The vent was still there. Still open. Swapping the torch to her left hand, she extracted the little spray bottle with her right. Pepper spray was illegal in Melbourne, but her cocktail of hairspray, olive oil and tabasco wasn't. She zipped up her bag, hunkered down and peered through the opening.

There were no cobwebs across the entrance this time. If only there were. That he'd crawled through here recently was obvious. How recently wasn't.

Was he still inside?

She had no way of knowing. What she did know was she had no other choice but to squeeze herself in and let memory guide the way. And when she reached the end, when she came out the other side, only smarts and sheer force of will would get her through the rest.

Chapter Sixty-Four

The sobbing gnawed at every fibre of Chase's nerves.

He gritted his teeth against words he'd doubtless regret once they were out. After all, if nothing else, Candace's very vocal distress provided the distraction he needed.

His shoulders bunched, wrists burning with the pull of the nylon, but he was nearly there. Why he hadn't thought of it earlier bugged the crap out of him. But he'd thought of it now, if only Candace would tone things down and give his throbbing head a break. Difficult to feel sorry for her when her predicament was of her own making. Still, he wouldn't be human if he didn't feel a modicum of unease at her suffering. That the bastard hadn't laid a finger on her yet didn't matter. It wouldn't be long until he grew tired with taunting and made good on every one of his threats. The large bolt cutters swinging from his hand the most obvious.

The metal patch snapped free of his waistband and he positioned it between finger and thumb, working it slowly against the nylon, sliding back and forth, blanking his expression even as both arms and shoulders screamed in protest.

The bastard circled their chairs, a hungry beast circling his prey, and Chase wrapped the metal in his palm. Fingertips swiped slowly across the back of his hand, then he watched Candace experience the same.

Her eyes were barely wet, but her sobs were loud and shafting. There were tears, but who knew if they were crocodile or not? The woman was as genuine as a Botox smile. Her gaze, when she met his, was granite.

At a guess, she'd moved from shouldering responsibility to laying the blame squarely on him. The woman was steeped in self-righteousness with no intention of finding a way out.

A leopard's spots changed as they aged, Candace Holland did not.

'Such pretty fingers.'

Candace jerked, eyes wider than Chase had believed possible.

His heart battered against his ribcage, his gaze bolted to the killer and his baby-soft hands wandering over hers, still trussed behind her back. His lips fluttered across her ear, his words so soft Chase had to strain to hear them. 'What a shame you can't keep them all. Any choice on which should go first?'

He kissed her neck, the base where it joined her shoulder and disappeared beneath the expensive silk of her top. She trembled. His hand wrapped over hers and the snap of bone shattered the air.

Candace howled. The bastard guffawed.

Chase wrenched against his bindings. 'You fucking asshole!'

'Oh, we've barely begun.' He twirled a lock of her hair about his finger, let the curl drop, then lightly brushed a tear from her grubby cheek. 'You act like such a big, bad girl, wronged by so many, paying it forward to so many more, yet you're nothing when weighed against the big, bad wolf.'

Wide lips spread thin across his bared teeth. Like the animal he professed to be.

'Scream as loud as you like, my little candy cane. Not a soul will hear or come to your rescue. And if someone tries, well, let's just say, they'll have one hell of a blast before they reach us.' A smirk slinked across his lips like a hyena slinks across its dead prey.

The pet name was as ironic as Chase's sympathy. Neither held the staunch of logic or reason.

The killer leaned in, his breath no doubt chilling Candace's neck. 'Time we started properly, don't you think?' He weighed the bolt cutters in his hand, snapped them purposefully just inches from her face.

She jolted. Whimpered. This time the fear in her eyes was real. No doubt so were the tears.

'Any last words before we begin?'

She swallowed. Sniffed. Her lips trembled. 'You said you l-loved me.'

'Ahh, yes. Words. Like orgasms. So easy to utter, and even easier to fake. You of all people should know they're as empty as your blackened heart.'

The blades cracked again.

Cricket-song broke out from somewhere nearby.

Raising his brows, he moved away and withdrew a mobile from his pocket. He tapped the screen, his grin slow-spreading and smug.

'And the fun begins,' he murmured, tapping the screen a couple times more. 'So deliciously predictable.'

The glassy gaze ripped across Chase, then Candace, then back again.

'Ever wonder how I knew your little ruse on the boat was a trap?' He dropped the bolt cutters onto the ground and extracted the gun from his waistband. 'It was too easy. I know Stacey. How the cogs in her mind work. What she'll say, how she'll react. How the little pulse on her neck races when she's excited, how the green of her irises disappears when she's aroused. How her lips quiver, then soften when she's kissed. How she moans when you come inside her.'

Metal sliced Chase's palm as his fist clenched. That the bastard was trying to rile him registered in the periphery of his mind. White-hot anger raged through his blood. What he'd do to silence the son of a bitch. Stifle every acerbic word before it left his lips. Leave him so he'd never utter a single word again.

'I know her better than anyone. And I'll keep on knowing her long after you're both gone.'

The implication rammed Chase's brain, even as his mind screamed in protest. The animal wouldn't lay a single, blood-stained finger on Stacey. Not while Chase still had the wherewithal to breathe. To batter him to a pulp.

Holding his shoulders still, he sawed the metal patch across the rope. The fibres weren't giving way yet, but they would.

'The universe has delivered.' The bastard glanced down at his phone. 'Things are about to get *very* interesting.'

He felt the ropes slacken. A *ping* as one of the coils snapped.

'But first …'

Ice-cold steel pressed against his temple. His heart hammered.

'Drop it, Durant.'

He froze. Eyes darting left to watch the killer's finger tense against the trigger.

Not now!

Chase's grip tightened around his make-shift blade. *He can't possibly know.*

'*Drop it!*' The barrel imprinted his skull. 'Much as I've anticipated the pleasure of drawing out our association, I won't hesitate to blow your brains from here to Hanging Rock if necessary.'

Chase let go and metal clanged against concrete. His best chance at breaking free now lay on the ground behind him.

Steel brushed across his brow, a cold caress. 'Good boy.' The voice softened, as if praising a tail-wagging companion.

Then the barrel retracted before sharp pain slammed against the back of his head.

A star-studded black filled his vision.

He blinked, fighting the draw of the dark.

Vaguely, he felt the pull of fresh nylon at his wrists. One final tug then the bastard stepped back, his gaze intent on his phone before it raised and slid between him and Candace.

Then he grinned. 'We're about to discover which one of you the charming Stacey Holland loves the most.'

Stacey's throat was so freaking raw, it was a wonder each breath didn't echo through the entire maze of tunnels.

Heat and dust coated her mouth, her dry lips cracking with the slightest movement.

She inched toward the muted light. Had long-since switched off her torch. No sense risking the element of surprise with a flickering light show.

Her shoulders bunched, her arms stretched out in front, one clasping her bag, the other her security spray. She pulled her body forward with her elbows, pushing at the ground with her toes. Her knees burned, the cramp in her left leg so intense she'd stopped trying to block it out, instead breathing and riding through the pain. It had nothing on what Chase would experience if she didn't get there in time.

She had to get there in time.

The outlet was only metres away.

Her chest was so tight, her heartbeat so fast. She'd never been so shit-scared in her life.

Chase's words haunted her.

I'm busy in the real world, solving real problems, catching real killers. I don't have time for pretend.

This wasn't pretend. Her keyboard no longer controlled the turn of events. If either one of them met with the wrong end of a knife or a gun or a serial killer's malice, there'd be no room for rewrites. No room for second-round edits or proofs.

They had one shot only. *Life or death.*

The thought shuddered through her control.

You can do this, Stacey. You know what makes a kick-ass heroine. Now all you have to do is be one.

The square of blue light widened as she closed in. Another minute and she'd be on the cusp. Then all she had to do was ease her way out of the vent, find a killer and stop him before he did something she'd regret for the rest of her life.

Regret because she'd lacked the guts to tell Chase "to hell with the circumstances, I'm going to love you no matter what". Instead, she'd pulled back and given in to fear. A fear that had nothing on what she was experiencing now. Fear that may have cost her the one chance to tell the man she loved how much he meant.

No.

She wouldn't think like that. Wouldn't let defeat take over, when the only thing between her and defeat was sheer will and smarts.

She blinked. Like she'd done the few times light had flashed. At first she'd thought someone else was up ahead. Then she realised it was like the flash of a camera. The knowledge squeezed at her heart, but not once did she consider turning back. She needed to get to Chase and keep him alive.

The cops outside would do the rest.

Even though the light ahead was a gloomy blue, it scorched her cornea after the murky dark in the vent. Grit caked her eyeballs and she needed a drink so badly she'd do anything for a drop of water.

Her mind raced, ideas on what to do next bouncing about like a pinball. She had to be the biggest fool around, walking – or more accurately *crawling* – into a hostage situation without a game plan, let alone a gun. She had a spray can and a handbag.

Fat lot of good they'd be if things turned bad.

Her fingertips reached the edge of her tunnel and she pulled herself forward, taking her first fresh gulp of air in fifteen minutes.

She blinked a few times, waited for her eyes to accustom to the light.

Focused.

Shit!

Much as she'd expected it, the reality rammed against her confidence.

Breath rasped against the back of her throat, and the world caved in, more claustrophobic than anytime during her crawl. Dank and sour filled her nostrils, the empty echo of dripping water the only sound.

Other than her heartbeat. That thrashed in her ears until she thought her eardrums might burst. Until it seemed as if the entire world around her might explode.

Her gaze dropped to the concrete floor – mere inches from where she'd frozen – and two perfectly shined shoes pointing straight toward her.

No need to wonder whether or where she'd find him. Her guess had been right. She had the location, she had the killer, and she'd even made it to the top of her own too stupid to live list.

She should move. Retreat back into the vent. Scramble out and run. Only every muscle had clenched into a gridlock.

He hunkered down, and then she saw the gun in his hand. The beastly grin on his face.

Her body began to shake.

'Hello Stacey. How nice of you to pop by.'

Chapter Sixty-Five

It would have been a smile if not for the predatory gleam in his eyes.

Realisation hammered through her already pounding brain – a dead man, greeting her as if it were the most natural thing in the world.

Des.

The Copycat Killer. Her assistant editor. The man who'd dragged her life and career through the mud. Murdered and maimed countless victims. Was perhaps planning to do the same to her, once he'd fulfilled whatever sick-assed delusions he had for her first.

Des plucked the spray from her fingers. Relieved her of her bag. Then proffered the hand not holding the gun. 'Let me help you up.'

She ignored the gesture and scrambled to her feet, her mind racing, searching for a plan.

What would your characters do?

Play along and wait for an opening.

It wasn't as if she had much choice. Plus, she needed to find Chase.

She rubbed her gritty, sweat-soaked palms over her thighs. His gaze followed their movement, then slithered over every inch of her, all the way down to her toes. Repulsion couldn't have hit with more ferocity if that gaze were replaced by a swarm of scuttling spiders. And no matter that she was fully clothed, he made her feel naked and exposed and so incredibly dirty.

His suit, the staid pink shirt and tie, were impeccable. Spotless. As if this were any other day. Any other meeting.

He met her gaze with brown eyes that had never seemed so chilling. 'You're just in time. We almost started the party without you.'

'We?' Did he mean Chase?

For the first time in too long, her heart leapt and filled with hope.

He's alive!

'Let's leave our guest list a surprise, shall we?' He waved the gun toward the left of the tunnel. A dead end lay to the right. An entire kilometre of Melbourne Rail Link and only *then* did planning figure out they'd got it wrong.

Des rested his palm against her lower back. She jumped, but he didn't seem to care. 'After you.'

Her sneakers padded against the uneven ground, her gaze flying every which way. Committing her surroundings once more to memory. Looking for something that might come in use when she and Chase made their escape.

Her mind flew to her research on hostage situations. The key was connecting with the hostage-taker. Building rapport. That they should already have rapport by the bucket-load made no difference. It wouldn't hurt to build on it. Make it more difficult for Des to hurt her. And as a consequence, Chase.

Getting him to talk seemed like a good start. And a distraction from the gun he was so carelessly brandishing her way.

'Why are you doing this Des?'

His head jerked back, brows arching high into his temple. 'You don't know?'

His surprise seemed genuine. She shook her head, biting her lip and words that could very well stop him from answering.

'I did it for you.'

'You killed my friends.'

'I assume you're talking about Jagger. He was a lowlife. Your ex wasn't much better.'

'And Ethan?'

'Ethan I did for me.'

'He was your brother.'

'And a constant reminder of my failings.' His lips curled around the words like a predator's talons curling around the charred remains of its meal. 'The favourite son. The perfect grandchild. The irresistible lover. He was a pissy do-gooder who thought he was too special to associate with the likes of his lesser brother. He deserved to die.'

Her stomach churned. That he could kill his own flesh and blood ...

What hope did that leave for her?

He slashed hand and gun through the air. 'Forget them. They're nothing. What matters is us. We make a good team. With your imagination and my skills, we beat any cliché ever written. Brains and brawn. A modern day Bonnie and Clyde.'

He grinned, and regardless that the humour bypassed his eyes, she could almost believe this was the old Des. The Des before the killer wielded control. Chatty, acting like their get-together was nothing more than a catch-up between friends. A fun day out.

'Bonnie was a writer. Did you know that?'

She nodded. Thought back to the evening he'd mentioned it. The evening before he killed Beth and Ethan, and slowly chipped away at her life.

The gun loomed in her face. 'I'm making conversation here. The least you could do is join in.'

This was not the Des she remembered. Easy going, funny, a little inappropriate, but damn good at his job, and to a point, a friend.

She swallowed. 'Yes. I remember you mentioned it at dinner.'

He nodded. 'Bonnie was married to some lowlife who ended up in prison. Clyde was the last and only true love in her life. After she met him, she never looked back.'

He was drawing parallels. Sick parallels. Was he so delusional as to believe she'd want to be with him – *fall in love with him* – after everything? Regardless of the scald that thought dragged up through her gut, she swallowed her disgust. His weakness might turn out to be her strength.

'You've always been a fan of Bonnie and Clyde.'

'More than a fan. We're going to bring their story back to life.'

She inhaled, breathing through her rising panic, trying not to lose whatever control she still retained over her nerves. She needed calm, focus. Needed to find a way out of this mess and Des's delusional fantasies.

The tunnel curved then widened. The intended location for Port Melbourne station, no doubt. Directly in front the tunnel forked, but that wasn't what snagged her attention.

A door. Metal reinforced. Double-locked. The one place they hadn't entered when Des and Beth had conducted their tour oh, so many months ago.

He flourished a set of keys. With a wide grin and double *click* the door swung open. 'Welcome to my domain.' He pressed his hand into her lower back.

She stumbled forward, away from his touch and into a room that ripped the band aid from her calm. *Her writing cave.*

The whirl of her mind almost hurled her to her knees. She braced, scoured the room again, slower this time. Not her writing cave. A replica, but with a difference.

Everything's real. The weapons, the props, the mannequin-like bodies slumped in the corner. *Ethan. Brad.*

Her throat constricted.

The writing cave had been Des's idea. He'd even helped with the design. But not once had he let slip he had a "cave" of his own.

He had it all; a locked cupboard, no doubt filled with weapons that didn't bear thinking about; a bragging corner, but where hers showcased awards, his featured news clippings and a photo array of victims, crime scenes, persons of interest. *Her.*

She ripped her gaze away and focused on the centre of the room. A desk. A stage. Two chairs facing the far wall.

She rushed forward, almost tripping up the stairs to reach him. The sandy blonde hair and broad, muscular shoulders were unmistakable. With his head bowed and blood glistening a trail over one ear, he looked anything but alive.

'Chase!'

His head jerked, and her heart jerked with it. He turned and she almost lost herself in those wondrous blue eyes.

A vice-like grip wrapped around her arm and her body jerked back.

Chase growled, wrenching forward against his restraints. Then his gaze shuttered. His nostrils flared. 'What the fuck are you doing here?'

Des yanked her in closer, until every inch of contacted skin crawled like she'd landed in a pit of worms. The skin beneath his palm stung, but it didn't hurt half as much as the venom in Chase's voice.

'What part of "back off" do you *not* understand?'

Her heart twisted, even as she told herself it was an act. The strategy made sense. Mask how much someone means to you and rob the killer of leverage.

Logic said the explanation fit. Emotions cut her heart into little pieces until her chest stabbed with every word.

'Trouble in paradise? How terribly cliché.' Des's slimy gaze flicked between them, then latched back to Chase. 'Am I to imagine you're less enamoured than you led Stacey to believe?'

'I did what was necessary to work the case.'

Des slammed Chase's temple with the butt of his gun. His head rolled back and a fine trail of blood wound its way over his brow. 'Shame your mother couldn't stick around and teach you some respect.'

'You bastard!' Her scream was accompanied by a caterwaul that froze her insides. The voice, so familiar. So shattering.

She whipped around, her gaze locking onto the other chair. The other occupant. Until now a mere blip in her peripheral vision.

The cement walls and ceiling and every terrifying, hideous thing in between began to spin. If she'd thought the weight of guilt couldn't drag her down further, she was wrong.

'Mum?'

Through all their differences – all the hurt and control, the constant bitching and nagging – one thing had never changed. The woman before her, all trussed up and dirty and bruised, was still her mother. Still the woman who'd cared enough to stick around and push her to make something of herself. Single-motherhood wasn't a breeze. Yet her mother had made it work and, at the end of it all, they'd both come out more than okay. Because she'd pushed herself and her daughter to succeed.

The sting in Stacey's heart swelled. Intensified.

Her mother had been thrust into the line of fire *because of her.*

She wrenched away from Des and this time he let her go.

Chase slumped in his seat, head lolling to one side. The front of his shirt gaped, revealing his beautiful chest and a patch of red, raw welts. What the hell had the bastard done? She longed to go to him, but instinct stopped her. Des was watching, and the more he witnessed their connection, the more he'd do to sever it. Translation – hurt Chase, or worse.

Her mother's face was grimy and tear-ridden. A purple bruise was darkening around her right eye and countless others scattered up her arms, disappearing under her silky grey sleeves.

Stacey wrapped her arms awkwardly around her mother's trembling body, her voice all wobbly and thick. 'Are you okay?'

Even now, with all that was happening, her mother's body stiffened. Unyielding. 'Why did you come, Stacey Marigold?'

The starch-stiffened shoulders shrugged inside her embrace. Her heart twisted as she dropped her arms and stepped away.

Only then did she remember the death-filled gaze scorching her back. 'I came to see Des.'

'How very touching.' His scorn-ridden voice slithered under her skin, zipping along her already frayed nerves.

Her mother barely glanced at Des. 'You should have stayed away.'

'Want to tell her why that is, Candace?'

Something in Des's words, his voice, affected her mother. Her expression turned furtive. Guilty, almost. 'No reason other than you being a sick sonofabitch.'

'Now, now. Is that any way to speak to your lover?'

Everything inside Stacey froze. 'What's he talking about, Mum?'

Beneath the bruises, the streaked blood and whatever makeup remained, her mother's face turned deathly white. She shook her head, but didn't answer. She didn't need to.

Her look, the rain of realisation in Stacey's mind, made everything all too clear. Insight was like a club slamming her head. *Her mother and Des.* All those visits to Thrasher. All those times her mother spoke of fostering a relationship between publisher and author. Instead she'd been fostering something quite different.

And worse – if that was at all possible – while he'd been fucking her mother, Des had been pursuing her.

She swallowed, hard. Fighting the churn in her stomach that threatened to overflow.

Would his level of sickness ever stop sinking toward rock-bottom?

'How *could* you?'

He sneered. 'Ever heard the maxim, it takes two to tango?'

'And all that time you pretended to be interested in me.'

'Oh, that was never pretend. Wanting you has always been very, very real.' He curled his fingers around her upper arm.

She tried to yank free. Unsuccessfully.

From the corner of her eye she saw Chase's eyes open. Rage flooded his expression.

She shook her head, barely perceptible, but hopefully he noticed. She wouldn't be the reason he suffered another blow.

She was here to rescue him, not the other way round.

And she'd do it. She just had to figure out how.

Des pulled her closer. 'You were a means to an end, Candace. Nothing more. Your heart's cold. Your body colder. A man wants a woman who makes him feel alive. Difficult when the woman's already dead inside.'

Red flooded her mother's cheeks. 'Bastard!'

'All this name-calling, it doesn't become you.'

Anger roared through Stacey's blood. She wanted to rip the sound of Des's voice from her ears. Rip the visuals of Des and her mother from her brain.

Rip the heart and life out of Des's hateful soul.

'You said you did all this for me. That you wanted me. Well, I'm here now, so you can let them both go.'

'What'd be the fun in that?' A burst of chirping cricket-song prevented her from saying more. And just when she wondered where the hell they were hiding, he pulled out his phone and tapped the screen. The chirping stopped. Another couple of taps, then he looked up.

'*Tut-tut*, Stacey. You forgot to tell me you brought friends.'

His grin shivered deep into her bones.

So he had cameras other than those in the air vent. He knew the cops were outside, yet his mood was more amused than worried.

The thought locked every muscle in her body. His expression said he had something planned. Impossible to wrap her mind around what. Or how bad it would be.

Whatever it was, she had to stop it.

She grabbed his sleeve, much as the contact made her skin crawl. 'There's still time to get away.'

'Yes, there is. *Plenty*.' He thrust his phone in her face.

The screen was on.

At the bottom, a large red button flashed, and just above, a video played – another air vent and a trail of officers crawling past a camera.

He wrapped his lips around a sneer. 'Why don't you do the honours?'

Everything inside froze. 'What honours?'

'Of giving us that time you mentioned. It's just a little red button.' The gun waved. 'Press it.'

She met his gaze – pure evil.

She locked her expression and glared back. 'No.'

Two steps and he thrust the barrel so hard against her mother's head, her other ear almost touched her shoulder. 'Do it, Stacey. I won't ask nicely again.'

Her brain screamed.

If she pressed, what would happen? How could she do it and not know?

His gaze narrowed, his lips thinned. He jerked the gun downward.

A blast shattered the silence.

Her mother shrieked, her face writhing, twisted. Blood gushed out from a hole in her foot.

With barely a blink, Des lifted his aim to her thigh. 'Shall I keep going?'

'No!' Stacey's body shook so hard she could barely see straight. She scrunched her eyes closed, held her breath and jabbed at the button.

A tear broke free. Then another.

Her heart pounded.

Not loud enough to drown out the distant roar. The ground shook, every shudder, every vibration, carving her control.

The big, ominous cupboard rocked, metal clattering against metal. No fake knives or weapons in there.

Her chest squeezed so tight, she could barely breathe.

What have I done?

'Good girl. Now we get to enjoy each other's company a while longer, what say we play a game?' He waved his godforsaken gun, grinning at each of them in turn. 'Who's up for Russian roulette?'

Chapter Sixty-Six

Fire lanced through Chase's skull. He blinked, then blinked again, and the multi-edged blur of his surroundings slowly merged into focus. It didn't help the scrambled-egg condition of his brain.

What the fuck kind of detective was he?

He should have been free by now. Should have been the one holding the gun, controlling the situation. Keeping Stacey and her mother safe. Instead, he was trussed up like a frigging pot roast. As useless as an MP40 without a magazine when the fucker fired *his* gun.

The blast ricocheted through his chest.

When Candace screamed, relief had surged through every locked muscle in his body. That it wasn't Stacey. That same surge made him sick to his stomach. Regardless of Candace's sins, a killer's bullet wasn't the right road to justice.

Then the ground shuddered and a bomb put pay to imminent rescue by Jayda and his team. Whittaker's smirk, the horror in Stacey's expression, confirmed as much.

He closed his eyes and cleared his mind. Not before one thought elbowed its way through. He'd do anything in his power to keep Stacey safe. *Anything.*

Funny that he'd spent most of his life waiting to die, but now, with the real possibility looming before him, it wasn't an option. Not when he'd just realised how much he had to live for. He couldn't leave Gracie without a brother and protector, or Jag Junior without an uncle and male role model; or *Stacey* without a whatever he'd be to her when they left this chaos behind.

His mind raced as he scanned the area – the concrete floor, the white-washed walls, the mannequin-stand-ins slumped against the far wall. Whittaker.

Then slowly, steadily, an idea began to take root.

No!

Stacey's heart shafted. She dragged air into her lungs, struggling for calm, struggling to tame the barrage of tears down her cheeks. 'This stops now, Des.'

'And why would I do that?'

'Because you have me. My attention. My approval. Isn't that what this is all about?'

'Is that what your pathetic psychology degree tells you?' His lip curled. 'You can't fit me or what I want into a box. I'm much bigger, much better than that.'

He was delusional. A narcissist suffering grandiose fantasies. How to rationalise with that?

How had she missed the signs? His obsession about her writing. *Her.* The whole Bonnie and Clyde fascination she'd believed to be whacky but harmless.

She scrubbed the back of her hand across her eyes and sniffed back another outpouring of tears. 'I won't play your game, Des.'

'You might want to check out the rules before making rash decisions.'

'It won't make a difference.'

'Oh, I think it might.' His teeth bared in what should have been a smile. 'You see, the lives of these two people, so very dear to you,' his gun waved from Chase to her mother, 'are at your mercy. I choose the weapon, you choose who gets a bullet and who gets to watch. It's really quite fun – like Cluedo, but with a twist.'

Her gaze darted toward the closed door, to a nearby ground-level vent, to the ceiling and a round, metal outline of a manhole almost directly above. She strained to hear. Something. Anything.

No sign or sound of approaching help. No chance of escape.

Not hopeless – she wouldn't believe that – but it came pretty damn close. Still, nothing would make her do his bidding. No way would she be responsible for the loss of another life.

She shook her head. 'Not happening. I won't do it. You can't make me choose.'

'You're right of course.' He cocked his head, a hyena calculating before moving in for the kill. 'But if you don't, they both die. At least if you pick, one lives.'

Her gut twisted.

What have I done?

My being here created this situation. This sick game.

Sharp nails cut into her palms, her fist clenched so tight her knuckles burned.

Stop!

This isn't on you.

This isn't your fault.

Chase's words and he was right – Des was the sicko, a psychopath and a killer. That meant he'd kill no matter what. With or without her books. With or without her there. With or without a reason. And if she hadn't turned up, both Chase and her mother might already be dead.

Her presence had saved them, and it would save them again.

All she needed was more of the same luck that kept them alive until now. More time to figure out how to set them free.

A delay tactic. A strategy, to talk Des out of the game, out of this madness. And a distraction, so he'd leave them both untouched and allow the remaining cops outside to live, while they both left the scene, together. A regular Bonnie and Clyde. Just as he wanted.

No sweat. Not.

Unless …

The idea hit. And thoughts of playing to Des's fantasies dragged a mass of centipedes, squirming and scuttling, through her stomach. But she wouldn't let squeamishness stop her. This wasn't about comfort zones. It was about saving lives.

One deep breath provided the fortitude to move.

Ignoring the gun he waved so carelessly, she rested her hands on his shoulders, leaned in and touched her lips to his.

He froze.

Moments stretched, timeless, heartbeat upon heartbeat, then with a burst of peppermint he kissed her back. The rough bristles of his moustache made her want to rip the scratchy skin apart.

Salt and bitter rammed her tastebuds, reality as distasteful as the idea.

Shudders racked through her. She blanked her mind. If for one moment she thought about what she was doing, she'd vomit and her distraction would be messy and oh, so over.

Somewhere in the background she heard a gasp. *Chase.*

She blocked him out, pulled back and forced her lips to curve upward. 'No need to worry about them. Let's leave before the cops arrive.' She pictured Chase, hoped her expression reflected love and not loathing as she stared into eyes of the devil incarnate. 'Then we'll both be outlaws, just like Bonnie and Clyde. And we'll be together.'

His gaze narrowed and shifted toward Chase.

She cupped his cheek and dragged it back to face her. 'Say "yes" and we can leave now. We can begin our life together while we still have the chance.'

Dropping her hand, she wrapped her fingers around his and tugged him toward the way they'd entered. It was like moving solid rock.

Des yanked back and her body slammed against him. His grip overpowered, tightened, driving her hand out and around, pressing it hard up her back and against her spine.

She gasped, pain shafting through her shoulder and down her arm.

Deep, dark chasms scanned her face. Probing. Searching for something she hoped he'd never find.

He glanced toward the door and despite the discomfort her heart leapt. He'd taken the bait!

His gaze dropped to her mouth, then his lips followed suit. She made herself respond, blocking every distasteful thought from her mind.

The kiss seemed never-ending, a purgatory that made hell look like a Sunday picnic. And when she thought she might pass out or pull away from disgust, he pulled back.

He forced her arm further up her back until it felt as if the ball might pop out from its socket. Water sprung to her eyes, her breathing short and sharp as she cried out.

Then, like a snake slithering across the desert sands, his lips slinked upward. 'No.'

'So, here's how we're going to do this.'

Whittaker dropped his hand from Stacey's back and curved it up over her hip. She stiffened, but her smile barely wavered.

Her eyes were still red-rimmed, but her tears had dried.

Chase yanked his hands, thunder rolling up through his chest, battering his brain.

Fucking useless!

The ropes scalded his already raw wrists, but the burn had nothing on the boil in his blood. He wanted to beat every perfect, pearly tooth from the bastard's smarmy grin. Rip his hands clean from his wrists so he'd never touch a single cell on Stacey's body again.

This from a man who believed – *profoundly* – in law and order. Who believed in the Australian court system and *not* the individual dispensing justice.

But the thought of any harm to Stacey …

Much as he knew what she was doing, knew why, it didn't stop the spectrum of hot-blooded emotions from ramming his brain.

The way she kissed the bastard, the loving looks …

Whittaker smirked. 'Now, now, never fear, detective.' He brushed a curl back from Stacey's face, eliciting the barest of flinches. 'Everyone gets a chance to play. Your turn will come soon enough.'

Chase's teeth clashed.

He bit back the diatribe threatening to spill out. He needed to keep cool. Had trained long and hard to do just that. But the sight of Whittaker's slimy tentacles on Stacey made it damn near impossible not to growl and want to tear the bastard limb from limb.

Thunder roared through the tunnel, shock and vibration racking up through his body.

Another explosion.

He tipped his head to stare at a metaphorical sky. If there was ever a time to wish for divine intervention, it was now.

Let Jayda and the team be safe. Let us all get out of this godforsaken mess alive.

Whittaker sniggered, staring at the door leading to the tunnels and yet another avenue of escape now obliterated. 'They never learn. As dumb as dog shit, every one of them.'

His beady gaze bored into Chase's. Then he made to step forward.

Stacey tugged his sleeve. 'They're closing in. Let's leave all this behind us and go. *Now.*'

Outwardly, she appeared as cool as the cold bastard beside her. But Chase detected the faint quiver of her lips. The enlarged pupils, the stiff line of her shoulders. The fact that she avoided his gaze, yet seemed hell-bent on saving her mother and him, at the expense of her own safety. Damn, but her brazen blew him away. His heart swelled, even while the prospect of watching her leave with Whittaker terrified the living bejesus out of him.

The hand at her waist tightened. She winced and Whittaker's grin widened. 'We'll be together. I promise.' He stared down into her eyes. 'But first I plan to give you the greatest gift one can give a writer.' He lowered his lips to her ear and whispered.

Her pupils all but swallow the green of her irises.

She gasped and pulled back. 'What do you mean, *experience?*'

'Until now, you've acted out every part of your scenes except the part that matters.' He withdrew his hand from her hip and held it out before him. 'You've never grasped someone's life in your palm and revelled in the power as you slowly, steadily squeeze the breath from their body.' His fingers curled into a tight fist. 'You've never pulled the trigger and watched the life-force spill from the wound, never felt the slide of a blade through living, pulsing flesh. Now you get the chance to appreciate all of the above, and more. This is what I give to you now.'

The bastard acted like he'd handed Stacey the world.

Her skin turned a pasty shade of green. Her fingers clamped, stiff and jerky, pushing a limp curl back from her face.

She swallowed. Blinked. Pushed a smile to her lips. 'Wow. No one's ever done anything like that for me before.'

Something sparked in Stacey's gaze. Something he'd label excitement if he hadn't known her better.

She gazed up into Whittaker's eyes with a warmth that burned Chase's gut. 'Thank you.'

The other man's gaze narrowed even while his lips curled, and he lowered them to hers. 'My pleasure.'

She didn't flinch. Didn't look the least bit repulsed as the bastard's mouth played over hers. Either her acting skills had suddenly improved or the anticipation lighting her eyes held substance.

Chase went with option one, because option two was just too …

wrong. It didn't lessen the slap of sour against his tongue. Or the crawl of his flesh every time Whittaker so much as looked at Stacey.

He tried to capture her gaze, to get some indication, some sense, of what she was thinking, but her eyes latched fast to Whittaker's.

She licked her lips. 'I never thought it was possible, but it is, isn't it?'

Whittaker nodded, fast, maniacal, the action a perfect match to the gleam in his eyes. 'Very possible, right now.'

'Now?' The flicker of uncertainty was so brief, he almost missed it. 'You mean I have to rush? That I can't savour the moment? Enjoy and record every second so I can write it later with reality?'

With Hollywood-type timing, a boom echoed through the tunnels outside, reverberating off each of the room's four walls.

Wincing, she once again tugged at his sleeve. 'Let's get out of here before it's too late.'

'Trust me. We have time.' He opened the gun, emptied all but one of the chambers. Then he snapped it shut and spun the cylinder. 'Ready to rock'n'roll?'

Barrel in hand, he offered the weapon to Stacey.

Her fingers wrapped almost reverently around the black rubber grip.

Chase's heart stalled. Stacey was armed.

Granted, she had one bullet and no idea where it sat in the chamber, but that didn't stop her from being one step closer to ending this mess. He braced in his seat, mind racing over what he could do to help. She lifted the weapon and weighed it in her hand, Whittaker watching with beady, avaricious eyes.

She flexed her fingers.

He saw the moment she was ready. Her gaze flicked to his before she tightened her hold.

He pushed up with the balls of his feet. The chair tilted, then he let the front legs slam down.

Whittaker's gaze bolted his way. Two strides and cool metal pressed hard against his temple.

Another gun.

How many did the bastard have?

'Just a little insurance.' He grinned. 'Be prepared, right? Not that I was ever a boy scout, but it makes perfect sense. And it hasn't failed me yet.'

He turned to Stacey. 'It's not playing out exactly like your scene, but then again, why shouldn't I benefit from writing my own ending?'

It took a moment for Chase's mind to wrap around Whittaker's words, then another moment to stop his jaw from dropping clear to the ground as he stared at Stacey. *You wrote this?*

Red seeped across her cheeks. 'It was cut from the final copyedit of *From Mishap to Murder*.'

Whittaker frowned. 'Not my choice. But of course, I wasn't your editor back then.'

The suggestion that he *was* her editor now, that he and Stacey faced a writing future together, was almost as sickening as Stacey creating the scene currently being played out.

'This is sick.'

Her head snapped back. 'That was the whole idea. It was *fiction* – you know, *not real* – and no worse than anything Karin Slaughter or Stephen King would create.'

Whittaker cocked his head. 'You say fiction, I say art. And really, is there any difference? But we digress.' He waved his gun toward Stacey's. 'Since I'm co-author of this scene, let's spice things up a little. Make it fun *and* educational. Ramp up your scene and make it better.'

What the fuck could he do to make it "better"? Translation – more sick and twisted.

'I know!' Whittaker clicked his fingers as if the idea just occurred. 'We'll have a quiz. I get to ask the question, Stacey gets to pull the trigger. Winner gets to live, loser gets a bullet … or not. Pure luck or bad luck, right? That'll be the fun part.'

Stacey stepped back. 'We're doing this now? With the police outside?'

'Trust me, they'll be a while.' His gaze hardened. 'Unless you'd prefer to dispense with the entertainment and kill them both now?'

'No!' She inhaled and let the air escape with a steady *whoosh*. 'Let's play. You're right. It'll be a blast.'

Again her gaze riveted to Whittaker and Chase couldn't get a gauge on what she was thinking. Or if she had a plan. Because dammit, he didn't. That slow-growing seed he'd hoped would sprout into one was dead before he'd had a chance to give it a try. With two guns floating around, anything he attempted was futile.

The term "sitting duck" seemed pretty fitting about now.

'Good choice of words.' Whittaker smirked, then switched his attention to the chair beside Chase's. 'Seems Mummy dearest is napping. And a game's no fun without at least two players.' He grabbed a water bottle from the desk, opened the spout and squeezed.

Liquid squirted into Candace's face. She sputtered, but her eyes remained closed. 'Wakey, wakey!' He slapped her cheeks. Once. Twice.

Her eyelids fluttered, then opened in a face so gaunt, so sunken, she looked barely alive.

The pain had to be agonising. A bullet in the foot wouldn't kill her, at least not straight away. But if she didn't get to a hospital soon, infection and shock could flip those odds. The flicker in Stacey's expression said she realised it too.

The Smith & Wesson trembled in her hand. Much as she had to be tempted to aim it at Whittaker's head, she had to know the odds as well as he did.

His unit had to be outside, had to be working on how to get them all out alive. They just needed to negotiate past each one of Whittaker's booby traps first. That'd take time. Something that was slipping rapidly through the hourglass.

'First question.' Whittaker's voice cut his thoughts back to reality. To the next bullet that might just as well be his, because either way, when it hit, it'd hurt like hell – anything that hurt Stacey, physically or emotionally, hurt him.

Whittaker squinted at the ceiling as if searching for a question he undoubtedly already had. 'What did Apollo 8 astronauts use to secure tools during weightlessness on their 1968 voyage to the moon?'

The answer popped into Chase's mind almost immediately, courtesy of a year ten school project.

But he wouldn't say it. Wouldn't force Stacey to pull the trigger on her mother. Wouldn't give Whittaker further satisfaction by playing his gruesome game.

He glanced across at Candace. No doubt she'd answer if she could, but her eyes were glazed and she was barely conscious.

'Answer!'

The gun smacked into his ribs and he flinched as pain lanced through his chest.

He levelled his gaze with that of a madman. 'No.'

Whittaker stilled, his voice cold, calm. Callous. 'Answer or I pull the trigger.' He redirected the gun to Candace's stomach. 'And just so you know, *this* chamber is full.'

What the fuck kind of choice was that? Answer and Stacey had to shoot her mother. Refuse and Whittaker would fill her stomach with a crap load of lead.

'For heaven's sake, just shoot me and get it over with, asshole. But leave Stacey and Chase out of it.'

Chase's head whipped toward Candace.

Difficult to work out what shocked him more – her voice or his name leaving her lips for the first time since they'd met.

Whittaker sneered. 'What would be the fun in that? Why don't we leave that decision to your daughter?'

A glance at Stacey showed the terror in her eyes. Her lips quivered. 'Say it, Chase. If you know the answer, *just say it.*'

He'd never felt so akin to a fish in a net. What choice did he have?

His lips moved, even while every syllable made him sick to his stomach. 'Soft putty.'

'Give the man a cigar. Or in this case, a reprieve.' Chortling, Whittaker turned to Stacey. 'You're up. Since this is your first time, you get to choose where.'

'I don't know if I can.' Her voice was so low, so lost, he wanted to wrap her in his arms and shelter her from this whole sordid situation.

Whittaker's eyes flinted like coal.

Stacey's gaze darted from wall to wall, finally latching onto the door behind him. Then her expression blanked, and panic transformed into appeal. 'I want to do this, really I do. But she's my mother.'

Whittaker shook his head, his *tut-tut* almost as loud as the roar of protest in Chase's head.

'Weakness is a choice, my dear Stacey, not a solution. It doesn't matter who gets the bullet. Point. Aim. Shoot. It's really that simple.'

She had to shoot her mother to give her any chance at living.

How fucked up was that?

Whittaker tapped the gun in Stacey's hand. 'Time to put that weapon to use and leap from good writer to great. Anything for research and a killer story, right?'

A grin slithered across his lips and she shuddered.

I can't do this!

The mess in her mind was like a town after a tornado.

If she pulled the trigger, maybe there'd be a bullet, and maybe there wouldn't. Either way, the thought of doing what she had to do made her want to close her eyes, bury her head and make the whole wicked world go away. *After* chucking her guts, that is. Yet, if she didn't do it, her mother was dead. Des would aim for her stomach and there'd be little chance he'd aim to miss the major organs or arteries. Then again, maybe if she played his game a little longer, he'd trust her enough to either listen and leave, or give her a gun with more than one bullet in the chamber.

If only she could count on her luck until then.

'Do it!' His gun was firm in his hand, and she didn't doubt he'd use it if she didn't act soon.

She aimed. Pictured what she knew of the body. Where a bullet could inflict the least damage. The location of major organs and arteries she couldn't afford to hit.

Then willing the shake from her hands, she slowly, gently pulled the trigger.

Chapter Sixty-Seven

C_lick!_

The hollow snap of an empty chamber echoed through the room. Stacey's body all but sagged.

Thank god!

'One down, five to go. Time for my next question.'

Her worst nightmare grinned, first at her, then at her mother and Chase. The rubber grip dug into her palm.

'You sick bastard! What the hell do you expect to achieve with all this?' Chase's face suffused with red and raw anger.

'Who said "achievement" was my goal? Can't a guy have a little fun?'

'Fun will be the least of your worries when I get my hands on you.'

'That, I'd like to see. Because Houdini you're not. And that's the least you'll have to be to get out of this alive.' Des stalked to the edge of the stage, then turned back. 'What is designer Chanel's first name?'

Stacey's heart sank. Chase wouldn't have a clue. The question was designed for her mother. As the first question had been designed for him. Des had designed a game with his rules, his sick brand of manipulation. One glance at Cookie Monster told her only half an hour had passed since she'd stumbled out of the tunnel and into Des's hands. Half an hour that seemed forever. Surely if the cops were coming they'd be here by now. A bomb wouldn't make them give up. It'd just make them go slower.

How much slower could they possibly go?

'Time's up! I need an answer.'

Her stomach vaulted into her throat as Chase shook his head. 'No idea.'

Des waved the gun. 'Candace, you're up.'

Her mother licked her lips, glanced from her to Chase, then licked her lips again.

'Cherry.'

'*Wrong!*' Des's gaze narrowed. 'But you already knew that, didn't you? New rule. If you fake a wrong answer, the other person automatically gets the gun.' Des's grin dripped from his lips, gleeful and ghastly. 'That means it's your turn, detective.'

Her mind whirled. Her mother's incorrect answer was deliberate. She could see it in her expression. Knew it instinctively. As much as she knew, she couldn't do it again. Couldn't pull the trigger. Couldn't bear the wait to see if she'd unleash a bullet or a click.

'I won't do this anymore. I won't shoot him.' Her voice wavered, but she wouldn't let that stop her. 'You say you care about me, that this is all for me, for us, so we can be together.' She waved her hand about the room. 'Well, if that's true, *show me*. Don't make me shoot people I know. Free them and let's go and leave all this behind us.'

Des huffed, too exaggerated to be genuine. 'I'm not sure you've thought this situation through, *my dear*. So let me think it through for you.' His nostrils flared. 'What's the one major downfall of any killer who eventually gets caught? Care to take a guess?'

He waited barely long enough for her head to board his train of thought before he answered himself. 'Witnesses.'

Before the last word left his lips, he turned and her mother jerked the same moment the blast echoed in her ears.

'I guess that means our little game is over.'

A cry caught in her throat.

Her mother screamed.

Grey silk bloomed with red, the hole in her chest so tiny it seemed impossible that it could wield so much damage.

She rushed to her mother's side, wrapping her arms around her shuddering torso. She didn't freeze, didn't twist away. Her body curled into Stacey's – it would have been a hug if she could have used her arms.

And Des stood back, watching, his expression oozing sick glee, as if he were taking in a movie and not the heart-wrenching reality of her mother dying in her arms.

'So sorry, honey. So … many things.' The words squeezed out through her mother's lips, gurgling, wheezing. 'This is … my fault.'

'It's okay, Mum. You're going to be okay.'

'Not okay.' She gave the barest shake of her head, her voice so weak Stacey had to turn her head to hear. 'Going to die … Can make my peace with that …' Liquid gurgled at the back of her throat, her voice barely a rasp. 'Need to make my peace with you, too.'

Stacey shed her jacket and balled it up, pressing it against the wound, flinching as a gasp wracked through her mother's lips.

The flow of her tears matched her mother's. The flow of blood, unstoppable.

She glared at Des. 'She needs a doctor.'

His lips twisted. 'Not for much longer.'

Her heart screamed.

Her mother had made choices – terribly misguided choices – but that didn't change the fact that love had been her motivator. That she'd always been there for Stacey. Had always urged her to be the best she could be. And for the first time ever, she was opening her heart, speaking to her in a way she never had.

She couldn't lose her now.

'Try not to talk, Mum. Just relax.'

'I messed up so many things … important things …' Another barely there shake of her head. 'Did what I thought was best … lost my way. Hurt you. Your marriage … not your failing. *Mine.* Everything wrong in your life was … my … failing. I pushed to make you strong … and instead I pushed you away.'

Stacey leaned closer, straining to hear the rasp of her mother's voice. Tears streaked through the grime and makeup on her face.

'Most of all …' She blinked, released a shuddering breath. 'I'm sorry my fears made me control you … I was wrong. To push your father away. To push you to be someone you didn't want to be. To make you feel less than the perfect person you are.'

She leaned into Stacey, brushed her lips over her cheek. 'Be happy. Find love and laughter and the freedom … to do and be what you want.'

Her breath hitched as she turned to Chase. 'I'm counting on you, detective. Look after her.'

Their gazes connected. Held.

Chase nodded.

Her mother released a sigh and returned her gaze to Stacey.

'I hope one day you'll remember me …' she inhaled a shallow, shaky breath, '… without regret. I have so many, but … you were never one of them.'

Brushing back a bedraggled clump of hair, Stacey pressed her lips to her mother's grubby forehead. 'I love you, Mum.'

She pulled back in time to see eyes so very like her own flutter, then roll back in her head. The weak breath on her cheek the only indication her mother still lived.

A throaty chuckle sliced through her pain. 'Bravo. *Bra-vo.* So *moving.* All that misunderstanding, all that forgiveness. Happy endings all around. And who doesn't love happy endings?'

Another chuckle. *Maniacal.*

Sobs wracked from Stacey's chest, the burn so great she thought her body would explode with it.

The chuckling stopped as abruptly as it started. 'Enough!' Des stalked forward, the .38 raised in his hand.

'No!' Chase jerked his chair forward. 'Leave them alone!'

Des swung his arm. The crack of metal against bone shafted through her chest as Chase's head slammed back. 'Don't forget your place, *detective.* You lost the right to dictate what happens when you lost your freedom.'

Then he turned back to her. 'Back away, Stacey.'

When she didn't move, he grabbed her hair and yanked. She yelped at the burn of her scalp, staggering backwards.

He growled. 'I said back away!'

'Leave her alone, you asshole!'

'We need to call an ambulance. *Please, Des.*'

'No, we need to leave.' He levelled his gun at Chase. 'One more bullet and we're done here.'

'No!' She leapt forward and knocked his hand away.

Before he could react, she raised her gun to Chase, pointed and pulled the trigger. At the hollow *click* she fired again. Chase jerked, his shock mirroring her own as the *boom* filled the room and blood soaked the thigh of his jeans.

'*Fuuuck!*' His glare was more hurt than angry, although the clench of his teeth and taut, drawn lines around mouth and eyes alike revealed his pain. 'You *shot* me.'

'I did.' A sharp nod. And if she'd had the guts to do it before, perhaps her mother wouldn't be dying right now.

Her heart twisted.

She swung round to face Des before she relented and ran to Chase, begging for his forgiveness. Not something she expected. She'd shot him, after all. Possibly damaged bone or nerves making it uncertain whether he'd walk again or continue being a detective, something he loved. Just days ago, he'd refused to be around her and a gun, and her actions made his concerns all the more founded. That she'd shot him to save his life didn't count. If not for her, he wouldn't be tied to that chair, wouldn't be facing death.

Wouldn't be bleeding out with no one around to stem the flow.

She couldn't think about that now. His unit was close, and she'd aimed to miss his femoral and other major arteries. She had to hope she'd succeeded.

The colour leeched from his face. 'I can't believe you did that.' His lips curled, angry. Disgusted. 'You're no frigging better than he is!'

Heart hammering, breaking, she glared at Des. 'Satisfied? I've done what you asked, now it's time for you to do the same for me. Bonny and Clyde, remember? We're a team. That means we work together. *Let's go.*'

Bang!

The door shuddered, another bomb blast that wracked through her body.

They were getting closer.

Des stared at the juddering metal and wood and bit out an oath.

This time when she pulled, he let her. Before he could look back, check on Chase, her mother, she tugged again, and held her breath until she was certain he wouldn't finish the job she'd started.

With a mutter, he followed, all the way to a drawer in his desk and enough C4 to obliterate a room of horrors and everything in it. He flicked a switch and, true to her deleted scene, the red digital numbers began to count down.

His expression dripped disdain, darting from the unmoving form of her mother to Chase yanking against his bindings, still bleeding, still beautiful.

The devil's claws clamped around her wrist, as if sensing her need to run to him. 'Soon you'll both be but a memory.' He sneered at Chase. 'And you get to spend your last moments knowing I won, detective. I got the girl.'

It was his turn to tug, fingers like claws digging into her skin. 'This way.'

Then without a backward glance toward the man and mother she loved, Stacey followed, unsure whether she'd ever see them again.

Mildew and burnt tar drenched Stacey's nostrils as she tripped her way behind the man squeezing her fingers so tight they felt as if they might break. Light from his headlamp bobbed and bowed, bloating their joined shadows into one grotesque monster.

Action replays reeled through her mind, no matter how much she willed them to stop. Those and every question around choices that could very well have maimed – or even killed – the man she loved.

Then there was her mother.

Her heart shafted.

And Ethan.

So much death and destruction.

Even Brad.

Numb seeped out from her brain and into chest. Her eyes dry, her body so heavy every step drained her energy until she had none to draw on.

After leading her through a doorway concealed at the back of his cave, Des now dragged her through a tunnel she'd never seen, either first-hand or on any existing underground map. Melbourne city had a myriad of World War II warrens and bunkers, none of which were documented in Port Melbourne. Not that the lack of records meant they didn't exist. It just meant the police were less likely to be looking for them here.

Which meant they were about to escape. Definitely not part of her plan.

Although, why should this moment break with protocol? It wasn't as if anything had run to plan since the moment she'd accepted the RuBY Award and her gaze had locked with Chase's.

He was the digression that injected her life with meaning. *Purpose.*

The man dragging her god knows where wasn't.

She dug her runners into the dirt and pulled back. 'Where are we going?'

'Where we'll never be found.'

Chills racked up her spine. The tunnel forked up ahead. Whichever way they turned, it wouldn't lead to anything good.

'Why go to so much trouble for me? Am I really worth all this?' She waved her arm around their dank, dark surrounds.

'"All this" meaning?'

'The killing, the bombs. The trail of dead bodies. An entire taskforce of police after us.'

'I've always had a predilection for the dramatic. Plus, I may have stretched the truth a little.' His smirk added to the shivers. 'I happen to enjoy the killing and the bombs. You, my dear Stacey, were an added incentive.' His fingers snaked along her arm and up over her shoulder to her cheek. 'You know, we're really not that different.'

His gaze locked with hers for seconds that seemed like grisly hours, then he urged her forward, the crunch of each step bouncing from stony wall to stony wall. The thought, his touch, burrowed deep into her stomach and wrenched.

She swallowed. *Don't lose your guts now, girl.*

Not when she was partway to convincing him he was winning her over.

She glanced at her wrist. Six minutes and the bomb's countdown would reach zero.

With barely a pause, he skirted toward the right tunnel. 'We each have a parent who deserted us.'

'Your mother died, Des.'

His gaze flared. 'She never fought hard enough to stick around.' The light on his forehead wavered, but he forged on.

Her gaze darted in every direction. There was no way out, and no doubt in her mind that if she ran, he'd capture her within seconds. What he'd do to her then, she had no idea. But the possibilities made her shudder. Her best bet was to keep him talking and somehow figure out how to outsmart him.

'And your father?'

'A stand-in for the sperm donor who couldn't be bothered to stick around. Instead, I landed a self-absorbed prick who didn't give two hoots about how mother's death affected anyone but him. He was supposed to be some fancy-assed doctor and he couldn't even save his own fucking wife.'

'The cancer killed her, Des. Neither one of them could prevent that.'

'What about gassing himself in our garage? Think he could have prevented that? Or his eight year old son finding his miserable, dead carcass?'

She gasped. 'Oh, Des. I'm so sorry.'

'Save your sympathy. He chose to rot six-feet under rather than be with me. I was better off without him. What he shouldn't have done was dump me with his holier-than-thou, stick-up-the-ass parents. Nothing I was or did was ever good enough. Much like you with your mother.'

The tunnel swerved to the right. His pace barely faltered, as if he knew his way, with or without the bobbing headlamp.

'Everything that bitch made you do was for her own satisfaction, not yours. But that stops now.'

He pulled up so fast, she bowled into him. She tried to mask the distaste as she stepped back and his gaze locked with hers. The glare from the lamp helped.

'You're free, like I was freed when the old farts carked it.' He reached for her hand.

She stifled a cringe, even managed to wrap her fingers around his and look into his eyes without disgust.

The gesture made him smile. 'I'm like one of those heroes in your book. Saving you. Sweeping the mundane from your life and giving you excitement. From now on, whatever you do will be for your own satisfaction, your own gain. We'll write books together. Fabulous books. Make history and world-wide news. And what's more, neither of us will have to do it alone.'

He started walking again and she followed.

'That all sounds,' she swallowed, 'amazing.'

'Doesn't it?' He glanced at his phone, then back the way they'd come. His thoughts had to be running along the same line as hers.

No bomb blast.

Oh god, please let it be so. Because that meant Chase had been saved.

Chapter Sixty-Eight

Chase guessed what was in the drawer even before Stacey mouthed the word.

Bomb.

Eyes wide, skin pale, she'd left – conflicted – but without a choice.

As she and Whittaker slipped away, his mind raced. His team was outside, of that he was sure. But how long until they found a way in? Stacey had silently flashed her hand at her side, twice. Did that mean he had ten minutes?

He planned not to waste a single one of them.

'Candace?'

Once a perfect fit for the pages of Vogue, the woman beside him was now a bedraggled mess, covered in blood, and either already dead or well on her way. He was doing this on his own.

Using the balls of his feet, he jerked his chair and slowly moved toward the desk. If there was a bomb, he had to see it for himself. See how long he had and find something to cut his bindings. Then he had to cut Candace free and get them both the hell out of there.

Just another day in the office.

Only it wasn't.

The ground clanked as he inched slowly toward the desk.

Death had always lurked in his future. And in some perverse way he'd accepted it. Why fight what you hadn't a chance in hell of beating? Yet now that menacing end was near, he found himself praying to a god he'd never believed existed for a life he'd never imagined he'd live long enough to enjoy.

He had to live long enough.

There was no Parkinson's in his future, but even if there was, he now realised he'd still have a lifetime – albeit small – to gather memories until his nerves gave out and his body gave in. Thinking about a life with Stacey made him want to enjoy every day, as if it were his last.

Something today would not be.

The drawer had been left open. Impossible to miss the four green blocks of C4 connected with wires of red, yellow, blue and green to a red digital counter.

Six-fifty-nine clicked over to six-fifty-eight.

He angled his chair, curled his finger through a drawer handle and pulled. It slid open easily revealing nothing but papers and post-its. The drawer above contained much the same.

One more remaining, then he'd have to look elsewhere.

His finger curled under the last drawer handle, his gaze scanning the room until it struck Whittaker's cabinet. The exterior was identical to Stacey's, but he'd bet the arsenal of weapons inside weren't polypropylene. Bound to find a knife or entire collection. The problem would be reaching the handle and opening it while he was still stuck in his chair.

A quick glance at the metaphorical heaven above, he opened the last drawer.

Pay dirt. A utility knife.

Digital red clicked to six-oh-six.

He lifted his wrists, reached back into the drawer and felt the prick as he located the blade. Sticky wet covered his fingers and he wrapped them around the handle.

Less than six minutes now.

He began to saw, wincing each time the blade skidded over the nylon and into his wrist. The knife slipped in his grip and he prayed he wouldn't drop it before the line was cut.

Bang!

The door shuddered. Then came another *bang*. A voice he recognised.

'I'm in here!' Not once did he stop cutting. 'There's a bomb. C4. Digital timer. Five minutes till detonation.'

The voice receded, then another told him to hold tight.

Not as if he had a choice.

One strand loosened, then another.

Four minutes to go.

He yanked his wrists. They parted, then stopped, two or three strands holding him back. Almost there.

Just a few seconds more.

The knife slipped. His heart dropped in sync with the knife and the room echoed with the sharp ping of metal against the cement floor.

Three minutes.

He yanked his wrists again. The nylon gave, then cut deep into his already bloody wrists.

Fuck!

He glared at the blade on the floor. The bomb in the drawer. Two and a half minutes to go.

He rocked. Again. Braced as the ground rushed up to meet him.

Sharp pain sliced through his shoulder. He ignored it. Ignored everything but the blade, just inches from his hand.

Pushing with his feet, he edged around until his fingers located the knife again.

Two minutes.

So close, yet so damn far.

He sawed. Once. Twice.

The knife slipped. Fire scorched his fingertip as the blade sliced deep.

The counting in his head said he had just over a minute more.

His shoulder throbbed, his head pounded. His fingers slowly lost sensation, even as they fumbled blindly and he prayed these seconds wouldn't be his last.

Was Chase still alive?

No bomb blast suggested it was a possibility.

Stacey's heart fluttered at the thought. Like a butterfly spreading its wings moments after leaving the chrysalis. Light. Happy. *Relieved.*

For the first time in too long, her lips lifted into a smile that tugged the strings of her heart.

There was hope after all.

The ground shuddered and pain sliced her eardrums. An explosion, wracking through her body, shattering her defences.

Minutes later than scheduled, but no less devastating.

She bit back a sob.

So that's it then.

'And then there were none.' The words carved through her dreams, leaving them in tatters.

She'd never thought to love again, yet now there was nothing she wanted more. With a detective, no less. She'd have laughed at the irony if she didn't want to bawl the crap out of her situation.

Happiness – for that brief, beautiful moment she'd lived it – had tasted sweeter than anything imaginable. The loss scooped out her insides until the gaping hollow consumed her.

Only one man carried the blame.

Steel leeched into her shoulders and hardened her heart.

The bastard would pay. That was one plan he wouldn't foil.

She blinked and refocused. Eyes almost as black as the soul behind them scrutinised her coldly.

She pressed a smile to her lips. 'Tell me how we're going to do this. How do we evade the cops?'

'New identities.' One last, probing look, then he started moving again. 'Everything's stashed at a safe-house. We just have to get there, then we're home free.' He glanced across at her. 'After today, Stacey Holland will be no more. Bonnie Elizabeth Barrow will be reborn, and married to yours truly, Clyde Champion Barrow.'

The absurdity of the names barely hit.

'Married?' Her voice squeaked, but he didn't seem to care.

'Of course. How could I expect you to accept anything less? Bound together until death do us part.'

She shivered.

'The ceremony's set for tonight.'

As if the baked clay walls hadn't suffocated enough, his words wrapped round her throat and squeezed.

He swerved left and she didn't get why until sharp pain exploded in her big toe.

Tears swam in her eyes as she sprawled forward and her knee cracked against the rock that put her there. Her palms burned.

She gasped for breath.

No way!

She wasn't leaving these tunnels with a psychopathic looney tune, and she definitely wasn't saying "I do".

'We need to keep going.' He hauled her up.

She lacked the strength to resist.

Thanks for the concern.

Another sharp breath and she forced enthusiasm into her voice. 'You've organised a wedding ceremony? For me?'

'For *us*.'

Thankfully he didn't look back, didn't see the horror that hijacked her expression as she limped after him, partly from pain, partly from a desire to slow their escape and give herself time to think.

'Six months ago I applied to become a celebrant. I completed the course and received my papers two weeks ago, in perfect timing. With Beth out of our way and no contract binding you to Thrasher, we'll be free and together.'

Bile rose up in her throat and would have made her gag if she hadn't managed to swallow it back down.

'All that's left is to wrangle a couple of witnesses,' he smirked, cementing doubts those witnesses would survive past signing, 'then my alter ego will oversee the ceremony. Not quite kosher, but for all intents and purposes, it's a marriage.'

She pulled her mind back. 'I don't have a dress.'

'I've got that covered. And the ring.'

'You know my size?'

'I checked out your closet.'

Was there any part of her life the man wouldn't violate?

It took every ounce of her remaining strength to sound as if his news wasn't her very worst nightmare. 'You're so thoughtful.'

'That's why we're the perfect fit.' He did glance back then, blinding her with the lamp so she stumbled. Again.

His hand shot out and he pulled her close. She didn't pull away.

'Careful.' He tilted the lamp and her eyes adjusted to find his face inches from hers. Peppermint wafted through the air between them. 'We're right for each other, Stacey. I just figured it out earlier and made the leap for both of us. You appreciate the little things, and I'm an attention-to-detail kind of guy. That means cupboards back at the house are already stocked with your favourite Aunt Milly's cookies.'

'Dark Chilli Choco-Sensations?'

'Of course.'

Difficult to fault his attentiveness. If only that didn't come with the psycho-killer tendencies and all-out creepiness, he'd be a catch.

She smiled, stood on tippy-toes, pressed her lips to his. 'Thank you.'

He smiled back. 'You're welcome.'

Twining his fingers in hers, he kept walking, kept talking. 'When we reach the safe-house, much as I hate it, you'll have to dye your hair. Blonde, I think. Perhaps we'll even cut it. But it'll only be for a while, until things die down and life can return to normal.'

He stopped suddenly, but this time she was prepared.

She'd been so focused on him, on every single shock announcement, she hadn't noticed they'd reached a dead end. Des looked skyward and she did the same. A narrow metal ladder stretched up three or four metres to stop just shy of a rusted manhole.

'Ladies first.' He waved toward the first rung and she noticed the gun in his hand once again.

She had no idea where they were. What she did know was the time and distance they'd walked would see them clear of the Old England Pub. And more, clear of the police perimeter.

Once she climbed that ladder and slipped through the manhole, she was on her own.

Any thoughts of rescue would be seeds in the wind.

Any chance of what she considered a normal life would be over.

Stacey shivered.

Pink and purple fingers stretched across the bay as daylight slipped with seamless elegance into dusk. Another evening and the shimmering seascape would have brought inspiration. A spark of romance. Ideas waxing lyrical that melted into a story.

'Faster!' Des waved the gun concealed in his jacket pocket, urging her between two old Colonial buildings, putting pay to any stray flights of fancy. Not that she had any.

Responsibility weighed heavy.

Escape was the coward's way out and a death sentence for anyone Des encountered after the fact. There'd be no more dead bodies to heap onto her conscience. Not when she was positioned so perfectly to stop him.

Nothing had come to her yet. But it would.

The cooling southerly slapped her cheeks and tussled about her hair. Her heart hadn't stopped racing since she'd seen the stack of C4 and the timer's diminishing red numbers. The pain in that very same organ she couldn't think about. Time enough to break apart when the man who'd stomped her heart to smithereens was behind bars.

She'd been waiting for a sign, an opening, to make a move, opting for cliché once again – she would end this or die trying.

Still limping, still maintaining the pretence that hadn't slowed them enough to be saved, she paused and winced, rubbing her thigh as if to ease the pain in her knee. 'How much further?'

'A couple more minutes and we'll be at the car.' He gripped her elbow and urged her on.

A couple more minutes and she'd be whisked so far away from the blockade of police there'd be no hope of rescue. Then what?

If only one of those uniforms would turn around and spot her. Just one – even the formidable Officer Stony-face Taylor – to skirt the blue and white tape and search further afield. Like between the Old Riviera restaurant and the hulking white building of the Royal Serviced Apartments.

She scanned the area for something – *anything* – that resembled a chance, and came up empty.

If only she could will it. Send vibes out into the universe and watch them do her bidding.

As if. Experience had demonstrated the fruitlessness of her efforts in the past.

She blanked her mind and sent a message out anyway. It wasn't as if she had anything to lose. All she needed was to capture attention without alerting Des and undoing all her trust-building.

Not much.

Just a miracle.

'In here.'

Her heart stalled.

He unlocked then pushed open a heavy fire door toward the rear of the apartment building. One she knew well. Stale cigarettes and fresh paint filled her nostrils. She scoured the well-lit entry, looking for her miracle. And found it.

Des turned and closed the door.

Eyes latched to the crisp lines of pink polyester across rounded shoulders, she toed her shoelace with one foot, lifting the other until the grimy white cord pulled loose. Then she lurched forward. Her fingers briefly contacted the small blue button before her elbow *thwacked* loudly against the wall.

'*Oww!*' She didn't have to feign the tears – funny bones connecting with hard plaster were no laughing matter.

But the pain was worth it. She'd activated the silent alarm, and now all she had to do was stall as much as possible and wait for help to come.

A little authenticity wouldn't hurt.

'Damned laces!' She kicked the wall. 'Damn, damn, damn!' Tears slipped down her cheeks. She swiped them back, wishing her acting skills were *that* good.

Dropping to one knee, her shaky fingers struggled to do something she'd mastered way before the age of five. Wily laces slipped through her fingers.

Des eyed the button, the ceiling.

She held her breath.

There was no sound. No flashing lights.

Please god, don't let him know the alarm's silent.

'Here, let me help.' He crouched down, placing the gun on the floor beside them. *So close.*

Her heart leapt.

She eyed the gun, the man, calculations of distance and the chance of success whirling through her mind. She measured the rigidity in his shoulders, the brace in his body. And did nothing.

Within seconds her laces were tied. Des wrapped his fingers around the weapon and helped her up. He met her gaze, a glint in his expression. *Triumph.*

She bit back a smile. The gun, the temptation, was a test. And she'd passed.

Des's trust was growing.

She just hoped when the time came, it'd be enough.

'Over there.'

Stacey's gaze followed Des's finger toward the far corner of the parking area. It slid over a cute green Coupe and stopped when it hit a large white van – built like a tank with tinted windows and god knows what in the back.

Every muscle from her shoulders down tensed.

The last thing she wanted was to get in, but what other choice did she have until help showed or another miracle in the form of an opportunity came along?

Scratch the miracle. One miracle a day was miracle enough.

Help was her best option. Assuming the alarm had worked, that is. Or was she waiting for something that had no chance of happening? She scoured the area, strained her ears for some sign they'd been found. A distant rumble came from the level above, a squeal of tyres, until it faded, leaving behind a loud, empty echo.

No rescue, then.

Even if the alarm had sounded, and even if the cops got wind of it, there was always a chance they'd assume it was kids mucking around instead of a plea for help.

If her heart sank any further, it'd reach Mexico.

She made for the van.

Des cupped her elbow and changed her course. 'The Coupe.'

That made her pull up, just for a second. 'Really? Since when?'

'They'll be looking for something less conspicuous. Flash is the perfect cover. Plus, it has surround sound and a full leather interior.'

Seemed all boys loved their toys, even those who were killers.

He popped the boot and dragged a blonde wig the colour of a pineapple out of a huge, brown duffel bag. 'Here. Put this on.'

Arguing would get her nowhere. Best to choose her battles and save her breath for the ones that counted.

Dipping her head, she wound her hair into a knot then slipped on the wig.

'And these.' He passed her a pair of large round sunnies that covered half her face – no doubt his intention. She had to look like a fly. A ridiculous blonde fly.

She pushed away a curl and scrunched her nose as it flopped back down. 'How far is the safe house?'

'Far enough to be safe.' His grin implied humour that missed its mark. But she smiled back, regardless.

'Can we stop for some food?' *And maybe a security camera or two.* 'I'm starving.'

'How about these?' He pressed two mini-bags of Aunt Milly's into her hands, a white choc and cranberry and a dark chilli Choco-Sensation. Thoughts of crumbly, melt-in-your-mouth incredibleness made her want to gag.

She swallowed. 'Wow, thanks.'

He returned to the back of the car and reached into the duffel bag again. Without shifting her gaze, she opened her hand and let a packet drop to her feet. A Hansel and Gretel clue left for anyone who knew her.

That deep in her heart she wished the "anyone" would be Chase may have been futile, but there it was. Logic seldom commanded emotion.

Des straightened and grinned her way. His wig was shoulder-length bleached-by-the-sun blonde, his cap and Ray-bans perfect accompaniments. Trading shirt and tie for something with slashes of watermelon red – perhaps to compliment her pineapple hair? – he looked ready to hit the beach.

He slammed the boot and was at her side in seconds.

'You dropped one.' He stooped, then handed her the crumpled cookie bag, his sharp gaze watching her too carefully for comfort.

She blinked back a sudden wave of tears. 'That'll teach me for not paying attention. Thanks.'

'Can't have you going hungry now, can we?'

He opened the car door. There was nothing for it but to get in. It took less than five seconds to realise there was nothing inside to use as a weapon. Nothing to help her end this thing and end Des's reign.

He slipped in beside her. 'I thought you were starving.' He looked pointedly at the cookie packets in her lap.

She ripped one open and sank her teeth into buttery sawdust. And tried not to gag.

Withdrawing another, she held it out for him. 'Want a bite?'

'Why not?' Capturing her gaze, he sank his teeth in and chewed, then turned the ignition. 'Ready?'

She nodded, pulling out a smile from god-knows where. 'More than.'

The engine revved.

A car backfired.

Des's head jerked to look behind. 'Bastards!'

She followed his gaze.

Her heart leapt. *Thank god!*

Armed officers formed a blockade at the exit ramp while two marked cars skidded to a stop behind them.

The moment she'd awaited.

Saved. Almost.

The easy option would be to open the car door and run like hell.

She flexed her fingers, then clamped them against her thigh. She wasn't going for easy. She was going for definitive, for ensuring every officer outside returned safely to their families tonight.

She steeled her expression. 'What do we do now?'

He revved the engine, one hand gripping the wheel, the other Chase's semi. 'Get out of here and take down as many of the bastards doing it.'

The car squealed over the black bitumen, stopping just shy of the parking space. He revved again, facing off the human barricade, pressing the window button with his elbow. Warm, fuel-infused air rushed into the car. His arm snaked out and he fired toward the officers, scattering their ranks.

He slapped a hand against the steering wheel, cackled. Lowered his foot on the gas.

She dragged in a deep breath, let it out long, slow. Then rested her hand on his thigh and squeezed. 'You can't drive and shoot. Give me the gun.' Opening her window with one hand, she offered her other. 'Bonnie and Clyde, right?'

Des froze. His fingers tightened about the trigger.

Her breath stalled, rocks catching in her throat. She swallowed. Willed her hand not to shake. Would he do it? Was the trust she'd fostered enough?

Each second was a lifetime flashing tauntingly through her mind.

'Don't we have a wedding to get to?' She reached over, kissed his cheek, then curled her fingers around the weapon. 'Let's take 'em for a lark, Clyde.'

She felt him stiffen. Knew he recognised Bonnie's very own words, even as she thanked the heavens she'd remembered them. She pulled slowly back, and as she did, his grip on the gun loosened.

She weighed it in her hand, tested the resistance of the trigger, then levelled it between his eyes. 'Take your foot off the accelerator, real slow, Des.' When he hesitated, as if he'd call her bluff, she curled her trigger finger just a little tighter. 'Do it! Or I'll blast your brains all over this damn fine leather.'

Chapter Sixty-Nine

'**F**ucking traitor!'

Red scorched Des's face, his teeth baring as if he'd like nothing better than to rip her apart.

Stacey fought the shake in her hand. There was no reason for it. Not anymore.

It's over.

She glared at the man who'd turned her entire world to mud. 'You better believe it.' Her grip on the gun tightened. 'No sudden moves, asshole. Turn off the engine.'

He raised his hands. Didn't even pretend he was about to do what she asked. 'You're going to regret this.'

'The only thing I regret is letting you into my life.'

He scowled. 'I was the best thing in it. The only one who gave a crap about you and your art.'

'Bullshit. This is all about you and your sick-assed delusion to become someone who matters. Well, newsflash asshole. You don't.'

'That's where you're wrong, Stacey. I've left a legacy people will never forget. And I've one more story to write.'

Before she could read the meaning behind his words, he lunged. Metal flashed. Her vision blurred and sharp pain sliced her stomach.

Where the hell did the knife come from?

With a leery grin, he pulled back, thick blood dripping from a long, thin blade. Her blood.

He lunged again.

Her hand clenched.

Boom!

The recoil rammed through her body.

Scorn slipped into surprise and Des slumped forward.

She shrunk back into her seat, legs and arms flailing against the smother of his body. Her stomach burned. Her eyes stung with tears she could no longer hold back.

The door beside her wrenched open and she jerked, waving the gun toward it.

'Whoa! Stacey, it's Jayda.' Warm hands loosened her fingers from their hold and somewhere in the back of her mind she registered officers pulling Des's lifeless body off her own.

Officer Taylor was there, taciturn replaced with worry.

'Paramedics!'

A sea of blue converged. Someone checked her pulse, her wound, firing questions she couldn't begin to follow. Something pressed hard against the sticky mess on her stomach and fire raged through her abdomen, making her eyes roll back in her head.

Then they were easing her out and onto a stretcher.

She blinked, forcing focus into the blur of activity around her.

A familiar face swam within the sea of others. She grabbed Jayda's wrist. 'Chase and my mother. Did you get to them in time? Are they okay?'

Before she could answer, the paramedic was back, asking if she had allergies, wiping something cool against the inside of her elbow, forcing cool liquid into her vein. His face swam, her thoughts a soup of nonsensical babble.

Then light transformed to dark, and the world around her was no more.

Stacey scrunched her eyelids against wakefulness.

I didn't save anyone.

The sting in her heart drowned out the throbbing ache from her stomach. Reality was a bitch when weighed against her ability to write her characters away from death.

She blinked, slowly allowing entrance to the bright, iridescent lights and white-painted hospital walls. Her body felt drug-heavy, her mind numb. The machine beside her bed whirred, its flickering LED heart proving she was indeed alive. That was the clinical assessment. The hole in her chest stated otherwise.

She had no idea what had happened after she left Des's cave of horrors. Had seen no one who could either confirm or deny her worst fears. Chase was supposed to be her future. A light at the end of this nightmarish tunnel. Now the nightmare was over, the elation that should have followed eluded her.

As a result of her refusal to shoot him, her mother had been shot in his place. Then she'd had no choice but to shoot him anyway, to save him, more than likely robbing him of a future in the career he loved. *If* he managed to survive the bomb blast and had any future at all.

Thoughts that carved at her heart, slice by aching slice.

And to top off all that warm, fuzzy crappiness, she'd lost every bit of pleasure for a vocation that had filled her up and made her whole after her failed marriage. Now emptiness filled her once again, leaving her without mother, lover or sanctuary and a meaningless future that loomed dark and dismal before her.

The makings of a damned rocking story. If only it wasn't her life.

'Stace!'

Her head jerked back, crinkling the over-starched pillow behind her.

A burst of energy and citrus perfume surged into the room. *Shazz. How'd she find out so fast?*

She pulled up just short of the bed, her normally sleek hair looking anything but, her stance uncertain, as if she had no idea whether to hug Stacey or whether hugging would break her further into pieces. 'I came as soon as they called. Thank god you put me as your second emergency contact.'

That explained it. A reaction in her post-divorce panic when asked to provide a name other than her mother's. Just as well. Her number one emergency contact was of no use now.

She blinked. Hard.

Shazz dumped a large shopping bag onto the trolley-like table, a handful of gossipy magazines and tub of Aunt Milly's poking out the top.

Nausea spilled up into her throat. Doubtful she'd ever eat, let alone enjoy them again.

Shazz's gaze slipped down to Stacey's stomach. So she knew about the stabbing. Her worry in that regard was unfounded. Des's aim had miraculously missed all major organs and blood vessels. The cut would heal. The rest …

Shazz grabbed her hand, avoiding the needle in her vein and heart monitor peg on her finger. 'How are you?'

Such a wide-ranging question. Anyone else, and they'd be referring to the stitched hole in her abdomen. But this was Shazz, and her expression said she was asking so much more – for Stacey to spill from wounds that once open, might never be forced closed again.

She willed up a smile. 'I'll live.'

One fine brow arched under a sleek auburn fringe. 'Well, that's a relief.'

Without letting go, she reached back and dragged up a chair before falling into it, her squinted gaze not once leaving Stacey's face. 'Now we've dispensed with the story you tell everyone else, we can talk about how you really feel.'

Stacey swallowed.

'Honey. It's me.' She squeezed her hand. 'Your editor was a serial killer, your mum's on life support and your – I don't know what to call him – is in a critical condition. When you're ready to unload, I'm here for you.'

She made to sit up and realised her mistake when fire raged through her abdomen. She barely acknowledged the pain.

Nothing else registered but one marvellous fact. 'Chase is alive?'

Shazz nodded, slowly. 'No one told you?'

'No one seemed to know anything when I asked.' Relief flooded her, followed by a surge of guilt. 'My mother?'

'Touch and go.' She shrugged. 'I don't know much – they won't share details with non-family members.'

She's dying because you couldn't shoot Chase. This is your fault.

'I need to see her.'

'She won't even know you're there.'

'But *I* will.'

She needed to live. *Please let her live.* Because then she could look at Chase without drowning in guilt that she was directly responsible for killing her own mother. For choosing Chase over her.

'In case you're wondering, Chase is in the ICU.'

She *was* wondering, although she had no right. Didn't deserve to have him in her life, have him love her. She readjusted her leg and despite the pain killers, everything ached. Most of all, her heart.

If only she could see him. If only they could pick up from where they left off before the plan and the perversion of events that changed *everything*.

Would he ever walk again? Work in homicide?

She tried once more to sit up and winced.

Dammit!

The pain sliced upward and the room eddied into doubles. 'I need to see my mother.'

Shazz stood and urged her back down against the pillow.

'You will, but not now. You've got a hole in your stomach the size of my fist and there's no way you'll be standing, let alone walking, any time soon.'

'You don't understand. I have to see her, Shazz.' Floodgates she'd kept closed until now, swung wide open and the guilt ripped right through. *'If I'd had the guts to shoot Chase, she'd be more than barely alive.'*

Shazz pulled back. 'You ... *you've lost me.'*

'Des invented some twisted game of Trivial Pursuit crossed with Russian roulette. I had to pull the trigger.'

'Shit!'

'Yeah.' Her voice croaked. She cleared her throat and tried to get it back again. 'I had to shoot Chase, and when I refused, Des shot mum in the stomach instead. Chase would have suffered the same fate, so I shot him. In the leg. *To save his life.'* The whisper wrenched from her chest so she barely recognised her own voice. 'And he probably hates me because he'll be stuck at a desk rather than out in the field. That's if he's even able to be a detective anymore.'

'Oh, honey.' Shazz perched on the edge of the bed and gave her a careful, Shazz-style hug. When she finally pulled back, her brows pitched into a deep vee. 'You've got to stop shouldering other people's failings. First Brad, now Des. They made their decisions and their actions were their actions, not yours.'

'But what if I'd done things differently? What if I'd come up with a plan that didn't involve playing Des's sick game and didn't involve shooting Chase?'

'And what if you did nothing and they both died?' She squeezed her arm. 'Stace, you've been through hell the past twenty-four hours and that makes you a victim, too. You did what you did to keep two people you care about alive. You succeeded, and because of you, a serial murderer will never kill again. You were amazing and brave and your actions mean both Chase and your mother have a chance.'

Shazz wrapped her up in another of her all-encompassing hugs. 'Now stop focusing on the "what ifs" and follow your doctor's orders – rest and get better and forget Des Whittaker ever existed. Because you're not in any condition to go bowling through the hospital to visit your mother – who, by the way, would only make you feel bad for wasting time visiting instead of finishing your next book.'

The irony was almost laughable. Just as well Shazz didn't know the extent of her mother's involvement. What would she say then?

No one needed to know.

Despite her actions, her mother deserved a second chance. A legacy linking her to a serial killer wouldn't change what she'd done. But giving her the opportunity to start again could change her future. Give them a future together. If she had one.

And that brought Stacey full-circle.

How could she find happiness with Chase if her mother died? Would there ever be a time she'd look at him and not remember? Not relive the guilt and pain and hopelessness of that moment when Des raised his gun and shot her in the stomach *because she'd chosen Chase over her.*

'What about Chase?'

Her mouth dried. 'What about him?'

Shazz searched her face then broke into a wide grin. 'You love him.'

She sucked in a deep breath and shook her head.

It was one thing to think it. Another to have it shouted out loud. She'd done what she swore she'd never do – fallen for a detective. And just to complicate things – because life wasn't complicated enough – she'd gone and shot him.

She'd tried to move past that. And failed.

He didn't have Parkinson's as he'd feared. He had a future in the force and a future outside it. What if her bullet had stripped all that away?

Shazz's grin dissolved into a frown. 'Stop that right now.'

'Stop what?'

'The second guessing. The wondering if you're doing the right thing, with the right man.'

For once Shazz was wrong. The question wasn't if Chase was right for her. She already knew he was. But where she'd believed that stopping Des would leave a clear path for their future, instead it had left a blockade.

And her mother stood dead centre.

She couldn't die. Not when they'd finally connected, after a lifetime of dissonance. Not when there was hope for their relationship, a chance to start again and build something great between them.

Not when dying would mean the death of any chance she had with Chase.

She had to see her mother. Save her.

Before it was too late.

Chapter Seventy

It was too late.

Unless …

Chase adjusted his crutches and rechecked the number. Two-one-four. *Right room.*

He peered inside. *Wrong woman.*

Thinning grey hair, pallid skin as wrinkled as an overripe grape. Another woman in the bed that was once Stacey's.

Damn!

He'd called Stacey every day for the past three days because he couldn't bear not hearing her voice. They'd talked, and although she'd seemed distant, he'd blamed it on the pain killers. Delayed shock. The fact that her mother was at death's door.

And he'd wanted to be with her through it all. Hated that he couldn't. If not for his damned leg …

He shifted, leaned more heavily on his crutches.

The prognosis wasn't great. Hell, it was shit on a stick served up by a doc who barely blinked as he'd stated there was no guarantee Chase would ever walk without a limp again.

Mentally he'd extrapolated. A busted leg meant no guarantee he'd be back in the field instead of stuck behind a desk. No guarantee he'd rejoin his unit. No guarantee he'd ever work homicide again. And yet the heaviness in his gut was less wrenching than he'd imagined. And so much less than it would have been at the idea of losing Stacey.

Not going to happen.

Whittaker was gone and nothing was stopping them being together.

He turned and made his awkward way toward the lifts. He'd head for the third floor, then the South wing and room 3155. Candace's room.

No doubt, he'd find Stacey there. She'd spent as much time as her doctor would allow at her mother's side. And why not? Her mother needed her, while he was up and well and on the right side of death.

He shouldn't resent the fact that he'd seen her for a mere five minutes since they'd been admitted – one visit, stilted and awkward and over before he could discover what was holding her back.

No. He wouldn't begrudge Stacey's time with her mother.

It was good they'd made their peace. That Candace had said what she said.

Most of all, it was good that she'd commanded Chase to take care of her daughter. Because he had every intention of doing just that.

'More read, Unc Chase!'

Stubby little fingers grabbed the closed *Hairy Maclary* book and opened it for the fourth time that morning.

Chase ruffled Jag's curls, his chest lightening in a way no one but his nephew could manage. 'Sure thing, buddy. What about a different book?'

Eying Chase's leg, as per his mother's strict instructions, he slid carefully down from the recliner, his bare feet slapping loudly against the wooden decking. Then two big brown saucers blinked as the ragamuffin shuffled impatiently from leg to leg. 'More 'clary?'

Who could say "No" to that face? 'Of course.'

His chubby expression lit as if he'd been promised a Super Soaker 300.

Chase couldn't help but grin back. 'Go on, bring back a couple.'

With a chortle, nappy and boy waddled toward Gracie's back door.

Warmth seeped through the chill in his heart.

That he'd been cajoled into staying while his leg healed wasn't all bad. The benefits were two-fold – he'd keep an eye on Gracie until the thugs who trashed her place were caught and he'd spend quality man-time with his nephew. Certainly not a hardship. And it kept his mind off other less-warming thoughts.

'No more, Jag.' Gracie's voice wafted out through the kitchen window. 'Uncle Chase needs to rest. He can read to you again later.'

A loud wail drowned out her final words.

He shifted and pain sliced up his thigh. His entire leg throbbed like fucking buggery. Only second in pain ratio to his sister's constant fussing.

The wail soon subsided, and in its place The Wiggles chanted the virtues of their Little Red Car.

'Cup of tea?' Gracie's head appeared through the kitchen window.

He winced. 'No thanks.'

'Coffee?'

He twisted, winced again. 'No.'

'What about something cold? I have lemonade and apple juice. Or you can have water with ice.'

The throb shifted to his head.

He closed his eyes. 'Water is perfect.' Better to accept something or she'd run through her entire pantry until he did.

He gritted his teeth.

Ungrateful bastard!

Was it so bad if Gracie wanted to take care of him? He'd scared her half to death. Escaped a burial. Only just survived a bomb blast and a bullet to the leg.

His mind moved to the woman who'd put it there, but he pulled it back. He wasn't ready.

It hurt too goddam much.

He owed Jayda and his team his life. And so much more. They'd disarmed the bomb, then stormed the parking building to disarm Whittaker and save Stacey.

A magpie cawed, swooping from a nearby apple tree to the large pear tree across the fence.

He rubbed his neck but the muscles remained locked.

Gracie's expression was forever carved into his mind, the moment she'd raced into his hospital room, grasped his hand overtight and stared down at him with wide glistening eyes. They were all the family they had, but that fact had barely registered when he'd bowled off after a psychopathic killer. That he'd fucked up royally on so many fronts was more than clear. He hadn't saved Gracie the pain of worry and he'd failed to save Stacey full stop.

'Here you go.'

His head snapped back to his sister stepping through the back door, and he did what he did best – severed his head from his heart and blocked all emotion from his mind.

'The service here is so good, I might never leave.' He forced his lips into a grin and accepted the cool, condensation-covered glass.

'Would that be such a bad thing?'

He sipped. Avoided her gaze. 'You and Jag need your space.'

'Say what you mean, little brother. You need yours.'

She was spot on. Not that he'd ever admit it.

'You don't need to monitor my activities, you know. I'm not an invalid, and I happen to enjoy reading to my nephew.'

She dropped into the recliner beside him, grabbed his hand and placed his next round of pain meds into his palm. 'You're tired and in pain. And it doesn't hurt for Jag to understand boundaries.'

There was something in her voice he hadn't noticed before. Something older, wiser, like he'd blinked for a second, and suddenly his sister had grown up.

He knocked back the pills, savouring the cool slide of icy liquid down his throat, and only then did he study the deep, dark lines on Gracie's face.

'You're a great mum, Gracie. I don't know if I ever told you that.'

Tears brimmed her lashes, but her lips wavered into the merest of smiles. 'I do what I have to do. And Jag makes my job pretty easy. He's a good kid.'

'Good kids only come from good parents.' He downed another swig of water. 'Talking about tired, you look like a break wouldn't go astray. You don't have to wait on me, you know. I can get my own drink.'

'I know. But I want to.' Her gaze darted to his leg and the thick white bandage still covering the bullet's legacy. 'When I heard what happened …'

He reached across and grabbed her hand. 'I'm sorry. I should never have put you through that.'

'It's not your fault, Chase. I know what you do is dangerous. That you face guns and bad guys every day, and that what happened has always been a possibility. I just blocked it from my mind.' She let out a deep sigh. 'Denial beats realism in spades, and I've always taken for granted that you'd be there for Jag and me, no matter what. You're the one constant in our lives and I can't imagine that changing.'

'Hey, I *will* always be here.'

Her lips wobbled. 'You almost weren't.'

Again bright green eyes and strawberry blonde curls nudged their way into his mind. The gun in Stacey's hand, the terror in her eyes. Her actions saved his life. Yet he'd barely had the chance to exchange two words, let alone his thanks.

Her mother was at death's door and she'd spent every waking hour at her side since her release from hospital. He got that. What he didn't get was her refusal to talk about *them*. Their future. As if she'd decided they no longer faced one together.

The knowledge seized his gut and twisted.

Gracie turned her hand, wrapping her fingers around his. 'Do you ever wonder what our lives would have been like if Mum didn't get sick? If Dad didn't spend every second caring for her when she was alive, then mourning her death when she was gone?'

He stared out over the small, square lawn and grass way overdue for a cut. How long since they'd discussed that part of their life? He shook his head. Too long ago to remember.

The pain in his leg had numbed. Other pains didn't, however, no matter how strong the meds.

'Sometimes. You?'

'The same. I thought about it a lot when I fell pregnant with Jag. Wondering if genetics meant he'd suffer the same fate.'

'And you don't still wonder?'

She shook her head. 'As soon as he was born I took the test.'

'Back then? You never said anything.'

'I got the all-clear so I didn't see the point. Plus, I assumed you'd done the same.' Her gaze narrowed. 'You did, right?'

His gaze slid left of hers. 'Sure.'

'When?'

What was the point in lying? 'Two weeks ago.'

'Two …? *Wow.*' Her expression turned thoughtful. 'That explains a lot.'

'What's that supposed to mean?'

'You never talk about the future. Never plan for it. Everything's about now. About your job. Nothing much else. I always wondered why.'

He dragged in a deep breath. 'I started showing symptoms about two years ago.'

'What? Why didn't you say anything?'

'Because it'd mean admitting it was happening.'

'So you did the typical male thing and stuck your head in the sand.'

'Pretty much.'

'And?'

'It was hyperthyroid, fixable with medication.'

A loud sigh escaped her lips. 'I wish you'd told me.' She tightened her grip round his hand and shook her head. 'You make this big deal about always being there for me and Jag, but you never let us be there for you. Like now. I had to fight for you to stay here. I even have to fight to bring you a drink, for god's sake. Seems you've locked people out of your life so long, you've forgotten how to let them in.'

'I let people in.'

'Who, Chase? Your squad? Your partner? You haven't spoken to a single one of them since you left the hospital. And if you did, what's the bet it was work related? Then there's your friends. I don't even know if you have any outside of your job.'

'Since when did this become a "crap on Chase" fest?'

'Since I want you to be happy.'

'I'm *happy*.' He masked the scowl from his expression. The pierce in his chest he couldn't stop. 'I've just been shot. Forgive me if I'm not cartwheeling through fields of clover.'

'You're alive, Chase. I'd have thought cartwheels *were* in order.' Every line in her body tensed. 'We need to talk about this. It's time you let Mum and Dad go and start living.'

His protest died as she raised her hand. 'Yes, parts of our childhood were crap. And yes, I wish Mum didn't die and Dad didn't pretend we didn't exist. But both those things happened, and life wasn't all bad because *we had each other*. Circumstances brought us closer together and I have an amazing brother who always looks out for me. What he doesn't realise is that the door swings both ways. I want to be there for you, too.'

Damn if his eyes didn't get all misty. 'When did you get so smart and grown up?'

'The smarts I got from my brother.' She grinned. 'The grown up part I got while your head was buried neck-deep in the sand.'

'Hilarious, Gracie.'

'Yep. And guess what. The humour is all mine.' She poked out her tongue with the same sass she'd given him back when they were kids. Back when she'd labelled his caring as "bossy" and paid him little or no mind. Some things never change.

She blinked the laughter from her expression, her lips flatlining into an I'll-take-no-nonsense-from-you frown. 'So, short of cartwheels, what are your plans until you're cleared for work?'

He'd barely allowed himself to think beyond the next meal, the next day. The next call that Stacey wouldn't return.

It wasn't over between them, not by a long-shot. But if she needed space, he'd give it. That didn't mean he had to like it.

He shrugged. 'Taking a well-deserved break. Spending quality time with you and Jag.'

'Bullshit, Chase. Since when did you take any kind of break?'

'A man can change.'

'Not that much. And you're still shutting me out.' Her gaze narrowed. 'What about your writer? You planning to do the same to her?'

'She's not *my* anything.'

'But you'd like her to be.'

'She won't return my calls.' He clamped his lips. *Hell!* The last thing he needed was to fling his dirty boxers all over the show in front of his sister. 'It doesn't matter. I'm handling it.'

'Handling it, how? By watching my pear tree grow and reading stories about some ridiculously hairy, cat-like dog? Get off your butt and see her.'

He huffed, more irritated with circumstances than with Gracie's meddling. 'She needs space. Her mother's dying.'

'Space, schmace! What a load of codswallop! She doesn't need someone who'll walk away when it's too hard. She needs someone who'll stand up and fight for her, beside her. Who'll be there, no matter what she says and does. If she's looking after her mother, who's looking after her? Damn straight, that person should be the man who loves her. *If* you love her?'

She speared him with a look reminiscent of their mother – piercing, probing, leaving him with nowhere to hide.

She nodded. 'I thought so. Don't let her push you away, Chase.

Decide if she's worth it. And after that, decide if you're worth it too.'

His neck prickled. It wasn't hot enough to blame the sun.

Denial tripped across his tongue.

Boppy music trilled from Gracie's pocket and he clamped his mouth closed. Her cheeks flushed deep red as she pulled out her mobile and tried to hide the screen. Too late.

Chris.

Why was his security man calling now his security stint was over? And why would his call cause Gracie to blush like a schoolgirl in love.

Shit!

He jolted forward. *No way!*

A metaphorical slap to his forehead didn't help. Perhaps a real one would do better.

He'd been so steeped in his own circumstances, he'd been oblivious to what was happening outside it.

Her gaze locked to the ringing phone. 'I have to take this.'

Before he could scrape his bottom jaw up from the jarrah slats, she'd dropped his hand and disappeared inside.

If Chris so much as laid a finger on Gracie …

From the look on her face, his old friend had laid a helluva lot more than just a finger on her. Before the thought saw him explode, he swivelled and dropped his feet to the ground, barely wincing at the thrum of pain up his thigh.

He braced to stand just as his own pocket began to sing.

He couldn't help it, his entire body tensed as he snapped the phone out. His racing heart barely slowed as he stared at the screen. Not Stacey, but it was the next best thing.

Then a thought gripped him.

He swiped a barely steady finger across the screen. 'Is Stacey okay?'

'Hi detective.' She chuckled. Actually chuckled.

The taut in his muscles relaxed just a fraction.

'It's been a long time.' The silky stroke of her voice should have sent his body into full-throttled awareness, but all it did was make him think of Stacey. Of why her friend was calling.

'Too long.' He scrubbed his jaw. 'Shazz, isn't it?'

'You've a good memory for names.'

'It comes with the job.'

'Of course.'

He leaned forward. Strained to read between the lines. Couldn't read a godforsaken thing.

He tried again. 'Is everything okay with Stacey?'

'Settle down sunshine. She's fine. Her mother, however, is not.'

His body stilled. The news wasn't unexpected – few people could sustain injuries like Candace's and come out the other end alive – but the source of the news was.

Not that the why's and wherefore's of her call mattered. He was just grateful she'd made it.

'Does Stacey know you're calling?' He swallowed, knowing the answer he wanted but doubting he'd get it.

'No.'

At least his instincts weren't completely screwed after a week off the job.

'How is she?'

'Angry, sad, overwhelmed. All the expected emotions. She could do with a friend right now.'

'And you think I fit the category?'

'Only you can decide that.' Papers rustled in the background. 'The funeral's tomorrow. Tell me if I should text you the details.'

'Has she …' He bit his tongue. Figuratively. Literally. And painfully. Wouldn't he sound just plain needy if he asked the question balancing on the tip of said muscle?

'Mentioned you?'

How the hell did she know?

'No. That's not what I was about to say.'

'Of course it wasn't, detective.' There was laughter in her voice, although the occasion didn't allow for more than a hint of it. 'Wish I could tell you, but then I'd have to kill you. And assaulting an officer just isn't my thing. Although the handcuffs … that's something else entirely.'

She was incorrigible, a woman who definitely matched those ridiculous heels.

Unlike his Stacey. She was in a class of her own.

His Stacey?

He stood and braced against the burn in his thigh. Stared out at next door's tabby perched precariously on the boundary fence, cleaning its paw.

'Text me.'

'Good boy. I knew you'd find those balls of yours again.'

He practically choked on the laughter. 'What made you think I'd ever misplaced them?'

'Just a hunch. And the fact you haven't pushed your ugly mug back into her life before now.' The jesting in her voice clicked over to professional. 'Good day, detective. I doubt you'll get more than one shot tomorrow. Make it count.'

Speaking of balls, Shazz had a steel set of her own. The woman was outrageous but she was a good friend of Stacey's and that counted for a lot.

He looked forward to becoming good friends with her sometime soon.

What was it Stacey said?

A relationship with me means having a relationship with my animals.

Surely the mantra included friends, too?

Chapter Seventy-One

The day was damp. Cold. Lifeless.

A perfect day for a funeral.

Stacey stood on the grass, dry eyes directed out over orderly rows of marble and rock – headstones that marked the end of an era. Life lost. Loved ones left behind. The air hung heavy with must and wet earth, mud squelching as mourners passed, payed their respects and slowly filtered away.

Shazz stirred beside her, and she turned, only to receive a brief hug and harried apology – something about the caterers. Or was it something else? Her brain barely registered and it didn't much matter. The world was a fuzzy old-time movie reel and she a spectator.

Marilyn Sotheby, her mother's best friend, wobbled past as heels – too long for solid ground, let alone soggy mud – sunk and then stuck. Stacey's gaze dropped to her chunky black boots – the more sensible choice for Melbourne's inclement weather.

Her mother would be mortified.

If that was something you could be when you were dead.

Her lips pursed.

A blackbird swooped over the crowd, settling on a headstone a few rows away, its song sweet, lilting, *alive*, ridiculously incongruous to its locale.

Her body knotted so tight she could barely move without every part aching. Least of all the hole in her stomach from Des's knife. Meds and time were caring for that. The rest? Well, there was no cure.

The wood in her expression mirrored the wood in her heart.

And the guilt wouldn't leave.

Where was the grief?

She'd attended more funerals the past fortnight than in her entire lifetime and it was as if her entire soul had been doused with ice, numbing her from the head down. She couldn't even lose herself in her writing. How could she, knowing lives had been lost because of it?

And worse, if that was at all possible, the one man who could make it all go away, who could make her *feel* again, was standing less than ten feet away, looking gorgeous and wonderful and oh, so distant.

And he could never be hers.

Again the guilt.

He hadn't approached her yet, and she wasn't sure what she'd do if he did.

What would she say?

I miss you. I want you. Please forgive me and can we go back to the time when my actions didn't break us, when you'd do anything to be with me, even hold a snake and hunt all night in the rain and the cold for my cat?

Why was he even here?

Of course the answer was obvious. He was one of the good guys. No matter her mother's sins, he'd been there during her last few moments of consciousness, had saved her from the bomb, and he'd come to pay his respects. She'd be a fool to read more into it than that. She'd barely seen him since their tandem hospital stay. Her choice. It had been better that way. *Safer.* Because the sight of him made her want to throw every emotion but impulse to the wind and bolt into his arms.

He stood alone – broad shoulders encased in a warm leather jacket, thighs encased in black pants that fit better than any glove – surveying the crowd just as she'd done moments before, a dark ash walking stick gripped in his left hand.

Her stomach clamped.

Then, as if he sensed her interest, as if he were as attuned to her as she was to him, his head spun round and his gaze clashed with hers. One look, and every muscle holding her upright began to dissolve. She locked her knees, willed herself not to fall apart.

The world faded.

Drumming filled her ears; Chase filled her eyes.

His body poised. Then, with shoulders squared and a sharp nod, he limped her way.

Any moment her heart would beat clear out of her chest. Rabid dry invaded her mouth. She tried to swallow, tried to cough life into her vocal chords.

Then he was there, invading her space, stealing her air. Smelling spicy and fresh and wonderful.

'Hi.'

Such a nothing word, yet from his lips it was so much more than a greeting.

'Hi.' Her throat croaked, but she managed the word, just.

His gaze burned. 'I'm sorry about your mum, Stacey.'

She nodded, sudden thickness cloaking her throat. 'Me too.'

Emotion rolled through her, blindsiding her like a hundred-foot tidal wave. She'd emerged days ago from a cloud of resentment and anger, and sorry didn't begin to cover how she felt about her mother now. Never really knowing her, yet knowing she'd teamed up with a serial killer. Had been complicit in murder. Beth's. Ethan's. So many others. Then witnessing her remorse. Her suffering.

Losing her before they could bridge the gap built by years of misunderstanding and resentment. Never being able to say goodbye, or that she loved her and forgave her, through all that had happened.

That was her biggest regret of all.

Barring the man standing before her. Here – *alive* – yet her regrets about Chase seemed so impossible to mend.

She searched for some semblance of ordinary conversation. 'How've you been?'

'I've missed you.' The unadulterated fervour in his expression chiselled at her control.

She nodded. Dropped her gaze to the cracked mud coating her boots.

God but she'd missed him too.

All the reasons she'd stayed away and avoided his calls hit her, wave by wave, and she couldn't dredge up the words to fix what had been broken between them.

Write yourself out of this, Stacey.

The more she hunted for words, the more her head pounded.

He sighed, glanced beyond her shoulder, then returned his gaze to hers. 'I've started my treatment.'

Her head jerked up. 'That's great.' Her gaze dropped, to the reason for a cane she knew he had to hate.

She pushed the hair from her face, curling it back around her ear. 'How's your leg?'

'Hurts like buggery.' He gave a wry grin. 'Only time will tell how well it heals, so I'm told.'

He blinked and something dulled in his expression, as if someone had flicked a switch and killed the light.

So many sorrys, so many regrets welled in her throat. Sometimes when life tossed you lemons, all you had at the end of the day were lemons.

His gaze narrowed. 'You were right, you know.'

She pulled herself out of her funk and tried to think of a way to end a conversation that was painful and leading her nowhere but heartache. 'Right about what?'

'Being an ace shot.'

She swallowed. Tried to think of a reply and failed.

He rubbed his thigh just above the hole she'd made. 'You missed pretty much everything that was important.'

'Pretty much?'

'Well, you didn't miss me.'

Heat spiked her blood, feeding the pound inside her skull. 'How can you laugh about it?'

He sighed. 'You're right. It's not funny. On the upside, I should be back at work before the end of next week.'

She knew what that meant. Desk duties. Twice in two months, both instances because of her.

He stepped in. 'Don't do that.'

She stepped back and mud squelched around her boot. 'What?'

'Blame yourself.'

She stared at him until the burn in her lungs reached unbearable and the breath she didn't realise she'd been holding rushed out. She couldn't do it. *Fight.* All her energy was sapped and she had nothing left to draw on.

She bit back the frustration. Every emotion he unwittingly unleashed. 'Why are you here, Chase?'

'Three reasons. To pay my respects, and to say thank you and sorry.'

She missed a breath. 'Those are my lines, not yours.'

'You saved my life, Stacey, when I should have saved yours.'

'I'm not a defenceless damsel who needs a man for that. I got us into that mess. It was my job to get us out.'

He frowned. 'That plan was both of ours. And I'm the one serving and protecting.'

'I'm the one Des was after.' She sighed.

The world was spinning and she wanted to get off. Fighting was the last thing she wanted to do with Chase. Problem was, everything else was off the table.

She tapped the mud with her toe. 'I'm sorry for shooting you.'

He quirked a brow. 'I'm sorry you had to.'

Their gazes locked. A moment that wrapped round her heart and tugged.

Her heartbeat picked up pace, her legs wobbled. 'Thanks for coming. I'm sure mum would have appreciated it.'

The words were automatic, as was the way she let him take her hand, let his thumb play across her knuckles.

Sensation bolted up her arm.

She yanked free. 'You should go now.'

His gaze narrowed. 'I'm not going anywhere.'

'I can't do this, Chase. I've just buried my mother.'

'I get that. I've been there. Remember? And I want to help. I told you before that I want to share my future with you. Nothing's changed.'

Her chest squeezed, followed by a rabid pounding between her eyes. 'Everything's changed. We can't be together. We can't be anything but friends.'

The moment the words left her lips, she knew her mistake. With Chase, being friends would be harder than being nothing at all. And "nothing" was like ripping her heart out and shoving it through a mincer.

His gaze burned. 'Friends isn't an option.' He shook his head, slowly, deliberately, his focus never once straying from hers. 'One of the many things you should know about me is once I set my mind on something, nothing short of *nothing* will make me change it. And, Stacey, my mind is set on you.'

Words, like a warm sudsy wash. Thick, foamy bubbles she wanted to sink into and soak in and never leave.

Fine if bubbles could last forever.

She braced. 'You need to unset it.'

'My heart might have something to say about that.'

'Then tell your heart to stop and move on.'

'Tell me why.'

She bit her lip until the pain was all encompassing, her eyes focused anywhere but on Chase.

Shazz stood a few feet away, watching, hoping, her expression as transparent as a swatch of cling film. She pulled her gaze away knowing her friend was going to be sorely disappointed.

A group of women from her mother's mah-jong group – who knew she even played the game? – hovered nearby, as if waiting for her tête-à-tête with Chase to be over.

It was.

'I can't do this now.'

The moment she stepped away, they surged forward.

Through a protracted exchange of mechanical handshakes, mechanical condolences and mechanical offers – as genuine as their Botox-powered smiles – she wished for the man beside her to give up and go.

As the last wire-haired woman squelched toward the stony path, Stacey's entire body drooped in a sigh. She should have realised Chase wouldn't give in that easy. Hadn't he told her, shown her multiple times, how stubborn he could be? Stubbornness that had saved his life. And her mother's – if only for a few precious days.

Somehow he was back at her side. 'Want to know the third reason I'm here?' His lips hovered tantalisingly close to her ear.

Her knees wobbled.

The hot damp of his breath shivered across her skin. Impulse would have her yell "*No!*" to his question, to her reaction. But what good was such an inconsequential word? She knew better than to expect him to leave before he'd said all he needed to say. So perhaps she should give him that – it was the least she could do – then he could go and leave her heart to shatter in solitude.

'Sure. Tell me the third reason you're here.'

'I thought you'd never ask.' A grin hijacked his lips and what remained of her knee ligaments. 'Come out for dinner with me this Saturday.'

'*Dinner?*' The word squeaked out through her hitched breath.

He nodded, stole a little more staunch from her knees. 'Yeah.'

'Like a date?'

'Not *like* a date. It'll *be* a date.'

'But I don't date.'

'I know.'

'And you're not my type.'

'I know.'

'I wear ridiculous shoes and I'm a danger to your health.'

He shuffled his left leg. Pools of deep tropical blue drilling into hers. 'I know.'

'And I told you, it's over.'

'And I told you the fat monkey hasn't sung a single, shrill note of that song yet.' He planted his feet, then grimaced, resting a little more heavily on the cane. 'Give me one chance, Stacey, to convince you we should be together and I'll give you one to tell me why not. Call it a date, call it anything you want, but let's have dinner. We can't leave things as they are, no matter what we end up being to each other.'

'Even knowing I want to break up with you, you still want a date?'

'More than anything.'

Her entire insides flip-flopped. *You don't want to say goodbye. Not yet. Not ever.*

Well that wasn't an option, but is one more evening, one measly meal, really that wrong?

Yes!

No!

Her tongue wouldn't move. Wouldn't unhinge from the roof of her mouth. And the carousel conversation in her head was unstoppable. She wanted this. One more memory. One more time with Chase before they said goodbye and split paths – he back to a job that meant the world to him, and her to, well, whatever was left of her life without him in it.

She closed her eyes, felt his gaze as if it were a real, tangible thing. Fingers brushing her over-sensitive skin. Lips butterfly-kissing her flesh into frenzy.

'Dinner, Stacey.' His voice wavered. 'Just dinner. I'll even let you choose where.'

She swallowed, stopped thinking and let her heart speak.

'How do you feel about Thai?'

Chapter Seventy-Two

Stacey surveyed the table for the umpteenth time.

The lights were dim but the silver gleamed like clear-cut diamonds – cutlery she'd polished until further polishing would have worn the engravings clear away. At the table's centre she'd positioned twin candles, their flames flickering between two perfectly placed settings – white china, crystal glasses, yellow serviette bunnies and a starched royal blue tablecloth. No effort spared.

It had to be perfect.

All the way down to the tray of Malatyan Turkish delight on the coffee table. Ironic that the surprise she'd ordered just over a week ago had arrived that morning, just in time for their dinner.

Her heart stuttered.

A week since the funeral. A week since she'd moved into her mother's Southbank apartment. A week since she'd last seen Chase.

And not once had she stopped questioning whether she'd made the right choice.

In answer to her question about Thai food, he'd mentioned a restaurant, she'd mentioned she made a wicked Penang chicken – of the vegan variety – and next thing she knew he was coming over for a home-cooked meal.

With a shaky hand, she smoothed the red silk over her hips while whorls of ginger and spice and fresh roti filled her senses.

It was too much. She'd gone too far.

Made it seem as if she wanted *this* – him here, *them* – more than anything.

She did.

But this was a goodbye, not a stepping-stone to something more.

Joe Cocker crooned about the night coming. Her mother's favourite CD. She swallowed. Glanced at her wristwatch, then the table.

Ten minutes before seven.

Crap!

Her heart raced.

Before she could think or question the rightness or wrongness of her decision, she flew into action. Snuffed out the candles, undimmed the lights. Snatched the meticulously folded bunnies, shook them out and refolded them into triangles. Slapped the stereo switch to off.

Silence bathed the room, smoky tendrils climbing the air above the table. She waved them away, felt the slap of crystal against her knuckle seconds before she heard the smash.

Murphy and his law had a lot to answer for.

By the time she'd tidied and replaced the glass it was a measly few minutes before Chase was due to arrive. Midnight watched, wide-eyed, from his cushioned basket in the corner. The tilt of his head said he thought she'd lost her mind. Not quite yet, but she was well on her way.

There was no terrarium nearby. No Cuddles to agree or disagree. He was gone, and Des had never revealed why or how before she'd ended his life.

Guilt wracked her for that. Just another notch carving into her conscience, regardless that it made no sense. Des had killed and hurt so many. He deserved to die. That didn't make it any easier, knowing she'd been the one to pull the trigger.

The bandage just above her waist pulled and the wound began to throb. So much for listening to her doctor's orders and taking it easy. Nothing in her life right now came even close to easy.

The room smelled of burnt wax and damp slathered her palms. She froze seconds before wiping them down her dress. Silk and sweat never mixed. A glance down at her outfit and her heart sank. The term "try-hard" flashed through her mind. And Chase's words – something about being who you are rather than who you think people want you to be.

The sexy outfit and shoes were Stacey Holland the author.

For their last dinner, the least she could do was be Stacey Holland the woman.

She kicked off her heels – so inappropriate for a home-cooked meal – and sped to the bedroom. She gripped the zip between her thumb and forefinger, then twisted and turned in front of the mirror in an effort to ease it down.

Crap, crap and crap!

There was a sharp rap at the front door.

Chase.

Double crap!

She wasn't even nearly ready. And that had nothing to do with the table or the food or her outfit. If she'd imagined the pound of her heart couldn't intensify she was wrong.

Her brain froze.

Breathe, Stacey. Take a deep, long breath.

This is who you are. What does it matter what he thinks – how you look – when you tell him you're never going to see him again?

Somehow, it mattered.

He knocked again.

She managed to gulp oxygen into her lungs. Enough to clear her mind and fuel her muscles into moving. With one last glance at her flushed cheeks and hair that had been smooth and shiny only ten minutes earlier, she skimmed her palms over her thighs, left the shoes where she'd dumped them, and made for the door.

She's not home.

Chase juggled the package in one hand, his keys and phone in the other, and waited.

He stuffed the latter two into his jacket pocket, tapped his foot, juggled again. Waited.

Knocked. Then waited some more.

She's changed her mind.

The black-and-white wrapping crinkled in his hand.

Two rounds of knocking. Was it worth trying for a third?

She never wanted to get involved with a cop. Least of all one who failed her so badly.

If she hasn't answered by now …

The door swung open.

His mouth dried.

All he could do was stare and hope he didn't look like a fool, jaw dropped, drooling like a teenager.

Filmy red hugged her breasts, draping across her body and fastening at a diamond brooch just above her waist. The gathers fell in waves to just above her knees, and his gaze dropped to her feet, bare but for the red-painted tips of her toes.

Her face was flushed, her chest heaving as if she'd run a marathon.

The ambient temperature spiked.

'Hi.' She gripped the door, breathless and blushing and gut-wrenchingly beautiful.

'Hi.' He swallowed the need to wrap her in his arms and never let her go. 'You look incredible.'

She glanced down and scrunched her nose, the red on her cheeks deepening. 'I was just about to change.'

'Why? That dress is … perfect.'

Again she looked down. 'This old thing?' Her hand skimmed over her thigh drawing his focus back to her curves. 'I wore it for cooking.'

She stepped back and opened the door. 'Come on in.'

He didn't even bother to question why she'd dress up to cook and then change for dinner. That'd be like asking why she alphabetised her kitchen or wore a blue monster as a timepiece. Quirky was but one of her charms.

He'd become quite partial to quirky.

Penang spices and coconut filled his nostrils. She closed the door behind them, her back so ramrod straight, her shoulders all sharp edges and determination, shunting any vestige of her softness into distant memory. As she moved further into a large, light living room, he watched the gentle sway of her ass wrapped in red and his mouth watered.

Now they stood mere centimetres apart, her gaze focused in every direction but his. She may have agreed to dinner, but it was obvious she wasn't enthralled with the idea.

She waved her hand at a stereo and nearby CD swivel-stand. 'Why don't you choose some music while I change?'

'You don't have to change on my account.'

Her wide green gaze shot toward him. 'I know. I'm changing for me.' She pivoted and headed toward a far door before she seemed to think better of it. She turned back, hesitated, then returned to his side. 'Can you give me a hand with the zip?'

She swept her hair aside and he stared at the creamy slope of her neck.

'Chase?'

He shook his head and thoughts of how the hollow between her neck and her shoulder would taste. 'Sure.'

Dropping the parcel next to the stereo, he moved in and dragged the zip slowly downward. He leaned closer and inhaled honeysuckle, his gut and below tightening as the gradual exposure of her back wrought havoc on his blood flow.

Her breathing deepened, the ragged rise and fall of her shoulders proving he wasn't the only one affected.

His finger brushed her skin. Accidental but not in the least bit regretted.

He wanted to do it again. And more.

His gut twisted. Damn, but he missed how they'd been before, how she'd melted into him with the merest of touches.

Now all she seemed to do was pull away. Like now.

'Thanks.' The tab slipped through his fingers as she dodged a cream leather couch and headed straight for the far door without turning to face him. 'I'll be back in a sec.'

The air thickened with things unsaid and events that could never be undone. How the hell were they going to get past that?

A door slammed, followed by a *thud* of something banging against it.

His gaze scanned the room until it landed on the parcel. A gift. Peace offering. Bribe. Whatever the label, he'd intended to hand it to her the moment she opened the door. And if the reality of her standing in the doorway hadn't hijacked his thoughts, he'd have done just that.

Just as well she'd elected to change. Keeping his head and his mind on fixing them would be difficult enough without the distraction of that dress.

He turned to the CDs and didn't make it further than what was already in the machine – a favourite and mellow enough to relax without being overly romantic. He didn't want to push the point, even though that was exactly what he wanted.

His glance slipped over the coffee table then lurched back. *Was that* ... He moved closer. Grabbed a square and popped it into his mouth. Icing sugar fizzed over his tongue, flavours of apricot, pistachio and Turkish delight exploding across his taste buds.

He chewed, smiling, savouring, his heart leaping, just a little.

She'd remembered. Made the effort to search for his "vice", then put them out tonight of all nights – it had to mean something.

'Hey.'

He swung round.

Forgot to breathe.

Turkish delight lodged in his throat.

He was wrong. The dress wasn't the distraction.

Sheathed in black, head to toe, the trouser and top outfit was understated, so unlike the woman wearing them. He could still see her curves, the contrast of pale, perfect skin against clingy fabric, the glow from inside that no clothing or cosmetic could mask.

His one regret? The disappearance of those toes into flat, black shoes.

She arched a brow. 'Joe Cocker?'

'Yeah. I'm a fan from way back.' He tried to read her expression. 'I can change it if you like.'

She opened her mouth, snapped it shut, then shook her head. 'No, it's fine.'

He tilted his head toward the table. 'You bought Turkish delight.'

'I did.' Her hand fluttered over her hip. 'I ordered it a week ago.'

She didn't finish the sentence. She didn't have to. He could read, even between lines so stilted they chopped his leaping heart off at the knees.

She'd bought the treat for him before they were over. At a time when she'd agreed to be a part of his future, before nerves and their plan made her change her mind.

It was his job now to change it back.

She still wanted him. And for as long as that feeling existed, he still had a chance.

He lifted the package from the shelf and passed it to her. 'Here. I got you something.'

Those wondrous lips curved upward, lightening the room. His heart. 'You didn't have to do that.'

'Great.' He snatched the box from her hands. 'I'm sure I still have the receipt somewhere.'

She grabbed it back. 'No way buster. You can't just offer

something then take it back.'

Her gaze widened, just a moment, then she seemed to recover. 'Can I open it?'

'That's the general idea.'

She dropped onto the white leather couch, balancing the present on her lap. 'Funny, ha ha.' She glanced up. 'Nice wrapping, by the way.'

The look, the words, made his hunt for black cat paper all the more worthwhile.

He joined her on the couch and watched her enjoyment. Three rips and the box was free of wrapping, the floor at her feet not so. He couldn't help but smile inside and out – the Stacey who'd captured his heart was back.

'Oh, Chase.' Her eyes misted, even as her lips trembled, no doubt remembering the snake she'd lost. 'It looks just like Cuddles. He's … *beautiful.*'

Beautiful wasn't a word he'd use. Horrendous, perhaps. But the moment he'd spotted the snake teapot online, he knew she'd love it. A bright green body coiling to form the pot, its head and open jaws forming the spout. Shipping it in time for their "date" had cost more than the teapot itself, but her expression, her delight, was worth it.

'Are you sure you like it?'

'I love it!' Her fingers stroked the coils as she lifted her gaze to his. 'Thank you. This is the best present, ever.'

His chest may have swelled just a little. 'I knew you had a Midnight teapot. It's only fair you have one for Cuddles too.'

Her lips twitched. 'Fess up. You were warming to him.'

'I'm warming to a lot of things.' He edged closer.

She jumped up. 'This is great.' She held the teapot in one hand, scrabbling to gather up the shredded wrapping in the other. 'I'll put it in the kitchen while I check on the food. I won't be long.'

Damn!

He didn't get it. The heat in her gaze proved she was interested. That she wasn't anywhere ready to call it quits. And he'd made it blatantly clear he was the same. What was holding her back? Something more than the guilt of shooting him. Something more than her mother's death. Something her weird and wonderful mind was stewing on but refused to share.

Something he'd have to change.

A rustle of fabric indicated she'd returned.

'I hope you're hungry.' She crossed the floor to the table and adjusted a crumpled bright yellow serviette. 'Hours slaving over a hot stove means there's an entire feast ready to be ravished.'

Her gaze widened, a flush of red flooding her cheeks. 'Eaten. I meant to say "eaten".'

He bit back a grin. 'Don't worry, I didn't take it as an invitation.'

She frowned. As if she'd wished he had.

He took a chance. 'That doesn't mean I don't want to, though.'

She clutched the back of the chair. 'I–' She blinked. Air whooshed out through her parted lips. 'I'll get dinner.'

Her hand dropped and she turned.

'Stacey.' Three strides and he grabbed her elbow. She tensed, but he didn't let go. 'Let's get rid of the elephant in the room.'

'*Elephant?*' She snorted, but at least she relaxed. 'I'd say there's an entire stampede of them in here.'

He rubbed his thumb along the soft stretch of skin inside her elbow. She shuddered, her reddened cheeks intensifying. But she didn't pull back – the first positive sign since she'd opened the door and stared at him as if he were breakfast, lunch and dinner all rolled into one.

He grinned at the thought. 'That's better.'

'What's better?'

'Your sense of humour's back.'

She pulled away, but not before the haunted look returned to her eyes. A look identical to those last moments before she'd left the tunnel with Whittaker.

'Aaand the elephant returns.' He touched his finger to her lips. 'We need to talk and I elect to go first.'

With a snap her teeth sunk into his finger.

He snatched it back. 'What the–!'

'You're terribly bossy all of a sudden.'

'All of a sudden?' His finger throbbed, more from shock than pain. He doubted she'd bitten it for any other reason than effect.

And seeing the return of her sass was worth it.

Her lips twitched. 'Okay then. *Again.*'

'Must be my macho superhero tendencies coming through.'

Her eyes sparkled with the semblance of a smile. 'Next you'll be wearing your undies on the outside.'

'Who said I'm wearing "undies" at all?'

Again a snort. At least she was starting to relax.

He dropped onto the couch and patted the cushion beside him. She eyed the spot without moving.

He sighed. 'We need to talk about what happened.'

She stepped back. 'No, we don't.' Her chin jerked up. 'Talking won't change anything.'

He fought not to match the spiral of her voice. 'No. But it'll change the way you view things.'

'What other way is there?' She shook her head. 'I wrote a story, created a killer that inspired my assistant editor to go on a killing frenzy, and what's more, he turned that and an obsession with Bonnie and Clyde into an obsession for me and committed multiple murders just to get my attention. So I shot him. But not before he shot my mother and I shot you.'

Only then did she take a breath – a long, deep, slow one – before she speared him with green orbs flecked with amber fire. 'Did I miss anything?'

Chapter Seventy-Three

Chase braced against the onslaught of every wrenching word from Stacey's lips. 'You pretty much captured it all except one thing.'

She raised her brows. 'Which is?'

'Whittaker made choices – clear, deliberate choices – that are the responsibility of no one but himself. Your mother did the same. As did you. The only difference?' He stood, ignoring the smart in his thigh, and moved in until honeysuckle surrounded him. 'Whittaker acted from hate. You acted from love.'

Her eyes widened, her lips parted.

He took her hand and brushed his thumb across her knuckles. She shivered.

'If you hadn't shot me, Whittaker would have, and dead certain if that happened I wouldn't be here right now. You saved me, Stacey. And not just in the tunnel but way before then.' He captured her gaze. 'You're the most amazing, infuriating, dazzling woman on this planet, and I want to be amazed and infuriated and bedazzled by you every day for the rest of my life.'

She froze.

A barricade slammed across her expression and she stepped back, twisting her hand free. Just when he thought he'd gotten through.

She shook her head. 'It can't happen.'

He clenched hands that wanted to grab her and pull her in and never let her go, and worked damn hard not to roar. 'Why? Just give me one good reason why?'

She swallowed, her eyes so wide they consumed her face. 'Whenever I look at you, all I think is my mother died because I couldn't shoot you.' Her lips wobbled. 'It's like I chose for her to die. Chose you over her. Do you have any idea how wrong that is?'

The most natural thing for him to do was step in and wrap her in his arms.

Her body stilled, inflexible, unyielding, until he dipped his head into her hair and rubbed circles slowly across her back. With a breath, she sank into him. His grip tightened. Given a choice, he'd hold her there forever.

'This is not on you, Stacey. None of it. Even your mother agreed. You. Are. Not. To. Blame.'

'I *am*. I …'

He kept rubbing. 'You, what?'

'You don't understand.' Her body tensed, short, shallow breaths converging in a gust that escaped through trembling lips. 'I'd do the same all over again. *I'd choose you.* Knowing her fate, knowing the consequences of my actions, *I'd still always choose you.* How can I forgive myself for that?'

She loves me.

The three words bombarded his brain as the woman who'd all but uttered them trembled in his arms. His heart ached and bloomed all at once. She may not have said the words, but the words she'd uttered said enough. She loved him. And it didn't matter a toss because her guilt – unfounded as it was – was tearing them apart.

Whittaker was still killing even after his death.

No! He tightened his hold.

He wouldn't allow it. Wouldn't let her go until she promised not to leave.

'Stacey, don't do this to yourself. To *us*.' He scrabbled for words, for something that would – could – make the difference. 'None of what happened was your fault. You didn't point the gun. You didn't pull the trigger. Whittaker killed your mother, just as he'd planned all along. And that game – that sick, demented game – was a ruse to get him off and drag out the inevitable that would have been two deaths – your mother and me.'

She pulled away until her hip collided with the table.

He shuffled his feet, his thigh aching like all hell. He should have brought his cane. Only he'd seen her reaction to it at the funeral. Seen the distress, the guilt. So, now he was paying the price for the trek between the taxi to her front door without it.

Not that he'd let on when it was already such a sore point between them. 'Don't you see? If you do this, if you ignore what we have and walk away, Whittaker wins. He wanted to destroy us, to have you for himself, and even in death he's doing just that. Your mother forgave you before she died. Don't you think it's time you forgave yourself?'

She shook her head, as if shaking away his declaration. 'What if I'd listened to your partner? If I'd stayed put and let the police do their job?'

His head hammered – a combination of waning painkillers, his leg and her stubbornness. 'Don't kid yourself it would have ended any better if you hadn't intervened. The only difference is I'm standing here today rather than lying in a cedar wooden box, and your mother got to make her peace, and she got to say goodbye. You made all that happen. Don't ever downplay what you did. You were smart and courageous and incredible.' He inhaled. 'If anyone's to blame, it's me. I should have saved your mother. And I should have saved you.'

'I don't blame you for any of this.'

'Like your mother didn't blame you. And neither do I. Don't you see? It works both ways.'

She slowly nodded, still contemplating, but the nod at least said she was coming around.

He almost sighed out loud. 'So, we're good?'

She stiffened. 'No.'

His head spun. 'No?'

'What about your leg?'

His head jerked back so he could stare down at her, dumbfounded. 'What about it?'

'I've killed your career.'

'No. You saved it. Along with my life.'

'So, you're telling me you'll be able to go back to your position in homicide sometime soon?'

'Does it matter?' He stepped forward.

'It matters to me. And it should matter to you.' She stepped back. 'You love that job.'

'And I love you more.'

Her jaw dropped as she crossed her arms.

He stepped forward. 'There's really no contest if I had to choose.

You'd win every time, Stacey.'

'You say that now.'

'And I'll say it forever.'

'You can't know that's how you'll feel when forever comes around. My mother loved my father once. Then in time she grew to resent him, for so many things. The biggest? She gave up a law career because of him.'

'That's not going to happen and I'll tell you why. Our story is different. *We're different.* And it has nothing to do with Whittaker or bullet wounds or my career. It's about a man who trawled through life without living it, without looking to the future.'

He rubbed his neck but the pound of his head didn't lessen. 'Until now, I avoided everything and everyone who threatened to yank my head out of the sand and my attitude out of my ass. Yes, my career was the most important thing in my life. *Because I didn't have anything else. Because I hadn't met you.'*

He watched her flinch. Watched her eyes open wide, her body tense, as if he'd backed her into a small, dark room and she had nowhere else to run. But he couldn't stop now. If he wanted to win her back, that meant pulling out all stops. He wouldn't kid himself he'd get another chance.

'You make the difference in my life. You make it worth living. So, leg or no leg, career or no career, I want to spend every day until my last one with you.'

He'd slayed every one of her objections. Easily pushed aside every obstacle she'd dumped in his path, and bowled on through.

He loved her and wanted to be with her.

She should be ecstatic.

And she was.

Even though it made what she had to do so much harder.

Logic had made a hasty retreat the day Chase Durant entered her life. And it held no place here or now. Emotion and experience did that to a person.

How he felt in this moment couldn't mean anything. It didn't make a difference. And in time, Chase would realise she was right. She just couldn't exist knowing that, when he did, her perfect life would be ripped right out from underneath her.

Hope slowly seeped from his expression. 'This has nothing to do with your mother or my leg, does it?'

She exhaled, slow, biding for time. 'You should sit down. It can't be good for your recovery to stand so long.'

He barely acknowledged she'd spoken. Didn't agree or disagree or move to take a seat. 'Stacey, please. Tell me what this is about.' And as she struggled to convert the boulder in her chest into words, his gaze hardened. 'After all we've been through, how can you not tell me? You owe me that much.'

'You're right.' She crossed to the couch and dropped into it, hoping he'd do the same.

The deep grooves bordering his mouth and eyes showed how much standing was costing him. She wanted more than anything to smooth them away. To brush each one of those lines with her lips until they softened and the chill in his eyes turned to heat.

Only she couldn't.

He stared at her, unmoving.

The man was all kinds of stubborn. And the reason for her racing heartbeat and sweaty palms.

Finally he huffed and dropped down next to her. 'So, help me out here. Why are you pushing me away?'

She drew in another deep breath, not that it made an iota of difference to her nerves. 'We can't be together, because when you leave I don't know how I'll survive.'

His entire body stiffened against the cushiony couch-back. '*When* I leave? Have you heard anything I've been saying?'

She nodded. 'Of course. *You love me.* The question is, which me is it you love? The real me or the me you think I am.'

He frowned, scratching at his chin and a shadow that was too distracting by far. 'I don't follow.'

'You were never interested in me – *really interested* – before all this *crap* happened.' She waved her hand. 'Sure, your sense of humour came out to play, you had some fun, partook in a little mindless flirting, all in the name of sport without substance. Then *wham*, enter a little danger, a little excitement, and I'm suddenly more interesting, more appealing than before.'

She raised her hand when he opened his mouth to argue. 'Please. You asked me for my reasons. Let me finish before you shoot me down.'

His lips clamped.

Damn but she was an idiot. And she hated that with every word she pushed Chase further away. She should be able to do this. Give them a chance. But every time she wavered, past failures underlined by Brad's ugly words battered against her happiness.

You're nothing. Will always be nothing.

… boring, empty, worthless …

… some namby-pamby book deal won't change that.

When Chase stripped away the surface, he'd find nothing but the woman behind the writer. The woman who wrote sexy, feisty heroines she longed to be but never could. She shook her head, shook the thought. Focused on what she had to do. 'When life is normal, I'm not interesting or funny or sexy.'

She dropped her hand and cleared the waver from her voice. 'I don't make smart, witty conversation. Don't wear sexy red dresses, seductive underwear or heels. I won't hold your interest or make you laugh or turn you on. And one day you're going to wake up and you'll realise that whatever it was that made you want me no longer exists. I wasn't enough for my father to stay. He may have left my mother, but he left me too. He never bothered to visit – his job and the booze held more allure than his five-year-old daughter. Something he told me, categorically, when I "borrowed" my mother's mobile and called him the day before my sixth birthday.'

She blinked away the tears of a rejection that shouldn't still hurt and shoved the hair back from her face. 'Then there's Brad.'

Barely pausing for a breath, she bowled on. 'In all the time we were together, I was never enough. Brad spent two years trying to make me into more. Into something he could love and respect. He never did, and it doesn't matter whose failing that was. Yes, I was the one who walked out. But the real Brad left me way before that. Because the person he loved and the real me weren't the same.'

Finally, she met his gaze. 'All those exasperating things that made you tear your hair out when we first met, they're me. And when life settles down and the excitement's gone, they're going to exasperate you once again. And you'll want to do one of two things – change me or leave me.' She swallowed and blinked back moisture that threatened to overflow. 'And either one is going to break my heart.'

Those deep, beautiful eyes held her gaze.

She had no idea what she'd expected. Anger. Disappointment. Impatience. Perhaps a combination of all three. Not … this. A return of the exasperation she knew so well.

'Ask me why I love you.'

Her head snapped up. Of all times not to take her seriously. 'That's not an answer.'

'It will be.' His gaze softened. 'Don't think I'm not taking you seriously. I am. And I want you to do the same for me. Just ask. *Please.*'

It was the *please* that did it. That and the uncertainty in his expression that melted her heart and the wall she so desperately needed to build around it.

She grabbed her mother's cream brocade cushion and hugged it to her chest. 'Why do you love me?'

'Because you're nothing like the person I imagined I'd fall for, but everything, and more, than I could ever want.' He shot her a shaky grin. 'You're funny and clumsy and have made the most ridiculous pet choices. Your kitchen is illogical and you're the only woman I know who can kill a mannequin in sixty-seven ways and get away with it. Your obstinacy drives me crazy and you leave cookie crumbs everywhere you go. You're stubborn and kind and loyal and principled, and the sexiest blue monster I've ever had the pleasure of being straddled by. You don't listen to sense and always have an opinion, and you drive me mindlessly to distraction. But I love you. Every bit of you. And I don't want to change a single thing.'

With every word her heart swelled just a little bit more. He'd hit on all the right buttons, and she wanted to believe him. Wanted it more than her next life-sustaining breath. But what if she did all that, gave them a chance, opened herself up to the beauty of a life with Chase and fell even more in love only to have him fall out of it?

What if he was the best thing that had ever happened to her, but she wasn't to him?

She wedged herself further into the edge of the couch and curled her legs tight beneath her. 'You say all that now.'

'Yes, I do.' He edged closer and pried her hand free to wrap it in his. She let him, dropping her gaze to their linked fingers, craving the contact while knowing each little concession would make it so much harder to pull away when the time came.

With a finger, he tilted her chin until she had no choice but to meet his gaze. 'I can't speak for the future. None of us can. All I know is that when I made decisions based on what I thought my future would be, my life became what I most feared. Empty. Lonely. A sad excuse for an existence.'

His grip around her hand tightened. 'I refuse to think that way any longer. And I'm going to do my damnedest to convince you to do the same. Not because I want back into your life again – much as there's nothing I want more – but because, beyond than that, I want you to be happy. And if your happiness means me walking away at the end of this evening, so be it.'

He leaned forward, so close he filled her vision, her entire world. 'But – and I need you to be honest here – if it's not, if your happiness is in some way tied to me like mine is to you, then all I ask is for you to give us one more chance.' He drew in a shuddering breath. 'Don't give up on something this good because one day it might turn bad. This is a choice. An opportunity some people wait their whole lives to find. And we have it – right here. Right now.'

He lifted their linked hands and she couldn't help but see how right they looked. How right the wrap of his fingers felt around hers.

He didn't stop lifting until his lips feathered across her knuckles. Indolent heat rolled up her arm, yet she shivered.

'We make sense, Stacey. Everything else in my life is surrounded by questions, yet when I'm with you it feels right. Perfect.' He kissed her once again, and his lips on her skin, the words from his mouth, they captured her very soul and squeezed.

'That feeling doesn't come around every day. I'm sure, for some people, it doesn't come around at all. Which means, when it happens, we need to grab hold and hang on for dear life.'

With a wince, he slid off the couch and onto his good knee.

Her breath hitched, her heart stuttering for one brief, beautiful moment. The room faded to nothing until her view was filled with Chase, his upturned face and her hand, still wonderfully joined with his.

'This is me hanging on for dear life.' He lifted her fingers to his lips, and her heart stopped beating altogether. 'Marry me.'

Chapter Seventy-Four

*Y*es!

Before she could stall her heart, it skipped and frolicked with possibility.

Her mind was slower to the party. What Chase asked was tantamount to a leap of faith. Could she do it? Discount her father? Brad? Their rejections still stung, but they didn't define her. She'd handed them that power in the past. Now she was about to relinquish her future as well.

Her heart screamed *no!*

Could she forget the past and rewrite her life anew?

Was she strong enough? Were *they?*

She'd faced a killer and come out on top. Why survive those horrors only to live half a life? And life without Chase would be just that. He'd asked her for honesty. Didn't they both deserve at least that?

She dropped to the floor.

Heart thrumming, she slid her hands over his shoulders, pulling his head down until his breath mingled with hers. 'This is me doing the same right back.'

She kissed. As if her life depended on it. As if he were everything and more.

Her every breath.

And she never wanted to stop. His hands scaled her hips to her butt, lodging her between his knee and raised leg. And he returned her kiss, as if he felt just the same. Time was meaningless. Seconds, hours, minutes, all blended into one mind-melting moment, and the promise of eternity with one man. He tasted of coffee and comfort, his arms around her like warm summer nights and snuggly woollen blankets.

There was no place she'd rather be.

Gasping for breath, he pulled back, cupping her face, eyes

devouring her like she was an entire box of Turkish delight. 'Is that a yes?'

'Yes.' She grinned, nodded, drank in every part of him through a cloud of happy tears. Covered his face with a trail of happy kisses, dropping her hand to his leg. 'Yes, yes, yes!'

He flinched.

She jerked her hand away. 'Oh, crap! I'm sorry.'

He grabbed her hand back, mischief sliding across his lips and a gaze of sparkling tropical blue. 'It'll be a great story to tell our kids and grandkids one day.'

'Kids?'

Her stomach flip-flopped as his palm curved a slow path across it.

'All ten of them. *And* grandkids.'

'Ten?' She might have squeaked. Just a little.

'Nine, then. I'm willing to negotiate.'

Just as well. Although the thought of a baby – part Chase and part her all rolled into one huggable bundle – was intoxicating and frightening and all-out, overwhelmingly beautiful.

'Two. One boy, one girl.'

'I won't go lower than six.'

'Four.'

'Done!'

Her gaze narrowed. 'Why do I get the feeling I've been had?'

He waggled his brows. 'Not yet, but I fully intend to.' He braced, then scowled. 'Dammit!'

'What?'

'When I planned this moment, I didn't think past getting down. Any chance you can help me up without popping your stitches?'

Laughing, she stood, took both his hands and braced. 'The big strong detective asking for help?'

He straightened, then pulled her into every hard inch of him. 'Wait till you see how I say thank you.'

Sensation rolled through her belly until she tingled head to toe. 'You're quite a wordsmith. You should have been a writer.'

His mouth quirked. 'And you've got guts by the bucketload, Miss Holland. You should have been a detective.'

Stealthy fingers tugged her top from her trousers and explored the skin underneath.

She shuddered. 'I'm sticking to excitement behind my keyboard from now on.'

'Hopefully not only behind the keyboard.'

One by one he released her shirt buttons, rolling his heated gaze over each and every quivering inch of her body.

Pure bliss.

'Well, I could be persuaded.' She reached for his belt, unhooked the buckle and slowly dragged down the zip.

His voice croaked, as if lodged halfway down his throat. 'And how would I do that?'

'I'm sure you'll think of something.'

'I'm sure I will.' He grinned. 'But first things first.' He reached into his pocket. 'What's an engagement without a ring?'

Her breath hitched, and didn't pick up again until he'd slid a chunky band onto her finger. 'It matches your watch.'

Tears pricked her eyelids.

A wide, Cookie Monster grin stared up at her from her left hand.

He squeezed the blue metal band until it fit. 'This'll do until we can pick something out together.'

Cats, butterflies, a whole party of them, danced across her heart. 'It's perfect.'

'*You're* perfect.' He cupped her cheek, kissing her lips, filling her heart.

His fingers slipped beneath her shirt, the reverent slide of his touch billowing and blooming inside her chest. She shrugged, dislodging the shirt from her shoulders, leaving it to fall down her arms and onto the floor. Cool air teased her skin until his warm, wondrous palms skimmed her waist, blazing a trail to her breasts.

Kisses feathered across her jaw, her neck, her collarbone, until sultry warmth covered her nipples, black lace and all, while his hands cupped and palmed and squeezed her to oblivion.

She moaned and lowered her hand, wrapping his hard, straining flesh into her palm. 'I need you, Chase.'

He dropped onto the couch and pulled her between his thighs, riveting her with turbulent blue. 'I need you, too. All of you.' Hot kisses feathered down her abdomen, gently skirting her bandage, raging a wildfire through her blood.

'Your body.' His fingers skirted her hips. 'Your soul.' He cupped her butt. 'Your laughter.' His palms slipped down further until his fingers slid between her thighs. 'Your love.'

Wet heat circled her belly button, his breath burning her up, inside, outside, everywhere in between. 'More than Turkish delight. More than my next breath. More than life.'

Easing both her trousers and panties down together, he released first one leg, then the other, before lifting his gaze from the throbbing flesh between her thighs. 'You are all of that, and more, Stacey Holland. You are everything.'

Flutters filled her tummy.

God she wanted him, the way he wanted her. In every way imaginable. For better, for worse, until forever and beyond.

He pulled her close, every breath a blanket of sensation rolling across her pulsing flesh.

She quivered, spearing her fingers through his hair, widening her stance, sinking into the barely there play of his tongue. Each lave, each lick, stole her breath, threatening to buckle her legs beneath her.

If not for his palms braced beneath her buttocks, she would have dissolved into a mindless puddle at his feet.

He raised his head, possession and passion filling his swirling blue gaze. 'Want to know the best part?' He grinned. 'That ring, our love, binds us together, for now, forever, till death do we part. Something I hope is a bloody long time away.'

Then he pressed his lips to her once again, and she was lost.

The world made sense.

Chase skirted the rectangular bandage on Stacey's abdomen and lost himself in burnished emerald. Gazes locked, he slowly, deliciously, slipped into her pulsing flesh.

It was like losing himself and finding himself all in one surreptitious moment. He dropped his lips to hers, adrenalin racing through his veins, his heart pumping out of control.

His leg jerked. '*Sonofabitch!*'

He rolled onto his back, gasping, his thigh howling like a banshee.

Stacey turned, her brows etched into a deep vee. 'Oh, god, Chase.

I'm sorry. Are you okay?'

He clenched his fist, cursed his thigh, dragged oxygen into his lungs before turning to face her, snagging her hand and bringing it to his lips.

'Don't ever apologise for turning me on.'

'But your leg—'

'Isn't half as painful as the throbbing here.' He directed her hand and growled when she wrapped him in her palm and squeezed.

The ache in his leg evaporated. 'Holy mother—'

'Start praying and I'll stop.' She chuckled.

'Don't you dare.'

He swooped down and swallowed her laughter. She tasted of everything he'd ever wanted but believed he could never have. She filled his heart, filled his soul, took the impossible and pressed it in the palm of his hand.

A lifetime with Stacey would never be enough. But it was a damned fine start.

She pulled back, her lips curving slowly upward. 'I'm feeling decidedly hungry, detective. What do you suggest?'

He quirked a brow. 'Pizza?'

Her hand moved and rational thought became a thing of the past. The slide of her palm, the cup of his balls, the skate of her body downward until she'd lodged between his thighs.

Her mouth just a breath away from—

Fuck!

Links from head to body severed, awareness arrowing to the hungry muscle between his legs. Her tongue rasping, the drag of her mouth. The building pressure in his balls until he could barely hold on.

He reached for her shoulders. *'Stacey.'*

She lifted her head, licked her lips and cat-got-the-cream smiled. 'That sure beats pizza.'

Before his addled brain could carve a response, she'd straddled his hips.

His subconscious took a moment of thanks that no kidneys were harmed in the process. His conscious mind went slowly mad as she rubbed her folds up and down his length. Then when he thought he couldn't take a second more, she tilted her hips and took him inside.

He sucked in a breath.

Lips pursed, tongue perched between her teeth, she braced her palms on his chest, lifted her hips, then sank slowly down.

'Feeling better now?'

He groaned. 'You have no idea.'

She moved again, her hair a wild halo about her flushed face. 'Oh, I think I do.'

She dropped forward, palms either side of his shoulders, nipples teasing his chest. 'And just so you know, Chase Durant.' Her lips melded briefly with his, sending his heartbeat into wild tumult. 'You are everything to me too.'

A racing drumbeat broke through Stacey's post-dream haze. She fought the call to wakefulness. Fought the drag from dreams of Chase and Cookie Monster rings and happy ever afters.

The drumming accelerated and warm breath fanned her hair. 'Morning.'

She shivered. Snuggled deeper into the body and arms surrounding her. Rubbed the plastic on her finger with her thumb.

Her heart stuttered. *Not a dream.*

She smiled. 'Morning.'

Her eyes fluttered open as taut skin and muscle contracted beneath her trailing fingertips. She circled lower until her palm located her prize. Hot. Hard. Already hungry.

'You're up early.'

He chuckled and the vibrations wracked her body.

'Pretty much unavoidable when you're around.'

She ran her hand up, then down, enjoying the feel of soft, satin skin stretched tight over hard muscle. Enjoying the catch of his breath as she increased the pressure.

His hands explored, his touch zapping places deep and damp, sparks flying over every inch of her skin. The lithe fingers roved deeper still, between her legs, circling her clit before sliding deep into her flesh. She gasped. Tightened her grip.

His voice strained. 'Seems you're suffering the same.'

Before she could take her next breath, he rolled over onto his good leg, his magnificent body hovering above hers. She moved her hips until his erection nudged just where she needed him most.

She met his gaze. 'What do you suggest?'

'A lifetime of research until we find a cure.'

She smiled. 'I like the sound of that.'

Slowly, wonderfully, he filled her. Completed her.

She moaned. Tilted her hips, wrapped her legs tight around his buttocks, swore to never let go.

Hands planted either side of her shoulders, he met her gaze. Then slowly, deliciously, he pulled back, then filled her once more. 'Happy?'

'Ecstatic.'

He thrust again. 'No regrets?'

She shook her head. 'None.'

Her heart stuttered when she realised it was the truth. She was ready to throw herself wholeheartedly into a future with Chase.

Happiness filled every wonderful facet of his face. He grinned and dropped to one elbow, his feather-light fingers brushing the hair back from her brow.

'And so, Miss Romance Writer, what would you have your hero do next?'

Her heart stalled. 'Take hold of the heroine and never let her go.'

His lips fluttered across her jaw to the throbbing pulse on her neck. 'A skill I intend to dedicate the rest of my life to perfecting.' He pushed back the duvet and his mouth moved lower with every tingling inch of exposed skin. 'Starting right now.'

ABOUT THE AUTHOR

Michelle Somers is a bookworm from way back. An ex-Kiwi who now calls Australia home, she's a professional killer and matchmaker, a storyteller and a romantic. Words are her power and her passion. Her heroes and heroines always get their happy ever after, but she'll put them through one hell of a journey to get there.

Michelle lives in Melbourne, Australia, with her real life hero and three little heroes in the making. Her debut novel, *Lethal in Love* won the Romance Writers of Australia's 2016 Romantic Book of the Year (RuBY) and the 2013 Valerie Parv Award.

Michelle loves hearing from readers, so please visit her at:
www.michelle-somers.com and sign up to her monthly newsletter
or follow her on social media:

Facebook:
facebook.com/MichelleSomersAuthor

Twitter:
twitter.com/msomerswriter

Pinterest:
pinterest.com/michelles3268

Instagram:
instagram.com/michellesomers00

YouTube:
youtube.com/channel/UCzqDkcerOgCocR_sEfPa9eQ

and **Random House Australia's website:**
randomhouse.com.au/authors/michelle-somers.aspx

ACKNOWLEDGEMENTS

'I've had so many rainbows in my clouds. I had a lot of clouds, but I had so many rainbows.'

Beautiful words from the very wonderful, very wise Maya Angelou.

What better place to mention my rainbows – the beautiful souls who have, in some way touched my life the past few years – than in this section of gratitude and thanks.

To those who have helped, in either small ways or big, to make *Murder Most Unusual* the book it is today – thank you.

Valerie Parv, my mentor, my friend, my inspiration. You are everything in a person and author that I aspire to be. Thank you for your unending wisdom and support, and for guiding me through the beginnings that have now become Stacey and Chase's story.

Robyn Grady, my mentor and friend, for showing me that an onion has more than one layer, and the more we peel, the more we unleash the tears.

My gorgeous critique partners – Lauren, Mandy and Cass. You girls are my sanity and my saviours.

My beta-readers Nena Drury, Ariel Moy, BJ Hooton, Ana Maree Ordway, Kathryn Jane and Cynthia Young.

As always, thank you Gordon for your fabulous insight into Victoria police. Thanks Kim-Louise for your weaponry expertise. And my medical gurus, Elissa Kennedy-Smith and Sarah Xanthos for sharing your knowledge. My zoo procedure experts, Amanda Tate and Nikki Logan. And Helene Young for her expertise on boats and sailing. Your knowledge has been invaluable, and all drifts from reality toward poetic license sit on my shoulders alone.

Much appreciation to those who shared their snakebite experiences – Stuart Parker, Amy Rose Bennett and Jenny White. And to Giusy Caporetto for sharing your fabulous *Pane, Vino e Peperoncino* recipe and your culinary know-how in making the perfect pasta sauce.

Thanks to Amary Chapman for providing *In Hot Water* with such a great name.

Acknowledgement to my talented editor, Ruth Kennedy. And to Lana Pecherczyk for your fabulous cover and creativity.

To Dorothy Adamek and Nas Dean for your advice and guidance through the turbulent waters that comprise the publishing world.

To the gorgeous women of Melbourne Romance Writers Guild (MRWG). Thank you for your love, fun times and never ending supply of chocolate rewards. And Romance Writers Australia (RWA) for your camaraderie, support and generosity of knowledge since the moment I joined your ranks.

And lastly, but by no means least, my family. My three exceptional young men, Josh, Nathan and Gabriel. Your enthusiasm lifts me up, your joy for life and the simple things keep me grounded. And your love keeps me going through the good and bad that life throws my way.

Danny. You're my very own real-life romance hero; the reason this story, my writing career, exists. Without your love, encouragement and belief, I would never have followed my dream, would never have succeeded.

And to all my readers, thank you. You give me reason to sit at my keyboard, day after day, and chase a muse that's sometimes more determined to hide than to come out and play.

Thank you.

LOVED MURDER MOST UNUSUAL?
THEN TRY MY AWARD-WINNING ROMANTIC
SUSPENSE,
LETHAL IN LOVE
Copyright Penguin Random House 2016

About the book

Homicide detective Jayda Thomasz never lets her emotions get in the way of a case. So when a serial killer re-emerges after 25 years, the last thing she expects is to catch herself fantasising over the hot, smooth-talking stranger who crosses the path of her investigation.

Reporter Seth Friedin is chasing the story that'll make his career. When he enters the world of swinging for research, he never imagines he'll be distracted by a hard-talking female detective whose kiss plagues his mind long after she's gone.

Past experience has shown Jayda that reporters are ruthless and unscrupulous. But when the murders get personal, will she make a deal with the devil to catch the killer? How far will she and Seth have to go? And do you ever really know who you can trust?

2016 winner Romance Writers of Australia Romantic Book of the Year (RuBY) Award
2013 winner Valerie Parv Award
2013 winner Indiana Golden Opportunities Award

'It's gritty, it's sexy and it kept me reading long past my bedtime two nights in a row!'
—Helene Young, award-winning romantic suspense author

'Michelle Somers is a powerful new voice in crime fiction.'
—Valerie Parv, international best-selling author

'Michelle Somers packs a powerful emotional punch with her passionate characters and gripping mystery. Lethal in Love is everything you want romantic suspense to be. Warning: you might want to read with the lights on.'
—Stefanie London, NYT bestseller

MICHELLE SOMERS

LETHAL IN LOVE

Prologue

*F*ools!

The fifty-inch plasma screen above the bar flickered.

Melbourne's beloved police. Futile. Inept. Buffoons, the lot of 'em.

His lip curled. And her… *especially her.* Thinking he'd falter, create hack-work like some wannabe ass-wipe. They didn't know shit. But they'd learn. *Soon.*

He lowered his bottle onto the beer-stained wood, adrenalin charging his veins. He'd be legend. Transcend death.

In-fucking-vincible.

Laughter hacked up his oesophagus. His breath caught, phlegm rising, spilling into his mouth. He gulped it back, along with a generous serving of blood. One of the good-for-nothing legacies passed down to him by the old prick.

Then there were others…

The pound against his skull slowed.

He knocked back a mouthful of ice-cold beer and rode the pain, a wildfire coursing down his throat.

His time had come. They'd pay. Every last fucking one. The bitch included.

He looked up. The camera panned, then zoomed. His gaze latched onto *her*, the woman behind the thick blue-and-white tape. Her eyes avoided the lens, her body drawn tight, erect, watching the shiny black body bag disappear into the back of the State Coroner's van. Then she turned, and he stared into the familiar green of her eyes.

He would carve his name into her heart, the way hers had been carved into his, day after day after day. But no more. Now he had no heart. No soul. None that belonged to him.

He flexed his fingers, cracked his knuckles one by one. Revelled in the pain. A final glance, then he shifted his sight to the woman nursing her nearly empty glass. The one he'd come for tonight.

His blood quickened, his groin tight. Anticipating.

He inhaled deeply, closed his eyes. The hunter. Testing the air, drawing on her essence, the very taste of it. Blind innocence. Youth. Vivacity. Before he drew each one from her like a vampire draws his blood fix.

He opened his eyes. Lips curving slowly upward, he cut his way around the bar. Her gaze lifted, his smile deepened. She liked what she saw. They always did.

Until that pivotal moment, when realisation speared through their bodies and death claimed them.

Fools. They were all fools.

He glanced at the wide screen, but the green-eyed witch was gone. No matter. He'd see her again. And she, him. Soon she'd do nothing but dream of him, in sleep and wakefulness. And then she'd be his.

Chapter One

'**B**etter make sure you keep your bra on.'

Jayda Thomasz shot Chase Durant a quelling look. As partners go, she could've had worse. She also could've had better. Still, one thing she did know – she could trust Chase with her life. That counted for a helluva lot when it was only your partner and his dependability standing between you and a whole lot of death.

If only she got a little less mouth from him. A little less interest, too.

'Don't worry. This sucker ain't coming off, no matter what.'

'More's the pity.'

Her jaw tightened.

Fellow officer Georgie Tanneras frowned, tweaking the thin wire that now lined Jayda's bra strap. 'How's that?'

'Perfect.' Jayda grabbed the silver lamé top from the bag at her feet and slipped it over her head. She straightened the neckline and tested the mic. Georgie nodded and moved away to twirl knobs and flick switches on equipment straight out of the space age.

Jayda grabbed Chase by the elbow and dragged him away from prying ears – almost impossible while in the back of a van crammed with tech equipment and the two techies that went with it.

Pressing her palm over the microphone on her chest, she forced her next words through gritted teeth. 'What was it about last week's sexual harassment talk that you didn't understand?'

'It's just that when we're talking about such a spectacular pair of –'

'Chase!'

'I was going to say speakers.' He held up the two earpieces. 'What'd you think I was referring to?'

Her face muscles clenched. She rolled her jaw to force it into relaxation mode. Not much she could do about the knots in her shoulders, or the war of butterflies churning her stomach.

'Your hair may have lost the red, but your temper hasn't. So tell me, is it really true what they say about blondes?'

She stared at the monitor and didn't bother with an answer. It was doubtful he expected one. The time when Chase and his wisecracks had seemed charming was long past.

He's not Liam.

She knew that. Knew this situation was nothing like before. But reason wouldn't curb her dread. She'd dodged the aftermath once. Unlikely she'd dodge it a second time round.

Ousting both men from her mind, she tugged an over-folded scrap of paper from her skirt pocket and skimmed the ten points she'd written last night. Each was a definitive check. Warmth frittered through her. She was ready.

Movement on the small screen above the control panel captured her attention and that of her three colleagues in the mobile surveillance unit. As she tucked the list into the bag at her feet, all eyes watched a couple, male and female, perhaps in their early thirties, pause on the veranda of 21 Brayside Avenue, then slip through the barely open front door.

Just a normal Saturday night in the 'burbs. A nice house in a nice neighbourhood, deep in the hub of Melbourne's northwest. Pleasant, quiet, happily dodging the radar. Until now.

She blinked, trying to ignore the unfamiliar scrape of blue-coloured contacts. Just one more facet of her multifaceted cover. A cover that could lead to a badly needed break in the case and stop a killer before he claimed his next victim.

It hadn't taken much to convince Hackett. She was lead investigator and the only woman in the Pacu task force who fit the victim's profile – age, build, apparent innocence. The one thing she'd had to change was her hair colour with a wig. Oh, and the green of her eyes. To a deep, bright tropical blue.

Images flashed through her brain; a young woman slumped against a dumpster, blue eyes gaping and vacant, her mouth a blistered, cavernous maw. She shook her head, wishing away the grasping, biting claws that snatched at her gut and squeezed every time the image appeared. A vision from crime scene photos, and – as of three weeks ago with the Night Terror's return – her ever recurring dreams. Or should she say nightmares?

The victims were all women, like her. The only real difference –

fate. And the unforgiving clutch of fingers around their throat. Impossible to imagine their terror in those last seconds as the oxygen squeezed from their lungs and they fought for existence.

Jayda blinked again. Looking in the mirror, it was difficult not to see the resemblance to her family that she'd longed for as a child. Sleek blonde hair. Blue eyes. When she squinted and tipped her head to the side, she could almost believe she was Bec's real rather than adopted sister.

'Jayda, you're good to go.'

'Thanks, Georgie.'

Her friend's lips tightened, her gaze questioning as it darted between Jayda and Chase. Fan-bloody-tastic. The force's 'non-fraternising in the ranks' policy may have been loose to the point of non-existence, but she'd learned the hard way how rumours – no matter how false – could turn a career into compost. Georgie was a friend, but others in the squad would be far quicker to comment. And judge.

Jayda's hand dropped to her hip, devoid now of her badge. It didn't matter that life outside the precinct had barely existed for her the past seven years. She'd matched her father's success, made detective before her thirtieth birthday. And she'd done it by keeping her head down and the fly of her pants securely fastened.

Thank you, Liam.

There he was again. Elbowing his way into her thoughts.

After seven years, the anger still lingered, a reminder of her promise never to compromise herself again.

Which made her stupidity with Chase all the more regrettable. One drunken night and a blind fumble between the sheets, which almost sealed the end to her reputation. With her partner. With anyone able to read between the tension.

And now she had so much more to lose than back then.

No excuse that she'd been celebrating Ian Trentham's twenty-year sentence for the cold-blooded murder of his family when her mother's news hit – her parents were separating, one week shy of their twenty-fifth anniversary. Both extremes of the spectrum – one high, one low – sending Jayda off on a deleterious tangent.

She'd drowned her disappointment in a string of tequila shots before falling into bed with the wrong man. Thank heavens sense had overthrown insensibility before she'd taken the plunge and slept with him.

Still, dodging the mess of a one-night hook-up hadn't changed that whole 'morning after' scenario, in which she'd stumbled out of his bed awash with mortification and regret, and a mother of a hangover. She'd regretted the slip ever since.

Better she stick to all work, no play. At least her job was the one scrap of her life she could depend on, where she felt safe.

Which was weird, considering what she was about to do.

The screen beside Georgie flickered, the house a fuzzy contrast of black, white and grey in the approaching dark. So sedate. Serene. Innocuous, even. No hint of what was really going on inside.

She could feel Chase's gaze at her back, his crystal blue eyes piercing, hankering for more than she was willing to give. They were partners, and that professional boundary should never have been scaled, would never be again. Regardless of what he thought he felt.

She stepped away from Georgie's over-alert ears, her hand shifting automatically to the mic on her chest. The familiar scent of spice assailed her nostrils as she whispered in Chase's ear. 'It won't happen again.'

'I know.'

'It was a mistake.'

He winced. 'I know.'

'We work together, for god's sake.'

'I know, Jayda.'

'Then stop with the wisecracks.'

'I only do it 'cos you're so easy…' he paused, his eyes sparkling, 'to wind up.'

She fought the rising boil in her blood. The job was her focus right now, not this wannabe stand-up comedian.

'Leave that to some other wise-ass who's not my partner.'

His smile evaporated. 'You know I've got your back, don't you?'

She play-punched his bicep. 'Yeah, I know, you big goofball. I trust you with my life.'

'Just not your heart.'

She searched his expression. Impossible to tell if he was still serious. She knew he was attracted to her, but love? That was a stretch of mega proportions. And top on her 'not in this lifetime' list. *Never date or fall in love on the job.*

'Chase, we've been through this.'

His expression lightened. 'Just kidding, Jayda. Geez, better loosen up before you go in. I've never met an uptight swinger before.'

'I didn't think you'd met any type of swinger.' She looked at him then. Really looked. They'd been partners for two years, worked together for the greater portion of that time, saw more of each other than they saw of their own families. Yet how much did she really know about Chase Durant beyond the odd snippets he'd shared?

Lately, something had felt *off.* If only she could put her finger on what that something was.

His gaze darted somewhere in the vicinity of her left shoulder. 'I haven't. Stop reading stuff that isn't there.'

'Now look who's uptight.'

'You guys ready?' The techie who'd been sitting silently beside Georgie turned in his chair. 'The private party's in the house outside, not my van.'

Sam Hathaway may have been joking, but it didn't stop the heat from finding and stamping Jayda's face. Or the alarm from filling her stomach as she imagined what he was drawing from their behaviour.

Paranoia wasn't a valuable commodity when you were about to go deep under cover. Chase moved away and slapped the other man's arm. 'Stop being such a grouch, Sam.'

'You try sleeping on the couch five nights running and let's see who's a grouch.'

'Christine still not talking?' Chase asked.

Jayda let out a sigh at the shift of spotlight, only half listening to the banter, her mind already on the job.

'Oh, she's *talking* alright. In volumes they can hear way down in Patagonia.'

Georgie's control panel crackled and all eyes zipped to the man who appeared on the second of the three screens lining the wall. 'Enough of the Oprah bloody heartbreak.' Detective Inspector Hackett's voice rumbled out of the speaker. 'We've got an op to run.'

Jayda sipped sparingly at her citrus martini, willing her racing heartbeat to match the sensual murmur of Marvin Gaye. Not a practised spirit drinker, she calculated she could afford one drink, two at a stretch. They were a necessity to blend in, but she also needed to be sharp. Razor senses were the order of the night. One lapse in attention could be fatal.

She closed her eyes, inhaling deep and slow. Reminding herself that if her nerves showed, it only served to cement her role here as a newbie. A first-time swinger looking to skirt the boundaries to a world where inhibitions and limitations didn't exist. Where lines were blurred and sex was free and easy and abundant.

Gaining admittance had been easier than she'd expected, despite the exclusivity of the club. She'd given Gina's name as a reference and while not necessary it had paved the way. They were expecting her.

She'd handed a wad of notes to Clara – the woman who'd answered the door in a black satin corset and stilettos – and won immediate acceptance, after the automatic condolences and niceties, of course. Gina's murder had hit the news two days earlier.

Another sip and she opened her eyes, allowing her gaze to skim the dimly lit interior. Low chandeliers flickered from high, cornice-edged ceilings, their shadows providing obscurity to the guests gathered beneath.

Occasionally she sensed interest, hushed whispers, blatant curiosity and awareness. But as yet, no one had approached, which was fine. It gave her time to scan the layout, get a handle on the group's dynamics. Work out if a ruthless killer could have wangled his way into their ranks.

Her gaze roamed as lemon zinged across her tastebuds, the icy vodka cool and refreshing but not nearly sweet enough. The sensation was, however, sophisticated. A perfect fit with the environment.

Unease shivered up her spine. Stifling the urge to bite her lip, she thrust her shoulders back and turned.

Premonition hadn't prepared her for this. *Him.* Martini clogged in her throat, now drier than the drink itself.

She swallowed, tried to drag her focus back. Failed.

Their gazes locked, and steely eyes the grey of a gun barrel charged the distance between them.

Chapter Two

The shaking had to stop.

Jayda gulped down a not-so-sparing portion of her drink and tightened her grip on the glass. This might be her first time under cover, but that was no excuse for nerves. Or the quiver sending her body into waves of hyper-awareness.

Intel was the only thing she'd be picking up tonight.

Get back in the game, Jayda girl. Don't lose it over something as shallow as broad shoulders and tight pecs. Or eyes with the power of a high-speed vortex.

Sand rasped her throat. She returned his gaze, with confidence and invitation she anything but felt.

His brow arched and he turned, revealing a scar that hugged the corner of his right eye. She shivered. What did Bec always say? *Bad boys make the best lovers.* Great advice from a sister who'd twice married a bad boy and was unashamedly hunting for a third.

She stared at the hunk in the corner, who was giving her more than just a once-over. A bad boy if ever she saw one. Although there was nothing about him that could be mistaken for anything less than a man. One who made her body react in ways it never had before.

It was the atmosphere. The low lighting, the sultry music, the burn of gardenia and orange blossom incense, the promise of culmination. The knowledge that just metres away, in nearby rooms, couples and groups were getting it on with an abandon Jayda had never before experienced.

Yeah, it had to be this place.

And yet, every brush of that penetrating gaze stroked flesh already aware and firing. Blood warming, nipples peaking, beckoning to be touched. *By him.*

A face sculpted from the gods. Brick-house shoulders. Firm, lean muscle.

His blue shirt hugged a chest broader than should be allowed for common men, tapering down to disappear beneath the waistband of his fitted black pants.

Her gaze roved lower still. After all, it was expected here. In a club of free love and free expression. If she really were one of them, a swinger, wouldn't she check out the merchandise? Unabashed. Confident. *Brazen*.

It was what she'd been sent here to do – fit in and evaluate the male clientele.

Not that she needed a reason to appreciate the cling of dark fabric against his thighs. No points for guessing he worked out. And she wasn't talking about weights. Something in his bearing hinted at passion: fervour, wild and unleashed. Hot, sweaty, back-against-the-wall sex.

The air shifted beside her. She dragged her gaze away from Bad Boy and towards the stranger moving in.

'Hi, I'm Brian.'

He was older, a couple of years either side of forty. Blond hair, eyes a cold, glacial blue. Your classic order of calculated good looks. Not something that had ever jerked, let alone yanked, her chain.

'I'm Shana.'

He took her hand and lifted it to his lips. 'A beautiful name. It suits you.'

She tried not to cringe, allowing herself a sidelong glance into the corner again. It was empty. The loss wasn't nearly as sharp as the disgust she directed her way.

Mind on the job and off your damn libido!

Bad Boy was attractive. So what? She could handle it, maybe use her reaction to her advantage. It was all part of the act. His presence just made acting all the more easy.

No matter how hot, he's a suspect, like every male here. Don't forget what happened to those other girls.

Images of cold, broken bodies assaulted her brain. Innocent prey to the devil. The grip on her hand tightened. 'Hey. Are you okay?'

She tugged free. *Game face on, Jayda.* 'Yeah.'

Brian's ice-blue eyes did nothing but chill her blood. A male version of the Night Terror's victims.

'I'm here to watch. It's my first time.' Words she'd been coached, tailored to allow observation without the pressure of joining activities she neither wanted nor needed.

Her gaze strayed to the still-empty corner. Several open doors led out from this main front room. He could be through any one of them, and what he'd be doing…

She shivered, met Brian's stare head on as she dragged in a deep breath. 'I'm a friend of Gina's.'

'I know.'

'You knew Gina?'

'Everyone here knew Gina.' The smile bypassed his eyes. She tilted her head, eyes wide. 'Oh. Why's that?'

He shot her a quizzical look. 'She was a party girl. Willing to do pretty much anything.'

Her heart quickened. 'Did you see her the night she… you know.' The contact lenses scraped as she blinked, stemming tears over a woman whose legacy should have amounted to more than Brian's snide assertion. No matter that the assertion provided new direction to the case.

'Died?'

She swallowed. 'Yeah.'

'What night was that?'

'Thursday. Two nights ago.'

His gaze sharpened, piercing her with razor scrutiny.

Swinger on, internal cop off, Thomasz. Slow down and quit with the interrogation steamroller.

She gulped. 'I can't believe it's been two days already.' Fingertips trembling against her lips, she blinked some more. 'I wonder if anybody here saw her. If at least she was *happy* those last few hours.'

Her hand tentatively touched his arm. 'Did you see her then? Do you know?'

He considered, covering her hand until she tugged it back.

'Don't believe I saw her. Difficult to remember. One night blends in with the next, know what I mean?' His lips twisted into what she assumed was meant to be a grin.

'And Joel?'

'Joel?'

'Her boyfriend. Did you know him?'

That razor gaze sharpened. 'First rule of the scene: no questions. Feel free to reveal whatever you wish,' his gaze poured slowly down her body, 'but personal details of other members are off-limits.'

Irritation made her blush genuine. More difficult to mask the look in her eyes. She lowered her gaze to her drink. 'I – I didn't realise.'

'I know you're new, so if you need any help… adjusting?' His look, his tone, made her feel dirty – as though a million centipedes crawled the length of her skin. She shivered again.

'You're cold.' He rubbed his palms over her biceps, his beer breath attacking her nostrils. Her first instinct was to pull away. But other eyes watched her reaction, assessing, analysing. This was a test she didn't dare fail.

'Just nerves.' She forced her lips to curve upward. 'Sorry for the questions. It's just… I thought Gina had only been a few times. And if I'd known it was without Joel, I might have come with.'

'How well did you know her?'

'Not as well as I thought.'

One palm remained on her arm, caressing her skin. 'Sure you don't want to do any more than watch?'

She suppressed a shudder. 'I'm sure. I…' Lip between her teeth, she lowered her gaze, performing a role not so difficult to feign. The innocent, unsuspecting, in search of a change. Her voice wavered and he leaned in to hear. 'I wanted to see what it was like. To see if I could do it.'

'And what do you think?'

He waited, sharp blue eyes appraising her, weighing every reaction, every word.

'I think I like what I see. So far.' Injecting just the right mix of shyness and innocence to cement her character, she bit her lip. Stared down at her smarting feet, and heels she couldn't remember the last time she'd worn. 'But I'd like to take it slow.'

'That's a shame, Shana.'

She startled at the use of a name that wasn't hers, barely stemming the reaction with a fumbled sip of her drink, using the movement as an excuse to step out of his grasp. If she was lucky, Brian and her other observers would chalk her reactions up to the nerves of a first-timer.

He indicated to her almost empty glass. 'Let me get you another drink.'

'Thanks.'

Brian slipped through a door to her left and she allowed her gaze to wander.

A delicious fusion of hot and cold rippled through her body as she studied the interaction of singles and couples. To get a feel for the place. Its workings. To understand how a serial killer could infiltrate this closed group simply to stalk and kill an innocent woman.

Now those facts had changed. How much had Joel Vance known?

Brian's words muddled round her mind, looking for a rightful space to settle. Gina was a regular. Not only that, she wasn't an 'innocent' like the vics who came before her. Which meant what? The killer had suddenly changed penchants? Not impossible, but all her instincts screamed it was highly improbable. Which raised questions about Gina's death and its connection to the other Night Terror victims. Something she'd get her head around when her mind could focus.

Brian and her refill never returned. Surveillance caught him stealing out the back and into his new model SUV. Before she could say a word, Chase was on it, ordering a tail on his car and a check on his registration. Leaving her free to return her attention to the room.

With Brian gone, she was seldom alone for long. Others approached, a mix of single men, women and couples, their conversations only serving to cement Brian's assessment of Gina.

Around her, the air buzzed, her senses buzzing right along with it. She watched with fascination – the come-ons, the blatant sexual displays, the *lust*.

And all the while, as she overtly studied the comings and goings, she couldn't help but covertly look for *him*. He was just as likely to be of interest as any other male in the room. And while too young to be the Night Terror, he could have knowledge useful to the investigation.

She had to follow every lead.

At least, that's what she told herself as she felt the hot burn of eyes at her back once again. Her goose bumps suddenly sprouted goose bumps of their own, and the hairs on her neck sprung to attention.

Slowly she turned, knowing exactly who she would find.

Beneath the muted glow of a nearby chandelier, Seth Friedin took his fill of the figure painted into her slinky top and short butt-hugging skirt. He didn't bother to hide his interest, or the obvious appreciation in his eyes, his body. The environment didn't require it. Tonight may have been about work but that didn't preclude him from enjoying the perks. The hottie before him included.

He watched the alluring pink of her cheeks darken, the flush spreading down her throat to disappear below the neckline of her top. What he couldn't see, he pictured. The generous scoops of flesh thrusting against the silky, fitted top – how they'd pucker and swell, fill the curve of his palm to perfection. Would her areolae be dusky pink? Or darker, the shade of sweet, plump raspberries?

His taste buds sprang to life with an intensity that surprised him, anticipating the flavour, the rich, ripe texture of her skin beneath his tongue. That wasn't the only portion of his body to spring into gear.

All thanks to the drought of recent months. It had to be. That and the sex-infused atmosphere of the house were toying with his mind. A mind that had been focused on work to the exclusion of everything else lately. Perhaps too much.

He raised his gaze to meet the unwavering fix of her stare. A pink tongue flicked over the arc of her lips triggering a keen jolt of muscle below. It was a challenge to his libido to ignore the invitation she offered. So he didn't.

She was too pretty, too soft and innocent to be in a joint like this. Not a woman he'd pick as typical to 'the scene'. But maybe that was a good thing.

He knocked back the rest of his whiskey and Coke before homing in on his target. After all, she might just be the one he was looking for.

Chapter Three

A panther-like tread brought his magnificent body to a stop before her.

'Enjoying your first time on the scene?' The voice matched the man; deep and rich, full bodied, sexy as all hell.

Jayda's shoulders stiffened. Inexperience was her cover, so she should have been pleased. Only, for some reason she found herself wanting to appear more worldly, more sophisticated for him.

Ridiculous. *Really!* Maybe more than disappointment and drink had led her to fall into Chase's arms. Thank God she hadn't fallen further with him. But that didn't mean falling was out of the question completely.

She made her body relax.

Once upon a time she'd clung to the misguided delusion of 'saving herself'.

Thanks once again, Liam. For pounding the final nail on that three-studded coffin, then leaving her without a backward glance. She'd never ventured down that path since. Still saving herself for someone worthy of her all. Just as her mother had.

Bullshit!

Knots squeezed at her chest.

That fabled life of love and wedded bliss was a lie.

If her parents could walk away after twenty-five years, what was she still waiting for? Perhaps it was time to tend urges other than that to succeed in her career. Time to take the bull by the horns and give him a big, hard yank.

A deep breath and she met that bull head-on. Grinned. Let every sexy, wicked thought swarm in that one look.

Feather-light fingers skated up her neck, the tips resting under her chin, raising her eyes to meet and melt in his.

God, she didn't want those fingers to stop. Wanted them to skate downward, touch every part of her that hadn't felt a man in way too long.

'No need to be embarrassed. We were all there once.'

A slow burn rolled out from beneath his touch, the soft murmur of his voice glazing her body, warm and thick like smooth, sinuous caramel.

Temptation. Not something that mixed well with the job.

Change might be the answer, but not here. Not now, with her unit listening in and so much on the line.

'You?'

He blinked and withdrew his hand. 'Yes, me.'

'How long since you started?'

'Swinging?'

She nodded.

He contemplated his drink. 'How long is a piece of string?'

She tilted her head. 'That's not really an answer.'

'No.' The admission was accompanied by a grin that dimpled his chin and made his eyes sparkle. 'But it's better than stringing you along with a lie.'

For some reason her heart stumbled. 'You make a good point.' Her gaze roved the surroundings before returning to him. 'So, help me out here. If no one shares anything personal, how do you work out whether you're compatible?'

'*You feel it.*' He took a step closer. 'Can you feel it, Shana?'

Caught between the wall at her back and temptation incarnate, she sidestepped, disregarding his question and the heat it aroused. 'H– how do you know my name?'

He grinned, undeterred by her evasion. 'I'm extremely resourceful.'

Their gazes locked. Impossible to drag her eyes away. *What else are you?*

It was a moment before she realised she'd whispered the words aloud. She refused to be embarrassed – the question was necessary, essential to playing a part. Regardless of the impulse that created it.

'I could demonstrate, but I understand you're only here to observe.'

She stilled fingers that longed to fidget with the stem of her glass. 'Yes. And to satisfy my curiosity.'

'Just your curiosity?'

His entire presence filled the room until there was only him and her and heat. Jayda remembered to breathe. 'So, what else did you manage to discover?'

He looked at her blankly.

She rolled her hand in the air. 'About me.'

His expression said he recognised the conversational ice-pack, but he let it go without comment.

'You're a friend of Gina's and a first-timer.' His gaze softened. 'I'm sorry for your loss.'

'Thank you.' She blinked rapidly, the contacts making the show of moisture in her eyes easier. Then she drew in a deep breath. 'Did you know Gina?'

'Not really. But in these circles, word gets around when someone leaves.'

'What word?'

'This and that.'

'More string, I take it?'

His grin completely dissolved her knee ligaments and she reached for the wall behind to steady herself.

'Something like that.' His gaze narrowed. 'What was she like outside of this place?'

She feigned hesitation. 'Fun, but private. In all our years of friendship, I never knew this side of her life existed.'

'That's not uncommon.' The tone of his voice dropped. 'Would you have joined in if you'd known?'

'I…'

This time when he stepped in, she stayed.

His thumb skimmed along her bottom lip, rubbing sensation across its circumference until she felt the rush of blood there and other deeper, darker places below. She let out a shaky sigh, eyes widening as he closed the distance and dipped his head, firm male lips ducking to meet hers.

She held her breath, allowing him in. Cementing her cover. This was for Gina, and all those women who'd succumbed to the hand of the Night Terror.

She smelled pine, a woodsy outdoors kind of scent, and man. Pure, virile, aroused man. Her eyes fluttered closed. She leaned in to meet him, heart gunning in her chest, blood thrashing through her veins, making her body heat and soften. His breath warmed her face, the last swig of his whiskey taunting her tastebuds as the whisper of his lips met hers.

A groan escaped. Hers? Or his?

Hand and glass dropped to her side. Thankfully, she'd drunk the last drop of martini well before he kissed her.

His tongue skirted her lips, sweeping away any last resistance, testing and tasting her as if she were everything. Warmth seared her hip as his palm brushed there, and lower, fingers sinking deep into her flesh, pulling her inward. Her body sighed, sank into him, meeting and melding with heat and hard male muscle.

All the while her body buzzed with the promise of more. Static shrilled in her ear. She flinched. Jerked back.

Room and reality shot into cruel, harsh focus, leaving what could have been and what was in a tug of war with her conscience.

Chase's voice echoed in her earpiece.

'Jayda, they've found another victim. We have to go.'

Her blood chilled, even while her heart still seemed determined to escape her ribcage. Her gaze darted towards the door.

'What's wrong?'

His hand left her chin as she fought for breath. And sense.

She grabbed his wrist as it drew away, 'Oh my god! The time!' She stared at the Omega watch face, the hot skin beneath her fingers zapping her anew, before she let go to grip her cool empty glass with two hands. 'I was supposed to meet my sister half an hour ago.' The practised words left her lips with superficial confidence.

'Really?' Left eyebrow raised, the word oozed scepticism.

'Bad enough that I'm late, she'll kill me if I don't show.'

Her tone was unequivocal, even as she searched for a place to offload her glass. There was none, of course. She thrust it towards him and those long, sure fingers wrapped it inside. His gaze never once strayed from hers.

'Thank you for – It was – I mean –' Yep, there was the unmistakable proof. Her entire unit listening in and she couldn't string more than three words together. Training hadn't prepared her for that kiss.

Not that she expected much when her entire blood supply had rushed south with the promise of –

She shook her head. If only her flustered innocence could be chalked up to acting. His gaze narrowed, and she pounced before he could call her bluff. 'See you around sometime.'

Her legs carried her to the front door, leaving her brain a few steps behind. She fumbled with the lock. Second try, it gave way. Steeling herself not to turn for one last mind-melting look, she slipped into the cool evening air and tugged the door closed behind her. The clatter of her heels down the front steps and over the pavement did nothing to calm her nerves.

A narrow escape, thanks to Chase.

Her mind whirled, spinning-top style. *Holy hell!*

This stranger with fathomless eyes and the scent of a forest meadow. She didn't know his name, but she knew she'd been willing to kiss him, and more. She was certain she would have done more. And she couldn't even blame the drink – she'd hardly had any. Was it the atmosphere in the house? She'd be kidding herself if she said yes.

It was her. And him. Her burning need and some indefinable, uncontrollable attraction. How could she have reached twenty-seven and not have experienced *that* before?

The ground rose before her as she stumbled. A crack in the pavement. Fatal and dangerous, if you didn't take care. Lessons she should well keep in mind.

She approached the black 'Antenna Solutions' truck parked just round the corner.

A cat skittered across her path and she froze, willing her nerves to get a grip. He had her unsettled, frazzled. Men didn't do that to Jayda Thomasz. Not anymore. She was unsusceptible to them, their wiles. She had a lifetime of fortification around her emotions to prevent exactly what had just taken place.

The job had been her single-minded focus for the past seven years. A moment's fancy couldn't be allowed to change that.

One slip. That's all it was. And Jayda was damn certain it would never happen again.

'What've we got, Teddy?'

Jayda braced her stomach as the stench of decomposing flesh hit her nostrils. The strong reek of urine from the adjacent lane didn't help. Or the overflowing dumpsters, a consequence of the council rubbish collectors' rolling strikes. The reason this victim wasn't found as quickly as the others. That and the fact she wasn't displayed so publicly and proudly.

Only the occasional car horn or rumble of a city tram disturbed the deceptive calm of the blind alley; reminders they were standing in the hub of Melbourne's city centre.

Medical examiner Rod Bearinger glanced up and nodded. 'Chase. Jayda.'

He pushed up with his cane, leaning heavily against the brass T-handle as his bespectacled gaze gave Jayda a once-over. 'Big night out?'

'I wish.' She tugged at the dipping neckline of her top. 'Undercover op. But because I'm lead on the case…'

'… you had to bail? Well, good for you. Your dad must be proud.'

'Thanks.' Warmth flooded her cheeks. She ignored the butterflies in her chest, gesturing instead towards the woman who deserved their undivided attention. 'Same MO?'

'Looks that way. Although she took longer to be discovered. I'd place time of death around seventy-two hours, possibly more. Which makes her victim number seven, not eight.'

He pushed back a strand of grey hair with his wrist and waved a gloved hand towards the victim. 'Proximate cause of death appears to be asphyxia by strangulation. Body propped up against the wall. Eyes open. Blistering around the mouth, white chemical burns on the surrounding skin. I'll get the lab to check it out, but from the look of it, I'd say concentrated hydrogen peroxide.'

'And the finger?'

Leaning heavily against his cane, he bent and lifted the woman's left hand. 'Ring finger severed. Surgical incision at the proximal inter-phalangeal joint. Only difference is what looks to be a nick in the proximal phalanx.'

He pointed to a small but clear indentation in the bone. 'Usually this kind of cut indicates hesitation. But I wouldn't have linked that with our killer. Maybe he had more difficulty with her, or was rushed. I'll know more when I get her onto my table.'

'Do we have an ID?' Chase's breath fanned the hair at the back of Jayda's neck.

She edged sideways, giving him space that didn't invade her own. The discomfort, she shrugged off. She was being ridiculous.

'Sure do.' Teddy's baritone interrupted thoughts better left till never. 'Angelique Sutton. Twenty-three.' He handed Chase an evidence bag containing a hot pink Cara Vinelli wallet, opened to reveal a Victorian driver's licence.

Jayda held down the hem of her skirt and crouched beside the body, eyes searching. Eventually he'd slip up. He had to. And when he did, that vital clue wouldn't escape unnoticed. She would catch this bastard and see he rotted in a steel six-by-eight until the end of his days.

Chase's hand shook as he handed her a pen. Good to know he shared her anger.

With the nib, she lifted a blonde curl from Angelique's forehead. The hair was coarse, dry, as if bleached without care or conditioner. Recently, too, considering the absence of dark roots to match the chestnut of her eyebrows and lashes.

She inspected lower. 'What's this?'

'Wondered if you'd notice.' Teddy leaned over the top of his cane again. 'Needle mark below the left earlobe, indicating an injection into the glossopharyngeal nerve.'

Jayda's gaze wandered beyond the body. 'I assume no needle was found at the scene?'

'You got it in one. Won't know what was injected until we do a tox screen. But lividity suggests she was killed elsewhere, then posed here.' Straightening, he pushed at his specs with the back of his hand. 'I'm all done here. Once you're finished I'll organise to get her back to the lab.'

Teddy limped towards the white coroner's van. Seemed his hip had flared up again. Weird that in a modern, non-wartime society, gout still existed. She'd always associated the ailment with older, ex-military men; Grandfather Joe's generation.

Chase moved to stand beside her. 'He's evolving. What's the bet it's propofol diluted with lidocaine again?' He rubbed his jaw. 'Two vics with needle marks. What do you figure that's about?'

She straightened, her mind racing.

First Gina Hennessey, then Angelique Sutton. Two deaths that didn't add up. Never had she been more certain.

'It's not the Night Terror.'

AND THERE'S MORE!

Like a free romantic suspense novelette?
Get a copy of COLD CASE, WARM HEART when you sign up to
my newsletter on my website
www.michelle-somers.com

ABOUT COLD CASE, WARM HEART

Three deaths, one clue and twenty-four hours before it's too late…

Homicide detective Calamity Dresden has twenty-four hours to catch
a killer before he kills again and disappears underground. Estranged
lover Sebastian Rourke wants justice for his murdered father and every
other victim of Melbourne's sadistic Trifecta Terror.

But when the two are forced to team up and danger closes in, can they
keep their minds on the case and their hands off each other?